MARY LA

was born in East Walpole, Massachu... brought home to Ireland by her paren... lived there ever since.

In 1938 she wrote her first short story, "Miss Holland", which was published by the *Dublin Magazine* where it was read by Lord Dunsany who gave her great encouragement and subsequently wrote an enthusiastic preface to her first collection, *Tales from Bective Bridge* (1942), which was awarded the James Tait Black Memorial Prize. Apart from two early novels, Mary Lavin has concentrated on the short story and the novella and has been held by many critics to be one of the greatest living writers of the short story. Her work, which has been widely translated, includes: *The Long Ago* (1944), *The Becker Wives* (1946), *At Sallygap* (1947), *A Single Lady* (1951), *The Patriot Son* (1956), *A Likely Story ...* (1957), *The Great Wave* (1961), *In the Middle of the Fields* (1967), *Happiness* (1969), *A Memory* (1972), *The Shrine* (1977) and *A Family Likeness* (1985). Stories from the above have also been collected into three volumes under the title *Stories of Mary Lavin*, and a volume of *Selected Stories* was published in 1984. She has also published one children's book, *The Second Best Children in the World* (1972), illustrated by Edward Ardizzone. Mary Lavin's novels are: *The House in Clewe Street* which was published in 1945 after serialisation in the *Atlantic Monthly* under the title "Gabriel Galloway", and *Mary O'Grady* (1950, also published in the Modern Classics Series).

Mary Lavin has been awarded two Guggenheim Fellowships, the Katherine Mansfield Prize, the Eire Society Gold Medal (USA), the Literary Award of the American Irish Foundation and the Gregory Medal, founded by Yeats to be "the supreme award of the Irish Nation". In 1968 Mary Lavin was made a D. Litt by her *alma mater*, the National University of Ireland. In 1964-5 she was the President of Irish PEN and in 1971-3 was President of the Irish Academy of Letters.

Mary Lavin was married in 1942 to William Walsh, by whom she had three daughters. After his death in 1954 she was a widow for fifteen years, until she married Michael MacDonald Scott in 1969. Her home is in Bective, County Meath but she also has a small studio in Dublin where she does most of her work.

VIRAGO
MODERN
CLASSIC

NUMBER
266

MARY LAVIN

THE HOUSE IN
CLEWE STREET

WITH AN AFTERWORD BY
AUGUSTINE MARTIN

Published by VIRAGO PRESS Limited 1987
41 William IV Street, London WC2N 4DB

First published in Great Britain by Michael Joseph 1945
Copyright Mary Lavin 1945
Afterword Copyright © Augustine Martin 1987

British Library Cataloguing in Publication Data

Lavin, Mary
    The house in Clewe Street. —(Virago
    modern classics).
    I. Title
    823'.912[F]   PR6023.A914

    ISBN 0-86068-718-X

    Printed in Finland by Werner Söderström,
            a member of Finnprint

PART I

Theodore and Cornelius

WHEN YOU are still several miles outside the town of Castlerampart you can see the spire of the church pricking the distant clouds. After that, with every step you take, the contours of the town rise higher, and if you keep your eyes upon it the whole town, with its steeple, chimneys, and irregular roofs, its ruined gables and jutting walls, will rise out of the flat fields in which it is set.

It is rarely, however, that the traveller can so keep his eyes upon the distant town, for along the way there are several distractions, which, in the monotony of the flat fields, attract attention irresistibly. Upon the left-hand side, just before coming to a crossroad, there is an iron gate leading into a plot in which all that is above the earth is bare and naked to view. This is the town cemetery; and although the ground slopes downwards ever so slightly at this point, causing people to hurry along involuntarily, the eye is nevertheless drawn to stare for a minute at the whitening headstones that lean to east and west, and at the damp mossy tombstones that solidly support their mountings of urns and angels. Even the simple grassy mounds of the poorer graves attract attention by their decaying heaps of laurel wreaths and their rusting tangles of glass-domed immortelles.

A small but energetic stream runs side by side with the road, and keeps it company with its noisy, rabbling waters. This energetic and rowdy stream, not content with attracting attention by its ceaseless chatter alone, gives a sudden twist every now and then and runs under the road, to come out again on the other side more noisy and boisterous than ever.

These sudden sallies on the part of the stream have resulted in the erection of brief, humped bridges that rise abruptly and descend even more abruptly still in the otherwise unbroken flatness of the road. These bridges have no geographical importance and appear on no known map. The traveller who goes over them in a wheeled vehicle, with any degree of speed, gets a jolt that is out of all proportion to what might seem to him the inconsiderable size of the obstacle. The fact is that, being of such slight importance, they were built by the ordinary road maker, without any great experience; and the sensation of going over them is that of riding over the carcass of an animal.

It is not surprising, therefore, that a traveller, meeting innumerable of these small bridges and receiving each time the disturbing sensation of riding over the back of a ram, spends more of his time looking backward over his shoulder than he spends looking forward at the road ahead of him. The town is upon him before he realizes, and upon his left-hand side the high walls of its ancient ramparts rise up sheer from the ground.

Under this rampart we must pass for a considerable distance yet, before coming to the entrance to the town. And meanwhile all trace of the steeple, chimneys, and ruins, the roofs and irregular gables, that he had seen from a distance has been completely blotted from view. All that can be seen, up over those ancient walls, is the tops of great and ancient trees that stretch their branches far and wide and press their muscular trunks against the masonry in which great fissures have been rent.

Viewed from beneath like this, the rampart looks like a great stone urn in which an overpowerful plant has expanded so much that it has cracked the sides of its container. Through one of these great cracks in the rampart wall a view can be taken of King John's Castle, a ruin which stands in the centre of a wild park, overgrown with trees. This park figures largely on the Ordnance Survey map of the district, and actually covers two-fifths of the area occupied by the entire town; yet it is vacant and waste land that is seldom entered by the people of the town. It is a silent and lonely place, with its great tree-shaded stretches of damp grass, its still pools of green-grown water, its creeping shrubs, and its heavy leafy boughs that dredge the grasses. There is a smell of dampness under the trees, and a damp, unhealthy brilliance in the greenery. Insects, wild birds, and wild creeping things are seldom silent.

In winter when the trees are bare, or at night when the lights are lit in the town, you can see beyond this park to the back windows of the houses in Clewe Street, but these houses are separated from the eerie park and its ruin by the town river and by their own long gardens that run up from the riverbank.

Indeed, river and rampart, which once protected their ancestors from dangers without, are now regarded by the people of Castlerampart as protecting them from dangers within. This change of attitude is suggested even more forcibly a little farther up the road by a cluster of poverty-stricken huts that shelter under the rampart, to which, particularly on wet and windy days, they cling as close as sheep to a hedgerow.

After sheltering these few poor hovels, however, the ramparts are no longer so strong. From this point onwards the fissures become gaps, and some of the gaps so great that in places there are more stones lying in the nettles than are resting upright upon each other, and through these gaps the town is once more fully exposed to view. It is from the town bridge, which was once a toll bridge, the ruined arch of which still remains, that the most comprehensive view can be taken of the town. From this point all its buildings are surprisingly clear, and each one by the simple nature of its architecture is immediately recognizable for what it is—the ugly

6

oblong schoolhouse with its high windows, the tall stone mill with its coating of slimy fungus and its carpet of bright wood shavings, the red metal bridge and buildings of the railway in the distance, the Friary ruin smothered in nettles, with its east gable blocked with cement to make a ball alley, and the spire of the church splattered white with bird droppings and ornamented by starlings as still as starlings carved out of stone. And between these prominent buildings are the ugly irregular blocks of shops and private houses, with their uneven levels of roof and chimney.

One afternoon in early August, Theodore Coniffe stood on the summit of the bridge leading into the town. He was standing with his hands shading his eyes in order to see against the slanted rays of the sun. But it was not over the town that he stared, but at the flat road that led into it.

Theodore Coniffe was a tall man. Although he was nearly seventy years of age, his figure was well preserved and straight. His face was thin, and he had the double advantage of good skin upon good bone. He had, moreover, the type of face, longer and wider at the temple than at the jaw, which presents a fine chiselled appearance without suggesting loss of character, as is the case with faces of similar shape where the effect is achieved by a medium-sized forehead with the chin falling away into a sharp and narrow point. His hair was of coarse grey, but in losing its colour it had not lost its vitality, and it shot up from his forehead, brisk as a brush.

This afternoon he was dressed in a black-striped suit, and was without an overcoat although there was already a sharp edge to the afternoon air. The neatness and cleanliness of his suit, and his leisurely attitude at a time of day when his fellow townsmen were usually most busy, seemed to indicate that Theodore had a generous adequacy of money. A glance at his smooth white hands, however, made it clear that, whatever way his money was made, it had not been by manual labour. Perhaps it was by using his intensely brilliant blue eyes that he was spared the necessity of using his hands too harshly.

On this particular afternoon, a moment after he had raised his hands to shield his eyes as he gazed out over the road leading into the town, there was a sound of horse hoofs coming up the bridge from the town, and before he had time to turn round a voice called out to him with great good humour.

"I see you are watching out for the Happy Pair!"

Theodore turned around in surprise to see Colonel Christopher Fanshawe crossing the crest of the bridge on a handsome bay mare.

Colonel Fanshawe was not much over thirty, but his skin was tanned to the colour of the saddle he sat upon, and his face had suffered more ravage from the weather than it had suffered from time. Across the bridge of his nose, and on the upper parts of his cheekbones where the skin was thin, there was a scratching of broken veins.

Between Theodore and Christopher Fanshawe, besides the obvious difference of age, there was another great difference, which strangely enough expressed itself by means of the very thing they had in common, well-kept clothes of a good quality. Both wore clothes of a good material, and the clothes in both cases were in good condition, neat, brushed, and pressed. But Theodore's clothes owed their respectability solely to the fact that they had never been submitted to hard wear, whereas it was clear that the clothes Colonel Fanshawe wore, from his green silk shirt to his yellow tie, printed all over with fox heads, had never been intended for hard wear.

The mare which Colonel Fanshawe rode had one white foot, a white star on her forehead, and a fringe of white to her mane. In the town she had suffered considerable annoyance when her master had occasion to stop and lean from his saddle to do business with one or other of the townspeople. When the time came to leave the town, therefore, she proceeded to do so with high spirit, and when they came to the crest of the bridge and she saw her road home ahead of her, between the beautiful free fields, she threw up her head with delight. It was just then that she felt again the tiresome curb upon the rein and she was forced to come to a halt once more. Sensing that it was due to the presence of Theodore upon the bridge that she had been forced to stop, the mare curved her neck and rolled her handsome eyes at him once in disdain, and then like a lovely but impatient woman she fixed her eye upon the indifferent fields ahead and regarded him no more. She was motionless upon her legs, but some involuntary nerves made her silk skin tremble over her rippling ribs.

Fanshawe had no sooner pulled the rein then he realized the impatience of his companion, and with a smile at her spoiled behaviour he gave in to her at once, and lifting the rein let her canter off once more. When Theodore turned around to answer what he thought had been a question, he found that it had been merely a greeting, and looking after the cantering mare he received another similar greeting from her rider who waved his crop and called out once more.

"Give my respects to the Bride!"

The Colonel was adept at remarks that sounded friendly and familiar without involving himself in any great degree of friendship or familiarity, and so, although Theodore was disconcerted at the abruptness with which he had been treated, he was gratified to think that Colonel Fanshawe had known and remembered that this was the day his daughter was coming home from her honeymoon. He stifled the last vestiges of his resentment by blaming the impatient bay. Colonel Fanshawe was very friendly and

8

kind, but the bay mare was a haughty piece. Theodore remembered with distaste the way she had rolled her eyes at him, but he appeased himself by reflecting that she was only an animal, and he turned back to the bridge; this time he looked in the direction of the town, refusing to follow the figure of the disdainful mare, whose cantering hoofs kept sounding in the air for a time, clearer, sweeter, and more insistent the further she went on her way.

Theodore stood for a few minutes upon the bridge, rather as if he had forgotten what had brought him there in the first place, and then he began to walk back slowly towards the centre of the town. Although he was somewhat distracted, nevertheless he kept turning his head continually and looking from one side of the road to the other. At some houses he stared with particularly keen attention. Others he treated with equally great indifference. From this alone it might perhaps be possible to guess the source of his income, but, when he turned into his own street—Clewe Street—it would be impossible to remain any longer unaware that Theodore derived his income from house property, for upon his appearance at the top of the street there was furious activity at the bottom.

From one window sill, upon which they had been sitting and swinging their legs, a group of children jumped to the ground. Some men who were talking idly outside a small cottage straightened themselves up from the wall on which they had been leaning. And from the gable of a house, near the end of the street, three boys who had been playing handball up against the gable end became so confused at the sight of him that they began to run in different directions like sheep, knocked into each other several times, and finally ran down an alleyway that led between two houses to the river, leaving their ball behind them in the gutter.

Clewe Street was a long, leisurely street, starting out, like all the streets in the town, from the market square, but blocked at the far end by a high wall, and shaded by it and by a pollarded oak tree, around the bole of which a wooden seat had been built, but upon which, owing to the dampness from the tree above it, no one ever sat.

The fact that no one ever sat on this seat was a sore point with Theodore Coniffe, for the somewhat simple reason that it was he who had put it there, and for the further reason that, although he had put it there to break his tenants of the habit of sitting upon their window sills, they still continued to sit upon them.

On this particular afternoon, as he turned into Clewe Street and saw the children jumping off the window ledges at sight of him, he gave an exclamation of irritation. Now, it happened that at that very moment Mrs. Finnerty, the wife of the new bank manager, was just stepping out of one of the shops at the top of the street, and hearing Theodore's exclamation she jumped to the conclusion that she had been the cause of it by startling him with her abrupt appearance before him.

"I beg your pardon, Mr. Coniffe. Did I startle you?" said Mrs. Finnerty, making an effort to step back into the doorway in order to let him pass upon the narrow footway, but Theodore had already side-stepped in order to give her precedence, and this time they banged into each other with even greater force.

In the explanations that followed, Theodore began to elucidate for Mrs. Finnerty the line of thought that had led to his exclamation.

Mrs. Finnerty was a bride—that is to say, it was exactly three months to the day since she had first arrived in the town upon the arm of Mr. Finnerty. Since the time limit for calling a bride a bride usually corresponded with the length of time during which she could manage to triumph over the other women of the town by producing new costumes, hats, jackets, and blouses, Mrs. Finnerty would soon be regarded as a mere wife, for not only had she begun to repeat her triumphs in such small matters as gloves and scarves, but, as she walked down Clewe Street with Theodore, she was wearing the very same costume she had worn upon her first appearance in the town, upon the arm of her new husband, and with it, moreover, she was wearing the identical hat that she had worn on that day, wreathed with rosebuds round the brim and speared with a steel hatpin in the shape of an arrow.

Indeed, even three months ago, when she first arrived in their midst, it had been difficult for the town to regard Mrs. Finnerty as a bride. There was something a little too thin, a little too dry, and even something a little too neat, about the new Mrs. Finnerty, which made it difficult to call her a bride, and even made it difficult for the people of the town to understand how the choice of the fat and red-faced manager had fallen upon her at all, unless it was assumed that his choice had been made at such an earlier date that the time that had subtracted from her charm had added to his sense of duty towards its memory. Everyone was agreed upon one thing, however : that Mrs. Finnerty was the most ladylike and well-mannered person that had ever come to the town. After the first few words he had exchanged with her, the morning after her arrival, Theodore had expressed himself as delighted with her. She had such a gift of dignifying the most trivial conversations with a polite precision of diction that it passed without notice that she never engaged in any others; and she was so diligent in getting to the bottom of every topic that she discussed, it passed without notice that the topic itself was always shallow. When talking to Theodore her sentences were laden with references to lintel and jamb, weatherboard and coping stone, and he always came away from his conversations with her convinced that she was the most intelligent women he had ever met. He was glad that she and her husband had rented one of his houses, and particularly one that adjoined his own house. As he often remarked, she was not a raw and inexperienced girl who would not understand the care and attention that was due to a house.

He was always pleased to meet her and engage in an intelligent conversation. When he ran into her, this day as they were both going down Clewe Street, he was delighted at an opportunity for airing his grievances about his less intelligent tenants.

"Yes, yes indeed!" he said, as they began to walk down the street together, after he had pointed to the window sill from which the children had jumped down on sight of him. "I had that seat built round the tree at the bottom of the street. But does anyone sit on it? Not a soul. The other day I saw no less than five children sitting on the window sill of Colgan's cottage, drumming their heels against the plaster of the wall, and singing at the tops of their voices. What do you think of that, Mrs. Finnerty?"

Mrs. Finnerty took time to think before she replied.

"All I can say," she said at last, "is that if window sills were intended for people to sit on them, why in the world were chairs invented!"

"That's what I was just about to say," said Theodore delightedly, although his delight was due to the fact that it was not at all what he had been about to say, being much better and more effectively expressed than he would have expressed it himself. "Would you like to know the reply I received from Mrs. Colgan? She said that she couldn't stop the children—if they wanted to sit on the window sill, they'd sit on the window sill."

"I would be interested to hear what reply you made to that, Mr. Coniffe," said Mrs. Finnerty, deferentially.

Theodore stopped on the pathway and looked at her.

"I need hardly tell you the reply I would like to have given!" he said, with dignity. "It was not the custom in my day for a mother to admit that she had no control over her children. But I restrained myself, and all I said was that she would have to find some way of keeping them off the window sills. That's what I said."

Theodore started onwards again. Mrs. Finnerty stepped alongside him, but she turned her head delicately towards him, with a politely interrogative air.

Theodore interpreted this slight gesture correctly and went ahead with his narrative. "Well," he said, "the very next day when I looked up the street, what did I see but a row of geranium pots ranged along the sill from one end of it to the other!"

From the tone of irritation in Theodore's voice, Mrs. Finnerty could see that for some reason or other he regarded the geranium pots with more

11

disfavour than he regarded the children, but her politeness was so great that she went one better than agreeing with him, and simulated instead a certain lack of understanding in order to give him an opportunity for explaining himself in full.

"I must be very stupid," she said, "but I don't see what harm the geranium plants could do. It seems to me quite a good idea for keeping the children off the window ledge. I'm afraid that I should have done the very same thing."

Theodore put his hand upon her sleeve.

"My dear lady, indeed you would not have done any such thing. You have far too much good sense. Why, flowerpots are the worst things in the world that could be put on a window sill. I would go so far as to say that it might be better to have people sitting on a sill than to have flowerpots ranged along it."

Mrs. Finnerty appeared unable to believe this.

"They look so pretty," she exclaimed.

"They do!" said Theodore. "But will they look pretty when the window ledge sags under them?"

"But surely, Mr. Coniffe," said Mrs. Finnerty, "a flowerpot is very light. How could it cause a window ledge to sag?"

Theodore was patient.

"Flowers don't grow without water, do they?"

"No," said Mrs. Finnerty.

"And I am given to understand that flowerpots will have to be watered from time to time?"

"Why, yes."

"I understand further that the water does not all remain in the pot, but after a certain quantity of it has been absorbed by the soil, the rest will escape from the pot?"

"That's right," said Mrs. Finnerty, entering into this byway of the subject with fresh interest. "As a matter of fact there are holes in the bottom of the flowerpot for the purpose of letting the excess water run out."

"Ha!" said Theodore, and he pressed the fist of one hand into the palm of the other. "I thought so. Precisely. And now let me ask you a question. Mrs. Finnerty. Where does that water go? Doesn't it run down on to the window sill?"

"Ah!" said Mrs. Finnerty brightly. "I see your point. The water is bad for the sill." She thought for a few minutes. "But surely the water from the plants cannot hurt the sill any more than rain?"

Theodore smiled tolerantly.

"You are forgetting," he said, "that the rain gets a chance to dry, but the water from a flowerpot is trapped under the pot and remains lodged

12

there, corroding the mortar and doing untold damage. When mortar is corroded, the stones loosen. When the stones loosen, the sill slips out of place. When the sill slips out of place, the whole window frame is thrown out of balance. And when any portion of a building is thrown out of balance, the whole edifice is in danger! Ah, my dear lady, you have to be constantly on guard. A small thing can start a lot of trouble." Theodore sighed. Mrs. Finnerty sighed too.

"I often heard my father say the same thing," she said. "He was always using those very words, talking to my mother. My mother used to be very fond of ivy——"

Theodore recoiled slightly in disbelief.

"Yes, ivy," said Mrs. Finnerty, giving a slight shudder. "My mother, poor thing, loved ivy. It seems when she was a young girl, before she met my father, she had a dress that she was very proud of, and this dress had a pattern of ivy leaves on the bodice. She was always describing it to me as a child. She said that she was always very much attached to ivy because it reminded her of the happy times she had in that dress. And when she got married and got a house of her own, the first thing she did was plant a slip of ivy at the gable end and begin to train it up the wall of the house."

Theodore was very interested.

"Your father put his foot down, I hope?"

"Oh, certainly," said Mrs. Finnerty. "He flew into a temper, I'm told, and tore it up by the roots and trampled on it. He was a man with a very strong character."

Theodore was not thinking about Mrs. Finnerty's father. He was thinking of her mother.

"How in the world could anyone like ivy?" he said. "I cannot understand such a thing."

Mrs. Finnerty put her head to one side. "Well, you may think it strange," she said, "but though I would never want to have ivy on my own house, I think I can understand how other people feel about it. There are some people, like my own mother, who think that ivy takes away the bare appearance from a house, and in the case of old houses I think people may be glad to have them covered with ivy to hide the cracks in the walls."

"Cracks! Hide the cracks in the walls!" Theodore became very excited. "If the ivy hides the cracks it's no more than might be expected from it, since those cracks would never have come if the ivy had not put them there! Ivy! Ivy! The enemy of civilization! It should be uprooted and destroyed every time it ventures to show its head. Have you ever considered the position of those foolish people who allow their houses to become covered with this poisonous plant? You haven't? Well, I have. I have thought for hours upon the subject. I never pass a house upon which ivy has taken its grip without shuddering to think of the way that it is pushing its way between mortar and brick, penetrating every crevice, dislodging the very cornerstones of the house. And this goes on night and day, day and night. Ivy never rests. Night and day, day and night, while the foolish people within the house are going about their business under the false impression that they are safe within four walls, the ivy they are so proud of is eating away their security, minute by minute, grain by grain! And all because the head of that house was ignorant of the attention that is due to a house. Ah, yes, a house is a delicate article. A house is ten times more delicate than the people that live in it. That is a strange thing, isn't it? But it's true. A person may suffer a bruise or a break, but the bone will knit and the skin will heal. That is not the way with a house. A house will not grow new mortar when the old wears out, nor grow new tiles if the old tiles are ripped off. When anything happens to a house, it is necessary to have workmen in to patch it up: and as all the world knows, when workmen are let into a house, they break as much as they mend. They do more damage with their feet than they are able to repair with their hands. I have seen a plumber bring down a whole plaster ceiling with a prod from his ladder. House repairing is a sad business. The only thing for a sensible man to do is to keep out of the way of needing such repairs by treating his house as gently as if it were a human being like himself—and a human being who was, moreover, more fragile and more delicate than himself."

They had come at last to the end of Clewe Street, and were confronted by the three tall houses of cut stone granite which Theodore owned and in the middle house of which he himself lived, having let the house upon the left to Mrs. Finnerty and the one upon its right to a certain Mrs. Molloy, to whose tenancy even after seven years Theodore had not yet accustomed himself.

Mrs. Molloy's house, although in size and shape it had every appearance of being an ordinary private dwelling, yet had a lamp suspended over the doorway, and a fibre mat spread in front of the doorstep, both of which proclaimed in large block letters that the premises were to be known as THE CENTRAL HOTEL.

These three houses were without doubt the most prosperous houses in the town, and if any assurance were needed other than the fine cut granite of which they were built, it could be found in the lavish additions that had been made to the exteriors in the way of bells and brass fittings, footscrapers, and wire mats. Indeed, Mrs. Molloy, having added every exterior adornment that her mind had been able to conceive, had at last resorted to making the inside furniture play its part in the outside appearance. In the front windows of the downstairs parlour she had placed a brass urn upon a pedestal, and in the urn was a large glossy-leaved eucalyptus plant, as plain to be seen from the street as if it were painted upon the glass, and no doubt difficult enough to see from inside the room, since it obscured a great part of the window light by which it might have been seen.

In the upstairs rooms, Mrs. Molloy had placed her great iron bedsteads in such positions of advantage that the large brass knobs of the foot rails shone resplendent through the window panes.

From somewhere within the Central Hotel there came forth a crashing noise which caused Theodore and Mrs. Finnerty to swivel around and stare at the windows, which still trembled with the resoundings of the crash. A moment later, as if, in her journey towards it, she had passed through the house like a whirlwind, Mrs. Molloy herself appeared at the front parlour window.

Mrs. Molloy was a large woman with several children and a small, meek husband. Although she was large and matronly in appearance, there were no grounds for assuming that her family was yet complete. And to those who marvelled that she should have taken upon herself the running of a hotel when she had already so many dependent upon her, she always replied that if a thing was worth doing, it was worth doing well. In addition to the humankind that were dependent upon her for bite and sup, Mrs. Molloy was always attended in her journeys from room to room by a large number of cats and dogs, and wobbling pups, that rubbed themselves against her ample ankles and constantly clamoured for attention.

It was quite understandable that the multiplicity of her duties had taken away any time she might otherwise have spent upon the niceties of the toilette, but unless we agree that human beings always find time for the cultivation of one vanity, it would be hard to understand how Mrs. Molloy had time to take care of her bright mass of yellow hair. This mass of hair was always washed, brushed, and brightly shining, no matter how much dirt was lodged under her fingernails and how dark the rim of her collar became. It was her sole pride and vanity.

So bright was this mass of Mrs. Molloy's hair that it would probably have attracted the attention of Theodore and Mrs. Finnerty had she but come to the window and stood there, but Mrs. Molloy took no such chance. Catching the brass finger grips of the window sash, she threw the window upwards with a great force, and sticking out her head she called to them in excitement, "Are they coming? Are they coming?" And without waiting for an answer she leaned out farther, her great bosom pressing against the granite sill, to see as far as she could up the street.

For a moment Mrs. Finnerty had not understood to whom Mrs. Molloy referred, but then she blushed in confusion.

"Oh, Mr. Coniffe!" she said. "How rude you must think me! I forgot to inquire about your daughter. I hear she's coming home today. What time do you expect her?"

But before Theodore had time to answer, Mrs. Molloy answered for him. "Don't expect that man to know!" she said. "That man never thinks of anything but his precious houses."

Mrs. Molloy winked once at each of them and then she leaned out farther over the sill and spoke more particularly to Mrs. Finnerty. "It's my belief they'll be here any minute. As a matter of fact, when I heard your voices in the street a minute ago, I was sure it was them. I nearly broke my neck getting to the window. I fell over half a dozen things. Isn't it awful the way everything gets in your way when you're in a hurry? Did you ever notice it? As I was saying, I thought that I heard them arriving and I ran here to the window as fast I could run. I wouldn't want to miss seeing them for anything. I always love to see a bride coming home. I like to see if there's any change in her. There usually is some change. Sometimes it's for the better; sometimes it's for the worse. Isn't that so?"

Mrs. Molloy paused for a minute to look up the street again. "They should be here any time now." She seemed to have a new idea. "Wait a minute! I'll come out into the street. Wait a minute!" And withdrawing her head again suddenly, Mrs. Molloy banged down the window sash so that the frame shook, and the glass shivered, and Theodore trembled with such irritation beside her that Mrs. Finnerty felt her own knees beginning to tremble slightly.

"That woman!" said Theodore. "That woman!"

Poor Mrs. Finnerty looked from Theodore to the window and from the window to Theodore, and the only thing that was clear in her mind was that she should at any cost escape before Mrs. Molloy came out into the street.

"If you'll excuse me, Mr. Coniffe, I think I'll step over to the door and inquire from Miss Theresa what time the travellers are expected."

Theodore nodded and she supposed that he had heard her. Smiling nervously, she walked over to the door of the middle house, and lifting the brass knocker she gave a delicate and discreet knock. Behind her back she heard the sound of Mrs. Molloy's voice raised in good-humoured quarrel with Theodore, and one or two phrases came to her ears.

"Who ever heard such a fuss about a bit of plaster! Two pennyworth of plaster!" she heard Mrs. Molloy exclaim, and another time she heard her roar, laughing, "Man dear, don't be talking nonsense. If ivy did harm, would the rampart walls be standing today? The rampart is hundreds of years old and yet it's so covered with ivy that you'd have to put your arm in, up to the elbow, before you could touch the stone. Ivy never did harm. Where did you get that idea?"

The timid knock that Mrs. Finnerty gave on the door was sharply contrasted with the determined sound of the footsteps inside the door as Mary Ellen, an elderly maidservant, came across the flagged hallway to answer the knock.

Mary Ellen was as tall as her master, and like him she was very stiff and straight. She wore at all times a blue-striped apron, starched until it creaked like a board, which emphasized by its vertical lines her unusual height and straightness. She had black hair, striped with grey, and her face was long and pale with a smooth yellowish colour and texture that reminded one at once of those dolls whose faces are carved out of soap. And like the faces of those soap dolls, Mary Ellen had a bright medallion of red upon each cheek.

It was quite clear, however, that in Mary Ellen's case these red medallions had not been applied with paint, for the simple reason that the same bright red colour was repeated again in a place where it is almost certain it would never have been artificially applied—the tip of her long nose. Perhaps in some moment of unusual excitement the blood had rushed to Mary Ellen's face, and when it began to recede again in a calmer moment, the supply that had flowed so easily to the tip of her nose found itself confronted with greater difficulty in the return journey, which was decidedly uphill, and had fallen back to remain there permanently.

As she opened the door to Mrs. Finnerty on this particular afternoon, the red medallions in her cheeks blazed very brightly, and the tip of her nose was afire.

"Good afternoon, Mary Ellen," said Mrs. Finnerty, smiling and preparing to step into the hall. "I called to see Miss Coniffe and to ask her at what hour she is expecting the return of the Happy Pair."

Mrs. Finnerty lifted her skirt and put out her small, neatly shod foot to step into the hallway, but to her astonishment Mary Ellen, although she was holding open the door, was herself blocking the ingress thereof, and instead of standing aside to allow the visitor to enter, she herself, after a backward glance over her shoulder, stepped out into the street, in her stiff blue-and-white-striped apron, and pulled the door out after her until the merest slit indicated that it was not closed entirely.

"You'll excuse me, I know, for taking a liberty, Mrs. Finnerty," said Mary Ellen, "but I think it might be as well if you didn't ask Miss Coniffe any questions. She's quite cheerful at the moment, decorating the table, and doing odd little jobs. She seems to have forgotten her troubles, but the least remark might upset her, and act on her nerves, and put us all to shame by showing a bad spirit when the poor creatures arrive."

Now Mrs. Finnerty had the reputation of being a tactful woman, and wishing to retain it, she judged it tactful to withdraw without asking any further explanation. Tact, however, is a fickle commodity. It is hard to say that anyone possesses it permanently. Because you have displayed it yesterday is no guarantee that you will display it again today. In other words, it might have been more tactful for Mrs. Finnerty to have delayed Mary Ellen further, and asked her a few questions as to why Miss Coniffe should be upset at the thought of her young sister's return from her wedding tour. For to have withdrawn so swiftly, and with such a ready understanding of the necessity for doing so, was an admission that, from one source or another, she knew only too well that the wedding of Lily Coniffe to Cornelius Galloway was a source of bitter mortification to her sisters, Theresa and Sara, but particularly to Theresa.

∾ ∾ ∾

The story behind Theresa's attitude was a long one, and to understand it fully the townspeople needed long memories, but those who did not have such memories were not without being able to profit from those who had.

As near as it is ever possible to say when a story has its beginning, this story began while Theodore Coniffe's wife, Katherine, was still alive.

Katherine Coniffe had borne two daughters to her husband, but had thereupon ceased to show any further sign of remedying this poor achievement by the addition of a son. Theodore made the best of things as they were, and when the two little girls were old enough to follow him up and down the street, he was flattered and proud of them, and his resignation turned into satisfaction. Soon his satisfaction became so great that he forgot that he had ever been dissatisfied, and on one or two occasions he was heard to say in public that a son only increased a man's responsibilities but that a daughter increased his pleasures. Before long, such sayings became habitual to him, and after a while it was noticed that he made a point of inquiring the sex of all the newly born children in the parish. If the infant was a boy he shook his head in sympathy for the unfortunate parents. Boys were difficult to rear. Boys were a source of worry and responsibility. The times were bad for bringing male children into the world. . . .

The small Coniffe girls were always dressed in their best clothes and they walked one on either side of their father when he went around the town to collect his rents. Now, a man will never allow himself the pleasure of telling a son how much money he has made for him, because it might, and indeed possibly would, give him an idea that, there being so much of it ready-made, there would be no need for him to make any more; but with a girl it was different: a girl would not be expected to work, and since all that she would have would come to her from two sources—from her father and from a husband—Theodore was determined that his daughters would never owe all their gratitude to the latter.

18

In short, there was no need to conceal from Sara and Theresa that they would some day be rich young women, and as he collected the rents from his cottages, he took them with him, giving them a coin apiece before he tossed the rest of the coins into his canvas bag secured at the top by two strings. And whenever he acquired a new property he took the little girls with him on the day that he took over formal possession of the house. As they stood beside him meekly and watched the signing of bonds and documents, he used to wink at old Jasper Kane, the solicitor, and pinch their ears and question them.

"Whose house is this?" he used to ask. "Is this yours, Theresa, or does it belong to Sara?" And very demurely, according to which of them the previous house had been allotted, the little girls would answer, until soon, when other children were sitting inside rainy window-panes, with old catalogues spread out before them, apportioning to each other the pictured objects, as all children do—"This is my one—this is your one!"— the small Coniffe girls might have sat at the attic window of their own fine stone house at the end of the town, and looking out over the roofs and chimneys of the town have played the game with real houses.

This was the state of affairs when Theresa was just about fifteen years old, and Sara thirteen, and Theodore was as satisfied with his lot as any man could be. The girls would soon be sent to boarding school and after that there would be a grand time altogether hunting down suitable husbands for them. Even Katherine, although she would prefer that they could remain children forever, was beginning to glow with the prospect of this sporting event that promised in the near future.

But the near future held a surprise for Theodore and his wife, and when Katherine began to experience symptoms of ill-health, some of which she had already experienced twice before in her lifetime, it was without recognizing their cause. After trying to remedy certain distresses with various brews and tisanes, she began with alarm to notice that her ankles were swelling and, worse still, that she was gaining weight with a dangerous rapidity.

Katherine Coniffe had always boasted a neat figure and had spoken with some contempt of those unfortunate matrons who lost control of their figures at forty.

"I'm only thirty-eight," she said with dismay to Mary Ellen, who was then only thirty-five herself, on one particular afternoon when she felt less well than usual. And taking Mary Ellen's yellow canvas measuring tape, she ran it round the formerly neat waist.

"Twenty-nine inches! Oh, Mary Ellen!" Katherine threw down the tape in horror and, running over to the mantelpiece, stared at her face in the looking glass. "I'm getting old!" she said with tears in her voice. For a few seconds there was silence as Katherine ran her hand over her hair in search of a grey hair, and closely examined her cheekbones to see if there were scratches of red. But although her eye flew to all the danger spots known so well to women, where age will first show itself, Katherine found nothing to worry her. The hair was black, the skin was light, the cheeks were soft and richly rounded. There was no sign of age. The face was beautiful, but better, it had still the beauty of youth.

"What good is a pretty face if my figure begins to thicken?" She bit her lip and then held out her hand imperiously. "Give me the tape again," she said, and when Mary Ellen handed it to her she passed it around her waist once more, drawing it tighter and tighter, and holding in her breath. "I may have made a mistake," she said, and she held it up again to correct the error. "Twenty-nine inches!" There was no mistake. "Twenty-nine inches! Oh, Mary Ellen. What will I do? Once a woman begins to put on weight, she gets heavier every day."

Mary Ellen had spent the last five minutes trying to convince her mistress that it was only her imagination that made her think she was getting stout. Now, in face of the evidence supplied by her own tape measure, Mary Ellen felt the necessity of taking a new attitude.

"It is not everyone that likes a thin woman," she said. "There are some people who wouldn't say thank you for a thin woman. I know a dressmaker and she wouldn't make a dress for any woman that wasn't a full thirty-six inches in the bust. She says that you might as well be making dresses for the palings and posts as dressing a woman that was under ten stone weight."

Katherine stuck her fingers in her ears. "Stop it, Mary Ellen," she said. "You're only saying that to console me. I feel worse now because I see that you think I'm a sight and you're trying to cheer me up. But nothing can cheer me."

"I never saw you look prettier," said Mary Ellen.

Katherine's spirits rose for an instant, but then her eyes rested on the measuring tape at her feet.

"Nothing will ever be the same again. I used to have the people turning their heads to look at me as I went up the aisle of the church on Sunday, but all that is over." The tears came into her eyes. "It's so unfair! It isn't as if I didn't take exercise. It isn't as if I overeat. I never eat much." She looked up at Mary Ellen, her lower lip caught between her teeth. "Lately I haven't eaten as much as a bird. I have such a distaste for food that I can hardly sit at the table."

Up to now Mary Ellen had only paid heed, out of courtesy, to the complaints of Katherine, but suddenly, when Katherine spoke of her distaste for food, Mary Ellen gave a start and for the first time during the whole conversation she gave a sharp glance at the waistline of her mistress.

"Perhaps it might be just as well to have a talk with the doctor," she said.

"Oh, not at all!" said Katherine scoffingly. "He'd laugh at me. Doctors are very heartless. They have no delicacy or sensitiveness. A doctor loves to see a person getting as fat as a pigeon, with cheeks blazing till they look as if they were covered with fire brash. There's no use going to a doctor and complaining that you're putting on weight. If I was losing weight, it would be different."

Mary Ellen said nothing for a few moments. Then she glanced once more at Katherine's waist. "There are times when putting on weight is just as bad as losing weight," she said, but further than this she dared not go.

Katherine, however, was without suspicions. "I wonder," she said. "I don't feel well; that's a certainty. Perhaps I might have a talk with old Dr. Simons."

"I think you should have a talk with him, anyway, ma'am," said Mary Ellen, and to her relief Katherine agreed.

"I will," said Katherine. "I will! I'd rather humiliate myself before him, in the hopes that he could do something for me, than allow myself to be humiliated before the whole parish—I who was always drawing attention to women who were a half ounce over average weight."

Katherine Coniffe might be condemned for her exceeding vanity, but there is much to be said in favour of a vain woman—for instance it spoke well for Katherine Coniffe that her mind could conceive no greater humiliation than that of thickening at the waist, losing the contour of face and limb, and being unable to smile with arrogance at the rest of the congregation as she walked up the aisle on Sundays upon the arm of her proud husband.

When a young girl glances in a mirror, there are people who cry shame on her for her vanity, but there are some women, and Katherine Coniffe was one of them, in whom vanity is so great that it cannot be altogether condemned, since it is the pivot upon which their whole life turns. Through the vanity with which she had decked herself in her girlhood, she had caught the eye of Theodore. Through vanity in his compliments she had gone to the altar with him. His delight in her body had more than paid for the pains of childbirth that had followed. And when her children were born her vanity was increased twofold, for while people began to compliment her upon new scores, they had no cause to cease their compliments upon the old. After the birth of her children she was more graceful and firm than before. Even when the little girls began to grow up, the glances of admiration that were cast on Katherine were more numerous when it appeared that she was their mother.

Perhaps if she had gradually lost some of her youthful attributes she might not have felt the loss of them so keenly, but with this sudden change in her weight she visioned herself as travelling rapidly down the road to wrinkles and old age. She began to think of the time when these two little girls that had formerly been measure for comparison would thereafter be used as measure for contrast.

She fancied then, with a stab of pain, that she saw the end of that pleasant time, when her children seemed to be reaching ever upwards out of childhood, straining to attain a harmonious likeness to their parents, and when every year that came carried parents and children forward together, towards the prime and fullness of life. She fancied she saw the end of that time, and that she and her little girls had come to the forking of the roads, when the years, although they would come as rapidly as ever, would henceforth carry them in different directions: the children still going forward towards the bright prime of beauty, but the parents, having overpassed their prime, would have to venture ahead alone, upon a dark and downward road.

∽ ∽ ∽

Katherine sent for Dr. Simons, and while she was expecting him she paced back and forth in the front parlour.

"I know that it's nonsense to see the doctor," she said to herself. "When age begins to set in, there is no stopping it. There is nothing Dr. Simons can do for me. I may as well give in to being an old woman."

And so well did she resign herself, in the half an hour before his arrival, and when Dr. Simons was announced she was listless and hardly inclined to answer his questions. She was convinced that he and his remedies were powerless.

While he took her hand and felt her pulse, she was looking over his shoulder at the pier glass on the wall, in which there was reflected from the wall on the opposite side of the room a picture of herself and Theodore taken on their wedding day. Her mind was filled with distractions, and when the doctor asked her questions she replied with an easy effortlessness that showed her lack of confidence in the estimates he might make from them. When she tired of looking at the picture reflected in the pier glass, she looked out of the window at the familiar street outside. But all at once, some question startled her into glancing sharply at the doctor.

"I beg your pardon, Doctor!" she said, because having sent for him through an impulse of purely secular vanity, he affronted her by asking a question of an intimate medical nature. There was a touch of hauteur in her voice. "Surely there isn't any need for a medical examination. All I need is a tonic. I just want something to brace me up."

22

She looked at the doctor with suspicion, but the old doctor looked back at her with equally great suspicion. Was she making a fool of him?

"Surely, Mrs. Coniffe, it cannot be possible that, having already experienced these same symptoms on two previous occasions, you are unaware of their significance now?" Katherine stared at him. There was a certain censoriousness in the old man's tone, upon which she spent her astonishment before she concentrated upon what he said. She stared at him haughtily for a moment and then, starting forward, her hands rushing to her cheeks, she comprehended in a moment both his words and the implications of those symptoms she had tried to diagnose without his help. Her youth, far from having begun to decay, had risen within her veins with new richness and fertility. She was with child.

Seldom had the necessity for making a psychological study of his cases arisen for Dr. Simons; and seldom as such necessity arose, it was never in a maternity case, which indeed he almost regarded as outside his province, relegating such cases to the district nurse, except where he was the family doctor, called in for this work merely among others. Having first thought that Katherine Coniffe was behaving with affectation, he was no sooner convinced that he was wrong on this score than he flung himself into another error.

"There is no doubt whatsoever, my dear lady," said Dr. Simons. "You need not fear any disappointment. Your case is rare, admittedly, but not altogether unusual. Your vitality and your youthful heart! I am glad to say you need not fear any disappointment. There is no doubt whatever." And then, looking around for his hat and gloves, he dismissed Katherine from his attention, and thinking of Theodore's pleasure, he was already moulding his face into congratulatory smiles, and rubbing his hands together with an unmistakable show of satisfaction. He was not looking at Katherine at all, and had just lifted his gloves from the side table when his attention was drawn back to his patient by a most astonishing outburst of sobbing, which made him turn in fright and drop the gloves upon the floor.

He was astonished. "My dear lady! My dear lady! What is this? What is this?" And he began to agitate his hands over the bent and sobbing figure with gestures as ineffectual as those he might make if trying to catch a moth in a circle of lamplight. "This is very bad for you. What on earth is the matter? Why are you crying? Calm yourself. Calm yourself." As he spoke, he wiped his forehead with his handkerchief, and then, seeing the bell cord hanging on the wall, he ran to it and, gripping it, gave it a violent tugging while he kept on exclaiming, "This is very bad for you. I can't understand this at all."

A moment later Mary Ellen ran into the room. Having heard the sound of sobbing and having been so impatient to reach her mistress, she would not have waited much longer for permission to rush into the room.

"Don't upset yourself, ma'am," she cried, "this is something to be glad about. You ought to be throwing up your hands for joy, and not crying. It's a great blessing. I often heard my mother say that a late child was God's way of blessing a house tenfold. There, now. Don't cry. Wait till you see, you'll feel better when you have a cup of tea. The blackest things are often the brightest when you've had a cup of tea. There, now. There, now."

Dr. Simons stood still during this excited gabble, and his hand still remained upon the bell cord, from which indeed he drew support. When he rang the bell, he had expected Mary Ellen, but he had hardly expected that she would arrive fully equipped and prepared to cope with the situation, and apparently endowed, moreover, with a full understanding of the situation with which it would be necessary to cope. And in his mind he wronged her, and decided that, although she had been with the family fourteen years, she was no better than others of her class and that she had prepared herself for this emergency by the simple expedient of listening at the keyhole. He did not realize that Mary Ellen was responsible for urging Mrs. Coniffe to consult him, and that she had so urged her because she had had a shrewd suspicion of what the result of his diagnosis would be, and further, more intuitive still, that she knew in advance the effect that that diagnosis would have upon her mistress. Whatever he may have thought of her honesty, however, Dr. Simons was glad to rely upon her efficiency, and as she comforted Mrs. Coniffe and coaxed her, with words of encouragement, he slipped out of the room and made his way down the hall to find Theodore and tell him the news.

Theodore was easily found. He was superintending the thatching of a house at the top of Clewe Street, and was himself holding the foot of the ladder upon which the thatcher stood, in case it might slip. " I saw a ladder slip one time during roof repairs," he said, talking up to Murty Rod, the thatcher upon the roof, "and it slashed down the front of the house and tore a gash in the mortar from the top of the wall to the bottom."

"What happened to the thatcher?" said Murty from overhead.

"Oh, it was a slated house," said Theodore impatiently. "It wasn't a thatcher that was working on it at all; it was a slater. And of course that was worse, as you can see. It was a two-storey slated house, and there it was with a gash down the face of the mortar—that showed up even after it was patched. It looked bad. There was no real damage done, but it looked bad." He shifted his weight from one foot to the other. "That is a thing that some people neglect to look into—the appearance of a house. But appearances count. Give me a good-looking exterior and I'll give you a good guess as to the interior." Theodore looked down the street, in order to pick out a house which he did not own himself, in order to illustrate the converse of this maxim, but when he looked he saw the doctor leaving his own hall door.

"My wife wasn't well these last few days," he said, talking upwards to Murty, but keeping his eyes on the doctor. " So I asked old Simons to step in and give her a tonic." Murty stopped his work and looked down the street at the advancing doctor.

"He's looking pleased with himself, anyway. It's fellows like that have the easy time. I suppose he got more for walking down the street than I'll get for doing the whole of this roof, and it will take me three days."

Normally Theodore would have suggested to Murty that he expected the job to be finished in less than three days, but his mind was occupied with Katherine at the moment.

"He must have found her well, when he's looking so pleased with himself," he said, watching the doctor advancing with a springing step and every appearance of eagerness upon his face as he drew nearer. Theodore wanted to advance to meet him, but he did not dare to leave the foot of the ladder.

"I hope he didn't find her too well," said Murty, and he selected another scollop of sally rod for the thatch.

Theodore looked up at him. He was friendly with the men that worked for him, but he felt that Murty had overstepped himself; but as the doctor was upon them he could not say anything to Murty, and instead he pretended not to have heard him at all, and waving his left hand to greet the doctor, he raised his voice so that he might overcome the distance that still divided them.

"Well, Doctor! I see you found the patient in better health than you expected."

Dr. Simons looked at Theodore and then he looked up at Murty, who was thatching away with great industry, having realized even quicker and clearer than Theodore that his last remark had been better unmade.

"If you could step a few paces down the road with me," said Dr. Simons, "I would like to have a few words with you, Theodore."

"I'd like to oblige you, Doctor," said Theodore, "but I'm afraid this ladder will slip. When someone comes along to hold it, I'll step over to your place and have a chat with you. I can see by your face that you're pleased with your patient. She was worried herself, but I knew it was nothing. Mary Ellen had me persecuted to send for you, but you know what women are. I knew there was nothing serious."

Dr. Simons wasn't satisfied. "Couldn't you put a stone to the foot of that ladder?" he said. "There's something particular I'd like to say to you." He lowered his voice.

Theodore sensed something unusual. He put his foot firmly to the base

25

of the ladder and leaned his long, thin body forward towards the doctor, indicating that the latter might care to lower his voice and impart the message there and then. But the doctor looked uneasily at Murty. Murty was twisting the sally rods with unusual concentration. Dr. Simons leaned very close and whispered to Theodore.

"What?" Theodore drew back. Murty stopped twisting the sallies.

"You don't mean it? Katherine? Is it true? Why on earth didn't she tell me? It can't be true. Are you sure?" And not waiting for an answer to any of these questions, all at once he let go the ladder and began to run down Clewe Street with no more apology to the man at the top of the ladder than to the man at the foot of it.

Now, a ladder will usually remain upright without being held, but like many a thing that received support when support was unnecessary, no sooner was Theodore's support withdrawn than the ladder began to slip.

"Watch out, Murty!" shouted the doctor, and he grabbed the ladder by one leg as it tottered, but it was too late; and although the ladder remained upright, Murty came slipping down the slanted pathway of the bright glossy straw of the thatch he had just laid, and in another moment was sitting, legs outspread, in the mass of rough black straw on the pavement.

"Are you hurt, Murty?" said the doctor, rushing forward. Coming so soon after the spiritual collapse of Mrs. Coniffe, the collapse of Murty, and the ladder upon which he stood, unnerved the old doctor completely. " Are you hurt, man?" he said. "If you are, you can take an action against Theodore Coniffe. He might have been the cause of your death."

"If I was killed, it would be yourself that would have been the cause of my death, Doctor," said Murty, picking himself up and rubbing himself reflectively. "If that ladder was nailed to the road, I'd have fallen off it all the same, when I heard the news you gave him. Do you think, will it be a son this time? Sure, the Almighty would never have let twenty years go by if He was only going to send the man another daughter at the end of them!"

∽   ∽   ∽

When Theodore ran down the street, his thoughts were in turmoil, but as he ran they settled into coherence and by the time he reached his own hall door he was in such a definite state of pleasurable excitement that he could not wait to get out a key and open the door, but began to hammer on the knocker, and when he heard a sound of feet advancing along the flagged passage inside the door, he rapped at the panels of the door and called out in a loud voice.

"Hurry up, Mary Ellen. Open the door. Hurry. Hurry!"

Theodore had taken the disappointment at not having got a son with exemplary patience and resignation, and had even, as we have seen, begun to argue himself into a belief that he was a lucky man not to have the responsibility of bringing up a male child. In the instant after hearing the doctor's news, however, such a gust of exultation shook him that it was ludicrous, looking backwards, to think that he had ever been reconciled. So, a child, running ahead of its elders in a hayfield, and covering itself with dry hay, will pretend to be a bundle of hay. While he is hiding all is well, but when after the elders have approached and he has sprung up with a yell, although they exclaim with mock terror and assure him that they were certain he was a cock of hay, the child himself is all at once abashed and has to keep his eyes averted from the scanty wisps of straw upon the ground which seem suddenly to have been a ludicrously inadequate costume of pretence. Resignation may be a fine thing, but it is only to be praised in a man after his death; for as long as there is life, there is a chance that it will undo itself and nothing will undo itself faster or more furiously.

Insensitive to the reactions of others, Theodore had run down Clewe Street and now, quite unaware of the anxious expression on Mary Ellen's face, he bounded past her and ran up the stairs and burst into his wife's room.

"Katherine! Katherine! What is this I hear?" he said, rushing forward with his hands outstretched and his face glowing. "But this is wonderful. I can hardly believe it."

Katherine lay on the day couch in her room, with her back to the window. Her figure was outlined in the light, but her face was obscured by the brightness of the sunlight shining on the windowpane.

Here she had lain upon two successive occasions and received the excited congratulations of Theodore. The scene was so exactly similar that, had he been in complete control of his powers of observation, Theodore might still have thought that this scene would be exactly like those other scenes, and that if there was any difference, the difference would be in the greater degree of his own delight and Katherine's satisfaction. He rushed forward and was about to throw himself down upon the rug alongside the couch when Katherine stood up suddenly and looked at him, the tears flashing into her eyes and her teeth biting into her pale lip, as if the mere sight of his delight were in itself the sole cause of her own distress.

"What do you mean!" she said. "What is wonderful? Do you mean to say that you can laugh and be delighted when your wife is to be humiliated before the whole town and made into a laughing-stock?"

The tears fell over her eyelids and ran down her cheeks. Her teeth bit deeper into her lip, and to the astonishment of Theodore she threw herself into his arms in a passion of weeping and convulsive sobbing. "Oh, Theodore! Why did this happen to me? Such humiliation! Such a disgrace! I will be ashamed to show myself outside the door. This is the most ridiculous position in which a woman could find herself. Oh, Theodore!"

Theodore was astonished. He could only hold her close in an effort to control her sobbing shudders, and patted her shoulders. His own delight was vanishing, but he tried to catch at the vanishing gleams in order to offer some consolation to his wife.

"But, Katherine," he said, "I thought you would be delighted. I thought you always wanted a son, as much as I did myself." He held her out from him, and began to rouse himself again. "Just think, Katherine, it may be a son!"

But his wife dragged herself free from him as violently as she had flung herself upon him.

"Is that the way?" she said. "Is that how you feel? You're thinking about your own selfish plans and not caring about me. Go away from me. Get out of my room. Men are all the same. Selfish! Selfish! Selfish!"

Theodore retreated backwards, greatly confused at the unexpected assault upon his madly erected edifice of joy. After he had closed the door he heard his wife sobbing but her feelings were still incomprehensible to him.

In the months that followed Katherine's outburst, it was made clear to Theodore in different ways that, although he might be secretly pleased at his wife's condition, it was better not to appear to be so, for there was, after all, something to be said for Katherine's attitude.

The state of pregnancy, although so common, is yet a state that excites more curiosity than the rarest phenomenon. Being a sensible man, Theodore was prepared for evidence of this curiosity as he had been upon the two former occasions, but as the months passed he could not help observing that there was a difference in the nature of the curiosity upon this occasion. The birth of a first child excites a certain sentimental interest in one's neighbours. The birth of the child is associated still, in a vague way, with the love-making of the couple, and all references to the birth have behind them semi-scandalous suggestions that create a pleasurable discomfort in those who are the object of them and a ripe amusement in those who make them. The interest that is shown in the birth of successive children is equally great but, by this time, the interest is more sympathetic, and inquiries are laden with a thousand significances. Curiosity centres now in the health of the mother, the sobriety of the father, the hereditary legacies of the child's ancestors, and the financial adjustments that its arrival will entail.

Theodore had experienced the inconveniences of both types of curiosity, but it was not until he came in contact with a third kind that he realized how preferable either was to the third. For in the arrival of a child, late in life, to a couple who have settled down to bring up their family in the assumption that it is complete, there is something faintly ridiculous. Although Theodore did not realize this at once, as the days passed he was made aware of it; firstly by his wife's continued lamentations, but secondly, and more surely, by the attitude of his neighbours, who strove to hide their curiosity, thereby indicating that the source from which it sprang was not altogether suitable for his inspection. So great was the effort made by the townspeople to conceal all traces of interest in the condition of Mrs. Coniffe that Theodore began to realize that there was perhaps some truth in his wife's suggestions that they were figures of ridicule in the town. Soon he became convinced of this and could not hear a laugh in the street, or come upon a group of people talking, that he did not suspect that he had been the subject of the mirth and the gossip.

But despite all this he retained his original joy in the thought that he might at last have a son, and so he kept up a continual barricade of words between his wife and her own bad humour.

"You are the envy of the town," he told her. "The Costigans are hardly able to bring themselves to speak civilly to me, when I go for the rent. I suppose they think it's a bit unfair that they have been married for twelve years and haven't yet given a sign of justifying their foolishness in having rented a house with nine rooms!"

"They're welcome to their envy," said Katherine, but she was somewhat mollified.

Mary Ellen, too, although well aware of the jokes and nudgings that went on around the town behind Theodore's back, was playing Theodore's game with Mrs. Coniffe. She was continually glancing out the window in search of some excuse for introducing the topic and putting her own construction upon it.

"Look out at that poor thing," she would say when she saw some spinster in the street, "you can hardly tell by looking at her whether you're looking at a woman or doll. She has herself painted up till you'd hardly think she was a human being at all. I like a woman to frizz her hair a bit, and give her cheeks a rub with a rough towel now and again to bring up the colour, but I think that that woman is going a bit too far. It's all very well for a young woman to add a bit of decoration to her countenance—what is it but touching up the colour that's already there?— but when it comes to painting a young look on an old face it's like putting a coat of white paint on a black coffin!" Mary Ellen turned. "Ah! If you're not young inside there's not much use trying to keep young-looking outside." She would give a flick of a duster to the back of a chair, and

29

take a sidelong glance at her mistress. "It must be a great source of annoyance to a woman like that to see a woman like you," she would add, if she thought her point was not made clear.

In short, almost everyone that had occasion to pass down Clewe Street was made an example of one kind or another, in order to impress Katherine Coniffe with the fact that she was a source of envy to the parish, that her condition was evidence of a great youth and elasticity of body and spirit, and that furthermore it would in itself be as good as a guarantee of a further and more unusual stretch of youth in the years ahead.

One day, as a stray tinker cart rolled down Clewe Street and drew up near the door of the Coniffe house, "Look at that tinker woman," said Mary Ellen. "Did you ever see so many children? It's surely a true thing to say that there is nothing like children for keeping the blood young. That woman could hold her own against half the young women in the town and I suppose, judging by the number of children, that she must be over forty at the very least, although no one could tell it from her face or her figure."

Katherine looked out listlessly at the young tinker woman with black untidy hair, and thin firm outline of figure and face, who sat on the cart surrounded by children. The children were mischievous and bold, and the young woman was under constant necessity to raise her hand in a slap, or to reach out and drag back a child by the hair. Instead of betraying irritation or the impatience of age, these gestures were so quick, so darting, and so unerring in their precision, that they heightened her appearance of youthfulness.

"I suppose it does keep a woman young to have a child later in life than she expected one?" said Katherine, half-heartedly. She sighed. "I don't seem to care so much, now, about looking young." She was silent for a few minutes. "Have the girls any idea that they're going to have a new brother?" She went on without waiting for an answer, "I think Sara will be glad. She loves mothering things. But I think Theresa will be difficult. Theresa will be jealous." She looked out the window. "I hate telling them. I suppose they must guess that there is something wrong. And yet I don't want them to be told by some child in the street. Girls are so sensitive. I think that they will be embarrassed." Tears came into her eyes. Mary Ellen was at a loss for words. Katherine leaned her face against the window pane. "No matter what anyone may say, Mary Ellen, this is a humiliating situation for a woman of my age. I no sooner argue myself out of thinking so in one direction than I find that I am humiliated in another way. There are so many things to be taken into consideration. The girls should be sent away soon. They shouldn't be here. They are too young to be of any help, but they are old enough to be curious. They must be sent away, but before they go someone should suggest to them that things will be different when they return. Oh dear! It's going to make a great change in the house to have a young child disorganizing everything."

Mary Ellen listened to the familiar lament, but with the wisdom of those whose knowledge of life has been learned mainly from studying people, she did not make any further effort to offer consolation. Instead she threw out what might have seemed to be a further subject for lament, but which was as skilfully chosen as the ounce of base alloy that goes into the melting pot to produce a good effect upon a fine metal.

"That's true!" said Mary Ellen. "And the worst of it all is that a boy is ten times harder to rear than a girl, and neither you nor I have any experience to help us in the matter."

Katherine brightened up almost beyond belief, and Mary Ellen relaxed.

"Do you really think it will be a boy, Mary Ellen? Sometimes I'm not so sure myself."

" Do I think it will be a boy!" said Mary Ellen. "As I said a hundred times before, what would be the sense of the Almighty having taken his time about sending the child along, if it wasn't to make yourself and the master more appreciative of the boy than you would have been if he came along in the early days. If this child isn't a boy I'll say there is no sense in the world!"

"Ah yes! I'm sure it will be a boy," said Katherine, completely mollified.

"The master is willing to bet me a pound note to a penny that it will be a boy."

Katherine smiled. Her momentary depression was gone. Her spirits were rising now to a point of arrogance. "Keep your penny, Mary Ellen," she said. "Mr. Coniffe is a man who never speculates without having a feeling that he is right. Keep your penny, Mary Ellen."

∽ ∽ ∽

Mary Ellen kept her money in her pocket, which was no more than what the other people in the town did, because although there was hardly a man or a woman in the town that wasn't anxious to bet on the subject there was no opportunity for laying money, because one and all were of the same opinion—that is to say, that the child would be a girl.

"It's well for you, Packy Hand," said Murty Rod one day to a lanky young man who spent the best part of his life sitting on the steps of the cross at the market square, chewing a blade of grass.

"How is that?" said Packy.

"You'll know before anyone whether it's a boy or a girl because it's likely they'll have you up to lay your hand on the child the minute it's born."

Packy Hand's father and mother had been killed by the train one night when Packy was only a small child, and the orphan was thrown upon the mercy of the town. He was pitied and petted by everyone while he was growing up but it passed without notice that he had ceased to grow and now at twenty-seven he was petted and pampered, pitied and protected, in exactly the same way as he had been at seven. He sat most of the day upon the steps of the market cross and only stirred himself to eat a meal. Since there were always several meals offered to him by different families he stirred himself oftener than this might suggest. Apart from the fact that he had been lucky enough to have been left behind in his cradle on the day his parents met their death, he had escaped death upon two other occasions, once by moving away from a wall a moment before it fell, and once by losing his ticket and being unable to travel on a train that went off the rails a mile outside the station. This and the further fact that he had one blue eye and one brown led the people of the town to believe that he was a child of luck, and in consequence of his luckiness he travelled free with all the local teams going out of the town to play a match, and was present at the foot of every wedding table, and upon the occasion of a birth he was often called in to put his hand on the child to bring it luck.

ഗ   ഗ   ഗ

"I'll split my sides laughing at old Theodore's face when he sees it's a girl," said Packy one afternoon as he sat on a window sill at the top of Clewe Street, looking down the street so as to be at hand if Mary Ellen summoned him.

It was a sunny afternoon in early July, and although the child was not expected for a day or two, Packy felt it well to be at hand.

He was talking to Murty Rod the thatcher and Oliver Sims the postman.

"I wonder will it be a boy?" said Murty for the thousandth time that day.

"Here's your answer," said Packy, looking down the street and giving a sudden shout. "I bet this call is for me to give my luck to the child!" For at the far end of Clewe Street, Mary Ellen could be seen standing out in the street waving her arms in their direction and beckoning with her hand. She had apparently been trying to attract Packy's attention, but having attracted it she put her hands to use in beckoning him onward, the urgency of her beckoning increasing the faster Packy moved his legs.

"I didn't think it was expected before next week," said Murty to the postman.

"Neither did I," said the postman. "My wife was certain that it was not due until next week at the earliest. I suppose I had better step over and acquaint her with the news. She's always complaining that although I carry around the news of the town in my canvas bag I never have a grain of it on my tongue!"

"That's a credit to you!" said Murty, idly.

"Oh, it wasn't meant in the nature of a compliment," said the postman sadly as he rose from the steps. "But I'll step across and give her the news; she might like to go down and offer her services to Mary Ellen!"

The postman walked across the street and went into a small house on the left with a slow, lurching walk which would not have drawn any comment from anyone were it not put into immediate contrast by the agitated gait of his wife, who came out the same door with such speed and precipitancy, and with such a short interval between her exit and her husband's entrance, that it might have seemed impossible that he had had time to deliver his news, were it not that the good lady instantly directed her feet in the direction of the Coniffes. She was moreover in such haste that small matters like the tying of her apron strings, the adjustment of her bun of hair, and the unrolling of her sleeves, had to be attended to as she went down the street. As she rolled down her sleeves over her wet, shining arms she shook off wisps of soapsuds that floated in the air behind her, and winked with iridescent gleams before they melted and vanished.

Murty looked after her, and he thought that it was a fine thing after all, that no matter what kind of a tongue she had in her head, no matter what havoc she had made of the life of a poor weedy harmless chap like Oliver, it was a good thing to have women like her around when there was need of a strong pair of arms. She'll be of great service to Mary Ellen, he thought.

Mrs. Sims sailed down the street, and the soap bubbles floated in her wake, but they did not float in a straight line, because on her way she made a curiously crooked progress, calling to the door of at least ten houses; now to one on this side of the street, now to one upon the other side. The purpose of these visits was not long in being revealed because as she sailed forward she left in her wake a troubled street. From every house at which she had stopped, the occupants began to emerge upon a variety of occupations, such as the sweeping of pavements, the cleaning of windows, the polishing of brass knockers, all of which occupations seemed to demand an identical posture and position, for all who engaged upon them faced down towards the bottom of the street, and all proceeded with their work whilst staring upward at the window of the room which was occupied by Mrs. Coniffe.

When, therefore, a short time after he had gone into the house, Packy Hand was seen to come out again, there was a great variety of people in the street and all were anxious to hear the result of the birth. Brooms were laid against the wall, dusters were thrown to the ground, and before Packy had reached the first house after Coniffe's, the occupants of the street were beginning to gravitate towards him as if he were an itinerant pedlar with wares to sell.

"Was it a boy? Was it a girl?"

33

"Did Theodore win his bet?"

"Is it all over, Packy?"

The voices clamoured in Packy's ears. "It's all over," he said. "I held the child for luck."

"The child! Do you hear that!" said Murty Rod. "Don't torment us! Is it a son or a daughter?"

"It's not a son," said Packy, but he said it without a smile.

They all looked at him. They looked at each other. This was the news that was to bring out the barrels. This was the news that was going to cause all the fun. This was the news that was going to give everyone an advantage over Theodore, and make the rent day a cause of silent laughing behind his back. But as the tenants of Clewe Street looked at Packy, they couldn't raise a smile. There was something flat about the news.

Packy began to push through the small crowd.

"Are you not going to tell us any more?" said Murty Rod in astonishment.

"I have to go down to the yard," said Packy. "I want to get straw."

"Straw? For what?"

Packy avoided all eyes. "Theodore told me to get straw and put it down on the street to deaden the noise of carts and the footsteps."

The small crowd broke asunder at once with exclamations of dismay and the people began to go back to their doors. They glanced up once in a while at the window of the room where Katherine Coniffe was lying.

In a short time afterwards they saw Packy Hand and Murty Rod coming down the road leading a horse and cart. The cart was laden with straw from which Packy pulled out tufts with a pitchfork. The feet of the horse were muffled with straw boots. Soon the street was spread with yellow straw and Packy was standing at the top of the street again keeping the children from making noise at their play.

Stillness came down over the street. And then, as if with the deadening of one sense the other senses became active, every action was noted and a significance given to it. A blind raised in a room gave a flutter of hope. A blind drawn made hearts fail.

A thin shaft of wind ran low along the street, and where it had not been trodden flat, the cold yellow straw stirred faintly. In the garden behind the Coniffe house the fragile leaves of a poplar stirred with a thin sound.

Before the sunset faded, Mary Ellen came to the door of the house and busied herself for a moment, her hands raised above her head. Several people watched her from behind windows. When she went into the house and shut the door with a bang the street echoed with the first loud human sound. But upon the door was pinned a true-lovers' knot of black crepe, the stiff ends lifting in the breeze as the loose yellow straw in the street lifted; lifted and fell.

∽ ∽ ∽

Katherine Coniffe left her child behind her; a girl child. The intrusion of tragedy upon the bawdy boards of comedy shut the mouths of the mockers. Theodore himself forgot his disappointment in the new grief of his wife's death. When he came back from his wife's graveside, however, he found that there was a great whispering of women in the hall. They were urging Mary Ellen to have the child baptized at once. It was pale and delicate-looking, and they were afraid to delay the baptism beyond that day in case it might die during the night. But Mary Ellen was afraid to take the responsibility of choosing a name for the child and still more afraid to ask her master for one.

At last Mary Ellen carried the child into the room to Theodore.

"It might be a good thing to have this poor creature baptized," she said.

Theodore waved his hand. "Attend to it," he said, and waved her towards the door.

Mary Ellen paused. Theodore looked up.

"Well? What are you waiting for?"

"It's usual to give a name to the child, sir, at baptism." Mary Ellen was trembling. She had dealt severely with her mistress but she had never come into close contact with her master.

"You can choose the name," he said, and then, as the small creature in Mary Ellen's arms gave a feeble cry, as if in protest against the hazard of Mary Ellen's choice, he relented. "Wait a minute! I'll give you a name for her." He went over and looked into the shawl at the pale face puckered with discomfort. He tried to remember some family names but he could not. The only name that came into his mind was the name of his dead wife and that he rejected without a second thought. Mary Ellen was watching him intently. He began to regret having undertaken to find a name. He put his hand over his face and determined to take the first name that came into his head, but no name came. His senses, however, were active; the silence of the room pressed upon him like a physical weight: the ticking of the clock in the hall seemed to be within his own head; and from around him a strange scent stole closer as the silence deepened. The mind when forced to concentrate at a time when the body is fatigued will often evade its task, and then, suddenly, take upon it some arbitrary task of concentration chosen by itself. As Theodore stood, apparently trying to think of a name for his child, his mind became busy with its own industrious efforts to identify the circling scent that swayed around the room. There was an odour of dust, but that wasn't all. There was an odour of damp from one particular corner of the room; but that was always there. The scent that puzzled him was not all over the room, it only threaded the air in places. At one turn of the head it was imperceptible. At another it pierced the nostrils. Suddenly he knew what it was. It was the scent of the lilies which had been piled up outside the window while the coffin was placed in the hearse.

"Would Lily be a suitable name?" said Theodore.

Mary Ellen bowed with relief, submission, and a desire to move her stiffened limbs.

"It's a lovely name, sir," she said, and she began to back out of the room.

Theodore sat down again in the darkened room. He could hear a suppressed whispering in the passageway and then the hall door opened and shut and Mary Ellen, with the infant in her arms, and a few of the neighbours accompanying her, passed by the window of the room on the way to the church.

Although, at the font, Mary Ellen had been careful to pronounce the name in full—Elizabeth—to Theodore his third daughter was always known as Lily.

The day after the funeral the two older girls were brought back. There was no longer any question of their going away to a boarding school as their assistance was needed with the baby girl.

The evening that they returned, Theodore called them into the parlour, and disregarding their tears he began to instruct them in the new life they were to live.

"You must take your mother's place!" he said to Theresa. "You must help Mary Ellen to bring up your young sister. Mary Ellen is a good girl and she will look out for the child but you will have to let her see that there are others interested in the child."

He turned to Sara. "You must love your little sister," he said. "You must love her so that she will never miss the love of her poor mother." He spoke to them as if they were themselves already beyond need of discipline and correction, and disregarding the evidence of their tears, he spoke as if they were also beyond the need of love and care.

They stood before him, in their black mourning clothes, docile and mute.

A few months before he had been anticipating the day when they would put off school clothes for the gay and pretty clothes of dancing and courtship. Now it seemed that he thrust them at once into the stiff costumes of adult responsibility.

The little girls took up their tasks earnestly, and soon their behaviour towards the baby sister was exemplary. They were serious and good and everyone said that their mother was watching them from Heaven, and giving them wisdom. But nobody seemed to realize that wisdom without

36

experience was a hollow gift. And even so, it was questionable whether their wisdom was altogether unearned, for when Lily at last reached the age at which they themselves had been left motherless, it began to appear that in mothering her, Sara and Theresa had worn their own youth thin.

And as for Theodore, the fact that at sixty-five he had a daughter with her hair still in a plait made him less conscious of years as they ran forward.

∽ ∽ ∽

One afternoon, when Lily, his youngest daughter, was sixteen, Theodore took her in to Draghead to see a dentist. Such jobs were usually undertaken by his other daughters but upon this occasion he had taken it upon himself. As they came back in the train Lily sat in the corner of the carriage with her hand up to her face from which a tooth had been extracted. Lily was an indefinite-looking girl with pale hair and a small pale face which took character directly from the clothes she wore. On this occasion she wore a plain dark blue coat, double-breasted, with plain pearl buttons in two rows from the neck to the waist. Her shoes and stockings were black, and on her tightly plaited hair she wore a straw hat with a dark blue band of ribbon. She was sixteen, but she looked even younger, and then too there is nothing like a toothache for reducing a person's dignity. With her palms pressed against her white cheek, and her blue eyes without lustre, Lily looked even more of a child than she was and Mr. Finnerty, who travelled in the same carriage with Theodore and herself on the return journey, ventured to make a remark which he trusted would not be interpreted by her, but which might amuse Theodore.

He leaned over and patted Lily on the knee. "How are the teeth? Are they better or worse?"

"Better," said Lily, faintly.

"That's right," said Mr. Finnerty. "I think, my young lady, that you'll have worse pains than this before you die." He winked at Theodore.

To his surprise Theodore took the joke coldly, so coldly that Mr. Finnerty was not exactly aware whether Theodore had missed his meaning or whether he had been offended by it, but remembering that he had papers in the pocket of his overcoat, which was on the rack over their heads, he stood up to cover his confusion and began to search for them.

"Would you care to see the paper?" he said, having found them, and tossing one of the papers to Theodore he himself opened out his own paper and, erecting it as high as possible between himself and Lily, began to read. The sight of her irritated him.

Theodore too opened out his paper, but he made no effort to read it. In fact, as Mr. Finnerty had used his paper to prevent him from seeing Lily, Theodore used his to take an opportunity of looking at her without her noticing that he was doing so. For, although he had heard, and understood, and resented as tasteless, the remark of the bank manager, it had nevertheless struck him forcibly that there was some justification for the remark and that his youngest daughter indeed was no longer a child. And, as the trees sped by the carriage window, as Mr. Finnerty rustled his paper, and as Lily herself sat and changed her chin from one hand to the other, and sighed and arranged and rearranged the folds of her blue coat over her thin knees, Theodore sat and stared at her. While he stared he remembered many things that he had long forgotten, or put deliberately out of his mind. He thought of the time before Lily was born, when he used to take Theresa and Sara everywhere with him. They, too, wore blue coats with pearl buttons and white straw hats, like the one Lily wore, and he remembered that he had been looking forward to settling them in life and making good marriages for them. Why had he not done so?

Lily was almost marriageable now. Why had he done nothing for those other daughters who were once as gentle, helpless, and dependent as Lily, and who had no doubt looked forward to the years ahead with hopes that had never been fulfilled? A sense of responsibility woke in Theodore and with it a sense of panic. He came back to where he was and as he stared at Lily, his eyes were anxious and strained, because it seemed to him, for an instant, that the rushing trees outside the carriage window, the sparks flown back from the engine, the rushing sound of the wind through which they travelled, and the pulsing throb of the engine, were all tokens of the speeding years of which he had lately taken such little heed.

"Is there anything wrong, Father?" said Lily, in concern, taking down her hand from her cheek and leaning forward in fright.

But the train had begun to slacken its pace, and with it had slackened the noise, the streamers of air, the rattling wheels, and even the trees outside the steamy plate-glass windows had begun to slacken in pace, till instead of flashing past, their images fell upon the windows singly, stroke by stroke, tree by tree, in a more normal way, as minutes of time strike upon the clock face. Theodore felt that time was resuming its more normal qualities. It travelled once more at a speed with which he could keep pace, but he was resolved, nevertheless, to remember that at times it could fly, and to make up, if it was still in his power to do so, the time that he had lost.

So, as the train slowed up, Theodore, while outwardly intent upon helping Lily to alight, was inwardly concentrating upon the problem in his mind. And then suddenly before his eyes upon the platform there appeared what might be a solution of his difficulties.

∽   ∽   ∽

When the train from Draghead drew up in the station at Castlerampart, there was seldom any stir or excitement on the part of Joss, the solitary porter. He knew from experience that the train rarely disgorged anyone needing his attention. The people who alighted from it were those who had boarded it that morning, and who had no need to be directed to a hotel or to be assisted to a cab. If they had parcels they had made provision for their transport before leaving in the morning, and a variety of children, shop boys, and servant girls stood beyond the white railway barrier waiting to cope with them. The porter stood with his arms at ease, leaning back against the closed doors of the waiting room.

As the train drew in this particular evening, however, and as Theodore was alighting, and helping Lily to alight, Mr. Finnerty, who was still in the train, desisted suddenly in his own preparation for alighting and stared at the platform.

"There must have been a stranger on the train," he observed to Theodore. There, sure enough, when Theodore turned around, he saw that Joss, the porter, was in a most unusual state of agitation. He had unfolded his arms and, after having obeyed a first impulse to rush over to the train itself, had darted back upon a second impulse, and kicked open the door of the waiting room. And, although the doors banging back against the boarded wall of the waiting room nearly drowned the efficacy of his whistle, he put his fingers between his lips and gave a piercing whistle at which the solitary cab horse outside the station gate pricked up his ears and neighed. Then, having attended to these things, Joss rushed over to the front of the train from which by this time it was seen, even by those who had not detected the fact from the previous clues, that a stranger had indeed stepped down on to the platform and was standing helpless in the centre of a pile of luggage, which, besides the conventional pieces of a gentleman's luggage, included several strange-looking green metal boxes, and a fat bulging brief case.

"He's not a tourist. It's the wrong time for tourists," said Theodore, musing aloud, and he looked for suggestions to Mr. Finnerty.

"It's too early for fishing," said Mr. Finnerty, "and moreover, this man has no fishing rod."

Together they stared at the stranger.

Then Mr. Finnerty clicked his fingers together in a businesslike way.

"I know who it is!" he said. "I heard there was a young solicitor coming to stay at the Central Hotel. He had a job in a Dublin office but he thought he'd set up on his own account in a country town."

"But why is he going to stay in the hotel?" said Theodore.

"He's not going to run the expense of an office until he sees if the town is suitable," said Mr. Finnerty.

"Is that so?" said Theodore. "That's a wise precaution. He must have a sound head."

"That's right," said Mr. Finnerty. " Caution is a great thing."

"Yes," said Theodore, absent-mindedly agreeing with a statement which he was about to disprove, at a blow, by his own words the next minute. "It's time we had a new man in the town," he said. "Old Kane is behind the times."

Mr. Finnerty looked back at the young man who was having his luggage carried out to the station cab. "I don't know if you're right there," he said. "Law is an accumulating business. It's experience that counts. Every case a man puts through his hands adds so much to his wisdom. You know your own business, Mr. Coniffe, but as for me, I'd sooner trust myself to an old man than to a young one." As he said this, Mr. Finnerty glanced involuntarily at Theodore's white hair and was perhaps hoping to remedy his tactless error of the train journey by a little subtle flattery but, had he read Theodore's mind, he would have reversed his remark. They were by this time out of the station walking up the town, and Theodore was impatiently waiting for the clip-clop of the station nag to pass them on the road until he should get another glimpse of the new solicitor. He replied rather gruffly.

"If everyone thought as you do, there would be no old men in the country, because they would have starved before they got old." Then, as the cab trotted by, and he caught a glimpse of the new solicitor, sitting up rigid on the seat with one of his metal boxes on his knee, Theodore wagged his forefinger at Mr. Finnerty. "I like the look of that young man and I'm going to try him out. I have a house in mind that I am thinking of buying if the present owners are agreeable, and I don't believe old Kane would get it for me if I was to wait forever. I'm going to put the affair into the hands of this young man. Yes, I'm going to give him a trial. Give youth its chance is what I say."

Theodore had no house in mind, and upon a deeper consideration of the matter he realized that there was, in fact, not a single house for sale in the town, good, bad, or indifferent. Since, however, the real purpose he had in mind demanded, as an essential step in its success, that he should meet the young solicitor with as little delay as possible, Theodore decided that if he could not buy a house he would turn around and sell one.

∽ ∽ ∽

Next morning bright and early, when the birds were singing gaily in the ivy of those houses which were not owned by Theodore, Theodore himself came out of his own door, whistling, and turned in the doorway of the Central Hotel. The door was open but Mrs. Molloy was not in sight, although a number of her hairpins were spilled upon the floor and an old yellow cardigan of hers hung on the hall rack among the hats of the hotel visitors. Theodore stood for a few minutes upon the fibre mat inside the door on which was written the word HOTEL and looked at the large brass bell on the open door, upon which was written the word Press.

Whenever he had business in the hotel it was his custom to walk right in through the hall to the kitchen where Mrs. Molloy was always to be found, superintending the activity around the big kitchen range. On this occasion he felt the need to be more formal, but he hesitated to ring the bell. All bells, knockers, and footscrapers in the town were consecrated solely to the use of strangers. However, he had no need to take such a drastic step, for the kitchen door opened and the kitchenmaid came out into the hall, wiping her hands in her apron. She was a local girl, and when she saw Theodore she smiled at him with good humour.

"Good morning, Mr. Coniffe," she said.

"Good morning," said Theodore stiffly. "I came to see the new solicitor."

"You want to see Mr. Cornelius Galloway?" said the girl, and her mouth opened. "I thought you always did your business with Mr. Kane?"

"Show me to Mr. Galloway's room," said Theodore, "like a good girl," and he gave her a stern look.

The girl raised her eyebrows but she went towards the stairs. "Mrs. Molloy is going to give him the use of the back parlour but we have to clear it out yet—he said there was too much furniture in it. Will you go up to his bedroom, Mr. Coniffe?"

Theodore hesitated again and then he said that he would go up. The girl went ahead of him towards the stairs. Her face was animated and pleasant, and her mood was conversational.

"This way, sir," she said, and she ran up before him. On the landing she waited for him. "Did you know Mr. Galloway before he came here, Mr. Coniffe, or is this the first time you ever met him?"

"I am calling on business, if that's what you mean," said Theodore, stiffly.

"Oh, I thought you knew him," said the girl disappointed. "I wanted to know more about him. He's very good-looking. Did you see him yet?"

Theodore frowned. It suited his purpose that the new solicitor should be a stranger to the town, that he should be poor, that he should be ambitious, for upon each of these things he could count as a help in carrying out his project of securing the young man as a suitor for Theresa or Sara, but that he should be considered good-looking was not necessary. It was, on the contrary, a disadvantage. For, might not a man who was considered attractive by any silly servant that he met upon the stairs, might he not be the type of young man who would have foolish notions about love and romance with which Theodore did not feel that he was capable of contending?

"I'll knock myself," said Theodore quickly, when the girl stopped out-

41

side a door on the front landing, and began to smooth her dirty apron and adjust her cap as a preparation for rapping upon the door. He gently moved the girl aside and rapped on the door himself, and when it was opened he hardly looked at the young man who opened it, so busily fixed were his thoughts upon closing the door so that the girl on the landing would have as small a chance as possible of seeing and being seen.

Cornelius Galloway had brought with him an adequate amount of office equipment, but this had not yet been unpacked and was piled up downstairs in the hall waiting for the back parlour to be made ready, so, apart from the bulging brief case, which rested against the wainscot, there was nothing about the room to inspire the confidence of a new client.

Yet, when Cornelius opened the door and ushered Theodore into the room, he disregarded the details of his surroundings with such complacency that although Theodore was forced to state his business while sitting on the side of a tousled bed, and staring at a wardrobe with a mirrored front which reflected his own incongruous position, after listening to Cornelius for a few minutes he began to feel an infinitely more professional atmosphere than he had ever felt in Jasper Kane's office, where three sides of the wall were lined with legal textbooks, where every available table, desk, and chair was piled with documents, and over the fireplace of which there was a certificate with heavy red wax seals announcing Jasper's claims to the confidence of his clients. Cornelius had a bearing.

Theodore looked well at him, and what had not struck him the night before at the station struck him forcibly in the early morning light, that Cornelius Galloway was perhaps too young a man for his daughter Theresa, or even for Sara, who was two years younger than Theresa. Cornelius was young but he was tall and thin, with a pointed face and sleek black hair. His nose, too, was thin and pointed and his clothes were sober and dark. After a few minutes' conversation with him, however, Theodore began to be reassured and to think that perhaps the difference in age between the new solicitor and his daughters was not going to be as great a barrier as he had thought at first. Cornelius looked young, but his manner completely neutralized his youthful looks. He had an elderly manner.

Anyone who doubted that a young man of twenty-seven could be able so completely to relinquish all the characteristics of youth could be convinced in an instant by introducing Cornelius into a company of genuinely young people, who were young in heart as well as in years, because then it would at once become apparent that youth is not altogether an affair of muscle and bone. In a company of young people Cornelius stood out conspicuously. His height became aggressive. His thinness

42

became austere; his pallor became puritanical, and his long thin nose became condemnatory. In fact, in a gathering of normal young people Cornelius looked like a dismal black crow. His long pointed nose resembled a beak, his black hair lay as sleek as feathers. His height caused him to stoop forward and while standing talking he made a habit of gripping a chair back with his long thin fingers. Add to this the fact that, from nervousness, he had developed a habit of looking away from people while addressing them, and therefore, like a bird, he was practically always seen in profile. The final, impossible touch was added to this impression he made of being like a bird when, having an unusually sharp mind, he anticipated what people were about to say, and darting upon their unfinished sentences he picked them up and completed them, giving one the same sensation of nervousness experienced watching a bird in a cage pecking at bird seed, with a sharp bill that may at any moment peck between the bars and stab the unwary fingers without.

That was Cornelius, and having engaged in a few preliminaries with him, Theodore broached the subject of having a house to sell.

The new solicitor was somewhat astonished at having secured a client so soon after arriving, and so early in the morning, but he began at once in a businesslike way to inquire for particulars of the house to be sold, whereupon Theodore was brought to the realization that, in his hurry, he had not yet decided with which of his houses he could bring himself to part, and he came to an embarrassed halt. Cornelius, then observing Theodore's hesitation in replying, jumped to the conclusion that the sale was necessary to extricate the owner from some pecuniary embarrassment and he tentatively suggested that, if this were the case, there might be some ways of raising a sum of money, if not too large, other than by the drastic method of an outright sale of property. To his astonishment Theodore gave such a vehement denial of the existence of any such difficulties that Cornelius took another look at his client's person, perceiving one or two details, such as the double length and thickness of the watch chain upon Theodore's chest, the silk-sewn clocks upon his socks, and the scent of pomade from his hair, and began to view him with more respect. He disregarded for the moment the projected sale of property, and set himself with a few questions to find out the exact position of Theodore's bank account, feeling that it would be well before he proceeded any further to estimate the worth of this client.

The result of his investigation was highly satisfactory to Cornelius, and Theodore, who was well aware of the purpose in the solicitor's mind, was not averse to having the information extracted from him, but a naturally combative spirit prompted him to make the extraction of the information as difficult as possible. A double service was performed by the questioning, for Cornelius obtained the information he sought and, from the dexterity with which he extracted a large amount of information by a small amount of questioning, Theodore obtained an increasingly favourable estimate of the young man's professional capacity.

Before Theodore left the hotel, the ostensible purpose of his visit had been disclosed to a point at which no further advance could be made until Cornelius had looked into the deeds of the house, and the real purpose of the visit had been advanced even further by the suggestion on the part of Theodore that since those deeds were in his own house and since Mr. Galloway had not yet set up in a regular office, and would be in any case without any of the conveniences of books, files, and folios, the next discussion might with equal suitability take place in Theodore's own house in Clewe Street.

"We'll have the benefit of a bit of fire in the grate at least," said Theodore, with that tone of self-depreciation with which a good host always promises lavishness, while he eyed with distaste the empty grate of the hotel bedroom, in which there were two large firebricks which indicated that if it should become at any time essential that a fire be lighted in it, the width and depth of the grate could be counteracted and the minimum amount of fuel would fit into the place. Meanwhile, no doubt in order to distract the mind of the visitor as much as possible from the original purpose of the fireplace and make such an eventuality as lighting a fire in it less likely to occur to him, there was placed in front of the grate a large blue vase with a high glaze, patterned with red roses, and filled with dried white honesty coated with dust.

"I'll tell my daughters to fix up a bit of a meal for you after the business is over, if you'd care to join us in a bite. A good meal is a treat when you're staying in a hotel. I remember when I was a young man, before I got married myself, that I used to have to hurry past the houses where there was a smell of cooking because I used to be so hungry. You hear people talking a lot about marriage, but, when all comes to all, I often think a man is only half a man till he's married, if it's for no other reason than that he gets proper meals, a good fire, and a warm bed. These are the things a man needs, if he's to get on in the world. What can a man do on an empty stomach?" And then, shortly after having made this remark, Theodore took his leave, satisfied that he had introduced a suspicion of his underlying purpose, but hardly aware that the grain of suspicion had been so large. He had omitted to count on the fact that Cornelius was trained to read the underlying purpose of every remark, and that, after the mention of his daughters, it was necessary only to make a few inquiries in the hotel to ascertain if his suspicions were correct. All that remained in order to turn suspicion into certainty was to see the daughters and see if he was mistaken or not in thinking that the Misses Coniffe were at an age when it was essential that it be not increased by many more months before husbands were found for them.

As for Theodore, he had arranged the affair with such satisfaction in his mind, and brought it to such a successful conclusion, that it was with great difficulty that he kept in mind that in reality the affair was yet in its very early stages.

And when next evening Cornelius arrived, it was with equally great difficulty that Theodore prevented the proportion of time spent on business discussion from becoming subordinate to that set aside for the meal, which was intended to be but a casual snack, but to the preparation of which Mary Ellen and the Misses Coniffe had devoted the whole afternoon.

The time came at last when the business might be considered to have been prolonged sufficiently to justify a respite for one night. Theodore led the way to the dining room.

The table was laid with a large white cloth that dropped to the floor at the sides, and upon it were set the best plates, the pattern of which however was completely obscured by the lavishness of the food upon them. On each plate there was cold chicken, cold ham, and cold tongue, overlapping each other like the petals of a flower and decorated with parsley and blobs of meat jelly.

While Theodore was introducing Theresa and Sara, he was eyeing the table with great anxiety, but when he took his place at the head of it, he glanced at his daughters with an even greater anxiety.

Theresa looked older than her years, he thought. He looked at her critically. Why did she scrape her hair back from her forehead in such a way that every grey rib was revealed? Well! It was frank anyway. Theodore had never taken much notice of what women wore, but he certainly did not like those tight pleats on Theresa's bodice, and the high collar that made her hold her head up stiffer than ever. And why did she wear black? Black was no colour for an unmarried woman to wear. It added years to Theresa. Still—Theodore looked at Cornelius—if a man had any wits he would be able to see that she was not as old as she looked, and what was more, it was not every man that wanted a young wife. A professional man, in particular, needed a wife who would be old enough to look after his interests. He didn't want a soft young woman that would fill his house with children before he knew where he was. Theresa was cut out to be a solicitor's wife. But would Cornelius think so?

When Theodore looked at Sara his spirits rose. Sara looked very pretty. He liked the silky stuff in her dress and the lace collar at her neck. She had a neat head, clouded with masses of soft brown hair that framed a small pale face. She had an old-fashioned look. Indeed her face, small, oval, and delicately pointed, was the kind that would be called old-fashioned by her contemporaries, no matter in what epoch of the world's history it chanced to make its appearance. He saw with relief that there was no grey in her hair, and no sign of wrinkles in her smooth skin. The colour had not gone from her cheeks. He liked the way she sat with her hands in her lap, palms upwards. He liked the simple way she looked from face to face as different people spoke. And yet he was dissatisfied and he felt that although she had every appearance of youth, from Sara, as from Theresa, the spirit of youth had undeniably fled.

Meanwhile the sisters, who had been nervous all day at the thought of having to endure the scrutiny of the new visitor, were made indescribably more nervous when they became aware that they were objects of scrutiny to their father as well. The effect of this nervousness was an intensification of personality until it seemed to Theodore that they caricatured themselves with every word and gesture. He saw that their differences in nature were contrasted with unfortunate effect. Theresa's strong and disciplined mind was revealed with every contribution she made to the conversation. As she spoke in her decisive voice, she made poor Sara seem foolishly ignorant and timid.

Yet this very timidity of Sara's, when in its turn it was revealed, made it seem all at once that Theresa had been unnecessarily strident.

Theodore began to realize that in bringing the young man to the house, and introducing him to his daughters, he had accomplished only half his task. While the meal progressed with stilted conversation, he himself, the only one who would have been capable of introducing a little vitality into it, was fussy with his own thoughts. He regarded the evening as unproductive and was resolved that upon the next occasion when the solicitor came to call there would have to be some important changes. For one thing the meal instead of being elaborate and cold would be simple and *hot*, and furthermore, the conversation, instead of being directed by Theresa, would be guided exclusively by himself into channels that would reveal the fecundity of the exchequer rather than the economy of the executive. He was determined to put all his strength into the next effort.

∽   ∽   ∽

Now Theodore, in resolving to throw all his weight into the task of obtaining Cornelius for a son-in-law, was like a man who, wishing to break his way through a door, musters all his strength together, laces his muscles, clenches his fists, tightens his lips, rises from the floor upon the balls of his feet, and, fixing his eyes upon the panels of the door, throws himself upon it with gigantic force, only to find that the door which he believed to be bolted had not been bolted at all. In other words, Cornelius had not only guessed, but had acquiesced in Theodore's plans. He had not kept up the fiction of discussion about a property that he knew would never be sold in order to gain time for a decision. He had made his decision. He wanted time only to accustom himself to it.

He called upon several evenings, and every evening he left the house with a courteous farewell to the ladies, a pat on the cheek to Lily as she sat struggling with her lessons, and a remark to Theodore that was always the same.

"I'll look up that item we mentioned and let you know the exact legal position in which you stand in regard to it."

Having disciplined himself into never regarding marriage without strict reference to its financial aspect, Cornelius had devoted all his attention to ascertaining the exact financial status which would be occupied in Clewe Street by a son-in-law. Having done this so carefully, and been so gratified by the result of his investigation before he turned his mind to the assessment of his emotional reactions, when the time came for him to consider that aspect he would have found it hard to relinquish the idea no matter what those reactions might be. This was an impregnable position from which to advance to meet Theodore, and Cornelius felt he was to be congratulated upon his self-discipline. There was only one matter to be settled, and that was to make a choice between Sara and Theresa.

Theresa and Sara were at this time, respectively, thirty-two and thirty, and although they might have been said to look more than this a week before the arrival of Cornelius, they looked considerably less than this a week afterwards, when it had dawned upon them that their father was intent on making a match for them, and, although they did not think for an instant that Cornelius would acquiesce with their father's plans, they permitted themselves to joke about the matter. When Theresa spoke of him to Sara she called him "your suitor" and when Sara spoke used the same pronoun with reference to Theresa. But it was all a joke.

As the weeks passed, however, the sisters realized that Cornelius could scarcely be unaware of the idea in Theodore's mind, and if he was aware of it he could scarcely be inimical to it, for where at first it had been two parts business in the small front parlour, as opposed to one part refreshment in the back parlour, the evenings were soon divided into two parts refreshment to one part business.

And then, one evening about a month after his first visit, Cornelius received a present of a large salmon from a country client, and when he did not know what to do with it, and when Theresa offered to have Mary Ellen cook it for him, and when Cornelius would only accept this offer on condition that they all partook of it together, there was an end to all pretence of business, and when Cornelius arrived he came in the hall door and passed the small parlour without a glance and walked straight into the long back parlour where the meal was laid.

Indeed, as a matter of fact, this was not the first time the pretence was dropped, because the night before, when he brought down the salmon to Mary Ellen, he stayed over an hour, helped Miss Sara to wind some crochet yarn, took a glass of milk in his hand standing up at the mantelpiece, and gave Lily some assistance with her sums before he left. Indeed, upon this occasion and again during the meal the following night he made one or two remarks that were considered very significant by Theresa and Sara, who stored them up and thrashed them out afterwards in their bedroom until they yielded their full grain of significance.

"Did you hear what he said to Lily last night when she was doing her home lessons?" said Theresa, as the two sisters were getting ready for bed.

"I saw him helping her with her sums," said Sara, "but I didn't catch what he said."

"He told her that she was counting too much on his help, and that he was not going to help her any more."

"He was right," said Sara.

"That's not all," said Theresa. "Wait till you hear! Lily answered him as saucily as you please. 'I didn't ask you to help me,' she said, 'you began it yourself, and if you've spoiled me it's your own fault, but you'll have to go on with it now.'"

"Isn't she a little bit too forward?" said Sara, timidly.

"Oh, never mind that!" said Theresa. "You'll be glad she was forward when you hear the reply he made! He turned his head aside and his voice was very queer. 'In that case, Lily,' he said, 'I think I shall have to take up residence here'!"

"He didn't say that!"

"He did! And what was more, you'd never guess what he was looking at while he said it?"

"I can't imagine," said Sara, and she clasped her hands in excitement.

"He was looking at the photograph on the mantelpiece!" said Theresa.

"What photograph?"

"Oh, stupid! Which photograph do you think?"

Sara tried to visualize the mantelpiece and visualize the photographs upon it, but she was too confused to do so. All that she could bring to mind about the mantelpiece was the brown velvet mantel border with the fat brown velvet bobbins.

"I don't know," she said, her mouth open.

"Why! The photograph of you and me!" said Theresa.

"The one taken with our hands joined, leaning against the tree?"

"Yes," said Theresa, triumphantly. Then, having moistened her fingers, she stretched out her hand to pinch the wick and quench the candle flame.

"Oh, wait a minute! Don't quench the candle!" said Sara. "I'm going downstairs to get the photograph. I want to look at it again. I wonder what he thought of it. It's ages since it was taken. I hope I'm not awful looking in it. I remember I wore a horrible dress with tight sleeves that day, and they pinched me all the time. I'm sure I looked strained in it." She slipped her feet outside the coverings and was groping for her slippers with her bare feet, while she struggled into her dressing gown.

Theresa left the candle lighted, but she sank down on the pillow.

"You've been looking at that old photograph every day for years, taking it up and dusting it, and yet you don't remember what it looks like!" Theresa stared up at the ceiling. "I can remember it distinctly. I look very well in it. I wouldn't have it there on the mantelpiece if I didn't!"

Sara paused at the door. "I don't exactly forget it," she said, "but you see I want to look at it again to see how it seemed to his eyes," and she ran back and took up the candle and ran out into the passage with it so fast that the flame blew backwards and was very nearly quenched by the draught.

As Sara came upstairs again with the candle in her right hand, and the photograph in her left hand, the door of Lily's room opened.

"What were you doing downstairs?" said Lily, coming out on the landing in her nightdress and bare feet, with her hair all loosened around her face. Her eyes fastened at once on the photograph frame. "What have you there?" she asked.

"You should be asleep, Lily," said Sara.

"I can't sleep," said Lily. "May I come into your room and talk for a while? I could hear you and Theresa talking since you came up to bed."

Sara hesitated. "Well, only for a few minutes, dear," she said.

Before Sara had time to turn the handle of the door Theresa, who had heard her footsteps, called out to her impatiently. "Did you get it? Let me have a look!" But when Sara appeared, followed by Lily, Theresa frowned. "What are you doing out of your bed at this hour?" she said, addressing herself to Lily. "Where are your slippers? Where is your dressing gown? Do you want to catch cold and be a nuisance to everyone?" She ran her eyes over Lily, travelling from her bare white feet to her tossed hair, that spread around her shoulders in a golden mist. "I thought you plaited your hair at night. Do you mean to say you sleep with it all loosened out around your face like that? It's most untidy!"

"It looks pretty, though," said Sara, and she lifted a strand of it in her hand.

"Pretty!" said Theresa. "I don't see anything pretty in it. It's untidy and unkempt and I'm sure it's a great waste of time teasing and tatting it out in the morning. Go back to your room, Lily, and plait it tight, before you get into bed." Lily looked at Sara.

"Let her stay and talk for a few minutes, Theresa," said Sara. "She can't sleep."

"I don't wonder," said Theresa. "No one could sleep with that cloud of hair about her face. Do as I say, Lily. Plait your hair nice and tight and you'll feel fresher and cleaner and you'll drop off to sleep at once."

Lily glanced desperately at the dressing table.

"Can I plait it in here with your comb?" she said.

"What is the matter with your own comb?"

Lily hesitated for a second. "The teeth are broken in it."

"I don't wonder," said Theresa again. "When you don't keep your hair sleek and tidy at night you can't expect a comb to remain unbroken very long. It would break any comb to pull it through snarled hair. Go back and use your own comb. I don't want mine broken!"

"She could use mine," said Sara, but Theresa cut her short. She said no more to Lily, but looked at her, and under her gaze Lily began to back towards the door. Just at the door, however, with her hand on the knob, she paused.

"I wanted to tell you what I heard in school today," she said, with a slightly pouting expression.

"Never mind till tomorrow," said Theresa, but even Theresa's clear strong voice was drowned by the sudden excited exclamation of Sara, who hunched up her knees in bed and spoke simultaneously with Theresa.

"What did you hear?"

Lily looked at Sara. "About Mr. Cornelius . . ." said Lily, and she began to come back into the room. Theresa opened her mouth, but Sara looked at her.

"Please, Theresa!" said Sara.

"Very well," said Theresa, impatiently, and she looked at Lily to give her permission, but Lily had interpreted the dumb dialogue between her sisters, and giving a toss to her tousled curls, and a laugh of delight, she ran across the room and sprang up on the end of Sara's bed, making the springs squeak and sing, and, continuing to fidget and jump while she told it, she broke into the story that had been keeping her awake.

"The girls were talking about him today in school. They're always talking about him. They think he's awfully handsome—in an awkward kind of way—but today when I came along they stopped talking and some of them got red in the face."

"Why?" said Theresa.

"Oh! Can't you guess!" said Lily patronizingly. "I knew at once. They were talking about you and Sara and saying that he was always calling here."

Sara blushed. "Oh, Lily," she said, and she put her hands up to her hot face.

Theresa hid her embarrassment more subtly, by pretending to be angry. "I hope you put down such talk," she said. "I hope you explained that he came here purely on business!" But over Lily's head, Sara and Theresa glanced at each other, and the glance was mutually appraising. They congratulated each other.

Lily snatched the photo frame from Theresa, gazed at it intently, and then suddenly lowered it and, glancing at her sisters, her eyes widened with a new and excited idea.

"I wonder which of you he will marry?" she said, and pursing her lips and linking her arms around her knees she began to sway backwards and forwards, while she contemplated them with a view to deciding which of them was the more likely to get Cornelius. Lost in her own speculations she did not notice the effect of her words upon her sisters, until Theresa, suddenly catching her by the arm, jerked her off the edge of the bed.

"You are not going to spend the night here," she said. "Get back to your own room," and then turning to Sara she spoke even more harshly. "I don't know why you encourage her, Sara. She should have been asleep an hour ago."

Lily pouted and went towards the door.

"Don't forget to plait your hair!" said Theresa.

"No," said Lily. "Good night, Theresa! Good night, Sara!"

Theresa uttered a curt good night, but Sara only nodded, because she had seen what Lily had missed—the sudden antagonism in Theresa's eyes, and she had felt, what was more disturbing, an answering antagonism in her own heart.

⌁ ⌁ ⌁

From the evening of Lily's very natural query as to which of them would eventually prove the choice of Cornelius, the Coniffe sisters began to feel a rivalry in their own hearts. Where, up to then, they had been inclined to drift into each other's habits, they now began to be conscious of their differences and to accentuate them as much as possible.

And so Cornelius, who had just come to the conclusion that their similarities were so great that his choice between them would be a matter of fortuity in the end, began to realize all at once that there were some differences to be contended with. In Sara he missed the efficiency that he found in Theresa, but the gentleness that was its substitute made him doubt if it was a loss at all.

He could not make up his mind, and finally abandoning all hope of being able to upset the equality of his regard for both of them he resolved to try a different method of coming to a choice, by investigating whether there was an inequality in the regard of the sisters for himself.

At last he decided to go away for a few days. He had an idea in the back of his mind that he might confide in a friend in Dublin. Whether or not he would do this, however, he would at least get a change of air, and when he came back he would have a fresh eye for the problem.

Theodore was at first somewhat sceptical about his going, but having ascertained judiciously that Cornelius was taking no more than a suit case with him as luggage, and that among his impedimenta left behind there were some articles of undoubted value, he encouraged him to go away, guessing probably at the idea in the back of the young man's mind.

The night before Cornelius left, as he said good-bye to the Coniffes, Theodore at the last minute came into the hall after him and asked if he would endeavour, while in the city, to bring back a sample of a certain new tobacco.

Theodore proffered the money. Cornelius waved it away.

"The least I might do," he said gallantly, "is bring back a present after my journey," and then as he spoke he looked back at the doorway of the house where Theresa and Sara were courteously waiting for him to take his complete departure before they shut the door, and the thought flashed into his mind that he would bring them back a present each. Perhaps in their reactions to his gift he might be able to detect their reactions to himself. "I'll do my best about that tobacco, sir," he said to Theodore. To the ladies he raised his hat. And to Lily, who came down the street with a crowd of other schoolgirls, he waved his hand and called out that he would bring home a big box of sweets.

At the thought of his return, laden with gifts, Cornelius felt conscious of a great feeling of generosity. The whole family would be indebted to him. They would look out for him with eagerness, and greet him with warmth. He felt that he was already one of the family.

"I must not forget anything," he said, and taking out his notebook he made notes in it.

Tobacco for Theodore. . . . Sweets for Lily. . . . He must on no account forget them. But what to bring Sara and what to bring Theresa he could not decide. The new problem began to absorb the interest of the old problem which it was to assist him in solving.

Cornelius spent only three days in Dublin. Once or twice the thought crossed his mind that it was foolish to have come. He had not much money to spare, and time hung on his hands. On the third day he had persuaded himself that his boredom with his own company was a desire for the company of the Misses Coniffe, and that day he took the train for home. Moreover he was somewhat impatient to see the effect he would create upon them with the presents he had bought. For Theresa he had bought a small gold timekeeper to pin on her bodice. For Sara he had bought a gold pendant, in the shape of a cross. They were made up in separate packages, and put into green leather boxes, with press studs of mother-o'-pearl. When you pressed the stud, the lid of the box opened and the gift lay before your eyes on a bed of crumpled satin. The crumpled satin fascinated Cornelius and when he fingered it and found that the crumples in the fabric were deliberately made and were kept in position by cardboard which was moulded into mounds and hollows, he was intrigued with this artifice, and on more than one occasion, in the train on the way back, he took out the boxes and snapped open the lids, just to finger the crumpled pearly satin. It is surprising that he remembered to bring back Theodore's tobacco, and not at all surprising that he forgot the box of sweets for Lily.

Yet, when Cornelius called with his gifts that evening there was no one at home but Lily.

"Miss Theresa and Miss Sara are gone out for a walk," said Mary Ellen. "But Lily is out in the garden. Will you go out to her, and wait there till the others come back?"

Cornelius smiled, and was about to slip into the hall when suddenly he remembered that he had brought nothing for Lily. He paused in the doorway with such an air of fright that Mary Ellen stared at him.

"Is there anything wrong, sir?"

Cornelius stared at her. "No, Mary Ellen," he said. "But I think perhaps I won't wait after all." He had an uncertain impulse to go up the town and buy some sweets and return. "I'll come back later," he said. Then he thought despairingly that Lily would recognize the sweets as having been bought in the town. It might be better to confess that he had forgotten them.

Meanwhile Mary Ellen held the door open. Cornelius swallowed and adjusted his collar by stretching his neck.

"As a matter of fact you gave me a fright, Mary Ellen. You see I brought two little tokens to Miss Theresa and Miss Sara. But Lily went completely out of my head and I forgot to bring her anything. I meant to get her a bag of sweets. I was wondering if I could get some in the town and pretend that I brought them with me? What do you think?"

"Oh, don't bother your head about Lily!" said Mary Ellen. "Tell her you lost them. Tell her you left them after you on the seat of the train. Tell her anything and she'll believe you. She's only a child. Don't fret yourself over Lily!" Mary Ellen could see no cause for concern at having to disappoint Lily. "She's used to disappointments," she added, as Cornelius did not seem reassured, and seeing that he was even less so after this remark, she ventured another—"You can promise her something instead. There's a circus coming to town next week. Tell her you'll take her to the circus." Cornelius brightened.

"That's right, Mary Ellen, I could do that. I could take her to the circus." He was sure that this would please Lily, and he felt it would be fun to have an excuse for going to a circus himself. Having forfeited most of the pleasures of youth, he had an unusually retentive memory for the pleasures of childhood.

He stepped into the hall, Mary Ellen was reassured. She looked at him slyly. "If the young ladies heard the whistle of the train they won't be long about returning!"

Cornelius laughed. "They didn't know that I was returning tonight."

"They may not know," said Mary Ellen, "but they'll want to find out, won't they?"

Cornelius laughed again.

"Lily is in the garden!" said Mary Ellen again. "You know the way out!"

"Yes, of course," said Cornelius, and he went down the passage towards the back door that led to the garden. The door was open, and at the end of the darkening passage the garden showed bright and radiant like the far end of a tunnel, although, outside too, the traces of evening were coming.

כ   כ   כ

The evening was coming, but not yet. The sky was darkening but the garden was still bright. Of the lavender shadows that fell upon the clouds, only the palest shadows had crept into the crevices of the shrubbery. Cornelius stepped into the garden and stooped to feel if the dew was on the grass before he crossed through it to the lower end where he thought he saw a figure sitting on a bench.

Lily was sitting on a green garden bench, and she did not hear Cornelius coming. She wore a lavender dress that was simple and unpatterned, and Cornelius noticed absent-mindedly that the skirt was sewn with fine tucks from the waistband down to the hem, which came just to Lily's knees. Her hair, which was not plaited, hung down over her face on either side, and this, together with the fact that she was straining her eyes by sewing in a bad light, made him forget the ceremonies of a visitor.

"You'll hurt your eyes, Lily, if you keep working in this bad light. What are you doing?"

Lily looked up briefly. She took no notice of the fact that Cornelius had returned before he was expected.

"I don't care if I hurt my eyes!" she said, but all the same she pulled the thread out of the needle and bending down she drew out a chocolate box from under the bench. From the box she took a piece of yellow flannel and into this she stuck the needle. She had been sewing little squares of linen, with pattern stitching. On one square she had a sample darn. Upon another she had a few sample rows of backstitch and cross-stitch and featherstitch.

At sight of the chocolate box Cornelius became uneasy for a moment, but Lily was so distracted with some grief of her own that he didn't need to worry. She had apparently forgotten that he had ever gone away.

"Won't you sit down?" she said, when she had put away the sewing.

54

She moved to make room for him on the bench. "My sisters will be disappointed at missing you," she said, with half-hearted politeness.

"They may return before I leave," said Cornelius, sitting down, and then hurriedly spring to his feet again, "That is to say, if you will permit me to wait with you?"

"I don't care," said Lily, ungraciously, and then, as Cornelius looked uncertain as to what he should do, she burst out confidentially: "I'm so unhappy, Mr. Galloway. Theresa and Sara are vexed with me. That's why they've gone out for a walk—because I vexed them! Theresa is furious with me. Even Sara is cross! Can you imagine it—even Sara!" The tears came into Lily's eyes.

"Perhaps you'll tell me what it was all about?" said Cornelius, sitting down again. Lily looked at him, doubtfully.

"Theresa and Sara are in the wrong, of course!" she said warningly.

"How do you know that?" said Cornelius, settling in to hear the whole story.

Lily was surprised at his question. "I know they're in the wrong," she said, "because I'm in the right!"

Cornelius, who was looking inattentively at the toe of his own shoe, looked up at Lily and took a good look at her expression before he threw back his head and laughed.

"What are you laughing at?" said Lily. "I think you're very mean!"

"I'm not laughing, Lily," said Cornelius, in between his fits of laughing. And then, unable to stop laughing, he put out his hand appealingly. "Don't be vexed with me, Lily. I haven't laughed like this for years."

"But what are you laughing at?" said Lily, somewhat appeased. Then, when he still kept laughing, wiping his lips with his handkerchief, she looked down at her hands and spoke softly, almost to herself. "I won't tell you anyway. You'd be sure to take my sisters' part."

Cornelius stopped laughing at once. His face looked more stern than ever. "Why should I take their part?" he demanded, almost angrily.

Lily said nothing.

"Why should I take their part?" asked Cornelius again.

Lily felt that her vengeance was sufficient. "Oh, it would be only natural," she said. "You're so much older than me."

Cornelius looked disconcerted. He had expected that she was going to make some remark like the one Mary Ellen had made at the door when he was coming in. That remark had given him a curious pleasure, but a similar remark from Lily would have annoyed him. Even the slight, but admittedly innocent, remark about his age piqued him.

"Suppose you tell me, Lily, first, and then see whose part I will take!"

Lily hesitated only another minute. "It's like this," she began. "I know I'm only sixteen, legally," (Cornelius found it difficult to refrain

55

from smiling again at this deference to his profession), "but I will be seventeen in two months' time. And besides that, I'm much older than my years."

She paused, as if expecting to be contradicted.

"Continue!" said Cornelius, gravely.

Lily sat up straighter. "Well, I was sent an invitation for the Annual Outing of the Women's Sodality!"

Cornelius made no comment. Lily lost patience.

"Can't you see!" she exclaimed. "I must be considered grown-up when I'm invited to the Annual Outing. I wasn't invited last year!"

Cornelius thought that he began to understand.

"Do they want you to stay at home? Does Theresa think you are too young?"

"Not at all," she said irritably. "That's not it. They'll let me go all right." Then her voice became very thin again, and to his astonishment Cornelius saw a bright tear in each eye. "They'll let me go, all right, but they won't let me get a new dress for it."

Cornelius experienced a feeling of relief. "Come now, Lily," he said, "you have several very pretty dresses. I think you could find one to wear at the Outing!"

"You don't understand," said Lily. "All my dresses are short dresses. I want to get a long dress! And they won't let me! They say it's bad taste to wear long dresses before you're seventeen!"

The bright tears welled over and fell. Cornelius did not this time make the mistake of laughing, but he made another equally great.

"It seems a small matter to me," he said. "I should think you would enjoy yourself just as well in a short dress as you would in a long one!"

"I knew you'd take their part!" said Lily, flashing a glance of bitter indignation at him, and feeling an even more bitter indignation with herself for having confided in him.

"I am not taking their part!" said Cornelius sharply. "But I think you could have just as good a time in a short dress as in a long dress."

"That's just like a man!" said Lily. "How could I expect you to understand?" She pursed her lips and tilted her head angrily. "I know the kind of a time I'll have in a short dress! I'll have a lovely time! I'll be sent on messages! I'll be told to stand up and let other people sit down! If there's a chair wanted I'll be sent to fetch it! I'll be asked to pass round the cake! The Committee will make use of me! Oh, I know the kind of a good time I'll have!" She stopped, and then she broke out again, "And on the way if there's no room in the wagonette I'll be asked to sit on Theresa's knee!"

Lily had barely time to wail out the last words before her tears began to fall in good earnest. Cornelius took his pocket handkerchief and proffered it. Viewed from this angle the matter was not so comical, and yet he was reluctant to take it seriously, her dismay was so comical. He forced himself to be serious.

"There must be something we can do," he said briskly. "What about your father? Did you appeal to him?"

"There's no use saying anything to him," said Lily. "Theresa's word is law in this house."

For a moment Cornelius was startled at this definite statement of Theresa's most outstanding quality, which he himself had been inclined to speak of more euphemistically as her efficiency, but he kept his mind on Lily's problem.

"Suppose you had money," he suggested eagerly, "would you buy a dress?"

"I have the money," said Lily, without any eagerness. "I have enough saved up in my black box. It isn't the money that matters. It isn't the money that Theresa and Sara mind." Then, as if she remembered something, Lily looked up at him swiftly. "They are awfully generous," she said. "Don't think anything else. They are the best sisters anyone ever had. They've been splendid to me. They've spent their lives taking my mother's place." Then she grew dull again. "No, it isn't money that matters."

"What is it so?"

"Theresa said 'it's the principle of the thing that matters.' We had a row over it tonight, and the last word she said was that I could make up my mind to wear one of my old dresses or I could make up my mind to stay at home."

"The dress you are wearing tonight is very pretty," said Cornelius. "It's a pity it's not a long dress."

He looked down at it and then, although he had glanced at it casually at first, he looked at it intently, and to Lily's surprise he lifted the hem slightly and examined the underside of the material. Then he let it fall again and looked up at Lily, and as he did so his face was boyish and full of mischief.

"I don't know much about sewing but I have a plan, Lily, and if it is successful we might be able to play a trick on Theresa and Sara." Lily was incredulous. "You could wear an old dress, and still wear a long dress!"

"You don't want me to sew a piece at the end?" said Lily sceptically, looking at him sideways and remembering that he had examined the hem of her dress. "I wouldn't do that. It would look silly."

"No. I was thinking of something more clever than that," said Cornelius. "Have you any scissors?"

Lily picked up the sewing box and took out a diminutive pair of scissors.

Cornelius lifted the hem of her dress again and bending close he pricked the stitching of the lowest tuck, the tuck nearest the hemline. Lily watched him for a minute. When he pricked a few more stitches she seemed to see what he intended. She gave a cry of delight.

"Just a minute!" said Cornelius, and leaving the scissors on the bench, he caught the cloth between his two hands and began to jerk it spasmodically. The stitches loosened and parted from the material. The tuck began to open out. The dress was lengthened almost half an inch.

"Oh, goodness!" said Lily, and she clapped her hands with delight. "I see what you mean. If all the tucks were let out, my dress would be down to my ankles! Oh, how marvellous. Give me the scissors!" And picking up the scissors she began to work with great excitement, pricking a stitch here and there, but in general the tucks needed only to be given a sharp tug and they ripped open.

"I can hardly see," said Lily, as the light failed minute by minute, but she kept on ripping the stitches.

"You'll hurt your eyes," said Cornelius, but he didn't urge her to stop, but only to hurry. "Hurry, hurry," he said once or twice, and while she worked, snipping and jerking the seams of the tucks, his excitement grew and he, too, in the fading light bent closer and closer to the work.

"Only two more to do," said Lily. "I hope the others won't come back for another few minutes."

"They won't," said Cornelius, with the confidence of irresponsibility.

The seconds went by, and as they went, the air darkened and the strange night insects began to issue from the shrubs, but faster than the minutes flew the stitches, ripping and breaking, and leaving little snarls of broken thread upon the grass, and causing Lily and Cornelius to bend closer and closer to the work, to breathe faster and faster, and even to talk and laugh faster and faster with the growing excitement in their hearts.

But once when Lily raised her head to rest her eyes and to take a deep breath Cornelius remembered something.

"Lily, I have a confession to make," he said. "I brought back presents to your older sisters but I forgot to get anything for you." He said it simply and he felt no need to placate her with lies about having brought her something and left it behind in the train.

Lily smiled. "I don't mind," she said.

"I wish I had remembered," said Cornelius.

"It doesn't matter," said Lily again. "I don't mind." She picked up the hem of her dress once more. She began to unpick the last few stitches.

Cornelius watched her. She had behaved so sedately and gravely over the present. She had not acted like a child at all. Of course, she was hardly to be called a child. As she said herself, she was nearly seventeen. He wondered how she would look if her hair was lifted up from her face and piled on the top of her head.

"I am nearly finished," she said suddenly, breaking in on his reverie. And in a few minutes, with her fingers nimbly skipping along, the last tuck was opened out flat and the work was done. "Oh-ho!" said Lily and she pushed her hair up from her face to cool her forehead. The gesture coincided with the thoughts that had been running in Cornelius's mind.

"Take away your hands," he said impulsively, abruptly, almost rudely, and reaching forward he caught up the light strands of her hair in his own hands and gathering them together in a soft mass he piled them loosely on the top of her head. Then holding her hair in place with one hand he strained back from her as far as possible and gazed at the effect.

"Lovely ! Lovely!" he said. "You'll make a lovely young woman, Lily."

Lily put up her own hands, and feeling in the soft hair for the clasp that had held it when it' hung down, she took it out and used it to fasten the new coiffure more securely. Then, moving gently so as not to cause it all to fall around her shoulders again, she took up the large bodkin needle with which she has been working, and ran it into the knot of hair as well as the clasp. Then she shook her head slightly, experimentally. It did not fall, nor loosen. She looked at Cornelius. She smiled at him.

"Stand up," he said, " shake out your dress!" And all the time he watched her face.

It was still the same small pointed face, pale and fragile, that he had seen with indifference so often. He was indifferent to it no longer. The long pale plaits that had hung down each side of it had made it seem too small, too pointed, too immature. Now, with the hair lifted away from it, the true and perfect balance of the face was seen in relation to the slender girlish figure. Like a statue that rests unnoticed on a sculptor's bench, awaiting but one more stroke to release it from the matrix and free it as a work of art, Lily's face needed but the lifting of her hair to show what the town would be most astonished to see, that she had both grace and beauty.

"Stand up!" said Cornelius, standing up himself, and filled with elation.

Slowly, and as if conscious that in shaking out the folds of the heavily creased tucks in her simple dress she was shaking out the lottery of the years ahead, Lily stood up, and catching the ends of her skirt shook it slowly. The tucks had been for a long time sewn tightly down. Many times they had been pressed closer and tighter by the flat-iron; held and thumped and stumped upon the damp ironing board by Mary Ellen's strong hands, so that even now, with the stitches released, they remained for a time in position in spite of the way the girl shook the skirt. Then, as she continued to shake it, the tucks began to give way, heavily and slowly opening, like the tucks in a concertina, and little by little the the hemline went lower and lower and lower until at last it reached her ankles and some of the longer, taller grasses reached up as far as it and striped and etched it like a dark embroidery.

The light had vanished from the garden, but stealing away so gradually from them that they had not felt it going, and the white moths and bright-bodied insects that had come out from the bushes dotted the dusk so generously that they did not notice the flowers fading from vision. Having been so near to each other, and so intent upon their task, they seemed still to see each other clearly, but it was probably only the vision of memory ; the sight of desire.

"You are no longer a child, Lily," said Cornelius. "You are a woman."

He looked about him, for not only the girl, but the garden around, and the night without, seemed to have taken on new qualities. Into the simple garden there had come some new influence.

"Isn't this a beautiful night," he said, in wonder. "I have never known such a night." He looked from side to side. "See the moths," he said once, and was silent again. And when from across the river in the Castle park a night bird cried fantastically, he spoke again, unaffectedly. "How sad that sounds," he said. "How strange, and sad, and beautiful!"

And then, turning back to where she stood, he could not at once see her. "Are you there?" he called out, urgently, for looking away from her his eyes had lost their focus. He could barely see the pale cloud of her dress.

"I'm here." She put out her hand and touched his hand. "It's very dark. We must go in. I think I hear the others coming in through the hall door." He turned and distinguished voices. Then he saw Mary Ellen come into the drawing room with a lighted taper. For a minute she came close to the window and there was a sharp tinkle of glass, but whether she had let the blind cord slap back out of her hand too quickly, they did not know. She must have applied the taper to the lamp because the window square lit up, after that, and her shadow came out across the grass, taller than life and fiercer and more stern.

"We must go in," said Lily, and her voice sounded frightened. Cornelius wasn't satisfied. He wanted to mark this evening out in some way from other evenings.

"I wish I had brought you something, Lily."

The path between the shrubs was too narrow for her to pass him by. She gave him a slight push forward.

"It doesn't matter," she said. "I don't care."

"I care!" said Cornelius, and he stood impassive as a tree. Then he put his hands into his pockets in search of something there. "Lily!" he said again, his voice lifting with excitement.

"Yes?" she said, her own voice rising in faint response.

"Supposing I gave you the presents I brought for your sisters and to-morrow I can get something else for them in Draghead?"

"Oh no! Don't do that!" Her voice was rich and authoritative now. "Don't do that," she repeated more gently, but there was genuine distress in her voice. He took his hands out of his pockets, but he made no attempt to move. This time there was distinctly a sound of voices in the house ; several voices. He felt rushed and confused.

"I want to give you something," he said impatiently, crossly.

"There's no need," said Lily. "I'd like to go inside." She put out her hands, and wishing to push him aside from the path he blocked, she laid her hands against him. The tokens on the chain of his watch rang as they hit together. "Oh dear!" she exclaimed, and he felt her breath in quick gasps on his face. "My finger's caught. Do something!"

He felt for her hand and caught her wrist. At first he did not know what had happened. Then a devastating elation filled him. Her little finger had caught on the gold ring on his chain. The scent, the dark, the beautiful fluttering moths, the stars that were coming out singly above them, all spoke, it seemed, in that moment. Holding her reluctant hand against him with one of his own, with the other he fumbled at the chain until he unfastened the catch that had held the ring upon it.

"I want to give you something. Let me give you this. Keep it," and pressing the ring deep down on her finger, he released her hand.

But instantly she dragged it off. "A ring!" her voice rang with dismay. "You're mad. I couldn't take that! Surely you're losing your senses." Here was the wise, the sane, the adult one.

Where was the disciplined man, with calm ambition and ordered voice? Who was this reckless, impatient young man, who ran his hand through his sleek hair and tossed it, and left it tossed?

"Lily," he cried. "What have I been thinking of? How nearly I missed you! To think that it was only by chance that I found you!"

"Let me go!" said Lily, although no one held her.

"Let you go!" He caught her by both of her slender wrists. "Let you go? Never! Never!"

Just then the door opened and a long shaft of light streamed out into the garden.

"Lily, are you there? Is there anyone with you?" Theresa stood, silhouetted in the doorway. Behind her, Sara was standing trying to rise on tiptoe to see out into the darkness. "Mary Ellen said that Mr. Galloway called!" said Theresa.

"You shouldn't have kept him out in the cold air, Lily," said Sara, gently upbraiding. "It's getting chilly. The dew is out."

"It was my fault entirely," said Cornelius, coming forward at once, with some assumption of his cool manner.

Lily hesitated and then, catching her skirts together behind her like a bustle in a vain hope of making them less conspicuous, she came slowly after him into the light.

All at once Theresa seemed to see her lengthened dress and her decorated hair, and more than that, her flushed and excited cheeks. But Sara, with a worse position for seeing, seemed yet to see into the very heart of the change that had come over Lily and, when Lily suddenly ran forward and burst into tears, it seemed that Sara's arms had been outstretched to receive her all the time.

Cornelius looked at Theresa. "Can I have a word with Mr. Coniffe?" he said, and he was stiff and forbidding, like a total stranger.

"Certainly," said Theresa, and she motioned him towards the front parlour.

He went forward in the dark hall to where the light spilled out from under the parlour door. And as he went he heard Theresa bending down to shoot the bolts in the garden door, and he heard Lily sobbing and he heard her saying over and over again :—

"I didn't mean it. I never dreamt of such a thing!"

He went along the passage and put his hand on the handle of the door, calm, resolute, well aware of the hurt and injustice of his actions, and of the pain and disappointment that he had caused, but fortified, upheld, exalted by the feeling that a force greater than himself had swept down upon him, and imposed its own will upon his sightless designs. He had been ready to make sacrifices for the sake of his ambitions. As a reward it had been revealed to him in a single moment that there were no sacrifices to make.

ᔕ ᔕ ᔕ

Under other circumstances, it might have been advisable to delay the wedding of Cornelius and Lily indefinitely, on account of her extreme youth, but owing to the sense of strain in the house in Clewe Street, the wedding date was settled, and the ceremony took place two weeks after Lily's seventeenth birthday.

The young couple left by train for a brief honeymoon. When they returned they were to take up residence with Theodore for a short time, until a suitable house could be vacated for them in the town.

It was assumed that they would return by train as they had departed, but on the morning of their arrival Theodore got a note from Lily to say that they would arrive some time in the afternoon, and that they were coming by road.

"They are hiring a coach!" said Theresa. "This is only the beginning! You mark my words, Father, that man will give himself luxuries with the money that you could hardly be persuaded to spend upon necessities!"

"We mustn't jump to conclusions, Theresa," said Sara, gently. "They may have borrowed the coach."

"I don't see why they couldn't travel in the train like normal people."

"Now what difference can it make to you, Theresa, whether they come by train or by coach!" said Theodore testily.

"It doesn't make any difference to us, Theresa," said Sara, timidly. It was to Sara that Theresa turned.

"If they were coming on the train there would be plenty of time for us all to sit down to supper together before Vespers, but if they come by coach, there is no knowing what time they will arrive, and I, for one, am not going to stay at home from the church to cater for the inconsiderateness of others!"

Sara stood rebuked. Theodore looked at Theresa.

"There's no need in the world for you to stay home from the church, Theresa," he said. "I'm sure Sara will be glad to stay home."

"That is a matter for Sara," said Theresa, stiffly.

Sara hesitated. "I'd love to stay at home, Father. I'm sure if it was anything else but church I wouldn't think twice of going, but it seems disrespectful to put pleasure before prayers. Doesn't it?" She looked at her father, and then at Theresa.

"Please yourself," said Theodore, "both of you. But whether you're going or staying be sure to have a good meal laid out for them. And you'd better start getting it ready now, because it may not be after the train that they'll arrive, but before it. I'm going to walk out to the River Bridge to see if there's any sign of them."

It was while Theodore was standing on the bridge waiting to catch a glimpse of the returning honeymoon couple that Colonel Fanshawe passed upon his capricious bay filly; and it was on the way back that he met Mrs. Finnerty, whose tactful dismissal by Mary Ellen from the door at Clewe Street must have seemed mysterious then, but should appear more natural now.

The evening train came in, however, before there was any sign of the coach, and Theresa and Sara, having given the finishing touches to the supper table, left Mary Ellen and Theodore to welcome home the travellers, for when the hour of Vespers came and there was no sign of them, they felt it their duty to set off for the church.

Theresa and Sara had not long left Clewe Street and were hardly in Church Street when old Theodore, who had an ear for sounds even when they were two miles off, went out into the street to confirm his conviction that there was a coach coming into the town. He stepped back into the hallway, and calling out to Mary Ellen he announced that the bride and groom would be into the town in another minute. Then he ran back to the door, and Mary Ellen after him, and by this time even Mary Ellen, who was said to be a shade deaf in one ear, was able to hear the sounds of horses trotting at as festive a pace as would be expected of horses that brought home a young couple from their honeymoon.

"They are passing under the town arch now," said Theodore, as the sounds deepened for an instant, being augmented under the arch with their own echoes. "They are turning into the square!" he said a moment later, when a cloud of sparrows flew up towards the steeple of the church from their more humble perches on the market square cross. "They're coming!" he shouted, as the horses' hoofs began to be less distinct in the mixture of sounds that accompanied them all the time, but which were too faint to be heard until the vehicle was near— a rattling of trappings, a flick of a whip, and a rhythmical creaking of straps that proclaimed the vehicle to be well and lightly sprung.

The next minute it appeared in sight at the corner of Clewe Street, and travelling at such a neat pace that the horses took the curve in a wide sweep, showing off the entire flank of the carriage as well as the frontage which alone would have been revealed had they kept close to the curb.

The carriage was black, in the main, but the wheel spokes, the door panels, and the shafts were painted with so light and so bright a shade of yellow that, although it was laid on with no more than the intention of relieving the sombreness of the black body, it struck the eye at once and gave the impression of a very fancy, very out-of-the-way, elaborate carriage.

From this carriage, out of each window, one at either side of the vehicle, there was a hand extended, waving already in acknowledgment of the waving that they expected would welcome them. Theodore threw up his hand and waved and ran forward to meet the coach.

Before it was brought properly to a standstill the carriage door opened and out jumped Theodore's youngest daughter, clothed in all manner of capelets and feather boas and wearing upon her finger the band of gold that would make such a difference in the distribution of authority between herself and her sister Theresa.

"We're back, Father! Just think of it. We're back!" she said and she hugged him. "Where are Theresa and Sara? Let me kiss them." And she kissed Theodore again, and running back in an afterthought to the other side of the carriage, from which Cornelius was not yet alighted, having engaged himself with putting out Lily's hatboxes and dressing cases before alighting himself, she kissed him too, as if this affection for those whom she had rejoined might not be supposed to make her forget that she now had another, and more immediate, claim upon her love. Then she ran into the hall, her voice coming back like a bell.

"We're back! We're back!"

Theodore, meanwhile, had gone around to the other side of the carriage. But the coachman having scrambled down from the box and piled in his arms the dress baskets and cardboard hatboxes that Cornelius was handing out from the interior of the carriage, it was difficult for Theodore to catch more than a glimpse of his son-in-law, much less shake him by the hand as he made an endeavour to do. Indeed the barrier of boxes was so high it was hard for him to feel they were within earshot.

"I'm glad to see you back," he shouted.

"I'm glad to see you, sir," said Cornelius, but he spoke less loudly, being preoccupied with getting a second armload for the man, who had returned after depositing the first load in the house. As the latter stepped forward, however, Theodore suddenly interposed himself neatly between the fellow and Cornelius.

"Here, give me those boxes," he said brusquely to his son-in-law, and as he bent down he whispered into his ear. "I know those fellows," he said warningly. "They take every step into account when it comes to settling the bill."

"Oh, that." Cornelius had conceded the boxes to what he had deemed a gesture of good will, but at this he adroitly took back custody of the tottering load and gave it to the outstretched arms of the coachman. "Don't bother about that, sir," he said to his father-in-law, as the man disappeared again in the direction of the house. "As a matter of fact every step he takes is a gain for us!" But seeing that Theodore failed to understand the full depth of his meaning he brushed the whole topic aside for the moment. "I will explain later," he said. Then, diving his head into the coach again, he brought out a little flowered parasol. "Here, sir," he said proffering it to Theodore, "if you wish you could take this for me," but as he handed it out he suddenly looked at it more intently and seemed to hesitate. "I don't think my wife ever uses that except when she is driving," he said, looking at it reflectively, as if trying to ascertain which, out of a great number of fairly similar parasols, this particular one might be. Making up his mind, then, with a determination all the stronger for the amount of reflection spent upon it, he took the flowered brolly out of Theodore's hand and threw it back again on the seat of the carriage. "We can leave it there. She will have it to hand when she needs it."

Theodore was startled. "But if someone else hires the carriage before you need it again, won't there be a danger of its being stolen?" he said, and he looked with perilous dread at the flowery parasol.

"Oh, there's no fear of that," said Cornelius, "no one will hire the carriage."

"What makes you think that?" said Theodore. "We may have more than our neighbours, but we are not the only ones to spend money foolishly. Don't think because they could be better advised spending their money on food and clothing that people won't have some to spare for driving around in a carriage. They will! And more often by far than their betters! Give me the parasol; it's better to take it out."

Cornelius coughed, and put his head into the carriage again to take up another armload of boxes.

"There won't be anyone using this carriage but ourselves, sir. I forgot to tell you that I thought it just as well to buy it. What was the good of paying for it in pieces, by hiring it every other day, as we would be doing, and yet this time next year, although we would have paid for it twice over, we would have no more right to stand on the footboard of it than if we had never put pen to paper to the tune of a penny! No! Indeed, that's not my method. The carriage is ours, sir!" And putting his hand on the top box to steady the lot as he passed in the doorway, Cornelius swung around so that his tailed coat spun in a curl as tight as a pig's tail, and disappeared into the open door of his new home in Clewe Street.

When Theodore recovered himself sufficiently from the surprise of his son-in-law's revelation, he made a tour of inspection from one end of the carriage to the other, and there wasn't a strap, spring, or panel in the entire wagon that he did not open, wrench at, or otherwise test to his satisfaction, and as for the door he tried it three or four times to see if the handle was working properly. When he had tried the handle for the fourth time, a field of further investigation presented itself and he stepped into the interior and sat down on the seat, from which place he not only examined the floor, the ceiling, the woodwork and cushions, but examined as well every button upon every cushion to see that all were tight to the leather, firm, well-sewn, and, furthermore, unlikely to alter their condition of perfection for many a year. Every button was tight. Every splinter of the bodywork was perfection indeed, and having failed to find a flaw in the carriage, old Theodore decided that it would be somewhat churlish to find fault with the man who, having had the recklessness to purchase a carriage, had still the good sense to choose one that was flawless and irreproachable.

Theodore sat in it a few minutes more, wondering at the temerity of his son-in-law in having spent so much of his father-in-law's money without consulting that father-in-law. And he wondered if perhaps he had misjudged the indications of Cornelius's thin face and had married into his house a man with more tendencies to spend than to make money. But his final feeling was one of pride. Here he was for the first time sitting in a coach of his own. It was a thing that he would never have contemplated buying, thinking that to do so would be to put himself above his position, and make himself a cause of laughter to his contemporaries. But it was a quite different thing altogether for his married daughter and her husband to have bought such a vehicle. And so, old Theodore swallowed his last misgiving on the price paid for the article, and upon the independence of this son-in-law in buying it without consulting him, and gave himself over to a last review of the coach, viewing it now, not as a critic, but as a fond possessor, and gradually the smile that had covered his face while he was waiting for the return of the couple came over his face again, and leaping down from the coach as lightly as his youngest daughter had leaped from it a few minutes before, he went into the house to hear news of the festive tour.

As he stepped into the hall, however, Theodore had to stand to one side abruptly as a figure came down the hall against him in the gathering dusk, but no sooner had this other become aware of Theodore than he in his turn sprang back against the wall.

"After you, sir," said the coachman.

The coachman? Theodore was rooted to the spot. He had forgotten the fellow. He glanced back through the doorway and the horse he had forgotten . . . the horse . . . he felt a nervous trembling in his limbs. Here were matters of more concern than the coach itself. The coach wouldn't have its hand out every week for a salary. The coach wouldn't eat them out of house and home. A moisture gathered on his brow and he glanced from the horse to the man and from the man to the horse. The latter looked as if it would know what to do with a queer lot of oats. "Though I must say the animal shows what he eats," he thought, with an involuntary flash of pride in the horse's glossy flanks. The man was another story. However, he turned and deliberately looked him up and down. But the coachman was a bit meagre in build. He didn't look as if he put away much food. Anyway, that was something. Old Theodore bent forward. He had not noticed the cut and dash of the fellow—black and yellow? Old Theodore peered close. Against his will he could not but feel an admiration for the finish that Cornelius put upon everything he did. Then, too, this fellow of his was certainly civil. He was pasted as flat to the wall as a shadow. With a shrug Theodore suddenly decided to avail himself of the fellow's civility. He passed down the narrow hallway and before he had reached the end of it the excitement that had filled him at first sight of the rapidly rolling yellow spokes had returned again with an unaccountable rush. Or had it something to do with the sound of happy voices in the back parlour through which there ran insistently all the while the little silver bell of Lily's laughter?

ᔐ ᔐ ᔐ

As the Misses Coniffe turned into Church Street, Sara thought for an instant that she heard a carriage echoing under the arch of the toll tower, and she mentioned the fact to Theresa.

"I think I hear a coach!" she said, slackening a little in her pace.

"What if you do?" said Theresa, without slackening her pace. Sara hurried to make up the lost inches.

"I thought that it seemed impolite to be out when they returned."

"I thought that we went over all that this morning," said Theresa, "and that we made our decision."

"Oh yes," said Sara, "but don't you think it makes a difference when they are *within hearing*?"

"I don't," said Theresa, "and anyway the church is *within sight*!" They were just nearing the church gate. "I know that I wouldn't turn around at the church gate and turn my back on the altar for anyone. But you may do as you please. You may feel differently about things. All consciences are not the same, I understand!" And saying this Theresa turned in the gravel path to the side-aisle door. Sara hesitated, but only for an instant, then she set out after Theresa once more at a brisk pace, and by the time they reached the side-aisle door she had put all her scruples behind her, and upon her face that was lifted eagerly forward from the frill at her neck, there was the same expression of satisfaction as that which had been upon Theresa's face since they set out from Clewe Street, and as they both reached out their hands for the holy water in the cold stone font, it could be seen from the vehement way they sprinkled the water right and left that they were not putting much penance upon themselves by this attendance at church.

The fact was that their nightly visit to the church constituted a major pleasure in the lives of the Misses Coniffe.

It is said that the number of poor plays, vaudevilles, and concerts that can continue to collect a crowd night after night owe their success almost entirely to the fact that women like to dress up and sally forth at night, no matter where they are going. The Misses Coniffe always wore their best clothes to the church "as a mark of respect."

This habit of churchgoing had developed long before the advent of

Cornelius, but there is no doubt that after the disappointments of his advent, they threw themselves into their nightly visits as into the only consolation available.

Although to both Theresa and Sara religion compensated in great measure for the fact that they were unmarried, yet for each one of them that compensation took a different form, and corresponded almost exactly with the pleasure that each would have derived from the state of marriage.

The strong example by which Theresa would have upheld a husband and family was not lost entirely for want of them, because as leader of the Women's Sodality she was tireless in the example she set to the rest of the congregation in such matters of devotion as the strict discipline of the eye, constant and rapid activity of the lips, and above all, in the inflexibility of her adherence to an upright posture while kneeling, a posture that allowed no modification either in the way of resting the arms upon the back of the pew in front or in allowing the hips to lean for support upon the seat of the pew behind.

Miss Sara, on the other hand, had she been married, would never have had time to think of setting an example, so busy would she have been with small fussing cares for the physical well-being of her family. This fussing care was not lost, however, any more than the upright example of Theresa, for as chairwoman of the altar society, Sara had taken upon herself, to the infinite relief of the town matrons, the laundering, darning, and general repair of all the altar linens and cloths. Upon this duty she lavished great zeal and devotion, and with the residue of her zeal she emptied and filled the flower vases, cleaned and polished the brass candelabra, and occasionally gave old Luke Humphries the sacristan a hand with straightening the pews when they had slipped out of line.

In consequence of these duties, the Misses Coniffe were privileged to remain in the church each evening, when the rest of the congregation had been reminded that it was time for them to depart, by such hints from the sacristan as the rattling of keys, the shutting of the side doors, the removal of flowers from the altar, and finally, the quenching of every candle except the one in his hand. When the church doors were shut Miss Theresa repaired to the sacristy and sat there at work upon the membership list for the Sodality, and Miss Sara busied herself with going from pew to pew with Luke collecting all beads, prayerbooks, and mortuary cards that had been lost during the day, and placing them on the high window ledge, where they could be seen and identified by the owners on the following Sunday.

On this particular evening Miss Theresa was in the vestry, working upon the Sodality list, and beside her on the table were a roll of red

69

silk ribbon and a box of medals. The ribbons were to be cut, and a medal sewn to each strip, to make ribands for the new members of the Sodality before Miss Theresa left the vestry. Therefore she did not pay much attention to the fact that Miss Sara was unusually long. Once she lifted her head as she heard another voice besides that of Sara in the chapel, but they were lowered in whispers and she could not distinguish them. She picked up another ribbon.

The new voice was that of Mrs. Molloy. Under her arm she carried a large prayer book, further enlarged by the insertion between its pages of dozens of holy pictures and mortuary cards. It was swollen and bulging to the resemblance of a large fat handbag.

It was one of these mortuary cards that Mrs. Molloy had lost and which she now came back to retrieve. It was astonishing that she could have missed one out of so many, but to Mrs. Molloy nothing was astonishing, nothing inexplicable.

"I've lost poor Lottie's mortuary card!" she said, calling out to the indistinct figures of Sara and Luke as she sailed down the centre aisle of the darkened church. "I missed it before I reached the gate!" she said, standing up on the front pew and groping on the dusty window ledge. "I wouldn't wish for the world to lose it," she said, retrieving a worn card, edged with heavy black paper lace, bearing a number of indulgenced prayers. "But, do you know"—she stepped down from the pew under the window and advanced towards the high altar, in front of which Sara was standing, having lacked the presence of mind of the sacristan, who darted away in the direction of the side confessionals and who was busying himself with some obscure occupation that necessitated the banging and rebanging of the confessional doors. "Do you know it's most extraordinary the way I missed it. I was walking along and I was looking at the way the gates of the churchyard are peeling for want of a bit of paint and I thought to myself that it was a wonder Father Drew didn't put a shade of paint on the gates. Now there are people who would say that the origin of a thought like that might be to be found in the fact of my daughter marrying a painter, but if you were to pause to consider the construction that would be put on your words in this town, it's seldom or never you'd get occasion to split your lips apart at all, and you might as well have them sewn up, as my poor mother, God be good to her soul, was always threatening on me when I was a child. Well! As I was saying—I was thinking it would be no harm at all, and might be said to be a good thing, if Father Drew was to hire some young lad, not meaning my own son-in-law, you understand, although it's my opinion that more is lost than is gained oftentimes by people being too backward about praising their own, and when it comes to a fine point if you don't do it yourself, others won't either, and if it comes to that, Miss Sara, your own poor mother that's dead and gone might have done a bit more than she did in the way of throwing out a hint about the fortune that would be left to you and your sister, Miss Coniffe, for if she did, you might both be married now and the fortune not rusting below in the vaults of the bank, although indeed, it won't rust for long when your new brother-in-law comes back from his tour, by all I hear—But that's beside the point and no concern of mine, although I wouldn't wish you to think by my saying that, that I regret having given you a hint in that direction, but only a hint, mind you, because he's a fine straight-standing man, and your sister Lily is lucky to have got him, because when all is said and done it's better to marry, no matter what kind of man you get, than not to marry at all, isn't that so?"

Mrs. Molloy rarely gave a person an opportunity of interrupting her by asking a question, but even the broadest bosom cannot hold an inexhaustible amount of breath.

"You were telling me about your cousin Lottie," said Miss Sara, desperately, while Mrs. Molloy was taking a fresh draught of air into her bosom.

"Poor Lottie!" said Mrs. Molloy. "That is true. Well, as I was saying I was looking at the railings and thinking to myself how badly they were in need of a stroke or two of paint . . ."

"And what happened?" said Miss Sara. This was the dangerous part in Mrs. Molloy's story where an apparently limitless number of side currents were waiting, and ready, to sweep her away upon their diverging courses. "What happened?" she said again.

"Well, as I was saying," said Mrs. Molloy reprovingly, "I was walking out the churchyard when I caught sight of the gates, and I said to myself, 'Those gates could do with a splash or two of paint!' Then I began to think of how bright and shining they used to be when I was a young girl. I remembered the day, when I was a child, if we saw a spot of mud on the railings we used to wipe it off with spits on our handkerchiefs. That's a fact. We used to do that! We were always playing around the church—those were the days before the new cemetery was bought—and another thing that we used to do was to walk around the graves back of the church and if there was any moss or dirt on a tombstone we used to get a bunch of grass and wipe it off. We were very particular about the churchyard. We took as much pride in it as if it was our own back yard. The older people used to laugh at us. All except one! And that was a cousin of mine, Lottie by name, who was the same age with my father although she was a first cousin of mine at the same time. Poor Lottie—not that I called her Lottie to her face, ever—I was too young for that, although young people nowadays haven't the same respect for names and Christian names that we had then—poor Lottie used to encourage me. She used to ask me where I was playing, and when I said in the churchyard, she'd say 'You're a good child; and when your poor cousin Lottie goes to her reward one of these days I hope you won't let any dirty moss creep up over the letters of her name on the headstone.' Even after I was grown up Cousin Lottie used to chat to me about the shortness of the time left to her on this earth. She often kept me up in her room for an hour or more showing me her shroud. Yes! Her shroud. She gave an order for one to be made and sent to her, and she kept it in a box under her bed, at the right-hand side so she could reach for it easily if she felt herself slipping away any night before she had time to rouse the house. She kept it in a box under the bed, but she often took it out and shook it and examined it and ironed out the creases and left it hanging up for a while to air. Whenever she did this she used to leave it hanging up till I came in to see her. 'I had my shroud out yesterday,' she used to say to me, 'and I didn't put it away because I knew you'd like to look at it, not like some other people I know who don't seem to remember ever having heard the saying that we know not the day nor the hour!' She used to give a queer, crooked look at her husband Matty when she said this because poor Matty couldn't stand the sight of the shroud, and even went so far, I'm told, as to pass some very disrespectful remarks about it. You could hardly blame him, in one way, seeing that he was a good ten years older than Lottie at the time. On the other hand, seeing that they didn't get on too well together, you'd think he wouldn't mind so much seeing her making her preparations for departure. And such preparations! The shroud was only the beginning. She went further than that. She had a cardboard box fitted up with a cross and a prayer book, and a tablecloth of linen, stiff from the mark of the iron, and a glass bowl and a towel—all the things that the priest would need if he was called in suddenly by someone that might not know the layout of the house, or where to put their hands on what he would need. Now this is a practice that I believe wouldn't be considered out of the way by others, although I myself would as soon think of cutting my own grave sods as I would of bringing myself that close to the thought of my own skeleton. But poor Lottie was never one to do anything by halves and, when she had cross and bowl, sheet, shroud, and corpse pillow all ready and laid out in a drawer, she began to get round her husband to let her order her coffin. But although Matty was a man that didn't draw the line where he ought to have drawn it, that didn't mean that he would go on for ever without drawing it somewhere. He drew the line at the coffin, and put his foot down on it too. There was a regular disturbance in the house for weeks over it all. And although it's not my practice to repeat the gossip of others, there were a good many people that said he should have let her get it and that if she belonged to them they'd be glad to see the coffin carried into the house to remind them of the day they'd be lifting it out again! But talk like that was only jealousy. That's my belief, and when the day did come for Matty to order a coffin for the poor thing the neighbours had good cause to be jealous because, seeing that the poor thing didn't die for a good thirty-seven years after collecting her funeral clothes and death baggage, they had the mortification of seeing better linen and worsteds on the corpse than they had on their own backs, for although everything changes they say there is nothing changes like the quality of textiles and you get no cloth today to equal that which was to be got yesterday. And talking about the change in the quality of textiles, there was a great change in the quality of paper too between those days and our days, and in respect to that article, too, Lottie was not behindhand in getting an advance on the times. When they opened her closet, what did they find, piled up as neat as you like, but a stack of mortuary cards, ready and printed, and a picture of herself on every one of them, as nice a picture as ever was taken of her, standing by the rosebush in her father's garden, years before she ever met Matty much less married him." Mrs. Molloy held out the card for Sara's inspection.

"Look at that black lace edging! You wouldn't get that nowadays. And look at the quality of the paper. There is no date on it, of course, and it doesn't say the age at which she died, but I remember something she said to me once about those things not mattering much if you had as many indulgenced prayers as the card would hold, although now that I come to think of it, it's a great wonder she didn't put a date on them, for she was always of the belief that she'd die before the year was out, every year! Well, anyway, every single one of the mortuary cards was in its envelope and addressed to the different persons of the town who would be expecting to receive one." Mrs. Molloy drew another breath. "Of course, seeing that she lived for so long after all, she might have spared herself the trouble, for the greater part of the cards had to be put in new envelopes, as the people they were intended for were dead before herself. However, there were a few that were still alive and they were sent their cards, although I believe that it was a cause of great consternation to some of them to get cards written in the hand of the woman whose death was announced on them. And one particular person—I won't mention a name because there was talk at the time, of a lawsuit being taken against poor Matty—as if it was his fault!—one particular person took such a turn at the sight of the dead woman's writing that she fell in a fever and was buried three days after poor Lottie herself!"

73

"Well just imagine that!" said Miss Sara, and into her voice she tried to put a tone of finality, as if she believed the story to be finished.

"I was telling you about the mortuary card, Miss Sara," said Mrs. Molloy, and into her voice she put an element of reproach sufficient to cover the hurt done both to herself and to the subject of her story. "I see you're in a hurry so I won't delay you, but I want to tell you something poor Lottie said to me once. 'I hope when I die,' said the poor creature, 'which event I don't doubt will soon take place, I hope that those that receive a card in memory of me will have the consideration to say a prayer for me once in a while. I intend,' she said, 'to have all three-hundred-day indulgences on my card, for I can't for the life of me see the sense in people wasting their time saying prayers that carry only one hundred days when there are others, no longer, that carry three times that number. Can you?' she said, looking at me. 'Don't be talking of dying, Lottie,' said I to her. 'I will talk of dying,' she said, 'and what is more I'm going to make you promise that you'll never look at my mortuary card without saying a prayer for me. Will you do that?' " Mrs. Molloy drew a deep breath. "I gave the promise," she said.

"Oh, a good promise, a good promise!" said Luke Humphries, who had come up to them at that point, in despair of Sara Coniffe's ever bringing the story to an end. But Mrs. Molloy fastened on him at once, and snatching up his words she wove them into the story to make it longer still.

"That's true for you, Luke Humphries," she said. "A good promise, but one, I regret to say, that has been defeated. Yes, defeated; and by the very thing you'd least expect—the black lace edging the poor creature put around the edge of the card! You see it was a bit awkward——" Mrs. Molloy lowered her voice on the last word, and then, in case she might be thought to belittle the dead, she hastened on, "In poor Lottie's day things were done on a lavish scale and the prayer books were as big as Bibles, and they left room, and to spare, for the lace edgings on the cards. But nowadays the prayer books have shrunk away to nothing, and the mortuary cards likewise, and poor Lottie's card wouldn't fit in my present-day prayer book, so there I had to put it into this out-of-the-way prayer book that I seldom or never use. But, here's the curious thing!—when I was coming out tonight I took a notion and what did I do but rummage for the old prayer book and brought it along with me. Now what made me do that, do you think? I have no doubt it was poor Lottie's soul trying to have a word with me. I have no doubt at all. But we are poor weak mortals at the best, and the dead have their work cut out for them trying to communicate their thoughts to us, for although I brought the prayer book with me, I didn't open it anywhere near the place

where the mortuary card was inserted and I never saw the card, nor
thought of it either, but just read a few gospels and then when I
looked around me I saw Luke putting out the candles on the side
altar, and I stood up to go out, because I'm not one to be anxious to
jump off my knees at the first excuse but against that again I'm not
one to stay praying on in the stench of the dying candles, delaying
people like yourselves that are giving your time to such matters. I
suppose that was the time that poor Lottie's spirit must have caused
the card to slip out on the floor. And still I didn't notice it! I went
out without saying as much as a prayer for poor Lottie although it
might be said to be her only chance of one prayer for a long time, for
I was thinking going out the churchyard that although times were
changing for the worse in most respects, the change in the size of the
prayer books was not one of the worst changes, and that I'd never
bring out this great awkward book with me any more. Poor Lottie
might never have got another prayer from me till the day I'd die—
and then, think of the shame I'd feel when I'd meet her face to face!
But thanks be to God, just at that moment I caught sight of the
church gates, and I thought how badly they needed a coat of paint, and
from that my mind jumped to the way I used to wipe them with my
handkerchief when I was a child, and from that my mind jumped
to thinking of the way we used to scrape the tombstones clean with
bits of grass—and then!—all of a sudden I remembered Lottie; like
a flash you would say, I went over all I'm after telling you, and I
remembered my promise. I opened the prayer book! There was no
sight of Lottie's card! I spit on my finger and turned over every page
but there was no sign of it! I ran back here, as you saw, and stepped
up on the pew to see if it was on the window ledge. And it was! Did
you ever hear anything stranger than that? Did you? And yet there
are people who will tell you that the dead are dead, and that they have
no powers after they go down in the clay!"

Mrs. Molloy drew herself up. "There you are! The dead have their
own ways of accomplishing their wishes. They may not be able to
speak but they have other ways. Depend upon it! Take my word for
it! They have their ways." And having come at last to the end of her
narrative, she brought into effect the gift of the second-best orator;
that is to say although she had not the salt of brevity with which to
season her story, when she came to the end of it she broke off with
such abruptness that even those most desirous that it should end were
disconcerted that it should do so with so little warning.

"Poor Lottie!" said Mrs. Molloy. "May the Lord have mercy on
her!" And saying this she dropped upon her knees, got up again, and
wheeled towards the aisle. "Good night to you both," she said with a

certain shade of severity in her voice, as she caught a glimpse of the clock in the sacristy and realized that half her night had been wasted, talking to the only two people in the town who had little or none of the small coinage of conversation with which to repay the prodigality of those who had.

᠎᠎᠎᠎᠎᠎ ᠎᠎ ᠎᠎

When Theresa and Sara came back from the church, although it was not very late, the bridal couple had retired for the night. It was the sisters' custom to drink a cup of hot water before retiring, and as they were waiting for the kettle to boil they sat in the back drawing room and discussed the adjustments that would be necessary in the house, but as Theresa spoke, she often stopped in her sentences and waited impatiently, with an expression of exasperation on her face, because, overhead, the ceiling occasionally shook, as Cornelius crossed the floor above, going from the dressing table to the chest of drawers, from the chest of drawers to the wash-hand basin. Every sound from overhead was an irritant that called forth a comment.

"We should not have given them that room. The floors in these old houses are not fit for heavy men's feet trampling them down. We'll have the ceiling down around our ears one of these nights!"

To Sara, however, the sound of Cornelius's feet brought no irritation. Perhaps she felt grateful that, having had the bad fortune to lose him as husband, she had gained him as a brother. Instead of crushing her affection for him she had set about adjusting it to his new relationship with her. Once or twice, however, she shivered slightly when the ceiling shook, although it was Lily's light feet that she heard running across the floor overhead. Another time she heard a chair turned over in the room above and there was a lot of laughing.

When the hot water had been drunk, and the cups rinsed at the sink, the sisters went up the stairs themselves. They were going quietly and without speaking until, suddenly, in the dusk, Theresa in passing the door of Lily's room struck her foot against something on the floor.

"What is this?" She held the candle up and peered down. On the mat outside the bedroom door there were two pairs of shoes, one pair of large tan shoes with strong, sturdy toes and heels, and a small pair of black calfskin shoes with high heels and pointed toes. "This is going too far!" said Theresa. "They were allowed to make this their home, but they need not think that they can make it an hotel!"

"Perhaps they forgot," said Sara. "Perhaps they thought they were still away. I'll give them a rub of the brush and we can speak to Lily privately in the morning."

She was stooping to pick up the shoes. Theresa caught her arm.

"You'll do nothing of the kind," she said, sternly. "Leave them there. When they find them unpolished in the morning they'll take the hint, and not leave them out tomorrow night." She drew herself up. "In the meantime I don't intend to let this pass. I see a light under Father's door. He's not asleep yet. I'll step in and tell him about this. It's a good opportunity to let him see the liberties that that man will take if he's given too much freedom. I was looking for an opportunity like this to say something of the kind to Father; to give him a warning. There are some people and the more you do for them the more they expect." She lowered the candle and advanced towards her father's door, but just as she reached the door, Theresa once again struck her foot against something on the floor, and at the same moment she thought she heard a smothered giggle from Sara. Looking down Theresa saw that outside her father's door, in the centre of the mat, were her father's muddy boots with which he had taken his bedtime walk in the garden. He had seen Cornelius's shoes and instead of adopting the attitude that his eldest daughter would have expected from him, Theodore had considered it an excellent idea and one from which he could profit himself.

To understand the sense of effrontery with which Theresa, and Sara too, although to a lesser extent, had suffered upon seeing the shoes and boots left outside the doors to be cleaned, it must be understood that in families of their class in almost every other town in the country, although there was always a servant, and often more than one, to do the services of the house, to cook, to clean, to serve the meals, to answer the door, and to do a thousand services in running from one room to another, from the attic to the cellar, it was the custom that these services must be in the communal interest, strictly dedicated to the running and ordering of the house, and that no personal services were to be expected by any member of the family as an individual. Hence, although the beds were made, the slops emptied, and the rooms dusted, the members of the family neither expected, nor thought of expecting, that anyone but themselves should carry up water if a bath was wanted. The womenfolk automatically rolled up the soiled sheets for the servant to wash, and threw them down over the banisters every Monday morning, but it would never occur to them to include their own stockings and underwear. These they washed out by themselves in their hand basins, and for the washing of them also, as for a bath, the hot water was carried up by themselves in a zinc bucket. The men expected the fires to be set, the grates leaded, the hearth swept, and the fire lighted, when the day began, but if they came into the room and the fire had gone down, it would not have occurred to them to do anything other than throw a coat over their shoulders and go out to the yard for more coal. And as for expecting Mary Ellen to blacken their shoes for them, not one of the Coniffes would have entertained such an extravagant thought.

The only time that such families became aware at all of the fact there was a class of society above as well as below them in life was upon the occasions when they saw some person exacting personal service from another. On the rare occasions when the Misses Fanshawe came into the town and Miss Theresa Coniffe saw their groom attending on them, retrieving a fallen glove, or hurrying to open a door for one of them, she always sniffed.

"She hasn't the strength to turn a door handle!" she said. "He had to hand her her pocket handkerchief! It's a great wonder to me that she has the strength to blow her own nose!"

Holding that view, it was of course a great shock to Theresa that Cornelius should leave out his shoes to be cleaned, and that Theodore encouraged him was utterly intolerable.

As the weeks went by, however, it became apparent that Cornelius had a totally different view from Theresa of the purpose for which money might be spent, and upon one or two occasions he pointed out to Theodore that there was only one real difference between people like the Fanshawes and people like the Coniffes themselves.

"And that difference is money! You don't need to tell me!" said Theodore, repeating one of the stock remarks that were used by everyone in the town when confronted with some evidence of the difference between their own manners and customs and those of the county families.

"I don't mean money!" said Cornelius, frowning at the interruption. "I have reason to know that your income, sir, is equal to that of Colonel Fanshawe, and that your capital is greater! The only difference there is between him and yourself is in your attitude to your money; in the uses to which you both put your money! With his money he has bought leisure and comfort for himself. He lives in a fine house and he has surrounded himself with beautiful things. He has not spent the money recklessly because his property represents a good sound investment, in which his capital is safe, and from the work of the farm land, and the setting of his cottages, he has a good steady income. Yet, because he is not ashamed to be seen in enjoyment of his money, he has shown an independence that has won the respect of the town. Even you yourself, sir, although you could buy and sell the man, are forced to respect him more than you respect yourself, and when he rides into town on his horse, you are flattered if he speaks to you. I think sometimes that it's a wonder that you don't raise your hat to him like Murty Rod and Packy Hand!"

The bluntness with which Cornelius made these remarks might perhaps have incensed his father-in-law against him had not his accidental reference to Colonel Fanshawe's horse stirred up some faint remembrance of that disdainful beauty's rolling eye the day that he had met herself and her rider up on the bridge some weeks before, and caused him to see a justice that he might not otherwise have seen in the remarks that Cornelius made about Fanshawe's arrogance and his own obsequious manner.

"Now take my office," said Cornelius, because it was apropos of which room he would apportion for his use that the topic had arisen on this particular occasion. "Take my office! I do not intend to have it become a stuffy place, with an accumulation of dusty and useless documents, like old Kane's office. I intend to keep my room more like a study; a calm, quiet place. I can never understand why it is considered likely that a client will be inspired by seeing evidence of a hundred other cases that are being dealt with at the same time as his own. I should imagine it would be quite the reverse and that a client would prefer to discuss his affairs in a calm and orderly room that looks clean and empty." Cornelius paused. Then he continued speaking rapidly. "And I do not think that I will put up a brass plate. What is the necessity for it? The town is not very large. People will know where I am, as well as who I am, without a plate on the door." As Theodore was about to say something, Cornelius put up his finger. "Consider it this way," he said. " A man may decide to buy a pair of shoes because he sees a good pair hanging up outside the shoemaker's, but it is not like that with law. A man will not enter into litigation just because he sees a brass plate on a wall."

Theodore scratched his head. "You know your own business," he said. He had been secretly looking forward to the brass plate. "But how will people outside the town know that you are a solicitor? Kane's practice is kept up more by the people outside the town than it is by the people inside it."

Cornelius had intended coming to this. "There's no need to worry, sir," he said. "I intend to make myself well known in the county "—he paused—"but not exclusively as a member of the legal faculty. I intend to become well known socially, and you'll find that according as people see that I am a person of integrity in private life they will automatically see that I have claims to their respect as well in my profession."

"I see your point," said Theodore, but it was quite clear that although he may have seen the point, he could not see beyond it.

"Take that coach I bought," said Cornelius. "Even that was a step forward. It lets people see that one is not to be dependent on others, that one is not afraid to spend today if it means a saving tomorrow, and above all that one has not a false opinion of the value of money. In short, it lets people see that I know what I owe to myself. Then there is this house! It is very well built, and I would like some day to have it as an office, but as soon as we can have a house built in the country I think that Lily and I should get out of town. Living in a town is in itself an admission that one attaches too great an importance to money-making. You should live in the country yourself, sir. In fact I am surprised that you have not moved out of the town long before now. I think that when Lily and I are having a house built we might as well make it a sizeable place, and all move out there. What do you think, sir?"

Theodore, however, was not thinking. He lived in an age and in a class in which it had been considered wise that the more money you made the less evidence you showed of it. Theodore would not add a new footscraper to his doorstep until he had made several judicious references to the dirt and mud that was carried into the house. He would make it clear to the whole town that the carpets were being destroyed and that if a new scraper was not bought there would be the expense of a new carpet. When the scraper eventually appeared, therefore, it would be an object of more commiseration than resentment, and instead of being envied for having it, Theodore would be pitied for having had to spend money upon it.

The Coniffes were so sensitive about appearing wealthier than their neighbours that when Theodore wanted to buy a new house he went to extreme lengths to justify himself for further augmenting property that was already large. Sometimes it was made clear that such and such a house was bought because, being next door to such and such another house that he already owned, the risk could not be taken of letting it pass into the hands of someone who might neglect the roof, or the painting, let ivy grow on the walls, or let it deteriorate in any way, since the deterioration of one house in a row could spread to all the others. Almost every new property acquired was therefore a cause of commiseration on some score or another until the townspeople quite lost sight of the fact that the new purchase indicated that the dividends from Theodore's previous investments were getting so big that it was necessary to convert them into capital again. When Cornelius came along therefore, with his plans and his notions for this improvement and that, Theodore suddenly saw that he could allow Cornelius to take the blame for all future extravagances and yet he, himself, could have the enjoyment of them.

"I don't know what this son-in-law of mine will turn his eyes to next," he said, when Cornelius bought an estate outside the town, and began to make plans for building a house upon it. "I don't want to cross him for Lily's sake."

And so the townspeople shook their heads and pitied Theodore every day, as he went out to superintend the clearing of the land and the laying of the foundation stones of a house in which he took more delight than Cornelius himself. And Theodore was grateful for their pity because it was expressed in prayers and blessings, and he knew that their envy would have been expressed in sneers and curses.

"Nothing will do these young people but pure cut-stone granite for the house foundation," said Theodore to Father Drew when the priest walked out with him one evening to see the house. "I'll be robbed."

"I hope the young couple will be grateful," said Father Drew. "I have no doubt they will. They ought to be happy in such a fine house. I have no doubt they will."

When Father Drew was gone, Theodore laughed.

"Be careful of that stone," he said to Packy Hand, who was giving the regular workman a little assistance. "Be careful of that stone, it carries the priest's blessing!"

There was one person in the town, however, who saw through these subterfuges of Theodore's, and that was his daughter Theresa. She was not deceived by his pretence. She knew that he was secretly pleased at this indirect way of asserting the claims of his money without breaking any of the customs of the town. She was worried, but she kept silent until the day Cornelius suggested that it would be a great help to him if he had a horse, and a great help to his reputation if he rode to hounds.

"If I were seen at the Hunt meetings I would attract the right kind of clients. Shopkeepers and poor farmers are not worth the trouble of catching their custom. I want to attract a different type of client. And I know where I can get a good chestnut filly for very little."

"You want to ruin us! That's what you want!" said Theresa, who came into the room unexpectedly in time to hear the end of the proposal. "You want to spend every penny we have. My father may be a blind fool—but I am not. I see what you're aiming at!"

"Who's a blind fool?" said Theodore, bristling at once, and swinging around to face his daughter with fury and indignation.

Theresa defeated her own purpose. She had provoked her father's anger against herself. Given a little time to consider the situation, there is no knowing the way he might have reacted to the new proposal, but in turning his anger upon herself Theresa had caused her father to become the ally of his son-in-law, and so before the young couple were four months married, Cornelius possessed, as well as the carriage horses, a thoroughbred chestnut mare with white fetlocks, a touch of white on the face, a longish mane, and a devilish temper.

෴ ෴ ෴

Two weeks after the Willful Filly was led into the yard, she threw Cornelius going over a ditch, and fell and rolled on him. The Master of the Hunt, Colonel Christopher Fanshawe, and three grooms, brought him home on a cart covered with coats.

"It's a shocking affair," said Colonel Fanshawe, standing in the narrow hallway, after breaking the news to Theodore. He was greatly at a loss for words. "This is the first fatal accident that I have ever seen on a hunting field, and I'm riding to hounds since I was seven years old!" He paused. A new aspect of the accident occurred to him. "You have to be bred to hunting," he said, " I always heard that said."

The grooms shuffled their feet and were glad of an opportunity to speak.

"That's right," they said. "You have to be bred to the hunting."

At the time that all this was taking place downstairs, the three sisters were sitting in Theresa's room which faced on the street; Theresa and Sara were sewing, and with their heads bent over their work they had not seen Colonel Fanshawe coming down the street. Lily was not sewing but sitting on a hassock at Sara's feet. She was turning over the pages of a catalogue that had come that morning from a furnishing establishment. When the knock sounded on the door below Lily was the first to look up.

"Oh, that couldn't be Cornelius home so early," she cried, but on the mere possibility that it might be, she threw down the catalogue, and raised her head to listen. "I hope Mary Ellen is downstairs," she murmured, getting hastily to her feet.

"Of course she's downstairs," said Theresa, " where else would she be, I'd like to know!" For she read clearly in Lily's flushed face her desire to run downstairs and open the door. Then as there was a sound of footsteps in the passage underneath Theresa took up her sewing again.

"Are you satisfied now?" she asked. "They got in, whoever they were!"

Lily stood irresolute still. For a few minutes she tried to dissemble her curiosity as to who had arrived, but at last she could not hide it any longer.

"I wonder who it was!" she said.

Theresa, to whom this remark had been addressed, said nothing, but Sara, who had only begun to be aware of the strain between the other two, felt compelled to say something.

"If it is anything that concerns us," she said, " Mary Ellen will come up and tell us, I suppose."

Lily turned to her.

"It might be Cornelius after all," she said. "He told me this morning that if they drew Colonel Fanshawe's cover he might be back early."

While Lily was speaking, Theresa had stopped sewing although she kept her head bent. This was partly to hear what Lily was saying, but partly, too, it was to try and catch what was going on below, for her own curiosity, although unmotivated, was not altogether inactive. As she could hear nothing from downstairs however she had been forced to concentrate entirely on what Lily was saying, and on hearing her young sister glibly and familiarly making use of an expression that would have been incomprehensible to all three of them a few months previous, an unspeakable irritation swept over her, and she threw down her work.

"And what if it was Cornelius!" she snapped. "Is that any reason for flying down the stairs two steps at a time? Let me tell you this, Lily Galloway! I may be an old maid but I know that being married doesn't put a woman beyond cheapening herself! Take my advice and don't be in such a hurry running after that husband of yours, or it's a poor opinion he'll have of you in the end; if he hasn't begun to have it already!"

"Oh, Theresa!" Sara half rose from her chair and looked in fright at Lily. But Lily was standing firmly on her two feet, and to Sara's surprise she had her chin held up defiantly.

"There's no fear of that," she said. "There are some people and you cannot make too much of them, no matter how much you try." And then and there she turned on her heel and ran over to the door. "It must be Cornelius," she said. "In any case I'll go downstairs; it's not very pleasant up here!"

Far quicker than Theresa, Lily's ears had caught the sound of voices below, and resting on the security of having her husband's support, she made for the stairs.

When Lily ran down the first flight of stairs however she paused on the landing. There were men's voices in the hall all right, and she could hear Theodore's voice among them. But she did not hear Cornelius. He must be getting out the decanters, she thought, and going down another step or two, she inclined her head in the direction of the dining room, and no sound came from there. Lily hesitated once more. Then to her relief she heard her father call Mary Ellen. She stood.

"Mary Ellen!"

Lily's lips parted slightly and she put her head to one side. Did she fancy it or was his voice peculiarly weak—old? And why was Mary Ellen not going to him? There! She heard Mary Ellen go into the hall.

"Mary Ellen." No. She did not fancy it; his voice was plainly odd. "Mary Ellen. Go upstairs at once and prevent the girls from coming down."

Lily put out her hand and caught the banister rail. Prevent them from coming down? There was something wrong. A strange beating started in her head. She clung to the rail and waited to hear more, unable to stir a step. Mary Ellen too must have been stunned for Theodore spoke sharply.

"Why are you standing there!" he said. "Do as I tell you at once. Keep them upstairs until I call you."

Lily came to her senses suddenly. Forgetting all that had gone before, her one thought now was to get back to her sisters. Turning around, not waiting for Mary Ellen, she ran up the stairs again and burst into Theresa's room.

"Theresa! Sara! There's something the matter. Something has happened!" she cried, and then incoherently she tried to repeat what she had heard.

Theresa and Sara sprang to their feet. Lily's confusion, more than her words, made them feel there was something wrong, but when a minute later Mary Ellen ran into the room what she had to say was no more enlightening than what Lily was stammering.

"Just a minute. Keep calm, both of you," cried Theresa, and upon Mary Ellen at least Theresa's words had some effect, for a great strain had been lifted from her upon discovering that whatever was the matter, the sisters had some inkling of it, and it was not left entirely to her to tell them about it.

"Not that I know myself," she said, turning in answer to Theresa. "All the master said was that I was not to let you downstairs. 'Keep them upstairs, Mary Ellen,' he said. Those were his words."

Sara sank back into her chair.

"Oh, it's something dreadful," she cried, and she put her hands up to her face.

Theresa, however, made for the door.

"Such nonsense," she said. "If there's anything wrong I should be down there." But as quick as Theresa got to the door Lily got there before her.

"Perhaps something happened to Cornelius," she said. "I'll go down too."

All at once an idea occurred to Theresa. She caught Lily by the arm and held her back. Then she turned to Mary Ellen.

"Just a minute!" she said. "If there was anyone needed my father would have sent for me. Tell me, Mary Ellen. Who is down there? Did you see anyone? Who was that who came in a few minutes ago?"

Then without waiting for a reply to any of her questions she turned to Lily with a cold and meaning look. "It may be," she said slowly, "that something has occurred that it is not suitable for us to see!"

"Why! What do you mean, Theresa?" cried Sara, starting up again and putting her hand to her heart. At the first hint of trouble she had been ready to faint, but this suggestion of something unusual acted upon her like *sal volatile*.

"I mean what I said," replied Theresa, and she looked directly at Lily.

"I don't know what you're talking about," said Lily, "but I suppose you're hitting at me!"

"Why should you think that?" Theresa asked, measuring out her words slowly and carefully. "If what I suspect is true then we'll all suffer the shame of it." She turned back to Mary Ellen again. "Well," she said impatiently, " did you hear me asking you? Who is down there?"

Taken by surprise Mary Ellen stumbled to get out her words this time before Theresa interrupted her again.

"I hardly took time to look," she said, "but I think it was Colonel Fanshawe."

Theresa smiled.

"I thought so!"

"What did you think?" cried Sara and Lily together.

Theresa ignored them.

"Was there anyone else?" she demanded.

"There were three other men," said Mary Ellen, "I don't know who they were." Then she thought for a moment. "I think they were three grooms," she said.

The smile on Theresa's face deepened.

"I think I know why my father didn't want us to go down," she said, and this time she addressed herself to Sara. To Lily she turned as if on an afterthought. "You may go down if you like," she said. "Perhaps after all it might be as well for you to accustom yourself to such sights!" She moved away from the door.

Lily stared at her.

"What do you mean, Theresa?" she begged pitifully, but instead of opening the door she moved back a few paces from it nervously. "What does she mean?" she cried to them, turning to Sara, to Mary Ellen. But they too were ignorant of Theresa's meaning although they had begun to suspect that it was unpleasant whatever it was.

Theresa meanwhile had sat down again and taken up her sewing.

"Colonel Fanshawe, you said, Mary Ellen?" she queried, as if absently, and then she made a soft murmuring sound, a kind of humming to herself, as much as to say there was something queer about that fact in itself.

A small flicker of pride came into Lily's face.

"Cornelius must have asked him home," she said. "He said that he intended to do so——" she faltered suddenly—"but he meant to our new home, I suppose."

"Oh, no doubt," said Theresa. "And I suppose he intended to invite Colonel Fanshawe's grooms!"

Lily bit her lip.

"I forgot the grooms!" she exclaimed.

"Well, I didn't," said Theresa. "As a matter of fact that was what first made me suspicious. Tell me, Mary Ellen, did you see nothing of Mr. Cornelius down there?"

Mary Ellen suddenly felt she was being made use of by Theresa to torment Lily.

"No!" she said shortly.

"You didn't hear his voice?"

"No!"

"That's rather strange, isn't it?" said Theresa, looking at Lily. "If Cornelius brought his friends home with him it's a wonder Mary Ellen didn't see anything of him."

Theresa, however, was dragging things out too much. Lily moved over to the door again as if she would be driven to end her suspense by going downstairs. Theresa was forced to shorten her method. "It looks to me," she said, " as if it was Colonel Fanshawe that brought home Cornelius, not Cornelius who brought home Colonel Fanshawe!"

For a minute no one understood what Theresa meant. Then all three of them understood at once. Sara and Lily glanced at each other startled. Then Sara glanced away and her eyes sought Mary Ellen's. But Lily faced Theresa.

"How dare you!" she said. "How dare you suggest such a thing. Cornelius never touches a drink. Why, even at our wedding he didn't even touch a drop of the port wine."

"That's nothing! That doesn't prove anything at all. There is always a first time for everything. And it's those that are least used to it that make the worst fools of themselves when they start."

But Lily only cried out her disbelief again.

"It isn't true, it isn't true," she cried, and to the astonishment of all of them, but particularly of Sara, she stamped her little shoe on the floor. "It's not true, it's not true, it's not true." And then, relying on the fact that no matter in what condition she might find him, unlike the others she had a husband downstairs to back her up, Lily stamped her small foot on the floor again and went one further with defiance.

"Even if it was true," she cried, " what business is it of yours, Theresa Coniffe?"

With that, tossing her head, Lily ran out of the room.

When she got outside the door, however, feelings that Lily had hidden from her sisters rushed into her heart. Just the same she continued to go down the stairs. But this time again she had gone no further than the first landing when a voice called out from below. It was Theodore again.

"Is that you, Mary Ellen?" he asked, calling up the stairs.

"No, Father, it's me, Lily. I'm coming down."

From below there came an exclamation. Then her father called up again. "Don't come any further," he cried in a voice that made her, against her will, stand still. The next minute he was coming up the stairs to meet her, his face so strained and drawn that she put out her hand reassuringly and patted him on the arm.

"It's all right, Father," she said, "there is no need to hide anything from me."

Theodore looked up somewhat confused.

"Did Mary Ellen go up to you?" he asked. "I didn't think she knew."

Lily's heart misgave her.

It must have been true after all what Theresa had hinted. She looked at her father. He had stretched out a hand to her, but she remained where she was, only raising a little on her toes to try and see beyond him; only elevating her head a little to try and hear if there was any sound in the lower rooms. But when she could neither see nor hear anything she looked down at her father with a pitiful expression on her small white face.

"Where is he, Father?" she said, trying to speak lightly. "Theresa guessed what was the matter, you——" She came to a halt, hating to bring out the words. Then she was determined to put a face on things, but she spoke so low he could hardly hear her. "She said there probably were refreshments served at the Meet and that——" she halted again and then hurried on—"and that perhaps Cornelius took a little too much; that it went to his head; that he——"

She said no more. Theodore waited to hear no more. With one step he was beside her, and he caught her in his arms.

"My poor child," he said, "my poor child."

At the same time there was a sound in the hall underneath them; a sound of strange people talking in loud voices and calling out orders to each other; orders that were incomprehensible to Lily.

"Mind! Mind! Watch out there!" said one voice.

"Gently. Gently," she heard another say. "Leave him down there till we see what arrangements have been made."

"Father!" she screamed.

"Hush! Hush!" said Theodore.

"It's Cornelius!" she screamed. "Let me go to him. What happened to him?"

But Theodore held her fast.

"Not now," he said. "Not now. You can do nothing. Later. Later. You can see him later." His voice was urgent and strong, but as he felt her relaxing in his arms his voice sank again. "My poor child," he said, and his tone filled her with terror. For another minute she stared at him as if she did not comprehend. Then as there was another sound in the hall she started back and put her fingers in her ears.

"Go upstairs. I'll be up after you," said Theodore. "I must go down now." He turned rapidly and went down the stairs, but at the foot of the staircase he turned around again and looked back, and when he saw her still standing where he had left her, directing his voice beyond her, he called up the stairs.

"Theresa! Mary Ellen!" he called, and then he had to turn and attend to the men in the hall.

Upstairs the three women had begun to be restless and curious, but until Theodore called neither Sara nor Mary Ellen dared to stir. Immediately upon hearing their father's voice, however, both sisters ran out on the landing.

"What is the matter, Lily?" cried Sara, even before she reached her young sister, but when she tried to put her arms around Lily, Lily drew back. Sara stood helpless. Then she looked over her shoulder.

"Hurry up, Theresa," she cried. "Hurry up for goodness' sake. I think she's going to faint."

But after the first glimpse she got of Lily when she came out on the landing, Theresa did not need to be told to hurry. With a rush she was beside her.

"What on earth is the matter?" she cried, and then, regretting but never doubting her own suspicions, she took Lily's arm and shook it. "Don't take on this way," she cried. "It's not the end of the world, you know."

"The end of the world?" Lily's face lit for a moment with the light of some secret thought within her. "Yes, that is it," she said, " the end of the world." And she gave such a strange moan that it could not be distinguished as either laughter or sobbing. Theresa got thoroughly frightened. Like Sara, but more awkwardly, she tried to put her arm around Lily. She had been unkind to her. She sought eagerly for some way to make up; to compensate her for the way she had treated her. Then, remembering that ever since Lily got married, she had treated her in the same way, as if she were no longer one of them, as if she were cut off from them, as if she were no longer a member of the family. Theresa tried in one rush to undo it. She would undo it. After all, it was Cornelius Galloway who was the stranger. She would draw Lily back from him into the Coniffe bosom.

"Never mind, Lily," she said, and forcibly she put her arms around her. "Never mind. Men are all alike. How dare he do this to you; to all of us, if it comes to that. How dare he?" And, as a sound of voices, now muffled, came from below, she raised her own voice in a shrill threat to be heard by all. "Why! I'd think nothing of going downstairs this minute and telling him to his face just what I think of him."

Something told Sara that Theresa had made an error. She did not know what it was but she put her hands across her own lips and stared down over the banisters in dismay. Lily looked down too but with a different expression. She looked back slowly at Theresa, measuring something in her heart, for her gaze was distant and secretive. Then all at once she gathered herself together, and summoning all the poor ragged scraps of courage that she had, she shook off Theresa's arm.

"Is that so?" she cried, and she pointed suddenly down the staircase with an imperative gesture. "Why don't you do it, then?" she cried. "Go down and tell him. Go on!" Her voice near the end broke into a scream. "Go down and tell him!" she screamed, and before Theresa, or the others behind her, had realized what was happening Lily Coniffe had put out her small cold hand and slapped her oldest sister across the side of the face. The next moment it seemed as if night had descended with a rush, for she tottered, put out her hand to grope a way, and, were it not for Mary Ellen, would have fallen on the stairs.

The radiance that shone over Lily was gone. Indeed, it had shone about her but so short a time it was almost as if it had never been. In the obscure days that were to make up the rest of her life, the short hours spent with Cornelius had been but as the summer lightnings that flutter for an instant in the sky ; now come, now gone.

As the long day passed, after the accident, it seemed that everywhere Theodore looked there was evidence of the failure of his son-in-law. There was the new coach in the coach house, and the coachman. There was the furniture for the new house. There was the foundation for the new house. And then, too, there was the Willful Filly stamping her foot in the stable.

A feeling of nausea came over him every time he remembered the words of Christopher Fanshawe—a man must be bred to horses. When those words came back into his mind, with them there came a remembrance of the odours that had emanated from the clothes of the huntsmen, and even from their grooms; a slightly scented, slightly camphorated odour of cloth preservative from their coats, mixed with odours of valet cream, saddle soap, and the faint by not unpleasant smell of sweat from a clean body. These odours began to symbolize something unattainable, for when the body of Cornelius was brought home covered over with the jackets and coats, gladly volunteered by members of the Hunt, from these coats there exhaled the same odours, while from the splattered clothes that were taken from the dead man, despite the racking they had received, it seemed to Theodore, as he threw them in a heap in the kitchen, that there was only an odour of newness, the smell of some tailoring establishment.

Cornelius was dead, and with his death Theodore felt that his son-in-law had been exposed as a sham, but the only sham that was exposed by the death of Cornelius was the one by which he had been deluding himself when he thought that the only difference between people like the Coniffes and people like the Fanshawes lay in the different uses to which they put their money. That this was not altogether so was shown by the way that Theodore and his family sank back at once into their old way of living. They had been bred too long in a servile tradition. Of Cornelius himself, however, it would have been true to say that money alone prevented him from leading a life of grace and dignity. In some characters Nature can accelerate, in a few years of perceptive adolescence, the effects that are not usually achieved without centuries of breeding and tradition. Many young men may have felt themselves in the same position as Cornelius, in fact cities are full of such young men, who feel that they were born for better things, but to most of them this is only a cause of hopeless despair and bitterness. They throw themselves into some literary or artistic movement, where they can eventually persuade themselves that their poverty is Revolt, and that their squalor is Reality. Cornelius was not one of these. He kept his ambitions clear in his mind, and he never lost the courage with which to pursue them. By failing to realize his ends, however, he had to lose the credit for many sound qualities.

After the death of her husband, Lily's authority was gone, she was dependent now in a way that she was never dependent before. Theresa found relief for her old resentment in glossing over the brief marriage as if it had never been. The privacy of Lily's room was no longer regarded. The sisters came in and out once more without knocking, and Mary Ellen was instructed to take away the second pillow that wasn't needed any more.

And once, when Theresa was particularly irritated, she said that Lily might just as well take off her ring, that it was only a mockery. "You might as well give up putting on airs as a married woman when you have no more to show for yourself than a band of gold on your finger. It makes me sick to hear people calling you Mrs. Galloway. Mrs. Galloway! You're as much Lily Coniffe as if that bragging pedlar had never darkened the door!"

Even Sara referred to her once or twice as Miss Lily. It was quite by accident, of course, but accidents that happen too frequently are indistinguishable from habits.

And Theodore, although he was not hard enough to be unkind to Lily, was not kind enough to prevent Theresa from deputizing for him in that respect. One day, however, when Theresa made some reference to Miss Lily, Theodore surprised her by pulling her up short.

"Give her her proper name," he said.

"I forgot," said Theresa.

"Well, you'd better not forget again," said Theodore. "In a month or two more it will look very strange to be calling her by her maiden name! You'd better take her to see the doctor!"

Birth and death. In the common pageant of human history, how monotonously these mummers appear. And when a man's life is over how few are the scattered incidents that will remain in the memories of those who survive him. They are not much more detailed than the brief records that would inevitably remain in the archives of town hall and church. Little remains of what the heart experienced in the indistinguishable moments. The story of each day is lost in the story of the parish. The story of the parish is lost in the national story, and even that great story is lost itself, in the immensity of the great story of the universe, until, like the leaf on the stem, the stem on the bough, and the bough on the tree, all, all, leaf, stem, bough, and tree, are lost at last in the immensity of the forest in which each had yet played its indispensable part.

From servants' gossip, young Gabriel Galloway will hear snatches of remarks about the past, but from the fragments of this gossip how simple the lives of those who went before him will seem! They will not give him any help in unravelling the complexities of his own life. They will not provide any deposit of experience from which he can supplement his own inexperience. They will only serve to accentuate the confusion of his own life. The pattern does not show up well until the carpet is worn.

PART II

Gabriel

SUNLIGHT flashed into the room as the clouds flew before the early sun. Tendrils of light played over the white ceiling, reflected from the water in the flower vase before the home-made altar on the mantelpiece. Master Gabriel Galloway, aged six years, opened his eyes and sat up in bed. He listened for a few minutes to hear the accustomed noises from downstairs, the shunting in and out of the dampers in the kitchen, the wheezing of the pump in the yard, and the tapping of his grandfather's stick on the flagged hall.

None of the usual sounds greeted him, and, although he cocked his head as he had seen a terrier do, in moments of doubt, he felt no better acquainted with what was going on downstairs than when he had first opened his eyes, so he kicked back the heavy blue-striped blankets, hopped out on the cold boards in his bare feet, and crossed over to the window to see if he could make any estimate of the hour from the scene outside. He stood at the window, small as he was, blocking the sunlight, and under his short white chemise his small flat buttocks were rosy-marbled over by the prickings of the frosty morning air.

"Perhaps I'm awake too early!" he thought, and then he exclaimed, "Oh, my goodness! Mrs. Molloy has let her dog out! It must be very late indeed." Because in Molloys' back yard he saw their spotted black-and-white dog, smelling among the matted grasses for offal. The dog was never let out of his shed until the hotel visitors had taken their breakfast and departed to their daily occupations. "It must be very late," he said, as he listened again to make sure he was not mistaken, and thinking that he might yet hear his grandfather's stick thumping on the floors below. "He must have gone out for his walk without me," thought Gabriel in bewilderment. "What happened to Mary Ellen?"

At eight o'clock every morning Mary Ellen came into Master Gabriel's room and woke him up with a big, slobbery kiss that Master Gabriel was at pains to wipe off with the corner of the rough blanket while Mary Ellen fussed about the room, gathering his clothes together and sousing the big pale-yellow sponge into the ewer that stood on the washstand until it came out a dirty brown colour, dripping water all over the floor. With this Mary Ellen would—as she said herself—"freshen up his face for the day."

But this morning there was no sign of Mary Ellen and when the frosty air became too vicious in its prickings on his sensitive hide, Master Gabriel ran back and jumped into bed again, hastening to nestle back if possible into the exact spot where he had lain all night in the hope of recovering the warmth he had quit so rashly.

Although Master Gabriel showed such solicitude for the comfort of his small body, he was evidently not without appreciation of the spiritual things of life, because, when he had wrapped the blankets tightly around himself and drawn the pillow close to keep out stray shafts of cold, he leaned up on his left elbow and stared out of the window with a steady and appreciative glance from his serious grey eyes.

From this position he could see the river, blazing with sunlight, and beyond it the great park of King John's Castle. The wide grassy stretches and the wide shady trees, the rambling shrubs and the still ponds, could be seen from Gabriel's bed as clearly as if his bed were in the topless turret of the ancient ruin, instead of in the plain stone house separated from the park by garden and river. Many, many times he had indeed pretended to himself, by standing far back in his room, so that the garden and the river were out of sight underneath, that he was the owner of the castle park across the river, and putting an imaginary gun to his shoulder he had fired innumerable, noiseless shots at innumerable imaginary pheasants.

Propped up on his pillow this fine sunny morning, having satisfied his desire for romance by looking out at the grass that was flossy with dew and glinting with every faint stir in the air, Gabriel began after a time, in sheer boredom, to stare at Molloys' patch. There, where there was little or no grass, the clay had been rutted and dug up in a score of places by the black and white dog. Near the back of the house empty crates and wooden boxes of all shapes and sizes had been piled from time to time in the hope that they would come in useful at a later date. There was a certain amount of squalid tidiness about these rotting crates on which fungi were beginning to sprout and grass to grow. Between these boxes and the far end of the garden there was a patch of tow grass almost as high and undisturbed as that in the Finnertys' garden. It was the extreme end of this garden, bordering upon the edge of the river itself, that was the most unkempt and untidy. Incidentally this was the part most clearly seen from the upper rooms of the Coniffes' house. Here, too, as in the Coniffes' and Finnertys' gardens there was a sloping declivity to the water edge. In the Finnertys' garden this slope was no different from the rest of the place, and was just as white with tow grass, which on windy days actually dipped and ruffled the water ripples. In the Coniffes' garden, the natural declivity had been graded and formed into grassy steps until it was a regular sloping terrace, so decoratively adorned with large white stones and plaster urns that, with the hedge boundary shutting out the view to either side, and the ruined park spreading leisurely away, it might be taken for the landing stage at some sweet river pleasance. But in Molloys' garden the slope at the end was a dumping ground. It suffered more from being far from the house than the rest of the yard suffered from being near to it, because its distance coincided with the throwing distance of Mrs. Molloy's arm, and every pot and pan, saucepan and kettle, that had sprung a leak, or lost a handle, in the last twelve years had been flung from the kitchen door to here; the new debris clattering down among the old debris, sending it rattling a little nearer to the water, and putting a few more chips and spots on such of the utensils as had been enamel, until they were as spotty as the spotted dog that ran among them continually. As the dog appeared again at that moment, Gabriel grew more impatient to be up and dressed for the day.

"What is keeping Mary Ellen?" he said, and this time he felt injured beyond words at her delay, and stretching out into the cold air again, and leaning down over the side of the bed, he picked up his small boot, with dangling laces and bright metal tips on the heel, and with it he beat a sharp and imperative tattoo on the boards of the floor which he judged to be directly over the room where his Aunt Theresa sat in the mornings to make up the accounts, and attend to her correspondence.

For a short time after he had rapped on the floor there was no response, but then there was suddenly a sound of feet running upstairs. Gabriel listened carefully. The footsteps were too heavy to be those of his mother or eitner of his two aunts, and too light to be those of Mary Ellen. He felt a slight, premonitory thrill that something unexpected was about to happen. But when the door opened and Mrs. Molloy ran in, for all the world as if she were a member of the household, he felt that the unexpected had overstepped itself, and he sank back into the hollows of the mattress until nothing could be seen but his thin silky hair, and his serious grey eyes.

It had been the constant dread of Mrs. Molloy's girlhood that her hair would darken with the years. To prevent this she had given it constant attention, washing, brushing, and combing it out more often than one could believe. Her hair had kept its colour, and every time she looked in her mirror she congratulated herself upon the fact, but she was always so busy looking at the tresses themselves that she never considered them in relation to her face and her general appearance. But her face had, alas, coarsened and reddened under the strain of her many activities, and indeed its complexion was hardly improved by the constant bending over the tub every other day, as she lathered her mop of hair and dried it in the sun, and so, as she rushed into Gabriel's room, she presented the startling spectacle of a red face under a yellow mop.

"So it was you that was making all the noise!" said Mrs. Molloy when she discovered him. "What in the name of God were you rapping like that for? I thought it was Miss Coniffe herself that wanted someone to give her a hand lifting the furniture or changing the beds!"

Mrs. Molloy turned, as if to go out again, but on another impulse she went over to the wall and ran her hand down the red surface of the wallpaper.

"Is that wallpaper or distemper?" she asked, and then without waiting for an answer she looked around the room again. "I was always wondering what these upstairs rooms were like. You can never judge a person's grandeur until you've seen their upstairs rooms. That's what I always say. It's easy enough to gather up a few carpets and picture frames, and an odd table and sofa, and put them in a room off the hall where everyone that comes their way is sure to see them. But it's the upstairs rooms, where no one ever puts a foot unless there is a death, or the like, that shows what class of person you're dealing with!"

Mrs. Molloy was a woman who never made a practice of talking to herself unless there was no other person present, which was seldom the case, as one of her children, her deaf husband, or the spotted dog was usually at hand. On this occasion, although there was no one else in the room, Gabriel did not feel that she was addressing him, from the way she looked from the wall to the ceiling and the ceiling to the mantel, all the time that she was speaking. Mrs. Molloy crossed over to the mantelpiece.

"Red velvet to match the walls! Can you beat that?" she said as she fingered the mantel border that ran around the mantelpiece and from which large fat bobbins of silk cord dangled heavily. "And what have we here?" she said, as she lifted the fat white china ewer from the hand basin and looked at the large fat roses that were painted on it in crimson with an overcoating of gold dust. "Roses on the ewer!" She looked at the sides of the hand basin before she set down the jug in it. "Roses on the hand basin!" she said, in further astonishment. She paused for a moment. "I bet they have a complete set!" She ran across to the bed and whisked up the edge of the chintz valance. "Doesn't that beat all?" said Mrs. Molloy, and she let the valance fall again almost reverently into its former folds.

"I'm glad I had the occasion to come up," said Mrs. Molloy. "I'll know now for sure what I am talking about, the next time I have occasion to speak of your Aunt Theresa's pernickety ways!" Mrs. Molloy went

95

over to the door again and was opening it to go out, when Gabriel found his tongue.

"I beg your pardon, Mrs. Molloy," he said, in a voice which he modelled as nearly as he could upon his Aunt Sara's voice, which he considered very genteel. "I beg your pardon, but could you tell me what is delaying Mary Ellen and why she hasn't come up yet?"

"Is that what you were rapping for?" said Mrs. Molloy, remembering the purpose for which she had come upstairs.

"Yes, m'am," said Gabriel faintly.

"Well, I know what I'd do with you if you were mine, making a row like that on the ceiling over people's heads, and they at their wits' ends already, without tomfoolery of that kind. I don't know what your aunt would say to you, but if you take my advice you'll have no more tantrums of rapping."

Gabriel stared at Mrs. Molloy, in doubt as to whether he should say anything else to justify himself, or whether it would be better to say nothing and wait till Mary Ellen came along. But her words about the people downstairs being at their wits' ends impelled him to say more.

"Will Mary Ellen be unable to come up?" he said, in as polite a tone of voice as he could achieve.

"She won't be up at all, if I know anything," said Mrs. Molloy. "She's run off her feet already. I heard your Aunt Sara say that the poor creature was up half the night. That's nothing to pass off in a joke, you know, losing a night's sleep, particularly at her age. I know that she's worked for the Coniffes since she was as high as her knee, but all the same it's not right to expect a human being to do more than he's fit for doing. Isn't that right?" Mrs. Molloy began to close the door out after her, and the only thing that saved her from clapping it shut at once was the fact that her eye was taking one last comprehensive glance around the big room, taking in every picture and statue, every bobbin on the mantelcloth, every chair and chest, every scallop in the curtains, and above all every spine on every rose that decorated the water jug and basin.

"Mrs. Molloy. Mrs. Molloy," said Gabriel, his words racing to penetrate Mrs. Molloy's consciousness before her eyes had completed their survey. "Mrs. Molloy! Mrs. Molloy! What about me?"

Mrs. Molloy's attention was caught at last. "What's that?" she said. "What is the matter now?"

"I was only wondering what I should do if Mary Ellen is too busy to come up to me. Will my mother or one of my aunts come instead, do you think? It's getting awfully late. I have several things to attend to downstairs, I should be up long ago!"

"I should think so!" said Mrs. Molloy. "You couldn't keep one of my lads in bed after the sun lets the first spit of light out of it."

Gabriel sensed an unfavourable criticism in the analogy. "That's what I say too, Mrs. Molloy. I say to Mary Ellen that it's a shame to be in bed when the sun is out. The day is so short and night comes so fast. But Mary Ellen says she has a lot of things to attend to in the morning before she attends to me."

Mrs. Molloy's hand slipped off the white doorknob. She came back into the centre of the room and stared at Gabriel as if she had only just seen him for the first time that moment. A new aspect of the situation had struck her. It had come to her with the speed of a stone out of a sling, and she seemed almost stunned by the ideas suggested. She even doubted her own deductions, and looked at Gabriel sideways before she asked any questions.

"Tell me this," she said at last, "why are you waiting for Mary Ellen?"

Gabriel's own face assumed a somewhat similar expression of incredulity to that on Mrs. Molloy's red countenance. He could not believe that anyone could be so stupid as to ask a question like that, the answer to which should be so obvious.

"I am waiting for her to dress me," said Master Gabriel Galloway, with dignity.

"Glory be to God!" said Mrs. Molloy, and this time she backed to the door, without any more glances to right or left, and as she went out she kept staring at Gabriel, who stared back at her with as much surprise as that with which she stared at him. Mrs. Molloy closed the door with almost the same reverence with which she had let the chintz valance fall back into its folds a few moments before, and when she closed it she stayed for a second or two in meditation outside before going downstairs again.

Gabriel listened to hear her go downstairs, and when he did not hear her go down at once he felt that help was still within reach, but when he heard her footsteps on the stairs a few seconds afterwards, he looked down at the chair beside his bed where his clothes were piled in a tidy heap, and putting out his hand he lifted them gingerly, one after another, and looked at them, leaving them there again, and lying down with a sigh.

All at once there was a sound of knocking on the hall door below, so loud that it reverberated all through the house, and the next minute there was a sound of voices raised in shrill tones and—yes, quite distinctly—a sound of crying! Gabriel raised himself up on his elbow and then curiosity began to itch at him till he jumped out of bed and ran across the floor and opened the door. From downstairs there came the sound of someone talking in a high voice, and then a sound of crying which was so real that Gabriel began to tremble with excitement. Something was going on downstairs. He was missing something! He ran over to his clothes, and, sorting them out, he began to dress himself.

At first when he began to struggle with the complications of his trousers and braces, Gabriel felt a great respect for Mary Ellen's intelligence swell into his heart, but as he grasped the general principles of the garment, his heart swelled with an even greater respect for himself.

It was with the great, swelling heart of a hero, who feels that he has conquered much, that Gabriel threw open the bedroom door some minutes later and ran out on the landing. "Mary Ellen! Mother!" he called as he ran, his footsteps drowning his voice. "Mother! Mary Ellen! I put on my own trousers!"

The awful words were no sooner said than Gabriel realized that something was wrong. He reached the lower landing and looked down. There below him, looking up at him with a most peculiar expression, was as big a crowd as he had ever seen in one house. There were so many faces staring up at him that he couldn't see to whom they belonged and they seemed nothing but great blobs of pink, floating in the darkness of the lower hall. Gabriel clutched the banister, and began to turn about to return to his own sunny room, when someone from below called him by name. With great reluctance he turned back, and the voice called again. This time the voice came from quite close to him at the foot of the stairs near the big mahogany knob at the end of the banister. He looked straight in the direction of the voice and saw the friendly face of Packy Hand. Packy put up a crooked finger and beckoned him to come down. At the same time he beckoned with his head, and even the bow of his tie began to bob back and forth on his neck, and beckon with a friendly motion. Gabriel's courage came back. A sense of familiarity returned to the stairs. By the very effort of concentrating on picking out Packy Hand from the rest of the pink, blobby faces, Gabriel discovered that he had clarified the whole atmosphere and he began to look carefully and slowly at each face, as Mrs. Molloy had looked around the door at the bobbins on the mantel border. Then, how familiar everything became! The hall lightened and the faces began to take a definite outline, and, best of all, he saw with relief that they were firmly attached to necks and bodies. Then he saw that there was another face he knew, and another. There was Murty! And there was Higgins who cleaned out the floors every Saturday. And there was Mr. Finnerty! There was Mrs. Finnerty! And Mrs. Finnerty was beckoning him, too. Gabriel changed his mind again. He took a firm grip of the banister rail and began to descend slowly.

"Poor child!" someone said, and then someone else took it up and soon the air was filled with the sentence as it was whispered gently around the hall.

"Is it me they mean?" Gabriel wondered and he began to get afraid again. He stopped on the third last step of the stairs, and stared at one face after another. Every face he stared at was staring at him, and he felt a terrible longing to be back upstairs, when all of a sudden the door of the front parlour opened and there was a great sound of feet shuffling as space was made for someone to pass.

"Who brought that child downstairs!" said a familiar voice, and before Gabriel could say anything, before he even had time to smile, he was lifted up in Mary Ellen's strong arms, and sinking into her big, soft bosom he was carried through the crowd of people in the hallway and brought into the dining room where his mother and his aunts were sitting, and the key was turned in the door.

ഗ   ഗ   ഗ

The three Coniffe sisters were alone in the front parlour, and all around the room, hanging upon coat hangers from the back of the door, and from the picture frames, were dresses and jackets of deep black mourning, sent on approval from the drapers. A choice from these had seemingly been made, as three dresses and three coats were hanging over the back of a chair, distinct from the rest, and from these Gabriel's mother was snipping off the price tags. Theresa and Sara were standing at the table, on which there were several hatboxes, frothing with tissue paper. From one of these boxes Sara had just drawn a black hat with black silk flowers upon it, and she had put it upon her head and was looking at herself with some approval in the mirror over the mantel.

"Put that hat away, Sara," said Theresa impatiently. "There's no use looking at one you can't have!"

Sara took off the hat and sighed. "I didn't think they would be noticed," she said, as she touched the silk flowers, in the hearts of which, she had to acknowledge with guilt, there were yellow silk stamens.

Mary Ellen rushed into the room, hugging Gabriel in her arms.

"What is to be done with this poor child?" she demanded. "There he was on the second last step of the stairs and they were all staring at him like bullocks staring at a frog. I'd like to order the whole lot of them out of the house this minute!"

"Speak lower, Mary Ellen," said his Aunt Sara. "They might hear you. You mustn't speak like that of the mourners. It was very kind of them to come!"

"Most of them came for want of something better to do if you ask me," said Mary Ellen.

Theresa Coniffe interrupted her. She put out a hand to Gabriel.

"Does the child know yet?" she asked.

"He does not," said Mary Ellen. "What does the like of him want to know about death?"

"He'll have to know sometime," said Theresa.

"Don't tell him until after his breakfast, Theresa," said his mother, and her eyes were red from crying.

Gabriel ran over and pressed his face close to his mother's thin silk knees.

"Nonsense," said Theresa. "Come here to me, Gabriel." The boy crept closer to his mother. "See!" said Theresa. "See, he is a coward already under your tutelage!" She looked from her sister Sara to the boy's mother. "Gabriel," she said, " stand up straight! Look at me when I speak to you. You may as well know now as later that your grandfather is dead. You won't see him any more!" Theresa Coniffe pursed her lips and stared at her nephew, ready to upbraid him for lack of courage when the childish tears flowed down his face. His mother and his Aunt Sara stared at him and sobbed noisily into their damp white handkerchiefs. Mary Ellen, at the door, spread her arms to hold her darling close when he ran to her in bewilderment. But Master Gabriel looked up, and interest flickered in his grey eyes. He loosened his grip upon his mother's skirt, and looked seriously at his Aunt Theresa. It was about time he was given some attention. It was about time that he was given some information. His aunt had begun the explanation, but she had only touched upon one of the strange troublous questions that the mysterious morning was raising in his mind. He moved over to her, more freely, and opened his mouth eagerly.

"Why are all those people out in the hall?" he said. He waited with interest to hear the answer to this question before he poured out others and others and others. . . . Death was only a word, and even in Theresa Coniffe's hard, unsympathetic voice it had no implications for the child. His mother took down the handkerchief from her nose and stared. His Aunt Sara sat down with relief. Mary Ellen busied herself with unlocking the door, to hide the smile of satisfaction that she couldn't control. But Theresa Coniffe tightened her lips.

"It's just as I thought," she said. "The child has no feeling. He is callous by nature, but he hasn't been assisted by the training he has got up to now! He is six and a half years old! He will be making his first confession in a few months' time, and he has no more idea of what death is than a bird on a tree!"

"But surely that is as it should be," said Lily Galloway. "Surely the longer a child is without that knowledge the better!"

"You speak like a pagan, Lily Coniffe," said her sister, who still continued to ignore wherever possible the fact that Lily had forfeited the family name. "It may be all right for some barefooted savages, living on fruit, and running naked in the sun, to have no knowledge of what end is in store for them, but for a child in a Christian home it is disgraceful, and it's a situation that I won't permit." She looked around at Sara. "And I suppose we may assume," she said, "that, being the eldest, I have the authority now that poor Father is gone?"

Sara, who had been glancing nervously from Lily to Theresa, and from Theresa to Mary Ellen, afraid of a more fierce dispute, was glad to change the subject. "Who else but you, Theresa?" she said. "Sure you were always the authority in the house. Poor Father himself looked up to you."

While the discussion about him was rising to dangerous heights, Gabriel himself had backed to the door and taken a firm grip of Mary Ellen's hand, listening intently in an endeavour to understand. He was mildly surprised to hear himself the subject of discussion, even in terms that he did not rightly comprehend, because times without number he had heard his Aunt Theresa herself chide his mother and his Aunt Sara for speaking about him in his presence.

"Do you want to give him notions?" she used to ask. "Lower your voice, or, better still, wait until he is out of the room."

On those occasions his mother always stood up and whispered to him and told him that there was a rosy apple hidden somewhere, and that he could have it if he found it, and that he could eat it all, every bit of it, unless he wished to give Mary Ellen a bite. And so, this morning, when he heard them talking about him he expected to be sent out every minute, and although the faces of the people in the hall had startled him and made him afraid a few minutes before, now he was anxious to go out and see them again. Instead of sending him away, however, his Aunt Theresa looked at him with a steady deliberate glance that took him in from top to toe.

"It seems as if I must look after everything," she said. "What is this child going to wear at the funeral? He will have to have a new suit!"

Gabriel's mother said nothing for a few minutes. She remembered vaguely a funeral of some obscure relation to which the three of them had been taken when she was very small. The scene at the grave came back to her vividly and she saw Theresa standing stiffly at the grave, as near as she could get to the edge, following the movements of the men who were filling in the hole with clay. And she remembered Sara, crouching behind Theresa, trying not to look at the grave, and turning aside as every shovelful of clay fell on the coffin.

"Don't you think he is too small to be taken to the funeral, Theresa?" she said deferentially, as if she were his aunt, speaking to his mother. "He might be frightened."

"Why should the child be frightened of a natural event that must come to all?"

Lily Galloway stood up. "As you say, Theresa! But the funeral is not today! Today he must be sent out of the house. Today he would be in the way. He must be sent right out of the house, Mary Ellen."

Mary Ellen had been standing alert, as one who was about to catch a thrown torch, and now she caught up Gabriel's hand, ready to hustle him away as soon as the destination was decided upon.

Gabriel's mother was rapidly turning over in her mind the different relatives to whom the child might be sent for the day. But the relatives would all be busy; they would be caught up in the confusion of the funeral preparations, and would not want to be bothered with minding a little boy. Then she remembered Mrs. Soraghan.

The Soraghans lived in a small cottage under the ramparts about half a mile outside the town. The family was large, and they were very poor. No one was ever very sure of how many young Soraghans there were in the family, because the number changed with such frequency, but whenever a woman in the town needed extra help about the house she sent a message up to Mrs. Soraghan and one of the Soraghan children was at hand as if by magic. There were so many of these children that it was hard to distinguish one from the other and people rarely knew whether they were employing Judie or Nonie, Chrissie or Lolly. Each one of them answered to the names of the others as well as to her own name and this fact, and the fact that they all made use of the same set of clothes, gave people in the town a pleasant and simple sense of uniformity and, instead of having to adapt themselves to new maids, they found the employment of the Soraghans almost as satisfactory as the impersonal cleaning service in a large city, with the important difference of course that it cost little or nothing to employ the Soraghans. The Soraghans were glad to get a meal, not to talk of anything else, and as for old shoes or raincoats, Mrs. Soraghan herself would call to say how grateful she was for them.

When she remembered Mrs. Soraghan, Lily was relieved. She spoke hurriedly. "Put on his coat, Mary Ellen," she said, "and bring him over to Soraghans', if you please, and ask Mrs. Soraghan if she will mind him until you go for him in the evening. Tell her that I will call to see her when all the fuss is over."

Mary Ellen, who, as we say, had been waiting for the word to snatch

Gabriel by the hand and hurry him out of the house, seemed to hesitate for a moment, when she heard where he was to be taken, but she rapidly put her scruples behind her, and taking him by the hand she whisked him round with a jerk of her wrist till he went through the door, more by the power of Mary Ellen's hand than by the power of his own feet.

When Mary Ellen and Gabriel were gone, Theresa Coniffe, who had said nothing in the last few minutes, put up her hand, and, unfastening the large gold brooch at her neck, took it out, and gathering the material of her dress into a lump between her fingers she replaced the brooch once more in the exact place where it had been before, but in doing so she jabbed the pin through the material of the dress with such determination and energy that one would be compelled to believe that a very important alteration had been made in the position. Sara and Lily looked at each other. There are slight gestures that pass unnoticed by a stranger, but which in a family have the weight of innumerable old associations, and they start more chilling apprehensions in the heart than the most outspoken words could ever do. Although her sister had said nothing, Lily stood up and went over to Theresa.

"You must admit that he would be in the way if he was here all day, Theresa!"

Theresa took her hands away from the brooch. "You are his mother. You have the right to decide. It's not for me to say whether he will be brought up sensibly, or coddled and deceived."

Lily pushed her hair back from her forehead. She listened to hear whether the hall door had been opened. She listened to hear if there were any voices in the hall.

"If you like, I will tell Mary Ellen that I have changed my mind. I thought it would be nice for him to spend the day with the Soraghans. He would be out in the air. He could run in the fields." She looked at Theresa, and began nervously to elaborate the theme. "The air is so fresh out there. The children run about in their bare feet! It would be good for him to see how poor people live. I hear they have only potatoes and milk. It will make him appreciative of what he gets at home!" She kept her eyes on her sister as she spoke, and at the last sentence, she laughed placatingly. "You always say that he doesn't know how well off he is!"

All the time Theresa Coniffe sat with her lips closed, in the intense attitude of one who listens in order to pounce upon the false notes. Then, letting her first grievance slip, she caught at another.

"I don't think our poor, dead father would like to think that his grandson would be sent out empty-handed to impose upon a family that have barely enough food for their own mouths! I have to think of everything!" She drew in a deep breath that swelled her thin frame into the semblance of a full bust, and went towards the door. "I have to attend to everything. I will give Mary Ellen a parcel of tea and some bacon, and on the way up the street she can get a bag of sweets for the children." She released a breath, and went out of the room, a tall thin woman, with a strong sense of right.

Soon after Theresa had gone out there was a noise in the hall and Gabriel's shrill voice raised in excitement. Then there was a loud bang as the hall door closed. Theresa came back into the room.

ဖ ဖ ဖ

Mary Ellen and the small boy were going up the street at a brisk pace. People who did not know Mary Ellen often received a mistaken impression of the weather when she passed up the street, because Mary Ellen went so fast that, no matter what way the wind was blowing that day, it seemed to blow against Mary Ellen, for her clothes swept back behind her from the force with which she strode forward. On this particular occasion, she went faster than ever, and the small boy who tried to keep up with her was nearly carried off his feet, and on one occasion he was actually lifted off the ground, and flapped for a moment in the air, like a rag doll, before Mary Ellen realized what had happened.

Gabriel and Mary Ellen went up Clewe Street, and up into the centre of the town, turned to the left at the top of the street and went down towards the river bridge, past the sawmill and the schoolhouse, past the ancient Friary, and finally passed out of the town under the remnant of the archway that had once marked the place of toll upon the bridgehead. The open country lay to the left, and the Soraghans' house was out of sight around the curve of the rampart wall. When they had crossed the bridge and entered on the country road Mary Ellen slackened her pace, and they went along more slowly.

As they went along, the small boy in his blue coat, Mary Ellen in her stiff blue-and-white-striped apron, between flat green fields and the tall grey ramparts, they formed a picture that was as simple as an illustration from a child's storybook, but to Gabriel the journey was very complicated. The town, as it seemed then to him, might be compared to a jigsaw puzzle. He was familiar with every piece of it, but he could not be said to have any idea of the general design made by those pieces. Sometimes, lying in bed at night when some small scolding or disgrace had roused pale rebellious dreams within him in the darkness, he thought that he would run away and, with a shiver of apprehension, he would set out upon an imaginary journey of revolt. First he would set off up Clewe Street, seeing every bit of the pavement as clearly as if it were under his feet, and then, very clearly, he would see the tollgate at the river bridge, leading out into the country, and beyond it he would see the stretching roads to right and left, but the essential connecting link between his own street and River Street, he never could see with sufficient clearness. He often tried hard to remember the places in between, and, although pictures would rise before him of the Friary smothered with nettles, the sawmill bright with planks of new wood piled against its damp walls, and the tall grey oblong schoolhouse, he could never see these buildings in quite the right sequence, and so he always sank back into the pillows in the end, cowed by the realization that if he lost his way in an imaginary journey what misfortune might not be expected to fall upon him in a real one?

On the day of his grandfather's death he followed every step of the way with careful attention, because in the back of his mind, as he hurried along, was the idea that if he did not like it there he might run away from Soraghans', and find his way home by himself. As they went further and further out into the flat green land outside the town, however, he began to enjoy the idea of spending the day in new surroundings.

"Do they live here?" he cried each time a new cottage came into view. He had frequent occasions to ask the question, for the low hills undulated so slightly but so continually that even houses quite nearly placed were often completely out of sight of each other.

Mary Ellen began to tire of the questions.

"You should remember the cottage," she said, "you went there once with your poor grandfather."

This visit had been made at least two years before and Gabriel did not remember anything about it, but an unendurable slur had been put upon his pride. He must not admit that he had forgotten.

"I am beginning to remember," he said, and then as the faint outline of a hay shed began to appear ahead he added quickly, "I think I remember a hay shed somewhere about here." He tried to stand to look around him, but Mary Ellen dragged him on remorselessly, although, when she herself saw the hay barn, a moment or two later, she looked at him suspiciously.

Gabriel pretended not to see the barn for a further few minutes and then, with a great show of astonishment, he pointed it out.

The game of anticipating the landmarks on the wayside, and profiting by Mary Ellen's shortsightedness, soon usurped even his interest in his destination. Trees, sheds, gaps in the rampart, were no sooner sighted upon the horizon than they were inquired after, innocently, as if they had been drawn from the reluctant clutch of memory. Mary Ellen was beginning to look with amazement at him, and to marvel at his astonishingly accurate memory, when all of a sudden Gabriel saw a flock of geese, cut out against the sky, as they crossed from one side of the road to the other at a point on the road which was slightly higher than the point which they had then reached.

"I think I remember some geese about here, somewhere," said Gabriel.

Mary Ellen laughed good-humouredly. "You don't expect a flock of geese to stay in the same place for two years, do you?" she said, and then, all at once, she raised her head, and there at the bend of the road was a flock of geese. Gabriel was elaborately examining the horizon at a different point.

"Hm!" said Mary Ellen, out loud, and, not deigning to correct such an obscure delinquency, she contented herself with shaking her arm violently in such a way that tremors and shivers shot through Gabriel, and he was made vaguely aware that all was not well.

At first Gabriel did not know whether to resent this anonymous form of punishment, and to resist it, too, by digging his feet into the road and yelling, or whether it was better to ignore it altogether. While he was trying to decide as to which course was the better, he was suddenly twitched so violently that he swung around in a half circle. He opened his mouth, without another moment's hesitation, and began to yell.

"Oh dear, oh dear, oh dear! What is the matter with this young man?" said an altogether strange voice, and Gabriel opened his eyes with a rush to find that Mary Ellen had swung him around as a mere accident, when she herself had swept around in a semi-circle to enter the gateway of the Soraghan cottage, and that he had already, without having noticed, passed within the gate, and was standing at the open door of the cottage with Mrs. Soraghan holding out her arms to him, and the faces of three or four of the Soraghan children staring at him from various points of vantage behind their mother's back.

"It isn't often we see you around this part of the world, Mary Ellen," said Mrs. Soraghan, when she had given sufficient attention to Gabriel. "Come inside at once."

As Mary Ellen and Gabriel went into the cottage, Gabriel felt a new unusual shyness come down over him like the snuffer over a candle. He no longer felt any desire to talk, and he was even afraid to look around him. He clung hard to Mary Ellen's hand and even the conversation between Mary Ellen and Mrs. Soraghan did not rouse him to any interest.

"I'm sorry for your trouble, Mary Ellen!" said Mrs. Soraghan.

"Thank you, Mrs. Soraghan," said Mary Ellen, "you're the first one today who had any sympathy for me. The people that are going nowadays don't have much understanding. There was such fussing and rushing as was never seen in Clewe Street this morning and not one of the hundreds that came in and out of that house had enough thoughtfulness to say what you're after saying this minute."

"A good master is a great loss. I know that," said Mrs. Soraghan. "But, of course you're all right, Mary Ellen. Miss Theresa will take over charge and everything will go on as before."

"No one can tell what Miss Theresa will take it into her head to do!"

"I suppose everything is left to her?"

"You may be sure it is. She was always going in and out of the old man's rooms these latter weeks. She hardly let Miss Sara or Miss Lily put their nose inside it for longer time that it took to say three words. I often saw them stealing in, as if they were trying to go into some place where they had no right. And if Miss Theresa came along and found out where they were she would go in after them and invent some excuse to send them out again about their business. Oh yes, I daresay Miss Theresa has the will arranged in the way most suitable to herself. Only this morning she began to lay down the law about this poor child!" Mary Ellen gave Gabriel's arm a jerk and Mrs. Soraghan, without waiting to hear any more of the story, swooped down and pinched Gabriel's cheeks together, with the fingers of one hand. Her coarse and hardened hand hurt him, but he felt that, although it hurt, this gesture was meant to indicate good feeling. He judged it wise to smile and, remembering the smile of the pink quartz angel over his bed at home, he smiled in a way that he hoped resembled the smile of the angel.

"You little angel!" said Mrs. Soraghan and she pinched his cheeks again, and, although it hurt him more this time, Gabriel felt a pride and confidence in his own performance. He let go Mary Ellen's hand and gave his hand to Mrs. Soraghan. "The little lamb!" said Mrs. Soraghan, and she caught up his hand and held it hard in hers while she begged Mary Ellen to continue her story.

"Miss Theresa wanted to keep him in Clewe Street today. Only for his poor mother the child would be there now, getting under people's feet the whole day, and as likely as not he would be in and out of the corpse room before the body was washed, or dressed, or readied for the wake! But his mother objected! It's a great wonder to me that she had the strength to resist Theresa. That poor creature hasn't the strength of a bird. And as for Miss Sara, that poor creature is nothing more than a bird either way you look at it, body or soul. I declare to goodness but it's a wonder Miss Theresa doesn't step on them some day in her hurry out to church and crush the life out of them! You'd admire Miss Lily, all the same, if you saw her this morning. She faced up to everyone. 'I want this child to get out into the country. I want him to have one happy day!' she said, and her face all flushed up while she was saying it and she looked at me as if she was imploring me to pick him up and run off with him before anyone interfered with her plans. 'Take him to Mrs. Soraghan, Mary Ellen,' she said, 'he'll have a happy day with the Soraghan children!' "

As Mary Ellen uttered the last words, a wonderful transformation came over the Soraghans.

They had been standing aloof, in the corners of the room, staring out at Gabriel shyly from dark angles between the dresser and the chimney, the chest of drawers and the settle bed, but as Mary Ellen pronounced the startling news that the little boy was to stay with them for the day, they began to look at each other and signal to each other, and Judy, the eldest, even ventured to emerge from her corner and approach nearer and nearer to him, till she could put out her hand and feel the soft nap of the sleeve of his coat and peer closely enough at the brass buttons on his cuff, from which the younger children had hardly taken their eyes, since he arrived, to be able to discover that they were embossed with the design of an anchor.

"He has an anchor on his buttons," she called back.

Even Mrs. Soraghan was transformed. Where she had previously spoken to him in an artificial coaxing voice, she looked at him now with a warm stare of proprietorship.

"Do you mean to say he's going to stay with us for the day?" she said. "The poor lamb! Why didn't you say that at once? Come here, child! It's too warm yet for that big topcoat." She began to rip off Gabriel's coat. "Would you like a slice of bread and butter?" She ran over to the dresser and caught up a big, fascinatingly crooked turnover of bread and began to slice it down into several thick cuts.

"One will be enough, thank you," said Gabriel politely.

"Did you hear that? One will be enough, thank you!" Mrs. Soraghan threw up her hands. "That's all you're getting, boy. But when one gets a slice of bread in this house, everyone gets one!" She waved the bread knife round and sure enough, all the young Soraghans, who had hitherto been but dimly seen in the darkened corners of the room, were advancing slowly but surely into the light of day, drawn by an irresistible fascination towards the glinting bread knife that flashed up and down through the bread as recklessly as if bread fell from heaven as free as rain.

"I must get back. They'll need me in Clewe Street," said Mary Ellen, and she looked at Gabriel with something like reproach. "Are you sure you won't be lonely, Gabriel?" she said, and the little boy took his eyes from the flashing knife and was about to give a reassuring answer when he felt another moment of intuition and looked up into Mary Ellen's face.

"I will try not to be lonely because I know that you and Mother want me to stay here," he said.

The tears came into Mary Ellen's eyes. Mrs. Soraghan threw up her hands again, but speedily lowered them to slap a very small Soraghan who had seized that opportunity to put up a hand too prematurely for his slice of bread.

Mary Ellen went out and as she passed along outside the small window of the cottage she darkened it momentarily with her great tall figure. Then she disappeared, and Gabriel was alone with the Soraghans. Already two new impressions had been recorded on his mind—that a person can hurt you when they mean to be kind, and that tears do not always mean displeasure.

The minute that Mary Ellen went out of the door Gabriel became aware that the restraint of the family had been due to her presence alone. Two or three of the younger children still held back somewhat, but Judy advanced and stood by her mother's side.

"Is he going to stay with us all day?"

"You have ears as well as me, haven't you?" said the mother, and her words were due less to discourtesy than to a necessity for keeping talk at the minimum in a house where there were so many tongues.

"Can I mind him?"

"You're not so agreeable when it comes to minding Onny," said her mother.

Onny was the youngest of the large brood, and Gabriel, who had already identified all the others by name, had not seen any sign so far of Onny.

Judy tossed her hair and walked across the room. She took up Gabriel's coat and began to look at it.

"Leave that where you got it!" said her mother. Judy threw down the coat and tossed her hair. The coat slipped on to the floor. Gabriel, who had been listening in amazement to this conversation which contained words with which he was quite familiar but from which in this instance he could take no meaning, felt uncertain. He looked around him, and when he saw that all the other children were looking at the coat where it lay on the floor he made a big decision, and stepping over he lifted it up.

"Wouldn't it be better to hang it up?" he said, advancing to Mrs. Soraghan with the coat.

Mrs. Soraghan, who had by this time buttered the bread, and was just about to pass it around, and who was indeed at that moment balancing Gabriel's slice on the flat of the knife preparatory to passing it to him, was so surprised that the slice of bread tilted and fell.

"Well, I never heard the like!" she said, and she took the coat in her hand. "There's a lesson for you," she said to the children. "There's a lesson to be learned from everything. This young lad has a half a dozen coats and he's as careful about them as a cat about his fur, while you—" she swung around in order that her reproaches might be scattered evenly among them—" you have hardly a coat between you and as often as not it's under my feet in the dirt when I walk across the floor." She went over and hung the coat on the back of the kitchen door, where so many old clothes were already hanging that the little blue coat looked like a sack on a haystack. "You're a good boy," she said then to Gabriel, and she took up a slice of bread from the table and put it into his hand directly, dispensing this time with the ceremony of passing it to him on the blade of the knife. "Come here, you," she said to the smallest of the children, and she pointed down at the floor where the fallen slice lay butter side under. "Pick up that and eat it," she said, and she turned back to the dresser and began to divide out the rest of the bread.

Gabriel was hungry. He settled down to enjoy his slice of bread. At first he found it very large and difficult to hold, but after adjusting it several times he finally secured a proper grip on it and took a big bite. Then he took another bite. He took three or four or five bites and chewed it politely with his mouth shut the way he was told to do at home. It was not until he came to the sixth or seventh bite that his hunger was sufficiently satisfied to permit of his looking around to see how the others were enjoying their bread. But when Gabriel lowered the big slice from his mouth and looked across it at the young Soraghans he nearly let the bread fall, because in front of him, watching him from every side, were the big bright eyes of the Soraghan children. Their eyes were fastened on the bread in his hand; and of their own slices no more remained than if they had never been given any. Gabriel held his bread, transfixed with his surprise, and Mrs. Soraghan, who was tidily brushing the crumbs down off the dresser on to the floor, and pressing them into semi-oblivion with her feet, looked at him sharply.

"If you don't want that bread there are plenty ready to grab it!"

Gabriel looked back at her, not knowing what answer to give, but after a moment he put the slice of bread up to his mouth and took another slow but adequate bite, his eyes still staring into the eyes of Mrs. Soraghan to see if she had interpreted his decision correctly. Whether she had done so or not, however it was clear that the Soraghan children had done so, for, one by one, they moved away from Gabriel, having no more hope that his slowness in eating the bread was due to lack of appetite.

Judy Soraghan was the last to move away. She went over to the dresser and began to pull at her mother's skirt.

"Can we take him out for a walk?" she said, and she jerked her head in Gabriel's direction.

"Will you be careful of him?" said her mother. "Remember the clothes he has on him cost more than you're ever likely to have jingling in your pocket. It wouldn't do for him to fall and tear them. It wouldn't do for him to get a ducking in the river."

Gabriel listened to the implied pleasures ahead of him with a slightly nervous air, and his mastication of the bread and butter was considerably slowed up at times, so that a person looking suddenly in at the window might have been astonished to see a small boy with his cheeks puffed out at one moment, his mouth open at another moment, and at yet another moment with such an appearance of having just swallowed something that it might have been a shilling piece, at least, that he had swallowed.

"I'll mind him, Ma," said Judy. "What makes you think I'd let him fall in the river?"

"You let Mollser fall in the river, didn't you, when she was only two and a half?"

Judy began to paw the cement floor with one foot like a pony anxious to be released from the embarrassment of a cart and trappings.

"Mollser saw Moran's dog running into the water after a stone and she ran in after him."

"Who threw the stone?" said Mrs. Soraghan absent-mindedly, her tongue furnishing, with astonishing simplicity, the inexorable logic which the mind does not always furnish.

"I promise I won't let him fall in the river, Ma."

"Don't go climbing on the ramparts either," said Mrs. Soraghan.

"Why can't we go on the ramparts?" said Judy. "The ramparts are all right. What's wrong with the ramparts?"

"Didn't you let Larry fall off the ramparts only a week ago? Have you no memory?"

Judy pawed the ground more restlessly than ever. There was irritability as well as restlessness in the scraping of her foot along the gritty floor.

"I didn't knock him," said Judy, "The wind blew him over."

"It was a good thing the wind was blowing the way it was then, because if it was blowing the other way he'd have gone to his death thirty feet into the stone and nettles."

As the dialogue between Judy and her mother went on Mrs. Soraghan was crossing and recrossing the kitchen with the darting energy of a woman for whom the day isn't half long enough for all there is to be done, and Judy was following her indolently. Before Judy was halfway across the kitchen after her mother, dragging her feet, Mrs. Soraghan was back again at the place she had just left and Judy was forced to take another direction. This happened so much that after a few minutes Judy's movements were more or less restricted to a few steps this way and a few steps that way, from a position which corresponded roughly with the centre of the room. Gabriel, whose eyes were getting as tired as Judy's feet, from following the darting journeys of the older woman, fixed his attention on Judy. In fact as she stood in the centre of the kitchen she was like an actress who has a long speech to make and upon whom a nervous producer has impressed the necessity of breaking up the speech from time to time with slight gestures of the hand and head, telling her to turn to this side as she says one phrase, and to the other side as she says the next. So Gabriel watched her, fascinated, and in time he forgot to eat his bread, and stared at the two women who were parcelling out his day for him. As the river and the ramparts were mentioned pictures of them rose before his mind. He thought of the river as he had seen it at flood tide from the bridge of the town, with twigs and branches of trees being dragged along its racing waters. He thought of the ramparts as he had seen them one day when his grandfather had taken him up on them and told him to look down. There had been a drop that went down, down, down, and at the end were rocks that had fallen with the passing of years from different places, and there was broken glass, and battered tin cans, and growing high among the tins and rocks and the broken glass were tall pointed nettles that had made him shiver more than the dizzy depths of the decline.

This was where Judy Soraghan was going to take him for a walk. He often went for a walk on the road with his aunts or his mother and all the time they held his hand. But Judy Soraghan didn't look as if she'd hold his hand for long. He looked at her bright eyes and her red cheeks, and he looked at her long legs that looked as if she would run away and leave you all alone in a field if she took the notion. He hung on every word that Mrs. Soraghan said, and he began to hope with all his strength that she would not allow Judy to take him out. His imagination pictured the scenes of misadventure that had come to Mollser and Larry and his fear altered the details until he pictured them being pushed about, and shoved into puddles, and knocked down into beds of nettles by their irritable sister Judy. He didn't want to go with her, but he didn't know how to get out of going.

"Can I take him, Ma?" said Judy. "Can I take him? I won't let him get hurt—I promise."

Gabriel stood frozen with fear. He looked to see how far he was from the door. For a moment he contemplated making a dash for the road. But the doorway was blocked by three or four of the smaller children and when Gabriel looked at them he saw that their eyes were once more fixed upon his bread and butter, which he had ceased to eat in his fear. He began to eat it again, hastily, and in this activity he forgot for a moment his fears of Judy, and as he was licking his fingers after the last bit of bread he heard one of the young Soraghans, Mollser, calling out to her mother from the doorway.

"I'll hold his hand, Ma." It had been decided that they were going to the ramparts. "I'll hold his hand, Ma," said Mollser again.

This was the first time anyone but Judy had spoken, and Mollser's example loosened the tongues of all the others. All together they began to talk, calling out to their mother in shrill voices, each one trying to penetrate the din made by the others. As well as Gabriel could make out, they were all of them eager to hold his hand. A great reassurance swelled within him. He was not going with Judy alone. They were all going together. With the relief that came upon him there came also a return of self-confidence. He spread his legs out wide and raising his voice he shouted out as loud as he could shout.

"I don't want anyone to hold my hand. I can walk by myself."

But as he opened his mouth to shout, the Soraghan children, whose eyes had never left him, all closed their mouths, some of them even in the middle of a word, and when Gabriel shrilled out what he had to say, it was into a silent kitchen that his words fell. He was halfway through what he had to say before he realized that he was shouting to penetrate a din that had ceased, and then it was too late to stop. He brought his sentence to an end with his cheeks blazing, and looked around with every expectation of seeing the Soraghan children nudging each other, sniggering, and poking their fingers at him. But looking around, in every face, from Mrs. Soraghan to Mollser, he was astonished to see a most deferential expression, and even upon the face of Judy there was a strange look of admiration.

The differences between the Coniffes and the Soraghans, between the inhabitants of Clewe Street and the inhabitants of the cottages under the ramparts, were many and great. These differences may have come from their different financial status, but time and custom had led the families in the town to consider things from a particular rather than a general attitude, and so it would not be surprising to find that Miss Theresa considered that she owed her position in the town to the fact that she wore a black silk dress at all times of the day. Mrs. Molloy felt that hers depended on her ability to live in the same street with the Finnertys and Coniffes. But Gabriel was near to discovering the real secret of the tyranny which Clewe Street exerted over the rampart cottages, the tyranny of the loud voices over the thin voices. This was the tyranny of the politician over the electorate, the priest over the sinner, the husband over the wife, the teacher over the child. It was even the tyranny of tinker over tinker; the real tyranny of Ireland, where, by a loud voice, all things are gained.

But Gabriel, blushing to the ears, not only failed to profit by the position he had gained with his shout, but actually regretted that he had shouted, and so in less than two minutes all the Soraghans, from the biggest to the smallest, had seen that his shout had been more an accident of the vocal chords than a trait of character, and, having found this out, as if they had actually discovered a weakness, they pounced upon him with one accord and began to hustle him into his coat and turn him this way and that. Whereas their former argument, as to which of them would walk at either side of him, had been confined to words, it was now more fiercely fought out by catching him by the sleeve and dragging him one from another.

The kitchen was filled with noise as they pushed each other and stamped their feet, and sometimes a wail arose as a slap, or a pinch in the arm, was administered by Mrs. Soraghan in a mistaken corrective to the general clatter.

"Are you ready now?" said Mrs. Soraghan, when at last some order had been established, and Mollser and Judy had placed themselves one to each side of Gabriel. "Are you all going?" She ran her eye over them rapidly.

"Judy, Mollser, Larry, Chrissie." She named them out, her eye checking them over as accurately as a machine. "Where is Matty?" she said then, suddenly.

"Matty's piling turf for Mr. Finnerty," said Judy.

"Where's Nonie?"

"Nonie is stirring jam for Mrs. Molloy."

Mrs. Soraghan's eye ran over the group once more. The worried look began to fade from her face, and she was turning away when suddenly she missed another of the children.

"Where's Onny?" she said, and hardly waiting for an answer she began to run into the inner room calling out "Onny! Onny!" as she ran.

Gabriel had paid little attention to the previous interrogations about Matty and Nonie, but he could not remain indifferent to the new note of anxiety that came into Mrs. Soraghan's voice when she sought to find out the whereabouts of Onny. Even the other children became excited.

"You were minding her," said Judy, turning upon Mollser, and raising her fist accusingly above her head.

"I told Chrissie to keep a hold of her hand," said Mollser, putting her two arms before her face to defend herself from Judy. Judy advanced a step.

"It will be your fault if she's lost." She advanced nearer. Mollser began to whimper.

Gabriel who was standing dangerously near Mollser, began to retreat also and was just contemplating putting up his own fists in protection when Mrs. Soraghan came running out from the inner room.

She stopped in the doorway. "Well?" she said, in a loud voice, and her face was damp and red. "What are you standing there for? Why don't you look for her? She's not in the room. I looked out of the window and she's not in the yard! Why don't you go out and look for her?" Her voice cracked on the last word.

The children stood grouped in the doorway, transfixed in the temporary postures of the moment. Judy had her arm raised. Mollser cowered with her hands over her face. Larry's hand was gripping the hem of Chrissie's dress, and Chrissie had one foot out of the door. Gabriel looked beyond them at the white sheets spread on the bushes and tried to see which way the wind was blowing, because for one long dreadful moment he remembered what Mary Ellen always said whenever he made a face at her. If the wind changed you'd stay like that for the rest of your life. But the white balls of dust were rolling down the hard bleached road, in the same way they had rolled before, and he felt some slight reassurance even before Mrs. Soraghan advanced and lifting the ends of her apron flapped it in the air with a violent sound like the crack of a whip, causing all the young Soraghans to leap into action and one after another to jostle a way through the narrow door. Chrissie, who stood behind Gabriel, was in such terror at the advance of her irate mother with the flapping apron that she judged it quicker to push Gabriel ahead of her than to try to get past him. And so in a second he was outside the cottage racing rapidly across the grass towards a gappy box hedge on which the day's washing of sheets and dresses, shirts and pillowcases, was spread to bleach. As he heard the angry flap of the apron behind him once more he turned and saw the rest of the Soraghan children scatter like hens to every side.

"Onny! Onny! Are you there?" shouted Mrs. Soraghan, putting her hands to her mouth like a bugle.

"Onny! Onny!" Soon Judy took up the cry from where she ran among the cabbages. "Onny! Onny!" Judy's voice was strong and heavy. It carried farther than her mother's.

"Onny! Onny!"

And as the cry of a bird in an aviary is taken up now by one bird, now by another, soon the small garden echoed and volleyed with the shouting of the Soraghans, and as the cries came from one side of him, at one moment, from the other side at the next moment, now high and shrill, now deep and penetrating, Gabriel, like a small and newly fledged member of the aviary, felt impelled to try his powers of imitation and soon he, too piped and in a high joyous voice, that took no heed of the sense of its sounds, but which pierced the air for the very joy of sound.

"Onny! Onny!"

Gabriel called for the joy of taking part in this game of sound and he didn't expect any results from his calls, but as he opened his mouth a second time to repeat them, he stopped with his mouth wide open— for on the other side of the small box hedge on which the linens were hanging to bleach, he heard a chuckling sound, and pushing aside the small pointed leaves of the hedge he looked into the field beyond it. There on the grass a small girl sat, and as he peered out at her through the chinks in the greenery she opened her eyes wide and shut them again and opened them again in an unmistakable but ambiguous acknowledgment of his stare.

This must be Onny. Gabriel ran back towards Mrs. Soraghan to tell her what he had seen but when he came up to her she pushed him aside and turning her back upon him completely she raised her hands to her lips again and called out once more louder and more shrilly than before.

"Onny! Onny!"

It was only then that Gabriel realized that the small girl must have heard them all calling while she sat on the grass in unconcern. Such independence astonished him. Into his small obedient soul a wilful breeze was blown. Admiration for Onny swept over him. She was such a little girl to be so bold. He ran back to the hedge and putting his eye to the chink in the leaves he stared at her as hard as he could.

She sat on the grass and with one hand she pulled out a curl of golden hair as far as it would go from her forehead and then she let it slap back against her face. Every time she pulled out the curl she stared at it with fierce concentration, but every time she let it slap back into its tight gold coil again she turned her head and stared at Gabriel's face that peered through the chinky leaves. Her big eyes were wide and blue and she neither smiled nor blinked.

As Gabriel bent down with his head half buried in the box hedge Chrissie came up and stood looking at him. After a few minutes Larry came and stood beside Chrissie.

In a family as large as the Soraghans the delinquencies or oddities in behaviour of any one member were sure to pass unnoticed, and so Mrs. Soraghan had not noticed Gabriel as he stood alone by the hedge. When she looked in his direction again, however, and saw the group of children standing there, she went over to investigate.

"What are you looking at?" she said, catching Larry by the ear and rendering him incapable of reply. "What are you looking at?" she said, reaching for Chrissie's ear, but Chrissie as she retreated out of reach pointed at Gabriel, who all this time remained motionless at his spy hole in the bush, unaware even of Mrs. Soraghan's great flat shadow that fell over him and the grass he stood upon.

Mrs. Soraghan was a tall woman. To see what absorbed Gabriel she did not need to look through the bushes, but leaned her great breast against the hedge, pressing it from her with her weight, and stared across it into the field beyond.

"Glory be to God!" screamed Mrs. Soraghan, and then she swung around. "Judy, Mollser! Come here. Chrissie! Larry! She's here!—The bold strumpet"—and then she leaned back and shook her fist at Onny over the hedge.

Judy and Chrissie ran up and began to scramble through the gap in the hedge.

"Bring her here to me at once," directed Mrs. Soraghan, and then she changed her mind. "Put on her dress before you bring her back," she said, and then she made another alteration in the command. "Slap her well, and put on her dress," she said.

It was only when these commands were shouted over the hedge that Gabriel realized that the small defiant girl who sat on the grass had discarded her clothes and sat there naked as the flowers, while a little way off from her there was a pile of pink and white linen folded as neatly as if it were folded on the end of a bed rail. Gabriel's former admiration fluttered to further heights. This was daring such as he had never even contemplated. He thought of the few shameful occasions on which Mary Ellen, coming into his room to wake him in the morning, had thrown back the clothes from his bed and finding that his nightshirt had wriggled out of place to such an extent that his middle was bared to view, had thrown the clothes over him again with haste and two bright spots had burned in her cheeks.

"Cover yourself, you wicked child," she had cried.

And now, here in the daylight was Onny Soraghan, sitting on the grass without a stitch of clothes on her. Gabriel clapped his hands together.

At the sound of clapping hands beside her Mrs. Soraghan looked down. For a moment she stared at Gabriel and then she stared across the hedge again. All at once she was struck by a new significance in the situation.

"Come away from that hedge," she said, making a rush at Gabriel, and dragging him back by the seat of his pants and the back of his collar. "Aren't you ashamed of yourself! What would your mother say if I told her about this!" Gabriel's collar was dragged so tight that he almost choked. The blood rushed up to his head. Mrs. Soraghan looked at him. "I'm glad you have the grace to blush at least!" she said and she let go his collar and gave him a push forward towards the gap in the hedge through which Judy and Chrissie were returning carrying a struggling Onny, whose golden hair was tossed wildly over her face and whose legs kicked frantically to free themselves.

The glory was gone from Onny. She was a cross little girl in a dirty dress, kicking her grimy legs. Gabriel did not understand why he was scolded and why he had been dragged from the hedge by the back of the neck, but he felt that something had gone wrong with the day and when he looked up at the sky he was faintly surprised to see that the gay sun still shone down.

And while the Soraghans dragged the reluctant Onny over to their mother, who scolded and slapped her roundly, Gabriel stared up into the sky and the tears came angrily into his eyes. He bit his lips and looked at the sun, and might have broken into loud grief if his attention had not been taken by the way the sun looked through his tears. It wasn't the same sun that he had looked at a moment before. It was spiked. It had piercing rays that ran right down to the earth. It had changed. It was a spider in a golden web. It was a bee with golden stings. It was a great gold-spitting gander.

A bee, a spider, a great gold-spitting gander. Gabriel's tears dried on his cheek. He laughed and ran over to Larry Soraghan.

"Look!" said Gabriel, pointing up into the sky, and Larry, for whom the sky was but the passageway of birds, lifted an imaginary shotgun to his shoulder and fired an imaginary shot into the air, once, twice, thrice. Gabriel looked at him with joy, pride, and satisfaction. Here was a man after his own heart. The confusing events of the past half hour passed away and he linked his arm in Larry Soraghan's arm and led him apart from the others.

As Gabriel and Larry went out into the road, linked arm in arm, Judy hastily liberated the screaming Onny from her mother and soon the entire band of Soraghans were trudging down the dusty road to a place some distance away, where the rampart wall was gapped sufficiently to allow foothold to be taken upon it.

The day was brilliantly sunny. The children went gaily along the road. Gabriel gradually lost his shy and separate identity, and with it he lost the ability to see the others as separate identities. Small threads of relationship were spun and when years afterwards he tried to remember that sunny summer day he could remember almost nothing of the hours that were spent on the rampart walls. He could remember nothing that happened after they passed out of the small garden, although every moment of the time before that was retained in his mind with great visual clarity. It is strange that the scenes of childhood in which we played a part are often dim in our memory, and those in which we stood apart from others, in fear or awe or admiration, retain their full lucidity.

One scene only of that long golden afternoon on the ramparts remained with Gabriel. The day was nearing an end. The clouds were wending their way towards the hills in the west, where they massed themselves together as if to block the passage of the vanishing day.

Satiated with play, the children were beginning to anticipate the intrusion of their elders, who would sternly call them in for the night. Impatience and regret put an edge upon their pleasure. They ran faster and the evening air seemed to flash brighter between them as they ran. They hid from each other more skilfully and the evening mists made their hearts beat fiercer with the dread of being discovered. They shouted louder and the evening silence, intensified by a trace of frost in the air, made their voices volley more loudly among the walls of the ruined towers that stood at intervals along the ruined walls. Everywhere sights and sounds became more accentuated. A horse with white forelegs released in a pasture away on the side of a hilly field dashed across the green stretch, diagonally, with a vivid gallop that held them all gazing, and the sound of his hoofs on the hard ground penetrated the stillness and beat a pattern of sound upon the air that made them hold their breaths. In the deepening silence a milk pail thrown down on the cobbles in a yard far away, and the voice of a girl singing, startled the ear with a simple sweetness of sound, as appealing as the single notes of a primitive flute coming after the complexity of a great orchestra.

"It's getting very late," said Gabriel, and he looked down the road towards the town. A few lights pricked the dark bulk of the buildings that a moment before had been inconspicuous. "Mary Ellen will be coming to bring me home."

"Will you come again tomorrow?" said Larry.

"How can he come tomorrow? He'll have to go to his grandfather's funeral!" said Judy.

Gabriel remembered his grandfather. He remembered the mysterious talk in the parlour earlier that day.

"My grandfather is dead," he said, importantly.

"Tell us something we don't know!" said Judy, tossing her hair. "It's because your grandfather's dead that you're sent out to us. I heard Mary Ellen telling my mother."

"Then perhaps I'll be sent again tomorrow!" said Gabriel.

"You will not. Tomorrow is the funeral. They only sent you today because he wasn't coffined."

Gabriel pondered this for a moment and decided not to betray his mystification, but Judy, watching him closely, divined it.

"They didn't want you to see him!" she said, lowering her voice ominously.

"I often saw him!" said Gabriel.

"You didn't see him *dead!*" said Judy.

Gabriel stared at her. She stood on a large stone fallen from one of the towers. There was something significant in the moment. The strange green sky beyond the ramparts seemed part of the moment's significance. The trees that had seemed so inoffensive all day branched out everywhere against the green sky, with desperate gestures. The other children, sensing something dramatic, clustered near and Chrissie caught Gabriel's hand. Gabriel was unable to part his dry lips, but a desperate longing for information finally forced them apart.

"What is it like to be dead?" he asked, in a terrified voice.

119

Judy looked around her nervously as if the silent empty fields had suddenly become peopled. The children drew closer together. Chrissie's hand was hot. Gabriel held his breath.

Judy bent and stuck her face into Gabriel's and put up her hands to her eyes.

"When you're dead," she said, "you get like this!" And pressing her fingers against the soft flesh under her eyes she drew down the lower lids leaving the eyes wide and strained and revealing the liquid inner flesh of the eye socket with its nauseating pools of pale blood.

"Judy! Judy!" the younger children screamed. Chrissie dragged at her sister's hands to tear them down from her face. Larry dug his fists into his own eyes to blot out the ugly sight.

Judy let her hands fall to her sides. She began to laugh. At her laughter the others were reassured and soon they were all laughing. In another minute they were all imitating her. Gabriel alone remained silent. And when they observed this fact, the young Soraghans began to dance around him, all of them pulling down their red eyelids and opening their mouths until the circling faces made his head reel, and breaking through the terrifying ring of faces, he began to run up the road in the direction of the lighted town, his feet ringing on the rough stones in the road, and the frantic trees on either side seeming to strain out towards him across the broken walls. All at once someone appeared ahead of him on the road, and even in the gathering darkness there was something familiar in the tall figure bearing swiftly towards him, her coat hem flowing back behind her.

"Mary Ellen. Mary Ellen!" screamed Gabriel, and he threw himself against the strong frame of Mary Ellen.

"What is the meaning of this?" she said. "Why are you out on the road alone at this hour of the evening? Where are the Soraghan children?"

The Soraghan children arrived at that moment, one after another, panting. Judy arrived first.

"We were running races," said Judy, defiantly.

"In that case it's a queer race if a boy of six can be ten lengths ahead of a girl of twelve," said Mary Ellen. "Tell your mother I'll call another day. Come, Gabriel!" Catching his hand she swung around in the road, the ends of her coat slashing out so furiously with the impetus of her turning that the Soraghans leaped out of the way, all but Larry, who got a slash of the heavy blue cloth in the eye, and as they went down the road it gave some measure of satisfaction to the elderly woman and a great deal of satisfaction to Gabriel, to hear the wailing of Larry.

As they drew nearer to the town, Gabriel's trembling ceased and when they turned into Clewe Street he completely forgot the death's-head faces that had danced around him when he saw the unusual brilliancy with which every window in the Coniffe house was lighted, in the upper as well as the lower story, and indeed, there were a great many lights to be seen in the windows of the Molloys and Finnertys.

"Why are all the lamps lighting?" he asked in a shrill voice of excitement, but as they were at this time passing before the open hall door of the Finnertys' house, Mary Ellen did not care to raise her voice in reply.

"Hush, child," she said, speaking rapidly and slowly, and gripping his hand tighter. Had it been possible to increase her pace, this she would have done. "I'll take you right upstairs," she declared, as she pushed open the hall door. "Pay no attention to anyone."

The hall inside the door was crowded with people, so crowded in fact that as Mary Ellen squeezed her way through it, with Gabriel by the hand, he had not room to turn his head, nor time to raise it, and when he reached the foot of the staircase the only impression he had received of the crowd was an impression formed entirely by dark trouser legs and dark skirts. The faces which belonged to the trousers and skirts he had not been able to see.

As they went up the stairs the door of the back parlour opened and his mother ran out.

"Is he back?" she cried, and she ran up a few steps of the stairs. "Did you have a happy day, Gabriel?" she asked and she caught him around the knees in a way that made him feel very insecure. He caught at Mary Ellen with one hand and with the other he steadied himself against the banisters. "Did he have a happy day?" said his mother looking at Mary Ellen, and then swooping her head down to kiss Gabriel. " What did you do all day? Tell me everything. Did you have a nice time? Did you miss Mother? Did you like the little Soraghans?" Gabriel pressed his face against her bodice but instead of the soft silken feel to which he was accustomed, the dress scraped his cheek. It was a harsh black tussore material with strands like fibre and it was embroidered with beads of jet that pricked him with their sharp edges. He drew back and put his hand to his cheek.

"Oh, you poor child," said his mother and she began to stroke his face, but the reminder that she had received of her mourning dress reminded her also of her mourning manners, and she gave a nervous glance over her shoulder at the room she had left where the people sitting around in silence seemed to chastise her with their eyes for her outburst of affection. She stood up. "Put him to bed, Mary Ellen, and leave a light burning in his room. I'll go in and kiss him later on."

Mary Ellen tugged at his hand. Gabriel climbed another step. As they turned the corner of the landing he could hear his mother explaining to the people in the hall that he had been very much attached to his grandfather. "Poor child," someone said, and then someone repeated

121

it, and as he went out of earshot the last thing Gabriel heard was " Poor child, poor child," in different voices, in different tones, eddying like a dying gust of wind in the rooms downstairs.

When he was tucked into bed and the pillows plumped up by Mary Ellen's vigorous fists, Gabriel remembered that his mother said he could have a night light burning in his room.

"Very well!" said Mary Ellen. "I'll light one, but I don't know why you want it. You ought to be asleep in two minutes after your day's airing in the country."

She tidied his clothes, folding them on the bed rail, and she lifted his shoes to take them away for polishing. As she lifted his shoes and saw the coating of white dust upon them she felt a great satisfaction with herself and with Gabriel's mother for having managed to outface Theresa Coniffe and send the child away from the house of death, where he would not have a chance of seeing the corpse.

Mary Ellen smiled at the dusty shoes as if they had shared in the complicity, and placing the night light in a saucer of cold water on the mantelpiece, she went out and closed the door, and went downstairs to take her turn sitting with the corpse of the master whom she had served for nearly forty years.

Theodore Coniffe was laid out in the small room beyond the parlour, where he died. When in the early hours old Theodore felt a strange sensation creeping over him the most obvious thing for him to have done would have been to knock on the wall and rouse his capable daughter Theresa, but it may have been that some intuition had come to tell him that not even the most capable person in the world would avail him anything then, and so he made his way down to the small back parlour where he knew he would find his gentlest daughter, Sara, still sitting over the fire dreaming.

It was therefore in this small room that he was laid out for his wake. All night long, willing neighbours had assisted the Coniffes in getting the room ready for the wake. The carpet was lifted, the floor scrubbed, and the windows were rubbed till they gleamed. The dark curtains were taken down, and white curtains, hastily borrowed from someone, were hung up, stiff with the folds of the ironing. The furniture was taken out, and Packy Hand was set to scour deal chairs from the three kitchens, Coniffes', Molloys', and Finnertys'. When these were scoured white as rope, they were set back in the room and ranged along the wall for the people who would come to the wake. The pictures were taken from the walls, and the mirrors were turned face inward. The room was transformed by the neighbours almost as greatly as the body of poor Theodore had been transformed by death. Both were washed and scoured and rigidly straightened, until there was such an exact relation between the corpse on the bed and the room in which the bed stood that the poor worn-out women who readied the room, and the undertaker's men who laid straight the corpse, were so out of keeping with their surroundings that, after wiping the sweat from their faces, and casting a last look over everything, they crept out and left the Coniffe women and their near relations to sit by the dead while they washed themselves at the pump in the yard and made themselves a hot pot of tea by the lively fire in the kitchen. It was towards daylight that Sara leant forward to Theresa and made her strange suggestion.

"Isn't it odd that we never used this room for anything," she said, indicating the silent room about them with one of her vague gestures.

It was on the tip of Theresa's tongue to say that after that night it was unlikely that room would ever be used for anything when something made her look at Sara. What was in her mind? Suddenly Sara spoke again.

"When everything is over," she said quietly, but without her usual timidity, "I think I will move my belongings down here. I always wanted a room of my own."

"Indeed!" Theresa glanced sharply at her. No matter what the circumstances she was not going to tolerate any nonsense. Then just as she was about to pounce upon her she recalled all at once the increasing frequency with which she was being wakened in what seemed to be the middle of the night by Sara who was only coming upstairs. It would appear for the first time really it would be as easy to have her out of the room.

"Please yourself!" she said suddenly and testily. There was nothing more said between the sisters till daylight brought their long vigil to an end.

Theodore Coniffe lay on snowy linen sheets, in a clean scoured room, his body straightened once more into the arrogant posture of youth, and his face wearing the white peace of a serenity such as even in youth it had never known. The lusts and passions of the years may fold the flesh but the bone retains the structure of God's hand, and so from this face had fallen away all the marks of age and there remained only the beautiful contours of the bone, with its thin covering of waxen skin. On the ground beside the stretched white bed the coffin was laid, one end tilted against the wall, to reveal the cold folded linens of the grave and the crimped linen frill that would be passed over the silent face. Death, here, displayed its dignity and as, during all that day, the people of the town and the people from the far-flung countryside outside the limits of the town came to sit for a few hours beside the corpse, it was life and not death which fared ill by comparison.

On the faces of the living there were the sweat marks of hard manual labour. Grime and dirt that was washed out of the young faces could not be dislodged from the wrinkles and lines upon the faces of the aged. Marks of lust, anger, greed, and ambition were visible on many faces, and even the tender-hearted, the nobler people, carried on their countenances, as blemishes, the marks of the qualities that gave them claim to greater nobility; gentleness had left the flabby cheeks, sensitivity had left the running eye. Best and worst these living people compared ill with the calm and grand dignity of the dead man.

Had Gabriel seen this vision of death it could have left no other impression upon him than a peaceful one. But in sending him away his mother had made a mistake that is all too common; all too human. We try to guard each other from scenes and incidents that will create a bad impression, without ever learning the lesson that although we can choose between the incidents to which we expose one another, we have no power over the impressions that they will make upon us. From a scene we think fearful, a lasting impression of beauty may be formed. From a scene that we think beautiful an impression of terror may be derived.

Gabriel was spared from looking on the white, chastened face of Theodore Coniffe, but as he lay in the large bedroom that night, with the shadows of the night light leaping from rose to rose on the patterned fabric of his counterpane, the impressions of the day ran together confusedly, as colours in a cheap fabric will run together when it gets wet, and it seemed to him that death was everywhere and instead of hearing the tapping of his grandfather's stick upon the floor of the room next door, he would hear the door handle rattle and in another moment his dead grandfather would hobble into the room, with gaping and polluted eye sockets in which cracked eyeballs rolled and pale blood eddied. Throwing the blankets over his face with frantic and impotent effort to protect himself from his fears he screamed for help, but one effort prevented the other from being effective, and his screams were drowned by the heavy blankets, so that at last, frenzied and fevered, with heartbeats that seemed to block the passage of breath in his swollen throat, he fell into a sleep of exhaustion in which the body reasserted itself over the mind and the sleeping limbs kicked off the suffocating covers. He lay there in the cold, twitching, and occasionally groaning out of his uneasy dreams until his mother crept in at a late hour to smooth down his bed and caress his sleeping body into a greater quietude.

Leaf by leaf, petal by petal, our impressions are laid down.

の   の   の

The next morning was wet. The year had reached that point at which one night of continual rain could transform the countryside into a scene of desolation. The day of Theodore's wake had been one of those warm sunny days which give a deceptive impression that the summer has not

124

yet gone, but that impression was completely destroyed by the night's rainfall. In spring or early summer a night of rain will often heighten the charm of the season. Then every leaf, bud, and blade, every pebble on the roadway, every ripple in the streams, will glitter and gleam as brightly as they did in the sunlight. But in the late summer, and early autumn, the rain shows up the decay that has been going on for some time under an artful disguise. The boughs of the trees absorb the wet and they take on a heavy sodden look. The rain soaks into the softened bark, causing it to give out an odour of rot and decay. On the bushes there are no pointed buds to which the crystal drops can cling. In the fields the grass is flattened. Sapless blades bend over and become matted together. And everywhere, logged in the fields, and pasted flat on the roads, are the leaves that had lately floated about in the air so freely. From them, too, a damp odour begins to rise, and waver in the air, like ribbons. But worst of all, stretching away and away, over the fields and roads alike, the eye can find no relief from the desolation. Everywhere there are the same bleak sodden trees, the same blenched and flattened fields, with the same pale sheets of shallow water flooding them. And everywhere, over the land, the low clouds seem to be no more than an arm's length above the sluggish earth.

It was upon this dismal day that Gabriel opened his eyes after his feverish night of tossing dreams. This time he had no cause to complain of any tardiness on Mary Ellen's part, because it was she who wakened him, letting the blind slap up against the wet glass of the window and throwing back the coverings from his shivering body.

"Wake up, Gabriel. It's nearly time for the hearse to arrive. Wake up, Gabriel, it will take a long time to get you into that new suit of yours. It's my belief it's too tight in the waistband."

And before his eyes had become clear and properly opened he was sitting on the side of the bed, gripping the cold brass rail, while Mary Ellen forced his legs into the tight trousers, and passed the cold braces over his head to slap against his back with a hard slap.

"Here's your shirt," she said, and she thrust the fresh linen with its icy gloss into his hands, while she caught up his foot and, turning her back upon him, with the foot under her arm, like a smithy with a horse hoof, drew the stiff new boot on to his foot and tied the laces so tightly that the tin eyelets were dug into his flesh through the stockings.

"Now your tie!" said Mary Ellen. "Now your clean handkerchief." And as one jerk superseded another, the desire to exclaim at one pinch was superseded by the desire to exclaim at another, so rapidly indeed that he was standing on the floor by the rose-patterned ewer and basin before he had exclaimed at all, and then the big yellow sponge dripping with icy sparkles of water was dabbed into his face and he could not open his mouth without danger of swallowing a mouthful.

"You're ready now!" said Mary Ellen, and hearing a horse in the street she ran to the window. "You're ready now, and not a crumb too soon, the hearse is coming down the street. Hurry now and keep your eyes downcast. Let the people see you're sorry for your poor grandfather, the Lord have mercy on him!"

Taking his hand she led him over to the door, and turning the handle with her great, definite gestures that gave her least actions an appearance of great portent, she launched Gabriel upon the landing and catching him by the shoulders she directed him ahead of her to the stairs.

The lower hall was again crowded with people, as it had been on the previous morning, but the fact did not surprise Gabriel this time, and coming slowly down the stairs he made a careful investigation of everything within the direct range of his glance. Mary Ellen's iron grip upon his shoulders limited the area of this glance by keeping him faced rigidly forward, but here and there among the vaguely familiar faces of the people in the hall Gabriel saw many kindly and very familiar faces. Once again Packy Hand was standing near the big knob at the end of the banisters, and once again Murty Rod leaned against the jamb of the cross door between the hall and kitchen. Mr. Finnerty and Mrs. Finnerty were staring up at him as he descended, in positions so almost exactly similar to those they had occupied the day before that it was hard to believe they had moved from them in the intervening time. Murty's face was usually round and shining as if made for smiling, but this morning, as on the evening before, it wore a forced appearance of solemnity and, as with people whose lives are spent mostly under the influence of one emotion, his expression had the temporary look of one who is merely making a grimace. On seeing Gabriel, Murty Rod's grimace of solemnity relaxed, and his eyes twinkled as if he might at any moment burst into his habitual smile, but he kept his cheek muscles in rigid control and the smile travelled no further than his twinkling eyes. Gabriel smiled back and descended another step. This brought him on a level with Packy Hand, and as Gabriel stared into his long, dull face Packy's wide lips twitched in an unmistakable grin. Gabriel grinned back, and impelled by Mary Ellen took another step downwards, but this time his eye had taken in the faces of Mr. and Mrs. Finnerty and Mr. and Mrs. Molloy, and divining suddenly that he would have to smile at each face in turn he lowered his eyes and began to devote all his attention to his feet.

Just as Gabriel stretched out his neatly booted foot for the last step of the stairs there was a sudden surge in the crowd in the back dining room and this in turn caused the people in the hall to surge nearer to the stairs. Down on Gabriel's small foot came the back of Murty's heel and then, quick as the wind, down came Mary Ellen's broad palm over his mouth to anticipate his yell of pain.

"Come back up here," said Mary Ellen, and she dragged him up three of four steps of the stairs he had just descended. Packy Hand and Murty stepped up on the step that Gabriel had vacated in order to leave room in the hall for the people who were streaming out of the back room. Gabriel put up a hand and pulled Mary Ellen's palm away from his mouth.

"Don't cry, like a good boy," said Mary Ellen, bending over him. "Your poor mother and your aunts are taking their leave of your grandfather."

The last person came out of the back room and the door was closed. The hall was darkened except for the faint blue and green and red rays that came from a panel of coloured glass in the door.

Packy Hand turned around in the small space at his disposal.

"Why don't you bring in the boy to have a look at the corpse?"

"Hush," said Mary Ellen and over his head Gabriel could feel that a mimic conversation was being carried on in gestures and motions of the face. A great fear clutched him. He gripped Mary Ellen's hand, but as Packy Hand shrugged his shoulders and turned back to his original position, he felt safe once more.

There were a few moments' silence then and the door of the back parlour was opened again. His mother and his aunts came out. His Aunt Theresa was dressed almost the same as usual but his Aunt Sara and his mother looked so strange and dismal in their black clothes that once again Gabriel felt a vague terror assail him. He strained out of Mary Ellen's hand to reach his mother but the way was blocked by tall silent men and women whose faces he could not even see and whose shapes were unfamiliar. As his mother passed through the crowd in the hall dabbing her pale face with a small wet handkerchief, Gabriel tugged at Mary Ellen's hand and was about to plead with her to take him after his mother, when there was a sudden noise in the room behind the closed door. A chair was pushed back, something fell, and all at once there was a stir among the people in the hall. Packy Hand straightened himself up. Murty blew his nose. Mr. Finnerty took off his gloves and shoved them into his pocket. The door was thrown open and there, in full sight of the doorway, Gabriel saw the long thin end of a bright yellow coffin with gleaming brass handles tied with bows of black ribbon.

"The bearers! Will the bearers please step this way now. The hearse is waiting." A small thin man with a bleached face who wore a soiled white apron was standing at the door and with the toe of his heavy hobnailed boot he was keeping the end of the coffin from resting with its full weight upon the ground.

Packy Hand stepped forward, pushing his way with ceremonious discourtesy. The lobes of Murty's ears grew fiery red and he looked uncertainly at Mary Ellen, who nodded her head vigorously at him and motioned him to go forward after Packy. Mr. Finnerty was hemmed in to either side, but he coughed discreetly and room was made way for him at once. With the activity of the bearers, restraint was lifted from the entire gathering, and people began to warm their feet by stamping first one foot and then another upon the hard flags of the hallway; heads leaned together in hurried conference, and from near the hall door a gust of cold air came streaming inward as the door was opened and people began to shuffle out on to the pavement, their voices that were freed upon the air coming back with guilty echoes into the dark house.

"Make way, please," said Mary Ellen, and Gabriel had but a moment to see the men who had volunteered for the job hoisting the pale yellow coffin on their shoulders and bending forward with the weight, before he was swept along with the crowd into the cold street.

The street was lined with black carriages, down the sides of which the rain streamed, and in front of which stood patient horses with dull black trappings. Small groups of people stood about in the street waiting for the allotment of seats in the mourning cabs, but here and there some of the stouter women of the gathering were choosing their own cabs and stepping into them with such great weight and determination that the springs squealed and the body of the vehicles leaned towards the sidewalk with a dangerous tilt. They were built, however, to give with the occupant and no sooner were the fat women established within than they tilted back again into their original position, merely rocking slightly from side to side, and only tilting again when the ladies saw fit to lean too heavily to one side or another in an effort to see that they had not missed anything by seating themselves soon.

Right in front of the hall door stood the hearse, with glittering windows of cut glass, which even in the cold wet light of early morning showed a tendency to catch the watery gleams and cast them back with prismatic rays. The hearse was drawn by four black horses whose trappings were black and silver and from whose silver headplates vast plumes of black feathers waved upwards. The horses stood remarkably still, but occasionally they shook their heads, and when they did this, the great feather plumes released a shower of silver raindrops.

Gabriel was fascinated. He wanted to stand and stare at the great glass carriage but Mary Ellen hurried him away from it and, catching him under the armpits, hoisted him into one of the dark wooden cabs. It was the first mourning coach and stood exactly behind the hearse, to proceed in that order when the funeral procession started. Gabriel was placed on the seat with its back to the horses, which meant that he would travel backwards all the way, but as soon as this fact was borne in upon his mind he climbed down and took his place on the opposite seat, facing forwards. He had not effected the change a moment too soon, because his two aunts and his pale-faced mother appeared again in the doorway of the house, and coming straight towards the first coach slipped into it and took their places. Theresa Coniffe, as the eldest of the three, was the first to step into the carriage, and as she chose the seat facing forward this meant that she and Gabriel shared it, while his mother and his Aunt Sara sat together on the opposite seat. For a moment Gabriel regretted his change but it soon occurred to him that he had not chosen too badly, for, sitting bolt upright, with her frame rigidly posed, her arms dug into her sides to maintain its strict rigidity, Theresa Coniffe could not see anything that was not within the direct orbit of her glance, and without taking up an entirely new posture she could hardly see him at all. That she would not alter her posture he knew almost for certain, because one of the things that his Aunt Theresa complained against most frequently was the fidgeting of others.

"Stop fidgeting, Sara! Stop fidgeting, Lily!" she said, a thousand times a day.

Gabriel felt that he had chosen his place well, if it were for nothing more than that he had the chance of smiling back at his sadly smiling mother.

"You are a very good boy," said his mother, leaning across and patting his knee. "I'm glad there are no tears."

"What did you expect?" said Theresa. "Did you expect him to cry? Why should he cry? Our father is gone to Heaven. He led a good life and a long one. He has gone to his rest. I don't see why anyone should cry." Without moving her head she darted a sharp glance at the red-eyed Sara. Sara felt that she had been addressed directly.

"I know poor Father is gone to his reward," she said, "but I cannot help thinking how much we will miss him around the house."

"It's not like you, Sara," said Theresa, "to put your own happiness before the happiness of others! Father is much better off where he is, than ever he was in this life. Indeed we will all be better off when we are laid in our coffins. What is this world? Nothing!"

Gabriel listened without much attention to the beginning of this discussion, but towards the end he became very attentive. Up to now he had been able to keep away all thought of his grandfather, as he now considered him to be, gaping-eyed and polluted, but as Theresa Coniffe spoke, the men were lifting the coffin into the hearse ahead of them, and through the window at the side he got a rapid glimpse of the yellow varnished wood. At once he seemed to see through the wood. He visioned once again the crude corruption that Judy Soraghan had mimicked in the evening shadows by the rampart, but now a greater grief came upon him because it seemed that to this end they all must come. Words that had drifted about him while he stood on the stairs came back to him again.

"There is no avoiding it. We all come to the same end. No one knows when his own time will come."

The terrors of the night before had been great but they had a nightmare quality and were dispelled by the reassuring presence of another person, but the cold dread that entered into the small soul of the child at that moment could never be dispelled. He looked at his lovely pale-faced mother and at his sad Aunt Sara, he looked with fright at his own pale reflection in the polished wood of the coach, and all the faces seemed to undergo a change, until it might almost be that he was back again on the rampart with the dancing urchins from the rampart cottages peering at him with polluted faces. He gripped the seat. He held his breath. He looked with terror at the side face of his Aunt Theresa. He was going to cry!

A moment before his mother had patted his knee because he was a good boy and did not cry, and now, a moment afterwards, he was going to do that very thing. His Aunt Theresa would be glad. She would blame his mother for his disgrace. She would say that his mother had put the idea into his head. And the more he resolved against crying, the more and more miserable he became, and the greater the danger of his doing so. Behind his eyes the tears were bright and feverish. Behind his tightly pressed lips a gale of hoarded breath threatened to burst forth. In his throat his grief was like a piece of glass. He could not keep back the tears. It was no use. In another minute he would have disgraced his dear mother. Gabriel stared at her in a frantic appeal for forgiveness even before he had transgressed.

But as Gabriel lifted his eyes to his mother, expecting to find an anxious anticipation of his tears in her gaze, he was surprised to see her smiling at him, so surprised that he let out his tortured hoard of breath, and, before he had realized that the danger was over, where the tears had threatened there rushed forth a flight of smiles.

Gabriel smiled at his mother and his mother smiled back at him. Outside the carriage, people were still sorting themselves into groups, and Mr. Finnerty was allotting them places in the other carriages. The coffin had been placed in the hearse and the men were busy piling up wreaths of lilies and yellow and white chrysanthemums upon the coffin lid. Gabriel felt more and more reassured. Several times he looked out of the window and several times he looked back at his beautiful pale mother and smiled secretly at her.

Gabriel was hidden from Theresa Coniffe but suddenly her attention was drawn to her sister Lily. She opened her mouth to say something and snapped it closed again.

130

Lily was smiling at her son and saw nothing, but Sara, nervously opening and shutting the metal clasp of her handbag, felt another necessity to speak.

"You were going to say something, Theresa?" she said.

Thesesa pursed her lips still tighter as if her former decision to speak had been one that would have added something to the situation and her later decision not to do so would deprive Sara personally of some benefit. But with her pursed lips she directed her glance at the smiling Lily who, indeed, on this occasion was actually wrinkling her nose in a whimsical way to put her small son still more at his ease. Sara knew at once that Theresa's decision to remain silent was not one that she would maintain for long and with her eye she measured the distance across the mildewed cushions of the cab which separated her from her sister Lily in a vague hope of being able to give her a slight dig in the ribs to make her aware of Theresa's displeasure.

As Sara's eye measured the distance on the mildewed cushion, Theresa's eye detected the thought behind the glance and her cold lips opened again.

"I should imagine that a mourning coach would be the last place for smiling and face-making."

Lily scarcely grasped the meaning of the words but the cold tone of the voice penetrated her consciousness and the smile was arrested. She remained, however, with her sweet short upper lip slightly raised from her small girlish teeth and she continued to stare at her small son opposite her.

It was upon Gabriel's face, rather than upon her own mind, that the meaning of the words was finally recorded. She looked up startled at Theresa. Theresa drew her arms close to her black silk sides.

"I'm sure I don't know how it will appear to the mourners to see the dead man's daughter smiling and laughing and bobbing her head before the funeral has left the death house!"

As quick as tears had given place to smiles in Gabriel's small pointed face, the smiles had fled from his mother's face and the bright tears glittered in her eyes.

"It seems tears are as easy as smiles with some people," said Theresa, but having desired to wound Lily, she had no sooner wounded her than she regretted it. Neither tears nor smiles came readily to her and it was with a strange envy in her heart that she chided those to whom they did come readily.

Theresa Coniffe looked out of the window away from the three faces upon which she knew she had brought a sadder shadow than death itself had brought. For a moment she stared out longing for some interruption to come that might break the silence she had laid upon them all.

Then, determined to break it herself, with a sudden impetuosity she

131

rapped on the glass of the carriage window with her hard thin knuckles, and following quickly upon this, she loosed the strap that held the window up and let it fall open with a loud slap.

"What is the delay?" she called out, directing her words towards Mr. Finnerty who still stood on the pavement with a wreath in either hand, but she attracted at the same time the attention of the entire cortege, to such an extent that even those who had entered their coaches put out their heads through the window and stared up at the first coach.

Mr. Finnerty hastily disposed of the wreaths and ran over to the window of the cab.

"I think everything is ready now, Miss Coniffe. We will be ready to start in a few moments." He lowered his voice. "The curate was delayed, I understand, but I see him coming down the street this moment. He's coming at a good pace. He's nearly tripping over his skirts. We'll be off now in half a minute, Miss Coniffe."

And sure enough, in less than a minute, Mr. Finnerty approached the head of the cortege once more and waving his hand downward two or three times, like a guard on the railway line signalling to the engine driver, he gave the driver of the hearse the intimation that he might begin to proceed.

Associating the gestures of Mr. Finnerty and a guard led Gabriel to believe that they would now proceed rapidly forward and it was with great excitement that he caught at the crusty leather strap beside him and pressed his shoulders securely into the hard pads of the cushion. But the hearse did not appear to move. It was some moments before he realized that it had moved but that it made such slow progress that one had to stare hard at the road to perceive the motion. There was a slight tilt in their own carriage just then, too, and they began to move forward after the hearse. It was only by looking out of the windows at the houses of Clewe Street as they were passed, one after another, that Gabriel was able to create a sense of motion which he hardly felt any other way, as the slow tread of the trained horses conveyed the cortege out of the town.

The countryside upon which they came at last was a dreary one. The gay and simple pattern of field and fence, road, tree, and hillock, was obscured by the rolling mists of rain that imposed their own monotony upon the entire landscape.

The cemetery was situated three miles outside the town, and situated at the crossroads. The crossroads was slightly sunk below the level of the surrounding country although the cemetery itself was on an upward sloping stretch of land that tended towards the far end to be a decided hill, crowned with a few solemn cypresses and a large wooden cross that could be seen for miles around. This rising ground obscured to a certain extent the fourth branch of the road which ran under the hill and disappeared in an unusually woody patch of the country. The other roads were plain and bare and could be followed by the eye from the crossroads to the rim of the flat fields on the sky line. A carriage or a solitary stroller who set out upon one road could be followed by the eye from either of the other roads from the moment he came into sight at the crest of the sky line until he reached the crossroads.

On this cold wet day, as the cortege of Theodore Coniffe stole out upon its sad, slack journey to the cemetery, the roads were bare, and over them, to emphasize their bleak and lonely emptiness, a cold rain-laden wind was blowing.

The three sisters had taken out their cold beads, and as they passed them stiffly through their fingers, their lips moved ceaselessly and even the necessity for the intake and output of breath did not interrupt that movement. But Gabriel stared out over the cold empty roads as the coach rolled slowly onward. Since they had left the town and entered upon the country road, the carriages had slightly increased their speed, and the bushes and stone walls flowed past the open window slightly faster than the big blocks of masonry had passed in Clewe Street.

Gabriel's eyes closed. The pace was gentle and underneath him the carriage swayed lightly on the straps by which it was slung from the traces. His eyes had closed against his will and when he forced them open again the daylight seemed to sear them. He closed them deliberately. This time sleep pressed on his lids and kept them pressed down. The sounds of the rolling wheels died away and instead the sibilant whispers of the prayers deepened, and as the whispers criss-crossed in the air, they seemed to become thin straws upon the wind, laid down one after another on top of him, covering him, securing him, shielding him from the daylight world. His head dropped.

Suddenly there was a sharp sound of harness and tackle being jerked. The horses' hoofs grated as if they were slipping on the wet road. The carriage jolted and came to a stop. Gabriel's eyes flew open and the whispered prayers of the sisters ceased as if they had been but the creakings of the leather. And there, framed in the window, was the sombre face of Packy Hand.

"What is the meaning of this delay?" said Theresa Coniffe, beating her black-clad foot upon the flooring of the cab as an angry accompaniment to her words, and increasing the tapping into a crescendo when her words had come to an end.

Packy gesticulated outside the glass and he said something which could not be heard. Theresa continued for a few minutes to tap her foot and then she shot out a hand and released the window strap, letting the window clap open.

"Packy Hand, are you out of your senses? What are you doing in the middle of the road, delaying a man on the way to the clay? Have you gone out of your mind?"

While Theresa Coniffe was speaking Packy Hand began to stamp his own great flat foot upon the road and when Theresa had finished and stared at him for an answer, he did not give it until he had beaten a further tune of angry taps on the wet road.

"It's easy seen that the man that is dead is no longer alive," said Packy Hand at last. "When a person came to ask a favour of Theodore Coniffe he was civilly received, let alone a person that came to confer a favour! I had better mind my own business I suppose," and there and then he turned on his heel and began to retreat towards one of the other coaches whence he had come. But Theresa Coniffe put her hand out of the window.

"Come back here, Packy Hand! It's a poor man that won't make allowances for the manners of those in trouble!"

Packy halted. "Miss Theresa, it's easy to make excuses for a remark provoked by a situation, but when a remark comes from the character there's no use excusing it. You had a hard tongue when you were only a sass of a girl flipping jackstones in the air as if the devil was jerking your elbow."

Theresa Coniffe clenched her two hands. "Did you put a stop to fifty mourning coaches and a hearse to pick a quarrel with your betters?"

"I did not," said Packy, "but I put a stop to it for another reason altogether about which you won't have the gratification of hearing now!"

"I demand to hear it," said Theresa Coniffe, and she put a hand outside to grasp the handle of the door as if she might alight and drag the answer to her question out of his mouth, but Packy set off down the road and was seen stepping into the third coach from the top. Since the first coach remained stationary, however, the entire cortege remained stationary, except for the glittering hearse which by this time had proceeded a considerable distance down the road, alone, the driver unaware that the rest of the procession had been delayed.

"Is that man mad?" said Theresa, sitting back on the seat and staring at the others. When she had stared for some time she began to tap her foot again on the flooring. Then she put up her hand and, dragging at the brooch at her neck, took it out, and put it in again, jabbing the pin through the material with greater determination and energy than anyone had ever seen her show before. And then, when she had done this, it seemed that she had exhausted all the courses of action possible short of jumping out on the road and going after Packy Hand. This would have been impossible, she realized. "Well!" she said impatiently, looking from one of her sisters to the other. "What do you suppose is wrong? What do you think we should do? Don't sit there staring like a pair of paper dolls! Say something!"

But her sisters had nothing to say.

Theresa turned suddenly to Gabriel. "I'll send the boy out to call Packy back!" she said. "Stand up, boy."

But just as Gabriel stood up there was a sound of argument further down the road, and before they had time to raise their heads to listen, Packy Hand appeared again at the carriage window. This time he stepped up on the foot block and put his head into the carriage. His purpose in doing this became clear at once when he turned his head in such a way that he had the back of it to Theresa. He addressed himself to her two sisters who were so conscious of the slight to Theresa as to be unconscious of the words that were addressed to themselves.

"I have been thinking things over," said Packy Hand, "and I see no reason why the discourtesy of the living should be revenged upon the dead!" He paused and this time he withdrew his head so that although still addressing the two younger women, he could see the reactions on the face of the older one. "I intend to give you my information. It has just been brought to my attention now that there is a man dead in the next town and that he is a native of this town!" He paused and stared at Theresa but there was no change in her countenance. Packy pursed his lips. "Does that convey nothing to you, Miss Coniffe?" he said at last.

"Nothing!" said Theresa.

"Does it convey nothing to you, Miss Sara?"

"I'm afraid it doesn't, Packy," said Sara, clasping her bag tightly.

Packy turned back to Theresa.

"Will it convey anything to you if I develop the subject further and tell you that this man died two days ago and is due to be put under the clay this very morning?"

There was no reply.

"Will it convey anything to you if I tell you that they're bringing him back to his native town to be buried?"

There was no sign that his words conveyed any particular significance although a vague dread of what that significance might prove to be had begun to show on the face of Sara.

"Ah! Times have changed," said Packy. "There was a time when people would cut off their right hands to ease the suffering of the poor helpless dead!"

Theresa Coniffe stiffened.

"Say whatever you're trying to say and be done with it!" she said, and she fixed him with her eye.

Packy Hand fixed Miss Coniffe with a still colder eye.

"Do you mean to say, Miss Coniffe, that you never heard tell that the last corpse into the cemetery must wait and guard the graves until the next corpse comes to take his place?"

135

"Packy Hand," said Miss Coniffe, "if you stopped my father's funeral to talk nonsense, you could have waited till we got to the grave, and even there I'd hardly have the time to listen to you and your superstitions."

"If I waited till then it might be too late."

"What are you talking about?"

"If I waited till then the other corpse might arrive before us, and if they planted him down before your poor father, your father'd be left to guard the grave. But if we get there first the other poor man will have to take his chance!"

Miss Theresa was disturbed. She didn't want to give in to Packy Hand's superstition, but she was afraid to disregard it.

"What can we do?" she said in a somewhat softer tone.

"We can hurry the horses, ma'am."

"Hurry the horses! I was on the point of tapping on the glass a few minutes ago to tell the driver to slacken his pace. There are people hereabouts that would judge your affection for the departed by the pace of your horses towards the graveyard. If you went above a snail's pace they'd say you were glad to be rid of the one that was gone. I don't want that to be said!"

Theresa Coniffe, although she was a thin woman, blocked the small window of the carriage, so that if the other three occupants had any opinions upon the matter they were not heard by Packy Hand. At this stage however Theresa Coniffe swung around and Packy saw that Sara had made so bold as to pull her sister by the skirt.

"Perhaps if Packy stepped to the window of each coach and explained the case, people wouldn't take it wrongly for us to hurry up the horses. After all it would be a dreadful thing to be lying awake at night thinking of poor Father's spirit standing at the cemetery in the cold and the wet, waiting for the next corpse to arrive."

"Father hated to be kept waiting at all times," said Theresa abstractedly.

"And there's no one sick in the town," said Sara, "and unless there's a sudden death, or an accident—the Lord between us and all harm—it may be months before there's another coffin brought in through the cemetery gates!"

Miss Coniffe sat back helplessly in her seat.

"It's all nonsense," she said wildly. "I won't subscribe to superstitious nonsense." She turned upon Packy Hand. "I don't know what business you had putting such thoughts into our heads in the first place."

"If that's all the thanks I get," said Packy, "for trying to do a service to the poor helpless dead, I might have saved myself the pains. All I can say is that if it was one of his daughters—God between us and all harm—that was being brought to her burial, and the poor dead man—God be good to him—that was in charge of the funeral arrangements, I have no doubt but that things would be different and some efforts would be made to save the spirit of the dead from an uneasy vigil."

Miss Coniffe sat up again. "It's all nonsense!" she said once more.

Packy Hand prepared to depart. "It might be better to be sure than sorry, Theresa," said Sara, in a courageous burst which was followed at once by a fit of weeping.

"Stop wailing, Sara," said Theresa. "How can I think with that noise in my ears?"

"If you're going to consider it, you'd want to consider it quickly," said Packy, and he pulled out a large silver watch, blackened and rusted, but ticking so loudly that Gabriel was emboldened to peer out at it under his aunt's elbow. "We've lost time already," said Packy.

"Of course we have!" said Theresa. "If you had stayed where you were we would have been at the cemetery by now and you would have had the satisfaction of your superstition and we would have been without the annoyance of it!" She leaned out and looked down the road. "The hearse is nearly there already," she said.

How things might have been settled it is difficult to know, because at that moment Gabriel raised his eyes from the ticking watch on the flat of Packy Hand's palm and glanced at the far edge of the horizon.

"Oh look!" cried Gabriel. "More horses!"

Packy Hand swung around. Theresa Coniffe threw up her head like a horse, and Sara and Lily strained to see out through the small chink under Theresa's elbow and over Gabriel's head. There on the grey horizon was the funeral cortege of the man from the next town.

There was a long line of black coaches and at the head was the pale hearse that carried the coffin. They were so far away that they looked like a string of miniature coaches such as might ornament a mantelpiece, or decorate the borders of a fancy plate. They were cut out against the grey sky and, although the distance between them and the Coniffe cortege was too great for the motion of the vehicles to be seen, the furious tilt of the carriages and the frenzied lift to the forefeet of the horses suggested at once that the other funeral was travelling at a great pace.

"Quick," cried Theresa Coniffe. "Don't let them get there before us! Quick!"

Packy Hand made a frantic signal to the coachman. He ran back to his own coach. There was a wild shaking of trappings and the flicking of whips on the wet flanks of the horses, and the cortege started again, with every ounce of the speed that Gabriel had expected to attend its departure from Clewe Street when Mr. Finnerty had waved his handkerchief.

Gabriel clutched the strap. The ladies on the opposite seat jolted together. Miss Theresa planted her feet apart to prevent such a contingency.

137

"Apart from the superstition," she said, "I hope we get there first. I wouldn't want to give anyone the satisfaction of saying that the Coniffes were kept waiting at the cemetery while they buried some man that nobody ever heard of until to-day."

"Oh, I wish the horses could fly!" said Sara.

"The others are gaining ground," said Lily. "Oh, poor Father! Poor Father!"

"Tap on the ceiling, Gabriel," said Theresa, sticking a long black umbrella into his hands. "It will make the man hurry more."

But no horse could hurry faster than the horses under the Coniffe coach, and no coach could travel faster upon its wheels than the coach they drew. Sara and Lily were thrown first to one side and then to another. First Lily knocked against the window on her side, then Sara against the window frame on her side, and then both of them were thrown towards the centre of the coach and crashed into each other. They were jolted upwards one moment, nearly hitting the ceiling, and the next minute they were so jerked that they lost their grip of the leather seat and were almost flung across on top of the occupants of the other seat. Their hats were knocked back off their heads leaving their foreheads bare, and they were no sooner adjusted than they were knocked forward nearly smothering their faces.

"Why can't you keep control of yourselves?" said Theresa. "How will you look when we reach the grave! Straighten your hat, Sara; Lily, your hair is coming undone. You look more as if you were on your way to a fancy fair than to your father's funeral."

For Theresa, in some mysterious mastery of the principles of gravity, was rolled neither to right nor to left. She suffered neither jolt nor jerk. When the coach tilted to one side Theresa tilted with it, so that although she slanted towards the road in the same proportion as the coach, she remained in exactly the same erect right angle to the seat upon which she sat. She might have been glued into an unalterable position like a top occupant of a top coach. Had the coach overturned it might well be believed that she would still retain her exact relation to the seat upon which she sat and that even if the coach lay upon its roof in the ditch, the horses kicking their legs in the air, Theresa Coniffe would still be sitting upon the seat with her legs up in the air, nothing altered in position, except, perhaps, her sleek black skirts, which might fall back to display her froth of virgin petticoats.

Gabriel, who at first had jolted as impotently as his mother and his younger aunt, had not been long in noticing his old aunt's mastery of the circumstances, and when his elbows had more than once come in contact with the wooden arm rest, and the back of his head had knocked with a resounding crack against the wooden backing of the seat, he overcame his fear and dislike for Theresa and, wedging his arm with great difficulty between the rigid arm and rigid body of the tall stiff woman beside him, he anchored himself securely to her side and soon shared her equipoise, and was able to divide his time between watching the pitching and tossing of his mother and his Aunt Sara and watching the rival funeral which galloped nearer and nearer, the distance between the two funerals being diminished with double rapidity as the horses tore along the roads and as the roads themselves converged toward the crossroads.

ல ல ல

The graveyard gates were wrought-iron, high-backed, and painted white. There were three gates, but the great centre gate was never opened. The side gates were opened so frequently that they had a tendency to swing open of their own accord on a windy day with a low wailing sound. Although the centre gate would have been wide enough to permit the entry of a hearse, the mourners always paid a last tribute to the dead by taking the coffin out of the hearse at the gate and shouldering it to its place of burial. This tribute was so universally observed that the great gate had probably never been opened since the day it was hung upon its great white hinges.

On this grey day, however, when the gravediggers had ascertained that the graves they had dug the night before were still open and ready for the coffins, they came down to the gates to watch the roads for the funerals. From this distance they were best able to ascertain the number of followers behind the hearse, and Milo Grimes, the oldest of the gravediggers, was said to have a complete record of the number of coaches that followed every corpse that had been buried in the town in the last sixty-two years, both in the old graveyard behind the chapel and in this new cemetery at the crossroads. In fact he was known to parcel out his deference to the people of the town, not according to their money or social position, but according to the total of mourning coaches that had followed the corpses of their relatives to the grave.

"Which funeral do you figure will arrive first?" said Ned Fell, a thin weedy youth who had been apprenticed to Milo a month before.

"Do you mean to say you'd have any doubt upon a subject like that?" said Milo, looking at him as if by his question he had betrayed a lack of intelligence, and one that would come against him greatly in his future career. "The Coniffes have been noted in these parts during the last sixty years for the splendour of their turnout upon a day of mourning. Never will you see more wreaths than you'll see on a Coniffe coffin. Never will you see a coffin with a better or brighter varnish. Never will you see more handsome handles. The pathway has to be scuffled fresh after a Coniffe funeral on account of the unnaturally big passage of people, and I've seen times when there were so many carriages after the hearse that they had no chance nor manner of turning in the road, and had to proceed straight on the way they were going until they got to a further crossroads two miles up the road and take the road back to the town by a roundabout way that sent them four miles out of their way and left them so late for the funeral feast that the women that were preparing it began to think the whole cortege, hearse and coffin, carriages and horses, people and wreaths, had ridden over the rim of the world."

Ned Fell listened to this long stretch of eloquence and when it was finished he went over it again, taking it up point by point, and still he found no answer to his own question in it anywhere. After a while he spoke again.

"It seems to me an elegant funeral like that would take a long time making its way here. I'm thinking maybe the other corpse will be here first!"

"It's easily seen you haven't much understanding about funerals," said Milo, "although I'll admit you have a good grip on a spade for a beginner. The more coaches there are, the more wreaths, the more men and the more women with white handkerchiefs, the more necessity there is for that funeral to arrive first when there are two funerals on the one day, as in the present unfortunate case."

"I don't see how you make that out," said Ned.

Milo looked at him suspiciously. "I hope you're not one of these people that have to have a remark explained to such a point that there's no life in it at the end? Can't you see for yourself that while it's easy for one small, unnoticeable hearse, with a few coaches, to pull up under a clump of trees near the gate and wait for their turn, a big turnout such as the Coniffes will have would look a fine foolish affair, stretching back from the gates to as-near-as-no-matter to the town it left! Do you think they'd let a thing like that happen even though there's only a parcel of women left in the place now to attend to such matters?"

Ned's face wore a worried expression as if he were not yet satisfied and were about to argue upon some point, when Milo looked up and immediately slapped his thigh.

"What did I tell you?" he shouted. "Here comes Theodore Coniffe!"

His old eyes, that could hardly read the name on his packet of snuff, had seen the hearse come out under the distant arch of the town gate and after it he could see, clearly enough to count them, the mourning coaches, as they appeared one after another, a long sombre fresco against the flat country.

Ned, greatly humbled, turned aside, refusing to take any further interest in the funeral and even beginning to whistle in order to drown the triumphal reckoning of Milo, who counted aloud as coach after coach came from under the arch, each one making the funeral fresco longer and more impressive, and counteracting in length for the reduction in size imposed on it by distance.

"Twenty-seven, twenty-eight. There were only twenty-eight coaches at the funeral of the stranger that was found dead in the bog hole! Twenty-nine, thirty! There can hardly be more than thirty. Thirty-one! There's thirty-one—thirty-two. This is a record in the history of grave-diggings. Thirty-three . . . Is it possible there are more to come?"

There were, as we know, seventeen more coaches yet to pass out under the town arch, but Milo's reckoning of them was interrupted at thirty-three by a pull at his sleeve. Ned was staring at the skyline where the Liscannor Road cut the fields with as straight a slash as the slash of a spade. He had seen a dark speck on the skyline and although he would have enjoyed calling out in triumph at the sight of it, he was afraid of being mistaken. Young eyes do not necessarily have the best sight when it comes to judging the shape of an article that old eyes have gazed and reckoned upon for nearly seventy years.

"Isn't that a funeral?" said Ned, pointing. It was.

"God in Heaven, this is a terrible thing to happen! They'll meet at the gates. It's only a matter of tossing a bone—knuckle to you, knuckle from you—which of them reaches the crossroads first."

"The Coniffes had a good start," said Ned, in whom argumentativeness had been but an artificial affair destined to pass the time, and which faded immediately before a genuine interest in the snails' race that had begun upon the horizon.

"Would you say there was any difference in the roads?" said old Milo. "It's a long time since I travelled the full length of either of them."

"There isn't a rut or a pothole of difference in them," said Ned, clapping his hands together. "As straight as spades, both of them."

"They're too far off to see what pace they're making," said Milo, "but there seems to be a great lift to the forefeet of the Liscannor horses."

"Do you suppose," said Ned, "that they can see each other as plain as we can see them?"

"I couldn't say. I think it's likely they're not thinking of looking from side to side. The ones in the first coaches are likely to be blotchy-eyed with crying and the general mourners in the back coaches are too busy telling yarns and smoking their pipes, and the women tittering and making eyes at those opposite them. They'll not be looking out the windows, I'm thinking."

"I think the Coniffes are keeping the gait they got at the start," said Ned, and then before the last word had rightly disentangled itself from the woolly grey breath that accompanied it out of Ned's mouth, he gave a loud significant whistle.

"What's that?" said Milo in alarm.

141

Ned put out a long thin finger which a caking of black clay made even more sinister-looking.

"The Coniffe coach is stopping upon the road!"

Milo could not deny that this was so. The motion which had been difficult to discern while it was in process became apparent as having previously existed as soon as it ceased. And to make it more obvious that the coaches had indeed stopped it was seen that the door of the third coach had opened and a figure had alighted from it.

"What in the name of pick and shovel is the matter with these people?" said Milo.

"The other funeral is gaining," said Ned, transferring his allegiance to the cortege which, if not the most advanced, was for the moment in a superior position.

"What are you thinking of!" said Milo, shaking his fist in the direction of the distant Coniffe cortege. "That's more like it," he said as the figure on the road went back to his coach and re-entered it. But the cortege did not move. "What's the matter now?" As the figure redescended into the road Milo became greatly agitated. "Get back into your box, whoever you are, and let us be on our way!" he shouted, and he turned his dismayed eyes upon Ned, who at the same time remembered that Milo and old Theodore Coniffe had gone to school together.

"The Coniffe hearse is continuing on its way anyhow," he said. "The hearse is nearly halfway to the gates!"

Old Milo looked at the lonely travelling hearse. "I don't know but that makes things worse instead of better. To think of poor Theodore travelling on his own, and his family gossiping on the road. I never heard tell of the like to happen in the best and longest of my days. I declare but I can't look on a sight so distressful!" And turning around he began to walk back up the centre of the cemetery. He had no sooner gone three steps, however, when Ned gave a shout.

"They've started again—" Old Milo, even then, did not have the heart to turn around. "They're moving forward," said Ned, and then something in his voice heartened Milo to look around. He began to retrace his steps slowly. Ned Fell began to leap into the air and beat his fists together over his head.

"They're travelling!" he said. "The Coniffes are travelling. They must have seen the others! Oh man! There's a race for you! They're moving! They're galloping! They're catching up on the hearse!"

Old Milo ran forward to the cemetery wall.

"A chariot race!" he shouted, slapping his sides. "Oh, man, but it's a pity old Theodore himself has to lie with his eyes closed while a sight like this is to be seen. He's the man would like the spirit of this." He put up his hands and formed them into binoculars through which he could stare

142

at his object undistractedly by any extraneous tree, or bush or brier. Once only did he lower his hands to gesture frantically in the direction of the other funeral. "Are the others gaining?" he cried, but in his anxiety for the Coniffes he dared not take his eyes from them.

"They are putting up their pace," said Ned.

"Come on, Theodore!" shouted Milo at once, raising himself on his toes.

"Come on, Liscannor!" shouted Ned, and in his excitement he stood up on a grave mound near the wall.

Old Milo saw him out of the corner of his eye. "Get down off that grave. Don't you know better than to stand on a consecrated grave?"

Ned got down, but his face wore a very sulky expression. "I don't see what harm I was doing. I only wanted to see the sport." He looked at old Milo's tall frame, which measured six feet six inches, although he only had the advantage in height of the six feet, being bent over to such an extent that the six inches went into the curve of his shoulders and neck. "We can't all be as tall as trees!"

The subtle flattery appeased Milo's ire for the dignity of the departed. He darted a glance at the headstone over the grave to refresh his memory of the occupant.

"Matthew Scrapes!" he read out, and then to Ned's astonishment he went over and began to pace the length of the grave edge with his big muddy boots. "Six foot!" he commented and put his fingers to his forehead to help himself in some mental calculation he was making. "I think it would be all right for you to stand hereabouts," he said, marking with the toe of his boot a space about two feet from one end.

"What difference does it make where I stand? Isn't it all the one grave?" said Ned grudgingly.

"Well, you see," said Milo, "poor Matthew, God rest him, was never over four foot five. It was always a source of scourge to his wife, the poor woman, God rest her too. She was a tall woman herself, and you could see it was a great mortification for her to have to walk up the aisle of a Sunday with him where everyone could measure to an inch the difference between them. He only came up to the bend of her shoulder. But when he died she was determined to rectify his deficiency and she gave orders to me, here on this spot in the pouring rain the evening I was digging his grave, that I was to make it a good long grave. I might dig it as narrow as ever I pleased, so narrow we'd have to wedge the coffin down into it with spades, and I might dig it so deep that I'd reach water, but I was to be sure to dig it the length of a tall man. It was just as well I gave in to the whimsicalities of the woman because when poor Matthew arrived, for his burial, he was encased in as long a coffin as you'd see in a year's planting.

She wasn't taking any chances so she gave orders to the undertaker to be generous with his measuring tape when he was making the coffin." Milo looked at the grave. "So there they are," he said reflectively, "and in after years people looking at the mounds will never know but that they were as well-matched as your spade and mine!" Taking Ned's spade he held it up against his own in illustration of the exactitude of his simile. Then he handed back the spade, and after a few moments he brought his mind back to the present problem. "So you see," he said, "it would be no disrespect for the dead if you were standing on the foot of the mound because there'd be nothing under you at that point but earth and just earth."

Old Milo had for the moment forgotten the object for which Ned had desired a higher eminence than that allotted to him by his own legs, but Ned had not forgotten, and as soon as the superior judgment had been pronounced upon grave-standing he sprang up on the green mound of Matthew's plot and, waving his hands wildly, took up his interest in the racing funerals.

"There's something happening! There's something happening," he shouted out, with such a fury of excitement that before Milo could control his shameful lower members that had been respectful of the dead for over sixty years, he himself had scrambled up on to the green mound beside Ned with such frenzied indiscrimination that he stood directly on the spot corresponding with poor Matthew's middle. And from there he made no effort to move, for something strange indeed was happening to the Coniffe cortege. The coaches had grown larger in the interval that had elapsed since Milo and Ned last looked at them and so it was particularly easy to see what was afoot when the third coach of the galloping cortege detached itself from its galloping followers and drew out on to the right side of the road.

"Somebody is drawing out," said Ned. "Somebody must have taken sick with the jolting and jostling."

"No such thing!" said Milo. "The man in that coach, whoever he is, must be a good friend to Theodore Coniffe."

Ned was at a loss to see why this should be so, but very soon it was clear that the third coach had pulled out with the very opposite intention in the world from the intention of turning back, which he had suggested. The third coach was so discontented with the speed of the preceding carriages that it was passing them out, intent upon setting its own lead. The feet of the horses were lifted so swiftly that it seemed as if they turned with the same speed as the spokes of the wheels, but although they gave a great appearance of speed it seemed to Milo and Ned a long time before the third coach crept up upon the two coaches before it, and, as they held their breaths tight, it seemed an age till it crept alongside the glass hearse and drew out past it into the clear roadway. However, no sooner had it gained the free road than it began to draw away from the cortege, leaving a considerably increasing gap.

"Good man!" said old Milo. "Whoever is inside that coach is a man with a head on him. You can't travel over a certain pace with a corpse without smashing the glass of the hearse to smithereens, but it doesn't matter whether it's the head or the tail of a funeral that gets to the gate first, it must be considered to have arrived. That man has a head on his shoulders!"

"They all have heads on their shoulders," said Ned, his heart leaping tumultuously, for suddenly heads appeared at the windows of all the carriages of the Coniffe cortege and a moment afterwards the orderly frescoed regularity of that body was dispelled and coach after coach pulled out to the right, and they began to pass each other out according to the rival merits of the animals in the shafts. In their turn, one after another, all the coaches overtook the hearse and increasing their speed to a frenzied pace they galloped topsy-turvy, sometimes two abreast. And soon the glittering glass of poor Theodore's travelling casket was as much behind the cortege as a short time earlier it had been before it.

"Good men! Good men!" shouted Milo, and Ned began to jump up and down in the air, his feet sinking so deep into the wet clay around that it was well he was standing at the end of the grave and not in the place where Milo stood, for judging by the depth to which his feet sank each time he landed upon the clay after a triumphant rise into the air, he would soon assuredly have crashed through the dry casing bones of Matthew Scrapes's ribbed skeleton.

Meanwhile, although they kept their eyes on the Coniffe funeral they were aware of the other one ever increasing in nearness.

"Is there any advantage in the wind, I wonder?" said Milo, putting up a hand to try and feel the direction of that fickle commodity.

"None!" said Ned.

"Is there any disadvantage in the way of a rise on the other road, I wonder?"

"Both roads are as flat as the palms of my hands!" said Ned, holding them out to show they were identical, which they were indeed, but their identity consisted rather in the number of blisters and calluses, equally sized and disposed, than in any equality of flatness.

"It's all in the hand of God, so, as to which of them will arrive first," said old Milo, and then upon a sudden thought he caught Ned by the sleeve. "Theodore's road runs almost straight for the gates," he said. "The other road runs past the gates!"

"What difference does that make?"

"Are you a fool?" said Milo. "That means the Liscannor horses can gallop their fullest until they leave the corpse level with the gates, but poor Theodore's team will have to slow up a considerable measure if they don't want to go crashing in through the bars of the gate!"

"They're beaten so!" said Ned.

"Beaten? Who said that?" said old Milo. "Theodore Coniffe and me sat on the same form in the same schoolhouse sixty years ago and it's not for me to see him disgraced on his last day, above all days. Come down here and give me a hand with these gates!"

And getting across the distance from the grass plots to the white iron gates, as well as his knotted joints permitted, Milo began to pull at the great white gates, and leaping behind him came Ned whose strength, when added to Milo's enthusiasm, succeeded in flinging back the great groaning gates that shivered like great white trembling mares as they hit the giant granite backstops on a level with the stone pillars.

The gates were not flung open a second too soon, for the great foaming horses of Packy Hand's coach came dashing into the open space of the crossway, and seeing the gates stretched open dashed between them, only coming to a stop when the whole coach, and the forefeet of the horses under the coach behind it, was well within the sanctified precincts. The way was blocked, and the Liscannor carriages that arrived a second later at the crossroads had to slacken their pace there and then, for the full cortege of the Coniffes was blocking the road and stood now in the same relation to the cross as the closed gates would have stood to the Coniffes themselves had Milo not sat upon the same lice-eaten form as old Theodore.

Packy Hand was the first to alight, his face covered with a foaming white lather which, before he brushed it away, gave him the terrifying appearance of a dog in rabies, but which, appearing also on the gentle face of Sara—who at that moment alighted from her carriage—and upon the small face of Gabriel and indeed upon the faces of most of the mourners, was soon ascertained to be but the flecks of lather from the horses, blown back by the wind upon their faces as they leaned out of the coaches to see how near the wheels were to the rim of the ditch. Indeed the black cabs were spattered all over with white foam, as if a sudden snowstorm had flown down the road. Even the curate when he stepped out of a coach near the end of the procession had his black cassock and biretta so flecked with foam that it was clear he had leaned out further and with greater danger than anyone else.

But from the furious red of Father Drew's countenance, on which the lather was melting like a snowball on the fire, it was soon clear that it was not from an interest similar to that of Packy Hand's interest in the race that he had leaned out so far and so dangerously. He had, in fact, been leaning out, waving his arms and even frantically calling out, in a vain effort to stay the unseemly gallop of the other carriages. But the noise of his voice was not only drowned by the beating hoofs of the horses and the rattling rims of the wheels, but, worse still, his waving arms were interpreted in several cases to be the fanfaronnade similar to that with which upon other occasions he encouraged the choir to greater vocal velocity. Some timid souls, who had felt they were actually taking their life into their hands, urged on their carriages solely because they believed that in doing so they acted in accord with the vehement mandate of the clergy. Furthermore, the horses under the curate's own carriage, hearing all around them the din of galloping hoofs, and maddened in particular by the sparks that were struck from the steel shoes of the horses directly in front of them, when they came in contact with rough stones upon the road, began to increase their own pace, and hearing the yells of the curate they remembered their young days and at once entering upon the competition with the fellow flesh they took a high-minded aim of being at least in the first six when they reached the finish, no matter how far away they might be.

But now, at the gates, alighting with irate face, Father Drew approached Packy Hand.

"Let me ask you a question, Packy Hand. Are you a Christian, or are you not?"

"Your meaning, Father?" said Packy, wiping the lather off his face and staring with a fatal fascination at the splatters of the same upon the priest's countenance. The priest put up a hand and lashed foam to right and left.

"It's only a pagan man would gallop a corpse in the way you've galloped this corpse to-day!"

Packy Hand raised himself up on his toes and stared out over the priest's left shoulder. Assured, he pointed his finger in the same direction his glance had taken.

"No one hurried the corpse at all. You're making a mistake, Father. Here comes the poor corpse now, travelling at his ease!"

The hearse was indeed at that moment only arriving to join the cortege it should have headed.

"It was you started this mad enterprise of galloping, wasn't it?" said the priest, unwilling to cede the argument, in which he had unfortunately made a bad beginning.

"If it was me started it, Father, I notice you weren't long about joining the chase!"

"Silence, Packy Hand!" said the priest, raising his hand, flat side outward. "You ought to know that it wasn't my fault if the horses took fright under me. In fact if I recollect aright you were the very man that told me those old horses of mine were a pair of point-to-pointers in their young days!"

"If they remembered those ancient days," said Packy, with the flourish of eloquence which accompanied heightened emotion, "it was seeing your own waving and brandishing of arms that recalled them to their minds."

"I was only waving my arms to put a stop to the whole outrageous situation," said the priest, showing a decided tendency in his vibrating muscles to repeat the fanfaronnade.

"Ah then," said Packy, "I heard tell that you had little knowledge of horseflesh but I can believe it now. You're the first man ever I heard of that thought to stop a rearing horse by rearing up alongside of him."

Father Drew's muscles began to vibrate inside his thin skin like cats in a sack, and turning upon Theresa Coniffe he sought to deal out her portion of censure.

"I cannot believe my eyes," he said, "that a member of the Coniffe family, a woman of maturity, the head of the Sodality, would allow her father's funeral to become a steeplechase! I never thought I'd live to see this day." Father Drew raised his voice deliberately in order that his words might carry to as many as possible of the funeral party and reach if possible the ears of the scandalized cortege from the next town, and while he spoke his eye travelled in a wide radius to see if he could judge by the expressions of the onlookers just exactly how wide was the radius ruled by his voice, but to his surprise a decidedly penitent and even frightened sob interrupted his peroration, and he was for a moment almost too astonished to look at the women before him because, as he knew Theresa Coniffe's social and ecclesiastical distinctions, he knew, too, the timbre of her temper and he did not expect such an easy capitulation to his attack.

Tears? He swung his glance back to the group before him, but there, staring him in the face, were the excessively dry eyes of Theodore Coniffe's elder daughter which were only shifted from his for a moment while she chastised her sister Sara.

"Stop whining, Sara," said Miss Theresa, for it was this mild-eyed creature who had capitulated to the curate's attack, and he could see by the red rim of her eyes and the blotchy patches on her cheeks that the tears he had caused were probably all too ready to fall and were no great tribute to the strength of his denunciatory powers.

"Excuse me, Father Drew," said Theresa Coniffe. "Before you waste your breath blaming the innocent, would you put some of it to better use by examining the information that is spread around your parish by some of your parishioners, to the effect that the spirit of a dead person must wait to guard the cemetery until the next dead man comes to take his place!"

"Who spread this nonsensical story?" said the priest, wheeling around.

"It is not who spread it that concerns me, Father," said Theresa Coniffe. "What I want to know is whether it's true or not."

Father Drew swung back to Theresa.

"Did you read this in the Catechism?" he said, and then, without waiting for an answer, "Did you read it in the Catechism Notes? Is it in the Gospels?" And then his eye fell upon the wide-eyed Gabriel. . . . He pointed his finger at him, and then fixed Theresa Coniffe with his gaze once more. "Aren't you ashamed to think of the impression that this scene of indecorous rowdyism is likely to make on the mind of that innocent child?" Before the severely pointed finger Gabriel began to retreat, step by step, behind his mother. "Where is the child's mother?" said Father Drew, and transferring his glance from Theresa to Lily he shook his head. "It will be a great task for you, ma'am, to efface this scene from the mind of this child. I hope that the task will not be neglected. How old is he?"

"He will be seven years in May, Father," said Lily, putting her arms around Gabriel protectingly, till they crossed his chest like banners of a scarf.

"In that case he's old enough to be sent to school where he can get a firmer foundation in the dogmas of his religion than he seems likely to get in Clewe Street. I'll tell the teacher to expect him on Monday morning."

And then, feeling that at last he had sent a straight shaft, he reached into his deep pocket for the bevelled ritual and advancing to the gate of the cemetery he began the prayers of reception for the corpse.

The sweetly smelling clay closed over Theodore Coniffe. The sods were in place again and the wreaths and immortelles were placed upon the mounded hump. The holy water was sprinkled over him time and again, as friend after friend advanced to the foot of the grave and dipped the slippy yellow brush into the pewter bowl and shed a shower of silver drops like the beads from a silver rosary over the grave. And then silently, walking backwards respectfully, the living drew away slowly from the place of the dead, and passed out through the gates.

∽ ∽ ∽

The coaches that now rolled homeward along the road were, however, long out of earshot of this final clanging chord of the burial service and were gay with that involuntary, utterly uncontrollable gaiety that marks the reaction of most people to the sight of an open grave. At a deathbed the general feeling is of sympathy with the departing soul, at a wake it is sympathy with the mourners, but at the brink of the grave it is generally the thoughts of their own inescapable fate in the matter of being closed under themselves one day that occupy men's minds, bring a pallor to their faces, and in the case of the women redden the eyes and cause those long sighs that stream upon the air like shreds of a thin dreary wind. Reaction sets in immediately they step into the coaches for the quick return to town.

In the Coniffe coach, the coach of the chief mourners, there was of course none of this gaiety; the only member who might have been able to shift the burden of death from his mind was oppressed with the burden of life.

"What is school like?" said Gabriel, the instant they were seated in the coach.

"No matter what it's like you'll have to put up with it the same as every other child," said his Aunt Theresa. "You've been long enough tasting the honey of life, it's time you got a sip of the vinegar!"

Lily's pale cheeks flushed. "Is this necessary?" she said, looking at Theresa, and then putting out her hand she patted Gabriel's bare knee.

"You'll have great times with the other boys, Gabriel. At the lunch hour I often listen to the shouting of the boys—it comes right across the town."

"You can hear the yelping of them too when they're getting a good slapping!" said Theresa.

"Really, Theresa, it's bad enough having to send the boy earlier than I intended without having you turn him against the thought of going."

"I'm only preparing him for the change," said Theresa. "It would be a strange thing to lift him out of his feathered nest and throw him to the cats without giving him a fair warning of what to expect."

Gabriel's eyes were getting larger and larger, and he stared from the face of his mother to the face of his Aunt Theresa.

At the first mention of school an exhilaration had entered into him, and fastly alternating visions of what might be ahead of him flashed before his mind. Passing near the schoolhouse he had often heard the lessons chanted in clear voices that sounded gay and companionable to him as he ran after a silent Mary Ellen whose desire to give him an airing was unconnected in her mind with any idea of giving him pleasure. Behind the schoolhouse there was a ball alley and sometimes the boys were playing in the ball alley, and their voices echoed back from the corners of the alley with as smart a volley as that with which the thud of the ball upon the concrete echoed the smack it had made when some boy hit it with a hard agile hand. These visions had largely made up Gabriel's picture of the school, but there was one in particular with which his fancy often occupied itself and with which the word "school" was inextricably associated. Upon their walks, on several occasions, Gabriel and Mary Ellen had passed the schoolhouse at lunch hour, and for a long time after they had passed it by, Gabriel had hung heavily out of Mary Ellen's hand and with his head turned upon his neck he had stared in frank admiration of the scholars as they partook of their lunch, sitting upon the wall of the schoolyard, their faces buried far into such thick slices of bread that Gabriel looked with critical distaste at the thin slices laid for him upon his return from the walk.

Now these visions faded and, staring from one face to another, he tried to read there the truth about this great adventure upon which he was soon to set out. The three sisters had forgotten him, but from the strange preoccupied look in their eyes it seemed to him that they were revolving his fate in their minds and he judged it best to sit quietly.

But the sisters were thinking of the last act of the day that had yet to be enacted, and which would take place at once upon their re-entrance into the house in Clewe Street. This would be the reading of Theodore's will. To one at least of them the will would make little difference, but the other two women were vaguely apprehensive.

To Theresa it sometimes had occurred with alarming accompanying images that her father might judge the matronly position of Lily to count for more than her own superiority of age. Though she never doubted for a moment that she would remain in exactly the same position even in such a deplorable eventuality, it nevertheless dampened her down considerably to think that she might suffer this setback in the eyes of the town. Though her position would not be changed her vanity would be considerably damaged.

Lily, however, having suffered already for the one flight of superiority which she had taken above her eldest sister, desired no such other flight for herself, but looking at her small son, of late years, she had begun to wonder how he would fare at the hands of Theresa were she left in entire possession of the family assets. It would be as likely for her to leave it, at her own departure, in the hands of the clergy as in the hands of a nephew who represented the perpetual evidence of Lily's own advantage over her.

There had been silence for a long time, but then as the carriage jolted going under the town gate, Theresa broke the silence.

"Get into the house as quickly as you can when the carriage draws up at the door. We don't want this business to be delayed. If anyone stops to sympathize with you, make it clear to them that there's not much thanks for sympathy that comes after the closing of the grave!"

"I wonder which coach he's in?" said Sara, timidly, and although no one had mentioned a name, both Theresa and Lily, knowing that she meant Jasper Kane, the lawyer, answered at once.

"He's in the seventh coach from the front!"

When they came to the turn for Clewe Street the Coniffe carriage turned to the right, and as it did so the rest of the coaches continued on to the main part of the town and only the near relatives and friends followed the Coniffe coach. Consequently when they alighted at the door Jasper Kane's coach was the second coach, and Mary Ellen had no sooner thrown open the door than Jasper was there to keep it open with the flat of his great bony hand and allow the three ladies in black to pass in before him, with Gabriel hustled somewhere between their skirts.

"Step this way, Mr. Kane," said Theresa, in her turn holding open the door of the front parlour, as he had held open the street door. And as he passed in she turned to Mary Ellen. "Take this child upstairs!" she said, and she gave Gabriel a tap on the shoulder.

Jasper Kane was well into the room and Sara and Lily were speaking together, both urging him to leave his hat aside, and to give them his gloves, but Jasper's keen ears pierced the twitter of gentle voices and he listened to the conversation in the hallway behind him. Wheeling around suddenly like a great crane wheeling in the air, he left the twittering ladies without a word and stepping back into the hallway he cleared his throat, and beckoning Gabriel with one crooked hand, he laid the other upon the bristling black alpaca coat sleeve of Theresa.

"I'd like the child to be present," he said.

"The child?" Theresa repeated faintly, her incredulity depriving her of the full force of her breath. "I was sending him upstairs. I've noticed lately that his ears are getting altogether too big for a child of his age!"

"The bigger his ears are the better on this occasion," said Jasper. "Give me your hand, boy," and stretching down, he took Gabriel's hand in his, and bowing to Miss Theresa he preceded her into the front parlour where Miss Lily and Miss Sara stood with their mouths still open after their unfinished sentences from which Mr. Kane had departed so abruptly.

"Sit down, please," said Jasper, with that temporary assumption of the duties of host which lawyers and doctors often assume. Sara and Lily, upon whom the significance of the situation had up to now rested lightly, sank back into the seats nearest them with such suddenness that they might have been blown backwards by a gust of wind. But Theresa remained standing long enough to dust off the table with a flick of her hand and opening the lid of the great silver inkstand endeavoured to retain over the superiority of the professional man, the superiority of the hostess. Gabriel ran to his mother.

"I have here, as you are aware, the will of your late father, Theodore Coniffe. It is my duty on this sad occasion to read this will for you, his sole survivors." Taking a stiff roll of parchment from his pocket he unrolled it slowly and kept it from furling up again by holding it at the top and the bottom.

Theodore had left his entire property to his grandson, Gabriel, with his mother and aunts to be trustees and later dependencies upon the estate. As these words were read out, Theresa Coniffe sat up straight in her chair, but in no other way betrayed any reaction whatever to what seemed to her the injustice of the will. When, however, in a later paragraph Jasper pointed out that the trusteeship was unusually long, and that Gabriel was not to come into control of the property until he was twenty-five, Theresa was unable to control her reaction to this, and she relaxed visibly, and an exclamation of satisfaction escaped her.

Jasper let go the end of the stiff parchment, which at once rolled up again into a neat cylinder.

A faint shadow may have fallen across his mind as he remembered the day that Cornelius Galloway had come to the town with his thin arrogant manner, or it may have been his customary remark upon such occasions, but as he looked around for his hat and gloves he made this remark :

"You are to be congratulated, ladies, on the excellency of your late father's will. He was a wise man."

ᔇ ᔇ ᔇ

The schoolhouse was a single-storied building made of grey granite that glittered in sunlight but which upon a rainy day became sodden with wet, and darker than the clouds from which the rain streamed. The windows were great windows with many panes but they were placed so high that curious people in the schoolyard could see no more of the classrooms than the frosted panels of the folding doors and the frigid white arctic regions as depicted in the great world maps stretching from floor to ceiling. The scholars within, on the other hand, could see no more than the sky, and the side branches of an elm tree that grew in a corner of the yard. They had certain advantages, however, for the elm tree was always changing its appearance, being different in sun and shower, in wind and in calm, to say nothing of its seasonal changes, and of the fact that in its branches, too, many a time strange dramas were enacted by the birds. As for the sky, it could be a never-ending source of spectacle to the idle-minded and the dreamer, for in its far sweet depths there was enacted the ceaseless silent ballet of the clouds.

Gabriel was for a long time so preoccupied with the inside of the classroom, staring at the other scholars and staring at the tall thin monitor, Philip Blake, that he did not desire any other spectacles. But the time came at length when this interest began to pale, and in the middle of a reading lesson one day he chanced to look up at the blue windows across which white clouds were travelling.

As he stared out, the monitor wrote the letters of the alphabet upon the blackboard, and with a long yellow cane, marked with rings of black at regular intervals along its length, he called out each letter and made the class repeat it. Gabriel's ears had grown as listless as his eye, but just as the listless eye had picked up its own interest upon the windowpane, his ear suddenly picked up a reiterated phrase that came thinly through the frosted glass partition from the older boys' classroom, where the master himself was in command.

"The world is round. It goes spinning around the sun"—there was a pause. "Is that clear to everyone?" There was another pause. There was no stir of interest.

The great solid scholars who sat upon strong forms in the classroom beyond the folding partition of frosted glass evidently found it a fact surpassing their powers of credulity to believe that they rested upon a furiously spinning globe. With mouths open and listless eyes they sat and stared at the master.

"I can see by the look on your faces you're not taking in a word I'm saying! Repeat what I said, Matty Soraghan!"

There was no reply. The master asked a few other boys to repeat what he said. There was no reply from any quarter.

"If you can't take it in you'd better write it out ten times and then perhaps you'll remember it even if you don't believe it. If you remember it till the inspector comes I don't care if you go to the full end of your days without believing it."

There was at once a scraping of chairs, and an adjustment of feet, proclaiming that the clumsy sons of the land were performing adroit feats with pencil and paper, and the master went over the geography lesson, slowly in dictation tone.

Gabriel raised his eyes to the high windows. The clouds were moving fast before the wind, and scudding across the windowpane, and as he stared a lightness came into his head and it seemed that it was the schoolhouse that moved, leaving behind the stationary sky and clouds, as a straw upon the river would stream past the wayside trees and ditches. The world was moving. The world was spinning around the sun. It would have been difficult for Gabriel at that moment to believe that the world stood still. Of course it was moving! He was filled with pride at his own perspicacity. He, Gabriel, who had been attending school for no longer than a mere five days, could see and grasp at once the lessons that the big boys were unable to get into their thick skulls. He turned back to the blackboard in his own class on which the hitherto incomprehensible calligraphs were still written.

"I'll repeat these letters once more," said the lower-school monitor briskly, "and then I'll ask any boy who thinks he can repeat them from memory to kindly raise his right hand."

Gabriel's attention was levelled upon the monitor. He could understand the geography lesson that the big boys could not grasp. He should have no hesitation in mastering a simple lesson in his own class.

The monitor read out the letters of the alphabet. Gabriel's eyes followed the yellow pointer. As the last letter was out of the monitor's mouth, Gabriel's hand was in the air, fluttering like a bird in a bush.

"Are you sure you can tackle it, Gabriel?" said the monitor, with a kindly glance at him. "We went over this several times before you joined the class."

For an answer Gabriel waved his hand still more furiously as he had seen Larry Soraghan do some time before upon being refused a first request to leave the room.

"Very well," said the monitor, smiling listlessly.

But the smile became an animated smile of encouragement as Gabriel made his way resolutely and with cautious pauses through the intricacies of the twenty-six letters of the alphabet.

"If you keep up this you'll be at the top of your class!" said the monitor as the triumphant twenty-sixth letter was enunciated clearly and correctly after a slight pause which may have been deliberately added for dramatic effect.

From this day Gabriel's mental faculties were sharpened and stimulated by vanity, and he rose rapidly from the middle benches where new scholars sat to the front benches where sat the students upon whom the lesson made some impression, and from there he soon progressed until a great part of the day he was out in the space between benches and rostrum, with the monitor's pointer in his hand, tapping the blackboard as he indicated to his fellows how simple the mysteries of learning were.

The places of the scholars in the classroom benches were not altogether indicative of their mental proficiency. There were other factors that had to be taken into consideration, and even these were variable and liable to alteration. On wet days, for example, all who came from a great distance were put sitting near the fire that they might dry out more rapidly, and, on days when an inspector was due, the clever boys were dispersed here and there through the room, much as gold threads are sewn into a coarse fabric, which is thus given a false appearance of costliness. On normal days, however, the setting out of the benches was determined by a very simple factor. It had originally been the custom for each scholar to bring with him each day a sod of turf for the school fire. This habit had persisted into Gabriel's day with one important alteration—those who could not easily procure turf were allowed to bring instead a halfpenny apiece. Since turf was not so easily procurable in the town, it was tacitly agreed that the town boys brought halfpennies and the country boys brought turf, and as a matter of fact the original reason for the distinction having long been forgotten, the town children, handing up their copper piece, had a pluto-cratic dignity in comparison with the country children who took from under their coats a large flaky sod of turf and, holding it up for the teacher to see, threw it into the reed basket by the chimney place. Those who brought turf sat on one side of the aisle and those who brought copper sat upon the other aisle. This difference was further accentuated by the fact that the town boys wore ready-made suits of varying dyes while the country children wore rough tweed suits made oftentimes by their mothers, and sometimes from the same length of tweed since it was procured from a pedlar's barrow that went from cottage to cottage.

The rough tweeds sat on the left side of the monitor, the serge suits sat upon his right. When to this distinction you add the complexity of mental difference you find Gabriel seated in the front row of serge suits and Larry Soraghan at the foot end of the rough tweeds. Separated as they were, therefore, by almost every conceivable difference, it might be thought that Gabriel's brief previous acquaintance with Larry would have vanished from the memory of both. Larry however on the first day had cast many glances at Gabriel and when the time came for the boys to take a run in the yard he came up to Gabriel and raised his voice loud enough to be heard by all the others.

"When are you coming over to our house again?"

"I don't know," said Gabriel. "I'll ask when I can go."

"Do you have to ask before you do everything?"

"I do," said Gabriel.

Larry was astonished. "Will you come out this evening after school?" he said, at last.

"Where?" said Gabriel.

"Anywhere," said Larry. "We could go down to the river."

"I'll ask if I can go," said Gabriel doubtfully.

Larry lowered his voice. "I'll be waiting for you under the arch of the bridge," he said.

"But the water goes under the arch!" said Gabriel.

"I know a way of getting down over the top of the bridge so you can creep on to a ledge under the arch without getting wet. No one else knows about it. It's my secret place. I keep a lot of things there in a crack in the wall. But I'll let you into the secret. And I'll show you how to get down. You climb on to the top of the bridge and sit on it for a while until you're sure there's no one looking, then you turn around and let your legs hang over the water. You have to hang by your hands but after a bit you feel your feet resting on the ledge under the bridge. Don't let go then, whatever you do, or you'll fall back into the water."

"What will I do?" said Gabriel, as breathlessly as if he were indeed hanging by his hands above the racing river, with his feet slipping and missing their foothold over an unseen ledge.

"You feel with your hand till you find an iron ring that's sticking out of the stone and you catch that at the same time as you let go your other hand. Then you slide on to the ledge," said Larry, "like this!" And swooping his right hand down through the air he slid it to rest, knuckles under, in the palm of the other hand. "I'll be there," he said, finishing the instructions, "but don't shout out. Take three stones and throw them into the water, plop, plop. plop. And I take three bits of cement off the wall and throw them in after your plop, plop, plop. That's the secret signal to show the den is safe."

"Safe from what?" said Gabriel and again he spoke as if the fears were imminent, and as if he would indeed be permitted to keep this rendezvous, a fact that he had good cause to doubt. As the day advanced his doubts grew, and, when Mary Ellen called for him at the school gate, and led him home at a swift pace while the other scholars dawdled along, chalking faces on the pavement and sailing boats in the rivulets of the gutter, he felt that he would not even have the courage to ask permission, much less expect it to be granted him.

When however he had been kissed by his mother, pressed to his Aunt Sara's heart, and called up before his Aunt Theresa to tell her all about his day, he felt a return of courage.

"Can I go out after dinner, Aunt Theresa?" he said.

Theresa was startled. Gabriel could see this and he could even feel that his mother and his Aunt Sara were startled, although they were behind him, with their backs to the light. He felt a rustling of skirts as they agitated their hands and exchanged glances.

"Where do you want to go, Gabriel?" said Theresa.

"A boy in school asked me to play with him," said Gabriel.

Aunt Sara advanced. "Isn't it nice that he made friends so soon," she said.

"Who is this boy?" said Theresa and his mother, both speaking at the same time. "Are you going to his house to play, or is he coming here to play with you?"

"He told me to meet him down at the river," said Gabriel.

Theresa stiffened. "Who is this boy?" she said, in quite a different tone.

"Larry Soraghan," said Gabriel.

"Larry Soraghan!" The three sisters repeated the words, but at slightly different moments and with slightly different speeds, so that all Gabriel heard was a vague sound that filled the air for a moment and left an aghast silence.

It had been one thing to put Gabriel under the care of Mrs. Soraghan for a day—the woman had been well paid for her trouble—but it was another thing altogether to have Gabriel choose one of the Soraghans for a playfellow.

"This is what comes of having to send him to the National school," said his mother at last. "The Soraghans are good children, biddable and clean, and they are good workers, but they're no company for Gabriel."

"I thought there was some distinction made," said Sara timidly.

"There can be no distinction in the National school," said Theresa, "although I understand they tried to keep the rough element apart."

Gabriel understood very little of this, but he gathered that he was hardly likely to be allowed down to the river, and since he was not to go, the dangers and hazards of reaching the ledge were lessened and he felt that he was being deprived of a wonderful adventure.

"Why can't I go?" he said, pouting his lips.

The sisters stared at him. Lily opened her mouth to give an explanation and closed it again. Theresa stood up.

"Gabriel, your mother and your aunts do not wish you to play with the Soraghan children. They are good children, but they are not fit companions for you. You will some day own this house and several other houses, and Larry Soraghan will some day have to take up a common position like—" she tried to think what demeaning future was likely for Larry Soraghan—"like a railway porter!" she finished.

Gabriel had not acquired the habit of disobedience. He accepted without questioning the discipline laid upon him, and although the fact that Larry Soraghan was destined to be a railway porter when he grew up added, instead of subtracted, from the glory that hung around this hero who made secret lairs in the dark arches of a bridge, Gabriel abandoned all hope of going out and resolved not to become engaged in any more speculative plans.

"He must have someone to play with," said Lily. "It's the only way to safeguard him against playing with the wrong kind of children."

"But who is there?" said Theresa, and it wasn't clear whether she agreed or disagreed with Gabriel's mother.

Just at that moment Sara, who was standing in the window, sighed, and although she frequently sighed there was a special weightiness about this sigh as if it had a direct reference to the conversation and was a definite articulation.

"What do you think we ought to do, Sara?" said Lily.

Sara turned around. "I was just thinking," she said, "what a pity that the two little Finnerty children are both girls." Pulling aside the curtains, she let her sisters see the two decorous little Finnerty girls, who with their nursemaid were passing down the street at that moment, arm in arm, their stiff white dresses slotted with blue ribbons, their short velvet coats fastened with bright pearl buttons, and their pale yellow hair brushed flatly around their ears with only the merest, and most decorous, suggestion of a curl at the end.

"That's the truest word I ever heard you say, Sara," said Theresa. "What perfect companions they would be for him."

"Perhaps—" said Lily, and she bit her lip. Mere aunts might think it silly to look as far into the future as she had looked for a moment when the two little girls had turned their heads, and, glancing politely in the direction of the window, smiled inwards at the ladies. "But I suppose they'll soon be going away to boarding school," she said sadly, speaking out of her thoughts. "Then we'll never see them."

"Nonsense!" Theresa threw up her head. "There was no talk of our going away to school at that age."

"Well," said Lily, "all I know is that their mother said children needed companions of their own age." At this, however, all three women recollected Gabriel's plight in this matter and the paucity of companions suitable to him in Castlerampart. Lily wrung her hands. Even Theresa felt the pressure of a certain anxiety. Sara alone was sanguine.

"Something will surely turn up," she said confidently, for it was by means of this assumption she had resolved herself, temporarily at least, out of every difficulty that had ever presented itself to her.

"I knew somebody would turn up," she said, a few days later, when she came in to report a piece of news that Mrs Molloy had reported to her.

"What are you talking about?" said Theresa.

"I knew a suitable companion would be found for Gabriel—I was talking to Mrs. Molloy and she told me that she is expecting a charming lady to stay with her as a permanent guest, and that this lady has a young boy only two years older than Gabriel. I'm sure he'll be exactly the right companion for Gabriel. His father was an artist and he died seven years ago. His mother is a perfect lady and she wants above all to give her son a chance to fulfil his father's promise, so she gave up her establishment in the city and is taking a room in the Central Hotel to keep down expenses and pay for the boy's education."

"What is the boy himself like?" said Theresa sceptically. Theresa opening her mouth to ask what use he would be to them if he was at boarding school, Sara hastened to add: "He'll be home at mid-term. Mrs. Molloy was telling me that's only three weeks away. We might invite him in to tea with Gabriel?"

ဆ ဆ ဆ

The three weeks which intervened between the repudiation of Larry and the determination to invite the new boy to tea were three weeks which Gabriel endured with mixed emotions. His initial vanity in surpassing his fellow benchers in the lower form had continued and he was soon undoubted leader of his class, but the hero of the bench is seldom the hero of the playground, and there Larry Soraghan had confided to the other scholars that Gabriel was afraid to come out after school.

On the day after his repudiation of Larry's generous offer Gabriel was startled at play hour when he went out into the yard to find a large circle forming around him, the boys holding hands as if for a game of ring-a-ring-a-rosy and all yelling at the top of their voices.

"Who's afraid of the ri-ver? Who's afraid of the ri-ver?"

Gabriel tried to break out of the ring but the children raised their clasped hands and the ring grew tighter. Before long, however, Philip Blake, the monitor, came out, and clapping his hands broke up the diabolical ring and making a feint of running, first at one boy, and then at another, he sent the entire crowd scattering about the yard and left Gabriel alone, his tears still valiantly unshed. Gabriel's gratitude was about to break out in place of his tears, but the monitor looked down at him with as much distaste as at the others, if not indeed with greater distaste since it was he who had caused the trouble, and giving him a push he told him to get away from the door and not to stay skulking under the windows.

"You can't expect to be treated well unless you treat others well, you conceited little whelp," he said and disappeared in the direction of the doorway. Before he had reached the door there was a sound of voices farther away and fainter, but singing the same refrain that the boys had sung a moment before.

"Who's afraid of the ri-ver? Who's afraid of the ri-ver?"

And there, on the high wall dividing the girls' yard from the boys' yard, were perched a couple of girls in rough dyed dresses of red, with white pinafores, their hands red and scratched from climbing, their faces red from the exertion of shouting and their hair lifting on the wind. "Who's afraid of the ri-ver?" they shouted and then all together they stuck out their tongues at Master Gabriel Galloway.

"I'll have those Soraghans strangled," said Philip Blake, and he made off in the direction of the green wicket gate in the middle of the dividing wall. Upon this he knocked with his malacca cane, in a manner which was apparently distinctive enough to be recognized as authoritative and not to be confused with the cracks and batters the door received at other times from accidental contact with the feet and elbows of the boys, for the gate was opened and in the gateway stood Nell Molloy, daughter of Mrs. Molloy, who was the monitress in the girls' school.

The eyes of all the boys were focussed at once upon the monitor and the monitress. The girls had disappeared from the wall, and a weighty silence prevailed, not great enough however for the voices of the adults to be heard even by those daring enough to edge near to them. Even upon one occasion when Larry Soraghan rolled a marble with remarkable exactitude right up to within an inch of the monitor's shoe, and having the excuse of going to retrieve it edged up close to the couple, he could not catch a sound. What could they be saying that could be so important? How the children wished they could hear, even one word!.

Indeed as they stared at times it seemed to the watchers as if the adults were not talking at all, for at least twice Miss Molloy put her hand up to the fair coil of hair upon the nape of her neck, and pushed home the errant hairpin with such expression of absorption in her blue eyes that if Philip Blake was saying anything at all it was certainly nothing of any great weight. And once they were undoubtedly saying nothing because Philip Blake began with the raised toe of his boot to design some irrelevant circles in the gravel at his feet, while Miss Molloy all the while stared down at her own pointed shoe of bright patent leather as if she considered it would be a much more efficient implement for such work.

While Philip Blake drew circles upon the gravel, and while Nell Molloy watched him, the girls appeared again upon the walls and judging that the consultation between the monitors either had no connection with them, or that their iniquity had become overlooked in the spontaneous development of more urgent matters, they shouted out again.

"Who's afraid of the ri-ver?" And the boys, taking up the cry, began to hold hands and advance again, but in the excitement someone caught hold of Gabriel's hand and soon he too was advancing and retreating with the others, and shouting out with them, "Who's afraid of the ri-ver?" and it was forgotten that the derisive question had originally been directed at him.

"Who's afraid of the ri-ver?" sang Judy Soraghan from the top of the wall, and the chorus was taken up by several other Soraghans of smaller size who hung by their hands from the wall, and by unseen crowds of girls underneath the wall whose fine serge dresses, embroidered with silk embroidery floss, could not be endangered by the rough wall in which bits of china and glass had been mixed with the cement to give its top an evil edge.

"Who's afraid of the ri-ver?" sang the shrill girlish voices.

"You are! You are!" shouted the boys.

"We are not! We are not!" sang the girls.

"You are so! You are so!" shouted the boys, and then with a new burst of inspiration someone added a new cry—"Red petticoats—red petticoats."

Now to this new cry Judy Soraghan apparently took a personal objection because she began to draw her long black-stockinged legs up on the wall and swinging them over on to the other side was about to drop down on the side of the enemy, her cheeks flaring and her lips pursed together angrily.

"Judy Soraghan!" Miss Molloy's face flushed rosily as she suddenly caught sight of her pupil, and in her excitement she ran into the boys' yard to head off the descent of the angry Judy. "Go back where you belong, you wicked, shameless girls," she said, and then, feeling as if her pupil had cast a reflection upon her entire sex, Miss Molloy's face flushed deeper and deeper, and feeling perhaps the necessity for retrenching her own position well within the walls of modesty and frigidity she hurried back through the gate in the wall with her head very arrogantly tilted and her stride so brisk that at least two hairpins were loosened and shed upon the ground.

"The time is up," she said, coldly, to Mr. Blake. "Will you please ring the bell?" For the bell that served for both the boys' and the girls' school, although hung directly in the centre of the schoolhouse roof, had only one bell cord which descended in a slant towards the boys' yard.

Mr. Philip Blake caught the end of this bell rope and instead of the customary three peals he gave the rope four vicious tugs, which not only added an extra peal but also a million minute tremors of sound that lingered in the air long after the scholars were seated within on the benches.

かか かか かか

The middle of the winter term came around at last and one afternoon as Gabriel sat in the back drawing room with pencils and crayons filling in the o's in his schoolbooks the door was opened and his Aunt Sara came running into the room.

"Oh, Gabriel, are your hands clean? Your Aunt Theresa and your mother have gone to call on the new visitor at the Central Hotel, and if her son, Sylvester, is home from school they are going to send him in to visit you. Now you'll have someone to play with you! Are your hands clean?" And taking out her cambric handkerchief Aunt Sara hastily moistened it with her lips and lifting up his hands one after another she wiped certain areas where the pencil might possibly have left a slight trace of lead.

While this operation was in progress a darkness came over the room, and looking up Gabriel saw a pale face pasted for a second to the outer side of the glass. A moment later there was a loud rat-a-tat on the hall door.

"It's all right to knock loud when you're invited," said his Aunt Sara, as if justifying some unspoken criticism, and dusting her own fingers with the moist handkerchief before secreting it under the lace jabot of her bodice, she went out quickly to open the door, without waiting for Mary Ellen.

"This is Sylvester," she said when she came back a second later, followed by a thin boy about Gabriel's own height, with a pale face, and straight, fair hair, thin and glossy like pale embroidery floss, and eyes which were a curious yellow colour. "I'll leave you alone," said Sara, and she nodded brightly to Gabriel. Her hand was shaking so much with excitement that twice it slipped off the glossy white knob of the door before she opened it and went out.

The two boys remained standing for a time. Gabriel felt a great shyness, but as Sylvester moved around the room taking up one object after another and examining it in silence, he recovered his balance, if not his speech, and going around in Sylvester's wake he picked up his own particularly admired curios and thrust them into the older boy's hand.

There was a large white shell, speckled all over with brown dots, and having a saw edge to its great pink lip. Gabriel like it, and when Sylvester put down the ivory replica of an elephant with jade tusks, he thrust the shell into his hand.

Sylvester looked at it and then he clicked the fingers of his left hand together.

"I have it," he said, aloud—"a dove; one of those pale doves with small heads darting from side to side."

Gabriel looked in amazement at the shell in Sylvester's hand. He failed to see any resemblance. Sylvester saw his amazement and he laughed.

"I don't mean that this is like a dove," he said, tossing it up into the air and just succeeding in catching it again as it came down. "I mean your Aunt Sara. Don't you think she's like a dove?"

"I don't know," said Gabriel.

"You're probably not observant," said Sylvester, and he picked up the crayon drawings with which Gabriel had been passing the time. Gabriel flushed.

"I never saw red smoke," said Sylvester, looking at it.

"I had no black," said Gabriel defensively.

"Smoke is blue," said Sylvester.

Gabriel looked at the chimney where the dark mounds of slack were pierced with a dull smoke. He pointed his finger at the grate.

"But when it comes out at the top of the chimney it's blue," said Sylvester, and he went to the window followed by Gabriel. Far off the rest of the town could be seen, and from one or two chimneys frail streamers of smoke rose up straight like blue quill feathers that had a jaunty twist to the tips. "Let's go out," said Sylvester.

Gabriel looked at him, and his heart beat fast.

"I'll ask my Aunt Sara," he said, "but I doubt if she will give me permission without getting the permission of my mother and my Aunt Theresa."

Up to this Sylvester had treated Gabriel with as scant an interest as that he had bestowed upon the speckled shells and the ivory elephant, but now he stared at him with genuine interest.

"Do you have to ask permission if you want to go out?" he said.

"My aunts don't like me to mix with people," said Gabriel. "That's why they asked you to come in and play with me."

"Play with you! What do they think I am—a nursemaid?" Sylvester started and looked around the room as if it had begun to contract and would soon close in upon him and choke him.

"I'm going out," he said, and then in the doorway he looked back at the pale and serious child whose face shone white in the dark room as human faces stand out in dark faded oil paintings. "Come on out. I'll leave you home again and if there's a row I'll take the blame."

Gabriel stared at him.

"Look out!" said Sylvester. "Your eyes will never close if you open them any wider. Come on. I'm not going to wait here all day!"

Gabriel glanced at the blue sky outside and he thought once again of the screaming and shouting he used to hear in the ball alley before he went to school himself, and he thought of the thudding echo of the ball, and although he had lately given up all hope of ever joining in those shouts, the hope flared up again.

He followed Sylvester into the dark hall, and without glancing backwards went out through the bright doorway into the street. He had only one moment of compunction as he thought of his Aunt Sara who was probably at that very moment spreading butter on neat slices of bread, shaking the ironed creases out of the stiff white linen tablecloth, and looking at herself in the silver teapot to make sure its polish was the very brightest polish possible.

"Did you never go out by yourself before?" said Sylvester, as they went slowly up the street.

"No!" said Gabriel.

"Didn't you ever want to go?"

Gabriel said nothing. He had so seldom contemplated going out that he had no views upon being forbidden to do so. Sylvester seemed to be waiting for an answer. Gabriel remembered the first day he went to school.

"I wanted to go out one day when Larry Soraghan asked me to meet him at the river," he said, " but I wouldn't be let go."

"Why?"

"My aunts didn't want me to play with Larry Soraghan."

"Why?"

"They don't like him," said Gabriel sedately.

"Do you like him?" said Sylvester.

"I don't know. You see I didn't speak to him since then."

Sylvester walked on a few steps. "I never take another person's opinion of anything. I find out for myself. If I were you I'd find out for myself about Larry Soraghan. If I didn't like him I'd agree with my aunts to save trouble, but if I did like him I'd face up to them and tell them so."

Gabriel's admiration made him sigh. He put his hands into his pockets in the way that Sylvester had his hands in his pockets, and when Sylvester took them out a moment later and began to bite his nails, Gabriel tried to bite his nails, but they had been so smoothly and finely rounded by his Aunt Sara's emery board that he could not get a grip upon them with his teeth and he had to forgo this detail in the emulation of his hero.

There was silence for a while and they came to the top of Clewe Street where it joined the butt ends of three other streets at a cross that marked the centre of the town. One street led to the railway, one led to the church, but the other led to the river. Sylvester looked speculatively down each of the streets.

"Why did Larry Soraghan want you to meet him down at the river?" he said.

"He had a secret lair under the bridge," said Gabriel, forgetting that the information was also a secret.

"Let's see what it's like," said Sylvester, and he started in the direction of the river.

The bridge which crossed the river at the end of River Street marked the town boundary in much the same way that the tollgate did on the west side of the town. On the near side of the river the houses straggled out until they were fewer and fewer, and their gardens longer and longer, and on the far side there were fields which, although somewhat urban in their dump hills of pans and buckets and broken wheels, were nevertheless actual fields and not mere gardens. A few yards beyond the river the ragged ramparts began their circle.

It was quiet near the bridge, and the water under it was, at the moment, running smoothly and with no sound. Sylvester strode along and Gabriel ran beside him, but coming near the bridge, Gabriel ran in front of Sylvester and assuming an air of importance, he put up a finger over his mouth for silence and secrecy. Stooping down, he picked up three stones from the ground and leaning up he dropped them over the parapet into the water and listened to the plop they made one after another.

"What is that for?" said Sylvester, and Gabriel put his finger to his lip again.

In a few minutes there was a sound of feet scraping on grit and a moment after the river surface was split into ripples again three times by the slow deliberate plop, plop, plop, of three pieces of concrete.

"That's the signal," said Gabriel. "We can go down now," but he looked with apprehension at the parapet which seemed hard enough to scale, without the further acrobatics that Larry had prescribed as necessary in order to reach the secret lair.

"How do we get down?" said Sylvester.

Gabriel was eager to see the theoretical instructions put into practice, and he rapidly and accurately repeated Larry's instructions, while a moment later Larry himself called them out again, his voice taking on a wonderful deep intonation from the concave dome of the bridge over him.

"Before I go to all that trouble," said Sylvester, "I'd like to see if it's worth it. Let's cross the bridge."

He strode across the bridge and climbed through the gapped wall of the first field on the other side. An old horse stood arrested in the act of grazing. Gabriel held back nervously.

"What's the matter? Are you afraid of the old nag? I'll fix him," said Sylvester, and lifting his foot he gave a kick to an empty biscuit tin that lay on its side inside the wall. The tin clattered into the sky, and at once the old horse threw up dry clods of clay and made off, with a mad mane, for the far corner of the field. The boys advanced into the field and jumping down into the rutted pits of grassy margin, they stood on the bank of the river so that the bridge was above them. They looked upwards at the black inner dome.

In building the bridge, the masons left rough stones projecting at either side of the piers, and upon these in recent years some vague architectural purpose had led to the placing of long boards from one side of the arch to the other, resting upon these rough piers. A small space, domed and dark, was thus enclosed, and from the long narrow aperture the face of Larry was seen in full, as he lay upon his stomach under the dome.

"Are you coming up?" he shouted, trumpeting his voice with his hands.

"Can you stand up there?" shouted Sylvester.

Larry felt an implied criticism in this question and scorned to answer it.

"You can't get up here any way only the way I told you," he trumpeted, his voice coiling and echoing in the dome behind him.

"What good is it up there if you can't stand up!" said Sylvester, and he turned away disdainfully. "Let's try and catch the old nag!" he said to Gabriel, and scrambling up the rutted bank he ran after the horse, waving his arms and yelling, until to the fascinated Gabriel it became impossible to distinguish whether it was Sylvester who with yells and waving arms chased the old horse around the field in circles, or whether it was the horse with rearing hoofs and frenzied mane, throwing up madly flying clods of clay, who chased Sylvester.

But whichever was the case, it was Sylvester who tired first, and ending his whooping circles at the gap through which they had entered, he beckoned to Gabriel and putting his hands in his pockets went out on the road again. To Gabriel's consternation he took the direction that led, not back to town, but away from it, but had he lifted his feet higher and trod away into the cold sky regions it is likely that Gabriel would have put all misgivings from him and endeavoured to follow him there.

When the mid-term holiday ended and Sylvester went back to boarding school, and when the consternation at the innovation he had introduced had died away in the hearts of the ladies in Clewe Street, two abiding changes had been made in Gabriel's life.

It became an accepted fact that he could go out to play after school as long as he did not leave Clewe Street, and although he was not allowed to play with him elsewhere he was allowed to play with Larry Soraghan in the schoolyard. But the liberty thus gained did not after all mean much to Gabriel, for, after sampling the friendship of Sylvester, that of Larry and his fellows was insipid, and Gabriel began to depend for real companionship upon the holidays that brought Sylvester back to Castlerampart.

∽ ∽ ∽

One day during the long summer holidays, when Gabriel woke up, Sylvester was sitting on the wall that divided the Central Hotel from the Coniffe garden, swinging his legs and whistling for him to come out in the sun. Underneath the wall, the spotted dog barked with impatience to be away. Gabriel sprang out of bed, and began to put on his trousers. Just as he did so, however, Mary Ellen came into his room.

"Why are you putting on your old clothes?" she asked. "Don't you know that to-day is a Holy Day? You have to go to church." And she went to the cupboard and began to take out his best serge suit. Gabriel did not know that it was a Holy Day. A feeling of bitter resentment rose up within him, and he dropped his old clothes to the ground. He felt that he had been imposed upon. It was not a Sunday. He was reconciled to the Sundays. They never took him unawares and interfered with his plans. But this Holy Day was a different matter. However, there was no way out of it. To church he must go. He picked up his best serge suit and began to get into it. But as he dressed his mind was filled with dismal thoughts.

As he dressed, he pictured to himself the interior of the church, with its mouldering wooden pews. The windows were so high that you could see nothing through them, and although there was a stained-glass window near the altar, it was darkened by the high trees outside, and he could never fully follow the story of its coloured fragments. Moreover this stained-glass window which was intended to throw a coloured light inward on a chapel interior only impeded the ordinary light, and gave the chapel a strange day darkness such as would be experienced elsewhere only in times of heavy fog.

Gabriel grew more and more dismal. Then he remembered Sylvester. Perhaps Sylvester was going to church too. And, at the thought of having his company up the street, and sitting in the same pew as he, he brightened somewhat. But when Gabriel was ready he found that Sylvester had already been to the early service.

"I'll be up the street with you, though," Sylvester conceded, and so they set off, but at the market square, Gabriel had to face down Church Street, while Sylvester turned off into River Street, the spotted dog at his heels and the sun picking out the lights in his flossy yellow hair as it picked out the points of the river ripples and made them shine like stars.

Gabriel turned into Church Street alone. Church Street was short and narrow and in the vicinity of the church was dark and sombre because of a plantation of tall trees that cast such a shade upon the great granite walls that there was a perpetual growth of green moss upon the lower sides of the walls, and upon the damp slates of the roof there were pads of green lichen. The gravel leading up to the chapel was covered at the sides with a green damp moss but the centre was worn smooth by the faithful feet of the townspeople. Gabriel walked along reluctantly, half hoping that he would be late for some of the ceremony, and half fearful that the hurrying people who shared the pathway with him might read this intention in his mind and tell his aunts or his mother about him.

How shocked they would be to think that he dallied deliberately on the way to church!

Then another thought struck him. If his mother and his aunts would be so vexed with him, what way would God regard him? Would God be terribly angry?

A further thought struck him. What would happen if he didn't go to church at all? Would God care? What would He do?

And with these questions a great curiosity came over Gabriel. "What would God do?" he asked himself. "Would God care?"

He tried to imagine how God would act, but he could only imagine God as a vague person, sitting on a great throne, miles and miles away up in the clouds, His arms folded together under a vast white robe and His eyes always shut in magnificent unconcern.

In spite of the way he dawdled along, Gabriel came at last to the gateway of the church, and faced inward with dragging feet. Then just as he was going through the gate he saw a familiar figure in a red jersey running up the street in a manner that proclaimed unmistakably that Larry Soraghan was not only arriving in haste but that in imagination he rode a furiously pacing steed which he lashed from moment to moment with a whip brought down from over his head in slashes of rage and fury.

It was only politeness to wait until this furiously charging companion drew rein beside him.

"I forgot my money for the plate!" he gasped. "I had to go back for it. I thought I'd be late." He gasped for breath. "It was good I had my horse," he said.

The last devotees, who were hurrying in at the gates, glanced sharply at the loiterers.

"We'd better go in," said Gabriel, as a vast wave of sound surged out from the church. The congregation were rising from their knees for the reading of the First Gospel. Larry nodded in agreement and went up the short path to the church door. Already they could see into the far depths within, where, by glimpses between the people's heads, they could see the candles glint. Then the gospel ended and the people sat down. The priest turned back to the altar with his arms outspread. A feeling of fatigue came over Gabriel as his eyes fixed on the wide-stretched arms. He put out his hand to dip into the holy-water font, along the bottom of which a slimy fungus loosened its strands and floated like human hair. Larry's fingers were dabbling the water with a last gesture of liberty before he went into the porch.

"Larry!" Gabriel caught Larry by the sleeve. "What do you think would happen if we didn't go in?"

"Didn't go to church?" Larry's hand remained poised halfway to his forehead, drops of holy water falling from his finger tips and tapping on the blue-black polish of his shoes.

Gabriel nodded. The suggestion had become too terrible to be further expanded in words. He threw a glance at the churchyard where a path between the tombstones of the dead pastors of the parish led to a stile in the wall. This stile led into a wide field where the parish priest's cow was grazing. Beyond it there was a high wall, the remains of the communal house of an ancient friary. And behind the high wall there was the ruin of the Friary Church, of which only the east gable and the twin gables of the transept still stood marking out their mullions and graceful architraves against the blue sky. Larry, who had no clear knowledge of church liturgy, moved back out of the view of the priest in case he might have occasion to turn towards the congregation again.

"It's a sin to stay away from church on a Holy Day!" But his alteration of position had already indicated a certain desire to discuss the suggestion. Then, as another thought struck him, he turned to Gabriel. "Do you know it's a sin?" he asked. "I do," said Gabriel. Larry's eyes widened. At that moment, however, a door was heard to open around at the back of the church. "There's somebody coming!" cried Larry, and the next minutes he was racing madly for the stile in the wall, taking no further time to weigh evil against retribution. He was followed by Gabriel, whose vague suggestion had hardly shadowed out such a drastic action.

Inside the stile the grass was high, and into this deep grass the pair tumbled headlong, to sit up a minute later quivering at their own temerity. Had anyone seen them?

It seemed that no one had seen them. They grew more confident. Larry raised his head and peered out over the wall. Then Gabriel stood up. There was no one in sight. "What will we do now?" he asked. But Larry was not listening. He was staring down at something he had been clutching in his hot palm. Then he held out his hand and displayed the moist penny he had been given for the collection plate. "Will I throw it away?"' It was a symbol of guilt.

For a moment Gabriel faltered too. Then he put his hand in his pocket and drew out his own penny for the plate. "Let's buy oranges with them," he said, "and climb into the Friary to eat them!" This time Larry gave in so readily he did not bother to make his agreement vocal. Instead he stretched out his hand. "Give me you penny, so," he said, "I'll get the oranges. You can wait here." For Larry was not so lost to practical matters as to forget his natural caution, and he felt that as a regular patron of the small hucksters' shops in Church Street, his custom at that hour would not be questioned as closely as Gabriel's. Gabriel was reluctant to fall in with a suggestion that seemed to put a slur upon his valour, but he was given no time to demur. Larry snatched up the penny, clinked the two coins together for an instant, and was gone. When he returned a few minutes later he was holding up two golden globes that shone in the morning sunlight with a bright illicit glow. And the next thing, with an orange apiece, they were racing through the field back of the church, startling the priest's cow, and climbing over the Friary wall to jump down intrepidly into the nettles within the ruin.

The Friary enclosure was no longer open for burials. Those who had been laid there might no longer lie in the expectation of new fellows to keep them company. And it was a long time since those who lay there had seen the light of day. The most vivid imagination could picture nothing beneath these serried headstones but a vast network of bleached bones. Meanwhile all was orderly and rigid, and no tombstone tottered however sunk the clay under it, for the graves here were so closely packed that they supported one another.

Within the abbey ruins itself more massive memorials still reared up into the blue air that came down through the roofless arches. The original flagstones of the Friary still remained in places inscribed with strange archaic letters that baffled the learning of the two lower-bench scholars as they wandered about, their footsteps echoing from the flags and their voices, which they hardly dared raise above a whisper, whispering back from the ghostly grey stones.

As they wandered around reading the lettering on the ancient monuments as if they were reading lessons upon a slate, they began to wonder whether the ceremony in the church was over or only just begun. When they looked back at the green field beyond the wall it seemed but a moment since they had fled across it. When they peered into the dim recesses of the ruin it seemed that they had been straying there for hours.

Meanwhile no aspect of the funeral purveyor's art remained un-examined, no weeping granite angel uninspected, no cold clusters of marble grapes unhandled, and there was no white urn, draped with pleated marble cloths, that had not been climbed upon, in case it might by any chance be a detachable vessel left on the top of the headstone by some careless previous visitor which might be allowed to pass into the hands of new owners on the ancient principle of finders being keepers. By degrees lethargy as great as any they would have endured in the pews of the church was beginning to descend upon them. All at once Larry put his hand in his pocket and exclaimed in surprise: "The oranges! We forgot to eat the oranges!" Gabriel dived into his own pocket. "Where will we eat them?" he cried, looking around him for somewhere to sit, but there and then Larry had seated himself on the curbstone of one of the graves in the very centre of what had once been the transept of the ancient sanctuary, and already he had begun to unpeel the flowing rind of the fruit. Soon a wicked fragrance rose to their nostrils, and a pagan saliva bubbled in their mouths.

But even before they broke open the pale heart of the fruit at all, there was a strange guilty feeling in their hearts as the luxurious scent and colour of the fruit filled the dead arches of the abbey. When Larry un-peeled the entire rind in one long unbroken spiral of golden orange he lifted his hand and, flinging it from him, watched it fall among the grey stones and green-grey nettles of the plot in the centre of the chancel aisle. Against this particular plot Larry had unconsciously harboured some resentment because it had been protected from their inspection by thick black railings, too high to be scaled.

Gabriel with his hand raised over his head was about to cast his own peel in the same direction when the sight of Larry's peeling struck him as indecorous where it lay within the railings.

"Perhaps we shouldn't throw away the peels?" he said, lowering his arm.

"Why not?" said Larry.

"They make a mess."

"Who'll see them!" said Larry, but even as he spoke a shade of arrogance left his face, and a half tone of arrogance was missing from his voice.

"We might bury them!" suggested Gabriel.

"That would be worse," said Larry, and he wriggled uncomfortably on the curbstone of the grave. "If you dug a hole in a graveyard you'd strike against *bones*," he said and his eyes grew deeper and wider.

"Perhaps we ought to eat the oranges outside in the field?" said Gabriel.

"And have everyone see us?" said Larry, in whom spiritual fears might stir, but would never, never utterly rout practical fears.

"If anyone put his head over the wall," said Gabriel, "he could see us here."

171

"We can move in more," said Larry, but he didn't move.

Instead he began to insert his thumb into the tight crevice at the top of the orange in order to split the fruit into halves. Gabriel put a hand on his arm.

"Larry, do you think *God* can see us?" he said in a whisper.

Larry's fingers remained pressed upon the orange. He shrugged his shoulders to shake off the unpleasant sensations that fell upon him with Gabriel's words.

"I don't care if He does!" he said, defiantly, looking up into the sky and splitting open the orange. But when Larry looked down at the fruit again he started to his feet with a scream, and, dropping it on the ground, he caught hold of Gabriel's arm.

"What's the matter?" said Gabriel, clutching his own orange till the juice squirted out into his face.

"There's blood in it!" said Larry, and with a blenched face on which the pale freckles stood out like measle pocks he pointed at the orange. It was the type of orange known as "blood orange." The pale fruit was splattered here and there with rich red splashes where some of the cells had swelled with richer juice than the others.

But neither Gabriel nor Larry had ever seen this phenomenon before, and Gabriel recoiled from the fallen orange even more violently than Larry had done.

"What is it?" he said.

"Blood I tell you," said Larry.

"Whose blood?" said Gabriel.

"I don't know."

There was a desperate silence. Then Gabriel thought of the religious pictures on the wall at home.

"Larry," he said, recoiling still further, "maybe it's God's blood!"

Larry stood rooted to the ground. Dumbly he pointed to the orange in Gabriel's hand. Gabriel held it out from him at once and was about to throw it as far as he could. Larry parted his dry lips.

"See if there's blood in yours too!"

Gabriel lowered his hand. He looked at the orange. Holding it far out from him he dug his fingers into it and split it open. There, too, on the pale yellow flesh of the fruit were the same ruby splatters of blood.

The orange fell from Gabriel's hand. Turning around without a word he fled for the open. Larry, his red jersey turned up over his head as if the Divine wrath were about to rain down upon him in torrents, ran after him with a scream. A minute afterwards they were both over the wall, running with scratched and bleeding knees across the field behind the church, and leaping over the stile even more quickly than they had leaped over it earlier they precipitated themselves one after another into the churchyard and ran out the gates barely a moment before the sacristan shot back the bolts on the side wings of the doors to give passageway to the congregation, who, although they had trickled into church in ones and twos, surged out, all together, like a mighty wave breaking on the shore.

∽   ∽   ∽

Larry and Gabriel stood outside the gates. Their hearts beat so violently they could hardly hear the thunder of feet as the congregation surged out around them, but with silent gratitude, they let themselves be surrounded and almost trodden under by the reassuring crowd of familiar human beings.

As the crowds came out between the church gates, talking and laughing, they snatched a false comfort and a fickle solace from the indifferent voices, but when the last person had come out, and gone upon his way, they looked at each other. Terror swooped down upon them once more.

"What will we do?" said Larry, and he looked as if he were going to cry.

Gabriel was torn by two emotions. He felt a sense of duty towards Larry because it was he who had made Larry stay away from the service, but the sight of Larry's pale face filled him with a great repugnance for the partner of his crime. This feeling of repugnance became so strong that he wanted to get away from Larry at once. He made a tremendous effort to stifle his own fears, and putting his hands in his pockets, he whistled a few nonchalant notes.

"I don't believe it was God's blood!" he said, defiantly. "I'm going home!" And with his hands still in his pockets he went off down Church Street, whistling.

For a few minutes Larry did not notice that Gabriel had gone. He was in such a state of nervousness that he was continually turning to either side, throwing rapid glances over his shoulder as if he expected every instant that Something would appear there, but in the course of one of these rapid turns he saw that Gabriel was not, as he thought, standing beside him, but was striding away down the street. He ran after him.

"Don't go home yet," he implored, and then as Gabriel strode on without replying, Larry ran after him again. "I'll go home with you and we can play in your yard," he said.

"My aunt wouldn't like me to bring you into our yard," said Gabriel.

"I'd sneak in! She wouldn't see me," said Larry.

"She sees everything," said Gabriel, "and anyway I'm not going to play in the yard, I'm going to play in the house."

Larry, whose temerity would have enabled him to dare an entry into the forbidden yard, flagged and failed at once when Gabriel said that he was going into the house. He stood still in the road, and made no further effort to follow his fellow sinner.

Gabriel strode onward, and only once he turned and looked back at Larry who stood where he had left him, in a dejected attitude. He turned away again in distaste. He felt that when he got out of sight of Larry he would forget all about the incident of the oranges, but strange to say, although he had repulsed Larry, and longed to be rid of the sight of him, he had no sooner turned around the corner leading into Clewe Street than he felt a return of the panic that had seized upon him in the Friary ruins. He was no sooner away from Larry than he wanted to be with him again. Perhaps the blood on the oranges was only a warning of something more awful to come? Perhaps, now at any minute, God would strike?

All at once Gabriel turned and ran back towards Church Street. Larry was not where he had left him. Where had he gone? For one terrible moment Gabriel thought that Larry had been stricken down and dragged away to another world, but just then he caught sight of the church door that stood open wide. That was where Larry had gone—into the church to ask God's forgiveness! Gabriel ran into the porch, and then, as he remembered himself, he ran out again and dipped his finger in the holy-water font. He thought with a pang of the time, such a little while before, when he and Larry had dipped their fingers in it together, just before the terrible thought had come to him of staying away from church. Oh, why had he ever had that wicked thought? He sprinkled the holy water lavishly, and then he ran back into the church, and ran down the centre aisle. But almost at once he saw that there was no sign of Larry. Gabriel proceeded nearer to the altar, over which the winking sanctuary light cast its nervous rays. The chapel seemed longer than it had ever seemed before, but soon Gabriel reached a point from which he could see down into the side aisles. There was no one at all in the left transept. He turned around calmly. Then he grew cold. Larry was not in the right transept. There was no sign of Larry in the whole church. Gabriel took one last fearful comprehensive stare around him. There was no sign of Larry in the transept, nave, or gallery. Pew after pew was idle and empty. The alleyways between the pews were empty. The stairway leading up to the gallery and choir, upon the steps of which the country lads stood at late Mass on Sundays, was empty. And then, as he realized that Larry was not in the church, another realization came over Gabriel. There was not a single soul in the church. He was all alone. A chance wind stirred the sanctuary lamp slightly, and it cast a moving shadow of red light on the flagged floor. It was like blood. Gabriel's heart beat with furious pace.

The chains by which the sanctuary lamp was suspended creaked slightly as it swayed. Gabriel tried to look at the Tabernacle, but he was unable to look with concentration in any one direction, so rapid were the inclinations that kept him looking over his shoulder, now to right now to left, to see if there was Somebody standing behind him. His feet were rooted on the floor. Then, once, as he jerked to look around him he saw, far off and brightly shining, the open door that led out into the cool white daylight. Somehow he took heart and made for the daylight and he did not stop running this time until he was inside the door of the house in Clewe Street.

But when Gabriel ran in at the open door, and banged it shut after him, the first thing that caught his eye was a large cardboard placard on the back of the door that told its legend in gold letters—GOD IS EVERY-WHERE. Gabriel felt his tongue stick to the roof of his mouth.

"What delayed you, Gabriel?" said Mary Ellen, coming out of the kitchen at that moment, with a large platter. "Hurry up and wash your hands, like a good child. The dinner is on the table!"

When he came to the table, Gabriel sat with his bib on his neck, staring at his plate, and he felt that he was not the same boy that had sat in that place the day before. He was different. He was marked out from the others. And when Mary Ellen handed him his plate of dinner, he pushed it back and felt that he could not eat.

"Eat your dinner, Gabriel!" said Mary Ellen, when she came into the room again with a covered dish of vegetables, and saw his untouched plate.

"Eat your dinner, dear," said his mother, urging him by lifting up his discarded knife and fork and putting them into his hands again.

"Don't fuss over him," said his Aunt Theresa. "If he doesn't eat at one meal he'll make up for it at the next."

His mother lifted his plate and handed it back to Mary Ellen. "Keep it in the oven for him, he may be hungry later on in the day."

"I hope he's not sick?" said Sara timidly, and then she stood up and went over to the sideboard. "Perhaps you'd like an apple, Gabriel?" she said, taking up a dish of red apples and bringing them to the table. At the sight of the apples Gabriel sprang up from the table, and bursting into tears he ran out of the room. The apples too might be sprinkled with God's blood! His guilt would be revealed to them all! He ran into the kitchen to seek the comforting ordinariness of Mary Ellen's company.

But the first thing that Gabriel saw in the kitchen was a picture which Mary Ellen had bought at the mission stand, a few months previously. Gabriel had enjoyed looking at it when it was new. He used to stand up on a chair and ask Mary Ellen questions about it.

"Can God stand on a cloud? . . . Why were His eyes shut?" For the picture represented the Ascension scene, in which the Deity appeared robed in white, midway in a patch of bright blue sky, His feet resting on white clouds, and from those feet, and in the palms of His outstretched hands, there were great wounds from which bright red drops of blood suspended, about to fall. Yes, upon this picture Gabriel had often gazed with the equanimity of the innocent, but as he walked into the kitchen now, he blenched at the sight of it. And yet he could not look away from it.

"I hope you're not getting sick," said Mary Ellen, as she looked at him critically. "Sit down there by the fire and rest yourself. You run around too much for your age."

Gabriel sat down, and tried to interest himself in Mary Ellen's activities, but his eyes were constantly drawn to the picture on the wall, and finally he had stared at it with such concentration that even when he looked away in another direction, details from it came before his eyes. Suddenly it seemed to him that the eyes in the picture moved. He stared hard. The eyes were shut. Surely they had been open? He blinked and looked again. He could not be sure. He wanted to ask Mary Ellen, and then the thought flashed through his mind that the eyes might be opening and shutting. God might be giving him another sign! His limbs began to tremble. He was afraid to look at the picture. For a few minutes he kept very still and did not look, then he screwed up his courage, and raising his head and lifting his eyes with a rush, he looked. His heart failed him. Did the outstretched arms move? As he raised his head with a swift rush it had seemed to him that the arms had altered their position slightly. The trembling in his own limbs grew greater.

"Are you sure you don't feel sick, Gabriel?" said Mary Ellen, stopping once more to stare at him. "Look at me!" she said, taking his chin in her hand. "Hold up your head! Stick out your tongue!" She let his chin drop. "I'll give you a dose in the morning. If you're not more lively after it, I'll make your mother call in the doctor."

Gabriel trembled more. The doctor! Perhaps that was the way that God would strike? He would get sick. They would get the doctor. The doctor would not be able to do anything for him. He would die. And after that? Gabriel's eyes turned instinctively to the great fire in the kitchen range, which Mary Ellen had poked until it blazed with a venomous roar. Tongues of fire licked the red-hot bars of the grate. Sparks fell like burning rain into the ash pit below. In the red depths of the fire there was a furious noise of flames as Mary Ellen pulled out the damper to create a draught. Fire and brimstone for all eternity.

From the earthly symbol of the damnation that he felt was stretching wide before him, Gabriel recoiled. He sprang up and ran out of the kitchen. He was suddenly as anxious to be out of the house as he had previously been anxious to get into it, but now he felt that no matter where he went, he would be confronted with shadows of his own iniquity and the doom it had brought upon him. God was everywhere. Yes! There on the back of the hall door was the placarded warning. GOD IS EVERY-WHERE! Before he dared step out into the street Gabriel put out his head and looked about him fearfully. The first thing Gabriel saw when he looked out reassured him so much that he drew a deep breath, before he banged the door behind him and advanced into the street.

Upon the seat, under the pollarded elm tree, Sylvester was sitting, whittling a stick. The spotted dog from the hotel was lying beside him on the ground. Sylvester would help him. Gabriel had always felt humiliated over his age when he was with Sylvester, but now, all of a sudden, he was glad of Sylvester's superiority over him in this respect, for Sylvester knew so much. He would tell him everything. Gabriel ran towards him and, when he got to the tree, he sat down and pulled the spotted dog up on his lap. He felt better with the dog's hot body close to his own.

But Sylvester was silent. He went on whittling the stick. Gabriel did not know how to begin. Suddenly he opened his mouth and blurted out a question.

"Did you ever see God's blood?" he asked, and he held his breath for the answer.

Sylvester didn't answer. He was frowning, and he seemed to be in a bad humour. Gabriel noticed that there was a brown paper parcel beside him on the seat, tied with ribbon, and fastened with a tag bearing his name. While he was looking at it, Sylvester raised his head.

"Today is my birthday," he said, and his voice was lifeless.

This statement was evidently intended to convey the cause of his misery to Gabriel, but when Gabriel said nothing, but merely sat in polite silence, hugging the dog, Sylvester looked at him, and then looked down at the parcel by his side. Then he picked up the parcel with a weary gesture and opened it. In the parcel was a black tin box in which were ranged dozens of small tinfoil tubes with different-coloured labels bearing the most peculiar names that Gabriel had ever seen in print.

Raw Sienna. Ochre. Cobalt. Gamboge. Umber.

He spelled out the letters of these extraordinary words, and then, spying a long thin brush, the uses of these strange tubes became clear to him suddenly.

"A box of paints!" he exclaimed with excitement, because all at once he imagined himself daubing his lesson books with stripes of red and yellow and green, and painting big circles of yellow and blue.

"Where did you get them?" he asked. "Don't you like them?"

Sylvester shrugged his shoulders. "You wouldn't understand," he said, and he kept his face averted. Suddenly he turned around quickly and snapped the lid down on the paints. "My mother will expect me to sit down and paint all day. She'll expect me to paint trees and birds and flowers and animals." He looked at Gabriel. "You see my father was an artist and my mother wants me to be one too. Sometimes when I'm sitting at the table with a pencil when she comes into the room, 'You're sketching, dear!' she says, delighted. 'I won't disturb you,' and she tiptoes out again. The other day when she came in there was an old catalogue on the table and it was raining and I had nothing to do so I was putting moustaches on the ladies' faces with a pencil. She came up behind me and she saw the figures. 'That looks very good,' she said, and she wanted to look closer at it. I put my arms over it." Sylvester paused and bit his lip. "She said that I was modest like my father. She said that he always said that the artist himself was never a judge of his own work. If the artist thought it was good it was sure to be bad, if he thought it was bad it was often a masterpiece. 'You're like your father,' she said." Sylvester bit deeper into his lip. "Today she gave me this box of paints," he said, "and every Saturday she puts money into a savings box to send me to Dublin to pay for studio fees for me. And you know," he said, turning to Gabriel, "I can't draw. I can't paint. At least I can't paint good enough to become a great painter."

Gabriel listened silently. He did not altogether understand the cause of Sylvester's misery but Sylvester's misery had reminded him again of his own, and under the double weight of misery he drooped. Suddenly Sylvester's spirits soared.

"Ah well," he said, "I won't worry till the time comes to worry." He lifted the paws of the spotted dog and stared at him. "Isn't that right, doggy? Don't trouble trouble until trouble troubles you"; and then he looked up at Gabriel. "What was the matter with you?" he said, dropping the dog's paws. "What did you say about blood? Whose blood?"

Gabriel looked at him. "God's blood," said he in a small faint voice, and he began his tale.

In the beginning Sylvester's interest was not very great, but as the story progressed his interest grew. Once or twice his eyes flashed, and once or twice he urged Gabriel on.

"What happened then?" he demanded. "What happened then?"

Nevertheless when the story was ended he took on a patronizing air. "I don't believe it was God's blood," he said, and then as the feeling of isolated identity came over Gabriel again and the tears began to shine in his eyes Sylvester made a concession. "I don't believe it was God's blood," he said once more, "but we'll have to make sure."

Gabriel's eyes widened. "How can we make sure?" he said.

Sylvester looked at him with pity for his slow understanding.

"You'll have to stay away from church again on Sunday," he said. "If it was God's blood, you'll see it again." His voice grew excited. "And I'll see it too because I'll go with you."

Gabriel's heart had failed him so completely upon hearing the first part of Sylvester's plan that even at the heartening news that Sylvester was going to brave damnation with him, he hardly felt any better.

"Do you agree?" demanded Sylvester.

Gabriel gulped. "What about Larry?" he said, taking refuge from reply in another question.

"Oh, Larry wouldn't have the guts to come with us!" said Sylvester, and Gabriel, feeling mollified at this implication as to his own courage, put his fears underfoot and began to listen to the arrangements that Sylvester was making for putting their plan into execution.

The next day was Sunday. There was only one night of suspense. But Gabriel had begun to lose his fears already. He began to doubt that God would give them another sign. Just the same he was not at ease. For he felt that if there was no sign, his own imminent terrors of damnation would be lessened, but so too would his stature be lessened in the sight of Sylvester.

ᔕ ᔕ ᔕ

Sylvester was the first to climb up on the Friary wall on Sunday. He sat astraddle on it and stretched out his hand to Gabriel, who was getting a foothold at the side of the wall.

"I can get up by myself," said Gabriel, anxious to show some capacity.

"Are you sure?" said Sylvester, and he turned around about to slip down on the other side to make way for Gabriel, who had indeed got a good foothold and was just about to hoist himself up to the top.

Just as Sylvester turned around, however, and was about to find a foothold on the other side of the wall he saw something in the distance that caused him to loosen his hands at once, and drop to the ground at the other side without breaking his fall by as much as an inch. He fell backwards into a bed of nettles and he was forced to spend the next few minutes in such concern at the blisters and burns that covered him, arms and legs, he forgot all about Gabriel. The rattle of loose pebbles that fell with him and a brief startled exclamation that he gave were all the warning Gabriel got, but even if he had had a more distinct warning he could not have done anything because he was at that moment hoisting himself to the top, and could see or do nothing until he himself was astraddle the wall. From there, however, he lost no time in looking around him.

Coming across the churchyard was his Aunt Theresa, making not for the church, however, but straight for the stile in the wall! She had seen them. Gabriel saw to his horror that his aunt was travelling at such a speed she did not bother even to lift the hem of her dress above the level of the wet blades. Even in his fright Gabriel noticed that she lifted it up too much, and revealed the frill of her white petticoat which was always dried on a clothes-horse in the kitchen, it being considered too indelicate an article to hang upon a clothes-line. When Theresa got to the foot of the

179

wall she said nothing for a moment, but fixed her eye upon her nephew, who sat speechless atop it. Then she opened her mouth. "I always knew there was a bad streak in you!" she said. She knew all.

Gabriel dropped to the ground, the balls of his feet tingling from the contact with the earth at such force. For a minute he thought that Theresa was going to strike him as she raised her umbrella, but instead of striking him she prodded him in the back with the point of it. When she gave him another and more violent prod it occurred to him that by this method she was urging him into motion. On the other side of the wall he heard a slight stir, and guessed that Sylvester was creeping away. He began to walk across the grass slowly, prodded moment by moment in the small of the back when he showed any reluctance to continue. And several times, indeed, he felt a great reluctance to continue owing to the fact that one or two people now lingered at the entrance to the chapel in order to see what the unusual scene might mean. They would soon know.

"It's a bad thing when a boy has to be driven to church with the point of a stick," said Theresa, when she got to the door of the porch.

Gabriel was overcome with shame. He dared not lift his eyes, and, as he made his way through the people around the church door, and went into the porch, he had only one thought and that was to hide himself soon in the crowded pews. But he was not to escape yet.

"Since when did you develop this contempt for the holy-water font?" said his aunt, dragging him back by the sleeve, and, not waiting for him to dip his fingers into the font, she dipped in her own fingers, and sprinkled him with a cold dash of water. A tendril of the green growth at the bottom came away on her finger and was dashed on his face, from which he dared not remove it.

The people near the door had turned around to stare at the sound of his aunt's audible whisper. As they looked at him Gabriel felt his cheeks burn. He looked at his aunt and made a gesture as if he would kneel down in a pew near the door.

"Go down to the front," she ordered.

And then, while his cheeks burned, she gave him another push forward, this time with her hand, and when he came to the second seat from the front she put her hand on his shoulder, pressing him to his knees so heavily that he nearly fell.

"Genuflect!" she said, and standing aside she ordered him into the pew.

From then to the end of the service, every time that he moved a fraction of an inch, his aunt shot a glance at him, until it seemed that every eye was upon him. It seemed that every tongue in the church would be busied with talk about him, as soon as the people rose from their knees and made their way out into the street. His mother and his Aunt Sara would hear about him. The teachers in the school would hear about him. The

Finnertys, and the Molloys, would look at him queerly. Larry Soraghan would jeer at him.

And then, at the thought of Larry Soraghan, he remembered the first day when he had stayed away from church, and he remembered his panic and his fears for God's wrath. Now those fears seemed unreal and far-away. He would never be silly and scared like that again. He was becoming aware in a vague way that there were more immediate things to fear. He had always been aware that his aunt had a vague antagonism towards him, but now he realized that he had given her an opportunity to bring her antagonism out into the open.

When the service was over, as he filed out of the church with the congregation, Gabriel saw Sylvester standing with an innocent face by the wall. Sylvester made a sign to him, and shrugged his shoulders. Gabriel understood. Sylvester had slipped away to put God to the test. But Gabriel knew without being told that God had not sent them a sign. It had been silly to think that He might. The Deity, with His thunder, and His power to walk on the clouds, seemed remote and fantastic, beside the fear he now felt at the scene that his aunt would make, as soon as they reached Clewe Street, and were once inside the door. He thought of the placard inside the door. He would like to turn it wrong side out. He thought of Mary Ellen's picture on the wall. It was only a picture. He thought of the way he had imagined that the eyes had opened and looked at him, and, with contempt, he told himself that the picture was dusty and smoked, and so blackened with fly blows that it was a wonder you could see it at all!

The power and might of God had dwindled. God was now no more to him than an idea in the mind of his Aunt Theresa.

When they reached the end of Clewe Street, however, and went into the narrow hallway, instead of turning upon him as he had expected Theresa Coniffe made her way upstairs just as it was her custom to do upon ordinary Sundays and ordinary Holy Days, when she made a point of carefully removing the clothes she had worn to church, and replaced in the side pieces of her hair the two metal curling pins which upon the lesser days of the week would not have been removed until the more seemly hour of supper.

Gabriel stared after her, uncertain as to what he should do under these peculiar circumstances. If only he could ask his mother or his Aunt Sara. But worse than he dreaded his Aunt Theresa's tongue, he dreaded to see the hurt expression that would come over their faces when they heard of his iniquity. The longer they were without knowing of it the better. Then, as he stood uncertain and perplexed on the mat at the foot of the stairs, he raised his head in surprise. At that moment there was a sound overhead, and Gabriel heard the door of Theresa's room open and shut again with a rapidity which would have left one in doubts that a human being could have emerged through it in such short time, if a moment later Theresa Coniffe had not appeared at the head of the stairs looking thinner than ever, for it was her practice when she was in haste to pin her skirts tight to her sides, suppress all bows and side curls, and to walk with her hands folded in front of her, thus anticipating the theories which in a later day were worked out in the construction of battleships and destroyers— the elimination of as many as possible of the surfaces which might otherwise have caught the wind and impeded the speed of her progress. Thus equipped for speed, Theresa advanced. Gabriel gritted his teeth and kept his stance, right in the middle of the mat at the foot of the stairs. Come what might, he would not flinch.

Step by step Theresa came down. And then on the last step she stopped and looked at him.

"Are you out of your wits," she demanded, "or what are you standing there for? How can a person pass up or down?"

And leaving him to gape after her, Theresa brushed him to one side with a sweep of her arm and advanced into the kitchen. For a minute he was baffled. Then he seemed to see clearly again. Why! Of course! She was going to tell her sisters about him first. Well, he reflected bitterly, they knew already! But just as he thought this the kitchen door opened and his Aunt Sara came out, the two sisters brushing past each other with the indifference of any ordinary day in the year. And as she passed him, the sinner, his Aunt Sara bestowed on him one of her usual sweet smiles. She didn't know after all! But would his Aunt Theresa let it go untold? Ah! He thought not. "Wait a minute, Sara," said Theresa, calling her back, while at the same moment she leant forward and looked into the kitchen. "Are you there, Lily? Come here a moment, please!" Gabriel gritted his teeth once more. But when Theresa opened her mouth again, the words of purely domestic import that issued from it were so incalculable as to be almost incomprehensible.

"Sara! Lily! On no account must we forget the parsley for the soup today. It was most insipid yesterday without it!" She swung around. "Gabriel! Go down the garden and get a handful of parsley this minute. No! Wait. Go up and change into your old shoes first, and then get it. You won't keep us waiting then after dinner."

After dinner? After dinner every Sunday it was the custom in Clewe Street for Gabriel to change out of his patent-leather shoes into shoes with heavier soles in order to accompany his aunts on the walk they took regardless of weather around the rampart road. And here was his Aunt Theresa freely making reference to such a walk that very afternoon, for all the world as if the morning had been any ordinary morning; for all the

182

world, that was to say, as if the whole day were to proceed with no further reference to its unlucky beginning.

Wasn't that his Aunt Sara's voice that he heard in the kitchen? What was she doing there? Sara was rarely or never to be found at the heart core of domestic activity. He listened intently. Wasn't that his mother's voice? His mother was in there too! They were all there! That was very strange! His Aunt Sara usually made the beds at this hour. And his mother usually sorted the linen at the press on the attic landing.

Instantly he jumped to the conclusion that their presence in the kitchen had something to do with him. Could it be that they already knew of his escapade? Could it be that some rumour of it had already reached Clewe Street, carried there even before he and his Aunt Theresa had arrived.

Mrs. Molloy? Suspicion of Mrs. Molloy shot through him and left him quivering.

Mrs. Molloy, as Gabriel knew, frequently had to leave the church before the end of the service because of a complaint from which she suffered at times, a complaint which was known to Gabriel by the familiar name of Pins and Needles, and of which every symptom and manifestation had been laid bare to him by Mary Ellen, the confidante of Mrs. Molloy, and herself an occasional sufferer from the same dreadful scourge.

Perhaps Mrs. Molloy had had Pins and Needles that morning! Gabriel shuddered. For, if Mrs. Molloy had had Pins and Needles it was beyond all doubt that she would have left the church earlier than the rest of the congregation, and, if so, it was still further beyond all doubt that she would have put her head inside the Coniffe door as she passed, if only to say that she could tell the inmates something of interest to them were it not for the fact that she made it a practice never to be the bearer of bad news.

Yes, Gabriel felt sure that the news of his guilt had travelled before him. He could picture how his Aunt Sara and his mother, having flown to Mary Ellen for comfort after hearing the allegations of Mrs. Molloy, would only wait Theresa's confirmation of the incident before they gave way to the violence of their distress. And when his aunt made no reference to the incident in the Friary before the sun went down under the rampart rim, he believed with absolute finality that all was to be forgotten and forgiven forever.

But Theresa Coniffe's decision to let her nephew go unpunished was drawn from a deeper well than forgiveness or forgetfulness.

∽ ∽ ∽

Theresa Coniffe had never forgotten that Gabriel was the son of the man who had slighted her to marry her youngest sister, although as a matter of fact she had rarely been able to vent her resentment on the child, because a more biddable and obedient child than Gabriel Galloway could hardly have been found. He not only did all that he was told to do, but as often as not he did not wait to be told. True, he was completely under her thumb, but it was a small triumph to have under your thumb a creature who submitted to you no more than he would have submitted to one of half your stature. It was small satisfaction for Theresa to know that Gabriel would instantly fetch his muffler if she ordered him to do so, when she knew that he would fetch his goloshes just as quickly if his Aunt Sara as much as mentioned that it was wet underfoot. When, therefore, she had come upon him in the Friary ruin, and realized that he was absenting himself from church, Theresa had experienced a curious sense of satisfaction. Here was an opportunity to humiliate Lily and to make more painful in the minds of all in Clewe Street the memory of Cornelius Galloway.

It was with this purpose of humiliating Lily that she had driven Gabriel across the churchyard and ordered him down the aisle in front of her, and her mind, for the first few minutes after they knelt down, was a turmoil of sayings and proverbs that pressed themselves forward as being one more appropriate than another for utterances as she would open the door in Clewe Street and lead the boy in to his mother with the story of his wickedness.

"Breed will show sooner or later. . . . Like father, like son. . . . You cannot make a silk purse out of a sow's ear."

She would fling the words out at Lily and Sara, leaving her meaning ambiguous until they were thoroughly ill-at-ease and then she would taunt them with the conduct of their pet.

Here in this very church she had suffered the humiliation of attending Lily's wedding; the elderly bridesmaid of a foolish young bride. Well, she was having some satisfaction now. Out of the corner of her eye she threw a glance at Gabriel.

But as her eye fell on him it rested there. Were his lips moving, or was he just kneeling there sullenly? She bent her eye to pry closer. His eyes, all right, were fastened on his prayer book, but his lips were idle and tightly closed.

Theresa drew a short quick breath. This was no attitude to adopt in the house of God. What would people think of him?

A new aspect of the affair occurred to her. She looked around her nervously. Perhaps this incident was but the first of a long series of iniquities by which this child would disgrace and abash his family?

She glanced over her shoulder again. Were people looking in their direction? She began to regret that she had made such a display of the boy. What were people thinking, she wondered. Were they laughing up their sleeves? She shot glances to right and left, looking obliquely out from under partially lowered lids. But the congregation was engrossed in the service.

The congregation was on its knees, engrossed in the service, but as Theresa glanced around the church her eye fell on the gaudy silken banners of the Women's Sodality, still hanging on their brass poles at the end of the pews from which old Luke had not had time to remove them since the Sodality meeting of the previous evening. At sight of the bright banners of the Sodality over which she presided as Leader, and over the members of which she had always exercised such a rigid and tireless example, Theresa's thoughts took another turn. Had the boy been altogether to blame? Had she herself been entirely blameless in the matter? After all was he not under her care? Was she not responsible for his guidance, for what use in that respect was his poor bird of a mother?

Theresa's heart grew tight inside her Sunday bombazine and she fixed her eyes once more on Gabriel. Instantly the fact that he was the son of Cornelius Galloway became insignificant beside the fact that he was also the grandson of Theodore Coniffe. When the service came to an end, Theresa had therefore suffered a complete change of heart. From being the child's accuser she intended henceforth to be his guardian. But since the first move she made in the new direction was to give him another poke in the back and tell him to get out in the aisle, it was not to be wondered at that Gabriel was for a long time unaware of what had happened. Moreover, even if he had been aware of all that had gone on in aunt's mind, it would have been a matter of small concern to him that his Aunt Theresa had constituted herself the guardian of his soul. Accustomed to have her examine the soles of his feet after he came in out of the rain in order to see if he had worn his goloshes, it was not much different to have her come into his room at night and take his trousers from the chair beside the bed to see if there was dust on the kneecaps to indicate that he had said his prayers. Accustomed to have her eye upon him at table to make sure that he chewed his food, it was hardly noticeable to him that she began to watch him also during the grace before meals in order to make sure that his lips were moving.

Once in a while, however, as the months went by, he got brief shafts of vision upon his new position in the house. For instance one day, when Sylvester was home on holidays, and when Gabriel himself was in bed with a chill, Sylvester had come up to his bedroom to see him.

Sitting up in bed, surrounded by books that his mother had bought for him, and complacently surveying the tea tray laden with iced cakes which his Aunt Sara had prepared in order that the two boys could have a treat, Gabriel felt, for once, that he was in a superior position to his friend. Remembering that Sylvester and his mother had exchanged their rooms in the Central Hotel only for a small house under the arch of the railway

185

bridge, he looked around with satisfaction at the rich red-papered walls of his room, at the glowing mahogany chests devoted exclusively to his small linens, and at the shelf over the mantelpiece which was burdened only with his own possessions, or such family ornaments as were promoted to that position by his own selection. Among the latter objects there were two which had been but recently acquired, and upon them Gabriel's eyes rested proudly. Sylvester would surely be impressed by them, he had given a certain amount of attention to them when they were still down in the parlour upon the first day of all that he had visited the house. These objects were the ivory elephant with the jade tusks, and the large white shell with the saw-edged lip that was speckled all over with brown dots.

This afternoon, overcome by his pride in them, although he was strictly forbidden to put his foot outside the bed, Gabriel was on the point of dashing over to the mantelpiece for one moment to alter the position of these precious ornaments, and make sure that they would not fail to catch the eye of his visitor immediately upon his entry into the room, when there was a sound of footsteps on the stairs and Sylvester's voice outside the door.

A moment later the door opened and Sylvester was in the room.

When Gabriel had lain complacently surveying his surroundings he had hoped that Sylvester would notice them. He had not dared to hope that his friend would examine the room corner for corner, which as a matter of fact Sylvester proceeded to do the moment the door had closed behind him.

"So this is your room?" said Sylvester, whose preliminary greeting to the invalid had taken the form of a nod. "Do you sleep here all alone?"

Without waiting for an answer Sylvester's glance ran over the furniture, resting particularly on the chest of drawers.

"Can you use all the drawers," he asked, "or are some of them locked?"

Simultaneously with the question he had asked, however, he had obviated the necessity for a reply by pulling out all the drawers one after another and revealing for himself Gabriel's ownership of the garments folded and piled therein.

At the ornaments on the mantelpiece Sylvester gazed not at all. And his eye when it fell on the rich red wallpaper seemed to darken as if with a frown.

"Don't you like the wallpaper?" said Gabriel, sitting up higher in bed. "Don't you think this is a nice room?"

But the mere fact that he was forced to ask the question, and to cast it into a negative form, showed that already some of his complacency had begun to flag.

Sylvester gave up his survey.

"Oh, it's all right," he said. "It's a good thing to have privacy." He nodded over his shoulder at the chest against the wall. "That's a good chest you've got there," he said. "Good, deep drawers; they'd be better, of course, if they had locks and keys to them, but that's a small job."

Gabriel allowed himself to slump down more comfortably into the pillows.

"Won't you sit down?" he said, with some remnant of the magnanimity with which he had intended to entertain his guest. He indicated a green wicker chair that Sara had placed beside his bed and on which she had put a fat cushion of red plush embroidered with yellow roses.

Sylvester was not however ready to sit down. He had not yet fully completed his survey of the room.

"On the whole, it's not a bad room," he said, and then just as he was preparing to sit down, an expression of great distaste came over his face.

What was the matter? Gabriel sat up again.

Sylvester's eye, at the moment when he shuddered, had been fixed on a picture that hung over the mantelpiece, and although he had hurriedly glanced away from it, it was to this picture that Gabriel's own eyes now flew in search of some reason why Sylvester should have behaved as he did. But the picture that had hung in that position as long as he could remember was so familiar to him that his eyes passed over it now with uncritical tolerance. It was a cheap print of a religious subject, executed in gaudy, facile colours, and differed only from those sold on a huckster's barrow by reason of the ornate and expensive frame in which it was confined.

Gabriel looked back questioningly at Sylvester.

"Why don't you take that down?" said Sylvester. "How can you stand it in the room?" And he nodded his left ear at the print, unwilling to submit his eyes to the strain of seeing it again.

Take down the picture! It would have appeared as easy to Gabriel to take down the wall upon which it hung. Immediately the feeling of proprietorship which had filled him with such pride a moment before vanished, and left him with the feeling that he was but a miserable tenant in the room with the red wallpaper.

"Will you have some tea?" he asked quickly and valiantly to keep his spirits from drooping. "We have only to press the bell and Mary Ellen will bring the teapot."

But the iced cakes, and even the gingerbread men that Mary Ellen brought up, hot from the oven, had lost their taste, and he could not stop his eye from wandering back to the picture, and his mind from dwelling upon Sylvester's criticism of it.

And after Sylvester had gone away, his mind was still upset, and what worried him most was that had Sylvester not shown him his error, he would never have noticed the ugliness of the picture. He looked up at it again. He had in fact liked it, and been rather proud of its gaudy splashes.

The day after Sylvester's visit Gabriel was well enough to get up and leave his room, and so the picture was not continually under his eye to annoy him, but every night and morning it was there to confront him when he went in with his candle, or when he opened his eyes at daylight.

For three or four days Gabriel bore his irritation about the picture but on the night of the fourth day after he had blown out the candle and lain in the darkness for a while it suddenly became insufferable to him to think that, although he could not see it, the picture hung upon the wall directly in front of him, outfacing him, you might say, even in the darkness.

All at once a spirit of daring and adventure came over him and made him tremble with excitement. He would do something about it. He would! With a shaking hand he groped for the matches and lit the candle. "I'll turn it with its face to the wall," he said. He jumped out of bed, and catching hold of the old wicker chair on which he laid his clothes at night, he dragged it over to the fireplace and sprang up on the seat of it, regardless of the creaking osiers. Then he caught the frame of the picture. It seemed but a matter of moments now to turn it around from back to front. But before his hands had rightly grasped the frame Gabriel became aware that all was not going as it should.

For a moment he thought that the chair had slipped from under his feet. In the next he thought that the picture had fallen from its cord, and at the next, with greater horror, he thought that the whole side of the wall was crashing down before him. For, no sooner had he put his hands upon the picture than, from under it, there began to scatter to all sides such a shower of leaflets, medallions, old letters, envelopes, and sprigs of faded palm, that it would be hard for the steadiest head to be sure of what in that room was stationary and what was in agitation.

At last the shower subsided, and Gabriel looked down at the jackdaw's collection that lay on the floor below him. Without another thought he stepped down and began to pick them up, stowing them away again in fistfuls into their original place behind the picture. For what use was there now in thinking to move it? Every time he touched it this shower would be whirled to the floor. Every time? Yes. For need it be said that although he intended to turn the picture to the wall he intended to restore it to its original position in the morning. Perhaps it was all for the best, thought Gabriel, as he stowed the last handful of leaflets behind the picture, got down from the wicker chair, and climbed in between the cold sheets with a feeling of defeat. For what would happen if, one morning, he should forget to turn the picture right side out again?

It was all very well for Sylvester to talk. He probably felt that he had to say what he said because his father was an artist, but this house wasn't the only one with holy pictures on the walls. Larry Soraghan said their house was filled with them.

"Ma says they bring a blessing on the house," said Larry, "and at the same time they help to hide the spots of damp on the wall."

Somehow or other, Gabriel felt better about the picture. Some of his former feeling of liking for it had returned, sharpened by feelings of defiance. Nevertheless, just before he put out the candle, when he glanced at the picture again, he fancied that in the far upper corner of the frame one fat pale angel looked down at him with a face that wore a smug and secretive smile.

About a year after the affair of the picture, there occurred another small incident of such a similar nature that it would hardly be worth recording, were it not that, this time, it was Gabriel himself who, without any hint from Sylvester, felt that Theresa's interference in some things was going a bit too far.

A mission had been held in the church for two weeks, one week being devoted to men and the other to women, and, before the greater humiliation took place at all, Gabriel had the humiliation of seeing Sylvester, and Larry and indeed all the fellows of his class, going off every evening to the men's mission, while he was kept back to attend the second week in company with his mother and his aunts.

To this humiliation he had bowed, but one morning, about a week after the closing of the mission, when he was getting up and dressing for school, his Aunt Theresa came into his room. He had just completed the curt task of brushing his hair, which was usually the last item of his preparations for the day. Theresa looked at him.

"Are you ready?" she said.

"Yes, Aunt!"

Thinking that she meant he would be late for school, Gabriel gave a hasty glance around him and made for the door.

"Just a minute, Gabriel! Aren't you forgetting something?"

Gabriel, who had almost reached the door, came to a stand. As he did so, he saw his aunt glance at the top of the cabinet in the corner of the room and he knew at once the cause of her vexation.

"Were those medals given out to lie about on the top of a chest of drawers?" she demanded, pointing her finger at a pair of blessed medals that had been distributed during the mission, and which now lay where she pointed, fastened together with the safety pin by which they had been secured to Gabriel's clothes upon the previous few days. Gabriel said nothing, but went over and took up the pin from which the medals dangled. But Theresa put out her hand and snatched them from him.

"Give me your coat!" she said, jerking it by the collar as she spoke.

189

"I'll sew them into it in such a way they won't be found lying about the house again."

Gabriel took his hands out of the sleeves awkwardly and allowed the coat to be snatched into Theresa's lap as she sat down abruptly on the side of the bed and, producing a threaded needle from under a pleat in her bodice, began to sew the medals into the lining of the coat. Gabriel stood indifferently at her side as the needle flashed in and out of the dark serge, and the medals hit together with a thin tinny sound. Then suddenly his eyes settled more steadily on his aunt's hands.

"Oh not there!" he cried agonizedly, as he saw that she was stitching the medals so near the flap of his lapel that they would undoubtedly be seen every time he stirred.

"Why not? Are you ashamed to be seen wearing them?" Theresa stopped sewing for long enough to stare at Gabriel; long enough for him to give a reply if he could, and then she resumed her stitching without breaking her thread.

A few minutes later Gabriel went out to school with the medals distinctly visible under his left lapel.

That was not the end of the incident however, for during the day Theresa took every opportunity of referring to Gabriel's forgetfulness over the medals and when dinnertime came, and he slipped into his place, she saw an excellent opportunity for upbraiding him.

"I see there are some things you don't forget," she said. "I see you don't forget to come to the table."

Gabriel moved about on his chair uneasily. Would she never stop talking, about those old medals, he wondered.

Now, as Gabriel squirmed about on his chair, although he did not notice it, his Aunt Sara seemed to be uneasy about something also, and she exchanged a significant glance with his mother.

Lily and Sara had always felt that Theresa was too hard upon Gabriel, even in the matter of his temporal welfare.

On one occasion Sara had even ventured to speak to Theresa.

"Aren't you a little too hard on him, Theresa?" she asked timidly.

Theresa, however, had had her answer ready.

"Hard on him?" she said. "I have to be hard on him, when you and Lily are so soft with him." Her face assumed an elaborate expression of patience. "Don't think I like to be hard. Let me tell you it would be far easier to be all smiles and gentle words. But I have a sense of responsibility if neither of you have one. It would be very nice for me to have Gabriel run to me, and throw his arms around me, and kiss me, but I know that if I encouraged him at the expense of discipline I would be taking the easy path; I would be avoiding my duties. If I am hard on him it is for his own sake. I want him to realize that as he goes through life he need not expect to find everyone as foolish and easygoing as yourself and his mother. I want him to realize that other people will not give way to him as you do. He will meet with reversals like everybody else, and he may as well get used to them at an early age. Of course I know the sacrifices I'm making. I know the boy will grow to dislike me—if he doesn't dislike me already—but I am ready, as I say, to make sacrifices. Some day he will thank me, and even if he is thankless, as most people in this world turn out to be sooner or later, I will still have the satisfaction of knowing that I acted as I thought right." All this was said in the quick staccato sentences which people use when any one of these sentences could have stood alone as an expression of their meaning. Then she sighed. "Ah, Sara," she said, "you little know how hard it is to be always stiff and stern. There are times when I would like to relax, but I would not permit myself such a luxury when a boy's character is at stake." At the sad truth of her own words, Theresa sighed again, a deeper sigh than before. "It's easy to be all smiles and soft words," she said.

Theresa's statement that smiles were easier to bestow than frowns was so indubitably true as applied to themselves that both Sara and Lily did not doubt that it was true when applied by Theresa to herself as well, and for some time after this conversation they tried by muscular contortion to assume the expression which, on their sister's face, came naturally out from within like measly pock. But as milk will not wrinkle unless it is sour, their faces were soon bright and blossomy once more and their lips were fluttering with smiles. No more was said for a time about Theresa's attitude to Gabriel. Before long, however, Sara began to feel uncomfortable once more as Theresa's interest in Gabriel's spiritual welfare doubled her occasions for correction and admonition. And so on the day of the disturbance over the medals she felt that something should be said. But this time she was careful to say it to someone other than Theresa.

"Lily," she said, "I'm worried about Gabriel." She paused and put her head to one side, choosing her words with extra care out of respect for the matter upon which she was about to speak. "I'm worried at the way Theresa harps on things, like for instance the medals this morning! I'm afraid that Gabriel might form a wrong impression about his religion. He might begin to think that God was harsh and unreasonable!"

"Harsh and unreasonable? God?" Lily did not understand.

"Oh you know," said Sara with timid impatience. "Like Theresa herself!"

"Oh, I see what you mean," said Lily, and she became very agitated. "But what can we do?"

"Well, I was thinking," said Sara, "that I might say a few words to him, if I get the opportunity. I might try to let him see that there is another aspect of religion; that God is gentle as well as stern, loving as well as just." Sara's face grew soft and happy for a moment, and then the habitual small frown of worry settled upon her faded face. "What do you think?" she said.

"I don't know," said Lily. "I suppose I should say something to him myself?" But she looked very scared at the prospect, and had no sooner made the suggestion than she saw a way for evading its execution. "These matters are so delicate I'd hardly know what to say. But you have a knack of putting things nicely. I think you'd better do it."

When this conversation took place it was about two o'clock and Gabriel was due back from school for his dinner in another few minutes. Before the two women were down in the hall, they heard him coming in by the front door.

Now when Sara said that she would watch for an opportunity of saying what she had to say to Gabriel it might be thought that she meant she would watch out for a moment when such intimacy would be rendered suitable by some mood of the boy's, some atmosphere in the house, or by a spiritual urge within her own heart. But no. What Sara considered a suitable opportunity was nothing more or less than a moment when Theresa would be absent, or out of earshot, and so, a few minutes after her talk with Lily, when she saw from the window on the landing that Theresa had gone down to the bottom of the garden with a basketful of wet clothes that would take at least ten minutes to spread upon the clothes-line, and when she heard at the same moment a sound in the hall that indicated the return of Gabriel, that was enough for her. With a quick pressure of Lily's arm which was meant to convey to her sister all that was in her mind, Sara sped lightly down the last steps of the stairs, and into the hall, where in the dim light she appeared suddenly to Gabriel like a wisp of spirit.

"Gabriel!" she said. "I wanted to say something to you! Don't worry about the medals! God will understand. He will never blame us for forgetfulness. It is only when we do something bad deliberately that He is hurt. Although of course we must remember that He watches over us night and day. 'Not one leaf shall fall to the ground,' He said, 'without my knowing it.' Isn't that a beautiful saying, Gabriel?" And then, hearing Theresa's voice at the back door Sara turned and sped away again, leaving Gabriel staring after her, surprised, and hardly aware of what she had said to him.

It was not long, however, before he noticed that his Aunt Sara had taken upon herself the task of counteracting the possible effect on him of Theresa's austerity. For as Theresa's vigilance over his soul grew more intense, Sara's whispers of balmy consolation grew more frequent, and more and more it became fixed in his mind that religion was another peculiar twist in the minds of the women in Clewe Street.

ᔇ ᔇ ᔇ

The friendship between Gabriel and Sylvester continued, although its continuance was a source of astonishment to Gabriel, who was always uneasy on the day that Sylvester was to arrive in Castlerampart. It did not seem possible to him that Sylvester could bother with him after the unimaginable distractions of the school term that lay between their meetings.

Once or twice Sylvester asked him why he never came to the train to meet him.

"You come to see me off!" he said.

"That's different," said Gabriel.

Characteristically Sylvester did not inquire the nature of the difference, he knew it to be some subtlety of mind in Gabriel which he would scarcely have patience to hear explained but which he appreciated just the same, and which he regarded as the personal flavour of Gabriel, a flavour he had not found in any of the contemporaries he met at college.

Gabriel did not go to the station to meet Sylvester because he was afraid that he would be imposing himself on Sylvester's attention. He preferred to wait and see if Sylvester would seek him out. But no matter how deep his doubts were at the end of each term, they would be dissipated a few minutes after Sylvester's train drew in to the platform, for Sylvester would take no more time than it took to walk in step with his mother to their rooms, and throw his case into the hall, before he would come whistling up the pavement and rap at the Coniffe door.

Sometimes after the opening of the door there would be a few moments of constraint still on Gabriel's side, because Sylvester was entering into those middle years of boyhood when every few months brought their own slight changes, and attitudes of maturity were beginning to show themselves. Sylvester, too, was apt for a time after his arrival to anticipate other traits of manhood which were not yet his by rights, but which melted away in a few minutes in the glow of Gabriel's affectionate admiration. There was no need to exert himself to an uncomfortable emulation of other people in order to impress Gabriel. Gabriel was sufficiently impressed already, and before he was ten minutes in the parlour at Clewe Street, Sylvester would have stowed away in his pocket a variety of articles, such as a yellow cigarette holder, a monster signet ring, and handkerchiefs of particularly violent design, all of which, during his train journey to Castlerampart, and his triumphant walk from the station to Clewe Street, had loudly adorned his person. Indeed, after a few minutes, instead of continuing to impress Gabriel, he would turn to minimizing himself and his friends at college, as Gabriel's weak questioning showed him the envy that was mixed with his admiration.

The truth was that Gabriel had no cause for jealousy, and that Sylvester was not as popular at college as Gabriel in his envy imagined. In school, where there was limitless choice of friendships, he had never formed a bond comparable with the accidental bond that had grown up between himself and Gabriel. And as a matter of fact it was his constant endeavour to make Gabriel return with him at the end of every term. Yet at the end of every term Gabriel went with him to the station only to see him off, and wave at him until he went out of sight under the tunnel beyond the junction.

"There's no use, I wouldn't be let," were Gabriel's words each time as he jerked along by Sylvester's side giving him a hand with his luggage strap.

"I don't believe you had the courage to ask!"

"Believe what you like!" Gabriel would reply.

For, knowing that there would be no use in his asking, he had indeed never done so.

Sylvester's disappointment took the form of irritation.

"It's ridiculous to think that with all the money your grandfather left, your education is going to be trusted to the mercy of that wretched Philip Blake. Ah well!" Sylvester would climb into the train. "It's your life, not mine. What's keeping this train? It's already three minutes late in starting!"

It was always the same.

As the train pulled out Gabriel would turn and walk back, his thoughts now flying after the shining rail with Sylvester, now turning over the last words he had said.

How contemptuously he had spoken of Blake!

Philip Blake, the former monitor, was now the Master of the Boys' School. Having married Nell Molloy, he was now no longer distracted by the sight of her shadow on the frosted glass of the partitions that divided the boys from the girls, but he had other causes for distraction in the increasing number of children that she was giving him, and the increasing strain that they were putting upon his pocket. Philip had frequently to resort to the thin subterfuge of giving his class transcription while he struggled with his domestic accounts on the back sheet of some scholar's copybook. The time that was thus lost by Mr. Blake was however easily spared, for the paucity of the curriculum was such that the knowledge available for distribution among the students had to be augmented by a triple enunciation of each item.

"Ireland is an island. Ireland is an island. Ireland is an island."

In his classroom in the early afternoon long before the hour for ending

194

school came round, Philip would grow tired of scratching on the board and of screaming at the top of his voice, and then the lethargy of the dying day would penetrate the small concrete schoolhouse, silencing even the most noisy and boisterous of the scholars, and soon scholar and master would be alike placated by the sounds that would reach their ears from the world without, announcing that the long day was coming to an end, the sound of the goods trains and the cattle wagons being shunted into a siding to make way for the evening passenger trains, the milch cows beginning to low complainingly in the distance, and the sounds of herdsmen in yards near by getting their tin cans ready for milking them. And lastly, dominating over all, the disorderly assembling of the birds, as they began to gather again in the trees, after their private excursions of the day.

As the clamour of the birds became deafening in the elms outside the window, Philip might perhaps shake off his lethargy for long enough to order his class to take out their dogeared primers to end the day with Reading in the Vernacular. Philip taking care to choose his readers cautiously from the best of his pupils so that corrections and interruptions due to difficulties of punctuation might be as few as possible, but as the afternoon flowed on, he would take the simpler method of choosing his readers by calling out indolently, "Next please!" And at the end of the page, "Next please!" until at last even this effort would become too great and the one voice would be allowed to continue for page after page, dropping lower and lower, until it became almost inaudible, and the reader might be supposed to be reading to himself, were it not evident from his monotonous incantation that even he himself was unaware of the meaning in the words he read, and was concerned only with the articulation of syllable after syllable.

In spite of Sylvester's remarks about old Theodore's money, it was not from a desire to conserve their resources that the Misses Coniffe kept Gabriel at home, and failed, year after year, to send him away to boarding school. The Misses Coniffe had other reasons for keeping their nephew at home. Wasn't he the grandson of Theodore Coniffe? Wouldn't he inherit his grandfather's position of eminence and authority in the town? What need was there for him to go away to school and put on false airs and graces? Above all, had they themselves gone away to school? They had not! Yet who was more highly respected in the town than the Coniffe sisters? And so, as one young fellow after another was withdrawn from the custody of Philip Blake and sent away to some college or seminary in Dublin, or its environs, the Misses Coniffe pulled in their waists and sniffed. It was a poor thing to have to try and puff up your family to give them the position that others had by natural rights from the time they were born. Even young Colgan the postman's son was said to be studying to be a doctor. Was there no end to the way people would try to push themselves forward?

Their Gabriel had no need to go away to be varnished and polished. He would take his place in the town as his grandfather did before him, and without any affectation or false manners either.

As the first of September came around each year and the young people in the town, including Sylvester, began to prepare for their return to college, Theresa Coniffe would congratulate Gabriel on his advantages over them.

"You may be very thankful, Gabriel, that you have no need to go off to one of those cold damp colleges, with bad food and lumpy mattresses. It's well for you! Lucky for you that you are who you are! Lucky for you that your poor grandfather left you with enough money to spare you from having to addle your brains, and maybe drive yourself into consumption as many a boy has done before now trying to fill his head with knowledge that might be more of a hindrance than a help to him as he goes through life. Although "—here Theresa shot a glance at Lily— "there was a time when, if things had not happened otherwise, there were some who would have seen to it that you didn't have a penny!"

It was not alone by the assistance which she gave Lily in trimming the grass upon his grave that Theresa kept everlastingly green the memory of Cornelius Galloway.

As a matter of fact, Theresa's determination that Gabriel should not go away to school was in itself connected with the memory of Cornelius.

And when Lily, who although she did not hold any different views upon the subject from her sister, would have liked Gabriel to go away to school —for such-like reasons as that he would then have striped blazers and ringed caps, which, for his sake, she envied upon the Sims boys and young Colgan, to say nothing of Sylvester, upon whom those trivial signia of college life sat especially resplendent, because of his long limbs, his bright yellow hair, and his blue eyes—she merely sighed and wondered.

"Theresa is so opposed to it," she said to her sister. "I can't imagine why!"

"I can!" was all that the timid Sara dared say, pursing her lips, for she did not want to hurt Lily's feelings by suggesting that Theresa might not want to take the risk of exposing Gabriel to the same system of education that had produced Cornelius Galloway, and which had been responsible for giving him such an erroneous interpretation of money and its uses that, as Theresa firmly believed, God Himself had had to intervene and correct him, by removing him from the scene of his errors—with the help of Willful Filly.

Of Gabriel's efforts on his own behalf there is no need to enlarge because, as Sylvester suspected, they were so fainthearted it is likely that Theresa did not notice them at all.

They consisted mainly in vague remarks about schools and colleges in general.

"I met Sam Colgan today," he might remark. "He says that they get jam on their bread in Clongowes."

To these vague remarks Theresa would make a pertinent reply.

"That will be something new for young Colgan."

But if she was aware of the purpose behind the utterance she gave no indication of it.

On one occasion only did Gabriel venture to give an opinion and even on this occasion he took care to give his words the cover of a certain subtlety.

He had just come in from school, and he put his satchel on the floor.

"Sit down, dinner is ready," said Mary Ellen.

He sat down. Theresa, Sara, and Lily came from their various tasks, appearing at the table at the same moment. Gabriel picked up a potato and began to peel it in order that his words might appear casual.

"Philip Blake says that I ought to be able to get a scholarship to a secondary school, if I got a bit of extra grinding in the evenings," he said then.

Now it is not at all certain that Philip Blake had ever made this suggestion. Gabriel threw out the statement merely as a means of getting his hearers by the ears. But if anyone was taken by the ears it was Gabriel himself, with the chorus of exclamation that broke out on all sides of him. The sisters, all three of them, tried to make themselves heard at the one time, and when they failed they turned upon each other and implored each other to give way.

"Please, Lily!" cried Sara.

"Please, Sara!" cried Lily.

While Theresa, louder and more imperative, called on both of them at the one time.

"Please! Please!" she exclaimed and held up her hands. Finally in the contest of voices Theresa's stridency won her the day.

"I never heard the like," she said, "I wouldn't think twice of going down to Philip Blake and telling him what I think of him!"

At this point, having discovered that they were all of the same mind, the sisters were better able to await their turn to exclaim.

"How Father would have been humiliated!" cried Sara.

"A scholarship!" cried Lily, and the tears came into her eyes. Pushing back her chair she ran over to throw her arms around her child upon whom the shadow of such a disgrace had been cast, but she had not gone three steps when her turn to exclaim had come around again and she ran back to her place.

"The impertinence of Philip Blake!" she cried.

Meanwhile Gabriel sat in his own place unable to stir a limb, unable to utter a word, his mind fastened, like a barnacle on a rock, to the awful possibility that these women would rise up in a flock and alight on the unfortunate Mr. Blake.

One thing only upheld him. In their distress at the effrontery of Mr. Blake, and in their desire to vindicate themselves from the charge of being unable to afford the fees of a secondary school, they might within the hour decide upon dispatching him to college. And so although they had taken it up by the wrong end, he might after all have used the right instrument for forcing his plans. He was not left long in the hope, however.

"Gabriel," said Theresa, "I want you to give a message to Mr. Philip Blake. Tell him from me that there is no need for the grandson of Theodore Coniffe to avail himself of charity scholarships in order to get a place in some finishing college. There is money and to spare for that, or any such-like purposes. But tell him, from me, that there is no need of your going away to any school, college, or institution, all of which, in my opinion, are only intended for turning out the like of himself, a miserable creature who has to earn every miserable crust that goes into his mouth." Theresa stopped to draw a breath. "School!" she said. "I know all about it. Bad food and lumpy mattresses."

This last information was not addressed to Gabriel, but rather to Lily and Sara, who nodded their heads vigorously in confirmation of the truth of what Theresa had said.

But as if their vigorous assent had irritated her, Theresa swung back to Gabriel.

"Tell him this too!" she cried. "He may be thankful that you're left in his schoolhouse, and that you are only left in it on condition that he keeps his place better, and sends no more insulting messages to those who could bring about his dismissal for a lesser thing!"

And then, as Theresa stopped again, it seemed to Gabriel that she was not sure but that her first idea had been the best, and that she should yet, even at this late hour, put on her hat and go down to Mr. Blake and give him the message straight from her own agile tongue. With the possibility of such a dreadful happening still hanging over his head, Gabriel felt that he might as well expose himself upon all flanks.

"But I'd like to go away to college," he said, and the first three words stood out like a shout from the rest of the sentence, merely because the rest of the sentence was almost inaudible.

Nevertheless it was heard.

"Ah, Gabriel," said Sara, "we cannot always do as we like in this world."

Gabriel looked across at his aunt. Seldom indeed were these words spoken by a person whose whole life gave a better illustration of their truth. He turned aside quickly to hear what his mother had to say.

"You might go later, Gabriel," said his mother, "but not just now," because in postponement she always took refuge—believing that if we cannot do as we like today, we might perhaps be able to do so tomorrow.

But even this feeble hope Theresa would not allow to sprout.

"Stop giving the boy false ideas," she said. "He ought to be made to realize how fortunate his lot has been, and not be allowed to fly in the face of Providence by wanting anything more!"

Theresa stood up and going over to the door that led into the kitchen passage she tapped on the panels with her knuckles. This was her way of letting Mary Ellen know that the meal was over and that she could come and clear the table. This day, however, she tapped on the panels with particular smartness and determination, as much as to say to those at the table that more than the meal was finished and that she wanted to hear no more, from any side, about this or any other topic.

Gabriel lifted up his chair and put it against the wall, as was customary for all to do after a meal. He went out then, and as he went he consoled himself with one thought—scholars were not retained in the local school after they had reached the age of sixteen. And he would be sixteen in the spring.

What would be done with him then?

On the one hand it seemed unlikely that Theresa would take him into the back parlour and hand over to him, then and there, the rental account books upon which she engaged herself for several hours each day, closeted close and permitting of no interruption.

On the other hand, it seemed more unlikely still that she would allow him to walk around the town with his hands in his pockets.

Had Theresa thought about this, he wondered, as he looked at her sideways once in a while, as the year wore on.

Theresa may not have thought about it as early in the year as Gabriel himself, but one day standing at the back door, looking into the yard where here and there thin grass had cracked a way between the cobbles, and where upon the crest of the stenching dunghill a few pale blades had pierced upwards to the light, Theresa Coniffe smelled the advancing spring. At once she turned and went indoors in search of her nephew.

"Gabriel," she said, as she came upon him, sitting at the dining-room table doing some of his homework before going out to meet Sylvester, who was at home again, this time for the Easter holidays, a full week before Philip Blake was due to liberate his scholars for the paschal season. "Gabriel, do you realize that you'll soon be finished school?"

There was a minute's silence and then there was a sharp snap as the point of Gabriel's pencil broke from the force with which he had unconsciously dug it into the page of his copybook.

"Yes, Aunt," he said then, and waited for an instant to see if he was meant to say more.

Lily and Sara, who sat at either side of the fireplace with their sewing in their hands, looked up and their needles were halted in mid-air.

"My Gabriel finished school!" cried Lily. "Can it be? It seems only the other day since he began!"

"How time flies!" said Sara, and she sighed sadly. But the sigh had hardly left her breast when she was caught up in enthusiasm of emphasizing this truism. "It seems only the other day since we went in to Draghead to get him a new suit of clothes for his first day."

"Oh," said Theresa, impatiently, "everything that ever happened to us seems only yesterday to you, Sara. As a matter of fact I have been thinking for some time about the problem of Gabriel's age."

"Problem?" At the sound of such an ominous word Lily and Sara lowered their needles and carefully stuck them into the cambric squares on which they had been sewing.

"Yes, problem," said Theresa, and she looked intently at Gabriel. "He's too young to assume the duties assigned to him by his grandfather's will, duties with which I have had to burthen myself, and with which I will, moreover, continue to burthen myself until such time as he is ready to take them over—not that I expect any thanks, but that's beside the point—and yet we cannot have him wandering about the streets doing nothing."

For a few minutes there was silence again, but this time no one attempted to break it, for everyone realized that Theresa was probably giving them an opportunity to see the nature and magnitude of the problem to which, in a few moments, she would undoubtedly produce a triumphant solution.

The minutes passed over their heads, one by one, marked out distinctly one from another by the hoarse tick of the ancient clock on the mantelshelf. Then, as if she had not intended to let so many minutes fly out from the clock, Theresa swung around upon Gabriel.

"Tell me!" she asked. "Are you good at figures? Are you quick at totting sums? Can you balance profit and loss?"

But these questions were shot so rapidly one after the other Theresa could not have expected an answer to any but the last of them, and before there was time for Gabriel to supply even that, Theresa went ahead triumphantly. "A young man in your position could not possibly know too much about money matters. I don't think we could do better for you than send you to do a course of bookkeeping at the Technical School in Draghead! You can go in there every morning on the early train, and be home again in the evening in time for supper. It will fill in your day nicely."

So that was Theresa's solution to the problem. Sara and Lily exchanged glances of apprehension.

"What do you think of that plan, Gabriel?" the two sisters asked, speaking together, and to each of them the sound of the other's voice stood instead of a reply from Gabriel, who was looking out of the window, forming in his own mind an almost similar question: "What will Sylvester think of this plan?"

"What does it matter what Gabriel thinks?" said Theresa. "It's for his good and that's all that matters." She paused. "Not that I doubt for a minute but that Gabriel agrees with me in thinking it an excellent plan!"

And taking care not to look at his dejected shoulder, where he sat looking out of the window, Theresa smoothed down the stiff front of her bodice and went out again to the yard to continue whatever job had been interrupted by the capricious waft of spring upon the green blades of the dunghill.

ဟ ဟ ဟ

Meanwhile Gabriel sat looking down at his copybook. What would Sylvester think?

That was the question that ran in his head. He even began to regret that Sylvester's holidays had begun so early for otherwise he could have told in a letter the news that he would now have to get out on his tongue. And all that day he hung back from the hour which was usually the most pleasant hour of the day, when he and Sylvester met on the town bridge, and walked out to the ramparts where they sat for long hours smoking surreptitious cigarettes, and talking.

ဟ ဟ ဟ

In places where it was still intact, about half a mile outside the town, the walls of the rampart rose to a great height over the road, and the sight of two young men sitting on the top of it, dangling their legs and taking their ease, would be a startling sight to a stranger who might not know that the ground inside the rampart was considerably higher than without, and that everyone who penetrated one of the long narrow fissures in the wall, further down the road, and nearer to the town, could walk along inside the castle park for some distance, then climb on to the rampart with the help of the long-armed branches of the trees and the thick ivy clusters, to sit astraddle upon it, and look down over a sheer drop of at least thirty feet.

The country people who customarily passed underneath the wall were however too familiar with the sight of the young men on the wall to wonder how they got there. They just nodded up to them and passed on in unconcern, while the young men themselves were so unconcerned with the people on the road that they rarely as much as acknowledged the nods. Sometimes, it is true, they intended to nod at someone whom they saw advancing along the road in the distance, but even then, as often as not, the person would be so long in travelling from the far point at which the young men from their eminence had first spied him, they would have forgotten all about him again before he arrived at the point under their perch, and he, too, would pass by without as much as a nod from either of them.

"Here come the two Finnerty girls," Sylvester said one evening. "I hear they are home from school for good; their education so complete there isn't room for a single new idea to be forced into their heads."

Gabriel looked down the road to where, in the distance, two small figures had appeared, making their way out of the town, by the river bridge, and coming in their direction.

Yet in spite of this display of interest in them, when sometime later Agnes and Hannah Finnerty passed under the wall, in the new hats and costumes they had bought for themselves in Dublin on their way home from school, neither Sylvester nor Gabriel saw them, so caught up had they become in one of the amicable arguments that gave zest to their evenings.

On the particular evening that Gabriel was to meet Sylvester after hearing his aunt's plan for his immediate future, instead of his finding Sylvester at the river bridge where they made it a custom to meet, the bridge was empty, and there was no sound but the sound of the water that ran idly underneath it.

Perhaps he was not coming this evening? Gabriel gave a vicious kick to a stone that lay in the middle of the road. There was no use in hoping that Sylvester would not come. There would be other evenings. And the humiliation of telling him about the course of bookkeeping would only be postponed for a few hours. He would wait a while and see if Sylvester would turn up.

Gabriel walked despondently over to the parapet of the bridge but he had no sooner put his hands behind him on the rough stone and hoisted himself up on it than he heard a long familiar whistle, and there at the top of the street was Sylvester.

As Gabriel looked up, Sylvester was about to put his fingers between his teeth again and give another piercing whistle, but seeing that he had attracted Gabriel's attention he took his hands down from his mouth.

Instead, however, of running down the street as Gabriel expected, Sylvester began to sign to him; jerking the thumb of one hand back in the direction of the town, he jerked the thumb of the other hand downward to the ground beside him where Gabriel saw with surprise a large yellow suitcase that he had not noticed at first.

Gabriel frowned. He could not make out the meaning of the signs. *What*? his attitude seemed to ask, as he strained forward on his hands and stared up the street.

But as quickly as he had appeared, Sylvester picked up the yellow case and turned back towards the town, walking very fast, and bending noticeably to one side as he balanced the weight on the other side. Gabriel looked after him, still straining forward, until Sylvester went out of sight, then he relaxed, and sat back more easily.

Sylvester would return in a few minutes. No doubt he had tried to convey this by the signs he had made. Gabriel crossed his legs and put one arm over the other as he settled into a comfortable position for waiting, his mind untroubled by any curiosity about the yellow case, which had, as a matter of fact, looked very much like the case that Mrs. Molloy used when she went to Dublin for a week. Sylvester had probably offered to leave it at the station for her. Not that he had heard any talk of Mrs. Molloy taking another trip to the city—she had indeed recently returned from there—but that was neither here nor there. He put the yellow case out of his head, and with it any feelings he had about the unusual behaviour of his friend.

But just then, as Sylvester came into sight again, this time without the case, and obviously hurrying to join him, Gabriel suddenly became alert to something so unusual about his friend that a kind of nervousness took possession of him and he was unable for an instant to tell whether it was in his clothes, or in his manner, in his attitude or in his expression, that Sylvester had effected a change. He could only stare at him with increasing uneasiness.

As Sylvester came nearer however it was apparent that although there might also have been some more subtle changes of which Gabriel had first become aware intuitively, there were several undoubted changes in his outer person. Firstly he wore a new suit, and in the dark serge cloth a bright stripe made his long legs look still longer. Secondly he had been to the barber, and although he had had no more than a trimming with the scissors, there was something about the way his hair had been cropped closer than usual at the sides which gave his face an older and harder appearance, and made the loose hair on his forehead look brighter and more yellow. Finally, he had a new handkerchief of bright yellow silk and a tie pin of light topaz, both so elaborately displayed that the eye could hardly have torn itself away from one to take note of the other, were it not that these objects were themselves shifted alternately into prominence by the jaunty side-to-side gait with which their possessor advanced into view.

Gabriel's heart rose and sank. He saw at once that there would be no need to humiliate himself by telling his plans to Sylvester. It was all too clear that if there were plans to be discussed, they would not be his miserable plans, but some exciting plans in Sylvester's head, plans which Gabriel sadly suspected were not unconcerned with the yellow silk handkerchief and the tie pin of yellow topaz.

When Sylvester came within earshot he ran forward eagerly.

"Gabriel," he cried, "what luck! Have you heard? I'm off to Dublin next week!" His voice was eager with excitement. "That's why I was late," he said. "I was down getting the loan of a suitcase from Mrs. Molloy." Then, as if he regretted having begun his story with the tale of the borrowed bag, he looked contemptuously across the river at the back yard of the Central Hotel. "I hope she gets it back some day. I must try and get it returned somehow."

"You're not coming back yourself?" Gabriel was hardly able to ask the question with surprise.

Sylvester saw that he had indeed made the wrong impression at the start.

"No," he said contemptuously, refraining from a further explanation.

"Are you going on to school from Dublin without coming back?"

"What school?" Sylvester was growing more and more irritated with himself for not having made a bolder splash with his news.

Suddenly Gabriel sprang down from the wall.

"You're not finished school?" he cried.

This was more like what Sylvester had expected. He nodded a casual affirmative, and then, offhandedly, he threw out a further explanation.

"The classes at the Art School begin after the Easter holidays."

The Art School! Gabriel was speechless. For in spite of the fact that the whole of Castlerampart took it for granted that Sylvester would follow in the footsteps of his father, and in spite of the fact that even the incredulous Theresa Coniffe had been known to say that he had the hands of an artist and that no one with Sylvester's long white fingers was ever known to lack an artistic temperament, nevertheless Gabriel had always felt there was something fraudulent about the talk, and that it was Sylvester's mother who was mainly responsible for it. Sylvester himself was seldom or never heard to refer to his gifts, nor for that matter did he ever show much interest in art at all. Then, too, apart from all this, another term had still to run before Sylvester was due to leave boarding school.

Yet here he was, with his new suit and his yellow tie pin, about to set off for Dublin inside a week.

"Well, you seem surprised," said Sylvester, as Gabriel continued to scrutinize him longer than seemed necessary.

"I am surprised," said Gabriel steadily, and he continued to stare.

"Well?" said Sylvester; then impatiently, "What are you thinking?"

"Oh nothing," said Gabriel, and he slipped down from the parapet of the bridge.

"Will we go out to the ramparts?" said Sylvester, still uneasy and awkward.

Gabriel began to walk along beside him without saying anything.

"I suppose you think I have no talent, is that it?" said Sylvester at last.

"Oh, I wouldn't mind that!" said Gabriel, looking indifferently over the fields to either side.

Sylvester was stung by the indifference.

"You wouldn't mind that?" he said, mimicking Gabriel irritably. "And why not?" he added, speaking sharply in his own voice. "It's fairly important after all to have some talent before you allow a poor widow to pay your expenses for five or six years, and set you up in a studio as well, with all you wanted in extra classes and equipment."

Gabriel was lagging slightly behind as they walked along the road.

"You have your reasons, I suppose," he said. "She's always talking about the day you'll have your own studio."

"Oh that!" Sylvester threw out his hand impatiently. "Poor Mother. I'd hate to let her down, but that's not the point. The point is that this is my only chance of getting a start in life. Do you think I'd have been sent away to school if it hadn't been for this notion she has about my gifts? Do you think she would have kept me at an expensive school after it had become clear, as it always did at examinations, that I was not an exceptionally brilliant scholar, and that there was not the most remote chance that I would assist in paying my way with either scholarships or prizes? No, Gabriel, Providence did not endow me very highly." All this was said with a peculiar tone of bitterness, of which Gabriel had once or twice heard undertones, but which had never sounded so clearly until now. As he watched Sylvester's curt upper lip carefully fashion each word, it occurred to him that familiarity had blinded him to a certain acid quality in his companion's face. But he liked it. He felt it quicken something in himself that was too flabby, too lifeless. Sylvester, who had been sullenly kicking a pebble along in front of him as he spoke, giving it only such force of his foot as would put it within reach of another kick a minute after, raised his foot suddenly and gave the stone a sharp kick that sent it flying through the air, up over the hedge at his left-hand side and down with a splash into the wet green ditch inside the field beyond. His moment of dejection had vanished. Something had put him back into the arrogant humour in which he had arrived.

"But wait, Gabriel!" he cried. "Providence may have failed to give me the gifts I deserve, but she did not do so badly by me, when she put in my way the opportunities that are usually accorded only to those with such gifts!"

He shot a glance at Gabriel who still walked somewhat laggardly behind, but Gabriel still plodded on with his head bent, looking at his feet as if he did not consider that Sylvester was finished. Sylvester kicked another stone on the road, and watched it as it ricocheted along in front of them for some yards. Then, accelerating his words, he spoke as if ending the matter once and for all.

"Let me once get into the city, with a few pounds in my pocket, a free hand with myself, and a year or two of liberty, and there is no knowing where I may end. My mother may be cherishing false hopes, but beside my own ambitions, her ambitions for me are pale and insignificant." He flung out his arms. "I have every confidence, Gabriel. I have every confidence. And in the vast sea of this confidence I drown whatever slight qualms I may feel at taking the money for my keep from my mother. I'll soon repay her, Gabriel. I'll find some place for myself even if it's not the place she would have picked for me. But I must get away by myself for a while. I must get time to think. I must get time to try out one idea after another; to meet people; to feel my way." He stopped and looked at Gabriel. "Where would I be, do you suppose, if I had been honest? I'd be inside a grocer's counter probably, or behind the desk of some poky provincial bank." He paused, and looking back over his shoulder gave an involuntary shudder. "I might even spend the whole of my days in some God-forsaken hole of a town like this one!"

As Sylvester said the last words, they had reached the gap in the rampart through which they usually made their way into the castle park. And so as they turned off the road and began to climb over the loose stones, Gabriel shut his lips upon his own plans. The life from which Sylvester was so determined to shake himself free was the life into which he was unthinkingly, unquestioningly settling down more steadily day after day.

What was the use, now, of telling Sylvester about the Technical School? His life and Sylvester's had only touched at odd points, here and there along the years, and now they were coming to the forking roads. What would Sylvester care about him? Was it not sufficient proof of his indifference that he had spoken as he did about the place where Gabriel would in all probability spend the whole of his days?

Sylvester was undoubtedly filled with excitement about his own plans, but Gabriel was wrong in thinking that he was indifferent about him. And, although they spent the whole evening on the rampart and night came slowly, with Sylvester talking and airing his plans without reference to Gabriel at all, the evening was not to pass without a significant moment.

They were coming home. They had left the darkening country road, and were turning into the short lane-like street that ran up from the rampart into the market place, when suddenly, for all the world as if

206

she had sprung up from the ground under their feet, a woman's form started up in their path, and after turning up a startled face for an instant, sped away into the dark with an unintelligible sound.

"Was that Doss Dolan?" said Sylvester, trying to see after the creature into the dark where she had vanished.

"Didn't you see her face?" said Gabriel, and he gave an involuntary shudder.

Doss Dolan was a poor creature who lived in one of the rampart hovels, and whose name was known to everyone in the town although there were some who had never seen her face, because from her infancy the poor creature had been afflicted by the most appalling facial disfigurement.

The whole lower portion of her face was perpetually inflamed and covered with running sores, while on the rest of her face and neck there were the dried scabs of sores that healed partially in summer only to break out again at the first frost.

Everyone in the town knew that this disfigurement was the result of an accident in infancy, but few could repress an involuntary shudder when they looked at the poor creature, and those who had occasion to speak to her had to fight against a feeling of nausea all the time. Lately, however, Doss had developed the habit of keeping within doors until dark had fallen before she ventured out for whatever messages she wanted in the town. And even then she had some child go into the lighted shops for her, while she waited to take the parcels out of his hand in the darkness around the corner, or at the head of one of the dark lanes.

Gabriel had only seen her two or three times and Sylvester never at all, yet they both knew at once who it was when she stared up in front of them in the lane.

She had been huddled close to the wall near the top of the lane, only leaning out to look up the lane in the direction of the shops in the market square, from one of which the youngster who was doing her messages had just run out into the yellow light, dragging after him her shapeless sack that made his feet clumsy with the drag of its weight.

In her anxiety over her messages she did not hear the young men approaching from behind, but when they had almost come upon her she started up and drew back with a jerk that threw her face into a short but ghastly prominence in the slanted light from the top of the lane.

There was an awkward moment as no one spoke. Doss ran clumsily into the street, stumbling as she crossed the gutter channel, and muttering something which the young men could not catch, but which they did not feel to be an utterance of ill will; rather on the contrary they felt conscious of inarticulate friendliness.

After they had gone on a few paces further up the lane Gabriel looked back.

"I never know whether it is best to speak or to pretend not to see her," he said, referring back to the encounter.

Sylvester shuddered in the darkness.

"Poor wretch!" he said casually. Then, after a minute or two he spoke again as if the incident had run in his mind. "What happened to her? I never heard. She must have some disease, no matter what people say."

"No," said Gabriel, stanchly. "It's not a disease. My Aunt Theresa told me what happened. She heard about it at the time. In fact I think she went down to the house when she heard about it. She said it was awful. Doss was only about a year old, and she used to be put to sleep at night in a box beside the fire because it was warm."

Gabriel stopped as if reluctant to go on.

"Well?" said Sylvester impatiently.

"That's all," said Gabriel illogically before he jerked out the climax. "That's all except one night a rat sprang into the box and attacked her. I suppose she screamed, because the father woke up, but before he got across the floor she was bitten all over the face." He shivered. "Then to make matters worse the doctor cauterized the bites to prevent pollution and this disfigured her more."

As he listened, Sylvester felt a nausea coming over him. He spat into the gutter. Then, as Gabriel finished, he hurried to bring the conversation back to a generalization.

"What a world it is!" he said. "To think of creatures like that cut off from birth from every phase of human happiness, doomed to spend the whole of their lives under conditions of miserable pain and humiliation. And yet they have done nothing, absolutely nothing, to merit such a fate."

They were crossing the market square, and would soon have reached the top of Clewe Street, and their parting place. Aware of this, Gabriel had already begun to lose interest in the conversation. Mechanically he added the few words that seemed necessary to conclude the topic, before saying good night.

"Poor creatures!" he said. "Ah well! They'll get their reward in another world. Such suffering should surely merit a special reward."

Although Gabriel's remarks were careless, and more or less meant to end the conversation, after a minute he felt that the silence with which Sylvester received what he had said was not altogether normal. He looked up. On Sylvester's face there was an unmistakable sneer. It seemed as if he had not spoken because no words could express his meaning as well as the sneer on his silent lips. But when Gabriel looked at him he spoke.

"What kind of second-rate talk is that?" he said angrily. "What kind of second-rate thinking?"

Gabriel was somewhat taken aback. Immediately he was conscious of having spoken facilely, repeating idly the words that he had heard others use whenever this poor creature was mentioned. He had not used his own mind. And in this he knew at once that he was wrong. But what exactly was wrong with the words that had come to his lips he could not at once see.

"Well," he said, lamely, "it seems hardly fair that she should have been born to suffer from the first year of her life, having done nothing to deserve such suffering."

"So her suffering is a mark of God's special predilection?"

"Well," said Gabriel again, as if he would explain further. But Sylvester made a gesture of impatience.

"Keep your balance," he said coldly. "Live with those foolish women-folk of yours if you insist, but don't accept all their ideas as if they were oracles of wisdom." He became more animated. "If, as you imply, it is a mark of special predilection to suffer in this world, and if such suffering here below will bring a reward in the other world, why then might I ask, reversing the position, should this creature be favoured as she was at the beginning of her life having done nothing to merit the special predilection any more than the special suffering?"

Then, turning his face aside, Sylvester disdained to listen to an answer. But Gabriel had no answer to make.

Once again, as on many occasions before, a spirit of sadness came over him, at the way in which Sylvester seemed able to pierce through falseness and hypocrisy and flash the light of reason into every corner of obscurity. Why had he, Gabriel, uncritically accepted as the truth this nonsense about Doss? For now it seemed nothing more.

And his admiration rushed over him like a flame. What would his aunts think if they could have heard what Sylvester said? What would Philip Blake think? What would the priest think?

Perhaps one or two of them, Philip Blake perhaps, or his mother when she was younger, might have dared to think such a thing, but to say it, out loud, as Sylvester had done, was something no one in the whole town would dare to do. Some superstition would have silenced their tongues.

It had not been superstition that had kept him silent. It had been his lazy mind. But now this mind was in a turmoil of activity. A thousand questions came to his lips at once.

Gabriel's mind burned with the ardour of his new thoughts. He had forgotten his own problems. He wanted only to discuss Doss and the problems she had created in his mind.

And so, when Sylvester suddenly brought the conversation back to their own plans, Gabriel was violently startled.

Sylvester, who had as a matter of fact intended all the time to speak on the subject, but had waited from moment to moment for an appropriate opening, felt that none could be better than the present.

"Gabriel," he said, beginning to speak quietly, but without being able to prevent his voice rising word after word, "Gabriel, why do you think that I was so anxious for you to come away to school with me?" He put up his hand to prevent Gabriel from answering him. "I wanted to get you away from those women in the end of the street," with a jerk of his head down towards Clewe Street. "I didn't want your mind to become debased to the level of those foolish superstitious women. But you wouldn't come. And now you make a stupid remark like that about Doss Dolan. This town is closing around your neck as tight as a bag."

At Sylvester's words, Gabriel could indeed almost feel a cord strangling his throat. But suddenly it seemed that he had a chance of getting in his news about the Technical School in a rather more favourable light than he could have hoped. After all, Draghead was not Castlerampart even though it was only eleven miles away.

" As a matter of fact," he said with a forced casualness, "I am starting a course of bookkeeping at the Technical School in Draghead. The town isn't closing around me as tight as you thought."

But the minute he had spoken he regretted his words. Quite rightly Sylvester sneered at him.

"So that is your Aunt Theresa's idea of being clever, is it?" he said.

Gabriel did not understand.

"What do you mean?" he said, stiffly.

"She's afraid that you may begin to see that you're tied, and so she's loosening the string a bit so that you can go as far as Draghead!"

Against his judgment Gabriel began to defend Theresa.

"It's all very well for you to talk!" he said. "But what would have been the use of my going away to school? It wasn't as if I was going to take up any profession or career. But this course of bookkeeping will be of use to me later on. You know I'll have to look after the property some day."

Put like this, all at once, it seemed to Gabriel that his lot was not so bad. Sylvester was not impressed. A quarrelsome mood sprang up in Gabriel.

"My grandfather was a better man than you're ever likely to be!"

"Your grandfather?" Sylvester looked at him. "He was! You're right! But I don't see what that has to do with you. I see no comparison. Your grandfather did a man's work, when he built up the property. It doesn't take much of a man to sit down and wait until it falls into his lap, and then spend the rest of his life going around the town collecting rents. Be sure you have plenty of small coin in your pockets. You'll need it to make change for your tenants." Sylvester paused. "I wonder what you'll be like when I come back—if I ever do—I suppose you'll never have stirred any further outside the town than you can go on a push-bike!"

Gabriel reddened with anger.

"Don't jump ahead too fast!" he said. "You forget that when I do inherit my grandfather's money I'll be my own master. Then I can do what I like, go where I like!"

Sylvester listened quietly.

"No," he said, "no, I haven't forgotten that, but don't you forget, Gabriel, that you have to wait till you're twenty-five for the money. And don't forget either that the desires you will have then won't be the desires you have now!"

Even in the heat of his anger, Gabriel felt the chill truth of these words steal into his mind. Still he prevaricated.

"You seem to think I'd be better off without my grandfather's money!" Then meanly he added, "Perhaps you're jealous."

Sylvester let the gibe pass. "Perhaps I am," he said carefully, "but at the same time let me tell you I wouldn't be in your shoes for twice the amount if it meant hanging about this town until I was twenty-five. Twenty-five! I often heard it said your grandfather made a clever will. I suppose he was afraid you might inherit some of your father's ambitions. He knew they'd have cooled down at twenty-five. But I don't think he need have worried. I don't think there's much ambition in you!"

"Oh stop baiting me!" Gabriel dragged himself away, as if Sylvester had held him by the coat sleeve, which was far from being the case, for Sylvester was walking along with his hands dug deep into his pockets. "Stop tormenting me," Gabriel repeated. "What can I do?"

"Make a stand against those women. Tell them you want to get out of this town for a bit before you settle down to manage their old property."

"They wouldn't listen to me," said Gabriel dejectedly. "My mother and Aunt Sara might, but Theresa wouldn't listen to a word."

"She might turn out to be better disposed to you if you showed some spirit!"

"Oh, talk is easy!" said Gabriel.

Suddenly Sylvester veered around. "I suppose there's something in what you say," he said. "And they'd hardly let you have any money if you went away against their wishes." He thought for a few minutes. "There might be ways of forcing them to give you money!" he said, thoughtfully.

"Oh no!" Gabriel shrank from such a thought. "How could I draw money from the property and know that my Aunt Theresa was carrying the burden of the rents and repairs?"

"Burden! Do you think it's a burden to her?" Sylvester laughed. "As far as I can see it's no burden on Theresa Coniffe to go around making clear to the town how much of it belongs to the Coniffes! In fact it's such a small burden on her I can't see her giving it over to you even when you are twenty-five! I'm sure if you took a stand against her she'd give you the money all right, and even if she didn't you could scrape up enough to go, and she'd hardly let you starve after that. Your mother or Aunt Sara would manage to send you enough to live on." Then as another thought came to him, Sylvester clicked his fingers together. "And what if they never sent you a penny! You could get a job and you're strong and young and able. I'm sure there are lots of jobs you could get." There was a pause while he sought around in his mind for some occupation for which Gabriel might be fitted. He felt that there must be several such jobs, but at that moment he could not name one. Slightly disappointed, he was about to see if Gabriel could think of anything for which he might feel himself fitted, when he was struck by a new idea. Grasping Gabriel by the arm in his enthusiasm he shook him violently before he spoke and when he did his voice was nearly incoherent with excitement. "Gabriel, why not come away with me? Why not come to Dublin with me next week? You could make a start! If your aunts didn't give you any money, we could get along for a while on my money. And you could look for something to do. There must be something you could do—and in the meantime we could get some advice about your affairs. There might be some way you could raise money on loan. There are lots of ways out of financial difficulty. The main thing is to face them!"

Almost carried away by his enthusiasm, Sylvester began to urge reason after reason in favour of his suggestion.

Gabriel stood silent. Although it was dark he kept his face averted towards the far fields beyond the town. For a few exhilarating moments after Sylvester had made his suggestion he had allowed himself to entertain the thought of going away, but as Sylvester paced up and down the road, excited, and gesticulating, and already, it seemed, so sure that his suggestion would be adopted that he was making plans for the day of their departure, the plan seemed suddenly absurd and impractical again.

Sylvester was clapping his hands together as he planned detail after detail of the adventure.

"You could have the old suitcase that I used to carry my books back and forth from school. You could bring down your things to me and I could pack them in it for you, so that you wouldn't need to have any luggage leaving the house. Your aunts would think you were coming to the train to see me off as you always do! The whole town would think it!"

Gabriel could stand it no longer. Turning suddenly he broke out with an impatient cry.

"It's absurd!" he said. "You know it is!" And facing towards Clewe Street he began to walk down it slowly, leaving Sylvester in the street alone.

∽ ∽ ∽

The week that intervened between the day of Sylvester's departure and the night that he had made his outrageous suggestion was one of strain between the two friends. Moreover, there were not many opportunities for lifting the strain because Sylvester was busy and frequently had to cut short his meetings with Gabriel.

The last meeting came at last and on that evening Sylvester made a point of keeping his time free for Gabriel. They walked out to the ramparts, and climbed up to their usual niche on the wall. But try as they did to be natural, there was something forced about the meeting. It was as if already they were trying to recapture an atmosphere of the past.

The moments went by with that rapidity they assume only when time is precious. The conversation on the contrary lagged, weighted down with the unnecessary and desultory topics that never seem to assert themselves as much as they do when there are other more important things lying unsaid in the heart. Long long silences fell between the young men, and awkwardnesses and embarrassments never experienced before cropped up between every sentence. Both were conscious of things unsaid, yet both felt handicapped by the thought that it was too late now to enter upon a discussion of any depth.

After a long time, in the distance, a train whistle blew shrilly in the night air. Sylvester raised his arms and stretched slowly.

"Tomorrow that whistle will be blowing for me," he said; taking advantage of the relevance of his remark he said what he had been anxious to say for some time past. "I suppose I had better be getting back to see about my packing."

He moved uneasily on the wall. Since the evening he had first made his proposal that Gabriel should go away with him he had not referred again to the subject, but now as if he felt that some reference should be made to it, he turned to Gabriel casually.

"Are you sure you won't change your mind?" he said, but he had no sooner said the casual words than he felt a return of his enthusiasm. He sprang down upon the ground at the inner side of the wall and began to pace up and down with rapid steps.

"Gabriel! Consider! A chance like this is not likely to present itself again. All you need do is to scrape up enough for the journey and after that I can manage the rest until you find something to do. Then, if you like, you can pay back anything you feel you owe me."

Gabriel smiled bitterly.

"Scrape enough for the journey! I have barely three pounds!" he said, but his face flushed when he saw Sylvester glance contemptuously at his thick heavy suiting, his strong shoes and his lisle hose with the silk clocking, for Sylvester's own suit, although it was new and sharply creased, was a thin blue serge, while his collar was ill-fitting, and his shoes had the glassy shine of cheap leather.

213

"The price of the suit on your back," said Sylvester, "would have paid for your ticker there and back three times!"

Gabriel flushed deeper because he felt that Sylvester must know that the suit had been ordered for him by his Aunt Theresa, and put down upon the family bill, and that he himself had never handled money save to deposit in his box the little gifts which rarely came from his Aunt Sara and his mother. And—the thought filled him with further bitterness— when he began his classes in Draghead, he would probably travel by means of a season ticket for which his Aunt Theresa herself would pay half yearly at the booking office.

Sylvester, who had ceased pacing up and down, came and stood in front of him. It seemed as if he were going to say something further, but suddenly, as if the expression of gloom on Gabriel's face made him realize the uselessness of any more persuasion, he shrugged his shoulders.

"Ah well," he said, "I can do no more for you, Gabriel. But remember if you should change your mind you can write to me. I will send you my address as soon as I am settled."

His momentary excitement had left him, and in the lull that followed he had nothing more to say to Gabriel. He even felt irked at the necessity of remaining any longer in his company. He remembered the luggage that was still unpacked in his room. He wished the evening were over, and that he was on his way. He looked across the wall at the dull fields. He looked back at the untidy outline of the town through the trees. The squalid cottages under the rampart were pouring out uncouth smoke in gulps. He wished that he was already gone.

"I had better get back to do some of my packing," he said again, trying not to sound ungracious and bored. "I don't suppose you're coming back so early?"

Gabriel bent his head. He knew that Sylvester was impatient with him and no longer wanted his company. Though the chill of the evening was coming down, and he felt himself beginning to shiver, he said that he would like to remain out a little longer. He not only knew the full extent of Sylvester's impatience, he understood it, and felt that it was justified. And a deep sadness settled over him as Sylvester sprang down over the loose rocks and made his way out on to the road. He watched him out of sight; and then with heavier steps he too climbed down on to the road and made his way in the same direction.

Yet as Gabriel walked along the road, some of the exhilaration that he had experienced when Sylvester first put out his suggestion began to stir in him again, and although he still felt that it would be impossible for him to leave Clewe Street, Sylvester had opened up a new world of dreams, and in it he wandered freely, as when, upon a summer day, the clouds are cobbled cities in which the eye delights no less to wander, because there the feet will never tread.

ᔕ ᔕ ᔕ

When Sylvester had disappeared down the road the night before his departure for Dublin, Gabriel felt that he had seen and heard the last of him. He believed that it would not be long until Sylvester's mother, the only link he had with Castlerampart, would follow her son, and make some attempt to set up an establishment for him. He was therefore surprised when within a week there was a letter for him from Dublin from Sylvester. He was at heart greatly pleased to get the letter, but he would not, even then, let himself believe that the letter was worth any more than the last wave of a person who waves the freer because he is confident that he will be out of sight at the next bend of the road. He was not going to answer it. But before a second week had passed a second letter arrived. This letter like the first was short and stiff, but from this fact alone Gabriel took sudden heart. It was not the letter of a person who enjoyed handling a pen. Sylvester's having written at all could only mean one thing—that he wanted to keep in touch with Gabriel.

All through the following months of the summer there was an exchange of letters between them, and at the end of each letter Sylvester always put the same query :—

"Have you changed your mind yet?"

But this query Gabriel always ignored and his own letters when he wrote were trivial and intended only to amuse.

It was in the course of one of these letters that Gabriel mentioned some amusing incident connected with one of the Finnerty girls. It was an incident he had heard someone relate. He had not even been an eyewitness to it. And he thought no more of it than that it would amuse Sylvester. He was therefore surprised to have an answer almost by return of post, from Sylvester, in which he showed annoyance at the story.

At the end of Sylvester's letter there was also a footnote :—

"Keep away from those Finnertys. If you get yourself involved with some local girl you'll never make anything of yourself."

This footnote so amused Gabriel that he laughed out loud as he read it. Nothing seemed more absurd than that he should involve himself with any girl.

"A girl!" he thought, and then he took the letter out of his pocket again on second thoughts and tore it up and put it into the fire.

"A girl!" It was amusing. But he would not want his Aunt Theresa to come across the letter. A girl! What would she say if she read that?

PART III

Gabriel and Onny

IN September, Gabriel began his classes at the Technical School. He had only been attending them for three weeks when a car was sent into Draghead to bring him home before the hour of the evening train. His mother was ill.

Lily Coniffe had been timid all her life, and she made no resistance to death when it struck her down suddenly as she was walking along the the passage at Clewe Street. She was dead when Gabriel arrived.

To Gabriel, the sorrow of his mother's death was the first of its kind that he had ever experienced, and between his gusts of grief he told himself that an incalculable change had come over his life with her loss. He made the mistake of measuring the influence his mother's death would have upon his life, by the depth of misery it caused him. But it is not necessarily the things that pierce our hearts most bitterly that will affect the material order of our lives, and when a few weeks after Lily's death, Theresa decided upon a change of domestic policy, Gabriel, lost in his grief, hardly concerned himself with it at all. Yet upon this change in the household there would depend far greater changes in his life than could ever have been effected by his pale, cloudy mother, whose love for him had been so inarticulate and ineffectual.

For a long time Theresa had intended to make a change in the house, but Lily's death gave her an opportunity for making it at once. She called Sara aside one evening.

"What is the use of keeping Mary Ellen?" she said. "There isn't enough work in this house for three women. We are only getting in each other's way."

"But surely you couldn't send Mary Ellen away now, after all those years?" said Sara, frightened at the mere suggestion. "Where could she go? She had no home."

"I have it all planned out," said Theresa. "The Colgans have not paid a penny of rent for the past three years, and yet I cannot put them out of the cottage without a good excuse. If I bring the matter to court I will get the worst of it. You can't turn people out unless you can prove that you want the house."

"But we don't want it," said Sara.

"Don't interrupt me," said Theresa, "I'm coming to that! Mary Ellen is getting too old to work. All she does is compare today with yesterday. I don't like her attitude, either. I never did. She seems to think that she had equal authority with me in this house. And besides that I think it would look badly in the eyes of the town for you and me to have a servant for ourselves alone. It was all right when Father was alive, or while Gabriel was a young boy needing attention, or even while Lily was alive, and there were three for every meal. But it's different now! I was thinking that this would be a good opportunity for getting the Colgans out of the cottage by saying that we wanted it for Mary Ellen. We could put her into it at a nominal rent, and give her some of the furniture out of these over-crowded rooms; things should not be kept after they have begun to fall to pieces. We could even give her a few shillings until she becomes eligible for the old-age pension. As well as that she could keep a few hens, and we could buy the eggs from her. It would be very nice to have fresh eggs that we could rely on, without having the hens in our own yard; they are such dirty things."

Sara felt sorry to lose Mary Ellen, but as well as that she felt sorry for Mary Ellen herself, and so she made an effort to influence Theresa in keeping her on.

"Who will clean the brasses on the hall door?" she asked. "Who will do the messages?"

But Mary Ellen was to go.

"I thought of that!" said Theresa. "We'll get one of the Soraghan children in for a few hours a day to do odd jobs."

Sara made a last protest.

"The Soraghans are all fairly big, now. I don't believe there is one of them young enough for our purpose."

"The youngest one of all is just the right age!" said Theresa, reprovingly. "One called Onny."

∾   ∾   ∾

Mary Ellen was gone one afternoon when Gabriel came home from the Technical School.

"She left a pair of boots after her," said Theresa, putting them into his hand. "If you like you can take them down to her, and see how she is getting on. See if she is getting things arranged the way she wants them. I hope the chimney is drawing well. The Colgans were always complaining about it, but they were a pack of whiners anyway, they complained about everything; about dampness and dry rot, weeping walls and broken windows I wouldn't mind what they said! It's a snug, tight cottage. However, see if she has any complaints. And tell her to come down to us for anything she wants." Theresa was turning away, but she turned back. "On second thoughts," she said, "I think you had better not say that. She might get into the habit of running back and forth between the houses. Tell her instead that I will send down the Soraghan child once in a while to see if there is anything she needs."

Gabriel went up the street to the cottage that had been given to Mary Ellen. He was looking forward to seeing her, and he was wondering, as he walked up the street, how she felt about the change. He intended to ask her. But when she opened the door he felt shy.

He had been thinking about her as he had always seen her, in the long blue-and-white apron, tied tight at the waist, and he was uncomfortable in the presence of this new Mary Ellen in a coarse black lustre dress, decorated with stitching and scrolls of braid. She was no longer his Mary Ellen. She was just an elderly woman to whom he must deliver a pair of worn boots. Even her manner, as she asked him to step inside, was not the manner with which he had been familiar. She had always adopted a slightly cross tone of voice with him, but now she was in her own house, and she laboured to be hospitable. She urged upon him the merits of one chair over another, and when he insisted that he was all right where he was, she bent down to make certain that the legs of the chair were firm. She thought he would be more comfortable on the sofa, and she pushed back the protruding springs, and covered them with a rug.

"I'm quite all right, thank you," said Gabriel, and then because the chair was uncomfortably stiff and hard, he leant his elbow on the table beside him. At once Mary Ellen, who had at last ventured to sit down upon the chair opposite him, sprang up and lifted the table around in case he might catch his sleeve on the tacks that held down the figured tarpaulin top.

Moment by moment he grew more ill at ease, and once, worst of all, he thought that when he turned his back to look at some picture, or calendar, on the wall, she whipped up the corner of her skirt and wiped her eyes. He could not be sure of this, but he felt more uncomfortable still. He wanted to get out of the cottage.

Mary Ellen, in the old days, had hardly ever taken time to devote all her energy to speech. Whatever she had to say was said as she rushed from one place to another, flicking crumbs from a table, brushing ashes under the grate, and, most characteristic gesture of all, stopping every other minute to tighten the bow of her apron strings. Now she sat, an old woman in a black dress, with her hands folded in her lap. He looked around the room to avoid looking at her, and as he did he saw with pleasure that there were at least some familiar articles, although even they looked strange in their new setting. There, on the wall, was the fly-blown picture from the Mission stall that had terrified him one day long ago. There, on the dresser, was the plate with the lacy china edge, and the hand-painted rose in the centre of it. Mary Ellen had often told him that it was a souvenir that had been brought back to her by his father and mother when they returned from their wedding trip. Along the mantelpiece, in frames of plaited straw and palm, were the mortuary cards of his grandmother and grandfather, his father, and, new and glossy, that of his mother. And in the centre of these cards on the mantelshelf was a small leather boot, stuffed with sawdust, and covered with red velvet to serve as a pincushion. This was the first leather boot that he had ever worn. It made him feel bad to see how she treasured these things. Had she no other life outside the life she had lived with them? He wondered about her. Where had she come from? Where did his grandmother get her? Had she no relatives of her own? Would they not come to see her? Had she even any old friends who would drop in for a chat with her now and then?

He resolved that he, at any rate, would drop in to see her often, and at the thought that he would do so he was reassured about her, and felt happier, and felt indeed that he might jump up any minute now and conclude the visit. He would come again! But this visit had dragged on long enough.

The first thing that Gabriel saw when he went out into the street was the new servant girl.

Onny Soraghan had often seen the Coniffe house from the street, and now, having done the few jobs that Miss Coniffe had given her upon her arrival, she had taken an opportunity of running to the hall door to see how Clewe Street looked from the Coniffe house. She had just stuck her head out of the doorway at the same moment that Gabriel came out of Mary Ellen's cottage, and he caught a glimpse of a tawny head, a bright red dress, and a rosy face, blackened already on one cheek by a streak of soot. At sight of him, however, the girl got frightened. He might tell Miss Coniffe she was peeping out the doorway. She ran back into the hall, and in her concern to shut the door behind her own back, she forgot that by doing so she was slamming it in Gabriel's face.

When Gabriel opened the door for himself a minute later the girl was standing up on a chair in the hall, taking down the globe from the hanging lamp, and trimming the wick for the evening. Mary Ellen could do this without a chair, she was so tall, and she had such long arms. Theresa Coniffe was coming down the stairs.

Theresa felt that Gabriel might be feeling bad after seeing Mary Ellen. She yielded to a rare impulse, and made him a concession.

"Gabriel," she said, "leave out your shoes tonight. Onny will give them a rub with the brush in the morning before you get up. You have enough to do in the mornings in order to get out in time for the early train." She turned to Onny. "Hurry up with those lamps," she said. "Lamps must be ready before dark. Your common sense should tell you that; if you have any. And when you have finished the lamps be sure you clean your hands carefully before you set the table!"

Clean the lamps. Set the table. Shine the brasses. Wash the dishes. What difference would there be between the duties of Mary Ellen and the duties of Onny Soraghan?

Onny? Where had he heard her name before? Gabriel had to wait until the girl got down from the chair before he could pass into the back parlour. Onny! He felt in the back of his mind that something in the past connected him, even ever so slightly, with the name of Onny. As he passed her she looked at him and his face reddened. He could not remember why the name sounded so familiar, but he felt that it had been connected with something not altogether pleasant; something that had shamed him, and made him hang his head. But that was nonsensical. He had probably heard Larry mention her name, or perhaps he had heard it shouted over the wall that divided the boys' school from the girls'.

"How is Larry?" he asked, on an impulse, as he got around the chair, which she held awkwardly with the legs sticking out in his way.

Onny said nothing. But that his remark had given her pleasure was clear from the way she bent her head and smiled. She gave a little giggle, too. She regarded his question about Larry as a compliment to herself, that needed no answer.

Gabriel, however, would have liked to hear news of Larry, who had recently got a job on the railroad, and was several stations down the line. He thought Larry's sister was a silly girl He went into the back parlour and began to wait for his supper. Mary Ellen would have had it on the table a minute after you came in the door. This girl was probably useless.

Yet he hated to hear his Aunt Theresa ordering her about as she did. Mary Ellen never had to be told what to do. She had known her job before Theresa had been born. But now Theresa's voice would be heard through the house all day, hardly ever stopping.

"Don't use that cloth on the floor, that is the dishcloth. Have you no eyes in your head? Don't touch that plate until you wipe your hands. What kind of habits have you? Lift that bucket up and never leave it there in the passageway again. Do you want someone to trip over it and be killed?"

Gabriel stopped his ears with his fingers, and sat waiting for his supper.

~ ~ ~

One afternoon, about a week after the coming of Onny to Clewe Street, when Gabriel came out from the Technical School in Draghead, he found that he was too early to go to the train.

The late sunlight fell on the old town, giving it a false glory. He was glad to wander in it. Apart from the main streets, and the section around the school, he was not familiar with the town, and as he passed the side alleys that led down to the docks, he stared into them curiously. Sometimes he caught glimpses of the reddened tips of mastheads in the estuary. To these, too, the fierce late rays gave prominence. He walked along the main street, and then, abruptly yielding to an impulse, he crossed the street and turned down one of the alleyways. He would stroll along the dockside until the train hour came, and it was possible that he would be able to find his way to the station through the back streets.

Idly he wandered along until he came to the first wharfs, and idly too his eyes wandered over the buildings and ships, noting the glory of the rich afternoon sunlight that lay on the top levels of the town, and still fell as low as the paving stones wherever it found passageway to that low level between the high wharf buildings.

All at once his attention was caught by a familiar figure ahead of him on the darkening side of the street. It was Agnes Finnerty. Since her return from boarding school he had seen her several times in the main streets of the town, but it needed a new setting to awaken his interest in her.

What was she doing in this locality? She had probably finished her shopping earlier than she had expected, and like himself was wandering here until it was time to go the station. Perhaps like him, too, she had been drawn down this direction by the reddened mastheads that rose over the squalid roofs. He followed her with his eyes, and then, more absently, he began to walk after her.

She wore a soft blue suit of some ribbed material, like velvet, and it clung close to her form, hugged tighter still by the way her arms were pressed close to her sides in keeping her hands within the small security of a little black sealskin muff. Her fair hair, usually so pale and blond, had taken some of the rich beneficence of the sun, and shone more brightly than usual under the small blue toque on her head. Around this hat a spray of soft feather lolled caressingly, one end of it hanging down her back a little way, and dancing upwards and downwards with every step she took, it seemed to defy the decorum of her gait.

She was walking with the same remarkable sedateness that characterized her older sister, Hannah, and watching her Gabriel smiled, because he was reminded of the way the swans on the upper reaches of the Boyne sailed onwards with such serious placidity that one had to glance at the banks along which they passed in order to perceive that they were in motion; nothing about their compact, calm demeanour suggested the furious activity of webbed foot that propelled them forward. With this comparison in his mind Gabriel glanced at the banks through which this particular swan was gliding, and he caught the eyes of a large buxom woman in a red skirt, who stood on the step of the public pump outside one of the squalid dockside houses, her arms crossing her ample breasts, as she contemplated the view from her gallery. He smiled outright into her bold brown eyes and, still aimless, continued to walk along keeping an eye on Agnes.

She walked along the dockside, apparently choosing her direction at random, since she once or twice took a turning which resulted in traversing the same ground twice. Then, with more deliberation, she entered one of the ancient archways that were tunnelled between the high warehouses, and made her way into a narrow street that in its turn led into a disused square where a rusting weighing machine, clogged with dried grain, once marked a centre of commercial activity.

He noticed with diffidence that the urchins playing with chalks upon the pavements withheld their games as she passed, and sometimes stood up to give her passage. There was a certain queenly quality in the way she went among them, not lifting her skirt, not altering her direction, yet seeming to take a clear passageway through them. At the door of one or two cottages there were women standing, leaning over the half-doors, rich in indolence. He saw their heads lift as she passed, and he saw them follow her form, line for line, from ankle to nape, with an appraising glance. Then as one or two of them turned their attention upon him he read all at once in their eyes the purpose that he had not read in his own mind. They were glancing from the figure of the young girl to the figure of the man following in her steps. They were connecting them, speculating upon them, linking them together with the fragile but beautiful strands of their own romantic impulses.

He still did not realize that he was following her with any degree of deliberation, but when, suddenly, she turned out of the square and took a direction that would undoubtedly lead back to the centre of the town, he, too, turned and, crossing the street to the other side in the hope of seeing her profile, followed her with a new quickening of the heart, which he yet dared not transfer to his pace.

What was there that was different about her today from the thousand other days that he had met her not only with equanimity, but even with a sense of apprehension that he might be burthened with her company in the train?

His mind played with these and other vague questions, and then fastened upon one of more immediate importance than the others. Did she know that he was following her? Had she seen him on the wharf?

He resolved to watch her carefully. When they came back into the main street, if she was going, as he supposed she was, to the station, she would be forced to cross the street once more, and once more her face would be in profile to him.

Back once more in the centre of the town, Agnes crossed the street in the direction he had predicted. As she lifted her foot to step up on to the rather elevated curb of the pavement he thought for a moment that she had glanced at him out of the corner of her eye, but he could not be sure. Her gait hastened certainly, and although the sun was descending rapidly now, and casting a blush over everything, it seemed to him that the small curve of her cheek that was visible to him had deepened in colour. She must have seen him!

He abandoned at once all idea of remaining longer in the streets. He, too, would go down to the station. There would be a long delay before the train arrived, but he was glad of it. He would speak to her. And after a conversation upon the platform what would be more natural than that they share a compartment on the journey homeward?

But they had some distance yet to walk before they reached the station. He wondered suddenly if she would be annoyed if he hurried now and caught up with her in the street. It would be nice to walk beside her. Then a more daring idea came into his mind—why not run and catch up with her and ask her to wait for a later train and have tea with him! The idea of such an adventure excited him. Even alone he had never remained over to take tea in Draghead. He could imagine them entering a teashop and seating themselves at one of the small marbled tables while the waitress brought along soft cakes iced lavishly all over the top with pink and white sugar. What they would say to each other was another matter, but he did not wait to think about it. He hastened his steps. But just as he did so, she turned to her left suddenly, and he saw that they were approaching the Cathedral. It was towards the Cathedral that she had turned, and the next minute she ran up the steps, taking them in one flight without stopping. Her ankles twinkled in their thin silk stockings, and the insteps of her shoes shone white where the leather had never been trodden.

Gabriel stood still. Could it be possible after all that she had been unaware of him? His eyes travelled after her up the steps, and, when she vanished into the dim recesses of the interior, he raised his head and looked, probably for the first time, at the cool grey spire, where starlings sat in crevices as neat and motionless as if they were part of the grey carving of the masonry. The spire travelled up into the skies so high that his neck ached in following its lanced pinnacle. He looked down again until his eye came level with the open door. In the depths of the darkness within he could see a faraway sanctuary lamp winking unceasingly. He had an impulse to go away. On second thoughts, he ran up the steps, and went into the Cathedral. He dipped his finger into the carved plaster shell that held holy water, thinking as he flicked the cold grey drops from his hand before carrying it to his forehead that there was somthing serious and impressive in entering the church. He blessed himself with holy water, although the impulse that led his feet there had been so capricious and profane.

He went into the Cathedral, which was quite bright within, although from the bottom of the steps it had seemed dim. He looked around to find the girl. She was kneeling far in at the end of a pew, and not in the direct ray of light from the doorway. He went as far up the aisle towards her pew as he dared, and even then, as he knelt down awkwardly, a splinter somewhere at the far end of the kneeler creaked loudly, and he felt rather than saw that she had looked over her shoulder at the sound.

He glanced around him. The church was narrow and tall, with arched columns, and in the interstices of the arches there were carved clusters of stone fruits, grape and acorn twined in their leaves of oak and vine. He looked at the thin pointed windows at the side, from which a frail shadow of purple and blue played downward for some distance on the pale plaster walls underneath. The high altar was bare and idle, but to each side the lesser altars were lit from the light of numerous candles of differing heights, set by penitents in the brass candelabra just inside the altar rails. From these candles in the calm air the flames pointed upward like flat gold-metal spades and, compared with their splendour, the reflections they cast on the glossy marble pillars were like pale dabs of winter sunlight.

He made no effort to pray. He kept watching the blue figure in front of him. When he had been kneeling for some time, however, he began to feel impatient. He moved his position and at once, like a splinter of glass, a sensation of pain ran through his knee. He wondered how she was able to keep so still, and her stillness gave her an air of mystery and remoteness. She was like a saint. All around the church, in every available niche, there were large plaster statues of the blessed dead of the Church. He could not identify any but the gilded-kirtled virgin near him, but he found a similarity between the posture of those unknown saints and that of the kneeling girl in the aisle across from him. Fragments of the gospel stories that he had not listened to with very great attention came back to him now, and he saw romantic scenes of Church history played over again between himself and this blue saint who knelt as motionless as the plaster statues around her.

But as the minutes went by, marked by the flickering shadows from the sanctuary lamp, he began to feel his knees stabbed again by splintering shafts of pain, as his muscles contracted, and his awe at her stillness gave way to a more active feeling of curiosity. He wondered if her lips were moving, were her eyes open or shut? Suddenly he came to a decision and stepped out of his own pew. Then moving on the tips of his toes, and taking advantage of the noises made by a charwoman who was clattering up the aisle with a rattling bucket of water and feet that flapped on the flagstones from loose shoes without latchets, he went up nearer to the altar, and knelt down in another pew a few yards behind the girl, but still upon the opposite side. He looked across at her.

Agnes Finnerty had her face tilted downward. She was not looking at the altar. She was too humble, he thought. She was probably staring at her folded hands like a very young child in the first fearfulness of religion. He glanced down. Her hands were not folded. One hand was clasped in the other and, quietly, without betraying another muscle in the action, with the small rounded edge of the nail of her index finger she was following the curve of the corresponding nail on her left hand.

All at once Gabriel saw the whole incident in a new light. All at once he knew that she had seen him behind her, had probably been aware of him ever since they had stood upon the wharf. She had seen him out of a side glance as he came after her, street by street, and she had read his intention when she had heard the quickening of his pace a moment before she had turned into the Cathedral. Why then had she turned? Watching her he knew, by an instinct that was corroborated by his own experiences in the last half hour, that she had come in here to delay the time of meeting with him, to postpone the climax of the chase, to make it more difficult, to make herself more precious.

And then at that moment Agnes betrayed herself. Having examined the fingernails of each hand carefully, minutely scrutinizing them, making imperceptible corrections in them by rubbing them on the soft pile of her velvet jacket, she came to a point in her own endurance where the strain she had been imposing upon him began to irk herself. He saw her lift her knee ever so slightly from the kneeler, and her short white teeth fastened upon her lower lip as the sensation of shooting pain caught her flesh. She moved the other knee. There was the same contraction of the knees betrayed again by the small white teeth biting into the red lip. Then distinctly he saw her, out of the corner of her eye, steal a glance at the back of the church, to the place where he had knelt a moment before that, and then, taken by surprise at not seeing him there, she raised her head abruptly and swung around to scan the whole back of the church. Finally, having failed to see him, she sprang to her feet forgetting in her hurry to genuflect to the Silent Host in the Tabernacle, and stepping out of the pew, she almost ran down the aisle to the bright doorway at the end. Gabriel let her go. He sat in the church and waited until she was well gone. And as he sat there, he looked around him once more. A burst of sunlight fell across the transept windows and the light came through the coloured windows in a shaft that fell directly in front of him, and in it the faint particles of dust that hung continually in the air became perceptible. They floated in unsettled directions, and he felt they were entering his lungs with every breath he drew. The plaster virgin over his head seemed tawdry in her painted robes with her tarnished gilt halo that had tilted slightly lopsided. The mock blue sky of the vaulted dome, with its blackening gilt stars, seemed a garish travesty of the real daylight.

∽ ∽ ∽

Gabriel missed the train. He had to wait for a later one. At the house in Clewe Street, his aunts, already dressed for the street, were going round securing the window fasteners, and closing the back door in preparation for going out to evening devotion. Sara pushed the door from her several times with her gloved hand, to make sure that the bolt was adequate.

"What delayed you?" said his Aunt Theresa, glancing at him so sharply that he looked away, and felt immediately that he was adopting a guilty attitude. "You'll be late for the church!"

"I was looking at some old books," he said, lamely.

"More shame for you! That's a fine admission to make! I suppose you had no tea!"

"Oh, it's all right, I'm not hungry," said Gabriel.

"Hmm! Not content with being deliberately late, yourself, you do the devil's work and try to keep others back from church. I'll have to stay at home and get you a meal."

His aunt drew off her gloves and laid her prayer book on the sideboard.

"Don't stay home on my account, Aunt Theresa, please," he begged. "I can wait till we come back, or Onny can get me something."

"Onny will do nothing of the kind. I know my duty to servants as well as my own, although she'd stay fast enough if she was allowed. She'd sooner spend her time on her knees scrubbing than praying."

Theresa turned to Sara. "Go ahead, you, Sara. Don't lose any more time. Hannah Finnerty is going to sing a solo in the choir tonight. Don't miss it. It will be worth hearing. There will be people in from the country specially to hear her. There's no need for both of us to be deprived of the pleasure." She glanced out of the window.

"How well the Finnerty girls can go into Draghead for the day and yet be back in time for the church! How well Mrs. Molloy with her eleven children can find time to say a few prayers before going to her bed, not knowing but that she might be whipped away in the wink of an eye during her sleep—God between us and all harm, this very night!"

Gabriel had eaten nothing all evening and although his stomach was empty, and long ugly noises sounded in its pit as spasms shot across his intestines, he felt the fast was preferable to the position of dependence in which he would place himself by accepting his aunt's offer.

He put his hand on her arm. "I'd rather not wait to eat anything. I don't want to be late for church myself," he said.

In his mind his contempt for Agnes Finnerty in the earlier afternoon became allied to a deeper and more bitter contempt for himself.

"Are you sure you won't be too hungry?" said his aunt, her manner changing, her better nature being able to afford some expansion now that the dangers that threatened her pleasure were removed.

His Aunt Sara, who had been standing in a state of nervous stiffness, relaxed too. She pulled off her gloves and ran over to the table.

"You'll have time to have a glass of milk, Gabriel. I'll get you a glass of milk and some biscuits."

"Oh, I can wait," said Gabriel.

"No, no," said Sara, pouring out a stream of sweet, white milk into a tumbler. "God does not expect us to do anything unreasonable. He does not expect us to jeopardize our health. You must have this."

She put the cold glass into his hand, and his hand tightened on it with irritation at the intimacy of her words. He lifted the glass and began to drink it.

"There's no need to wait for me. I can run and overtake you," he said.

"That's right," said Sara. "We can go on ahead. Are you ready, Theresa?"

She put on her gloves again, and straightened her hat once more, and never doubting that Theresa was waiting for her, she sailed out into the hall to join her. But, as Sara opened the hall door, to Gabriel's dismay his Aunt Theresa continued to stand in the hall. Was she going to wait for him? He gulped the milk with distaste. But before he had come to the bottom of the glass he heard Theresa striding down the hall again in the direction of the kitchen. "This is going too far!" he heard her exclaim.

"Don't lose your temper, Theresa!" cried Sara, running after her. Gabriel lowered the glass in surprise and then, as Theresa lifted her umbrella and smote upon the door of the kitchen, Sara ran into the parlour to Gabriel.

"It's that dreadful Onny!" she said. "It's like this night after night. She keeps us late. I do believe she does it out of spite!" And through the frightened patter of Sara's words the cascade of blows from Theresa's umbrella upon the kitchen door could be heard distinctly. "The dreadful girl!" said Sara again.

There was the sound of more rapping. "Onny Soraghan! Open this door at once! What do you mean by delaying us in this manner?"

Gabriel listened. He turned to the frightened Sara.

"Why does she lock the door?" he said.

Sara straightened up. She coughed. She assumed a look of delicacy and then she lowered her voice.

"She washes herself at the sink," she said, modestly and doubtfully, but as Gabriel roared out in a loud laugh she spoke more confidentially. "I think it's nice of her to want to clean herself before going to the church, but we believe she makes it an excuse for dawdling and delaying. Theresa says she is not content with being late herself, she wants to keep others late as well!"

Sara's voice was drowned once more by Theresa rapping on the kitchen door.

"If you're ashamed to be seen with the sweat of honest work on your face you should stay at home! It isn't to waste our soap and water that we pay you your wages, Miss Soraghan."

"I'm coming, ma'am." Onny's voice sounded frail and far away, as if she were bending down and her voice had to travel through curves and pathways as well as through the wood of the door.

"She changes her stockings, I think," said Sara, confidingly. "That's going a little too far. Who is to see what she has on her in the dark of the church? It's not about her legs she should be thinking."

Just then the door opened and Theresa stood aside like a jailer to let out a prisoner, and as Onny slunk out abashed, the first thing that Gabriel looked at was her legs, and laughed at the bright yellow sheen that came from the cheap silk stockings. It was almost impossible for anyone with sight in his eye to avoid seeing that they covered a shapely limb. He turned to make a joke with his Aunt Sara, but when he looked at her he was startled for a second by the similarity to Theresa that was creeping, with age, across her face. Upon both faces as they stared at the offending Onny there was the same expression of indignation. Age was souring Sara.

He looked away in distaste and looked back at the offending Onny as she stole out the hall door, her blue coat tight around her, as if in shutting out the cold she shut out also the criticism that was showering down upon her from Theresa Coniffe's tongue. The yellow-clad legs flashed as she went down the hall, the dark coat was deepened in a ray of blue light from the glass lamp shade over her head, and under her red cap the tawny hair had a defiant gleam in it.

"Hurry up. Hurry up," called Theresa after her, but an awkward slowness of movement was imposed on Onny, by either embarrassment or defiance, and not until she had stepped over the threshold into the night air did she make any real effort to hasten. Then, poised for a moment in the doorway, she threw a glance backward at the group in the hall and, turning swiftly, she broke into a run and they could hear her feet in the silence even as the sisters noisily rearranged their clothes with little pats and pulls, and, coughing, started off again for the doorway.

"You'll overtake us, Gabriel," they said, and went out banging the door.

Gabriel listened till the feet died away in the distance, and then he began to smile. He recalled all the details of the scene. He recalled the way Onny had slunk out of the kitchen, her face bright from a rough rubbing with the towel, her hair with the rude trace of the comb still in it, and her glittering cheap stockings. He recalled the way she had stumbled over the mat, hit against the hall stand, and made the long mirror in the hall tilt to one side in her embarrassment. Her ignominy in being driven like a heifer by the prodding of Theresa's umbrella served as a butt for the laughter he could not turn upon his own almost similar position, and he laughed out loud, leaning against the jamb of the kitchen door.

Then he remembered the way Onny had remained for a second on the threshold of the door before disappearing. The door might have been one of those inexplicably placed doorways that one sees sometimes in the upper storey of an old house, or mill, with no apparent balustrading or stairway leading down from them, for it seemed as if she had stepped out in the air and been caught up into a swift flight, so great a grace was there in her figure at the moment when it met the night air. She had taken an imperious freedom of flight, away from the dark hallway through which she had stumbled so clumsily, as a strange sea bird would rise in beauty from a lump of greywacke, where it had perched grotesquely.

Gabriel glanced at the clock. It was hardly worth while to go down to the church now, but he finished the milk and, taking a pair of gloves from the hall stand, went out the door and turned in the direction of the church.

As Gabriel came near the church, the darkness of the evening was splintered by the long shafts of light from the narrow, pointed windows. He went into the churchyard and stood outside the centre door looking down the main aisle. All the heads were bent, and it was the moment at which the priest himself bends over before raising the monstrance.

Then he hurried round to the dark side door, finding his way with difficulty, because his eyes were temporarily dazzled by the blaze of candles on the altar. The shafted windows were so high they cast their light too far for guidance to those on the pathway and there was no light from the side door. He put his hand on the handle of the door, and then, just as he was about to push it inwards, he glanced up at the sky.

It often happens that on a dark night, our eyes blinded by some sudden glare of artificial light, we grope among trees or bushes, or among low buildings, while, all the time above our heads, did we but raise our eyes, the sky itself is luminous with stars, and against it the very objects among whose bases we stumble make a vivid pattern, being themselves the cause of the darkness. So, on this night, the branching trees, the belfry, and the tall, thin steeple shot up darkly into a sky that was seeded over with brilliant stars, and in which even the shredded clouds were visibly floating towards a misty quarter in the distant levels of the sky where a moon might break through at any moment.

Gabriel took his hand from the doorknob and stared upwards reluctant to go indoors. While he was staring upwards, it seemed to him, suddenly, that he was not alone, that he was being watched, if only by the still small eyes of an animal, the agile eye of a bird, or even the fierce eye of a rat measuring his chances of security before darting across the grass.

Gabriel, feeling this sudden sensation, looked around first of all to see if anyone had followed him up the path, then he looked into the churchyard with a sense of distaste that anyone should be lingering among the graves upon a night of such living beauty. There was no one in sight. On one headstone there was a graven figure of a human form, lifelike in silhouette against the sky, and, although he did not remember having seen it before, he was about to give allowance for some distorting element in the starlight, when the figure raised an arm, and all at once the sensation of being watched became a certainty.

"Who is there?" said Gabriel, stepping nearer.

At once the figure slipped from its perch on the headstone. Gabriel ran over instinctively. The desire of the other person to conceal its identity had aroused an unthinking impulse in him to discover that identity.

"Come back; I won't hurt you! Who are you?" he called out as he ran into the wet grass in the direction that the figure had taken, but there was only a rustling of wet grass and, although he had measured with his eye the exact position and the exact headstone upon which the figure had been perched, when he had run a few paces into the churchyard one headstone seemed like another and he lost all bearing. Only by looking back at the church continually could he see in what direction he was proceeding.

He ran from headstone to headstone, clambering among them, grasping their cold stone surfaces to propel himself forward over the mounds; but, just as he was about to abandon the chase, there was a sound of fabric catching on something and ripping with a harsh sound, a figure started up like a hare almost from under his feet and sprang past him out on to the clear path again. The figure had almost brushed against him, but its nearness had baffled identity, and, instead of reaching forwards towards it, he had been thrown off his balance and, taking a backward step, found that his foot had crashed through the glass dome of an artificial wreath.

Gabriel freed his foot from the wreath. The sound of running feet played on his nerves. He tried to rearrange the wreath into something of its former state, and placed it back as nearly as he could judge to the place it had originally reposed, and then he started down the dark pathway after the running figure. He was out on the road and had nearly reached the first of the lighted patches on the sidewalk that came from the shop windows, when he drew near enough to the person he pursued to hear the heavy breathing as clearly as the running feet. It was a girl.

Another step and he drew abreast of her and, reaching out his hand, caught at a coat sleeve, bringing both himself and the girl to a stop in the patch of yellow lamplight that flooded out on the pavement from a small sweetshop to their left.

It was only when he felt the fabric in his hand that he realized the impertinent quality of his pursuit, and a feeling of chill descended on him, making the cold moisture start from his flesh and stream down his spine. But, as he looked at the struggling creature in his grasp and heard the gulping laughter, he began to feel that the pursued had taken the whole affair in the same spirit as himself. Her head was bent as she struggled away from him and, since in order to do this more effectively she had turned in his clutch, and was using her head and shoulders to push him away from her, he was still unaware of her identity, but from her laughter he guessed that it was someone he knew. Nevertheless when he wrenched her arm around and flashed her face into view he was unprepared for the shock of seeing Onny Soraghan's face laughing up at him with a full consciousness of the incongruity of his position, and in his astonishment he let go his grasp. She stood up straight for a moment, took a gasping breath and pushed her hair out of her eyes, laughed at him again, and without saying anything ran away in the direction of Clewe Street, while behind him there was a murmur of voices, and casually moving footsteps and the people coming out from the church began to come down the streets of the town.

Not wishing to return to the house until his aunts would have arrived there before him, he turned abruptly down River Street and sat on a bridge for a time, until he felt sure they would have returned home. Yet he had walked with the speed prompted by upset nerves, and so, although he had travelled a good mile, he arrived back at the house only a few minutes after his aunts, and they were still taking off their hats. The shadows, as they raised their hands and lifted off their finery, were silhouetted on the street in the bright squares of the window light, and, while he watched the sham scenes of their actions, he smiled to himself and seemed to see the asperity of Theresa and the timidity of Sara emphasized more fully in this dumb show than he had ever noticed before.

With this in his mind he turned rapidly to look at the back windows, particularly the kitchen window, his mind filled with a new speculative interest in Onny. He thought, perhaps, that he might be able to make some such simplification of her character too from a pantomime upon the window blind. But Onny had drawn the buff-coloured blind and, although upon such buff blinds silhouettes are notoriously clear, so thick a coating of turf smoke and finger grime had been laid on with the years as to make it an effective lantern screen, and so it was only a vague blur that moved across it from moment to moment, giving no idea of the persons within, much less of the actions upon which they were engaged.

He went in. The kitchen door was open. Onny was cleaning shoes. Upon the scrubbed white boards of the table were a row of shoes with the shape of the owners' feet still in them, and Onny, as she lifted shoe after shoe, gave it a dab of the thick blacking from a tin which she had left upon the table. The air was scented with the heavy polish.

"If I were you, I would have polished the shoes before I scrubbed the table," he said, seeing that the white boards were already streaked with the blacking. But he spoke only from a desire to speak.

"There is an order in this house and it is not to be disturbed," said Onny, in such an exact imitation of Theresa Coniffe's voice that Gabriel looked at her sharply to see if she was deliberately imitating his aunt, but her face was bent over the shoe in her hand which was the first to have received its dab of blacking and was now getting a more severe rubbing with the polishing brush. Onny was rubbing the brush back and forth with such vigour that her whole body shook, and so the hand that held the shoe was almost as violently agitated as the one that held the brush, and she looked like one of those mechanical toys which are made so that the maximum number of the limbs move, in order to give a semblance of life, but which, since they all move in the same rhythm, give an effect that is entirely lifeless.

"Why don't you hold the shoe still, and rub the brush up and down?" said Gabriel, and when she made no answer he laughed, "Or you could hold the brush still, and rub the shoe up and down."

Onny caught her rich lower lip in her teeth. Apart from the one repetition of Theresa Coniffe's remark she had said nothing. Gabriel began to feel unwelcome. He picked up a pair of his own shoes. They were covered with mud.

"What's the use of shining those? They'll be just as bad tomorrow!"

Onny went on vigorously rubbing the other shoe.

"Will I throw them under the dresser?" he said taking them up.

Onny stopped rubbing. She went over and took the boots out of his hand and left them back on the table from which he had taken them. With one thumb she jerked upwards where there was a sound of footsteps going back and forth on the old flooring boards. She jerked her thumb from the ceiling to the boots and then towards herself with such a comical urgency, her lips still compressed with the energy with which she had wielded the polishing rag, that Gabriel laughed. He sat up on the edge of the table. Onny put down the brush she had held in her right hand, and began to jerk her thumb again in a dumb indication of the door. Then, putting down the shoe she held in her left hand, and catching him by the sleeve, she made it clear that she wanted him to leave the kitchen.

Gabriel resisted. He gripped the ledge of the table with his knees, and caught the edges with his hands.

"What's the matter? Have you lost your tongue?"

Onny shook her head from side to side in denial of this. She looked up at the ceiling again.

"What have they got to do with you?" said Gabriel.

Onny hesitated. "I was told not to encourage you coming into the kitchen," she said at last, reluctantly.

Gabriel began to laugh. "Do you always do what you're told?"

Onny picked up another shoe and began to rub it.

"What about tonight?"

She stopped rubbing. "What about tonight?" she repeated, truculently.

Gabriel began to feel a sense of achievement at having made her speak.

"What would my aunt say if she knew you didn't go into the church for the service?"

"Who's going to tell her?" Onny stared at him hard.

"Well," said Gabriel, drawing out his words, slowly, and watching the increase of anxiety in her face, "well, I am not in the habit of interfering with other people's business." She released her breath. Then he added quickly, "Of course, I'm not sure but that this may be a case where it would be my duty to interfere!"

The long breath of relief that Onny had expelled left her mouth open and now she remained with it open.

"This is not an ordinary situation, you know," he said, slowly. "You kept my aunts waiting deliberately while you were titivating and getting ready. They were very impatient, but they waited for you because they thought that you did not want to appear in the lighted church with a dirty face, but I wonder how they would feel if they knew you were washing your face and putting on silk stockings to tantalize the ghosts in the churchyard?"

Towards the end of this interrogation Onny's face began to relax and as she began to realize that he was teasing her a softer, shyer look came over her face.

" What were you doing?" she ventured. "You should have been in church yourself."

"Oh, it's different for me," said Gabriel. "I am my own master."

Almost as soon as he had said it he realized that it was both untrue and unkind. It was the unkindness that he regretted most, however, and he looked at her quickly to see if she had taken offence. To cover up the error he hurried on without choosing his words.

"Why didn't you go into the church?"

"Because I wanted to stay out."

"Are you putting me in my place?" he asked.

"There's only one way to put a fellow in his place," said Onny.

"What way is that?"

"Slap his face."

"Why didn't you slap my face?" he said, delighted at the incongruity of the idea. Onny gave him a scathing glance.

"Did you want to?" he persisted.

She looked more scathingly at him. "Have you lost your tongue again?" he asked.

Onny began to collect together all the shoes in her arms and started to walk towards the door.

"Are you mad with me?" said Gabriel, slipping off the table and opening the door for her.

She was going to pass through it without answering him when he shot out his hand and barred her way.

"Let me go," she said, and at the same time she raised her head like a startled foal, as there was the sound of a door shutting upstairs. "Let me go," she repeated frantically, pressing against his outstretched arm as at a barrier that might be expected to break in the middle. The boots and shoes dug into his arm. Her eyes were large and childish, and to his amazement he saw that she was frightened. "Oh, let me pass. Let me pass," she cried.

He held his arm out another fraction of a second. His lips were parted with a desire to say something, and still he could think of nothing to say. Then, quite suddenly, he remembered her truancy from the benediction.

"I think you were splendid to have the courage of your convictions," he said.

He wasn't sure whether she had understood him or not, but he let his arm fall. She burst out of the door and, as he stepped back into the kitchen, he heard her run up the stairs. A second later he heard her stop, and he knew that she was standing aside to let his aunt pass down. From the delay he could imagine his aunt examining the shoes, and then, as one shoe fell and then another, he knew that his aunt had passed downwards and that Onny's tension had slackened only then from the fierce tight embrace of the hard leathers. With an instinct quite unanalysed he slipped across the kitchen floor, taking advantage of the noise of falling boots, and, as his aunt passed across the hallway into the kitchen, he crossed it at the other end and went into the back parlour where supper was laid.

In his mind lay an unassorted heap of new ideas, all trivial and common-place, but all the more welcome for that reason. They afforded him respite from the strange troubled thoughts about his own future that had occupied him during the past few weeks. He sat down by the fire and, taking up the poker, idly began to poke at the glowing coals.

How contradictory had been the behaviour of the little servant. She had been in terror of her life at the sound of his aunt's footsteps descending the stairs, and yet an hour before she had sat defiant and cool on a headstone in the dark churchyard.

And, even with himself, she had behaved with a curious servility. As he chased her in the churchyard and wrestled with her in the lighted square of the shop window he had glimpsed a real person, but in the conversation over the kitchen table there had been no reality. She was choosing her words and gestures.

There was only one way to put a fellow in his place, and that was to slap his face. She had said that, but she did not consider that he was a real fellow.

He thrust the poker into the fire again with fury, and broke the coals until every cinder in the grate released its tongue of flame and blazed like a furnace.

"What is the meaning of this?" said Theresa Coniffe, as she came into the parlour. "Do you want to set the chimney on fire? That grate was banked so that the fire would last for the whole evening. Now it will burn out in half an hour and more coal will have to be brought in."

Sara came in. "Oh, the heat? Why is there such a blaze?" and she pressed her two hands against her face.

"I'm sure I don't know," said Theresa. She went to the door and called out to the kitchen. "Before you get the supper, Onny, bring in some more coal for this fire."

A few minutes later Gabriel heard a shovel grating in the dark yard outside the window, and it occurred to him that his thoughtlessness had laid another task upon Onny's shoulders which must surely, he thought, be weary. He thought for the first time of the long distance she had to travel between Clewe Street and the rampart cottages. He thought of the thin fabric of the coat she had worn to the church. He thought of the darkness and loneliness of the rutted roads outside the town, and a new comprehension of the difficulties under which other people laboured came into his mind, but it did not strike deep enough to make him any the more satisfied with his own lot, and, as he took his place at the table, he thought of Sylvester and wondered what he was doing at that moment.

Onny came in with the tray containing the supper. Gabriel looked at her with amusement. She had taken off the stockings she had worn to the church and her legs were bare. They were white and hairless, and the dirty white canvas shoes into which they were thrust were down-at-heel and slopping wet. They left a trail after them with every step she took. Her red dress too had become drabbled with dishwater and looked more sloppy than ever. But as he followed her with his eyes he was surprised to see how attractive her form was, in spite of the repellent clothes. Under the sloppy red dress her body was firm and perfect. As the sloppy rags swayed back and forth ill-fittingly over her ample hips he thought suddenly that she was like the simple white statues that stand in the porchways of museums, with a few garments caught together across their limbs.

He pictured her getting up in the morning, yawning, brushing her tangled hair from her face and stepping out on to the cold boards of the floor naked, and humped forward with a kind of instinctive modesty, that resented the touch of the air, the light. And he thought that, as she pulled a shrunken discoloured chemise over her head, she must have much the same attractive incongruity of those same statuaries when a dust sheet is thrown over them by a charwoman before she mops down the walls.

When the meal was over Onny came into the room again. Gabriel, who had left the table and taken up a book, sat with it in his lap, but he followed her movements, raising his eyes without raising his head, as she went around the table collecting the soiled crockery and piling it up precariously in her arms. She had the inscrutable look of a woman who performs routine work which demands not the least attention of the mind. He wondered where her thoughts were, and tried by the very movement of her limbs to trace the path taken by her thoughts. There was undeniably a peculiar rhythm in the way she swept up the cups and saucers, lightly yet surely, and there was an undeniable character in the kilting movement of her skirt as she went around the table from one side to another. It might be, he thought, that her mind was far off in a free field, and that in her thoughts she filled her arms with branches of lilac boughs and that her skirts were kilted high because she stepped through high and tangled grasses.

He kept looking at her face, and all at once he felt piqued that her thoughts should desert them all so completely that she could walk into the room where they sat and not have the slightest curiosity, not look their way, not be perhaps even aware that they were there. He remembered that, in all the times that she had crossed back and forth between the door and the table since the meal was finished, she had not once looked at him even with the most cursory curiosity. And he remembered that on at least two occasions she had stepped across his legs that sprawled out in her way, when she wanted to put the cutlery in the drawer of the sideboard, in much the same way as one would step over a sleeping dog. He felt an impulse to say something to turn her eyes on him for a moment, but before he had yielded to it he felt suddenly that, although Onny's eyes were following the faraway visions of her heart, there were a pair of eyes watching himself and watching him steadily. He swung his head upwards and sidewards with such swiftness that his aunt, who had been staring at him for so long a time, could not avert her eyes quickly enough before he looked straight at her. She had been watching him for a time past, and, as she watched him staring at Onny's movements, her mind had speculated on his thoughts as his had speculated upon the thoughts of the servant girl. He returned the stare of his aunt with a cold stare, and decided in his mind that she could not possibly have read his thoughts. She might perhaps, and no doubt did, attribute some lewd thought to him, but she could not possibly have known that in his thoughts he had but garlanded the girl with blossoming boughs and piled her arms with sheafs of bloom-laden lilac.

He felt so secure in the secrecy of his dream that he looked deliberately away from the cold elderly eyes that continued to watch him, and deliberately looked down at the bare white legs of the servant girl.

"Onny! Do you know what time it is?"

The girl started violently as the harsh voice split the air. It seemed to Gabriel that she was expecting the next words, because she seemed to toughen perceptibly, take a firmer stance and close her lips aggressively.

"Hurry up, please," said his aunt. "I want you to be gone out of this house at a respectable hour. I'm willing to be responsible for you in the daytime when you're under my eye, but I won't be responsible for you after you leave this house. I don't want your mother coming up here moaning and crying over you, one of these days."

If Gabriel had complained that the girl had stepped over him like a sleeping dog he had no cause to complain now. Her glance flew from his aunt to himself and he saw the struggle in her face as she wondered whether to be silent under the shame of the unnecessary reproach or whether to brazen it out with a back answer. He thought that he would spare her some embarrassment by going out, and he tore a piece of red-fringed paper that decorated the shelf under the mantelpiece and put it into the book to mark the place before he closed it. He threw the book up on the mantelpiece and went out without saying anything.

Gabriel went up the street and turned down River Street, past the sprawling whitewashed cottages where the sleepy children leaned in the doorways and played lackadaisically. He crossed the bridge and walked out past the rampart cottages where Onny lived, until he came to his favourite sanctuary on the rampart wall. He flattened a place for himself on the tow grasses that grew up between the stones as coarse as wire, and taking out a cigarette he lit it and sat smoking.

The incident in the dining room at Clewe Street had disturbed him even more than he realized, and it was with genuine surprise that he noticed a tremor in his hand as he put the cigarette to his lips. He felt that it was his stupidity, his culpable recklessness that had brought the ugly rebuke upon the girl. He remembered with pain the flush of shame that had stained her cheeks when she looked at him, with her lip caught in her teeth till it was blenched in an angry white streak. His glances at her body had been almost in the nature of a quizzical joke with himself; he had, he admitted, at the time that he was staring at her, a cheap feeling of familiarity. There had been no more personal feeling in his thoughts about her than he would have felt had she danced above him behind footlights in the local theatre, providing paid entertainment. But as her face came before him again with the flushed cheeks, the blenched lip and look of resentment, he thought about her for the first time as a human being. He felt a great pity for her. And he made a resolution to put something pleasant in her way, if it was within his power to do so, to recompense for the insult that he felt himself directly responsible for bringing upon her.

As he sat there, thinking and smoking, the stars came out and a brisk wind sprang up to lash the branches of the trees. As he walked back along the broken ramparts sometime later his eyes were constantly drawn upwards from the uneven stones from which it was dangerous to look aside, because the great beauty of a starry night lay open to him, where the bright

237

sky stretched like a field, and the branches of the trees threshed the stars.

~ ~ ~

It seemed to Gabriel that a long time had passed before he climbed down from the rampart and made his way back to Clewe Street, but, when he went in, his aunts were still sitting by the flagging fire in the parlour, and as he entered they both called out to him.

"Is that you, Gabriel?"

He wanted to go upstairs to his room, but there was an excitement in their voices. When he went into the room they both spoke at once.

"Where were you? We were longing for you to come in. We had such a pleasant evening."

Then the sisters disentangled their words and Sara, running ahead, caught her hands together and exclaimed :

"They're so charming!"

"Who was here?" said Gabriel, and without hearing he began to detect a scent in the air of the room that he had not at once noticed.

"The Finnerty girls!" said Theresa. "I had no idea they would turn out to be such charming girls. Agnes is very pretty."

"Hannah is a very good-mannered girl," said Sara, and all at once, looking at Sara's eager upturned face, Gabriel knew that his Aunt Theresa had spoken about the way he had been staring at Onny. He knew they had been talking about him and that they were beginning to worry about Onny Soraghan. This was her way of trying to remedy it.

The next evening about seven o'clock, before they went up to get ready for church, his aunts were busy plumping up the cushions in the parlour, straightening the picture frames. Sara took the two candles out of the candelabra on the piano, which, although they were never used, she replaced by two fresh candles, the old ones having a dirty appearance from a thick coating of dust. And as he passed the kitchen he saw that Onny, who had her back turned, was polishing the silver tea service, and pieces of it lay upon the table catching in their pale silver surface the bright red gleams of the fire.

"Is there anyone coming?" said Gabriel once, looking up from his book as Sara came in with the old dusty candles and began to look around for some place to leave them.

"Why do you ask that, dear?" said Sara, uneasily. "It's nice to be prepared. It's nice to have the house looking good if anyone should call unexpectedly."

As the house was always spotless, this remark was suspicious. Gabriel wasn't satisfied. He went out to the kitchen again.

"Is there company expected, Onny?"

"How do I know!" said Onny, and she rubbed the silver more vigorously.

238

Gabriel pointed at the teapot. "Why are you shining up the silver?"

"Silver has to be shined up now and again, as everybody knows," said Onny.

"But why are you doing it now? Couldn't it wait till the morning?"

Onny shrugged her shoulders, and looked at herself in the bright surface. She laid down the teapot and lifted the cream ewer.

"That's done," said Gabriel.

"No," said Onny.

"It's just as bright as the teapot."

"All on this side of the table is done, all on that side is to be done."

"I don't see any difference," said Gabriel. "They all look equally bright to me." He lifted the sugar basin and looked at himself in it, his face elongated grotesquely. "Oh, I say, look at yourself in this, Onny!"

Onny took it out of his hand. She glanced disdainfully at her image, but when she saw its distorted proportions, she laughed and stuck out her tongue at herself. Gabriel moved nearer to see better, and put out his hand to steady the improvised mirror for his gaze. Onny stopped laughing at once, lowering the sugar basin. She gave it a rub against the skirt of her dress.

"You'll mark it with your fingers," she said, accusingly, "and make a show of us before the very people that have the sharpest tongues of the town in their heads."

"So there is someone coming!"

"Maybe there is!"

"Onny! Who is coming?"

All of Onny's answers up to now had been given with an abstracted air as she rubbed the silver and held it up to see the glow of the fire in it, but now she turned around with a sudden twist that sent her red skirt hem swirling around her legs.

"If you don't know who's coming, I don't know who should know!"

And, catching up the pieces of the silver, she rattled them on to a silver tray and clinking them together as carelessly as if they were made of tin, she flounced out of the room, her skirts kilting angrily, and left Gabriel standing in the kitchen. The firelight flickered erratically, its shadow flames irritably licking the ceiling and walls, and a spate of sparks going up into the chimney minute by minute.

Gabriel felt an irritation growing within himself, and he sat on the table edge recalling all that Onny had said, and then, with a sudden comprehension of her meaning, he laughed. He had a good idea who the visitors were, and so had Onny. Onny was jealous of them.

At eight o'clock there was a rap at the door. The light brass knocker never emitted more than a weak metallic sound, but on this occasion it gave only a thin sound like the dropping of water into a tin vessel. Nor-

239

mally so light a sound would have passed unnoticed and the visitor would have had to resort to tapping on the windowpane of the kitchen to attract Onny's attention, or as Mrs. Molloy did, to the disgust of Theresa, open the letter box and call upon the Coniffes by name, proclaiming at the same time her own identity and even her object in calling. This was a vulgarity which never ceased to infuriate Theresa. It caused her upon numerous occasions to state that she would put That Person in her place one fine day.

On this evening, however, the light knocking which Gabriel had not even heard penetrated the ears of Miss Theresa and Miss Sara so simultaneously that they both sprang to their feet at the same moment, which was also the identical moment at which the knocker struck its first weak rap upon the door.

"A knock at the door! Who can that be?" cried both ladies together, but unfortunately with such simultaneousness that it was at once apparent that they were both expecting the callers. If this fact was not lost on Gabriel it was not lost upon the sisters themselves either, for with a look of reciprocal displeasure at having betrayed themselves, they both sank back into their chairs again with a show of false indifference more revealing than their sincerity of a moment before.

"Will I answer the door?" said Gabriel, looking from one to the other.

"That would be very nice," said Sara.

"That would be very nice," said Theresa.

Both looked as if, at the moment at least, nothing nicer could be expected from life, by either of them, than that their nephew should answer the door to their callers. Seeing an opportunity to tease them, Gabriel stood up and then, lifting his head exaggeratedly, he appeared to listen for a sound.

"Are you sure there was a knock?" he asked.

"Why, of course," said Sara.

The thin knock sounded again.

"There it is again!" said Theresa, holding up her hand for silence.

"I don't hear anything," said Gabriel.

"You must be getting deaf," said Theresa irritably. "We heard it distinctly."

"I think sometimes that I *am* getting deaf," said Gabriel. "One of the lecturers at the Technical School was saying the other day that people should have their ears tested every year, and if there is the least trace . . ."

"The door, Gabriel!" said Miss Sara. "I don't wish to interrupt you, dear, and I'm very interested in what the lecturers say, they are the people who know what is right and what is wrong." Sara's interruption threatened to be so lengthy that it would defeat its own end. Miss Theresa's shoe began to tap out its familiar warning of irritability upon the floor.

"Is the door going to be opened, or is it not?" She gripped the arms of her chair and assumed an attitude which suggested that if motion were added to it, she would herself be out in the hallway in another moment.

Gabriel went over and courteously pushed Theresa back into the depth of her chair.

"I believe you are mistaken, Aunt. I don't believe there was a knock at all."

"Of course there was a knock!"

"It must have been a poor, feeble-spirited knock if so!" said Gabriel. "If it's anyone of importance let him knock out loud and clear so that we may be sure, and not have us running to the door every other minute upon false errands. There is nothing I dislike more than a watery, weak knock at a door. Let us ignore it, I say."

Sara, who was easily nonplussed, dropped her hands to her sides and began to stare in the direction of the hallway as if all that were needed now to complicate the situation to the point of tears would be a repetition of the knocking. Theresa, however, fell into the trap.

"How smart you are!" she said contemptuously. "Do you expect the young ladies to break down the door? They are not blacksmiths, are they? They are not savages, are they?"

"Oh, I beg your pardon, Aunt," said Gabriel. "I did not know you were expecting anyone in particular. That's quite a different matter."

Having satisfied himself, he laughed and went out to the hall. The sisters stood up and went out after him, and when Gabriel pulled back the door all three of them were framed in its threshold to welcome the Finnertys.

The instant the door was opened, there was a flutter of voices, as the four ladies began to speak all together, but there was a certain cadence in the flutter, since the two elderly ladies and the two young ladies were saying exactly the same thing.

"Come in. Come in," cried Sara and Theresa together.

"So nice of you to ask us!" said the Misses Finnerty, also speaking together; and then, as Gabriel stepped back and held the door of the parlour open, the ladies began to engage in that most delightful of all feminine imbecilities, helping each other to discard hats and gloves and scraps of scarves.

"Won't you take off your hat?" said Theresa to Hannah Finnerty, and instantly, as if to protect herself from the danger of having it forcibly dragged from her head, Hannah's hand flew to her hat.

"I think I'd prefer to leave it on, Miss Coniffe, if you don't mind."

"Oh, not at all, my dear. As you please," said Miss Coniffe, whose hands had indeed been outstretched with terrifying eagerness.

"But I think I'll take off my scarf!" said Hannah, compromisingly, and she began to unwind a wisp of silk from her neck, and turned to hand it to Miss Coniffe. Miss Coniffe, however, had just become engaged in helping her sister to cope with the belongings of Agnes Finnerty. For Agnes had immediately complied with Miss Sara Coniffe's suggestion that she remove her hat and had taken it off and put it into Miss Sara's hand, only to find that when she unwound her scarf, Miss Sara was unable to manage it, having difficulty in holding the hat without damaging her eye with the long blue feather in it.

Agnes withdrew the hand that was stretched out with the scarf.

"Don't bother, Miss Coniffe," she said. "I'll leave it anywhere," and she began to look around her vaguely and apologetically.

"Theresa," said Sara, appealingly, "would you hold Agnes's hat for a minute, please, while I take her scarf?"

"Certainly!" said Theresa, with a smiling graciousness which might have seemed unusual, were it not realized that she regarded this civility to Sara as indirectly penetrating to the visitors. "Give me the hat," she said. "What a pretty hat! I was admiring it the other day when you passed up the street. It's very becoming to you."

"It was not that one you saw," said Hannah. "This is the first time she has worn this hat. She only bought it yesterday."

Hannah still held her scarf awkwardly in her hand and had entered the conversation merely in order to draw attention to herself that she might be relieved of it. Her plan worked admirably, because both of the Misses Coniffe became simultaneously aware of the scarf that Hannah held in her hand.

"Hold this, Sara," said Theresa, passing Agnes's hat back into Sara's hand and going to reach for Hannah's scarf.

"Oh, mind the feather!" cried Hannah, nervously, as her sister's hat made a perilously quick transfer from Theresa to Sara. "I'll hold it," she volunteered, but just before she took the hat she threw her scarf to Agnes. "Hold my scarf, Agnes, please," she said.

Agnes took the scarf, but, as she had been in the act of withdrawing her gloves and had already removed one glove, she held the scarf with extreme reluctance. It prevented her from taking off the other glove.

For a moment or two then the situation became desperate as gloves and scarves and hats and purses were handed from one person to another. And in the middle of this pleasant confusion Hannah Finnerty decided to change her mind about her own hat, and instead of leaving it upon her head, as she had intended, seizing a moment when her own hands were free, she put them up to her head and took off her toque. She held it precariously poised on the tips of her fingers and looked almost at once as if she considered that her former decision had been wiser, and this decision a downright mistake.

"Oh, dear me," said Sara Coniffe, seeing Hannah's expression. "This hallway is so narrow. There's no room for a hall stand. We should have asked you to come upstairs!"

At this exclamation from Miss Sara, however, both Agnes and Hannah burst out together, in an effort not to appear fussy.

"Don't worry about the old things," they said. "Throw them anywhere." But as they spoke they looked around then with ever greater apprehension.

"I'll make room for them on this table," said Theresa, and she ran over and lifted up a large flower vase from a small table in a dark corner of the hall. "Now we have plenty of room!" she cried in delight, surveying the empty space she had cleared upon the table. "Now you can give me your hat, Agnes," she said, "and I'll leave it here."

Before the situation reached a frenzy the younger ladies became suddenly aware of the fact that the door of the front parlour was ajar and that although Gabriel had gone in there, and was out of sight, he was not out of earshot. Now, in fact, a faint cough recalled his presence to their minds. Instantly their difficulties vanished, and the hats, gloves, and scarves were disposed of as if by miracle, and the young Misses Finnerty were entering the parlour, their feet reluctant, but their eyes eagerly trying to pick the most advantageous seats in the room.

As Agnes came into the room slowly, hesitatingly, in advance of her sister, Gabriel felt a capricious desire to suspend criticism, and to arouse, if he could, the feelings of attraction he had felt that day.

"I hope you won't feel the room chilly. Where will you sit?" Sara pulled out one chair and then another and appealed to Theresa. "Which chair do you think would be most comfortable?"

"Oh, anywhere at all," said Hannah, looking covetously at the stool near the fire.

"Anywhere at all," said Agnes, looking nervously at, and actually shrinking away from, a stiff leather chair which was placed rather too near the window.

Sara pulled out a chair near the piano. "You'll have to play for us, you know!" she said to Anges.

"Are you out of your mind, Sara," said Miss Theresa impatiently, "to talk of playing while they're frozen with the cold? Sit over near the fire, girls," she said, and kneeling down she pierced the coals with a long poker, sending up gay sparks which almost made up for the lack of conversation for a moment, so brightly did they jostle each other up the chimney, and so ardently they shone before they disappeared in the blackness of the flue.

Gabriel, who had up to now said nothing, could feel his throat swelling with embarrassment. He no sooner moved in one direction to accommodate Agnes than he found to his dismay he was blocking Hannah's passage to the fire. He stepped backward, once or twice to find himself jabbed in the back by the corner of the piano, or in such a bad position with regard to the lamp that he not only shaded everyone in the room, but cast his own shadow over them in grotesque proportions.

"Where will you sit, Gabriel?" said Hannah at last, speaking to him directly, and his gratitude was so great that he sat down on the edge of the lounge beside her although, even in his previous confusion, he had been aware that there was room also at the other end beside Agnes. He sat down beside Hannah, who smiled and looked at him, her whole face bright and alert with readiness to co-operate in conversation, but bearing at the same time unmistakable signs of unwillingness to be the first to open the conversation.

Gabriel's embarrassment rose in his throat again, and apart from being unable to think of anything to say he felt that even if he had the most delightful things to say he would not be able to articulate them.

At that moment, so great is the mechanical element in us, the words that he had heard darting back and forth in this room for the past few minutes came back into his mind with a rush and, before he could prevent himself, he heard himself speaking.

"I hope you were not long knocking at the door? We thought we heard a knock but we weren't sure."

When the words were out of his mouth he bit his lip with vexation at his own stupidity, but to his surprise, instead of giggling as he thought they might easily have done, Agnes, leaning forward swiftly across her sister, and with unnecessary interruption, took up the jaded remark as if it were as fresh as a flower, and with an animation in her face which came from some inward significance that she attached to her words, she answered him before Hannah had time to do so.

"No! We weren't long knocking, only a moment. We had just come up to the door. We barely tipped the knocker when the door was flung open!"

And then, having said what she wanted to say, she leaned back again with a resumption of her former indolent manner and listened to what the Coniffe sisters were saying about the piano, which Theresa polished with her sleeve as she spoke, and along the keys of which Sara ran a provocative finger without, however, daring to press it firmly enough to evoke any sound.

"We never play now," Theresa said.

"We used to play all day long, when we were your age," said Sara.

"Of course, music is something you never forget," said Theresa.

"Like riding a bicycle," said Hannah Finnerty, and she nodded at Gabriel encouragingly, to draw him into the conversation. "I always hear my mother say that although it is thirty years since she sat on the saddle of a bicycle, she could jump on one any time she chooses and pedal down the street as fast as the wheels would go round!"

Gabriel smiled. There was a humorous picture presented to his mind by the thought of Mrs. Finnerty pedalling down Clewe Street, but he did not feel like smiling. The moment of mental indolence with which he had welcomed the feminine talk had vanished. He kept looking at Agnes Finnerty, trying to understand a mind that showed its shallows so obviously. Why has she striven to tell an unnecessary lie about a trivial circumstance? Why had her vanity been so quick, so sensitive to deny that she had been kept waiting one moment more than another at the hall door? What did she hope to gain by it?

The conversation went its way, flowing evenly in its insipid channels. There were no swift interruptions, no exclamations of surprise, no irrepressible contradictions, no accompaniment of gestures, such as mark the progress of a living conversation fed with thought and emotion. He listened and gave his answers when his turn came, and with every remark made by Agnes Finnerty, with ever gesture and with every look she gave him, he measured her character carefully, and from word, look, and gesture, decided that his estimate of her as vain and shallow and worthless was a correct one.

The evening wore on. After a long time, it seemed, of idle talk, Agnes was prevailed upon to play. She stood up, shrugging her silk shoulders in deprecation of something, possibly her own talent, possibly her audience. Then she sat down on the piano stool and ran her forefinger lightly along the keyboard, before breaking into a pretty piece of music that rippled and trilled this way and that. Gabriel closed his eyes, and it seemed to him that he was listening to several birds flying irresponsibly this way and that, singing and chirping, now one at a time, now all together, but the image was not pleasant, for it seemed to him that they were the fluttering and chirping of limited freedom.

He opened his eyes a slit, without appearing to do so, and he could just see the arched wrists coming out of their lacy sleeves, rising, descending, rising, descending, and he transferred the image from the music to the frail white hands. They now were the imprisoned birds, that must rise and fall, rise and fall, within the caged limits set to them by the vanity of their owner's soul. By raising his head imperceptibly, he looked higher and higher, and he followed the line of the young girl's body, noticing for the first time the deliberate cut of the cloth, the tightening of the seams, the intricacy of the stitching, and it seemed that the whole making of the dress had been one long unconscious lascivious thought. And yet the seductive disposition of bows and embroidery failed to touch him. He looked around at Hannah, at his aunts, and suddenly he felt sickened to see that on all of them the dresses were all equally capriciously planned and cut. He felt that they were dressed with a design that shamed his own manhood. He thought deliberately of the women he knew, bringing them before his mind, incongruously paired, as the music rippled onward with an almost imbecile regularity. They were all the same—even poor old Mary Ellen, they had all about them this extraordinary deliberation of dress.

And then as he paraded the women of the town before his eyes, striving to include in his procession the most incongruous of types, he was startled, as if it were indeed a real procession of people which was passing before his eyes, when, slowly, her gait impeded by the badly broken shoes upon her feet, a last figure strolled across his screen of vision, in a loose, ill-fitting red dress, her ruddy face smiling at him with a mixture of contempt and respect which was only too sincerely expressive of the feelings she had for him, as a man and as the master of the house. Her dress was utterly shape-less, serving but one purpose, to cover her body, and at the thought of its sloppy appearance, Gabriel smiled.

"Did you like that?"

The music was over. Agnes twirled on the revolving music stool.

"I enjoyed it very much," said Gabriel, and standing up he lifted a pile of music from the piano top. "Can you play some of these?" He sorted them rapidly and carelessly, barely listening to her replies, in his anxiety to have her play again, and keep playing, that he might indulge in watching the Onny of his vision, and stare at her, in a way he did not dare to do when she was present in the flesh.

But after she had played another piece, Agnes looked across at Hannah and raised her eyebrows in what was meant to be a secret signal that it was time for them to leave. So obvious was this signal, however, that Theresa Coniffe interpreted it even before Hannah, and, jumping up, she caught the little red enamel clock which stood upon the mantelpiece and turned it with its face to the wall.

"It's too early to look at the clock," she said. "You are only here a few minutes."

"And you must have a cup of tea before you go," said Sara.

"Please don't bother, Miss Coniffe," said the two girls together, and once again Agnes raised her eyebrows significantly as she looked at Hannah.

"I'll take no excuses!" said Theresa, again answering the signal which Hannah was endeavouring to have repeated by elaborately raising her own brows to indicate that she had not comprehended what her sister wished to convey.

Sara was edging past Gabriel, whose knees seemed to protrude a long way into the room, although he sat far into the corner.

"The tray is all ready. The bread and butter is cut. The kettle is boiling!" she cried, as she made her way to the door, excusing herself excitedly, now to Gabriel, now to Theresa, now to Agnes, as she made her way out, and once indeed to the edge of the piano, against which she banged her elbow in an effort to avoid tilting the table upon which the lamp rested.

"It's a shame to put you to such trouble when we live so near," said Hannah.

"No trouble at all," said Theresa, as Sara went out and closed the door.

"You're very silent tonight, Gabriel" said Theresa. "There must be some reason for that!" She looked from Agnes to Hannah and smiled.

"He couldn't be shy of us when we have lived so near all our lives," said Hannah, looking at him with the unattractive practicality of a plain woman.

"He wants us to think he is deep," said Agnes.

"Do you think I am really very shallow?" said Gabriel.

"I'm sure I don't know," said Agnes, whose idea of conversation was that it ran in couplets; a sentence brought forth an answer but did not necessarily start a chain.

"If you think that I am trying to appear deep, then you must also think that I am in reality very shallow." Gabriel leaned nearer. "But why should one wish to appear something one is nót?" He hoped to make her blush. He hoped to remind her of her petty deception in the chapel, but Agnes, although she did not see the trap he had laid for her, did not, for all that, fall into it, but assuming that he had some flirtatious significance underlying the words she tilted her head towards him slightly and smiled up at him from the corners of her bright-irised eyes. Gabriel sank back in his chair.

Sara came in with the tray, laden with an unnecessary amount of china, and a teapot on which there was pressed a large padded cosy covered in red silk.

"What a pretty cosy!" said Hannah, and then, with one last look at Gabriel, who was staring at Agnes, she relinquished all hope of attracting him to herself and began to foster the cause of getting him for a brother-in-law. "My sister Agnes embroidered a beautiful one at school last year. My mother says it is too artistic to use every day. We keep it on the sideboard." She addressed herself to the Coniffe sisters, turning elaborately from one to the other, but out of the corner of her eye she watched Gabriel.

He was staring at the tray, but whether at the tea cosy or at the silver teapot she was not sure. A moment later it was clear, however, that it was at the teapot he was staring, because he leaned out and lifted it slightly and held it up in front of Agnes.

"Did you ever admire your beauty in a mirror of this kind, Miss Finnerty?" he asked, holding it nearer within her range of vision.

"No, thank you!" said Agnes, waving it away, having already caught an involuntary glance at the distorted image of herself in its brilliantly shined surface.

"Do look!" pursued Gabriel, holding it nearer. "I assure you that this is a most excellent mirror, and one which the parish priest would never condemn you for gazing upon at any hour."

"Don't tease Agnes," said Theresa, but it was clear that she was pleased at this form of teasing which seemed to her, from comparison with dim memories of long ago, to be a prelude to courtship.

247

Agnes was rapidly losing her temper. The glinting silver was coming nearer and nearer and nearer. From the spout a topaz drop of tea suspended perilously. "Do be careful of what you are doing," she said at last, pushing back her chair and rising; "you will spill the tea on my dress."

"Be careful, Gabriel," said Sara, but she felt the injustice of correcting Gabriel when in reality it was Agnes who was at fault, for losing her temper over such a trivial thing.

Sara looked apprehensively at Theresa, who looked back at her without being able to do anything either. It seemed that Gabriel and Agnes were not so well suited after all. They both looked at Hannah, and Hannah, divining with a flash that all was not well with the cause of Agnes, saw that it might not be so disloyal after all to enter the lists.

"Let me look, Gabriel!" she said, stretching out a hand.

Gabriel lowered the teapot. He looked at Hannah's broad white face with its overweighted cheekbones and long thin nose.

"There is no need in your looking, Hannah," he said, with a mixture of contempt and kindness, as he laid the teapot down again upon the tray.

Sara took it up rapidly and began to pour out the tea, but Gabriel's eyes followed it as it glinted and lit with the reflections of the firelight, and in it too he seemed to see again the ruddy cheeks of Onny Soraghan as she had held it up in her hands that afternoon and impudently put out the tip of her red tongue at her own comical image.

It was now the end of October, but the weather was still warm and summery. When he came back from Draghead one evening, Gabriel took a book and went out into the garden at the back of the house. The light was beginning to fade and he would not be able to read for long, but it made him feel less aimless to clasp the book under his arm.

The garden was still and empty. He passed down the centre path to the slope at the river edge. On the way he noticed a small wet handkerchief spread to dry upon one of the hedges. It was white, with a border of blue dots around the hem. He didn't remember having seen it with either of his aunts. It must be Onny's, he thought.

When he reached the end of the garden Gabriel opened his book, but he had no real inclination to read. He sat listening to the soft noises of the water and left the book open upon his knee.

The river was low, being nearly dried up, and although in the middle of its course a swift stream of bright water ran freely on its way, the rest of the river bed was filled with such a pale shallow wash of water that the pebbles and stones on the bottom, which in winter were not to be seen, were now bared to view, and moreover portions of the larger stones rose above the water level, dry as bones. Lancing high out of the water there were grasses and waterweeds which normally grew high enough to penetrate the surface of the stream, even in winter, but which, in that season, were never allowed to strike up vertically, because the swift currents bent them under and dragged them as far as their roots would allow in the direction they travelled themselves.

There was also a strange collection of things that had been thrown from time to time into the river and which moved along for a short distance and then sank, only to be revealed after strange changes had come over them; an old black shoe lay on one side, as if it had just been cast off by the owner, but in its rich blackness under the water it wore a greater shine than the hand of man could have brought upon it, and from out of its rusted eyelets, from which the laces had been eaten away by minnows, there was a beading of silver drops that would have made it a shoe for a king, could it but be preserved. There were old pearl buttons, rusted safety pins, and a small unrusted wheel with mitred edges that might have come out of a clock. There were pieces of broken china, on which gay patterns of rose and leafage still remained. And over all this the water was flat and serene, like the plate glass that covers the showcases in a museum. But under this glass cover from time to time a small minnow would flick from under a stone and shoot, with the speed of a nerve in the body, through the beautiful debris, to take cover under another partially exposed stone. Gabriel thought of all the times that he had sat as a child by this river, content to dream and idle, but now as he sat there he felt impatient with himself and he wanted companionship outside himself and his own dreams.

He looked across the river at the lonely desolate park of the ruined castle. The summer light that lay richly on the shallow water and deepened the distant vista only penetrated the lawn across the river in thin bars between the trees, but this light, like the light that penetrated a dark room through the slits of a wooden shutter, seemed more rich and tantalizing than the outer light. From where he sat Gabriel could just see the dark outline of the ruin, and beyond it again the broken rim of the rampart. The great loneliness of the place settled slowly into his mind and his own personal loneliness became as nothing beside it. But as the evening came on, the colour in the sky deepening as the colour on the earth faded, he heard a faint sound of music lift on the wind for a moment like a streamer, and after a few minutes he heard it again. He lifted his head to catch it and hear where it came from, and at the same time he thought that it was followed by a sound of laughing. But there was only silence. He bent his head to his book again. Again a streamer of music flagged faintly on the wind, and this time, unmistakable, after it, came human laughter and the clear ringing of human voices, calling out, one after another, in the far-off roads beyond the rampart.

Gabriel raised his head. The voices came from the cemetery cross-road, where the wide arc made by the cemetery gates, added to the space made by the joining roads, tempted the young people of the town to linger if groups of them met there while out walking.

Crossroad dancing was forbidden by the parish priest, but the cross-roads was still a meeting place. Here the young shop boys and servant girls of the town met on bright nights and, although they did not dance in couples, there were often jigs and solo dances to the tune of melodeons, mouth organs, and jew's-harps. To this music also there was a continual activity of handkerchief snatching, hair pulling, and impudent pinching, which was in itself, although it followed no measured pattern, like an elaborate figure dance of erotic import.

Gabriel listened, and although he could see nothing, or perhaps indeed because of that fact, he was filled with an envy of the companionship that the voices suggested; even to listen evoked a faint feeling of gaiety in his heart.

The evening deepened. It was that hour at which the light no longer beats down upon the earth, but the colours of all things seemed deeper for that, as if the sun had over-illumined them, and now without that bright glare on them they showed the full depth of their own colour. The trees were a richer green, the sap had risen fresh in the blades of the grass. He looked back at the house; even the old stone house was a richer, warmer shade than when he had last looked at it.

He did not think that he had been sitting there long, but once when he looked around him he saw that the little dotted handkerchief that had clung so limply to the hedge was stiff and dry. Then, a minute or two after he had turned to look at it, he heard the back door open, and looking around again, he saw Onny come out into the garden. She made straight for the hedge, and picking up the handkerchief began to fold it carefully, matching corner to corner with such care that she might have been folding it upon a laundry board. She did not see him. She was dressed with a particular care this evening, he noticed. She wore the same ample and badly fitting red dress, but to it she had added a green silk bow that plastered her bosom like a great dead bird pinned there. Over the dress she wore a bright blue coat. Now, from her sister Judy, Onny may have heard that it was incorrect for a lady to wear more than three colours at the same time, and so she had resisted the temptation to wear her yellow cap, but the rule that restricted a lady to three colours alone took for granted that the lady in question would have a somewhat quiet taste in hosiery and that her natural colouring would be somewhat quiet as well, yet under the red skirts Onny's legs were clad in her stockings of glittering amber, and above the green silk bow and the brilliant blue coat her ruddy cheeks and her bright curls added just the same touch that a poster painter might add if he were painting a bill of attraction for a coming circus.

Gabriel took in every detail of the festive attire which Onny wore, and he was well aware that it had a great tastelessness in its many conflicting details, but, although it would have horrified the tastes of the averagely sensitive person, there was in his nature a depth of sensitiveness that analysed further than most people, and he felt that in the general picture created by the different garments there was not after all such a tastelessness as at first seemed, for Onny was dressed for an evening of gaiety, and unless she wore the traditional costume of motley, she could not have worn anything more festive than her ill-assorted garments. He looked again at the sparkling patent-leather shoes with their bright steel buckles; at the lolloping swirls of the wide red dress, the spreading silk of the great green bow, the glittering stockings, the blue coat and the rusty hair, and he felt a spirit of gaiety rise in him till he could no longer control it, and slapping the book on his thigh he laughed outright.

"Oh God!" said Onny, springing away from the dimming bushes and letting the folded handkerchief flutter out of her fingers. "Oh God, you gave me a fright!" she said, as she saw him.

Gabriel stood up. "Why are you all dressed up?" he said, more closely inspecting the details of her finery.

"It's my free evening!" said Onny, dropping back into a deferential manner and beginning to edge away towards the house.

"Are you going without this?" Gabriel stooped and picked up the blue-dotted handkerchief.

Onny put out a hand for it speechlessly.

Absolutely unable to cease teasing her, he put it behind his back. "Shame on you, Onny, going out for the evening with a handkerchief that isn't ironed!" He held it out and shook it, holding it by a corner, and revealing the crisp creases that had dried into it. Onny said nothing. "Now, if you were the fine lady you'd like to think yourself, Miss Onny, you would delay a moment and heat up an iron to make this piece of cambric a docile folded square that would do you credit with the young men of the town, should you have occasion to display it in public. This crumpled cloth, with the prick of the bushes still upon it, will do you no credit in the matrimonial markets."

While he spoke Gabriel advanced and drew the fluttering handkerchief before Onny's wide eyes, over which the lashes fluttered nervously. He liked looking at her. She made him feel gay. He felt an impulse to keep her there. He spoke without listening to his own words, thrusting the handkerchief nearer and nearer to her face each time, fascinated by the way the eyelashes fluttered, and wondering how long her patience would endure the torment. Watching her so closely he did not catch what she said when, bending her head suddenly, a tear splashed out of her eyes and fell on the silk bow at her neck, making a dark stain on the gaudy emerald silk.

"Onny! You're not crying! Onny!" He stopped waving the handkerchief. "I was only teasing you. You shouldn't mind what I say, Onny!" She kept her head bent and he saw her short, white teeth bite into the soft fluid flesh of her lips. "Onny!" He did not know what to do. He looked foolishly at the handkerchief in his hand. "See," he said, stretching it out towards her. "See, here it is. I don't want it. I was only teasing you." He held it out foolishly, and then seeing that she had no intention of taking it he leaned across and tucked it into her belt. Onny put up her hand, and taking it out of her belt crumpled it up and put it into her pocket.

She turned around and began to walk back towards the house with her head still bent in a way that made her sloped shoulders look childish and unhappy. His desire to keep her out in the garden had been only a whim, but now he wanted to delay her until she had recovered her good spirits. He remembered how happily she had run across the grass a few minutes before and he wondered at his own stupidity in having made her unhappy. But still he could not think of anything to say which would delay her without making himself look foolish. Then just as she was nearing the house he remembered that she had said something which he did not catch just before she began to cry.

"Onny!" She stopped when he called her name but she did not turn around. "Onny! Come back!"

She turned around slowly and came back. The tears had dried on her cheeks. Her eyes were bright again. But her short teeth still bit into her lips and her whole face had the sorrowful look of a child's face which, although we know the hurt that has caused it, gives us an uncontrollable desire to smile. Tears from the pallid and weary we expect, but upon red cheeks they are an incongruity. Gabriel controlled his features and putting as much concern as possible into his voice he spoke to her gently, coaxingly.

"You said something about the handkerchief before you began to cry. What was it?" The short teeth released the red lip, which fell open, gleaming redder where it had been tightly caught.

He saw that she was afraid of being teased. With a sudden remembrance of days long ago, when he had played with Larry Soraghan under the river arch, he put his two hands to his face, the tips of his fingers pressing against his lips, and blowing a kiss into the fading evening skies, he smiled at her.

"I swear I won't laugh at you, Onny. What did you say? Please say it again."

She had followed his gesture with infinite attention, and when he had raised his finger tips towards the sky she had stared up into the blue for a moment with such intensity that she seemed to follow the kisses of heavenly propitiation as they travelled into the evanescent skies. Then looking down at him again she smiled with perfect trust and simplicity.

"I said that I like the smell of the bushes," she said, and then she sighed as if she had vindicated some great charge that he had made against her and could rest now in the security that his opinion of her had changed.

But Gabriel did not understand. He looked at her sharply to see if she were not teasing him, but she looked so completely happy and serene that he knew this was not so.

"The bushes? The smell of the bushes? What do you mean, Onny?" He felt ridiculous to think that he had dragged this remark out of her only to find it incomprehensible. "I don't understand. What did you mean?"

Onny's lips went together again tightly as if she were going to cry once more. He didn't understand!

"Don't cry, Onny. I'm sure it was very sensible whatever you meant. Just explain it a little more, will you?" He coaxed her with gesture and voice and eyes.

Onny drew a deep breath. "You said it was a shame on me not to iron the handkerchief," she said falteringly.

"Yes? Go on." Gabriel had forgotten the handkerchief. What on earth was in her mind?

"You said it was all crumpled. . ."

"Yes. Go on."

"You thought I was too lazy to iron it!" Onny was gaining confidence.

"I didn't *say* that, did I? You shouldn't try to read people's thoughts."

"But you *thought* that?"

Gabriel felt that he was gradually falling into the inferior position. The colour was as bright as ever in her cheeks. He saw only one way to extricate himself from his position and that was by teasing her again.

"Well. That was the reason, wasn't it?"

The colour brimmed over in her cheeks. "No, that was not the reason," declared Onny, with all the righteousness of one about to deliver a crushing reply. "I never iron my handkerchiefs because I like the smell of the bushes on them! So there!" And then, entirely restored to the good spirits of a short time before, she stood in front of him, wreathed in

253

smiles, her head moving slightly and involuntarily with the slightly tipsy sensation of triumph.

For a moment more Gabriel could not understand what she meant, and then, leaning over, he took the piece of crumpled linen from her pocket and pressed it to his face. He breathed in the sweet wild scent of the air that clings to clean-washed cool linens as it clings to nothing else, and in breathing it a new sense of sweetness and simplicity in life seemed suddenly to come to him, and Onny, herself, as she stood, with her toes turned in, upon the dampening grass, seemed nearer and more in harmony with the earth than anyone he had ever met.

"Where are you going, Onny?" he asked, with more real curiosity in the question than there had been in any other he had asked. And then, before she had time to answer, the need to do so was removed, because from across the river, once more, but this time louder and clearer in the bolder air of the later evening, came the stranded music of an accordion, and the voices of young people, singing upward into the air, laughing and calling out gaily. "Are you going over to the crossroads?" he said.

She nodded.

"You would be there by this time if I had not kept you?"

He felt compunction for having kept her here in the dull garden which he had himself thought of as a prison a short time before. Her time was so short for pleasure and she worked so hard. He wanted to atone for having kept her there, for having made her cry, for having perhaps put a shadow upon her anticipation of pleasure. But he could not think of anything to do to remedy what he had done.

"How long will it take you to get over there?"

He thought of his bicycle, and of how short a time it would take him to bring her over there, if she were perched on the handlebars, but with the thought he realized the impossibility of his lowering his dignity like that, passing through the main streets of the town.

"Onny!" His face lit up with excitement. "I have an idea. I'll tell you what to do! You'll be over at the crossroads in the twinkling of an eye, if you do as I say."

Onny looked at him. She was doubtful.

"The river is nearly dry," he said. "You can get across on the stones!" Onny looked down with a mixture of credulity and fear. "It's a great idea," said Gabriel. "Come, I'll show you. You can cross in a minute. I'll help you and then you will only have to run through the park, climb over the rampart, and you're there! Come!"

He caught her hand and, making her run too, he ran down the sloped grass to the edge of the water. As Gabriel ran his excitement grew. The thought of helping her to cross upon the stones seemed to carry with it some of the excitement with which he had sailed out floating paper boats upon it as a child. It held something of the old make-believe qualities that gilded the days of childhood, and yet her hand in his had the new pulse of reality.

"I couldn't cross that!" said Onny, pulling back, as they came to the fringe of the water where a breeze had ruffled the shallows slightly, making faint noises of sighing and lisping.

"Of course you can," said Gabriel, still holding her hand, and jerking it, with a mixture of impatience and encouragement.

He looked at her and saw that with the jerk to her hand an alteration had come in the colour of her cheeks. He was amused. He jerked her again, more gently.

"Of course you can," he repeated idly, because he was watching her face, where the colouring shifted slightly again with the force of the jerk.

A great careless gaiety came into his heart. He looked around him quickly and examined the stones with a glance, putting out his foot and trying to see if this one was steady, if that one was steady, if it was possible to reach from either of them to another one, which was more isolated and further out in the stream.

"Put your foot on this one," he directed then, stepping back on the bank, and pulling up a stem of green sally from the boundary hedge, he pointed to a large stone, smooth and slate-coloured, which was flat like a chiselled steppingstone.

Onny hesitated one moment more, and then biting her lip in her teeth she put out the tip of her foot nervously and tried to stir the stone. It did not move. She gained more confidence, and leaning forward so that her weight fell on the foot which pressed against the stone, she pressed it several times, allowing her other foot to rise from the bank until it barely tipped the security of the ground and was merely a symbol of the fact that she had not yet given her full confidence to the idea.

"Go on. Why are you afraid?" said Gabriel, and with the leafy end of the sally rod he tickled the yellow silk ankle of the foot which still rested on the grass.

"Oh! My stockings! Be careful, you'll tear them," said Onny, looking over her shoulder in a far greater concern for the silk covering upon the left leg than she had displayed for the security of the right foot poised upon the stone.

Gabriel continued to tickle the silk ankle with the soft tufty leaves of the sally rod.

"I'll tear it if you don't move on," he said, and he began to trace the stiff line of the coarse seam upon the stocking with the small sensitive fingers of the twig.

"They'll tear! I'll be a show with my stockings all torn," wailed Onny.

"You know what to do!" said Gabriel.

With one last look of appeal, to which Gabriel remained un-susceptible, Onny drew in an abrupt breath, and shifting the right foot slightly upon the stone made way for the other foot, which she brought across with such a jerk that the stone rocked slightly.

"I'm falling!" she called out, but she at once threw out her arms and righted herself, and this time, owing her courage to the reassurance of her own balancing, she began to enjoy the idea. She looked for another steppingstone and began to try it with the point of her shoe.

"Not that one!" called Gabriel, each time, as she stirred a stone and sent a slow ripple of water out from under it.

"Look, try this one," he called at last, and he pointed with the sally rod to a rough, edgy stone of a granite discoloured by the yellow waters that had covered it all winter.

"I want a flat stone," said Onny, looking at it distrustfully.

"Do as I say," said Gabriel. "Put your left foot on that one, and only touch it lightly and spring from it to that big stone beside the reeds."

"I won't be able to reach that far."

"Try it."

"I'm afraid."

"Try it."

Onny drew another breath and sprang from the yellow rock to the large flat stone among the reeds.

"You're nearly halfway across now," said Gabriel.

The stone that Onny stood upon was the last large stone in the shallow waters. Underneath it on the far side, the river ran deeper, with the only current which carried the fresh water onwards to the main river. The current was slight, but in comparison with the flat and stagnant waters under the bank, it appeared to be very fast. Onny stared down at its swiftly running ripples.

"There's no stone to step on!" she said.

"There's a stone on the other side of the current," said Gabriel. "Stretch your foot across!"

"It's too wide!"

"Jump then!"

"It's too deep, I might fall."

Onny's voice was faltering. She stared at the running water and she began to follow certain ripples with her eyes, until new ripples attracted her attention and she looked back, only to follow them. Her gaze seemed to ride along a little way with each ripple that passed, and then run back again to follow another. Fascinated, her head began to sway in rhythm with the ripples.

"Stop looking down!" called Gabriel. "Look up! Onny."

Onny tore her eyes away from the water and looked up into the sky. Over her head the evening clouds were moving onwards in the same way as the water, to their haven in the west. She looked down. She looked up again. Below her the world was moving. Above her the clouds travelled. Her head began to reel. The stone under her was for a moment the most secure rock on the surface of the earth but, almost at once, she began to have a sensation that the water was still and motionless, that the clouds were painted fast to a motionless sky, and that it was the rock she stood upon that was travelling. The rock was moving! And she was poised on it, with foothold enough only to stand, and nothing to grasp. She stared in a last desperate hope at the banks to either side of her. Both were now equally far away. And, slyly and meanly, the banks were gliding away from her too, with a vicious waving of the grasses that fringed their sides.

"I'm falling!" cried Onny, and she threw out her hands and tried to balance herself.

"Keep your head, Onny," shouted Gabriel, and he looked at her.

There was something inexpressibly comic in the attitude of the girl, perched on the sturdy rock, secure and safe, but in her excitement tilting forward, more and more, to the rippling waters, and waving her arms, more and more wildly, like a bird flapping its foolish wings as she became more and more fascinated by the water and more and more unbalanced by her fascination.

"If you keep on like that you will fall in for a certainty," he shouted. "Keep your head, Onny. Stop waving your arms."

But even while he spoke he felt an irrepressible impulse to laugh at the thought that she might topple into the shallow river. He could imagine the splash. He could imagine the cry of consternation. And above all he could imagine the draggled girl, being helped out on to the bank, her hair hanging lank and her clothes stuck to her skin as wet fur sticks to a drenched dog.

"You'll fall, all right, Onny," he said, and this time he doubled up on the bank and laughed, holding his sides. But all at once, when he heard his own loud laughter it seemed coarse and unnecessary, and through it he heard a small agonized voice, from the middle of the stream.

"My shoes. I have my good shoes on me. And my coat. My good coat!"

And at once the figure that had seemed so comic to him became so tragic that he caught his breath. The pitiful red dress with the green bow, the bright blue coat, the dotted handkerchief, and the shiny black shoes with the silver buckles seemed in an instant to represent all that was gay and courageous and festive in the dull walled town, and the waters that ran sluggish and clogged seemed to be but another force of the oppression that daily waylaid his own heart.

"Hold on, I'm coming," he shouted, and splashing into the water, not caring whether he landed on them or not, he leaped from stone to stone, and just as the last vestige of control departed from the dazzled Onny and she tilted forward with a gasp, he landed on the stone beside her with one foot on the outer edge and the other foot between Onny's patent shoes, and throwing out his arms, he caught her against him and bound her tight to himself and to the security of his steady nerve.

Onny faced outwards to the far bank. Gabriel faced the same way, his breast pressed close to her thin shoulders. Against the frame of her body he could hear his own heart beat, and the great gasping breath that he created stirred the light down on the back of her neck. Onny said nothing. Tears of relief had come into her eyes and he could hear her give short childish sobs that shook her slightly. He held her closer and tried to make his own breathing more even.

While he composed himself he looked around to see what he would do. From the position in which they stood it might be easier to continue across the stream than to try to get back to the bank they had left. It would be difficult to get Onny to turn around. His breath came more evenly.

"Are you all right, Onny?" He slackened his hold upon her.

"How will we get back?" said Onny.

"You're not afraid now that I'm with you?" said Gabriel.

"I don't know!" said Onny.

This was such a challenge that Gabriel took a last long breath. "Do as I say now," he ordered, and gripping her tightly around the waist, he called out " Jump!" and literally lifting her in his arms he leaped across the moving water and came to a slippery foothold on a large horny stone in the shallows on the other side of the current. Onny's feet brushed against the reeds as they landed. They hardly touched the stone. "Ready?" said Gabriel, and he leaped again, this time landing securely on a flat stone and bringing Onny's feet down upon the safe and even surface, with a reassuring laugh.

"Now, I brought you safe. Didn't I?" he said, as he took his arm from her waist, and twirled her round to face him. "We are beyond the dangerous part." For it seemed, now that they had crossed it, that the crossing of the river had been a hazardous and dangerous operation, and that saving the black shiny shoes from a wetting in the river was an achievement worthy of self-congratulation.

"We can pick our way out from here without any difficulty."

But he put out his hand and caught Onny's hand as he stepped from one stone to another, and as he guided her he looked with amusement once again at the changing expressions that flitted across her face, as a stone tilted slightly, a pebble loosened and rolled over on the river floor, or a ripple created by a loosened reed that pierced the surface set the waters murmuring softly.

"I thought you were a great adventurer!" he said. "I thought you did not have an ounce of fear in your whole body." And then the old inclination to tease began to rise again. "Is this the girl that was not afraid to play hide-and-seek in a graveyard?" He sprang up on to the bank at the other side, giving such a jerk to Onny's wrist that when she was lifted up beside him she was very close to him and he could see the tear marks on her flushed face. "Now your face is dirty," he said.

Onny took out the spotted handkerchief. She turned around and dipped it in the stream behind her and began to wipe it gently over her face while the fresh tears began to run down in the tracks of the old.

"You are a funny girl!" said Gabriel. "Why are you crying now?"

"I'm all dirty and my dress is splashed. They'll all laugh at me, when I get to the crossroads."

At the mention of the crossroads Gabriel's own face fell. In the excitement of negotiating the stream, and in his amusement at his companion's expressions, he had completely forgotten the object of the journey across the river. He had forgotten that he was only a casual agent in helping Onny to take a short cut to her destination. He forgot that it was for her companions at the crossroads that she wore her festive colours and her glittering slipper buckles. He forgot that, now, once she was set securely upon the far bank, she would be bidding him good-bye and leaving him to his loneliness while she sped off through the damp evening grasses in the direction of the darkening skyline from which the silver evening voices volleyed through the trees.

And looking around him at the darkening spaces of the old park, where the colours were deepened with that last desperate depth of colour that the earth takes on before night descends, he felt a passionate desire to enjoy the evening and to be gay, to be lighthearted. The bank of the river which he had left was like the shore of another world; a dull world of routine and convention. Crossing the river he seemed to have stepped into an enchanted land where everything wore a new shape, a new colour, and where the sounds of the earth were different.

He listened. Low sounds stirred in the dead beech leaves under the wild laurels. A flight of dark birds agitated the dry leaves in the tree tops. And from somewhere in the wet grass a pheasant gave a lonely cry.

He had stepped into the enchanted land towards which he had yearned in childhood, when standing far back in his bedroom, his chilled feet upon the cold floor, he had raised an imaginary gun to his shoulder and fired innumerable shots at innumerable imaginary pheasants. This was the estate of which he had dreamed himself the ruling lord. This was the dark, secret place where he had set the living scene for every story

259

he had read. This was the unreal land. This was the land of impossible dreams and impossible actions.

He looked back at Onny. He looked at her face rubbed red with the damp linen of the handkerchief she had dipped in the river. He looked at the decked-out bodice of the red dress. He looked at the glittering shoe buckles. He looked at the riotous unruly curls of the heavy copper hair. He looked at the bright eyes that were regaining their saucy twinkle. She was no longer the kitchen drudge. She was young. She was decked for a fancy evening. She was pleating the folds of her dress and looking out towards the crossroads where young men and women were taking the full advantage of their youth in gaiety and laughter.

"Onny! I'm going with you! I can dance as well as any of your friends. I can sing. I can play a mouth organ if necessary."

Gabriel caught up a reed from the edge of the river and blowing along its lacerative edge he raised a thin note that yet was sweet and piercing.

" Show me!" Onny pulled the reed from him and blew along it. There was no sound.

"There is an art in it," said Gabriel, and he bent down and, leaving the reed still held in her hands, he put his lips to the outer edge and blew a thin breath along it.

There was again a piercingly sweet wail upon the air. As he listened to it he stared into Onny's eyes over the cold edge of the river reed.

Onny's eyes widened. "You cannot come to the crossroads!" she said.

"Why not?"

"Because!"

"Don't you want me to go?"

"It's not that," said Onny.

"What is it?"

She tore her eyes away from him. She looked away into space but she jerked her head backwards to indicate the other side of the river where the back of the Coniffe house stared across at them with its blank windows.

"Your aunts would hear about it," said Onny. "It's only shop boys and lads from the farm that go over to the crossroads."

"What do I care about my aunts?" said Gabriel, for the river seemed to have widened until he felt that never again would he recross it and go back to the old flat life of obedience and self-abasement.

"If they found out you came with me I'd be sent home," said Onny.

Gabriel looked down from the grey façade of the house across the river. "How would they find out?" he said, seeking eagerly to be deluded, to have the truth of her words erased by a recklessness that would carry his own recklessness forward beyond hope of control. But he knew that she was speaking the truth and that his aunts would be bewildered and insulted if they heard that he had gone to dance at the crossroads with the servant girl from their own house, and those of her class who met her there.

"Bad news travels fast," said Onny. "There are plenty of people that are ready to spread a lie without giving them a chance to spread a story that's true!"

She began to move away slowly in the direction of the rampart where, even at this distance, a gap could be seen leading into the lighter fields beyond that led out to the cemetery road.

"Onny! Wait!" Gabriel ran after her. "Were you ever up in the ruins of the old tower?"

"It's ghosty!" said Onny.

"I thought you said that you wouldn't be afraid with me?"

"You can't get up there! The stones are loose. The steps are broken."

"I was up there a few times. I dragged myself up on the ivy. I'd pull you up after me."

"Why do you want to go up there? It's only an old tower. It's all crumbling to pieces."

"You can see out over the whole town; over all the ramparts and over the fields. You can see your cottage. You can see the cemetery. You can see the dancers at the crossroads and you can hear the music floating up through the air."

"It's too dark to see anything at this hour," said Onny, and she looked up at the first pale stars that were piercing through the sky above them.

"Well! What better could we have to look at than the stars?" said Gabriel, and he looked up at them himself.

Onny looked at his throat that arched with the terrifying strength of a man under the thin skin of a boy.

"I'd get light in my head up there on the broken stones looking at the stars," she said.

Gabriel looked down at her.

"I'd hold you!" he said. "I'd hold you tight so that you couldn't fall."

And while he spoke he put out his hand to her and drew her arm through his arm, and led her slow feet across the dark grasses towards the tower. He was unable to speak, because the memory of holding her against him while they stood on the stone in the middle of the river had returned to intoxicate him in a way that it had not done while they stood there in the flesh. He could feel again the beat of his own heart against the rounded curve of her shoulders and he began to hasten his steps, for already his blood was busy with anticipation of the moment when he would draw her up beside him on the crumbling ledge of the cold glassless castle, and his pulses throbbed with a pitiful violence when he felt the full significance of the fact that this time it would be her soft bosom that would be pressed to his breast.

∽ ∽ ∽

After the first evening that they spent in the old tower, Gabriel met Onny Soraghan there every evening when he came back from Draghead and when her work in Clewe Street was done. She brought him distraction from the discontent that Sylvester had planted in his mind. The hours took wing, and day flew forward after day.

From the first, Gabriel was aware that his aunts would bitterly disapprove of his meetings with Onny, but he had gradually lost confidence in their judgment of conduct, and whatever misgivings he may have had from within, vanished after a few meetings and it seemed to him that he was justified in taking his own decision in the matter.

As time went on however and their relations became more intimate, Gabriel was no longer able to delude himself that he was innocent. Yet, he justified himself, and as he looked at Onny sometimes in the kitchen in Clewe Street and saw her wretched poverty of attire, and her unkempt hair which she had hardly ever time to drag out with a comb, he asked himself if there was not still something to be said for the way in which they had come together, for if he had not grown familiar with her rich warmth, and her impudent vitality, in the dark hours in the old tower, he would never have seen in her any more than his aunts saw, a miserable servant girl, unkempt and ill-clad.

It must not be thought that Gabriel had any ideas about free love, or the independence of the sexes. Such ideas were unknown to him, he had neither heard of them nor read of them. He only knew that Onny Soraghan never would have come into his life if his meetings with her had been confined to those that convention permitted. They would have been less than strangers; two people familiar with each other's appearance, but ignorant of, and uninterested in, anything that the other might possess in the way of a soul. And it never entered his head to doubt the wisdom of things as they were.

There was need for a great discretion in their meetings, and so, immediately after supper, Gabriel went out, ostensibly for a walk, and, making his way out of the town, he slipped inside the rampart wall by the same fissure through which he and Sylvester used to make their entry. Instead, however, of walking along inside the wall and climbing up on to it, as he had done with Sylvester, he threaded through the damp grass and thick undergrowth and made his way to the tower. There he sat waiting for her.

Onny herself had more difficulties in making excuses to get out. When her work at Clewe Street was finished she ran home and let her mother know she was free. Then upon one pretext or another she evaded the tasks that were awaiting her there and slipped out again. One night she would say she was going for a walk. Another night she would say that she was going down to the church. And yet on another night she would say that she was going back to do some late work for Miss Coniffe. But whatever excuse Onny made it was sufficient for her to escape from the door of the house, for once outside it was only a matter of a minute to reach the rampart wall and join Gabriel. She did not have his need for care in entering the rampart. She could go as boldly as she liked, for the young Soraghans had always been seen playing in and out of the long cracks in the high wall behind their cottage, and no one would wonder at seeing her in that vicinity. Even if her mother had chanced to come to the door after Onny had gone out, she would not have noticed that Onny went in the opposite direction from that in which she was supposed to be going, for Mrs. Soraghan was a woman who was so weighed down with her work that it was a matter of complete indifference to her whether she was within or without the house.

As she went about her chores, Mrs. Soraghan ran in and out of the house as often as she ran from room to room. Now she would dart over to the fire and pull back a kettle that was boiling over with a spitting noise. Now she would dart over to the back door and throw out a basin of dirty water into the yard. At one moment she would run into the bedroom off the kitchen to gather up a few socks and shirts for the washtub, and a few minutes after she would dart out of the door again to fling the wet garments on the hedge to dry. She would no more have thought to look to either side, to pause and glance at the surrounding country, than she would have thought to stop up in the middle of the kitchen and admire the wallpaper roses of red and orange that still persisted brightly on their smoky background.

Once within the rampart, however, Gabriel and Onny were both secure. And yet so great was the pressure of their secrecy upon them that hardly a bird stirred in the brushwood, hardly a rabbit ran through the stiff green grasses, and hardly a branch stirred in the far tops of the trees, without causing them to lift their heads in fright. Never again could they risk crossing the river at the end of the garden, because what was done without thought of danger could never be repeated again with the same spirit, and the back windows of the house in Clewe Street that had seemed like vacant and blind eyes upon that first evening seemed now, even when they gazed at them from the far, secure distance of the old tower, to be jealous, living eyes, that pierced the stone walls of the tower and the dark mists of the night that came down around it before Onny was able to break away from him, and wrap her old threadbare coat tighter across her breast, and say that if she did not go home her mother would be out looking for her.

"She'll be out at the gate looking up and down the road!"

"Is it the mother of fourteen children?" Gabriel said. "If half of you were to fall in the river she wouldn't miss you for a week!"

There were times when Onny could not know from Gabriel's words whether he was teasing her, or whether he was in earnest. If she was able to see his face she could usually tell from the sparkle that he could not keep out of his eyes, but knowing that, Gabriel always tried to hold her against him so closely that she could not stretch back her head to look up into his face. However, in the weeks that had passed since they crossed the river on the stones, familiarity had shown them that no matter how numerous or how various the tyrannies they imposed upon each other, they were both of them subject to some tyrannical influence that made them eager to meet and loth to part.

"It's early—you don't need to go so soon!" said Gabriel. "Listen! The birds are not quiet yet; it can't be very late."

The birds had long since silenced their songs but a faint rustling of the decaying leaves in a tree top near by would give him a pretext for enforcing his will on her.

"It's very late. The lights are gone out in the hotel!" Onny would struggle.

"But the light is burning brighter than ever in Finnertys'!" Gabriel would hold her closer.

"The lights in the presbytery are gone out!"

"The priests go to bed with the flowers!"

"They do not. They stay up playing cards until all hours. My mother used to wash up the dishes for the Canon when his housekeeper was ill last winter and she said . . ."

"Yes? What did your mother say?" Gabriel would begin to stroke her hair, absent-mindedly.

Onny would jerk her head. "You don't care what my mother said! You just want to keep me here! Let me go! They'll be looking for me I tell you!"

"It will be a good thing to bring your poor mother out of doors. She looks as if she never got a breath of fresh air. I think sometimes that she's tied by the leg to that cottage."

"A lot you care about my mother!"

When Onny struggled against him her determination was roused more by his resistance than by real desire to leave him. His struggles to hold her against her will had a sweetness for her that the earlier caresses of the evening lacked entirely. In the intervals between her struggling, when she had to rest, she laid her head against his shoulder and accepted his

264

kisses, but this docility lasted only as long as it took to renew her breath and her strength.

For her this was the exciting climax of the evening, but when, through the slits in the old tower wall she saw that not merely windows of the old and cantankerous, but all the windows in the town were darkening, one after another, steadily, and beyond doubt of their implication as to the lateness of the hour, she made no further attempt to struggle but gave him instead some reminder of the consequences that would attend his foolishness.

One evening when she had told her mother that she was going back to help Miss Coniffe with some jam making, she foretold a particularly dire consequence that might attend them if Gabriel did not release her quickly and let her go home.

"My mother might come out looking for me. She might call to ask Miss Coniffe what time I left Clewe Street!"

Somewhat to her surprise Gabriel at once released his hold. Her suggestion was one that sounded very credible—Mrs. Soraghan if she missed Onny might indeed call at Coniffes' to inquire about her—but it was not the suggestion itself that made Gabriel drop his hands to his sides and turn away so abruptly; it was a sudden anger that he felt towards Onny herself for using this threat to force his will. Keeping his hands straight down by his sides, he looked at her coldly.

"Why did you say that, Onny?" he said.

"Say what?" Onny felt at once that he was angry but she did not see why he had been angered and so she pretended not to remember what she had said.

"You know what I mean. Why did you say that your mother would come to Clewe Street?"

Onny hesitated for a moment. She was tempted to deny that she had said any such thing and to persuade him that he had not heard her rightly, or at least that he had misunderstood her meaning, but in a spirit of defiance she flew to the opposite extreme and not only answered him that she meant what she said, but proceeded to reaffirm her words.

"What I said is true!" she said, doggedly.

"That's not important," said Gabriel. "As a matter of fact it's very likely that she might come, and you had better get home as quickly as you can, but—" and here he put his hands firmly upon her arms— "but before you go I want to know why you said it just then?"

Onny shrugged her arms to free them. His fingers tightened.

"I forget why I said it. A person doesn't remember every word he says."

"Did you say it to have a hold over me?" Gabriel pressed his fingers deeper into her arm.

"You're hurting me!" said Onny. "I don't know what you mean!"

"Did you want to humiliate me?"

"Let go my arm!"

"Did you think I would be afraid of what my aunts might think?"
Onny bit her lower lip.

"Did you want to shame me?"

"I don't know what you're talking about," said Onny.

What was the matter with him, she wondered. She knew hate, and she knew love, she knew fear and she knew joy. She knew all the simple emotions of the human heart, and she could read their expression in the human face, but before this strange complexity in the heart of Gabriel, which left his cold face inscrutable, Onny was helpless and humbled. She knew nothing of the complexities of the heart that form in the long hours of a lonely childhood. In the Soraghan family solitude was unknown. Even in the fastness of the night there was always a child tossing and moaning in the dark. And in the Soraghan children, as in their father and mother before them, all traces of temperament and individuality were early brought under the discipline of hard toil and sweat.

"I don't know what you're talking about!" she said again, pitifully. And suddenly Gabriel believed her. He made a great effort and conquered his desire to probe her heart further. "I want to go home!" she said.

"You may go, Onny," said Gabriel. Then, when she stood hesitatingly without speaking, he took her hands in his again. "I was very hard on you, Onny, but I had a reason. I wanted to show you that you must never have any feeling underneath the words you say to me. Say whatever you like to me. Be bitter! Be condemning! Accuse me! Cut me! But never say one thing and mean another. Never say something, as you did tonight, that seems simple and inoffensive at the time that it is said, but which when it is remembered afterwards may reveal a sting." He looked down at her seriously, doubtful whether she understood him or not, but as he saw her beginning to relax he continued. "I want everything to be clear between us, Onny, as clear as the stars up there above us!" And he lifted her face and tilted it upwards towards the starry sky. Then, patting her cheek and taking her by the hand like a small child, he spoke in a quite different voice. "I'll go down first," he said, "and I'll lift you down." He slipped down over the stone rim of the tower and lowered himself cautiously, seeking a foothold on a ledge beneath. "Give me your hand," he said. "Be careful." And he began to guide her. When he had reached the grass below and she was still on a ledge above him on the level of his chest he called out to her gaily. "Jump!" he commanded. "Jump!"

And then as he set her down in the grass, he put his hand under her cheek again and stared into her face. "I'm going to walk out to the road with you," he said. "I don't care who sees me."

Usually when they reached the rampart wall they spent some time looking up and down the road to see that they were unobserved, but on this occasion Gabriel strode towards the gap boldly and helped Onny to climb through it. He was just about to follow her when she turned suddenly and gave him a gentle push that put him back into the grass in an effort to balance himself, and when he had clambered up again she was gone, and he could hear her footsteps ringing on the hard road, and hear her voice call out to someone whom she had encountered there.

He waited until he heard the ring of the iron gate in front of the cottage and then he went out on to the road himself and began to walk back towards the town.

His mind was uneasy. He knew that she had had some taunt behind her words and it worried him to think that there might have been some cunning in her heart. The suspicions she had roused threw their shadows over him as he walked along, and he tried to recall her face as she had spoken. But the memory of her impudent face, with the bright open cheeks and lips and the bold eyes, was as potent as her presence to silence his suspicions. He had given in to the influence of her memory so much that he felt the same humility before her simplicity as she herself had felt before his complexity, and, added to the mystery of sex that held them together, there was a new and meretricious mystery of mind.

∽ ∽ ∽

The winter set in at last. The nights were dark without relief of stars, and even at the hour at which Onny left Clewe Street there was a dark journey ahead of her, out of the town to the cottage.

For this reason Miss Sara Coniffe tried to let her finish her work as early as possible, and urged upon her from time to time, as she went round her tasks, the danger of delaying so long that it would be dark upon the roads.

"You have no idea of the dangers," said Miss Sara, without, however, making any effort to enlighten her, as the girl hurried to brush the sweepings into the grate, and fill the coal buckets to leave ready for the long night by the fire.

"I don't know why you keep urging Onny to hurry," said Theresa, when they sat sewing, after the girl had gone home. "I never in my life saw anyone more anxious to put off her apron than that girl."

"I wouldn't blame her too much for that, Theresa," said Miss Sara, timidly. "She does a long, hard day's work, and then she is very young."

"It's because she's young she's hired to work," said Theresa testily.

"If she doesn't work now she won't have money when she's too old to work."

"But I think she gives all her money to her mother," said Sara. Theresa Coniffe stared pityingly at her sister.

"What do you expect!" she said. "Do you think she should spend it all on herself, and the family crying for bread?"

"Oh no. No!" said Miss Sara. "Of course I want her to give it to her poor mother. How could you imagine that I would want anything else, Theresa? It was only that I thought it hard for the child to work all day long and never have a few hours to rest, or even a few pence to buy hair ribbons."

"Hair ribbons! Are you getting soft in the head? What would the like of her want with hair ribbons? She's bold and brassy enough without decking herself out like a circus queen. If you ask me, she gets back a good few of the pence she gives up, and it's not on her hair she spends it. She'd go stark naked rather than go without a pair of flashy stockings on those bold legs of hers."

"I used to love stockings, myself," said Miss Sara, sighing, "and when we were her age there was hardly anything of our stocking seen at all!"

"Well, let me tell you! There's more of Onny Soraghan's seen than fashion caters for—the girl is man-mad."

"You cannot blame her, Theresa, if she thinks of having a home of her own. It's only natural. I suppose she has an admirer!"

Theresa tapped her foot on the carpet. "Sara Coniffe, it's a strange thing to hear a woman of your age romancing about things that ought by right to be beneath your notice. All I can say is that I hope you will keep your romancing to yourself, and not put ideas into the head of one that has too many similar ideas already!"

Sara lowered her eyes. She picked up the dull-coloured linen table centre, on which she was embroidering a green and yellow dragon with a red tongue. She jabbed the needle into the tip of the dragon's tail, with a venom of industry most unlike her usual patient stitching.

"After all she's not much younger than Gabriel, and think of all the liberty and pleasure he has compared with her!"

"Gabriel is a gentleman!" said Theresa. "And there can be no comparison, except in the head of a fool, between the son of a gentleman and a slut of a servant with flashy legs. You don't open your mouth very often, Sara, but when you do it's hard for a person not to say that it's a good thing you keep it shut for the best part of the time."

Sara would hardly have made any answer to this criticism had she been listening, but at the moment her attention had been carried away by a sound at the door. "It might be Gabriel," she thought and she was about to exclaim her thoughts when she stopped. There was no use in drawing Theresa's attention to the hour.

For some time past while they were sewing and talking, Sara had been aware of the lateness of the hour and of Gabriel's absence, but every minute she was hoping that Theresa would stand up to go to bed.

In spite of her general conformity to her sister's habits Sara had made a stand on one small point. She went to bed at whatever time she chose, and it was always a later hour than that at which Theresa was in the habit of retiring. As a girl, as a young woman, she had had this habit of staying up until all hours; sitting by the fire in winter or by the open window in summer.

"I can't understand it!" Theresa said, time and again. "What is the use of sleeping bolt upright on a hard chair when you can lie comfortably in your bed?" For unless Theresa was actively engaged at something, sewing or talking, making up the accounts, she wouldn't be two minutes sitting in her chair until she was nodding to sleep. Theresa knew nothing of the dreams that Sara wove when all the house was still and the night outside was dark and peaceful. And Sara had not given up her habit even when the bright dreams of the future had changed to sad memories of the past. Long after Theresa had yawned, folded up her work, and gone stiffly up the stairs, her younger sister sat in her chair, sat there till long after eleven, till midnight, sometimes till later still. And so, it was natural that even in Theodore's time, when she was still very young, Sara had been given the care of locking up the house for the night, securing the windows, seeing that the lamps were extinguished and the fires dead. In those days of course Lily sometimes stayed up with her, but this ended with Lily's marriage. After her marriage Lily always went upstairs at the same time as Cornelius. And afterwards, when she was a widow, she nearly always had to stay upstairs with Gabriel for so long a time, trying to put him to sleep with songs and stories, that she usually lay across her own bed and fell asleep. When she woke up it was often dusk and the simplest thing was to undress and remain upstairs for the night. Later, when Gabriel grew up, for the first time Sara had someone to keep her company at night because Gabriel liked to read for a while before he went to bed. Sometimes he took a walk, particularly if Sylvester was at home, and even alone if the evening was fine. "You won't be gone to bed, Aunt Sara?" he asked.

"Oh there's no fear of that," Theresa said if she had not already gone upstairs herself, and in the opportunity afforded her of condemning Sara's late hours she overlooked the implication about Gabriel. Sara herself overlooked it also for a long time. It was pleasant to sit quiet in the empty house as she had always done, and yet not to have the feeling that she was the only one stirring in the town, but that her strong young nephew would come down the silent street in time to help her in bolting and barring the doors. In fact she had begun to count on his help because of late the heavy iron bars that had to be drawn across the shutters seemed heavier than they used to be. Gabriel was so strong; he was able to draw them across so easily, without straining. But for some time past Sara, in spite of her own bad habits in this respect, had begun to feel uneasy about Gabriel. He was staying out too late. At first he was only a little later than usual, but in the last month or so even she, even she, had begun to yawn and feel sleepy, and on at least two or three occasions she had not waited for him to help her but had locked and barred the house herself in order to be able to go right up the stairs the minute he came in the door. But instead of being cross she had been apologetic.

"I don't know what is coming over me. I usedn't to be like this, Gabriel, but tonight I could not keep my eyes open. Why long ago I could have sat and watched for the daylight. I suppose it's not right to expect to be always the same."

And Gabriel had been contrite.

"You look tired, Aunt Sara," he said with real compunction. Sara's main concern, however, was to hush him.

"Not so loud, Gabriel dear!" she cried, putting her finger to her lips. "You'll waken your Aunt Theresa."

For the only danger that Sara saw for either of them in the late hour that Gabriel came home was the danger of Theresa's detecting it. As it was Theresa knew nothing of it.

"She wouldn't understand, you know, Gabriel," Sara continued in a whisper, "Theresa is so wonderfully practical and sensible. She has no time for dreamers like us." She smiled at him. "It isn't everyone who can appreciate solitude," she said, for except when she knew him to be out with Sylvester, it never occurred to Sara but that her nephew spent his time out of doors in much the same way in which she spent hers within doors. True, once or twice, she had found a suspicion entering her mind that he was not altogether as simple as they thought. For instance the evening that she had spoken about solitude. She fancied he reddened that evening. And after that she sometimes wondered about him. Could it be that there was a romance in the family which they had not discovered? Her mind flew at once to explore the possibility of this, but it alighted on the nearest and most convenient perch. What about the Finnerty girls? She was never satisfied about them; never convinced that Gabriel could be indifferent to them. Agnes in particular was such a sweet girl. Something about her always reminded Sara of her own youth. She used to wear blue too. This fancy reassured Sara for a few nights. Theresa would not be so annoyed at Gabriel's behaviour if it meant that he was suffering from a romantic attachment to Agnes

Finnerty, or even to Hannah. And who else was there in the town in the least likely to take the eye of a young man like Gabriel? Still it was hard to see how even this could keep him out so late. The Finnerty girls would never be allowed to stay out one part as late as the hour at which Gabriel had returned on some occasions. And they would hardly permit Gabriel to visit there so late either. In fact, Sara recalled with alarm that his footsteps came from the opposite direction and although she could attribute this to romantic motives also, she was gradually, night after night, becoming more and more uneasy. And this particular evening, when above all things Theresa had stayed up unusually late, to finish a corner of her embroidery; Sara had grown almost feverish in case it should come to her attention that Gabriel was not yet home.

To her relief, however, the sound she heard was made by Gabriel. It was he coming up the passageway. And although it was late Theresa did not seem to be aware of it. On the contrary, accustomed to go to bed early without seeing Gabriel after his walk, it seemed to her now that he had come home early. And so greatly was she relishing the topic under discussion with Sara that she was even sorry he had come so soon.

"I hope there will be a different topic on your tongue before him!" she said impatiently when Sara started to her feet and exclaimed that it was their nephew.

And then as Gabriel walked down the passage and came into the room, she raised her voice in a bright, clear tone, easily recognizable as the tone adopted when hurriedly changing the subject of conversation. "It was a very nice day," she said. "Such sun! But it's. getting chilly now." She did not look up at Gabriel when he crossed the threshold of the room, but when he walked over to the fire, and threw a shadow across her sewing, she looked up, and in an even brighter voice, like that of an actress in a third-rate company, she let her sewing drop.

"Oh Gabriel, there you are! I didn't hear you coming in!"

A blush stole over Sara's face. She bent her head closer to her sewing. Gabriel glanced at her. He needed only to confirm his own suspicions of Theresa by looking at Sara, because, although habit and discipline had long ago brought her words and gestures into harmony with the words and gestures of Theresa, her sensitive heart was still undisciplined and when there was insincerity in the air that heart sent out its message of blood to the pale cheeks.

Gabriel smiled mechanically at Theresa and sat down by the fire and held out his hands. After a minute he withdrew them and picked up the end of Sara's embroidery square.

"Is this a dragon?" he asked. "Why is he green and yellow? Are they the right colours for a dragon?"

271

"I think they are nice colours for one," said Sara, striving to justify her choice of embroidery floss without going beyond the limits of truth.

"They may be nice colours, but I am sure they are not the correct colours. I am surprised at you, of all people, Aunt Sara, trying to distort the truth!"

Miss Theresa Coniffe listened to this conversation. She felt slightly nervous of stepping into it herself. Gabriel and Sara skated over it easily enough, but it seemed to her that its surface had a dangerously brittle quality that she was afraid to try. Yet she did not relish standing silent on the bank, so she prepared to step forward on to the ice. Boldness was the right attitude under the circumstances.

"There is no such thing as a dragon!" said Theresa emphatically. "There are no real dragons. They are like unicorns and mermaids. They are only found in fairy tales!"

Gabriel winked at his Aunt Sara.

"Oh, they are real enough! Aren't they, Aunt Sara!" He turned to Theresa with mock seriousness. "Aunt Sara has, in fact, made a study of them. She knows all there is to be known about them; their habitations and their inclinations. Although I regret to say she is terrified out of her wits of them!"

Sara blushed red to the tips of her ears.

"Don't mind him, Theresa," she said. "He's only joking!"

"I can tell a joke when I hear one, as well as anyone, and without help from others," said Theresa, trying to smile, but not with great success. Then she regained her usual confidence. "As a matter of fact, Sara, now that you remind me, I may as well tell you that you should cure yourself of that very irritating habit that I have noticed you falling into of late, the habit of explaining things to people who, as often as not, have more understanding than you have yourself. I only mention this for your own good, because a habit like that would make you very conspicuous, and very unpopular. People would laugh at you, and imitate you behind your back. I only mention it for your own good. I'm sure Gabriel will agree with me?"

Theresa turned to Gabriel, but first she shot a glance of triumph at the green-and-yellow dragon because in the reference to the dragon she had been able to detect, if not to interpret, some vague criticism of herself.

Theresa's correction of Sara had brought a silence on the room. Gabriel stared into the fire. It was, of late, as Sara had said, unusual for him to come back to the house early enough to sit by the fire with his aunts. He felt the strain of having to talk to them. He began to wonder how best to get himself out of the situation in which he was involved. His real reason for returning so early had been to see if Onny had by any chance been delayed there. For the first time since he had begun to meet her in the evenings she had not turned up at the meeting place.

Since the winter had set in they no longer went into the old tower. It was sufficient now to meet inside the broken rampart, on the fallen stones on which Gabriel would sit to wait for her, without fear of being seen. They could even venture, on cloudy nights, to walk along the road, as the other strollers that they met there were in all likelihood as anxious as themselves to remain unknown. The young men might mutter a greeting in a dulled voice, but the girls always passed with averted heads and did not speak.

Under the new circumstances Gabriel felt happier than when the devices of concealing their relationship devolved entirely upon themselves, although when, on moonlit nights, it was necessary to go back to the old arts of concealment, he was all the more unhappy and oppressed. But even then Onny was usually able to change his mood before long. With a change of mood there was always a change of opinion. The secrecy that had seemed evil when he thought of it himself began to seem better when he thought with Onny's mind.

"I wouldn't want to be seen walking with a fellow, even if I was to be married to him in the morning!" said Onny on those occasions. "I think there is something common about linking a man in the broad daylight. Some girls like it, some girls would give anything to be seen walking with someone. Agnes Finnerty is always walking slowly coming out of the chapel so that some of the fellows will have to catch up with her unless they walk like snails. And she doesn't care any more for them than the feather in her cap—if she cares that much at all—but it's only that she wants to have the people see her with a man walking beside her."

A mention of Agnes Finnerty always made Gabriel vindictive.

"I wouldn't compare yourself with Agnes Finnerty, Onny. You could find better than her for your comparison!"

"I'm not comparing myself to anyone; I'm only trying to show you that you have no need to be sulky and dull, just because there's a moon out and the roads are white. It's on a moon-bright night that most fellows are in good form, but a moonlight night only puts you into worse form than other nights."

"Perhaps you'd prefer to be out with some other fellow—as you say —someone who would be in such good form that he'd make the moon seem dim, he'd raise such sparks on the road with the tips of his shoes!"

When a person is moody and sullen, it is a step forward for them to become cross. Onny would clap her hands.

"You're getting into better humour," she would say, and laugh at him till he laughed himself.

But on this particular moonlit night, when Gabriel went to the meeting

273

place, there was no sign of Onny. He waited as usual, thinking that she had been delayed, and then when more than a reasonable time had passed he began to wonder if she had come ahead of him, and stepped deeper into the park to avoid being seen. He jumped down and whistled, with a thin cautious whistle. There was no reply. The park was as bright as by daylight. The shadows of the trees fell across each other everywhere, and his own shadow, as he came out from under the wall, was outlined on the pale grass.

He wondered with concern if she could have gone to the tower alone, but as he sprang down and ran across to it he began to wonder, with a still greater concern, if she had remembered his displays of bad humour on other moonlit nights. She might have grown tired of him. She might have decided that she'd leave him alone with the moonlight. He remembered that she had spoken of the other fellows she knew, and of how gay they would be on such a night.

"You couldn't hold them," she had said. "They're half out of their minds on a moonlight night. They're ready for anything. You'd break your heart listening to the things that they'd want to do. There is no stopping them. They'd want to walk to Draghead one minute, and the next minute they'd want to hire a sidecar and go to a dance ten miles away!"

He began to run towards the tower, although he did not now expect to find her there. The cold dew began to soak into his socks at the ankles when the longer grasses brushed against his running feet. He felt sure that she had grown tired of him. He was absolutely certain that she had felt the need for gayer company, and then, at the very moment when he put his hands on the chilled ledge of the old tower and drew himself up, calling her name, there was a faraway sound of voices, voices of young people male and female, raised in a sound of singing; and when he pulled himself up into the tower, and looked in the direction of the voices, he saw a sidecar, clear as day, with a smart trotting horse, going out along the Draghead road, rocking with the gaiety of the occupants who were singing, their voices raising echoes. He could not see who they were, but he felt an absolute certainty that Onny was with them and he held hard to the stone until the sound of the singing had died away. And long after it had died away, his ears, strained with the force of concentrating for so long and so intensely, betrayed him with false echoes of the singing, and the fake singing echoes sounded more mocking and more bitter than the real.

Although he was almost convinced that Onny had grown tired of him, and had not come there at all to meet him, he continued to call her name, as he went through the trees, and at times he almost persuaded himself that he heard her answering him faintly, but he scoffed at himself for his foolishness. When he came again to the gap of brightness in the rampart and climbed out into the road, however, he was struck with another thought. Supposing that she had come there earlier than usual and when he had not joined her there at once, her imagination had become fired as his own had done, and remembering his ill-humour on other moonlight nights, she had convinced herself that he was not going to meet her. She might have hurried home in humiliation.

The imagination can furnish us with a picture so detailed in particulars, so vivid in presentation, that we acquiesce at once with the likelihood of its being a picture of the reality, yet should we have reason to doubt its veracity we are no sooner convinced of the error than we blot out the picture and start to sketch a fresh one, equally detailed, equally vivid, equally convincing. The picture of the galloping sidecar rolling along with its cargo of singing carousers was blotted out and in its place there came a pitiful picture of a humiliated girl, running along the road, the tears streaming down her face.

This picture so impressed itself upon his mind that he began to run forward in the direction of the Soraghan cottage, his hands slightly spread before him, as if the black bars of the elm-tree shadows, thrown down by the moon from the banks on the side of the road, were real barriers that came between him and his destination. What he would do when he reached the Soraghans' cottage he did not plan, or think about, because one of the outstanding disabilities of the over-imaginative mind is that it wastes in anticipating scenes of possible distress the time that should be spent in plans to cope with their eventuality.

When Gabriel reached the Soraghans' cottage he came to a sudden realization that he had no plan in his head for finding out whether or not Onny was within.

At first a reckless impulse came over him to go up to the door and ask for her, pretending that he had a message from his aunts. This impulse, however, was not strong enough to carry him through the physical acts of opening the gate, walking up the cinder path, and lifting the iron knocker. It is said that our bodies have a certain power of reasoning and that when the mind is ready to spring forward rashly, the limbs will refuse to do so. So Gabriel's hands grew limp at the thought of opening the squealing latch of the gate. His thighs trembled at the thought of walking up the pathway, and his whole body, from the delicate membrane of his stomach to the high levels of his forehead, ached at the mere thought of banging the iron knocker down upon the dull door of the cottage.

He stood for a moment irresolute and then he set off past the cottage at a brisk pace, swinging his arms, and giving a perfect impersonation of one who was so lost in the beauties of the night that he was careless of his destination, and utterly unconscious of his surroundings. When he had walked a few yards down the road, with the sound of his own footsteps ringing in his ears, he became aware that his fine display of indifference was played to an even more indifferent audience, for there was nothing human in sight, to right or left, behind or before him, and the trees, the stars, and the travelling moon were all alike apathetic to his purpose—hidden or otherwise. Even the windows of the Soraghans' cottage, when he looked back at them, were shuttered with heavy curtains and gave that almost insolent appearance of indifference which a woman can give by lowering her lids and studying her finger tips, her thoughts withdrawn within her secret heart.

He stood still again, and then he turned back towards the cottage, walking cautiously on the soft rim of the road, and when he came in front of the cottage he drew into the thick bushes on the other side of the road and, bending his head, tried to interpret the shadows that fell upon the yellow blind. He might yet find out if Onny was within, at no cost of exposure to himself, and without any profit of vanity to her. He sat down on the bank, as close as possible to the sheltering and concealing bushes, and he had no sooner done so than the door of the cottage opened suddenly and Judy Soraghan was framed in the lighted strip of the door. She looked out into the night and uttered an exclamation and her voice carried to him across the road, although she turned her head backwards to the room behind her when she spoke.

"There's no sign of her coming down the road, Mother."

Gabriel was startled. There was no name mentioned. It might not be of Onny that Judy spoke—and yet he felt that it would be too great a coincidence that his own anxiety about one member of the family should coincide with Judy's anxiety about another member of the same family. He waited, not daring to stir in case a dried leaf might rustle and betray him, or a piece of the gritty cement, that joined the blocks of stone upon the wall, should fall to the road and cause Judy to look up in that direction.

There was a sound of voices inside the cottage, and then Judy looked down the road again.

"If she's not here in another hour I'll slip down to Miss Coniffe's and ask if she's there. They might have kept her working late."

This time, Judy's voice was not so clear because evidently the person to whom she had been speaking had come nearer to the door. A second later another figure appeared in the strip of light, and Mrs. Soraghan stood beside her daughter Judy, resting one hand against the low lintel, and leaning forward to stare down the road without stepping up from the hollow of the sunken kitchen to the level of the pathway that led up to the door. As they stood in the gilt light, they were like the figures in ancient ecclesiastical mosaics, not set against a background of scenery, but against a background of plain gilt tiles, that neither tree, nor flower, nor blade of grass would distract from the simple gravity of their human forms.

After a few minutes' silence, Mrs. Soraghan spoke.

"Theresa Coniffe is a hard person to make you work, but she will never give you cause for any other kind of complaint. She will make your back ache, but she won't give you cause for worry and anxiety if she can avoid it. She would never have kept Onny working after her usual hour, without sending her home first to tell me that she would be late. I wouldn't want you to insult Miss Coniffe by sending down to ask if Onny was there! You may take it from me she is not there. It's some devilry of her own that has kept her late." The woman turned to the girl. "Do you mean to tell me that if I wasn't here to put you wise, you'd be stupid enough to go down to the Coniffes' and let them find out that Onny was out gallivanting somewhere, and that her own mother didn't know where she was, or who was with her? Would you be as stupid as all that? Would you put the words into their mouths for them to use next day when they'd send her packing home, as they would for certain? Have you no sense at all? If Onny has put this worry on her mother, that's no reason for her mother to let the whole town know about the business. Take care would you go to Coniffes'! Take care would you let on you were worried about her!" Mrs. Soraghan leaned further out across the threshold. "She'll get a good trouncing for this worry she has caused me. She won't do it again, I can tell you. My own mother used to say that she welcomed the first time a person did wrong because there is always a first time, and the sooner it comes the sooner you can make it clear that you don't want to hear of a second time!"

She moved out of the stream of light, and her next words came from the depths of the kitchen and could not be heard in the road. Judy moved over until she filled the centre of the gilt mosaic.

"All the same, Mother, if she doesn't come back before half-past eleven I think that some of us should go out and look for her."

She leaned further out into the darkness, and then the silent watcher saw that she too shrugged her shoulders and turned back into the kitchen, leaving the path of gilt light as vacant and untenanted as the stretches of blue moonlight that lay across the grass to either side of it. Someone within the cottage must have made a complaint then against the open door, for in a moment Judy reappeared, moving swiftly, and closed the door with a bang that showed as plainly as her words that her mind was not at ease, that her nerves were on edge.

Gabriel had found out all, and more, than he had sought to learn, but

277

he waited a few minutes longer in the shade to make sure that he would not be caught by another sudden opening of the cottage door as he stepped from behind his protective bushes and began to regain the road.

He had now no doubt as to Onny's whereabouts. He felt with absolute certainty that she had been one of the singing girls on the tilting sidecar that had gone out of the town, out along the Draghead road, while he stood at the ramparts waiting for her.

He stopped once in the middle of the road, as the thought occurred to him that it might be a good idea to wait in his cover under the trees and bushes until the sidecar returned that he might enjoy the spectacle of her punishment at her mother's hands, which he longed at that moment to have the pleasure of inflicting himself but which he knew from experience he would not have any desire to do when once confronted with her presence again. Then he put the thought from him, and went on homeward. It had also occurred to him that in the event of Onny's not returning soon, her mother might indeed be prevailed upon to call at the house in Clewe Street to make an inquiry for her. In that case it would be just as well if he were there when she called; otherwise there would be little difference between the real incident of her visit and the scenes that he and Onny had imagined with fear and misgiving upon many occasions. Remembering those misgivings Gabriel could not resist a feeling of satisfaction at the thought that although she had delayed with him on the tower, evening after evening while the stars wheeled higher into the sky and the lights in the houses dimmed, and were quenched, one by one, a spirit of good luck had hung over them, and the Soraghans had never begun to worry about her late hours. Now, however, when she had gone off on a cheap joy ride, although it was not yet very late, not even as late as she had been on many a night when they were together on the tower, her mother had by some chance grown uneasy about her. He felt pleased that ill-luck of this nature should have attended her escapade, since he had not shared it with her.

の の の

Gabriel let his key fall outside the hall door and had to scuffle with his foot on the dark pavement before he found it again. His foot hit against the door and the old doorframe shook, and as he found the key and placed it in the lock he smiled to think of the way his aunts would prick up their ears at the sound of his unusually early home-coming, and the clumsy manner of his entry. Their hearts would leap with fear that he had at last succumbed to the temptation of taking a drink. This was their great fear. He smiled at the thought, and stepped into the cold hall with a steady foot.

There was a sound of voices raised to a tone that would make it seem that the sisters had been arguing, although it was hard to imagine Sara raising her voice in any cause. When he was halfway down the hallway the voices dropped as suddenly as the wind falls in uneven, blustery weather. Then there was a spate of whispering and Theresa's voice broke out again with false brightness, and Gabriel knew that they were trying to hide something they had been saying, and trying to create the impression that their conversation had been altogether impersonal.

"It was a very nice day. Such sun! But it's getting chilly now," said Theresa Coniffe.

By making silly remarks about the embroidered dragon, Gabriel had hoped to distract himself from his thoughts, and when the conversation about the embroidered dragon became too thin to support his attention he introduced a little undertone of meaning into his words that they might convey more to his mild Aunt Sara than they would to the over-alert Theresa. By this simple device he hoped to make the conversation flow deeper than it might seem to those who heard only the surface ripples. But if Theresa was not quick enough to catch the undertones, she was quick enough to put an end to all conversation, and soon the silence in the room was as deep as the night outside the windows and Gabriel's thoughts intruded themselves upon him once again.

At last, however, his aunts began to look at the clock, and Sara took down the tin alarm clock that she kept under the mantel border, and began to wind it until its sharp imperative ticking filled the room. Gabriel wondered if Onny had returned, and some of the elation he had felt at the thought of the reception she would get upon her return began to die away, and give place to fears that she might not yet have returned at all.

Theresa Coniffe went upstairs. Sara began to go around the lower rooms, examining the bolts to see that they were truly shot home, and examining the latches to see that they were latched, the hasps to see that they were hasped.

"I'll hold the lamp for you, Aunt Sara," he said, rising to assist her.

"It's all right, Gabriel, thank you," said Sara, holding on to the lamp, but shielding it with her hand at that moment to look around the room and see that no truant spark had leaped from the grate to await the silence and darkness before it flared into a vicious flame. Gabriel followed her from room to room, but every few minutes he raised his head, and once or twice he asked Sara if she thought she had heard a noise. For with every minute it seemed more certain to him that if Onny had not yet returned one of the Soraghans would come to the house to inquire the hour at which she had left there.

"I think everything is all right now for the night," said Sara, and she raised the lamp above her head and gave a last glance around the lower hall. "Are you coming to bed now, Gabriel?"

The light fell on her face in such a way that her brow, and the tips of her lashes, and the wings of her wide nostrils, were lit with the soft light, while the rest of her face was obscured by the shadows these features threw. In the play of light and shade her face took on a swift grace. Gabriel stared at her with sadness. He had never thought of her youth but he realized with a rush that she must have been gentle and lovely. He forgot to answer her question, and continued to stare at her.

Sara did not repeat her question. The expression on Gabriel's face had awakened some lonely dream in her heart, and she let his eyes revive the illusion of the past in her heart as the lamp revived the illusion of youth on her brow.

Such still moments come to all quiet people, and it is a matter of wonder how long such moments of enchantment would last if interruption did not come from without, for with every moment that passes the mood of the mind gains power over the body and an inertia possesses one limb after another. Perhaps it was in one such long, mesmerized gaze that Lot's wife turned into a pillar of salt. Perhaps people who are found dead in some posture in life, sitting in a chair or leaning against a gate, may have let life slip from them in some such way. But for every one such person, of dreaming nature, there are thousands of busy active ones, and the interruption that the dreamers cannot bring about themselves comes from without.

So, as Gabriel stared at Sara, blazing with lost beauty in the illusory light of the upheld lamp, and as she gazed back at him, there was all of a sudden a sound of feet outside in the street, feet that ran urgently in the darkness, and ran in the direction of the house.

When the imagination teases us with what we think to be real, there is nothing that will show these sounds up to be fake like the introduction of a real sound. A hundred times Gabriel had fancied that he heard footsteps, and found it hard to convince himself that he was mistaken, but when the real sound came, before the running feet had reached the door, he had run towards it, and the sound of a body flinging itself against the door and a hand grasping for the knocker hardly came a second before the door was opened wide, and Gabriel, with Sara beside him, faced the person in the doorway—a person whose face was so blotched with the heat of running, and whose breath was so strangled, that it was almost a minute before even Gabriel, who might have guessed at her identity, could see that it was Onny's mother.

"Mrs. Soraghan! What is the matter? Come in. Come in."

Sara put the lamp down on the hall table and ran forward to draw the panting woman into the hall.

"Is Onny here?"

When she had said this Mrs. Soraghan had to gasp to regain the breath that she had lost in saying it.

"Is she here, is she here?" she repeated, and as if she would not be able to understand the reply, but would have to use the evidence of the only sense that was not distorted by fatigue and anxiety, she ran over to the kitchen door and opened it to look into the empty room, where the fire had long died out into a waste of white ashes.

"She's not here," she said, answering her own question and relieving the trembling Sara from having to do so. "Oh where is she at all?" and she sat down on the chair in the kitchen. "My daughter Judy wanted to come two hours ago and ask if she was here and I wouldn't let her. I was afraid it might give you and Miss Theresa a bad opinion of the girl. Wasn't I the wicked woman to put the thought of a few pence above the thought of Onny's safety?"

Miss Sara put out her hand and rested it on Mrs. Soraghan's shoulder. She gave little timid pats to the shoulder and muttered soothingly whatever came into her head.

"There now, Mrs. Soraghan, Everything will be all right. Calm yourself. Everything will be all right."

But over the bent head she looked at Gabriel with terrified eyes, and forming some urgent words noiselessly with her lips, she gave him a nod in the direction of the stairs which indicated that he was to call Theresa down again.

Gabriel went out to the stairs and went up deliberately and without undue hurry. He felt a great anger and resentment against Onny, for having drawn this attention on herself, which would surely result in her being put under a more severe control at home. She would not be able to meet him so often; nor risk staying with him as late as she had done before.

Upstairs Gabriel raised his voice and called his Aunt Theresa.

Theresa was sitting up in bed in her flannel nightdress which was designed with even greater modesty of cut and pleating than her outdoor clothes. She was combing her long hair which, although when it was set and piled over her head, displayed a great predominance of grey hair displayed when down around her shoulders a greater proportion of black hairs. The blackness of these long thin strands, however, did not give her back any appearance of youth because of the great contrast between the hanging hair and the hard, thin face it framed. Gabriel told her that Mrs. Soraghan was downstairs looking for Onny. Theresa sat up straighter.

"What do we know about Onny, after the time she leaves here?" said

Theresa, her instinct bringing a defence of herself to her lips as quickly as Sara's instinct had brought out a cry of sympathy.

"It appears they thought that we might be able to give them some information."

"She left here at the usual time," said Theresa. "How dare they think that she was kept here till this hour? Where is Mrs. Soraghan? I think it very impertinent of her to come inquiring here about a girl that leaves sharp to the minute every evening at the hour that was originally settled for her to leave, and which was never altered from the day she first set foot in the house. Where is Mrs. Soraghan?" And putting first one foot and then the other outside the crackling white bedclothes, she motioned Gabriel to go down. "Tell Mrs. Soraghan that I will come down to speak to her," she said.

But Gabriel as he went downstairs was careful to allow his imitative powers to lapse, and when he carried the message to the kitchen, although he delivered it in the exact words of Theresa, he did so in such a different tone of voice from the tone in which it was delivered to him that Sara looked up at the ceiling over their heads where the sound of Theresa's feet were plainly heard upon the boards.

"There is no one like Theresa for turning to when you are in trouble," she said.

"God bless the both of you," said Mrs Soraghan. And when Theresa herself came into the room a few minutes afterwards fully dressed as in the daytime, she was so disconcerted by the way Mrs. Soraghan ran up to her with gratitude and dependence, that the hard words she had prepared to utter died on her lips and the same impulse that had impelled Sara to offer sympathy took possession of her, with the important difference that although she was slow to offer sympathy, when she offered it, it was of a more practical nature than that extended more freely and more liberally by others.

"Sit down, Mrs. Soraghan," she said, "and tell me the details. Did she not go home at eight o'clock as usual?"

"We didn't see her since she left the house this morning, Miss Coniffe, and only for my not wanting people to know she was getting into bad habits, and staying out late, I would have sent the children looking for her earlier in the night. But once it went past half-eleven I sent them out all over the town."

"They didn't come here," said Theresa.

"I told them to leave this house until the last, and that if anyone came down to this house I'd be the one to come. I wanted to speak in a way that wouldn't put you against the girl, Miss Coniffe, and be the cause of her being sent from your employment, because as I and my husband know it's a good employment for a girl, and if it was nothing more than the training a girl would get in this house, to say nothing of her pay, it would be worth doing a lot to see that she didn't lose her job."

Mrs. Soraghan had spoken with the headlong speediness of a wheel which, once started, will roll down a hill, but which, once it reaches the flat ground again, will falter, and depart from the straight path it followed to wobble now to one side, now to another.

"What will I do?" she said. "Where will I go? When I saw the night thickening every minute, and the lights going out in every house, and the moon itself getting thin and going behind the clouds, I didn't care if she was never to do another hour's work if only she was safe and in her bed. Where can she be? What would keep her out till this hour?"

"Is there any house where she might visit? There might be dancing or singing, and she might let the time slip."

"She never went anywhere to a dance but at the crossroads and there was no dancing there this long while back. The priest put a stop to it."

"Where did she spend her evenings?"

"She spent most evenings in the best place they could be spent," said Mrs. Soraghan. "She used to be hardly settled down to the table for her evening meal when she'd be up again she was so anxious to get to the church. I think she spent the best part of her evening there, and after that she used to go for a bit of a walk."

"Who did she go walking with?" said Theresa.

"She went by herself, Miss Coniffe. She was queer and quiet in her ways. I often said that it would be a nice thing for her to have a companion of her own age, and I thought some of the girls that went to the schoolhouse with her would be nice company for her. When I was a young girl I was always with a crowd of other girls walking along the road and laughing and making a jeer out of everything that passed. But her father used to say that as long as she had no wish for a companion not to be forcing one on her, because when Onny took a notion for company it wasn't likely to be the company of another girl she'd want."

Mrs. Soraghan sobbed, and it was not clear whether it was with regret for having heeded her husband's advice, or for not having heeded her own, that she sobbed.

"I don't see what is to be done," said Theresa, and she went over to the windowpane and cleared aside the curtain. "The moon has darkened," she said, "there was a moon when I was getting ready for bed, but it has gone behind the clouds."

"Oh my little girl! My little girl!" said Mrs. Soraghan, and she rocked backwards and forwards, with her feet pressing now on the ball, now on the heel, as if it were her sorrowful task to treadle an invisible spinning wheel.

Gabriel looked at her and where her complaining voice could not touch his pity something in her attitude awakened a desire to ease her sorrow. He had remained all during this scene in a state of indifference which sprang directly from his continued and obstinate belief that Onny had gone off on the carousal with the gay boys of the town, and a feeling that she deserved all the punishment she would receive, although it would be for a reason which her judges would not suspect—her disloyalty and caprice towards him. The sight of the worn creature before him, however, racked with a grief that he felt it in his power to dispel with a few words, finally prevailed upon him and he decided to mention the sidecar that he had seen canter under the evening stars in the direction of Draghead.

Before Gabriel could relieve the sorrowing woman, however, as he believed he could, he would have to weigh up whether or not it would seem to Onny that he had betrayed her through jealousy and vindictiveness. Her mother would be sure to bring up his name in connection with the source of her information. This consideration was one which did not altogether antagonize him from mentioning the matter since it would be as good a way as any other for him to acquaint Onny with the fact that he had known all about her escapade and that, having seen her depart, he had not, as she might have spitefully supposed, been waiting for her for hours in the damp undergrowth of the park. On the other hand, it had also to be taken into consideration that the situation was grave enough to justify his speaking, and that if Onny's mother was not relieved soon of the anxiety which threatened to scatter her wits, his disloyalty might become a matter of small moment in the serious consequences that would follow.

That he still delayed, after turning over these considerations, was due to the fact that he hoped at any minute to hear the running feet of another messenger from the cottage with the news that Onny had returned, and the revelation of whence she had come, which would spare him the necessity of revealing whither she had gone.

The time wore on, and although he could tell by the tilt of his aunt's head, as she stood at the window, that she expected the same message as himself, he could no longer delay in revealing his knowledge.

Now it often happens that when we cogitate for long as to the wisdom or folly of a certain course of action, when we come at last to a decision we find that we have only surmounted half the difficulties. When Gabriel opened his mouth to speak he realized that he must approach the topic in a careful manner, and let his information emerge as the mere idle speculation of one not greatly interested in the situation, in case it should occur to his listeners that it was a queer thing for him not to have spoken sooner.

His Aunt Sara, however, by good luck noticed his silence at the time when her notice of it was most welcome.

"You are saying nothing, Gabriel! Have you no suggestions to offer poor Mrs. Soraghan?"

"Ah don't bother poor Master Gabriel!" said the woman, but nevertheless she turned her eyes up to him hopefully. He might have a suggestion to make.

"To tell you the truth I'm not worried about her," said Gabriel. "She's probably gone off on some joy-ride, and she can't come home until the rest of the crowd are willing to return." When he used the word "joy-ride" it was impossible to restrain a sneer from appearing on his face. It was this sneer on his lips as much as his words that made Mrs. Soraghan stand up.

"Onny is not one to go joy-riding without telling her mother!"

"There's always a first time for everything, Mrs. Soraghan," said Theresa Coniffe, and although Mrs. Soraghan felt there was something vaguely familiar in the words, as if she had heard them recently, she did not remember that it was she herself who had used them. "That may be true for some people," she said, "but I brought up my children in a way different from most people, and God knows I had experience enough in bringing them up before Onny arrived!" She turned to Gabriel. "What makes you think, Master Gabriel, that my Onny would go joy-riding with a crowd of people who could see no difference between the day and the night when it came to enjoying themselves?"

Gabriel felt cornered. He saw no way out of the difficulties so he plunged deeper into them.

"As a matter of fact I wouldn't have mentioned the subject at all, knowing that you would hardly be pleased to hear such a thing, only that I wanted to relieve your anxiety, for it's better to know the truth, even if it's unpleasant, than to remain in ignorance and anxiety." Not only Mrs. Soraghan but Theresa and Sara were staring at him. He went on. "The reason I spoke about joy-riding was that I saw a sidecar laden with fellows and girls going out the Draghead road early this evening and the car drew up within a few yards of your cottage. It came into my mind at the time, and recent events proved the truth of my suspicion, that Onny must have gone with them!"

His hurt and resentment stirred in him again as he spoke, and he stared into the fire, which Sara had revived with the bellows, seeing again in a random gallop of flame the toppling sidecar that had become a symbol of all that was treacherous and disloyal. As he stared into the fire he did not bother about the effect of his words upon Mrs. Soraghan. If he were interested at all in what that effect might be, he would have supposed that the climax of the scene was over and that Mrs. Soraghan would have taken herself up and gone home, with no other worry now than the worry of finding words strong enough with which to greet the erring Onny when she came to the latch in the dawn. She wouldn't come back till dawn he supposed, and his mind was about to create other, and more humiliating pictures of Onny with the aid of the volatile flames of the grate when he became aware suddenly that instead of causing an easing of the tension, his words seemed to have heightened it to such an extent that his Aunt Theresa had dropped into a chair behind her without as much as glancing to see if it was free of dust, much less giving it the usual flick with her handkerchief, as was her custom with chairs both at home and abroad. She dropped back into the chair, and threw up her hands. Miss Sara gave a small cry of concern, and Mrs. Soraghan put her hands up to her face and all that could be heard from between the hard knotted fingers, bitter with dirt and crooked with age, was the name of her daughter Onny.

"Oh Onny! Onny! Onny!" she kept saying over and over again. "Oh Onny! Onny! Onny!"

Gabriel looked at his aunt. "What is the matter? Did I say something to upset her? I don't see that it was such great harm after all for the girl to have gone for a ride! The hours slipped by. She didn't feel the time pass. There's nothing to be upset about."

Theresa looked at him with contempt. "Didn't you hear what Mrs. Soraghan said?"

"What?"

"Onny wasn't on that sidecar. Mrs. Soraghan saw it when it went past the cottage and stopped nearly outside the door to pick up Ned Naylor. There was no one on it but Joss Carty, the Beales and Lily Bell, and the two Dockery girls. Onny wasn't on it."

It was a few minutes before Gabriel was able to take in the significance of this information. It might have been easier for him to relinquish his error of the eye, but it is hard to admit the errors of a jealous heart.

"Is that true, Mrs. Soraghan? Are you sure that she couldn't have been on the far side of the car, the side away from you, where you mightn't have seen her so well? She might have kept her head down so you wouldn't see her, in case you might stop her going."

Mrs. Soraghan looked up. "A few minutes ago you were taking her part and saying that she must surely have forgotten to let me know where she was going, and now you'd have me think that she'd pass me on the road outside her own house, and duck down her head for fear I'd see her. It's easy to see that words to a person in trouble are the first words that come to the tongue and that a person may look neither for rhyme or reason in them! I saw every inch of the car. Didn't it drive up almost on a level with the cottage, and the red-headed Dockery girl singing her loudest, and Sammy Beale with his arm around her playing the mouth organ, and then when they heard Ned Naylor running up the road after them, and calling for them to stop, they turned the car around on the road and gave me every chance of seeing the party sitting on the other side, Joss Carty, and the black Dockery girls, bold and double, their legs hanging down as long and as plain as his! Ned was put sitting up in the well of the car and then they turned again and came past me the second time, and galloped away up the road in the moonlight, till they rose over the hill and their figures were cut out against the sky like the figures carved out in the altar rails—God forgive me for such a comparison!" Mrs. Soraghan turned to Theresa. "I'm glad to say that Onny wasn't with those hooligans."

But as she realized that she did not know where Onny was, and she could perhaps be in worse places, she began to moan again. Theresa and Sara looked commiseratingly at her, but when Gabriel ran over and began to shake the woman, pushing her back and pulling her towards him with a fury of temper, they sprang from their chairs again as abruptly as they had fallen back into them.

"Have you gone out of your mind, Gabriel?" said Theresa, trying to pull his sleeve.

But Gabriel was shaking the woman and calling out questions to her as if she were stone deaf, or as if he believed that in her case, as is said to be the case with some animals, although they do not understand the human tongue they can interpret words from the tone in which they are delivered.

"Why didn't you say that long ago? Why didn't you mention that, when you first came in? Are you keeping back any more information? God Almighty! Do you realize the seriousness of this? Do you know the time it is?" He glanced wildly around the room in search of that information for himself. "It is nearly two o'clock in the morning! Did you tell the Guards? Did you tell the priests? The town should be awakened. There should be a search."

"Gabriel, control yourself. What has come over you?" Miss Coniffe was stiffened at the thought of the publicity that was threatening to be drawn down upon them. "You took the affair very easy up to now. What's come over you? Control yourself!"

"I thought she was on the sidecar. I was sure of it!" He ran his hands through his hair. "Why should I blame the poor thing?" he said, looking down at the limp form of Mrs. Soraghan, who had fallen forward like an old rag doll, and who moaned with a continual sound that showed

287

that her last effort to cope with the situation had been made and this was all that might be expected from her now till she was brought face to face with her child. The thought came into Gabriel's head that she might well have cause to moan more bitterly when that moment came, but he put such a thought from him with horror. All his former feelings, from the first moment that he had decided Onny was not coming to the tower, fell away from him as fast as a flock of starlings at the appearance of the hawk. New feelings of guilt and terror and an itching urgency for action came over him.

"We must do something," he said, and he threw out his hands to Theresa.

"It's not for you to do anything; it's for her brothers to do whatever is to be done," said Theresa.

"There's no time for making minor distinctions like that now," he cried, and ran into the hall to get his coat.

Theresa went after him and her grip on his arm was as strong as her will.

"This is no small distinction," she said. "Think of the consequences if you find her—" she faltered for a moment before the harshness of her thoughts, but went on with grim determination—"and if you should find her corpse, God between us and all harm, what excuse would you make for being the one to go looking for her in the middle of the night?"

For a powerful moment the truth hung on Gabriel's lips, but he held it back.

"Did your fine preachers below in the church ever get time, between asking for money, to make any mention of Christian charity?"

Sara came forward at the sound of the voices.

"Lower your voice, Gabriel, lower your voice," she said. "You can be heard in the streets."

"Keep out of this, Sara," said Theresa, and she turned back to Gabriel. "Kindly leave religion out of this," she said.

"It's you who are doing that!" said Gabriel, and he jerked himself free. "What would you have me do?" he added in a fierce curiosity of anguish.

"There is only one thing to do, although I expect you will sneer at it." Theresa turned round. "Come, Sara," she said. "We cannot do any more. Let him go as he chooses. We will give poor Onny the only help that is in our power, and wherever she is, and whatever has befallen her, our help will be the kind that will avail her most."

Gabriel pushed his arms into the sleeve of his coat. His hands sweated with fear and they went into the sleeves clumsily. One arm caught in a torn lining and he dragged it out again and opened the door without waiting to put his arm out in the right armhole. As he banged the door behind him he just caught the intonation of his aunts' voices, with the weak voice of Mrs. Soraghan, as they knelt up on the kitchen chairs to pray for Onny's safety.

∽ ∽ ∽

When Gabriel ran out under the bright night sky he had no clear idea of what he was going to do, or where he was going to go. And after he had run through the three or four main streets of the town he came to a standstill. A country town consists of little more than streets. If Onny was not to be found in one of them, where was she?

How small the town looked as it lay under the moon—a few streets, a shabby station, a gaunt church, and the straggling ruins of an ancient friary. That was all. And beyond the town the country stretched out wide to every side, field beyond field, the land rising and sinking with its ancient furrows, visible although unharrowed for hundreds of years. There was no use looking in the fields. The fields were infinite. They stretched away to the hills, and the hills stretched away to the hills of other countries, and they in turn stretched down to the fringe of towns of which Onny had never heard the names, even when she was a flighty youngster sitting on the schoolhouse bench.

Gabriel stood and looked around him at the silent empty houses. In the whole town there was not a single soul abroad. And in not one single window was there a gleam of light. Only the roofs of the houses were lit, and they were lit with the cold indifferent light of the moon.

"Onny! Onny!" he cried despairingly, and he did not know where to turn.

Onny? An incongruous thought took possession of his vacant mind. What was the right form of her name? For Father Drew would have been unlikely, he thought, to pour waters of baptism over a name of such anonymous quality as Onny.

"I must ask her what name she was given at the font," he said, speaking aloud, and at the thought of her pert face, and the pert answer she would be likely to give him, he lost some of his anxiety. "Perhaps she is safe at home all the time!" he thought, and the idea that this might be so had no sooner come into this mind than he grasped it, and clung to it.

"I won't waste any more time in suspense that may be needless," he said. "I'll go out to the cottage and make sure that she isn't safe in her bed while I'm making a fool of myself here."

Somehow it did not occur to him to go to the castle park. Having waited for her there in the early part of the night it did not occur to him to go there again. And even as he passed under the rampart walls on his way to the cottage no thought of climbing up there came into his head. But suddenly, just as he was coming near the Soraghan cottage in which the gleam of a light made his pulse beat faster because he could not tell whether it was a good or a bad sign, over the high wall of the rampart from the depths of the park within, there came the sudden scream of a frightened night fowl.

At once, as the scream pierced the air, Gabriel's heart was besieged with its desperate implications. His body trembled, suddenly aware in every limb of the savagery and terror of the earth and its creatures.

He looked up at the towering walls. Why had he not searched there in the first place? Onny had not been there when he went to meet her at the ordained hour. But might she not have gone there after he had left? Might she not have waited there thinking that it was he who was late? And while she was waiting there, what might not have happened? He stood still on the road, his heart beating furiously.

Once again the strange bird screamed with terror in the dark.

In another moment Gabriel was running towards the familiar fissure in the wall, and before the echo of the bird had died upon the air he had clambered up over the rough stones and dropped down into the inner ring of the keep.

The moon no longer shone out bright and clear and blue, as it had shone earlier in the night, but even behind the banks of cloud that hid it, it still gave some luminous quality to the air. Nevertheless it was difficult to see. He stretched out his hands to guard against running into a tree trunk, but he was guided mainly by the instincts of his heart. In a few minutes the lower tower loomed up before him.

Gabriel gripped the lower ledge of the stone parapet, put his feet into the familiar footholds, and shafting his arm through a long spy hole, he drew up on to the crumbling platform. From here he could command as wide a view of the park as the darkness of the night would allow. From this high vantage point he would be able to disentangle from the mournful noises of the night creatures that ran in the depths, and stirred in the branches of the trees, any noise that might help him in his search.

The moon came through the fragmentary clouds from time to time, but its light was more of a hindrance than a help; flashing out as it did with the swiftness of a white nut breaking free of the silken kernel, it stayed in sight only for a brief instant, and the shadows of the trees that it cast upon the ground were moving shadows that maddened and deluded the watcher by their likeness to human figures, flying across the grass, too fleet to be followed and captured.

Upon one part of the night scene only did the moon shed light with any permanence, and that was upon the surface of the river that ran so roughly that its broken surface caught the light as brightly as broken glass. Upon this broken river that ran wildly down between its banks, Gabriel gazed with a sad remembrance of the first evening that he had crossed it, and a goading grief came over him to think that in the idle impulse of that evening the seed of this bitter moment was sown. He looked at it, wondering suddenly whether it would be possible to cross back from here in the other direction and avoid retracing his steps through the park. But he dismissed the idea as madness, for although the river was not at full peak, it had a wild streak in it that sent it hurrying along jerkily, and the jostling ripples often rose up like the crack of a whip to a height as great as any it ever attained. He gazed down at the bright water; a fascination seemed to come over him, and he slipped down from the tower and went down through the trees to the nearest point of the river. This point, directly opposite the tower, was further down the stream than the point opposite the house where he and Onny had crossed in the summer. Here the river, having passed beyond the reach of those whose back gardens gave them the right to tame it with weeding scythe and water rake, wore a wilder aspect than might be expected at such a short distance from the town. Here too it was diverted from its straight course by heaps of stones from the ruin that had fallen into the river bed, possibly blown there by one of the first blasts of gunpowder used in Ireland, and never lifted since. Here too the dense shrubbery, ash and willow, although growing in the dry soil on the bank, had dipped its branches over gradually into the water until they reached the surface and were like woodland girls bending their heads to wash their tresses in the stream. These shrubs had settled together, and they in their turn had caught the dust and dirt that lay on the top of the water, and the clots of soiled foam that had formed where the ripples dashed against the stones, and although all this debris was deposited at floodtide, slowly, imperceptibly, like the building of a bird's nest, when the river level dropped, there was displayed upon the curving branches such a weight of rubbish and dirt that at times it was hard to believe that a human hand had not hung these branches with bundles and clots of rags, as the tinkers load the bushes with sundry articles when they make camp by the roadside.

It was upon one laden bough in particular that Gabriel's eye fell as he was turning around to trace his way back along the riverbank.

One might almost think it was a human form that was caught in those treacherous boughs, he thought, the body caught in the lower branches, the arms thrown over an upper bough, the head hanging despondent as the water dragged at the heavy sodden clothing, dragging it more violently and more successfully each moment. The moon shone white again from the kernel of cloud—it was like a woman's form, he thought! And then, with a wilder thought, he started forward frantically. The clots of dirt upon the other branches were shapeless and colourless. Whatever was caught on this branch had shape and colour, for although the moon is no respecter of colour, painting dark things dark, and light things light, he saw with horror that it was Onny's red skirt that caught on the weighted branches!

Rushing forward, his heart beating louder than the rabbling of the waters, Gabriel ran to the place on the bank nearest to the spot in the river where the tree hung out over the water. The garments were Onny's. The human figure, that was slung like a rag doll upon the dangerous branch, was the body of Onny. But whether the garments clad a cold and sodden corpse, or a body in which the breast still lifted to the living heart, he could not from this distance tell.

His first impulse was to cling, himself, to the horizontal bough, and by its weight support himself while he dragged himself forward towards her. But at a glance he knew that her frail chance of survival depended upon her remaining within his reach, and her remaining within his reach depended on the way her clothes were accidentally caught upon a branch which the slightest stir might dislodge. If it were dislodged and she was carried away, hope of recovering the body would be removed, and without a shadow of doubt there would be removed all possibility of recovering it with the life still in it. If he tried to run out through the waters, his feet slipping between the unseen rocks over which the water jostled, he might lurch against the bough and achieve the same disastrous result. Time seemed to cease. Past and present seemed to become one interminable moment in which a rushing wilderness of water flowed between him and the girl.

Then he began to think again. Back from the bank around the ash tree, which as well as casting this branch out over the water had filled a good ten yards of the bank with branches and overground roots, skirting them scrupulously so as not to shake any portion of them, he came upon the bank of the river again, but this time the current that divided him from Onny was flowing towards him so that any clumsiness of his that might dislodge her and throw her into the stream would carry her towards him, and not away from him. And if his arms were not strong enough to drag her to safety, they would be strong enough to bind her to him, and if she was to be rushed over the broken rocks and sucked under the surface of the waters, he would be with her.

Gabriel pushed aside the small evil fingers of the twigs that tore at his hair and skin, and plunged his feet into the icy water, tumbling and falling and catching at boughs. He felt the river rising and his own feet sinking in weedy mud, but he threw the weight of his body forward and with one arm he flung a wild embrace upon the rough, knotted bough, while with the other he caught at the sodden hem of Onny's garments that spread taut upon the lesser branches. One precaution without the other would have been useless and vain, for as the weight of his body shook the tree, Onny's limp body slipped from its cleft in the fork of the branch, and the well-worn cotton of the dress that had hung taut upon the knots gave way with a tearing sound, and upon his arm that held the other end of the clothing there came such a violent strain that he was nearly dragged from his own security upon the tree. Steadying himself, with muscles that seemed as if they would crack, he dragged the dead weight of the girl towards him, and then, grasping her with his thighs, and using them like a vice, he held the wet form firm until he could put down a hand and catch a secure grip of her arm, afraid to trust the worn wet clothing any further.

But from the moment he clasped her wet arm, a flash of triumph had run through him to encourage his perseverance. Even with his scant experience of death, Gabriel knew from the limpness of the body clasped in his arms that he was no longer alone in this terror, but that another living being, breathing and pulsing, was there with him in the darkness.

Slowly, cautiously, he dragged himself along with one arm, though his flesh was bitten and seared by the bark, and with the other hand he dragged the girl until they came into shallows that made it possible for him to let go his hold of the tree and gather her against his breast so that they both together fell upon the bank.

As they fell upon the riverbank, for a long time Gabriel's breath tore at him as the water had torn his clothing. His hands, that hung down limp, were numbed and unable to lift themselves. But rolling over he managed to lift his head so that he could look at Onny. He stared at the white face in its tangle of wet hair. And then, suddenly, while he stared, with a swift lifting of the lids the eyes of the face opened. Deepened and darkened by night and by the terrors of the previous hours, the eyes stared into his for a moment, and there was a recognition in them that could only come from a person still well within the shores of the living.

"Oh, Onny!" he cried. "Onny, Onny!"

He fell beside her, and having no knowledge of how to treat a dying woman, he treated her like a living one, and with his arms he clasped her close and caressed the curves of her shoulder and throat. In the warmth of his embrace the glorious vibration of nerves was set up once more in Onny's numbed body, and as he in his turn felt her responding to him, his own confidence came back and he felt a new ability to cope with the situation. Pulling off his coat, he wrapped it around her and, lifting her in his arms, this time putting one arm around her waist and the other under her knees, he began to run across the grass in the direction of the gap in the wall, her weight as nothing now.

Although the Soraghan cottage was only a few paces from the rampart, Gabriel's only thought was to get the girl home to Clewe Street. For whatever he might think of his Aunt Theresa in other respects, there was no one in whom he would have greater confidence when it came to ministering to the sick or wounded.

Although he halted many times in the journey from the ramparts to Clewe Street, he seemed to make the journey in a short time after all, and soon he was crossing the river bridge that led into the town. Looking up at the houses, scanning window after window, he was surprised to find them all as blind and dark as they were when he last looked at them. He had expected that some of the town at least would have been aroused, and a searching party set up to look for the missing girl. But no light shone from any window until he reached Clewe Street. There the light shone out upon the pavement from the yellow blind, and between the light and the window blind a stiff figure knelt casting her rigid shadow out upon the flagged path. Staunch, rigid, unalterable in her fierce determination to dominate destiny with her own will, Theresa prayed, still kneeling upright on the hard wooden chair. Gabriel freed one hand and struck the window glass. The silhouetted figure crossed herself as calmly as if she knelt at casual evening prayers, and an instant later the door was opened.

"I knew that prayer would be answered," said Theresa, and she went before him throwing open the kitchen door. "Is she hurt? Is she all right?" she asked. "Where in the name of God did you find her?" And looking contemptuously at the other two women, Theresa went over and gave a shake to Sara, who had not heard the knock, nor noticed her sister leaving the room, but who still knelt up on the deal chairs, her arms propped on the chair back and her head bent over her arms. "Much good your chatter of prayers would be!" she said. "Gabriel is back! Get up and don't make a fool of yourself!"

And upon Mrs. Soraghan she looked with contempt too great for word or gesture to increase, for after the door had opened and Gabriel had come well within the room with Onny, who still dripped with mud and drops of water, Mrs. Soraghan still knelt on the wooden chair muttering responses to unvoiced prayers, toneless, and of no more account than the words that rise upon stupefied lips when sleep has overtaken the body in a posture that keeps it from relaxing completely into unconsciousness.

ᕦ ᕤ ᕦ

When Theresa's harsh voice penetrated the wearied consciousness of Sara, she raised her head, and looked around at Gabriel who still held Onny in his arms, and at whose feet there was now a wide pool of water from their sodden clothes. She stood up from her knees, slowly and stiffly, and went over to Mrs. Soraghan.

"Get up from your knees, Mrs. Soraghan," she said, " Gabriel has come back. Our prayers are answered ; he has brought back Onny."

Mrs. Soraghan raised her eyes, scarcely comprehending Sara's words. Sara put her arms around her, and assisted her to change the posture that had cramped her bones into the rigidity of wood. She put her sitting on the chair facing the chair on which Gabriel and Theresa were settling Onny.

"See! Onny is safe!" she said. "Theresa and Gabriel are taking care of her."

Theresa, who was dragging up a second chair to put under Onny's feet, swung around at this point.

"Stop wasting your time with that foolish creature," she said, indicating Mrs. Soraghan with a jerk of her head. "Attend to me! Get me a hot jar. Put a saucepan of milk to heat on the fire! Is there nothing to put under the girl's head?" Whatever views she might hold on the incident as a whole, Theresa was not going to neglect such an opportunity of taking command. "Hurry! Stir yourself, Sara!" she cried. But although Sara rushed forward at the first of Theresa's orders, her sister's contemptuous dismissal of Onny's mother as a foolish creature was hardly justified, for, as the orders multiplied, Sara became confused and stood irresolute, and it was Mrs. Soraghan who, coming to her senses all at once, rushed to the assistance of Miss Coniffe.

"Here!" she cried, and she caught up a big red cushion from the chair behind Sara, and handing it to Theresa she helped her to hold Onny upright while they wedged the cushion behind her back.

"She's all right," she said, reassuringly.

"Of course she's all right!" said Miss Coniffe testily. It was to herself however that Mrs. Soraghan was speaking, for, although Onny lay back exhausted, with closed eyes, the mother's true eye had taken in everything from the even rise of the girl's bosom to the returning colour in her cheeks, and her concern was diverted all at once to giving Miss Coniffe all the help in her power.

"The saucepan!" she said, springing to her feet again. That was another thing Miss Coniffe had called for. She ran over to a cupboard in the corner. "Is this where the pots and pans are kept?" she asked as she threw open the doors of it, but before she searched for either vessel or milk she ran back to Sara who stood wringing her hands and looking down at Onny. "Blankets!" she cried, catching her by the arm. "Didn't you hear Miss Coniffe? She wants blankets and a hot jar!" Then as she ran back to the cupboard she gave an exclamation of impatience. "I wish I knew the layout of the house," she said half to herself and half in apology to Theresa for Sara's delay. "How much milk will I heat?" she added, but without waiting to be told she poured out a long stream of the milk Theresa had set for the breakfast into the saucepan.

"There was no need for the top of the milk to be used," said Theresa, and then she jerked her shoulders impatiently. "What is Sara doing?" she said. "That's the wrong saucepan!" But it was too late. The milk was in the saucepan; the saucepan was on the fire; and Mrs. Soraghan had run to the door of the kitchen to meet Sara, who was returning with the blankets, the hot jar, and an old dressing gown of her own of faded blue flannel.

"I'll take them from you, Miss Sara," she cried, but Theresa shot out an arm.

295

"Give me those blankets," she said, "I'm long enough waiting for them."
The rebuke was not for Sara, however, and she darted a critical glance at
Onny's mother. "Give me the dressing gown too," she said. If she had
had another hand free she would also have snapped at the hot-water jar.
This however fell to Mrs. Soraghan, who lost not a minute in unscrewing
the stopper.

"Please! Mrs. Soraghan!" said Theresa, throwing down the blankets
and the dressing gown. "Those hot jars have to be carefully handled. Your
daughter Onny cracked one already since she came to the house. The
water should never be put into them until the boil has gone off it!" And
she caught the jar so roughly that it nearly fell on the floor.

In short, if Theresa had rashly complained of having no assistance
before, she had cause now to complain of too much. And yet things
weren't done.

"Look," she cried, "the milk will boil over! Who is supposed to be
watching it?"

The dig was lost on Mrs. Soraghan, however. Indeed she was unaware
that she was being addressed because she found cause for complaint herself
with the way the fire was drawing.

"What kind of dampers are these?" she exclaimed as she noisily pulled
out one after another. "This fire is nearly out." She turned around to
where Gabriel stood, still in his wet clothes, leaning against the mantelpiece watching Onny. "Run out and get an armful of sticks," she said to
him, "this fire will never heat the milk."

Did she hear aright? Theresa, who was at that moment stripping the
wet clothes from Onny, straightened up. Did her ears betray her? Or did
she hear Mrs. Soraghan giving orders to Gabriel just as if he were her own
Larry? This was the last straw! She opened her mouth. But at that
moment another aspect of the situation struck her.

"Are you here all the time?" she said, turning on Gabriel himself. "Have
you no shame? Get out of here at once. You should know enough for that
without being told." She turned around to Mrs. Soraghan. "To think that
you stood there looking at him, and didn't call my attention to him. What
kind of mothers are going nowadays!"

Gabriel flushed deeply and went towards the door. He had hardly been
conscious as he stood there in the kitchen, his eyes fastened on Onny,
grateful for all the fuss that was being made of her, satisfied to be left
alone.

"I'm sorry, Aunt Theresa," he said, averting his eyes and going towards
the door.

From the far corner of the room, Sara, slow at some things, but quick
in heart, took in the situation, and as she saw Gabriel flush, the colour ran
into her own cheeks.

"You can come back in a minute, Gabriel," she called out after him, and catching up the flannel dressing gown she thrust Onny's bare arm into it, and drew it across her. "You shouldn't have stood around in your wet clothes," she said. "It was a dangerous thing to do. Go and change at once."

"Thank you, Aunt Sara," said Gabriel gratefully. He went out into the hall. He had hardly gone down the hall passage however when Theresa's voice called out after him, ordering him back as peremptorily as she had ordered him out.

"Gabriel, get those sticks before you go to change your clothes," she said. "I thought the milk was ready. Instead of that the fire is almost out. Only a fool would have tried to heat a saucepan on it. There's no doubt about it that where there are too many people doing a thing it's never done right."

For it was not with her nephew Theresa was irritated. When he came back with the kindling wood and threw in into the fire she was at pains to let him see this. "I didn't get time to look at you at all," she said, "are you all right? You must tell me all about it to-morrow. I hope you won't be any the worse for your adventure. You'll have to take a cup of this milk." For the milk, after all, was ready. "Although it's a wonder it is!" she said, lifting it from the fire, and lowering her voice to a whisper. "There's no need at all for that woman to stay here," she said. "It's bad enough having to keep the girl here for the night, but I don't see the need of having the whole family here!" She poured the milk into a cup and put her other arm around Onny. "Come, Onny. Sip this like a good girl. Take your time. Don't try to talk. Just take a sip of this nice hot milk. I'll hold the glass for you. Keep your hands under the blanket. You're safe and well now. There's no need to be frightened. You'll be as right as a fiddle in the morning. Sip this!" And as she coaxed Onny, Theresa still found time to throw remarks to the others.

"What are you standing there for, Sara? Where is this girl going to sleep?"

"There's no need to put those things away, Mrs. Soraghan. I always find it's no help to have people who don't know the habits of the house poking around and putting things in the wrong place. It only makes more work in the long run."

And so with one thing and another there was soon such a state of activity in the room that as the various occupants rushed from the fire to lift the boiling saucepan, to the dresser to fetch a cup, from the improvised couch to the table on which bottles and vessels and towels were rapidly accumulating, they were inclined to knock into each other, and soon there was such a fuss and excitement that it was only natural that without the aid of spirits or friction Onny would have come to a full realization of her surroundings, and the troubled memories of what she had endured would be defeated by the sheer noise and commotion of the reality around her.

For some time her eyes had been opening, with heavy fluttering of lashes, and dropping closed again, as if from the weariness of their own exertion. Her lips had opened in somewhat similar ineffectual attempts to speak. Soon, however, in the noisy altercation between Theresa, her mother, and Sara, she opened her eyes with a wide steady stare, and taking in the safety of her surroundings from a slow observation of each familiar object in the kitchen, and putting out a hand to grasp the blankets over her, and establish, by touch, that they were real, she realized, with far greater speed and certainty, that she was safe, than she would have done had the others been watching her, and hovering near to assure her, with a babble of talk, that she was all right; that she was safe; and that she need have no fear.

Settling herself more comfortably on the clumsy stretcher, Onny soon came back to her senses so thoroughly that she was able to enjoy to the full the fact that Miss Coniffe and Miss Sara were waiting upon her hand and foot, and that upon Miss Coniffe's stiff black pleated bodice there was a slop of hot milk, and on Miss Sara's skirt there was another big stain. She sleepily planned to tell her mother of this phenomenal change in the relationship between herself and her mistresses when all of a sudden she thought of her mother's anxiety, part of which had tormented her in the harshest hours of the struggle in the dark river.

"My mother," she said suddenly, out loud. "I must go home to my mother!"

After her first furious activity Mrs. Soraghan's energy had not after all been a match for Theresa, and she had finally sunk back into a chair which, placed at a slant from Onny, put her out of the girl's direct range. Hearing her daughter mention her however, she sat up again with a start.

"I'm here, Onny," she said, springing to her feet. "I'm here!"

Onny turned around. She stared uncomprehendingly at her mother, and then looked at her mistresses. In a dazed and drowsy way she had accepted her surroundings as familiar and therefore natural, but now at the sound of her mother's voice in the unaccustomed setting, she got confused.

"Where am I?" she asked in a frightened voice, and began to whimper.

Sara and Gabriel ran to her side at once.

"You're here in Clewe Street with us, Onny," cried Sara. "Don't you know me? And your mother is here too. She came looking for you."

"You're safe with us, Onny," cried Gabriel. "Don't try to think. My aunts are looking after you. You're going to stay here with us to-night."

But Mrs. Soraghan, after the strain of the past hours, was overcome by reaction.

"She doesn't know me," she cried, and she threw up her hands and began to wail in a loud voice.

Theresa's opportunity had come and she was not going to lose it.

"Don't be nonsensical, woman," she said. "Of course she knows you. The girl is bothered with all the fuss and noise. She ought to be in her bed. And as long as there's no question of her going home at this hour she might as well be put to bed at once. But there's no need for you to delay any longer, Mrs. Soraghan."

Mrs. Soraghan's wailing stopped short.

"She might like to have me beside her," she said. "She might be lonely in a strange house."

"A strange house!" Theresa sniffed. "And what about your other children, Mrs. Soraghan?" she asked. "Have you forgotten them? It seems to me a queer thing for any mother to run out in the middle of the night and leave a cottageful of children all by themselves in a lonely place. There's no knowing who might be lurking around those ramparts! If I were you I'd think of your other children and not be worrying about the only one of them you can be sure is in good hands at this moment!" Miss Coniffe crossed herself. "God between us and all harm," she said. "Who knows what you may find before you when you go home?"

But her strategy almost overpassed itself. Mrs. Soraghan, who had risen at the first of this outburst, sank back on her chair again near the end of it, paralysed with fright.

"Oh, Theresa, you're forgetting Judy," said Sara, "and Judy is old enough to look after the house." She put her arm around Mrs. Soraghan and assisted her to her feet. "If Onny feels lonely," she said, "I can sit up with her till she falls asleep."

"There, you see," said Theresa. "My sister will look after her." She took Mrs. Soraghan by the arm again. "Where is your coat? Oh, you didn't wear one? Very good. What about a hat? You didn't have one, did you?"

"I just rushed out as I was," said Mrs. Soraghan.

"Well is there anything else here belonging to you?" said Theresa, and she guided her towards the door.

"Are you sure you'll be all right, Onny?" said Mrs. Soraghan, straining backwards to look over her shoulder.

"Oh, I'm all right," said Onny quickly. She was hardly heeding the talk. She was staring at Gabriel.

"Come and help me to get rid of this tiresome woman," said Theresa to Sara in an undertone.

Sara and Theresa took Mrs. Soraghan one by each arm and led her out

299

into the hall from whence her voice could still be heard, although less distinctly, looking for assurance that they did not need her.

Gabriel walked over and knelt down beside Onny.

"Onny!" he said, and he looked into her eyes. Then he slipped his arm under her shoulders and drawing her into a more upright position, he drew her slightly sideways at the same time, so that she was leaning against his shoulder. When the door was banged at last on Mrs. Soraghan Theresa heaved a sigh of relief.

"Is there anything being done about getting a bed ready?" she said, and Sara hurried away towards the stairs. Theresa herself came back into the kitchen and she advanced to Onny with a rapid stride. "Don't be frightened, Onny!" she said, with a gentleness that Gabriel could never have believed was possible for her. He looked up with gratitude, but, as he did, Theresa saw his arm around the girl. She drew up with a startled air. "Take away your arm!" she said. "There is such a thing as going too far!" And turning she looked at him with irritation. "What possessed you to bring her here at all? Why didn't you take her home, where she belonged?"

Sara came back into the room. "You can make up a bed for yourself in my room, Sara," said Theresa. "I want to put Onny in your room." She flashed a look at Gabriel which he felt was intended to convey more than he had energy to interpret. But when Sara lifted Onny and he made a gesture as if to assist her, Theresa again gave him the same fierce glance. "Keep back, please!" she commanded, and clearing him from her pathway by a gesture, she began to move towards the door, Sara with difficulty helping to support the girl.

With an awkward gait they went down the passage and when they had entered Sara's room there was a creak as Onny was let down upon the old bed. A minute later, Theresa came to the door and slammed it shut.

Gabriel sat down on a hard chair by the fire for a few minutes longer, disturbed by the noises that came from behind the closed door. He turned over the details of the evening.

After a time the door opened and his Aunt Theresa came in again. "What's keeping you up?" she said. "Get to your bed!"

～ ～ ～

When Onny was established in the big bed in Sara's room, and Sara had carried blankets and bedding and aired them in front of the kitchen fire, before making up a bed for herself in Theresa's room, the sisters prepared to go upstairs. The great yellow-cased clock in the hall struck the hour of four.

"This is an unfortunate affair!" said Theresa, as she turned Onny's wet clothes over before the dying fire.

"The poor child!" said Sara. "I hope she's all right!"

"She's all right. Depend upon it!" said Theresa, and she heaped ashes over the remaining blaze in the grate. "Oh, she's clever! She's as clever as a fox. She was not half as bad as we thought, but she played up to us nicely till I saw what her game was!"

"I don't understand!" said Sara.

"Of course you don't," said Theresa. "If it weren't for me the hussy might get away with her plans, but since I'm here she'll get a fine surprise in the morning if I decide to send her packing."

"Send her packing? But why, Theresa? Why should she be sent away because of an accident? An accident is an accident!" Sara put her hands up to her face in surprise. "Oh!" she said. "We forgot to ask her what happened to her in the excitement."

"I didn't forget," said Theresa. "I'm not likely to forget things that affect our welfare, Sara, even if you have very little head for such things."

"Oh! And what did she say?"

"Don't pull me up in my sentences like that, Sara, I wasn't finished what I was saying. I was going on to explain that I didn't forget to ask her what happened but I deliberately refrained from asking her, which is quite a different thing. I deliberately refrained from giving her an opportunity for putting the sin of a lie on her soul. I well knew without asking her that nothing much happened to her at all."

"But she fell in the river. We know that much. She was all wet, and her dress was torn. Those scratches on her arms!"

"It's my opinion that that was all arranged. It was a queer thing for the mother to come down here looking for help. It was a queer thing that Gabriel should be the one to be sent out looking for her!"

"But what was to be gained by it, if it was so?" said Sara, her eyes wide with interest.

"Can't you guess?" said Theresa, disgusted at Sara's lack of intuition.

"No, I can't. What could she possibly gain by such a terrible trick?"

Theresa drew herself up. "There are several people in this town who might think it worth risking a great deal to have a chance of putting you and me out of this house."

"Out of this house?" Sara was dismayed.

"Wouldn't it be a fine thing for Miss Onny to be taking over these keys?" Theresa rattled the keys at her belt. "And how would you feel, Sara Coniffe, if you had to be going to Miss Onny Soraghan, and asking her permission to open the larder if you should happen to take a fancy for a cup of tea during the day, as you often do, in your own father's house! Of course she would not be Miss Onny Soraghan then, but Mrs. Gabriel Galloway. Lord, doesn't it sound well! It's the name of a lady! It would sit well on that slut from the rampart cottages!"

"But Gabriel wouldn't be so foolish," cried Sara. "Gabriel will have his choice of a score of girls, girls with money, girls with good family connections!"

"It's the men that have a wide choice that make a narrow picking," said Theresa.

Sara began to cry quietly.

"There's no need for tears," said Theresa. "If I was gone from you, Sara, and you were left to deal with the situation all by yourself, I have no doubt that you'd be cast aside with the back of the hand, and then you'd have cause for tears. But not now! I'm still head of this house, thank God, and I am still mistress of my own servants. As soon as she puts her foot on the floorboards in the morning, I'll let her see her true position in this house."

The clock struck half-past four. They went upstairs, and Theresa took the blankets from Sara, and began to make up the spare bed in her room.

"I've had some suspicions before now that she was trying to shape things to her own designs, but I didn't see through to-night's affair until I saw Gabriel demean himself by putting his arm around her waist when she was on the stretcher by the fire. To do such a thing before us all; before her mother! It was as good as putting the raw material for a breach-of-promise action into their mouths!"

Theresa had laid the blankets on the bed and tucked in the sheets, spreading the coverlet over them, and catching the pillow by the ears she propped it up against the head rail. The bed was dressed with its usual daytime perfection.

"Thank you, Theresa," said Sara, and then, mechanically, she began to take off the coverlet again and fold it on the foot rail, to roll back the top sheets and to put the pillow flat on the bed.

"Did you bring up your nightdress?" said Theresa.

"Yes, Theresa!" said Sara, and taking it out she began to shake it out of its folds, but her mind was on other things as she shook out her nightdress, and she suddenly turned to Theresa.

"Theresa, what about Gabriel himself?"

"What do you mean?" said Theresa, taking down her hair.

"Supposing that he liked Onny? Supposing that it wasn't only Onny who was fond of him, but that he was fond of Onny?"

"What difference would that make?" she inquired, as if Sara had asked a more than usually stupid question. "What difference would that make?" she repeated, and began to give her hair the brushing that Gabriel had interrupted early in the night.

Theresa's question had been merely a flourish of rhetoric, but, had it been one that required an answer, it is unlikely that Sara could have given one from her inexperienced heart. Yet it was a question well worth answering, had there been an impartial voice of wisdom in that room. There would

302

have been a great difference in the destiny of both Onny and Gabriel had Gabriel loved her so ardently that he would allow no obstacle to come between him and his right to love her lawfully. And, on the other hand, if he had cared less than he did, things might have been better still, but between love and lack of love there are many middle courses, and Gabriel and Onny had involved their impassioned blood, and vulnerable nerves, in a relationship which knit them together by a thousand bonds of secrecy, guilt, and wretched loyalty.

∽　∽　∽

In his own room Gabriel heard the footsteps of his aunts, as they came upstairs at last, and through the wall that divided their room from his, he heard their muffled voices as they undressed. As the voices continued longer than might have been expected at that hour of the night, he began to grow anxious. He began to think that Onny might have made them suspicious by some unthinking word, let slip through sheer fatigue.

Then his thoughts centred on Onny herself, and for a moment he hoped that his aunts had indeed become suspicious. It might make things easier. It might bring nearer the difficult time when he would have to tell them about Onny. He remembered with great distaste the way his Aunt Theresa had turned upon him reproachfully, saying, "Why did you bring her to this house?" He remembered the way he had been ordered from the room when they were taking her wet clothes from her, and last of all he remembered the way the door had been slammed shut after they had carried her into Sara's room. And why Sara's room? He could not help feeling that there was some significance in putting her on the ground floor. At that moment he could see the door of the room where Onny lay rise up before his mind, with its unequal panels, its peeling white paint, and its broken crystal knob. It was a symbol of all the closeness and secrecy that had become part of his life, since the first night that he had crossed the river, and taken Onny up to the tower.

Behind that door Onny lay in the dark. She was probably awake. Was she frightened, he wondered. Someone should have stayed with her, at least until she fell asleep, to reassure her that she was well, and safe, and prevent her from falling into frightened dreams that she was back again in the struggling river.

Gabriel could not sleep himself. He longed for daylight. He leaned up on one elbow and looked out the window. It was nearly daylight already.

While Gabriel leaned upon his elbow he thought that he heard a sound in the room below him. He listened. Onny was awake too. He heard the springs of the bed twang, as she tossed from one side to another. Then he heard a slight cough. Yes, she was awake!

He sank back into the hollows of his own bed, where the sheets were crumpled with his tossing and turning, but all at once he sprang up again.

In all the excitement of the night, no one had asked how the accident had happened. How had she fallen into the river? He felt that he could hardly wait till morning, and then as suddenly as it had risen his excitement died, and a slow, reluctant fear began to take its place. Was it an accident?

When they had first begun to meet in the tower Onny had been impudent and saucy. She had been gay all the time, but of late, he remembered, she had begun to droop under the constant pressure of his desire for secrecy. Before he had claimed her company, her evenings had been spent at the crossroads with the boisterous young people of the town and countryside. He had taken her away from those gay companions. Even as late as to-night, when he thought she had gone off without him for what would have been, after all, a harmless joy ride, he had been ready to accuse her of every baseness, to punish her by nights of moodiness and complaints. He had basked in her sunshine, but over her he had cast his shadow. Perhaps it had become unbearable to her. There might be strange complexities in a girl's heart. To them life might not be as simple as it was for a man. Onny might have confounded secrecy with guilt, and solitude with shame. She might have thought that he was getting tired of her. She might even, with her passionate way of veering from one extreme to another, have felt that if he was tired of her, the best favour she could do him would be to get out of his way for good!

The cold sweat broke out on him. Onny! Onny! He could not bear to think of the torture she might have been enduring for weeks without confiding in him, until, tonight, she could not bear it any longer. He sprang out of bed, and ran across the floor, pulling an old coat around him, and going out on to the landing, not troubling to close the door behind him.

Had he yielded to his earlier impulses to go down to Onny's room he would have crept down with the stealth of one who knows the creaking board in every floor, looking back over his shoulder every moment, starting back from his own shadow, and stopping short at the sound of his own heartbeats, but now, running out on to the landing, he made no effort to avoid noise. The buckle on the belt of his coat hit loudly against the banister rails. He ran down the stairs two at a time. He did not care whom he wakened.

But such is the luck of the dauntless, no one awakened.

There was a night light burning in Onny's room and it spread an arc of light over the brass-knobbed bed, with the white counterpane, in which Onny lay with her arms stretched along to each side of her outside the bedclothes. The bed was large and in the centre of it she seemed a smaller and more pitiful creature than she would have seemed in her own bed in the cottage, which she shared with Judy and Chrissie, and over the outer edge of which, at times, she overflowed so much that it was necessary to place a chair against the side of the bed to prevent her from falling out on the floor. Here too, in Miss Sara's room, the gentle yellow light from the small wick at the bedside threw a great shadow of the bed upon the wall, with all its brass knobs and crossbars, and there was also a shadow of its occupant when she sat up at the sound of the door opening. Against the striped wallpaper the gigantically enlarged shadows made the real Onny smaller still. Gabriel felt abashed. He felt awkward and clumsy. He had opened the door and he was staring at her, but he was unable to speak. At length he managed to open his mouth.

"Can I come in, Onny?" he said, and a vast humility came over him and was expressed in his low voice and in his very attitude as he remained in the threshold without advancing further.

"Come in," said Onny, her voice unconsciously echoing the formality and shyness of his voice, but her face lighting up with interest as she beckoned him forward with a warm gesture, patting the side of the bed for him to sit there.

Gabriel advanced nearer. He came to the edge of the bed, but he did not sit down. He stood looking down at her. She was still wearing the old blue flannel dressing gown that Sara had put on her, but she had it pinned tightly across her chest with a safety pin. His eyes followed every flow of her body under the pliant sheet, then he lifted the hand nearest to him, as it lay against the cold counterpane, and he kissed it, palm and finger tips, before he laid it back as gently, and spoke to her.

"Do you mind my coming into your room, Onny?" he said, and waited for an answer.

The moment was greater than Onny knew. It was greater than any moment she had known before, although, without its customary cloak of passion and intensity, it might be understandable that she did not recognize it. She only kept herself from tittering at his diffidence because she was afraid that her mistresses might hear them, and that at any minute Miss Theresa Coniffe might swoop down upon them, fully clothed in her austere black satin raiment, as a bird would swoop, fully feathered, from the branches of sleep to pounce on the first red worm that dared to break the soil at dawn. Had she been able to overcome that fear, and yielded to her natural inclination to laugh at him then, there might still have been a pause in the downstroke of their destiny, but it is only in the light of what subsequently befalls that such moments become illuminated.

As it was, Onny was not only afraid to yield to her impulse to laugh, but she was almost afraid to open her mouth in this dangerous silence. She shivered when Gabriel himself spoke, and while he was speaking she kept her finger pressed against her lips to warn him that he must not raise his voice. Beside her on the wall loomed her shadow, making the same gesture, It was as if she were trying to silence the words upon which, if spoken, so much would rest. But this was not Onny's motive. And when Gabriel opened his mouth to speak the words were hardly coherent. Onny leaned forward and put her hand across his mouth. Her eyes blazed with absolute terror.

"You'll wake your aunts. You'll wake them. You'll wake them!" she cried, raising her own voice in her anxiety. "Miss Coniffe will come down! She'll turn me out of the house!"

Gabriel caught the hand that was pressed across his mouth.

"Hush, Onny, hush! Don't say such things. No one will turn you out of this house. From now on things will be different. In the past I may have been secretive but I say from now on things will be different."

Onny listened with her lips apart. She had expected that he would come to her room. She argued in her own mind that he who had encountered so many obstacles in order to meet her every single night, if only for a few minutes, would hardly fail to come down to her when she lay in a lockless room in his own house. But she did not understand this new method of love-making, that held back more than ever before, yet at one and the same time offered more than ever before. Then with a flash of intuition she realized that there was something in his mind which she did not understand. What could it be? She glanced at him narrowly out of lowered eyes, and listened more carefully to what he was saying. And all at once she knew what he had been thinking. Rapidly she adjusted her own thoughts to suit this new aspect of affairs, and in a moment she was picturing herself, walking down the front stairs of the house, with Theresa Coniffe's keys dangling from her belt, and her ample young limbs moulded into a stiff pleated dress of black satin like the one that Theresa wore. She saw herself giving orders to a servant girl like herself, and she pictured Miss Sara Coniffe passing her out apologetically on the landing, and telling the servant to take good care and give no cheek or back talk to Mrs. Gabriel Galloway. She was recalled by Gabriel's voice questioning her in an urgent whisper.

"Onny, how did you fall into the river?"

It was as she had guessed. He thought that she had thrown herself into it. She hesitated for a moment and then, believing that a lie could only be made by the tongue, she gave him no answer, but put up her hands to her face, as if to cover shame and confusion. From his exclamation she knew at once that he had jumped to the conclusion that his suspicions were right.

"Oh, Onny, you cannot know how the thought of what might have happened to you terrifies me. You poor thing! You were so frightened and so lonely! I made you feel that you were guilty and wicked. I made you feel that our meetings were deceitful and wrong. I made you feel that I was ashamed of you. Oh, Onny! I blame myself so much! Thank God I have nothing worse for which to blame myself! Forgive me! All that secrecy is gone forever. I will never be ashamed to claim you in public again. I will let the whole town see that I am proud of you."

Upon the wall of Onny's room at home in the cottage there were several fly-blown pictures, but there was one that hung just over her bed, to which she was much attached as it was her own belonging, having been given to her as a child. This picture represented a girl with golden hair and bare feet, who walked blindfold through a land where brier brambles hung out to either side of the paths, and reptiles crept from under stones, and where at every step the ground gaped with great fissures and ravines. But through this perilous land the golden girl trod her way with safety, because at her side there walked her guardian angel, a youth clad in shining armour, bearing a sword; a youth who was not at all unlike Gabriel himself.

Onny thought of the glossy print, as she listened to Gabriel's words. He vaunted his desire to protect her as the angel vaunted his sword. She began to wish that she had indeed thrown herself into the river, that she might really merit this romantic protection. She lay back against her pillow and listened to his voice, but then, as she listened, she began to lose confidence in him. She looked up sideways again. In the same way that she had been only pretending so too might he be only pretending.

"If it was true," she said, "I might have been drowned before you got to me. And what would you do then? You couldn't do me much good if I was drowned!"

Gabriel was about to beseech her not to mention such a terrible possibility, when he pulled himself up suddenly and repeated her words to himself.

"If it was true," he said. "What do you mean by that? If what was true?"

"If it was true that I threw myself in the river."

Gabriel's hands fell to his sides.

"Isn't it true?" he said, stupidly.

Onny bit her lip. She saw that she had made a slip. She began, too, to see the evil of deception she had played upon him, but still the lie she had given with a gesture did not seem to her as bad as a lie of the tongue, and her whole attitude was so different from his that she would have been as quick to forgive such a joke as to play it herself.

"It's not true," she said, "but I wanted to see what you'd say if you thought it was true!"

"Oh, Onny. How could you joke upon a subject so serious?"

Onny tilted her head angrily.

"You're always teasing me."

"Never by a lie!"

"I didn't tell a lie," said Onny. "I just said nothing."

"That is as bad as a lie!" said Gabriel, but he was already somewhat softened. "Oh, Onny, you badly need someone to guide you."

He wiped his forehead on which the cold sweat had gathered, and he sat down on the side of the bed. Already he was reacting to the news, always welcome, that although he was ready and braced to face all manner of dangers, the dangers had, all at once, taken themselves away. But even in his relief a slight worry yet remained and he felt that some purpose had been served by the fright she had given him. He realized that he was travelling a dangerous road with Onny. Their secret was safe to-night. But a day might come when nothing could save that secret from being known. A day might come when it would be laid bare as inevitably as the leaves came on the trees. This night might give them warning of a truth that was hidden, but active, and thrusting itself towards a real disclosure. Events that are to happen often are intuitively apprehended at a too previous date, and the emotion they would arouse is dissipated on the false event.

Gabriel sat so silent that Onny began to get frightened. She began to realize something of the fright she had given him.

"Are you mad with me?" she said, in a chastened tone, and when he answered her so abstractedly that it was hardly an answer at all, she was overcome with perplexity.

"Do you mean," she said, "that you wish it was true? That you wish I was in trouble?"

Her mind, stored with tales of other girls who had met with misfortune, told to her many a night in bed by her sister Judy, was utterly perplexed before this new revelation from Gabriel that it would not have been a misfortune at all.

"Why would it be a misfortune, Onny? Was it a misfortune to your mother when you were born?"

"But my father married my mother!" said Onny.

"That doesn't make any difference," said Gabriel in a lordly way that was easier to sustain when there was no great pressure of emergency.

"If anything like that was to happen I'd like to have a wedding ring," said Onny, reluctant to cede a point even upon an issue of speculative interest.

"Don't cross your bridges before you come to them," he said casually, and he stood up. "Look, the sky is lightening," he said. "Listen to the birds!"

He went over to the window and opened the casement, and then stepping back into the room he quenched the spluttering night light. The room was no darker than when the feeble flame had struggled up from the colza oil, because the first pale strands of light from the new day were streaming into the room.

"It was a weary bitter night, Onny!" said Gabriel, putting an arm down on the window sash and leaning his head upon it. "But it's over now, and such a night will never come again. I feel older and wiser and better than I felt yesterday, and perhaps this that has happened is all for the best, because you will know in future that I am nearer to you than anyone and that if you are afraid of anything or anyone you must come to me." He came back to the bedside. "There are people in this town that wear wedding rings and were married out of the priest's breviary, with deacons and acolytes and servers, as thick as sheep in a shearing pen, and yet they are no more surely married than you and I."

Onny lay back on the pillows. She saw that she would have to give up her dream of being able to issue orders to Miss Coniffe, but she preened herself on having come well out of the night. She had never thought that Gabriel would marry her, but neither had she thought that he would stick to her if she were involved in what she still preferred to call by its familiar name as a disgrace! And she had enough wit to divine, further even than Gabriel, that the valorous course he chose would demand such changes in the situation of things as might amount to as much, and more, of a triumph than marriage! They would have to go away. She had heard tell of girls that did that—went away to a new country and didn't come back till years afterwards, and when they came back they were dressed with such finery and style that they were too much above everyone for anyone to look down on them!

"I didn't tell you what really happened tonight," said Onny, sitting up higher and bolder in the bed as the light brightened.

"It's getting very bright," said Gabriel, nervously, looking out where the dark leaves that had been silhouetted against the window space were beginning to gleam with green. The explanation of the accident seemed of little matter now. He hardly listened to her voice.

"I went home at the usual time but my supper wasn't ready and there was no one in the house so I went out to the ramparts. I was too early and I thought I'd hide in the trees and pretend that I wasn't coming. I wanted to see what you'd do. But as I was hiding I thought I heard you coming and thought you saw me. I ran out and I heard a man laughing and it wasn't you! I got such a fright! I screamed and ran to another tree, but he ran after me. I kept running from tree to tree thinking that he might lose me in the shadows."

Gabriel straightened up.

"Who was he?" he demanded. "It was bright. Did you see his face?"

"I didn't take time to look! I was running so hard, I ran from one tree to another. I tried to keep going a way that would bring me back near to the gap but he was gaining on me and I had to run straight not to lose any time. I ran without looking where I was going, breaking back the branches if they were in my way, and then all at once I saw why he was running to the right of me—he was driving me down to the river."

Gabriel broke into her words.

"Did he catch you?" he said sharply, and gripped her wrist.

"If he did it wouldn't be my fault! " said Onny, wincing with the pain of his fingers. He relaxed.

"Of course not, Onny, forgive me! Tell me what happened."

Onny looked up at him. "I thought of the day that you made me cross over on the stones," she said.

"But the river was low then, it was nearly dry."

"I didn't think of that, I didn't think of anything, but I ran into the water and began to wade out."

"What did the man do?"

"He called out to me—'Come back you little fool'—but I kept on going. The rocks were nearly covered with water but I could see them all the same. He was standing on the bank yelling at me. 'Come out and I promise I'll go away and leave you alone,' he said. I stood on one of the stones and I looked back at him standing there. He was a poacher I think. He had rabbits slung over his shoulder. He was a stranger, I never saw him before. His face was as white as a sheet. He was afraid I'd drown." Onny chuckled.

"Don't laugh like that; you might have been drowned, Onny," said Gabriel gravely.

"I might for all he did to save me!" said Onny, breaking off her laughter. "I was on the edge of the current and I remembered the way you leaped across it. I could see the stones at the other side where the water wasn't flowing so fast.

" 'Don't attempt that,' said the poacher, and that was the last I heard because my foot slipped when I leaped off the stone and I felt the water carrying me away, and the sound of it roaring in my ears."

Onny caught Gabriel's hand as she remembered the rushing water.

"And what did he do?" said Gabriel.

"I don't know," said Onny. "I think he ran away."

"Coward, coward that he was!" said Gabriel.

"Some men are afraid of their lives they'll get involved in something that will have their names all over the paper," said Onny, repeating a dictum often expressed by Mrs. Soraghan.

"Men are poor creatures, Onny!" said Gabriel, and he felt proud of the feelings of purity and modesty and loyalty that had made Onny risk her life.

There was a far faint sound of a bell ringing in the frosty air.

"That's the bell in the convent," he said absently, "the nuns are getting up. I must go back to my room."

He looked again at the window, at the strange early freshness of the scenes outside, where the underleaves of the trees in the garden were grey with clinging, frosty dew, and where the birds gave a clear note and flew through the branches, showering drops of water from their shaken perches and scattering them in the air with their fidgeting wings. The sky was lit by the sun that yet had not come above the rim of the earth, but cast a clear green light that was sweet and piercing—a shade seen rarely in the evening, and never then so deep, with the brightness of the stars to break the green intensity.

He opened the door softly and closed it. The hall, not having the benefit of a window opening upon the east, and lit only by the fanlight over the hall door and by such light as came down from the landing window, was still dark, and he began to walk on the tips of his toes, having lost the careless recklessness with which he had defied the doors and creaking footboards a short time before. He went up the stairs slowly, looking downwards to make a careful choice of step, and guard against stumbling. He did not want to waken his aunts. Now that he was determined to marry Onny, he saw more than ever the need for keeping their relationship secret until he had made some plans.

He was going to marry her, but there was no great hurry. It was absolutely necessary to see about getting some means for supporting her.

There was only one thing that could force his hand. If his aunts had become suspicious of Onny he would have to come out into the open. He would have to make a stand against them. And this he would do! He was determined upon it. But he hoped that the necessity for such a stand would not occur. Before he went into his own room he stood outside his Aunt Theresa's door. Was she asleep, he wondered? How much did she guess? Then he moved away. The morning would tell.

∽ ∽ ∽

Next morning when Sara Coniffe wakened, the events of the night before came back to her and she lay with terror, thinking of the action that her sister Theresa planned to take. She had a longing to get up and rush away from the house out into the early morning air, away, away, anywhere, anywhere. But another impulse to stay and perhaps soften the blow that was to fall on Onny made her get up, and dress quickly, and hurry downstairs.

Theresa was already astir. Sara could hear her firm steps in the rooms below. Perhaps the interview with Onny was over. Perhaps Onny was gone! There was a trembling sensation in Sara's limbs and she gripped the handrail of the banister tightly. But when she came to the landing she saw that Onny's door was closed. She felt a regret that she would still have to witness the humiliation of the girl, but she felt a relief for the girl's sake that her humiliation had not yet come upon her, and this was strengthened when she thought that some unforeseen event might prevent it from coming at all.

She went into the kitchen.

"Good morning, Theresa."

Theresa looked up from the table.

"I'm glad you came down," said Theresa. "I want to say a few words to you before Gabriel gets up."

Theresa was preparing a breakfast tray while she spoke, and putting a piece of bread, and a toasting fork, into Sara's hands, she told her to make toast while she herself was pouring the water into the teapot.

"I lay awake for some time after I went to bed," she said, "and it appeared to me that it would be adopting an altogether wrong course to turn the girl out of the house. That would be the very worst thing to do. It would arouse Gabriel's sympathy. There's no knowing but that we might be simply throwing her into his arms. I have decided against sending her away. I have other plans." She put out her hand. "Is that toast ready? I'm bringing Gabriel a cup of tea in bed. I want to gloss over the slight harshness I showed last night. It is most essential to my plan that he doesn't think that I suspect him of any interest, above the ordinary, in Onny. I don't want her to suspect that I know either. That will put her into such a position that she won't know where she is!" She arranged the toast in the toast rack, and lifted the tray. "I intend to let things go on as usual for the present, but I am going to make use of every opportunity to show her up, so that he will be forced to see her in her true light!" She held the tray bosom high, and went towards the door determinedly. At the door she paused and looked back. "Remember, Sara, I don't want you to be ugly to the girl; not in any way! I don't want her to suspect that I am observing her!"

Sara stood looking after her sister as she went up the stairs, carrying the tray high, so that she could see to pick her steps on the stairs. She felt the trembling sensation in her limbs again. She stared at the closed door of Onny's room, and an unaccountable dread came over her. She felt that, although for Onny the situation had changed, the change had been for the worse.

But Gabriel was her nearer concern and suddenly, rolling all her timidity up into one ball, she ran out into the hall and called up the stairs after Theresa.

"Theresa! I want to say something." Her face was flushed and excited. Theresa lowered the tray and looked down at her.

"Well?" said Theresa.

Sara almost faltered, but not quite.

"I was just thinking," she said, "that it might be no harm if Gabriel had some loose change in his pockets now and again!"

"Why?" asked Theresa inexorably, determined to pursue the thought behind Sara's words, and bring it to light quicker than it would otherwise come.

"Well, I thought it would be nice for him to be able to give a cup of tea to Agnes Finnerty, or Hannah, if he ran across them in Draghead."

"Oh I see." Theresa considered the suggestion for a moment. "There's something in what you say," she said grudgingly, and then she looked down at the tray in her hands. "I can't delay to discuss it now," she said, "the tea is getting cold." She caught the tray up close to her chin again and began to mount the stairs once more. But the idea certainly had its points. On the landing she felt compelled to turn around. "I won't decide anything rashly, Sara," she said. "And above all I must pick my time. I don't want him to see what's behind the idea!" Then, turning around again, Theresa went up the rest of the stairs with great confidence. Her plans were all complete. She opened the door of Gabriel's room

"I brought up your breakfast," she said, anticipating his surprise, and glossing it over by giving him an order to draw up a chair on which she might place the tray. "I thought you would like to stay in bed for a while this morning after the terrible strain of last night. I hope you slept?" She put down the tray and began to assist him in pouring out a cup of tea. "I never knew such an upset. You can't imagine the tension while you were out, trying to keep that poor woman from going out of her mind with anxiety. The poor thing! I was hardly able to keep my patience with her. I know she was a very pitiful object, but at the same time there is some kind of a barrier between us and a poor creature of her class. No matter how one wants to help them, there is always some barrier. I don't believe in class. I hate the word. I never use it. But when there is an occurrence like last night's you recognize that there is something that divides people like us from people like the Soraghans. It is not that they have to work— work is honest—but it is some inferiority in the blood that makes it impossible for them to be dignified. Goodness knows I was as kind as I could be to her, I made her a cup of tea with my own hands, and gave her one of Sara's shawls to put over her shoulders, but the barrier remained. It was she who kept it there. She was every minute humbling herself; ingratiating herself. She was a servant first, and a mother second. They have no dignity. People can work, and yet be proud if they are not servile by nature. Ah well!" Theresa drew herself up into her familiar posture, with her arms crossed and each hand gripping the inner side of the other forearm. "Ah well, one should be thankful to God that one is born of sound upright stock. There is no need to be proud of your position, but to be proud of your personal integrity is another thing altogether. Have you everything? Would you like your tea stronger?"

"I'm all right," said Gabriel, and he hesitated. "Is Onny all right?" he asked, faintly.

"I didn't call her yet," said Theresa. "I let her sleep. I'm afraid I was harsh with her last night, towards the latter end of events. I was quite worn out with worry and fatigue. But your Aunt Sara is going to take her in a cup of tea before she gets up. Indeed, if she shows any signs of a cold I suppose it would be a charity to let her stay in bed for the day. Although hardship seems to be nothing to those Soraghans. They are hardly like human beings at all. The way they all live together in that hovel is example enough for anyone. The air must be foul there, when they are all inside at night. God forgive me, but it's my belief the ducking in the river will do her more good than harm. I hope you're all right, Gabriel?" She altered her tone to one of greater concern, and looking at him closely, she said, "I've seen times when a young one like Onny got into mischief and dragged another person in to her assistance, and although she herself would be as well as could be, the other person would suffer. I dread to think of what might have happened—a worthless piece like herself might have come out of the adventure safely, and a fine young man, like you, with the prospects of a good, profitable life, might have been lost on account of her." She was at the door by this time, and she was about to turn the knob when a thought seemed to strike her. "I just remembered that there was no nightdress left out for Onny! Ah well, I don't suppose that mattered much. I don't think they look very closely into the refinements of life where there is such a houseful as in the Soraghans'! I feel sorry for poor Sara having to give up her room. I wouldn't care very much to have given up my own room. I'd never feel quite the same about it again. The sheets, of course, will be sent out to the wash at once, but there is no way to treat the mattress. I suppose the child is quite clean, but all the same one has an uncomfortable feeling about people like that. It's very silly, I suppose, but it is an instinctive feeling and there is very little that can be done about it. It's good to remember that she had that douse in the river. If Sara feels uncomfortable about the mattress, I must remind her about the dousing in the river."

Gabriel was drinking the tea with downcast eyes. A resentment against his aunt's words stirred him so violently that he longed to dash the cup on the floor, and order her out of the room, but he felt a politic desire to hide his feelings. Controlling his voice, however, he broke in towards the end.

"I think Onny is very clean. I hear you complaining that she is always washing herself in the sink in the kitchen!"

"A cat's lick! She dabs the towel in water and rubs it over her face, and around the rim of her neck. The person who is always dabbling in water is not always the clean person. Cleanliness goes deeper than that. Ah, well, the poor child! I hope I'm not turning you against her, Gabriel. I hope that you won't feel my disgust about having her in the house. I wouldn't want you to worry about your meals, or your linens. Let me hasten to assure you that you have no need to worry on those scores. I see to everything like that myself personally. I never let her hang over the beds, or tamper with the food. I just let her do the rougher work. Sometimes you may see her peeling the potatoes, or scraping the vegetables, but remember they had to be boiled after that, and boiling kills all germs. There is no need for you to worry! I am very particular about things like that. And so is your Aunt Sara. You need not feel the least distaste. And of course, the poor child is learning. Already she has lost some of her bad habits, but most of them I am afraid are rooted too deeply for me to eradicate, and as well as that I don't like to keep always nagging at her. Of course I wouldn't want for the whole wide world that she should hear what I have just said about her to you. I may be harsh, but I would not want to hurt her feelings. It is impossible not to take her to task when she does something particularly stupid, but I hope I would never hurt her feelings about anything personal, for which after all she cannot be blamed. She was brought up that way. She was bred that way." Theresa bent down and caught up the tray. "Are you finished with the tray? I may as well take it down, as I am going. I only intended to leave it with you and come up for it again, but here I am, talking for goodness knows how long! How did we ever start such a conversation? And at this hour of the morning! To think of all I have to do, downstairs, and yet here I stood, for all the world as if it were the middle of the afternoon. I must go downstairs at once. Stay in bed as long as you wish. Would you like to read? Shall I hand you a book?"

"No thank you," said Gabriel, and he put his hands behind his head, and lay looking up at the ceiling. Theresa glanced at him sharply. She was afraid that she had gone too far. She felt inclined to stay for a few minutes longer and lead the conversation into a totally different channel before she went away, so that he would not brood too much on what she had said. But there was something remote about Gabriel's posture, as he lay looking up at the ceiling. It was as if he were already lost in his own thoughts. For good or bad she felt that she would have to leave things as they were. She went out and closed the door.

When his aunt had gone out Gabriel unclasped his hands and lowered them. They were torn and scratched. Every limb in his body ached. He felt utterly disinclined to get up, but greater than the disinclination of his limbs to undertake the duties of the day was the disinclination of his mind to dwell upon the incidents of the night before. He could not remember the details of his talk in the early morning with Onny, but he recalled the fact that they were going to be married. The relief that he had first felt when he had come to his decision had now settled down into an insipid resignation. Last night he had shaken off his old worries. Today he knew that he was facing others. He would have to tell his aunts of his plans. He had seen, only too clearly, through his aunt's words this morning. They had been intending to turn him against Onny. He would have to speak to them before their campaign had gone much further, because already, although he despised the intention that underlay Theresa's remarks about Onny, he felt there was perhaps some truth in them.

Gabriel did not get up that day. Next morning his Aunt Theresa once more brought him a cup of tea in bed, but he forestalled any conversation by saying that he was getting up at once, and asked her to leave the cup of tea on the mantelpiece. He prepared to throw off the blankets. Theresa went out.

When he went downstairs to his breakfast he was prepared for meeting Onny, but when she brought in his breakfast his aunts were in the room and he was unable to have any conversation with her. Still he managed to catch her eye as he asked her if she felt any the worse for her adventure, and with a penetrating stare he tried to counteract the formality of his words. He remembered that he had told her that henceforth he would claim her openly. He hoped that she would understand that a change could not be made too abruptly.

Onny did not seem, however, to have expected that he would behave any differently from usual. She continued to act her usual part of indifference to him, as she adjusted the knives and the forks on the table, and put the cream jug and sugar basin within his reach. He saw that her cheeks were pale, and that there were scratches on the backs of her hands, but her voice was normal, and her body was as free and limber as ever. She answered him casually.

"It's hard to kill a bad thing," she said airily.

Gabriel could not decide whether her indifference was put on for the benefit of his aunts, or whether it was the natural indifference of a healthy animal to whom safety and warmth bring back a rush of vitality, no matter what the body had endured.

When Onny went out of the room, Theresa came across to the table. "Is your breakfast all right? Your Aunt Sara cooked it." She leaned over the plate. "Excuse me," she said, "I hope that Onny's hands were clean. I notice that she sometimes puts finger marks on the rims of the plates."

Gabriel jerked his plate away from her inspection.

"It's all right!" he exclaimed. "Why do you keep her if you find so much fault with her?"

"We keep her because we can get no better!" said Theresa. "You have no idea of the way times have changed, Gabriel, even in the last few years. A short time ago the country girls were glad and willing to take work in the towns, but now they will only work in the cities. They used to think it a good thing to get paid for doing the work they had to do for nothing at home, but now they are ashamed of housework. They think it more respectable to work in a factory, or get a few shillings in an office. Mrs. Finnerty says she doesn't know what the world will be like in another few years. She says there won't be a servant to be found, no matter what salary is offered. But I don't agree with her. While there are different types of human beings in the world, I say, there will also be plenty of servants available. No matter how the world changes there will always be the servile type that cannot elevate itself above the level of scrubbing and pot scouring. There will always be people like the Soraghans. And when nothing better is to be found, I for one am glad to have a substitute. But it's beyond the power of human endurance not to complain once in a while."

Gabriel caught his aunt's skirt and jerked it to indicate that Onny was coming along the passage towards them. His aunt nodded significantly to indicate that she too had heard the girl, but she went on speaking without appreciably lowering her voice, and when Gabriel's face flushed, she glanced at him scathingly.

"She won't understand what we are saying!" she said, and then she repeated deliberately, " There are always people of the type we mentioned." She was about to say more when Onny walked into the room.

"I am finished, Onny," said Gabriel, speaking quickly, to interrupt his aunt, and lifting his plate to hand to the girl.

Theresa bit her lips. She did not attempt to finish her sentence, but she caught Onny by the arm as she was clearing the dishes from the table.

"Don't rub up against the clean tablecloth with that dirty apron!" she said. "I don't know how you get your aprons so filthy."

Gabriel's heart sank. He sat back from the table and watched the girl as she moved around collecting the plates and scraping them, before she piled them up on the tray. It was not so long ago since he had sat, his heart filled with pity, and watched her while his aunt gave her humiliating orders. Then his feelings had been pure and disinterested. Now he felt that he was no longer the spectator of her humiliation and degradation, but that he too was humiliated and degraded. The situation was unbearable. He would have to speak to his aunt. But, looking again at Onny's dress, and at her soiled canvas slippers flapping wetly on the floor, he felt an unreality in the situation. He felt it impossible to believe that by speaking to his aunt he would have transformed the situation so that it would no longer seem ludicrous to regard Onny as Mrs. Gabriel Galloway.

317

Just then Onny came slopping up the passage again in her wet canvas shoes. She handed a bundle of letters to Theresa, and went out. On the way out she made some signal to Gabriel, nodding at him behind his aunt's back, but he could not catch her meaning.

"There's a letter for you, Gabriel," said his aunt after she had sorted the bundle. She handed him a thin blue envelope. "Who is it from?" she asked, and leaving her own letters unopened she sat forward in her chair in the expectation of hearing the contents of her nephew's letter. In the passageway outside there was a sound of quick small steps and Sara came to the door, her face eager with interest.

"I saw there was a letter for you, Gabriel," she said. "The postman handed the bundle to me, but my hands were wet so I gave them to Onny to deliver."

She pulled out a chair, and sat down like Theresa upon the edge of the seat, to hear the contents of the letter.

The handwriting was Sylvester's. Gabriel recognized it at once, but he hesitated to open it.

"What are you looking at it for? Aren't you going to open it? Here is a hairpin!" said Sara, eagerly drawing a long tortoise-shell pin from her hair. "Slit it open with this."

"I am not going to open it just now," he said, and he looked up at the clock. "I'll be late for my train," he said. "Will you excuse me?"

Standing up, Gabriel brushed past Sara and went out. He went straight to the hall door, but as he passed the door of the kitchen, which was open, he saw Onny. She too looked up questioningly as he passed out. He knew that she wanted to speak to him, to ask him what he intended to do, but a bitter independence possessed him, and he guarded himself from her as from his aunts. He went out and closed the heavy door. As he passed by the kitchen window he kept his eyes on the pavement, because, as he expected, Onny had come to the window and her face was pressed close to the glass.

He put the unopened letter into his pocket. He would read it in the train, but before Gabriel had gone more than a yard up the street he heard the door open behind him again and Onny ran out into the street. For a moment he thought that she was outfacing everyone and he was about to speak sharply to her, but before he had time to say anything, Onny called out to him.

"You're to come back," she said. "Miss Theresa wants you."

When he went back Sara and Theresa were standing in the hall, but as soon as they saw him, Theresa beckoned him into the front parlour. Sara turned to go upstairs, about her business, but her face wore a knowing look. Theresa shut the door after them.

"I won't keep you a minute, Gabriel," she said, and she went over to

318

the black tin box in which she kept her money. "Your Aunt Sara and I were saying the other day that you might like to have some small change in your pocket, particularly now that you are going in and out of Drag-head. You might like to take a cup of tea occasionally, if you have to wait for the train. Or you might like to give some young lady a treat! We don't forget what it is to be young, you know!" Theresa smiled archly, and then looking at the clock she opened the box hurriedly. "I don't want to keep you late though," she said, and she pulled out a ten-shilling note, "Here, take this," she said, " and I'll give you the same every week. There's no need to spend it all, of course, but on the other hand don't stint yourself. And as I say, if you should want to treat anyone!" Once again Theresa gave him an arch smile. "We won't mention any names!" she said, and then, cutting short his confusion and thanks by closing the lid of the box with a snap, Theresa threw up her hand. "Is that the whistle of your train, Gabriel?" she asked, and as he started up she went ahead of him and threw open the door. Gabriel took up the note from the table.

"I'll be in time," he cried. "There is always a delay in the morning."

ɷ　ɷ　ɷ

Gabriel got to the station in time to drag open a carriage door as the train pulled out of the station. In another minute the town was behind him, shrinking smaller and smaller, until it was only a cluster of houses bound by a broken rampart, and pierced by a single spire. He leaned out of the window of the train. How small it was! Again this thought struck him forcibly—and yet around it the winds lashed; winds that had travelled across plains and seas, and lifted the pennants of cities a thousand miles away. He withdrew his head, and sat down in the empty compartment, fixing his eyes upon the dusty carpeted seat. He had not yet opened Sylvester's letter.

The truth was that he dreaded to read it. Lately Sylvester had ceased to inquire what he was doing. He had ceased to ask if there was any chance of his coming to Dublin. Instead the letters were full of his own activities. In the last of them he had given a description of the new rooms he had taken. They were in Kildare Street, a street near the Art School. There were three rooms. In one he slept. In the other he cooked and ate his meals. The third was a lumber room. It would come in useful some day. But at the moment he had no use for it. The boards were not very good. The light was bad too. But it was a decent size. So the letter had run on, occupied with the writer's own concerns.

Why does he keep on writing to me? thought Gabriel irritably, as he took out the unopened letter and prepared to slit the flap of the envelope.

Lately Sylvester's letters made him unhappy. In spite of the curtness and abruptness with which they were written, it was clear that Sylvester was more than satisfied with his lot in Dublin.

And look at the mess I've got myself into here, thought Gabriel. He stared out of the carriage window at the speeding fields and hedges. Why didn't I go away with him as he urged me to go?

For, in comparison with the difficulties into which he had got himself in the last few months, the difficulties that had stood between him and going away with Sylvester seemed so trivial he could not remember them, much less understand how it was that he had not attempted to overcome them.

Then all at once he remembered at least one of those past difficulties, and one that was not the least important—money. But as he thought of it his hand flew to his pocket, where, carelessly crumpled up like the paper off a caramel, was the ten-shilling note his aunt had given him. Ten shillings! And another the following week; and every week after that. It wouldn't take long to save up a small sum.

An idea suddenly began to form in his mind. He had only three pounds at the time Sylvester was urging him to go away. Now he would have a little money, regularly. He was in a difficult situation here. How better could he solve it than by going away?

In a few minutes his plans took shape. He would have to write to Sylvester first. And then of course he would have to wait long enough for the ten-shilling notes to amount to something. He calculated quickly on his fingers. By the end of the summer he should have more than ten pounds. Ten pounds ought to be enough to get to Dublin, and pay for a week or so in a lodginghouse while he was looking for something to do. Like Sylvester, he now had every confidence that he would find some form of suitable work in a big place like Dublin. And if he had to avail himself of Sylvester's offer to put him up for a few weeks he would be able to repay him in a short time.

Sylvester, of course, did not know about Onny. For a moment Gabriel was daunted by this thought. But his confidence was great enough to sweep away all obstacles. If necessary he could go alone, and send for Onny later. At any rate there was no need to tell her about his plans until it was nearer to the time for putting them into execution. The less she knew the better.

But although he kept Onny in ignorance of his plans all through the following weeks, Gabriel's determination to take her with him grew more steadily.

Time and again, as he saw her driven about the house by his Aunt Theresa, he told himself that he could not bear to go and leave her behind him, but deeper in his heart he was sometimes forced to acknowledge that it would be easier to take her with him than it would be to send for her

320

if he was once away from the immediate magnetism of her person. But whether she went with him, or whether he sent for her afterwards, the only way that he could see of discharging his duties to Onny was by taking her out of Castlerampart. For with every day that passed, Theresa found new opportunities of showing how poor a breed Mrs. Soraghan had raised in the cottage under the ramparts.

The only real change that came after the episode of the river was that Gabriel made up his mind not to meet Onny by stealth any more. This meant that their meetings in the tower came to an end. Instead they went for walks along the roads. But it was not the same. They were all the time meeting people, and in spite of Gabriel's determination not to be secretive, Onny would insist on lagging behind, or walking hurriedly ahead, behaving in a manner intended to make it seem that their meeting was accidental. On bright nights she was particularly difficult, and once or twice when he went out to meet her she was with one of her sisters, and passed him by with a nod, telling him next day that she could not get rid of other people unless they went some place quiet like the tower. She could not understand his attitude.

"It's for your own good, Onny," he protested, when she pouted and complained.

But with a surer instinct Onny felt that her hold over him was dependent on a degree of familiarity and intimacy that was impossible in meetings in any other place but the old ruin in the deserted park. And Gabriel himself at times, after listening to Theresa's jibes at her all day, found that not seeing her, or a stilted meeting under the observation of other people, was not enough to take away the uneasy feeling caused by his aunt's words. But it would all be different when they went away. That seemed still to be the only way out of what he was coming to regard as an awkward situation.

∽   ∽   ∽

Gabriel planned that he might be able to leave Castlerampart about the end of August, but one day in May his plans came to a head overnight.

He had been counting over his money, which amounted to nine pounds, and he was just putting back the box in which he kept it under the chest of drawers beside his bed when his Aunt Sara knocked at his door. She came in almost at once, and on her face, which was always soft and smiling, there was an unusually benign expression. Something about this expression on Sara's face seemed familiar to Gabriel, and indeed, there seemed to be something familiar to him in the very way she knocked at the door, the very way she came forward at once upon his calling out to do so, and above all in the provocative way in which she advanced towards him with her hands hidden behind her back.

Why, of course! It must be his birthday.

And sure enough, Sara had no sooner reached the centre of the room than she fixed her eyes on him playfully and put the old familiar question, by which, year after year, she had marked his birthday out from the rest of the days in the calendar.

"I wonder what day it is today?"

Gabriel smiled.

His birthdays did not mean much to him. The fact that they were unfailingly remembered by his aunts, who both made a point of giving him gifts on that day, did not make the day much different from the other days in the calendar, because Theresa and Sara always gave him articles of clothing: ties, socks, pyjamas, or other wearables, which although they were tied up with flowered paper and fancy ribbons were scarcely any different from the packages of similar articles which were ordered for him in Draghead from time to time, and which arrived in plain brown paper, tied with ordinary string. The gifts by which they commemorated his birthday were different from the things they regularly bought for him by reason of their wrapping alone. There was no element of surprise in them. And if his aunts should by chance forget to draw his attention to the fact that it was his birthday, Gabriel himself would never notice their omission.

This day, however, when Sara came into his room with her hands behind her back, whatever she had for him was smaller than usual, for not a vestige of wrapper or package could be seen to either side of her. And indeed, so small was it that when, a minute afterwards, she wished him many happy returns of the day, and brought her hands from behind her back and clasped them together over her bosom, she still concealed whatever was tightly clutched in one of them.

For the first time since he was a small child, Gabriel felt a glow of excitement.

"What have you for me, Aunt Sara?" he cried, and he went to catch at her hands.

"Wait, wait!" cried Sara, and she backed away from him.

Her confidence in the success of her present was beginning to ebb away.

"Now, my dear boy," she began, "if you don't like what I have for you, you have only to tell me. Remember that you have only to tell me, and tomorrow you'll have something else." Sara clasped her hands tighter together and drew back towards the door. "I don't believe I'll give it to you at all," she cried. "I'm sure you won't like it. I'll wait and get something in Draghead tomorrow." Gabriel was about to protest but Sara held up her hand. "Don't interrupt me, dear," she said. "You see, what I was going to give you would not be a surprise, and I always think a present should be a surprise." She paused. "You think you're getting a pair of socks and what do you get but a box of handkerchiefs. It's the surprise that counts. Oh, dear, why didn't I buy you something! What gave me the foolish idea that you would like this?"

With her left hand Sara tapped at the gift which was still clutched in concealment in the fist of her right hand.

"But, Aunt Sara," cried Gabriel, "I don't know what you have for me, but I can tell you that I was never so curious about anything in my whole life. Whatever it is it will be sure to give me a bigger surprise than anything you ever gave me before now."

Sara regained a small shred of confidence.

"Do you think so?" she said, and then she faltered again. "I wouldn't want you to think that I let the time pass until it was too late to buy you anything, and that that is why I am giving you this!"

Sara stretched out her hand suddenly and pressed her gift into Gabriel's hand. He looked down. In his hand he had a five-pound note.

"Oh, but Aunt Sara! This is far too much to give me," he exclaimed. Sara blushed.

"Oh, why should you say that, Gabriel?" she said. "It's less than I would have spent if I bought you something, but somehow or other five pounds seems more correct to give as a present than six or six pounds ten, don't you think, or is that stupid of me?"

Gabriel began to uncrumple the note and fold it into regular sections.

It was probably true, although he had never set much value on them, that the shirts and pyjamas his aunts gave him would cost this much money and more. But how provident that Sara should have given him the money instead of spending it on more clothes of which he had a surplus already.

How provident! In his mind he began to add this sum to the sum he already had in the black tin box, and Sara, watching him, was fully assured that her present was appreciated.

"I'm so glad you are pleased, Gabriel," she said, and she pressed his hand.

But at the gentle pressure of Sara's soft and timid hand, Gabriel suddenly felt suffused with shame. How hurt she would be when she discovered that it was with the help of her money that he ran away with the servant girl from her own house. Sara above all. If only it had been Theresa who had given it to him, he thought, how small a trouble it would be to him to use it in a manner that would aggravate her.

He was almost shaken in his purpose for a moment, as he looked at Sara's face wreathed in the smiles of contentment. But his mind was upset and one thought intruded upon another.

Supposing Theresa was planning to give him money also. His heart leaped. And his distress over the disillusionment he would cause his Aunt Sara was scattered to atoms in the joyful excitement of the new thought.

Sara, seeing the leap of excitement in her nephew's eyes, decided that he was already springing ahead with plans for spending her gift, and that she should go away as fast as she could.

"I'm so glad you are pleased, dear," she said again, and pressing his hand once more she went over to the door, instinctively going on tiptoe so as not to intrude by as much as a footfall on the plans she had made possible.

After Sara went away, Gabriel stood in the centre of the floor. The sisters usually came along with their gifts within a few minutes of each other. Theresa ought to be at the door any minute. He wondered if there was time to get down on his knees and take up the tin box, because his hands itched to hold in one fist the whole of the sum that was now in his possession.

"Fourteen pounds!" And if by a miracle Theresa were to give him another five pounds?

If she did! If she did! He looked around the red-papered room. If Theresa gave him another five-pound note he wouldn't sleep many more nights in this room.

"Can I come in, Gabriel?"

There was a sharp knock on the door, followed by this concise request. Gabriel ran to the door.

"Come in, Aunt Theresa," he cried, cordiality in every word and gesture, but Theresa had no sooner come inside the door than his face fell, for although, like Sara, Theresa kept her present for him behind her back, to either side of her thin black figure there protruded the end of a glossy draper's box. When Theresa went out Gabriel opened the tin box and took out its contents, and folding the new note in among the old ones, he put the money into his pocket. He would write to Sylvester at once, and tell him to expect him at the end of the week. He would have gone the following morning, but he felt that he had better wait to give Sylvester time to answer his letter. And until he had that answer he would not tell Onny anything.

On Thursday morning when Gabriel came down to breakfast there was a letter from Sylvester. In it Sylvester made no mention of Onny. In general the letter was cordial enough. Sylvester said he would meet the evening train, presuming that was the one on which they would travel. Gabriel as a matter of fact intended to go on the morning train, as he could leave the house in the normal way at the normal hour that he would be going to Draghead, and Onny, too, would be more likely to get to the station unnoticed at an early hour in the day. He decided to stick to his first plan and go by the early train. They could walk about the city and go back to the station in the evening to meet Sylvester. He stood up from the table. He had to see Onny.

Onny had gone upstairs with his aunts to do the upper rooms, but after a few minutes she came down carrying the brass water cans to fill them and bring them upstairs again. She found Gabriel waiting for her at the foot of the stairs.

"Onny" he said, "you'll have to be ready to come away with me tomorrow"

Onny was surprised, but she tried not to show it.

"Are we going to be married?" she asked.

"Of course we are," said Gabriel impatiently. "We'll be married later on. But there's no use thinking we could ever live here. People would never let you forget that you once worked in this house as a servant. We must go away. We couldn't be married here anyway, you would have to get your mother's consent!"

"My mother would give her consent!" said Onny eagerly.

"I have no doubt she would," said Gabriel dryly, but then he spoke more persuasively. "If your mother knew about it it would soon come to the ears of my aunts and I can assure you that we wouldn't get their consent so easily. My Aunt Theresa would do all in her power to stop us."

"Well, what are we going to do?" said Onny.

"This," said Gabriel, and he outlined his plan. "Now you must put together whatever few things you want to take with you, and get a suitcase for them; then tomorrow morning, you must steal out of the house, and go down to the station."

"Tomorrow?" said Onny, who had forgotten the beginning of the conversation. "The station! A suitcase!" She stared at him with her lips apart.

"Yes, yes," said Gabriel, impatiently.

He had spent so long preparing his plans and they had become so acceptable to him that he did not consider the effect they would have upon Onny. As he heard his aunt's footsteps overhead he hurried his words. He considered that everything was settled, but he repeated a few points.

"You don't need much luggage," he said, "but be sure to be in time for the train. Above all, don't tell anyone anything; we can't risk being stopped."

"My mother will get a fright when she finds me gone," said Onny, clinging to anything that held her back from a final decision.

"We'll send messages home as soon as we are safely on our way," said Gabriel. "How would you like it if your mother sent the priest after you to drag you home, and disgrace you before the whole town?"

Onny gave in. Gabriel drew a deep breath. He turned to go up the stairs.

"Where are we going?" said Onny, running after him, and pulling him by the sleeve.

"It's better for you not to know till tomorrow. You'll have no temptation to boast about your destination!" He loosened her hand from his sleeve. "I've a lot to attend to, Onny," he said. "I may not see you again until tomorrow morning."

Onny's face fell at his words, but she remembered Sylvester's letters that had been coming with increasing frequency. She remembered that one had arrived that morning. She clapped her hands, and was about to call after Gabriel, but on second thoughts she ran over to the mirror, and pushing aside her hair from her face, she smiled into the glass.

A decision, even a wrong decision, brings a certain peace of mind with it. Gabriel went up to his room and began to select among his possessions the articles that he intended to take with him.

∽   ∽   ∽

Next morning Gabriel was up early, and in his anxiety to get out of the house with his suitcase without being seen, he did not have time for misgivings at leaving the house where he was born. He walked slowly to the railway so that the train would be in the station when he arrived, and there would be no danger of his encountering Onny on the platform. He had timed his pace well, and he arrived at the station just as the train pulled into it. He stepped at once into an empty carriage, and began to watch for Onny. He did not feel any different from the way he felt on other occasions when he had taken the train to the Technical School. The strong odour of the dust stored in the thick pile of the red plush cushions, the stale smell of steam, the taste of smoke in his mouth, all assorted their associations upon him. It was hard to feel that this was a new epoch. Then he saw Onny running into the station.

Onny wore her best clothes, gaudy and bright. At first he thought she had no luggage, and he thought that perhaps she had changed her mind about accompanying him, but then he saw that she carried a small carpet-bag, of a bright red colour with a cross-stitch design of pink roses on it, and it was bulging with things. She, too, looked around her for a moment, saw him, blushed, and ran down the platform to the other end and disappeared into a carriage. The guard banged the door after her, a whistle blew, and the train began to steam out of the town.

Some time later, when they came to a small, quiet, country station, Gabriel jumped out on to the platform, and ran down the train to Onny's compartment and jumped into it.

Onny had been talking animatedly to the other occupants of the carriage, but when she saw him she blushed and stopped up in the middle of what she was saying. Seeing her embarrassment he winked at her, and putting his case on the luggage rack sat down in the far corner, without speaking to her. He saw at once that she was relieved, but she was still considerably quietened by his presence. In the carriage there were two large women, with pale faces, sitting on the same side as Onny. They were country-women with shawls and baskets, and one of them had on her lap a large wicker basket in which there were live hens. In the corner opposite Onny there was a tall man, possibly a commercial traveller, and one who, while adept at starting a train conversation, was equally adept in retiring from it to sit back and enjoy the efforts of others, with only an intermittent contribution when it flagged. After Gabriel's entry into the carriage, the conversation went on without interruption, although Onny's contributions had dwindled to yes, and no.

"I hate travelling!" said the woman with the basket of hens. "But I have to go to see my sister. She hasn't been well lately. I got a letter from her, asking me to send a few chickens. I thought that I might as well bring them to her myself," she sighed. "Nature is nature," she said. "If we don't take care of our own, who will take care of us?"

The commercial traveller shifted his legs.

"Don't talk about travelling!" he said. "In my job you get your fill of it. I'm on the road nine hours a day, and I lie in a strange bed every other night."

"I hope you're careful!" The second woman leaned forward. "I hope you see that the sheets are aired? That is a thing I am always in dread of —damp sheets. Damp sheets are the cause of more deaths than people imagine. I am always saying that, and no one listens to me. People should look into the question of damp sheets. If I were you, young man, I'd never sleep in a strange bed without testing the sheets."

At this point Onny could not keep out of the conversation any longer. She was caught up into it again.

"How would you test them?" she asked, leaning forward.

"Well," said the woman, "I'll tell you what I do myself. I light a match and hold it over the sheet. If the sheet is damp you will see the steam rising from it! Of course, you can't always do that. Sometimes a sheet is not properly aired, which comes to the same thing as being damp, but in that case you won't see any steam rising."

"If I have any doubts I sleep between the blankets," said the woman with the hens.

"Oh, I wouldn't do that!" said the other woman. "It's not healthy to sleep between blankets. It's almost as bad as sleeping in damp sheets! I'll tell you what I do myself. I usually take my sheets away with me!"

The palms of victory were about to be tossed in her direction when the woman with the hens snatched them almost from the air.

"That's all right if you are only going away for a short stay," she said. "But what would you do if you were going away for two weeks? You can't let two weeks go by without a change of sheets; if it is only the under sheet, although I myself like a change of upper and lower sheets!"

Her opponent was dashed to the ground, but she rose to a feeble protest.

"Two weeks is a long time to be away," she said. "It's well for a person who is able to stay away from her home two weeks and not worry at the way it's going to rack and ruin in her absence. I wouldn't trust my house for two weeks!"

Gabriel wondered how Onny could listen to such talk: how it could interest her. Beyond the carriage windows the fields sped by, acre after acre, widening the rift between past and future. They had begun to go through the midlands, where the fields were flat and wet, with muddy lanes; everywhere there were ugly limestone cottages and badly constructed houses, built to a contractor's plan. Some of the houses were settled in flats of mud, trodden indiscriminately by cattle, humans, and mud-splattered hens. This mud was often splashed half-way up the walls. And above these squalid farms, there rose the gorgeous architecture of the clouds.

Their travelling companions got out, one at a time, at different stations along the way. Gabriel stared indifferently at the scenes. They were always the same. A porter in plain clothes ran out from a low station house as the train drew into the platform; as he ran, he snatched an official cap from the damp window sill of the waiting room, and still chewing the last of the meal from which he had been called away, he waved a stick on which a piece of green cloth was tied. A dog chased up and down the platform. A boy with a running nose had a few tattered magazines in a wicker basket, but he did not proffer them for sale, unless someone whistled at him. At stations where passengers descended there were the usual scenes: women kissed each other, and helped with baskets.

At last the carriage was empty. Gabriel went over and sat beside Onny.

"Well, Onny?" he said. "I was laughing at you! You must have given your cheeks a great scrubbing this morning. You're as clean as a corpse! Why on earth did you enter into conversation with those foolish people?"

Onny pulled away from him. "Are you going to find fault with me?"

"I'm not finding fault, Onny. To wish to correct slight imperfections in a person who is dear to me is not finding fault."

"But I don't try to correct you!" said Onny.

"I don't think you have occasion to do so!" said Gabriel, somewhat stiffly. Then, more curious, he added, " What fault do you find in me?" Onny did not answer.

"I don't suppose I'm perfect," said Gabriel, "but I hardly thought that my faults were visible on the surface for all to see! Tell me, what faults have you discovered in me?"

Onny bit her lip.

Gabriel became more and more interested.

"I'd hate to think that you had seen faults in me and kept them hidden from me. I prefer that if you had seen anything in my character, or rather in my manner, that you disliked, that you would have corrected it, Onny. It is not sincere to hide a person's faults from him. Tell me one of my faults, Onny!"

"I can't think of one now," said Onny.

Gabriel frowned. "I hope that you did not make a rash statement just to get your own back. That would be spiteful and petty. But if you were sincere, then I am glad you spoke, because I want you to remember, Onny, that if you ever see me do something that you do not like, you must correct me, just as I correct you. In that way we will benefit each other. Will you do that?"

"All right," said Onny, at once. "I'll tell you one thing I don't like. I don't like being corrected!"

"Oh, Onny!" Gabriel gave in with an exasperated laugh. "I give in," he said. "Tell me about this morning. How soon do you think you will be missed? What luggage did you bring? Is this all you brought?" He looked at the red carpet bag, and drawing it towards him he was about to open it and delve among its contents.

"Stop that!" Onny gave his hand a sharp slap. "That doesn't belong to you."

"You belong to me, and what belongs to you belongs to me."

"I don't belong to you!"

"Oh, yes, you do!"

"I'm not your wife!" said Onny defiantly.

Gabriel laughed. "I see!" he said. "You want the privileges of a wife, and the liberties of a free woman." Then his face grew more serious. "All the same, Onny, I want you to know that I regard you as bound to me just as much as if we were already married." He moved nearer to her and caught her hands. But Onny had seen something through the carriage window. Snatching her hands away, she exclaimed.

"Oh, look, we're coming into a big station!" she cried, and so they were. The train was drawing into the city of Dublin, running along a high overhead track, from which the backs of the houses were exposed with all their squalor. In some houses the blinds were being let up, and dull, unwashed faces stared out for a moment, mechanically. It was impossible to say if they stared out to ascertain the state of the weather, to look upon the passing train, or just merely stared in front of them as they let up the window blind.

Onny sprang up and ran to the window.

"Oh, look at the man!" she cried. "Look at the woman!" And impudently she waved a hand at a dull face that stared out over the upper half of a window just outside the railway siding. "Cranky old thing!" she said, when the indifferent face evinced no interest in a naïveté with which it was no doubt only too familiar.

⌒ ⌒ ⌒

It was still early when they reached the city, and after claiming their luggage they began to walk around the streets of Dublin. They had a long day to pass before it would be time to go back to the station to meet Sylvester. Although it was unlikely that they could have been traced, even supposing that their plans had been discovered sooner than they imagined, Gabriel, nevertheless, thought it wise to avoid the larger restaurants and hotels, and they had a small meal in a cheap café on the quays. Onny enjoyed it, exclaiming continually and speaking to the waitress enthusiastically at every opportunity, but Gabriel felt oppressed by the third-rate quality of the room and the food, and was glad when they wandered out into the sunlit streets again. He had a small guidebook that he had bought self-consciously in Draghead one day, and he was anxious to study the buildings and monuments which were described in it. He had no very clear idea of what constituted an architectural beauty, and his interest in history was not very keen, but he had noticed that Sylvester, in his letters, frequently had spoken of the fine edifices in the city, and he was determined that he would practise his eye upon them without delay. When they came out of the restaurant he consulted the guidebook. "We will go down this way, Onny," he said, and led her across the street.

Perhaps the best guide to any city is one who is himself a stranger; one whose eye is still bright for detail. Gabriel wandered round the city, with Onny hanging from his arm, and to the passer-by he might have seemed an experienced guide, from the assiduity with which he pointed out building after building, steeple after steeple, to his young companion, putting his face down level with hers at times, to assist her in focusing her gaze in the exact direction in which he pointed his finger, but in reality his attention flew from place to place capriciously, and when he pointed it was with a childishly impulsive gesture as some new feature of a building caught his eye. For he was, himself, somewhat dazzled by the pinnacles and domes, pillars and statues, steeples, towers, and glittering vanes on which the early morning sun still shone resplendently, and over which the clouds of smoke and soot had not yet had time to accumulate.

The people who jostled them in the street were merely a nuisance to him, and they came between him and the vistas down which he stared. When he stopped to gaze up at a building, they ran against him and he lost the page in his guidebook. When he stood out in the street to get a better angle of vision on some church tower, a lorry driver yelled at him to get back on to the footpath. Indifferent to the crowds that swarmed around them, his eyes sought only carving and cornice; his ear listened only to the deep rhythmical voice of the city; and his nostrils distended with recognition of the city's hidden industries, as the strong odour of malt came through the air from the breweries, and the smell of stale brine washed up the Liffey tide from the dockyards.

He wondered once or twice what impression the city was making on Onny, who had come to it unprepared even by the slender preparations of the imagination. She had never been to Draghead. She had never been out of her own town, or never any further out of it than she had gone upon her own two legs, wandering the roads as a child, picking nuts, or gathering blackberries.

"What do you think of it all, Onny?" he asked. "What do you think of Dublin?"

"It's lovely," said Onny, and she hugged his arm closer.

"What do you think of this?" he asked as they looked down the Liffey towards the frail arc of the Metal Bridge, that had once been a toll bridge.

"Lovely!" said Onny. "Lovely!"

Everything was lovely—buildings and statues, bridges and steeples. Everything was lovely. The glittering tram rails were lovely. The monuments and fountains were lovely. The ornamental lamp standards were lovely.

"Lovely! Lovely! " said Gabriel at last in exasperation. "Have you no other word in your head, Onny?" He drew her attention to something else. "Don't say it's lovely," he warned. But as they wandered on, he drew her attention irresistibly to right and left, and irresistibly it seemed the same word rose to her lips.

Gabriel found it more and more hard to control his irritation. He made the common mistake of thinking that where feelings are unexpressed they are non-existent. He looked at her face from time to time. It was bright with excitement, but he could not fathom it further. The human face can express great depths of emotion, and were life all intensity, words might never have been invented, but what of the thousand subtle shadows that play upon the shallows of the soul? The face cannot always reflect them, so fleetingly they fall. To express them the facile lips must open and the heart itself must speak. But if, like Onny, one is without any great gift of words, one is likely to be written down for a dull person indeed.

Onny had no words with which to appraise this panorama of masonry, these intricacies of architecture. But for the things with which she was familiar she had words enough, and so, as the day stretched out, and as her shyness left her, she began to seek out the things that interested herself, and soon it was she who pulled Gabriel's sleeve and called forth his attention, it was she who pointed with an eager hand, it was she who demanded to know what he thought of this and that.

Strangely enough, in this city of unfamiliar sights, it was the familiar that attracted Onny's attention. The vast towering buildings, the bridges, the steeples and monuments, could not hold her eyes while there were gulls in flight over the water, horses striking the cobbles with a patient foot, dogs running in the gutter, and people, people, people.

"Oh, look at the horse, Gabriel," she would cry, when far away in the traffic she saw a dray horse coming towards them. "He's like the old horse in the field opposite our house." The familiar outline had attracted her attention, but her attention, once held, began to employ itself in picking out small differences. "Look at the way his tail is tied! I never saw a horse with his tail tied like that before, did you?" And then before Gabriel would answer she had twisted around in another direction as a sea gull wheeled angrily inland from the docks, giving a piercing scream.

"Look at the bird!" she cried. "Why is he screaming like that?" She looked around at the hard pavements in concern for the bird's welfare. "What do those birds get to eat?" she asked. "They can't pick worms here."

But above all else the people that passed them by in the street interested and excited her. Gabriel was embarrassed at the way she stared at them. She was continually nudging him and whispering.

"Oh, Gabriel, look at that fat man. Did you ever see anyone so fat? He's fatter than Mr. Finnerty. He's fatter than anyone I ever saw in my life." She turned to look after the fat man.

"Hush, Onny, he'll hear you," said Gabriel, agonized with embarrassment, but when she desisted, it was usually because her attention had been drawn elsewhere.

"Look at the man with only one leg! Look at the priest! Look at the lady with the little dog! Why is she carrying him in her arms? Can he not walk? We had a cat one time and it had only three legs but it could walk as good as if it had four. It could climb trees better than another cat we had that had four legs. Oh, look, Gabriel, there is a woman like your Aunt Theresa, she has the same way of walking, as if she could walk through a wall if she had a mind to do it."

People, people, people. Faces, faces, faces. Walking along the streets she looked from side to side. Over her head the city soared into the sky unheeded. Her heart expanded in this new city, but it expanded only to new variations of the things that it had always known.

One thing alone had any power to distract her from her embarrassing habit of staring at the faces around her, and that was the sight of the city-bred pigeons that strolled about the pavements, bolder than themselves. These pigeons made their way between the wheels of the vehicles in the street, and between the feet of the pedestrians on the pathways as if they were indifferent to the one, and superior to the other. In their agility they showed better adaptability to their environment than was shown by many of their human fellows in the city.

To Onny these birds were fascinating. They captivated her. She wanted to stand continually and watch them. They probably presented the perfect example of the familiar object with interesting differences. She was accustomed to all manner of birds, the swallows that swooped down into the yard at Clewe Street, the great black crows that hovered over the fields of corn, the flocks of starlings that swept across the roads like a spate of rain, but all, all had fled from humankind, and had to be netted and limed in order to be caught or tamed. It astonished her that these pigeons should allow people in the street to approach so closely to them, and that when they wished to put some distance between them and anyone particularly hurried or awkward, they did not lift themselves and fly away, but were content to take a few paces to one side or another on their delicate, pink toes. They did not deign to fly except in cases of emergency, and then they flew low, spreading their wings out noisily and showing off every feather on their soft underwings. She could watch them for ever, she felt. The sight of them gave her the same exciting mixture of credulity and incredulity that a child feels reading its early tales of dogs that talk and cats that laugh, and jackdaws that walk about in waistcoats.

"Oh, Gabriel, look!" Again and again she stopped to watch the pigeons display some further example of their docility and intelligence.

"Come along, Onny, there is a lot to be seen yet," he said, several times.

"Just one minute!" begged Onny, looking back over her shoulder.

"This is College Green," said Gabriel, when they came out on to Dame Street, after looking at the Cathedral. "There is Trinity College, and there is the Bank of Ireland." He consulted the guidebook. "The Bank of Ireland was once the House of Parliament. Aren't they fine buildings, Onny? I expect they are nothing like what are to be seen in other cities, but they are very fine to us now. How massive they are, and yet how graceful!" He stared up with delight at the fine old Georgian piles, shining with the peculiar brightness of their granites, and shadowed so indeliberately but so beautifully with their accumulations of smoke and grime. He pointed to the strong parapets and columns and to the gracile garlands that were carved out of the stone. He pointed to the figures that were niched in the walls. "Look, Onny!" he cried. "What do you think of this?"

"It's lovely," said Onny, and she was about to add something else, but she did not say it.

"You were going to say something?"

"Oh, nothing," said Onny. She had been about to ask if they were going to spend all their time in Dublin as they had spent today, standing about in the streets, staring up at old stones.

"I'd rather you'd say whatever you were going to say, Onny," said Gabriel, earnestly.

"All right," said Onny, "I'll say it. I'm hungry." Gabriel laughed.

"So am I," he said, "but we may as well wait now until we meet Sylvester. As I said, I don't think it is wise to go into the restaurants. You'd never know who we might meet that we knew." He put his arm through her arm. "It's only a short time now to wait. You'll have patience, won't you?" While he was speaking his eyes had been glancing back at the buildings. "Do you know what came into my mind a moment ago?" he asked. "I'll tell you. It was something fantastic. Do you see the way the soot and smoke has lodged in the crevices of the masonry, between the rails of the stone balustrades, between the clusters of the stone fruits, between the armpits of the carved figures, and in the spaces between the pillars? Do you see? Look at how black those crevices are compared with the bright white appearance of those parts of the masonry that protrude into the air: the sides of the pillars, the ribbons of the garlands, the outer folds of the garments on the figures, and the more prominent of their facial features—the brow, the nose, the chin. Do you see? Well, as I was looking at them it came into my mind idly that the whole building might have been unearthed this moment from the excavators' pit, the crevices still clogged with clay and the outer surfaces merely freed by the shaking of the excavation and the rude brushing of the excavator's hand!" Gabriel waved his own hand, as if he too were about to brush away some of that black deposit. He turned to Onny. She too was staring raptly at the parapets above them. He was delighted. He had won her interest at last. He had captured her attention by playing upon her imagination. He looked at the grime-shadowed walls of the massive granite buildings.

"Perhaps a day will come when people will stand here where we stand today, but their feet will be sunk in a mound of upthrown clay, broken with wild grass blades, and they will stare on this very building, glassless and deserted, dug up out of a forgotten city, and they will try to imagine the life that was led by the unimaginable people who inhabited it in its time! Can you imagine the scene, Onny?" He lowered his own fascinated eyes, and looked into her face, but at the moment that he looked her expression changed. Her hands flew to her cheeks, and she gave a cry of dismay.

"They will fall and be killed!" she cried, and, looking swiftly where her eyes had flown, he saw that on the ledge of the high gray parapet, where he had not noticed them in his enthusiasm over the carving, there were five or six pigeons, walking round following each other's movements with strange bird rites. He saw the cause of her concern. On the narrow ledge two of the birds were about to pass each other. For a moment Gabriel himself forgot their winged protection against disaster, and held his breath while they delicately negotiated their pathway. Then he turned on Onny with annoyance.

"Were you looking at the pigeons all the time I was talking about the architecture?"

"What if I was!" said Onny. "I want to look at them, and you won't let me, you keep walking on and dragging me with you. My feet are tired, and I have a pain in my neck looking up at stupid old buildings." She broke away from him, pulling her arm from under his arm. Gabriel softened.

"I forgot, Onny. But I want you to do whatever you please. What would you like to do? Tell me. What would you like to do?"

But Onny had not waited to hear him! Breaking away from him she had run forward along the path to where a few pigeons were walking here and there, keeping out of the way of the traffic, and out of the direct path of the pedestrians, effecting this by stepping up on the path as a car passed too near the curb, and stepping down again into the road if the people on the footpath became too numerous. At this moment the street was particularly quiet, and after Onny had run forward a little way, she began to walk, and to walk cautiously. As she went she crouched lower and put out her hands. To his amusement, Gabriel realized that she hoped to catch one of the pigeons—and it seemed as if she might. Near her, one pigeon of dark blue plumage, with iridescent gleams of peacock green and magenta, put its head to one side, and looked with surprise at the girl as she advanced, but it did not move. Accustomed to having the indifferent skirts of the city-goer brush over it, the pigeon did not at once divine Onny's intention, but it was suspicious, and so just as she was within arm's reach of it, as a precautionary measure it lifted its delicate pink legs and took two or three steps that carried it out of her reach. Onny moved after it. It was once again within arm's reach. Once again it put its head to the side, and looked at Onny, its head feathers gleaming purple and green, and again it stepped out of reach. Gabriel gave a roar of laughter. The pigeon rose into the air with a flap of wings.

"There now, you frightened him," said Onny.

"Catch this one," said Gabriel, pointing to a very pretty pigeon behind her back. It was a pale pearl-coloured bird, with wings of deeper colour, and tail feathers of dark brown. On its pale pearly neck there were gilt and bronze feathers, and when it turned its head these feathers glinted brightly.

Onny turned round. She no sooner saw the bird that she crouched down and stretched out her hands to it. Her face was radiant. Looking at her, Gabriel felt his tenseness stream away. His heart lifted, and he felt happy in her happiness.

All day since they had left home, Gabriel had been uncomfortably aware of the way Onny differed from him in manner and vocabulary, in interests, in gestures and in demeanour, but now, watching her display a difference deeper than any of these surface differences, a deep difference of nature, he felt again that curiosity and tantalization that he had felt the night that he had come upon her sitting on the headstone in the churchyard, outlined against the sky, defiant and indifferent to a discipline that had deadened and discouraged him. His interest and enthusiasms were renewed, and he looked around for a clock.

"It is time to go towards the station," he said. "Come along, Onny!"

The way back to the station led through the poorer sections of the city. They had time to spare at starting out, and so they made their way on foot. The back streets through which they passed were busy with commercial traffic and the people they met on the streets were mainly working people and wearing their working clothes. There were few residential houses in the quarters through which they passed, but here and there between the high warehouses there were small houses abutting on the footpath, and nearly all of them displayed placards which announced that board and lodgings might be had for the night, or that hot and cold meals could be produced at a low charge.

"We could have had our dinner here!" said Onny, to Gabriel's surprise, as they passed one of those houses, which, although neat and respectable, was even smaller and more humble than the rest. He looked at Onny. Did she want to save their money? he wondered.

Onny's interest in the boardinghouse seemed to depend upon other causes, however. As they passed it she hung back out of Gabriel's arm, and stared at every window. And after they had turned a corner, she still spoke about it.

"I wonder do they get many people to stay the night?" she said. "I wonder do many people go there for their dinner?"

Gabriel stared at her. He could not understand her taking such interest in a cheap boardinghouse, while she had only glanced casually at the hotels in the main streets.

Onny suddenly gave him her reason. "My mother was thinking of putting up a sign on our cottage to say we'd give teas in the summer. She said lots of people would stop and she'd make a lot of money. She said she'd put tables out under the ramparts, and put tablecloths on them!"

To Gabriel's consternation, Onny's voice thickened at the end of the sentence and when he looked at her he saw that she was biting her lower

336

lip. When she had agreed to come away with him, she had forgotten this great family project that threatened in the future. He looked at her anxiously. What would he do if she got homesick?

There was no need to worry. Onny had no sooner closed her mouth with a tearful pout than she had cause to open it again in an exclamation of admiration.

"Oh, Gabriel, look at that girl!" she cried, as down the street in front of them, leaning against the jamb of a boardinghouse similar to the one they had left behind them, was a young girl of about Onny's own age.

"Stop staring at her, Onny," said Gabriel, quickly, as they drew near to the doorway, and he saw that Onny had not taken her eyes off the girl. "You must not stare at people like that. They resent it."

"I can't help staring at her," said Onny. "Look at the lovely shoes she has. Look at her handbag! Look at the fur! I'll be a show in these old clothes!"

Gabriel was about to give her the reassurance of a quick denial, but when he looked at the girl in the doorway, he had had an immediate misgiving himself about Onny's appearance. He hesitated for an instant, and then he compromised.

"No one will know you, except Sylvester," he said, "and he won't expect you to look like a peacock."

"Won't he?" said Onny, satisfactorily distracted from the inadequacy of her raiment. "What is he like, Gabriel?"

"Oh, you'll see," said Gabriel. "You'll like him, Onny. And I am sure that he will not trouble about how you are dressed. He will see your true self as I saw it. Do not be shy of Sylvester."

But when, a few minutes later, they went into the station, and Sylvester, who had been waiting on the platform for the train from Draghead, turned around suddenly and saw them coming towards him, Gabriel saw with misgiving that his eyes flew at once from the top of Onny's head to the tip of her shining patent shoes, and that his glance was sharp and critical. Even in the taxi which his friend had whistled to the curb in an instant, Gabriel saw that Sylvester was unable to keep from glancing sideways at Onny's attire from minute to minute, until they arrived at his apartment where, he told them, tea was all ready for them.

Gabriel was awkward and ill at ease. He wanted to ask Sylvester's opinion of Onny, but he knew that he must not do that, now or at any time. He sat stiffly in the taxi, saying nothing and listening to Onny, who, on the contrary, was fully at ease, prattling to Sylvester about all she had seen during the day.

Gabriel wished that he had bought her some new clothes. He thought of the money in his wallet, and wondered if he could afford to spend some of it on getting her a new outfit, but he felt that it was absolutely necessary.

to see first what he would have to pay for lodgings. Yet, at the mere mention of the word "lodgings," Sylvester had intervened. He had something to say on the subject.

"Lodgings? Nonsense! You are not going to look for lodgings tonight. You're going to stay with me! And you're welcome to stay as long as you like. I have a large apartment with a studio and two living rooms. I eat in one room and sleep in the other, but the studio, as you may imagine, Gabriel, is always idle. You can have the studio. I have a day couch there. You can manage with that, I should think."He looked at Onny. "It may be a tight fit, but Onny looks very plastic!"

Gabriel flushed. The remark struck him as indelicate. But when he saw the studio, a few minutes later, his heart sank utterly.

Sylvester's apartment occupied the entire top storey of a dark building in Kildare Street. The rest of the building was deserted after five o'clock, the other floors being used for offices and showrooms. Away at the end of the street, in a bright shaft between two buildings, the gardens of Stephen's Green could be seen. The two rooms of Sylvester's looked out over the front street, and from these rooms the public gardens could be seen when the window sash was thrown open.

The studio was at the back. It ran the entire width of the building and could be entered directly from the landing. It was a large, cold room, practically empty, with bare floorboards, and it was lit by a sizable skylight of northern aspect that shed green and penetrating light. In one corner there were a heap of rubbish, a broken chair, a few discarded utensils, some empty paint tubes, and a miscellaneous collection of statuary and unfinished canvases. In the far corner there was a day couch covered with a faded red material, burnt in places with cigarette holes. This couch, a rickety table, and a strip of worn carpet emphasized the vacancy of the rest of the room, and gave it a more desolate air than if it had been entirely unfurnished. The cold glare from the skylight spilled down upon that part of the room which was filled by the jumbled pieces of furniture. The other end of the room, that nearest the door, was ill-lit, and the objects that were strewn about at this point were uncertain and anonymous. At this point, however—that is to say, directly opposite the door that led in from the landing—there was a heavy, red curtain drawn across that might have been an alcove, or even a cupboard. Gabriel's eye came back to it once or twice in curiosity, and seeing this Sylvester went over to it.

"You have a window here," he said, drawing the curtain across with a jangle of brass rings. "The curtain is usually left undrawn because the prospect isn't very good. You can do as you please!"

The window revealed a near view of the adjacent roofs and chimneys of the city. It was a vast panorama of slates and tiles, most of which were old and broken, and some of which were lifted by grasses that sprouted between them or peculiar pale fungus growths that pushed them out of place. All were whitened by bird droppings, and littered with bird's feathers. In his short rapid glance in that direction Gabriel saw a piece of gray fur sticking to one of the slates, fastened there by a smear of blood.

"Cats!" said Sylvester, seeing the direction of his glance. "They fight like tigers on the roofs at night. That's another reason for keeping the curtains drawn."

"It keeps out the sounds, I suppose?" said Gabriel, unenthusiastically.

"Yes, and the smells too," said Sylvester, laughing. Onny joined them in the laughing. Sylvester drew the curtain across the window again. While he had not known there was a window Gabriel did not find the darkness so bad, but when he knew there was one, even with such a poor aspect, he felt stifled and ill at ease, when he looked in its direction.

Sylvester spread out his hands with a foreign gesture.

"Now I have shown you the worst features," he said, "and I have told you the worst disadvantages, but, having satisfied my instincts of honesty, I still recommend you to avail yourselves of the place to save money, because you may as well harvest whatever money you have." He turned directly to Gabriel. "By the way, are you all right in that respect? Do you want anything?"

Gabriel rushed into assurances that he was all right, that he had enough money for their immediate needs.

"I saw to that in advance," he said, almost stiffly. He did not wish Sylvester to appear in a superior light to Onny. Sylvester pointed to the canvases on the floor.

"Don't pay any attention to this stuff. I'll clear it all out when I have time. As a matter of fact I did not need to take a studio of my own, I never work in it. I do all my work in the class studio at the College."

Gabriel, who was not sure whether Sylvester was genuinely painting or not, was somewhat relieved to hear him mention his work. Sylvester noticed his relief. "Actually," he said, "I'm getting on fairly well. It appears that I have a good hand. Or is it a good eye? I think I have some capacity. I may not be the genius we thought I was when we used to talk about things long ago on the ramparts, but perhaps that's no harm! Genius might be a bit of a handicap to a fellow like me! I care less now about making a name than I do about making a fortune. It seems to be one or the other!" He turned on his heel abruptly. He said nothing about the statuary in the studio. "I will put on the kettle," he said, as he opened the door. "I'm sure you are both hungry. Tomorrow, if you like, we can buy some kind of a spirit lamp and you can fix up your own meals in here." He went out.

After Sylvester went out Gabriel looked around the studio once more.

The plaster figures, heads and limbless trunks, the plaster casts and the clay blocks, gave the place the impersonality of a museum. He flung out his hands.

"I hate to have you sleep here, Onny," he said. "I knew we would have to economize, but I thought that we would begin with a week, at least in pleasant surroundings."

"I think this is all right," said Onny. "After all, Sylvester knows the city. He knows what would be best for us to do. And I think he was right about buying some new clothes for me, don't you? I'm not just thinking of myself, Gabriel, but in the street I saw people staring at me, and one man laughed when he looked at my legs."

"I'm sure you were mistaken, Onny," said Gabriel, halfheartedly.

"I was not mistaken," said Onny. "I stared back at him as much as to tell him he had a cheek to laugh at me, and I saw him say something to the woman that was with him." Onny put her head to one side meditatively. "The woman laughed too, but wasn't it queer, Gabriel, she was laughing at you? I suppose she thought it queer to see you walking with me in these old clothes, and linking my arm as if I belonged to you!"

Gabriel looked around the studio once more with distaste.

"Oh, come on!" said Onny, shaking him. "This place isn't so bad. I think he was very decent to let us come in here. And it's only for a while."

"Yes, it's only for a while," said Gabriel, forcing himself to shake off his depression. "I know that: but it's such a pity that the first night we are alone together should be spent in a place like this! Onny, don't you realize how important this night is to us? Our first night together!" His heart ached, and he stretched out his arms to her.

"Oh!" said Onny, springing up from the couch on which she had sat down. "Do you suppose that Sylvester thinks that we are married?"

"I don't know," said Gabriel. "I don't think he cares whether we are or not."

"Are you sure of that?" said Onny, and her face had become frightened. "He might not have let us use his studio if he knew that we weren't!"

Gabriel tried to put his hand over her mouth before she finished her sentence.

"Hush, Onny," he said. "Sylvester feels as I do about things. Sylvester understands."

But Onny was not listening.

"He could have seen that I had no ring on my finger," she said, and Gabriel saw that she was going back over the events of the last hour to see if anything had been said that would show whether or not Sylvester was aware of their relationship.

Gabriel took her hand. "Would you like a ring for your finger, Onny? Would it make you feel happier?"

Onny laughed. "If Sylvester doesn't care, I don't care," she said. "I'd rather have a new pair of shoes than a ring. We can ask Sylvester! I think we ought to ask him, don't you?" She went over to the door and opened it a crack to peep out on the landing. "I wonder if he is going to call us when the tea is made, or if he meant us to go in when we were ready?"

"Oh, haven't we had enough of Sylvester for a while? He'll call us when he is ready. Come here to me, Onny." He sat down on the couch. Onny went over to him reluctantly, but when he drew her down beside him she put up her hand and smoothed his hair.

"Your hair is thicker than Sylvester's," she said, "and your skin is smoother." She drew back and looked intently at him. "You're thinner than Sylvester too; much thinner."

"You sound as if you had just seen me for the first time," said Gabriel. Onny did not answer him.

"I suppose there are some people," she said, "who would consider that you were better-looking than Sylvester!"

"Sylvester, Sylvester! I'm tired of Sylvester. Let's forget him."

"But we've only just met him!" said Onny, pouting so prettily that Gabriel argued no more, but began to kiss her and toss her hair.

Yet, later, when they had left Sylvester for the night, and when the great pale moon shone down upon the skylight in the studio and Onny lay asleep, Gabriel was awake, staring at the pale plaster heads and broken limbs that lay about on the green-lit attic floor. Sylvester had not said anything about them. Were they the creatures of his hand? He felt that the soulless eyes were watching him. And he felt also that something had gone wrong with his plans, and that he should not have agreed to stay in the studio. He had to tell himself over and over again that it had been a matter of expediency.

∽ ∽ ∽

Next morning they all went out to buy Onny's new clothes. Upon this errand Sylvester seemed to expend an energy and interest even greater than Onny's own. He appointed himself captain of the expedition and led them from street to street and from shop to shop. Onny was enraptured with every shop, and in every shop window they passed she saw something that appealed to her taste. It was in his efforts to relate this taste to his own taste that Sylvester's energies were expended. To Onny, the brilliant colours made an immediate appeal. Black she would not look at, and from the pale colours which Sylvester liked she turned aside with a flounce. At first she had been shy in the shops, but she soon saw that the shopgirls, although they glanced contemptuously at her upon her first entrance, rapidly changed their attitude when they saw that she was escorted by two good-looking young men. In fact between Sylvester's easy sophistication and Gabriel's obvious discomfort at finding himself in the ladies' department of the shop, the assistants looked forward to a pleasant interlude in the day's routine, and took every trouble to help Onny make her choice. Onny became less and less shy, and soon she began to make a double issue of the shopping. While she carefully raked the counters for things that appealed to herself, and was exacting in her requests for hand mirrors and side mirrors, she lost no opportunity of making the shopping an entertainment for Gabriel and Sylvester by picking up the most ridiculous hats and putting them on her head at a tipsy angle, and parading up and down the shop. By means of this pantomime, she amused the young men and at the same time succeeded in imposing her own taste upon them, for when she put on a hat that pleased her she twirled and pirouetted, lifted her face up to the light, and held her head at such a flattering angle that it displayed her best features to her escorts. When, on the contrary, she tried on a hat which they had suggested and which did not please her, she was careful to put it on at a silly angle, to tilt her head just a shade too much, and, as she walked over to the mirrors, to swagger so comically that the shopgirls began to laugh and against their will Sylvester and Gabriel had to laugh too, and declare themselves wrong.

At last, Sylvester had to admit that the pastel colours which he would like for Onny were not suited to her colouring, and that he had better relinquish his efforts to rule her choice of colour, and confine himself to guiding her choice of cut and line. When they finally emerged from the shopping centre and made their way to a café, Onny was dressed in almost the exact shades of brilliant blue and red that she had worn earlier in the day, but this time the garments fitted her closely, and the glances they drew in her direction were different from those that had fastened upon her earlier in the day.

"Now, for refreshment," said Sylvester, as he led the way across the street to a café where a large green-striped awning threw a shade across the green metal tables and chairs, which would have otherwise been too hot to lay a hand upon. "Sit down," said Sylvester. "What will you take, Gabriel? What will you take, Onny?" He whistled for the waiter. But when the waiter came he did not see him; he was staring at Onny. "Now, you look effective, Onny," he said. "You were only a bundle of clothes when you got off the train; but now you are a woman. The test of a well-dressed woman comes when a man can look at her without being conscious that she is clad; when nothing distracts from the sense of being in the presence of the fabulous female form."

Gabriel broke in harshly. "Are you going to give the order?" he said.

Sylvester turned from Onny and gave the order with nonchalance. He turned back as if he might continue on the same strain. Gabriel was determined to interrupt.

"Sylvester," he said, plucking him by the sleeve. "We were talking last night, Onny and I, and we wanted to ask your advice about something delicate."

"I prefer giving advice about something indelicate," said Sylvester, and he looked at Onny and laughed.

Onny lowered her head but she began to smile.

Gabriel addressed her. "You wanted to ask his advice, didn't you, Onny?"

"I don't think it matters," said Onny.

"It matters a great deal," said Gabriel.

Sylvester saw a strain coming in the situation.

"Get it off your mind, Gabriel," he said, patting him on the shoulder.

"It's about Onny and me," said Gabriel, and he hesitated. He found a difficulty in explaining what he wanted to say. He tried to remember the words Onny used when they had discussed the affair the night before, but this confused him more. "We were thinking that you might perhaps have thought we were married. We're not."

Sylvester gave a laugh. "You didn't need to tell me," he said. "I knew at a glance."

"How?" said Gabriel and Onny together.

Sylvester laughed. "Is that the face of a wife?" he said, and he put a hand under Onny's chin and tilted it up to the light.

Gabriel winced at the words, but Sylvester was irrepressible.

He turned and looked at Gabriel himself, and putting out a rapid hand he tilted Gabriel's chin. "Now, if I had to judge by looking at your own face," he said, "I should perhaps have made a worse guess. You, Gabriel, I am sorry to say, have certain features of the husband in your face, but no doubt we will be able to disguise them in a brief space."

Gabriel tried to smile. Onny looked at him, and he could see that she wanted him to unstiffen.

She put her elbows on the table. "What is the face of a wife?" she said. Sylvester leaned back in his chair, and allowed his legs to stretch so far under the table that Gabriel had to curl his legs round the rungs of his chair to make space for him.

"To begin with," he said, "a wife's face is usually plain."

Onny laughed. And Sylvester began a long jocose monologue, to which she listened with a mixture of credulity and incredulity, looking anxious one moment, in case a remark might be applicable to herself, and the next moment clapping her hands with amusement and naming people in the town at home to whom she herself could apply the descriptions.

Gabriel interrupted. "I'm sorry, Sylvester, but I may as well tell you

343

that I consider that Onny is my wife just as surely as if we were married in twenty churches."

"Look at him now, Onny!" said Sylvester. "Now he is the picture of a husband!"

"I consider that I am her husband," said Gabriel, his sense of humour deserting him more and more each minute.

"All right, all right," said Sylvester, placatingly, "but I hope you will come to me for advice when you want to get rid of her." He was looking at Onny while he was talking to Gabriel.

"This may be a joke to you, Sylvester," said Gabriel, "but I am serious. You seem to like Onny. In that case you might show interest in something that concerns her even more than it concerns me."

With a visible effort, Sylvester brought his eyes to rest on Gabriel.

"We were wondering whether she should call herself Mrs. Galloway," said Gabriel, "and whether we should buy a ring. I hate deceit; but, if you thought that not having a ring would cause anyone to regard her slightingly, I would be willing to buy one!" He sat forward. "In fact, although I believe that before God we are as much married now as if we were married in a church, rather than have a single sneering remark made about Onny, I would marry her at once."

Sylvester sat up. He leaned across to Gabriel. "Why did you come to Dublin? Why did you leave home? You did so, I presume, because there you had to cut your actions to the pattern of your neighbours' conscience. Well, you've left home now. You're in a strange city. What you do is your own business." He took the bill from the waiter. "And anyway, the crowd you'll mix with here will never get as far as knowing your surnames. You'll be Gabriel and Onny to them from the first minute they lay eyes on you." He turned back to Onny. "Surnames are so rare in the crowd I mix among that in some cases a surname is only used once; on the lid of your coffin! By the way, Onny is not your real name, is it? It's a nice name; it's saucy and impudent like yourself, but I cannot imagine any Irish priest sprinkling holy water on a name like that! What is your full name?"

"I am only called Onny for short. My real name is Honor. I was christened Honor."

"Honor!" Sylvester slipped down into his chair again. "I don't believe it!" he said, and he began to laugh and the tears streamed down his cheeks. "That's the funniest name I ever heard. Why didn't you tell me, Gabriel? Why did you keep the secret up your sleeve? I have met queer names in my time; but that beats the funniest."

"What is so funny about it?" said Gabriel. "I often heard it before."

"I was always ashamed of it," said Onny herself. "At school when the inspector read it out, the whole class began to laugh."

344

"I'll tell everyone," said Sylvester. "Oh, Onny, you'll never hear the end of that. That's the kind of a name that will make you notorious all over Dublin."

Gabriel felt a great humiliation that he himself had not known Onny's full name. It was left for Sylvester to discover it. His regrets were all the more bitter because he did not feel as Sylvester felt about it. He thought it a beautiful name; a name that should make her proud. It would have given her dignity and distinction. If she had been introduced to Sylvester as Honor in the early formal stages of their acquaintance he would not have dared to make fun of the name, even if he had thought it strange. And Gabriel greatly doubted that the name could have been so strange to him. It was uncommon, but not unknown. Gabriel felt that it was himself and not Onny that Sylvester had ridiculed, when he laughed at the name. And he anticipated that he would suffer a great deal of joking about it from Sylvester's friends when he met them. Nevertheless the thought of meeting those friends was pleasant to him, mainly because he felt that by making other contacts he would eventually see less of Sylvester himself.

It was becoming hourly more difficult for him to understand the desire that he had had to renew acquaintance with his former friend. He was anxious to establish new contacts as quickly as possible, and to find some work to do which would give him a livelihood.

∽ ∽ ∽

Sylvester's friends came around to the apartment that evening. As they were preparing to meet them, Gabriel and Onny heard them coming up the stairs at odd intervals, and heard the din growing greater in the rooms across the landing.

"Come across when you feel like it," Sylvester had said. Gabriel did not look forward to the moment when they would have to go over. He felt apprehensive at the thought of meeting so many strangers, but Onny, bent down towards the small mirror that she had set up on the window ledge, combing her hair with absorption, only delayed from a desire to make herself more and more ready for inspection. She was wearing the new clothes that they had brought in the morning, and she had combed up her hair into a more tidy style than she had worn it before. Looking at her Gabriel realized that these changes would probably give her a self-assurance that he himself lacked, in meeting the strangers. She could feel that she was herself in some way different from the girl that had left home the day before. He looked down at his own familiar clothes, and he looked at his familiar face in the mirror. He felt that he was imprisoned in some atmosphere of gaucherie and provinciality. When would he shake it off?

They went out to the landing and crossed over to the larger of the two rooms on the other side, the room in which Sylvester ate his meals, and entertained his friends. The door was open, and already the cigarette smoke had filled the room with a blue mist, through which the red and green and yellow dresses of the girls could be seen dully. Tendrils of blue smoke stole out to the landing, and the voices of several people, speaking all together, gave that concerted effect which is always so embarrassing to a stranger, who feels at one moment that if he is to be heard at all he will have to put his hands to his mouth and shout, and at the next that the whole room may become silent at his least utterance, leaving him with the impression of having shouted into a void. Gabriel hesitated. Onny gave him a push forward.

She was all eagerness to get into the room. To her there was no embarrassment in the situation. In Clewe Street her duties of setting and clearing the table had often necessitated entering the dining room while there was in progress a conversation in which she was not intended to take an active part.

"Go on!" she said, pushing Gabriel forward with a dig in the ribs.

They went forward. There was only nine or ten people in the room after all. It had seemed that there were many more. Still Gabriel and Onny were unnoticed for a few minutes after their entry. Sylvester was in the far corner, bending down over the table and slicing a large loaf of bread, from which a shower of white crumbs were flying like sawdust from a mill saw. He did not see them, but a small thin girl in a red dress, with bobbed black hair and light china eyes, not only saw them but, as she looked over the shoulder of the man to whom she was talking, stared at them from head to toe. She apparently said something to her companion, for he turned round once and glanced at them too, but without any great interest, because he continued, after a moment, to talk in a high excited voice, and began again to reinforce his statements with vigorous gestures. The girl did not listen. She stared at them over his shoulder.

"Will we go over to Sylvester?" said Gabriel, to whom the moments at the door were interminable.

"Wait a minute," said Onny, who was making good use of her position to stare at everything and everyone, and who looked as if she had achieved her object in getting into the room, and that a further acquaintance with its occupants was not necessary to her pleasure, if only she might stand there indefinitely and look about her.

Gabriel, far from wishing to stare at anyone, was fearful of raising his eyes to the level of anyone's face. He looked up at the ceiling and down at the wainscot. He looked at the legs of the table, and finally fastened his gaze upon the flame of a spirit lamp in the corner of the room. The flame pulsed with life, and made energetic efforts to escape the confines of its metal container and consume the small kettle that it was supposed to bring to the boil. Even in the din of voices the pulsing voice of the small flame could be heard, and every now and then it spluttered and altered colour, as if from vexation at the number of people crowding into the room, and a thin, vicious tongue of fire licked up the sides of the kettle.

Then, quite suddenly, as he stared at the flame, Gabriel felt that there was someone else staring at him, and immediately raising his head he looked instinctively to his right. There, across the room, he saw a fair-haired girl in a pale dress, sitting on the window sill, and he looked straight into eyes that were fixed on him too intensely for their owner to shift her glance before its intensity was noticed. A faint flush of irritation came into the girl's face, but she was too self-possessed to glance away at once; instead she altered her glance to a more indifferent stare, and then, concentrating it on his clothes, she gave him such a feeling of uneasiness about their correctness that he glanced down involuntarily at his own person. When he looked up again the girl had looked away, and he realized at once that she had tricked him into releasing her own eyes. But he felt warmed and pleased at the slight interlude. There had been all the difference in the world between this involuntary stare and the deliberately insolent stare of the dark girl with the red lips that had discomforted him when they first came in. There had been interest and kindness in the eyes that had stared at him from the window, and in the ensuing game of glances there had been a hidden smile. As he was thinking these things his estimate of the girl's kindness was qualified, because she leaned slightly forward and caught Sylvester's sleeve, nodding in the direction of Gabriel and Onny, and then, as Sylvester dropped the bread knife and, looking up, saw them, she leaned back again against the window and stared down into the street below.

In a few minutes Sylvester had brought them forward and given them brief introductions to the more prominent people of the crowd. It was some time before Gabriel's attention was free again to wander over to the window ledge; and, when he looked there, the slim fair girl was gone. He was surprised at the feeling of disappointment he experienced, and was going to turn around and search the room for her, when Sylvester suddenly jerked him by the sleeve. "And this is Helen!" Sylvester said. Gabriel turned around. Beside him stood the girl who had sat upon the window ledge. There, her back had been to the light and he had not seen her clearly. He had had but a vague impression of her fairness, and a strong impression of the intensity of her eyes, although he could not have told their colour. He might have hazarded that they were dark, because depth of expression is usually associated with dark eyes, but Helen's eyes were not dark. They were blue. The iris of the eye was, however, delicately etched with darker markings, and fringed with dark lashes. Moreover, they were set in a small pointed face, pale and delicate, where the other features, particularly the small pointed chin, seemed to have been deliberately ill-proportioned to give them emphasis. Even her hair was exceedingly pale, and honey-coloured, and light and thin like a young child's, so light in fact that when she walked it lifted slightly with the movement of the air around her. Today, and as he was to learn almost always, she wore an indefinite-coloured dress, a kind of buff colour, that gave the last and final accentuation to her enormous eyes. From this buff-coloured dress, from the pale pointed chin, from the light honey-coloured hair, the eye that beheld her glanced back all the time to the beautiful eyes. Gabriel had a full moment in which to gaze at those lovely eyes because Helen was looking at Onny, not at him, and, more formal than anyone else had been, she stretched out a pale hand in which the blue veins showed, and shook Onny's hand. Her voice when she spoke was formal, too, but her words were quite informal.

"You're not a bit like what I imagined you would be!" she said. Then she turned to Gabriel himself, and held out her hand. "Now, you are exactly as I thought you would be!"

It was clear that she was trying to put them at ease by letting them know that she had heard about them in advance; that they need not regard themselves as strangers. An impulse of gratitude quickened Gabriel's first impulse of attraction to her. So he was like what she had imagined! It was pleasant to feel that she had been thinking about them. He wondered in what way was Onny different from what she had imagined.

"I suppose Sylvester gave you a description of us?" said Gabriel. "Although he could hardly remember Onny. He could only have seen her once or twice."

"Oh, I wouldn't let him describe either of you!" said Helen. "That would take away the fun of making my own descriptions. He just told me a few things about you; things that you had done and things that you had said"—she hesitated and then went on carelessly "—and the reasons you came here! Then I told him what I thought you would be like in appearance." She turned to Sylvester. "I was right about his colouring, wasn't I?" But Sylvester had taken Onny by the elbow and was leading her across the room to the table where he had been slicing the bread. He did not hear Helen because he and Onny were laughing. Slightly disconcerted, Helen looked after them, then she turned and smiled at Gabriel, and together they stared after the others.

Onny and Sylvester were some time before they stopped laughing at whatever joke they shared, but reaching the other end of the room, Onny, without waiting to regain her seriousness, caught up the knife and began to slice the bread that Sylvester had left uncut.

Sylvester stood looking at her for a few moments in amusement and was then going to walk away, but she pulled him by the tail of the jacket. With the bread knife she indicated the crumbs on the floor. "Get a brush and sweep those crumbs!" she said. Sylvester stared. Someone laughed. Onny tossed her head. "Is there any butter?" she asked. "I want someone to butter the bread. Here, you!" She prodded the blunt end of the bread knife in the ribs of an exceedingly tall and heavy young man who was holding up a canvas and explaining something about it to the girl with the bang of black hair on her forehead. "Make yourself useful!" said Onny, handing him a plate of butter and a knife.

Slightly dazed at the arbitrary tone, the painter let down the canvas against the wainscot and took the packet of butter in one hand and the knife in the other.

"Look at Telman!" said Sylvester, coming over to Gabriel. "If Onny makes that fat pig do a stroke of honest work she'll have more than my admiration."

"She's industrious, isn't she?" said Helen, looking at Gabriel. "Domestic skill always brings a woman immediate success. It is only people like myself, who have not taste for the natural duties of their sex, who try to achieve a false success by bad sculpture."

She had deliberately let him know that she had heard an account of them from Sylvester. Was it deliberately or accidentally that she let him know now that she was aware of Onny's humble origin? He decided that it was accidentally that she had made the reference.

"Are you a sculptor?" he said, wondering uneasily whether his use of the word was correct, when applied to a woman.

"Didn't you know?" she said, lifting her brows in a slight arc. "You must have seen my things. Sylvester has stored some of them here for me, I believe." She began to move back towards the window as she spoke. Since there was no one there towards whom she might be moving, Gabriel felt that she intended him to follow her. He did.

When she had first begun to speak he had wondered that she should speak so clearly and distinctly in a crowded room where so many could overhear her words, but soon he realized that although the clear voice was distinctly audible in the din of the room, no one heeded it, or heard it. So too, in a noisy park, above the din of children screaming at play, and the bark and yelp of dogs that frolic after them in excitement, above the talk of the people who congregate at the fountains, above the whistle of the park keeper as someone strolls on to a forbidden patch of green, and above even the incessant sound of the traffic beyond the railings, with its whistles and motor horns, its jarring of brakes and rattle of wheels, there pours forth, all day long, unheeded and unheard, the piercing sweetness of a bird's song.

When she reached the window, Helen sat up on the window ledge again.

Gabriel stood waiting for her to speak. After a while, looking down into the streets below, with her cold profile close to the window-pane, she spoke so casually as to be almost insulting, as if she were merely keeping alive a pretence of conversation while her thoughts were far away, flying among the leafy branches of the trees in the public park. "I'm sure you have seen some of my work; heads and plaster casts." She turned and looked him straight in the face. "You must have seen them," she said, coldly and distinctly. "They are in the studio. You sleep there, don't you?"

"Yes," he said, confusedly, "yes, I saw them."

Gabriel felt the blood rush up to his temples. All around them was laughter and talk, aimless and careless sentences looping and crossing like clothes upon a clothesline on a windy day, but every word Helen said seemed to be sharp and clear and deliberate. Did she mean to humiliate him by letting him see how complete was her knowledge of his affairs, or did she hope to put him at ease by that same means? He wished earnestly to know which was her motive, but yet he shrank from trying to find out. She was so outspoken he was afraid of what she might say if provoked. She might say anything. She might ask any question. And although he felt excited at being in such new and strange company, he wished for the present to make his escape from this strange, penetrating person in whose company he was made so conscious of the insecurity of his position.

"I think I had better join Onny," he said, slipping down from the window sill. "She may feel out of place here among so many strangers."

But before he had time to turn away, Helen glanced across the room and he saw that she was smiling peculiarly.

"I don't think you need worry about Onny," said Helen. "She seems to be very much at home here." But although she smiled with apparent amusement as she nodded her head slightly towards the other end of the room, Gabriel felt that there was a criticism of Onny underneath her words. He turned around.

At the other end of the room, the bread had been cut, buttered, and piled on plates. From the opposite corner a cloud of steam from the kettle was puffing into the air unheeded. Onny, who had evidently cut the last of the loaves of bread, was brushing the crumbs to the floor with a sweep of her elbow. Her cheeks had flushed an even deeper red than they had been when she first entered the room, and her hair, that had been moistened slightly by the steam from the kettle, was beginning to curl untidily around her face. Sylvester, standing behind her, was brandishing a large knife.

"Who is going to make the tea?" he cried, over the general din.

It appeared that everyone was taking part in the preparation of the meal, but from the laughter and the noisy banter, and from the fact that the helpers were picking at the food, and putting the bottles to their mouths as they opened them, it was clear that the preparation of the meal and the consumption of it had become inextricably mixed. They were all passing food to each other, their own mouths full, and sometimes the large painter, in laughing, spluttered crumbs to right and left, and the girls skirted aside with expressions of good-humoured disgust. Onny was enjoying herself immensely.

Gabriel turned back to Helen. The excuse he had tried to make for leaving her had been taken away from him. But when he looked at her again she seemed to have undergone some change. Her face was more indifferent now, and she had withdrawn herself still further into the corner of the window sill, and turned her face towards the cold glass. When she spoke it was of indifferent matters. He no longer felt the need to be alert and watchful in answering her. After a time he, too, sat up on the window sill and, like his companion, he too looked down into the street below. The street was more grey and empty than it had been a few moments before. In the alleyways there was a faint mist and a deeper mist at the end of the street hid its far confines. In the public park the greenery had a cold harsh glitter, and looking up he saw that the sky had taken on its grave, evening shades of blue and green. It was this cold light that gave the leaves their hard glitter. Stretching away into the deep mist the tram rails glittered too.

As he looked, suddenly, the lights went on all down the street, lamp after lamp lighting up swiftly one after another as if a flock of brilliant, golden birds had flown down the sky, and alighted on their perches with nature's swift impetuous precision. Daylight and lamplight shone together over the city, but even as he stared downward, the strength of the lamplight seemed to vanquish the day, the green light vanished from the sky. Only the branches of trees that came within the arc of lamplight retained their colour, which was brightened, heightened, and jewelled till it surpassed their daytime colour. Over all the distant park, too, darkness had settled softly, deepening where the trees were thickest. And over the city dark purple clouds advanced like fabulous creatures part man, part beast, part bird.

"Evening," said Helen, softly. "How silent the room has become."

With a great effort Gabriel looked away from the window. He longed to strain his eyes after the vanishing day, still to be glimpsed in the spaces between the far roofs and tree tops. When he turned back, however, the room was dark and was no longer noisy and rowdy. Sylvester's guests had taken up different positions, some sitting on the top of the table, some crouched up on the sofa, some sitting on the floor. They were talking now in different groups, and the bright points of their cigarettes pricked the darkness with ruby stars.

Evening had imposed its gravity on the room, and Gabriel and Helen came under its influence too. They became more and more silent as time went on, and listened more to the voices of the others. Near them, sitting on the floor, Sylvester was telling a story. Then, as if their silence attracted his attention where the voices had been unheeded, Sylvester interrupted his story and called out to them.

"Helen! Gabriel! Are you two still sitting on the window ledge? If you are will you open the window? The room is getting infernally hot. But don't fall out."

Gabriel threw up the window and the fresh night air came in with a rush, like a rush of wings, laden with the scent of the dew-moistened trees. In the distance a chiming clock began to strike the hour, cutting the air like silver hammers. Gabriel leaned his face close to the glass. Below him the street was silent. The trees under the window dredged the lamplight with their jewelled leaves. Upon the pavement below the trees, the tracery of the leaves was thrown in silhouette, and when a faint stir came in the air, the leaves and their shadows moved together in harmony. A solitary person came into view walking along the empty street, his solitariness giving him a temporary significance. Gabriel followed him till he vanished again, his feet echoing even then in the quiet street. When he heard the last echo of the stranger's feet he turned round again to see where Helen had gone, for he had felt her slip down from the window ledge and walk into the centre of the room, but in the darkness he could not tell where she had taken up her new position. If he could not see, he could, however, be seen, for the lamplight in the street below made the window paler than the rest of the room and he was silhouetted against it. A voice called to him.

"Sit down here, Gabriel!" said Onny. Her voice came from quite near him. "I came over to the window. It was too hot where I was," she said, and she put out a hand and drew him down beside her on the floor. He wondered if her coming had sent Helen away. He sank down on the floor beside her, and she drew his arm through hers. After the cold air that had blown across from the park, he felt the sweetness of her warmth, and from the pleasant chill of his clothes and from his cold face Onny derived relief from the feverishness caused by excitement.

"Are you happy?" said Gabriel.

She nodded for reply. They listened quietly to the talk around them, no longer needing to take part in it, forgotten, perhaps, now that they were hidden in the darkness.

The time filtered slowly away, as time might pass through the filter of sleep, and the dim figures in the room moved and spoke with the fragmentary and illusory quality of people in a dream. Onny fell into a light sleep against his shoulder, and when she wakened again she made no effort to take up the thread of what she had been saying, as people do in an effort to conceal that they have nodded to sleep. When she wakened she said the first thing that came into her head.

Gabriel's mind turned on many things. He wondered how soon his absence had been noticed in Clewe Street. He wondered how soon it would be connected with the absence of Onny, which would probably be sooner found out. And he once or twice, involuntarily, wondered if he had been wise to take Onny with him without first making some effort to secure a livelihood for them. The words of the girl on the window sill came back to his mind, and he recalled the expression on her face when she looked at Onny. Why was she so critical of the way Onny adapted herself to her new surroundings? He himself had only worried in case she might be awkward and embarrassed.

Just then Onny stirred against him drowsily. He put aside the worries that Helen's words had raised in him. And instead he set himself deliberately to think of the squalor from which he had taken her. At home, at this hour, she would be huddled into a close and badly ventilated room, smothered in hot bedclothes, between Chrissie and Judy. He had taken her away from that life. He had brought her here to this city, and this was only the beginning of the great changes he would make in her life.

A far bell chimed. Below in the street doubtless the leaves still threw their shadows on the asphalt. The lateness of the hour, the height of the room above the street, the gathering of strangers, all combined to give him a feeling of freedom. Tomorrow was Sunday. But the day after that he would begin to look for work of some kind or another to ensure that he would be able to keep his freedom. He had no regrets for the life he had left. Although, looking back, even at such a short interval, it seemed to him that the annoyances he had suffered in it had not been so very great. He resolved to send his aunts a telegram to say that he was safe, and that they were not to worry about him. But he knew they would. And his last thought that night was one of pity for them.

෴ ෴ ෴

Sunday morning dawned bright and clear as Sunday morning should. Gabriel opened his eyes and looked around the studio. In the morning light it was shown up at its worst, but nevertheless he looked around him with a feeling of satisfaction. He recalled the previous night and the air of freedom that had characterized the actions and speech of the people he had met. As Onny opened her eyes he sat up, and leaning over on his elbow, he looked at the tin clock that stood on a box beside the bed. The

353

clock had been one of Onny's treasures and it had come out of the embroidered carpet bag.

"Eleven o'clock!" he exclaimed. "Onny, can you believe it? Eleven o'clock on a Sunday morning, and no one shouting up the stairs and rapping at the door to tell us we'll be late for church."

Onny crouched down lower into the bed.

"Oh, how sleepy I am," she said. "I could sleep for a week."

Gabriel laughed. There was something comic in the way Onny buried her face in the pillow only venturing to open one eye at a time, and that but narrowly and reluctantly.

Gabriel slumped down again between the warm sheets.

"I'm sleepy myself," he said. "It's a pity it's Sunday."

This time it was Onny who sat up. She sat up suddenly and opened her eyes wide.

"Why is it a pity?" she asked. "What difference does Sunday make?"

"All the difference in the world," said Gabriel, indolently staring at the ceiling and contemplating the disagreeable thought of getting up again. "All the difference in the world," he said. "We have to get up!"

But Onny still sat bolt upright.

"Why?" she said, and something in her tone made Gabriel look at her sharply.

"We're going to church, aren't we?" he asked.

This was evidently what Onny had feared he would say.

"You can go if you like," she said, "but I'm not going." Catching up the clothes she threw herself down again under the covers, and pulled them tight across under her chin. "There's no one to make me go!" she said.

Gabriel lay still. He was startled, shocked even, at Onny's attitude. He looked at her. She was not fooling or teasing him. She had rolled over on her side, and with eyes squeezed tight against the daylight was trying to recapture the warmth and darkness of sleep. He stared up at the ceiling.

In Clewe Street the preparations for church had begun as early as Saturday morning. All day long his aunts had been busy upon small personal preparations for the next day. As soon as the fire in the kitchen was well established and bright, Theresa would go upstairs and bring down her own and Sara's Sunday garments to air them and examine them against possible deterioration or dust, moth, or damp. And Sara, having washed a pair of yellow chamois gloves shortly after getting up, would spend a considerable part of the day going back and forth to the clothes line in the garden to examine them, to turn them, to stretch them, and to feel how successfully they were drying. Several times he himself would be netted into the general preparation.

"How are your shoes, Gabriel? Are they all right for tomorrow? You don't want new shoelaces, do you? Because tomorrow morning is not the time to attend to those matters. Are you sure you have a clean handkerchief for tomorrow, Gabriel?"

All day the small preparations continued until at last on Saturday night the sideboard in the back parlour was cleared at one corner, and here were placed, in readiness for the next day, the gloves, the clean handkerchiefs, the hatpins, the veils, the brass-bound prayer books, and all the other accessories of churchgoing which in less orderly households might have caused confusion and delay by having to be sought up and down the house in different closets and cupboards. And on the sideboard with these articles there were unfailingly three neat piles of coppers: one for Theresa, one for Sara, and one for Gabriel. They were the coppers for the collection plate that would be passed around during the service. No laggard could seek an excuse for being late on the grounds that he was trying to find change at the last minute.

It was of course essential to have the right amount for the collection because to have given a larger coin than was necessary would have meant getting change in return and this, Sara feared, would be "taking money from God," and was not to be thought of for a moment. So the piles of coppers were made ready every Saturday night.

And when Sunday came, the day would no sooner have dawned than there would be a rap at Gabriel's door.

"I knew you'd want to be awake in good time, Gabriel," his Aunt Sara would say, putting her head around the door for an instant.

And after that, at intervals of five and ten minutes, as she had occasion to pass by his door, she would stick in her head again with a nervous inquiry.

"Is there any danger of your falling asleep again, dear?"

He used to lie doggedly in bed until the latest possible moment for getting up with any hope of reaching the church gates before the last bell ceased to peal, while his aunts would continue to rap at his door, even to call up to him from the foot of the stairs with the information that they themselves were on the point of leaving the house. Oftentimes indeed he had not sprung out on to the floor until the door had banged after his aunts. While they were in the house urging him to hurry and to watch the clock, he seemed to be powerless to move, so intense was his irritation at the fuss and interference.

But—and Gabriel glanced again at the sleeping Onny with surprise and curiosity—never at any time had the thought entered his head that he would stay away from church if he was outside the reach of his aunts' warning voices.

Once again Onny had outstripped him in the courage of her convictions.

But on this occasion he did not feel the admiration he had felt for her on former occasions. He felt instead the twinge of worry and uneasiness. He wondered if he would rouse her again and appeal to her to get up and go out with him to church. But looking at her, and she had indeed fallen back into a fast sleep, he decided that she had had unusual excitement and an unusual expenditure of energy in the last three days, and that he could, without scruple, let her sleep this morning. And then, with a feeling of recklessness, he himself sank back into the bedclothes. They were neither of them fully recovered yet from the effects of the journey and the strangeness of the new life. He would not want to make a practice of this laziness, of course, but for this morning it was surely excusable. And, as Onny had said, there was no one to make them go.

Sometime after noon Gabriel and Onny got up, and since they were still taking their meals with Sylvester, they went out to the other room to find him and see what was to be had for a meal, and what plans Sylvester had made for the day.

Sylvester was going about his room in an old dressing gown, and he was not shaved, but when they came in it seemed to Gabriel that he was surprised to see that Onny was wearing her loose broken-down slippers, and that he himself was wearing a short shirt with an open collar.

"Were you not out of doors yet?" he asked, and although the question was vague, Gabriel knew that he was wondering that they had not gone to church.

Before he had time to answer, Onny burst out with an impetuous explanation.

"He wanted to go to church," she said, jerking her thumb derisively at Gabriel, "but I told him not to be silly," and flouncing her skirts, Onny went over familiarly to the food cupboard in the corner of the room. "What are we going to have for dinner?" she said. "Shall I start getting it ready?"

Sylvester looked at Gabriel with a strange smile.

"I see your disciple has outstripped you," he said, and then, as Onny clamoured again to know what they were to have for dinner, he turned around and called out something to her which Gabriel did not heed.

Onny was all earnestness however, and in response to a direction from Sylvester she was straining up at the top shelf of the cupboard, raised on the tips of her toes and bending forward until her skirt rose higher and higher up the backs of plump calves.

"I can't see anything," she cried.

Gabriel was about to step over and help her, when by the help of his few additional inches in height, looking up at the shelf he saw without moving that it was bare and empty, and was covered with a coating of dust that had been undisturbed for many a day. He was about to tell

Sylvester that he was mistaken and that there was nothing on the shelf when, looking across at him, he saw that Sylvester, who evidently knew well that there was nothing on the shelf, was staring with silent amusement at Onny's fat calves and at the hem of her skirt that ran up and down over those ample calves according as Onny raised or lowered herself on the toes of the broken-down slippers. The irritation that Sylvester had set up in him the evening of their arrival, and which had been forgotten on the previous evening in the confused excitement of making new acquaintances, came back now with a rush. He was about to say something but on another impulse he walked over to the window.

In the street below the people were passing in unusually large numbers. He glanced back at the clock on the mantelpiece behind him. The last service was over now in all the churches. The people were returning from their devotions. He looked down more attentively and saw that many of the people below were carrying prayer books in their hands or under their arms. He stared out. So many people; and all, all unknown to him. He was overcome by a sudden feeling of his own temerity in having come among them; come to swell the already swollen, overwhelming number of human beings. The thought that in the morning he would have to venture out among these crowding numbers, to look for work, to seek what seemed to him to be an incalculable favour for himself, was a thought that filled him with depression.

But suddenly, as he stared down despondently into the street, among the crowding strangers, his eye was caught by someone who seemed slightly familiar

Along the street, on the opposite side, a young girl in a dark blue coat was walking with rapid steps that contrasted with the easygoing stride of the rest of the people on the pavement. She was just passing opposite the window where he stood at the moment that he caught sight of her and so he had only a moment to identify the vague familiarity of the figure. But the moment was enough. Under her small dark blue hat he saw a small pointed face, and a loose strand of honey-coloured hair, and recognized the Helen of his conversation the night before. He looked after her. She had in a moment outstripped three or four of the more indolent people who were going in the same direction, but before she had reached the top of Molesworth Street and turned sharply down it, Gabriel saw with a certain surprise that under her left arm, tucked close and inconspicuous, was a small prayer book which might have escaped even his attention, but for the fact that the gilt bevelling glinted suddenly as she turned abruptly around the corner

For some time after Helen had vanished, Gabriel looked at the corner around which she had gone, and his thoughts were of a mixed nature. First he was surprised to think that anyone whom he had met in Sylvester's company of the night before should be so strict an observer of the Sabbath, and, secondly, he wondered if he would have been likely to have chanced upon the same church as Helen if he had persisted in going out himself as he had originally intended. And would he have spoken to her? That was another thing. Would the short acquaintance of one evening permit him to stop her if they met in the street?

These vague questions eventually settled into the more definite question of whether or not he would be likely to meet her again with Sylvester. Compared with the others she seemed to have been very distant and cool with Sylvester, and yet he could not help thinking that this coldness in her manner was due to some strain of intimacy rather than to unfamiliarity or strangeness. And then, too, she had said that the statues in the studio belonged to her. Why were they there? And why—the question that had bothered him last night came back again—why had she deliberately let him know that the pieces of statuary belonged to her?

To settle these questions the natural thing would have been to put them to Sylvester and get the answer from him, but some instinct kept Gabriel from doing this. Sylvester might take on the jocose manner which he, Gabriel, hated so much and with which he had never come into contact until now.

If I had noticed it before, he thought—that stupid sneering at everything—I would have thought twice about coming here.

But, as a matter of fact, his despondency was not as great as it had been a few minutes before, and the sight of the familiar face of Helen passing in the throng of unknown faces had given him a curious impulse of lightheartedness. She had seemed like an omen of good.

The day passed indolently. It was late afternoon before they had finished the meal that made up both breakfast and dinner, and after that Sylvester threw himself down on an old couch that lay along the wall and yawned loudly.

"You're a born cook, Onny," he said "I never ate such a good meal in my life. I'll spend the rest of the day recovering from it."

Onny's face beamed with pleasure and pride. "I'll wash up the dishes now," she cried, and clattering up an armful of cups and saucers she looked around for a basin in which to put them.

There was a cold tap in the corner of the room, but no sink

"Where's the basin?" she demanded. "What did you do with it?" and her tone of housewifely peevishness made Sylvester laugh heartily. After a minute, however, he sat up.

"Leave those dishes, you little fool," he said. "I'll wash them up later, or you can do them yourself tonight, if you want, but go out now while the sun is out. You've hardly seen the city yet." He turned to Gabriel. "Take her out," he said, "and show her around."

"Won't you come?" said Onny, who was ready to abandon the dishes at the first word.

Sylvester lay back on the couch.

"No," he said flatly. "Not even for you, my dear Onny, could I bring myself to endure the streets of Dublin on a Sunday. On weekdays I ask nothing better than to jostle my fellow men on the pavement, because on weekdays they are all individuals; men, women, and children, they are going about their own affairs. But on Sunday!" Sylvester shuddered. "On Sunday the individual is effaced. The gregarious instinct holds sway over the city. Such individuals as have managed to preserve their individuality, like myself for instance, skulk indoors. The family man is abroad in all his glory.

"First, however, let us take the potential family man: the lover. Sunday is, above all other days, his day. See him as he walks along, by the side of some dressed-up doll; every vestige of man's dignity as a separate human soul has vanished from his countenance, with every glance and every gesture he shows that he is no longer a man, but a slave. Watch him. See how he glances to either side, how now with pride and now with apprehension, he watches to see the effect his pretty doll will make on other men, as they pass by with what he considers to be very inferior possessions. Ah yes, the lover is a degrading sight as he parades the street on a Sunday; but"—and here Sylvester, who was being carried away by his own eloquence, sat up and flung out his hand dramatically in the direction of the public park whose topmost trees could be seen in the distance—"take the married man, the man of family. In his cheap Sunday shoes and his cheap Sunday clothes he walks along beside his mate, surrounded on all sides by peevish offspring who pull and drag on him, and one of whom is always lagging behind. Unlike the lover, the family man will not be looking from side to side, but will most likely have his eyes cast to the ground, for now, alas, there is no reason to be either proud or apprehensive of the glances that fall upon his bedraggled mate. And even the children are in their own way pitiable and degraded." Sylvester made a deprecatory gesture with his hand. "And speaking of dogs," he said. "Why, the very cur that ran neglected and starving through the streets all week is, on Sunday, caught by the scruff of the neck and forced into a collar and strap that he may be paraded as part of the family. Yes! On Sundays even the dogs are family dogs."

As Sylvester was talking Gabriel was looking at him with amusement which was all the greater when he chanced to glance at Onny and saw that to her Sylvester's words appeared as serious. When Sylvester was finished he laughed wholeheartedly.

"Come, Onny," he said, "we must get out into the streets and see these sights for ourselves."

Onny turned around.

"I'm not going out," she said. "Go yourself if you like."

"But why not, Onny?" asked Gabriel, still laughing at the comical scene that had been pictured for them by Sylvester. "Surely you would like to see these people for yourself?"

Onny looked at him scathingly.

"I wouldn't mind seeing them," she said, "if we could see them from a window, but can't you see——" her voice became sharp with impatience—"can't you see that if we go out in the street we'll be just like them!"

This time it was Sylvester's turn to laugh, and at the expense of Gabriel.

"There's wit for you," he said admiringly, but as Onny again clattered up an armful of crockery, he urged Gabriel's cause. "No, Onny. You must go out," he said "Gabriel is right. It will be good for you to go out in the sun. Don't mind what I said. I was only joking. I'd go out with you myself but as a matter of fact I'm expecting Telman Young in the afternoon. He's giving a party for us some night next week and he wants to talk about it."

"A party!" said Onny. "Oh, couldn't we stay and hear about it?"

"No," said Sylvester again, firmly and decisively. "It's to be a surprise for you. I shouldn't have told you at all."

"Who is Telman Young?" asked Gabriel, turning to Sylvester.

"Oh, don't you know!" cried Onny impatiently. "He's the big tall man we met last night; the painter. How can you be so stupid as to forget?"

Gabriel smiled indulgently.

"Come on, Onny," he said. "Get your coat and hat."

"I don't want any hat," said Onny, and she ran out on to the landing to fetch the coat.

Onny and Gabriel started out from the apartment in good spirits. Onny was filled with excitement at the thought of the party Telman was going to give them, and her conversation was mainly made up of questions which she put to Gabriel without the least concern at his being unable to answer them.

"Do you think there will be many people at it?" she would ask. "Do you think we'll meet some of the people that were at Sylvester's last night?"

But as Gabriel answered them more and more indifferently she gave up asking them aloud. It was clear, however, from the detached way in which she passed through the unfamiliar sights and scenes of the city that her mind was still turned inwards and that the questions were still forming silently in her heart.

And after a time Gabriel's own thoughts turned inward from the scene around them, and he began to put questions to himself as difficult of answer as those that Onny had posed. Would he be long in finding work to do in this city? What kind of work would he get? And soon the attention that he had given to the fine buildings of limestone and granite between which they passed as they wandered aimlessly from street to street, became limited to those portions of the buildings around the doorways and porches that were placarded with brass plates indicating the varieties of trades and professions that were carried on within the walls.

After a time, however, both the scene before their eyes and the thoughts that filled their minds began to grow tiresome, and to their unaccustomed feet the hard city pavements became wearisome and burning.

"Let's go back," said Onny, all at once, stopping up abruptly and planting her feet firmly together as if refusing to go another step.

Gabriel was no less anxious to return, but happening at that moment to catch sight of a clock that hung out from a building over their heads, he saw that it was only four o'clock, and that they had hardly been out an hour.

"Sylvester's friend will hardly have gone yet," he said. "I don't think we could go back so soon."

Onny pouted. She saw the expediency of Gabriel's observations, but her feet were hurting her and she was irritated by an inner conflict of self-interest against self-will.

"I think you might have found something better for us to do than walk about the streets!" she said. "We could have gone and sat in that park near the apartment."

"Would you have liked that?" said Gabriel, surprised. "Why didn't you say so? We could go back there now for an hour or so." He began to look around to see what direction they would take in order to make their way back to Stephen's Green.

"An hour!" Onny gasped. And then she too looked around her. "It's miles away," she said petulantly, and as they began to walk back she dragged her feet and finally hung out of Gabriel's arm so heavily that he hardly knew what weight bore down on him the heavier, the weight upon his arm or the weight of her ill-humour upon his heart.

The park, when they reached it, was crowded, and it was hard to find room on the seats, but at last after walking up and down for some time, they came on a seat that was quite deserted, probably because it was situated on the east side, in a damp spot overhung with heavy shrubs that shut out at one and the same time the light and heat of the sun, and any hope or prospect for the eye.

"We'll go back at five," said Gabriel, hoping by this suggestion to make it more endurable for Onny to sit for the rest of the time on this dull viewless seat.

They sat down. As Gabriel spoke a clock in the distance began to chime. Onny, who had just sat down, sprang up again.

"Listen!" she cried. "It's five o'clock now!"

The chime pealed out, however, no more than four dulcet tones.

"It's only half-past four," said Gabriel reluctantly, and he took her hand. "Perhaps we won't wait till five. Perhaps we'll go back at a quarter to the hour!"

But Onny, in spite of her ill will against him for not being able to employ the time more agreeably, was just the same determined not to go back.

"You know Sylvester said he didn't want us there with Telman," she said, and she sat back again on the seat, with her face set resolutely to stare in front of her at the dusty bushes on the other side of the path.

Gabriel sat staring at the same dull prospect. For a few minutes they said nothing, and then involuntarily Gabriel spoke out of his thoughts.

"Doesn't the day seem endless when you don't go to church?" he said, and not expecting any answer he was about to make some further remark, when suddenly to his surprise Onny sprang up from the seat, and when he looked up at her as she stood over him, his surprise turned to astonishment when he saw that her cheeks were red and angry and that it was, apparently, his words that had inflamed them.

"Well!" cried Onny. "It's bad enough to have to sit here in this stupid place, but if you're going to start preaching you can sit here alone!"

And turning on her heel she set off down the path in a state of determined anger which no longer took into account the tenderness of her feet about which she had so lately complained.

Gabriel, although he had been taken by surprise, sprang up and hurried after her and caught up with her in a few paces.

"Oh, Onny," he cried, "how could you think that I was preaching! I was only making a simple statement. You said a few minutes ago that you never found a day so long and tedious."

He drew her arm through his and glanced at her uneasily to see if her anger was in any danger of breaking out with the same intensity, but Onny gave her arm a jerk and drew it free from under his, and looking ahead he saw that they were entering upon the sunnier spaces of the park where there were consequently an increasingly greater number of people sitting along the seats by the sides of the path. There people found their entertainment in watching those strollers who passed in front of them, and realizing that Onny had withdrawn her arm from his in order that they would not be diverted by the evidence of such intimacy, he judged that she would scarcely give them the greater diversion of seeing a violent quarrel. He felt reassured, and began to explain himself in a low and quiet tone of voice. Onny would not listen. Instead she made her own comments.

362

"Sylvester wasn't at church!" she said. "And those other people we met in the apartment last night, I'm sure they don't trouble themselves about such things."

She tilted her head in a way that Gabriel would have found amusingly arrogant if he were not uneasy in his mind about her.

"They are enlightened people!" she said, and at the thought of these charming people she tossed her head with some return of good humour.

"That's where you're wrong," said Gabriel energetically. "When I was looking out the window this morning, I saw one of the girls we met last night, going along the street with a prayer book under her arm."

Onny seemed surprised for a moment, but then she exclaimed depreciatingly:—

"Oh, I expect it was that girl called Helen. I wouldn't mind her!"

There was such a note of contempt in Onny's voice when she mentioned Helen that Gabriel turned around in surprise to stare at her and, forgetting all that had gone before, seized on Onny's last words in an effort to understand how Onny, who seemed to him to be so young and inexperienced, could have spoken in such a tone about a girl who had, or so it appeared to him, at least a dozen attributes that a girl like Onny might have admired and striven to attain.

"You wouldn't mind Helen," he said, repeating her words incredulously. "What do you mean, Onny?"

Onny jerked her shoulders upwards as if she were shaking off some imperceptible burden.

"Oh, she's one of those tiresome saints that are always preaching and prying into other people's business," she said.

"Why, Onny! How do you know so much about her?" Gabriel asked. As far as he could remember Onny had not been talking to Helen for more than a moment or two when they were first introduced to each other by Sylvester.

"Oh, Sylvester told me all about her," said Onny, easily and lightly as at the same time she put up her hand to try and grasp a branch of trailing shrubbery that overhung the path.

"What did he tell you?" said Gabriel, curious, and somewhat astonished that the questions that had run through his mind about the strange girl should be answered by Onny of all people.

"Oh, he used to like her one time," said Onny, her voice still casual, as, having caught at the branch and dragged off a handful of foliage, she was busy fastening the spray in the front of her dress. "He thought she was wonderful when he first met her. But he got tired of her."

"Why?" said Gabriel.

"Oh, he couldn't stand the way she was always getting at him about not going to church and that kind of thing. He said he had no time for Holy Mollys!"

Gabriel listened to this gratuitously offered piece of gossip with an interest that was twofold, but not the less keen for that. He had already felt that there was something strange in Helen's manner towards Sylvester, and it had roused his curiosity. Here was an explanation which, if not altogether reliable in the form in which it came from Onny's glib tongue, must be at least partially true since it was Sylvester who told it to Onny.

But he was astonished to think that, while he, who was Sylvester's friend, had not had a moment's conversation with him since he arrived in the city, Onny had found time to discover information of this intimate nature. He was surprised and his mind dwelt on the subject for some time as they made their way back to the apartment, but it did not dwell exclusively on this subject, for long before they turned into Kildare Street he had gone back to thinking about Helen in the light of what Onny had said about herself and Sylvester.

Ever since he had first looked up in Sylvester's room and seen her with her serious eyes fixed on him, his interest in her had been growing hourly. The way his interest had flared up in an instant recalled to him the way in which once, long ago, the sight of Agnes Finnerty in the street in Draghead had roused him suddenly to such a curiosity in her that he had followed her, street by street, like a common corner boy. How quickly that bright spark of interest had been quenched; he wondered if this too would be blown out in a moment. For it did seem to Gabriel that these capricious flares of interest had no lasting significance. In the two important relations of his life, his relationship with Onny and that with Sylvester, he had experienced no such lightning stroke of attraction, but by gradual daily intercourse he had been bound to them slowly and surely.

In other words, as Gabriel walked along by the side of Onny, he felt there was no disloyalty to her in the thoughts that ran through his head about Helen. Helen, like Agnes, was a stranger, fascinating for a moment, tantalizing and occupying the mind, but Onny was part of him, a possession of every day. Onny belonged to him. And so far was he from forgetting this was so that when they came to the building, just as they were about to go up the dark stairs to the apartment, he turned on the doorstep.

"There are three things I must do tomorrow," he said, breaking the long silence. "I must write to my aunts. I must start to look for work." He paused and caught Onny's arm. "And I must see about getting some priest to marry us."

Onny, whose ill-feelings had lifted as soon as they had entered Kildare Street, turned around with her old affability, and her old smile of robust good humour.

"There's only one thing I have to do," she said, "and I'm going to do it right now." And leaning her weight on Gabriel's arm, she stooped down and drew off one shoe and then the other, and slinging them together by the laces, she laughed up gaily into Gabriel's face, and ran up the stairs ahead of him in her stockinged feet.

∽ ∽ ∽

The three matters upon which Gabriel proposed to engage his attention next day turned out on further reflection to be of such a nature that they could not be accomplished in the order in which Gabriel had enumerated them to Onny. In fact it became clear that the order of their accomplishment was a very important matter.

For example, it was of small use to write to Castlerampart until the letter could give the news that he and Onny were married, because whatever the reaction of the Coniffe sisters might be to the news that Onny had gone with their nephew, that reaction could only be made more bitter by knowing that they were not even married.

That is the matter I must attend to first, thought Gabriel, as he awoke on Monday morning, but before the day had lengthened itself by more than an hour, he had changed his mind, and decided that his first necessity was to obtain some kind of work that would give him independence, and give to Onny the privacy of her own apartment. For the original plan of setting up a separate household in the studio was not yet put into practice, and Gabriel was beginning to feel that Onny's habit of running back and forth between Sylvester's room and their own was one that would be hard to break even if they had crockery and utensils of their own. Further, although the gas ring was communally situated on the landing, the water tap was in Sylvester's room. Onny ran in and out of all the rooms at will, and at times her energies brought her from one place to another with such darting frequency that she found it expedient to leave all the doors wide open.

"We'll have to get a place of our own," said Gabriel to Sylvester, when they had taken their breakfast together in Sylvester's room. "And in order to be able to do that I'll have to earn some money somehow."

"Why such hurry?" said Sylvester. "Aren't you all right here?"

"Oh I don't know what we would have done without your help and hospitality," said Gabriel, "but we don't want to make ourselves a nuisance." He pointed to the door behind them, which Onny had left wide open in her last excursion to the gas ring. Through the door they could see across the landing to the other room, which presented an untidy appearance of early morning disarray. "It's not very pleasant for you," he said.

Sylvester stood up from the table.

"Don't think of me," he said. "Think only of yourselves. After all,

I'm benefiting by this arrangement." As Gabriel looked at him in some surprise, Sylvester nodded his head at Onny who had come back into the room only to gather up the soiled dishes and take them into a corner to wash them and put them away in the cupboard. "As long as you stay," he said, "I have a servant without having to pay wages."

Gabriel felt his cheeks flush foolishly and he looked at Sylvester quickly and then at Onny. He could not say whether Sylvester was aware or not of the stupid blunder he had made. Sylvester, however, was leaning back in his chair blandly, and had even called out across his shoulder to Onny.

"Isn't that right, Onny?" he asked, and Onny, although she said nothing, and stood with her back to them, had every air of being pleased and even complimented.

Gabriel stood up.

"Well, anyway," he said, "whether we stay or not I must start to look for a job. What do you advise me to do, Sylvester?"

He was hurt that Sylvester had shown so little interest in his plans, and that since he had come to the apartment Sylvester had shown no desire to have any conversation with him alone. He takes more notice of Onny than he does of me, thought Gabriel, but he consoled himself by thinking that Sylvester did this in order, indirectly, to make things easier for them all. After all, he thought, he might have behaved very differently. He might have been annoyed with me for having brought her here with me.

This morning, however, he was determined that he would discuss his plans, and not let another day pass over him without getting something settled.

"You said it ought to be easy for me to find something to do," he said quietly as Sylvester's attention seemed likely to stray back again to Onny, who was making a somewhat distracting din with the rattling of the dishes in the basin.

"Oh, I expect there are several things you could do," said Sylvester easily, but he seemed disinclined to go into the matter any closer. "I have to go out now anyway," he said, "I promised to give Helen a hand with moving some of her statuary. She is showing some of it at an exhibition in Duke Street, and there are a few pieces too heavy for her to carry." He stood up. "I'll tell you, though," he said, as an afterthought, "why don't you come too? You can carry some of the stuff, and we can discuss your affairs on the way. As a matter of fact, Helen may have some ideas. She's a good hand at helping lame dogs over stiles."

Taking his suggestion as accepted, Sylvester took up a shoe brush and began to rub his shoes.

"You can stay here, Onny," he said, "and get the dinner."

Onny, who had begun to dry her hands at the first mention of the expedition, did not nevertheless show any signs of disappointment.

"All right," she said, turning back to the dishes, and then almost immediately turning around again, she spoke excitedly. "I think I'll give this whole place a good going-over while you're out," she said. "It looks as if no one put a hand to it for a year. Look at that," she cried, pointing to a cobweb in a corner. "Look at that"—she pointed to the coating of dust and dirt on the paintwork. "Look at·that—look at that."

In a whirl of energy she flew from place to place, lifting cushions, and shaking curtains, and showing that her energy in discovering such dirt was only to be equalled by her determination to rout it.

"Good girl!" said Sylvester, and taking his hat he put his hand under Gabriel's elbow. "Come on," he said. "This will be no place for us in another few minutes."

He led the way out on to the landing. On the top step of the stairs, however, he stopped, and going back to the door of the room they had left, he called in to Onny.

"Put on your old clothes before you start your work," he said, "we don't want to come back and find you as bad as the night you arrived."

∽ ∽ ∽

Helen occupied a large room on the ground floor of a house in Molesworth Street within a few yards of Sylvester's abode. Gabriel looked forward with interest to seeing this room, feeling that a further revelation of her character was likely to be given by the background against which she lived. From Sylvester he understood that Helen, unlike himself, had taken an empty room which she had furnished with articles of her own choice.

"She has taste, there's no doubt about that!" said Sylvester hastily as a last word on the subject when they were within a few yards of the house. "I was with her when she bought some of her furniture."

There was no time for Gabriel to make any remark, but before they had pushed open the hall door, which was ajar, there was just time for his mind to turn over Sylvester's words, and to ask himself with surprise if Sylvester's opportunities for appraising Helen's possessions had been limited to the occasions that he had helped her to buy them in the shops? This seemed unlikely when he considered her frequent visits to Sylvester's studio and still more so when he remembered Onny's stories about their former friendship.

Only a minute marked the time in which these thoughts ran through Gabriel's mind, and in the next minute they were inside the hallway of the building.

The building in which they found themselves was bright and spacious, and in the distance the sound of a typewriter and overhead the sound of feet tramping about showed that there was a great variety of people housed under the one roof, and that a great variety of occupations were carried out within slight radius of each other. At the end of the hall, however, there was a closed door upon the panels of which there were none of the smudges and finger marks that marked the other doors on the landing, and at the base of this door there was not a single blemish in the paintwork, whereas on all the other doors there were large patches where the paint was entirely removed, and in places indeed there were actual dents in the woodwork which showed that those who came and went through those doors had no scruples, when their hands were occupied, in opening the doors by a kick. There was a public character about all these doors: use was made of them by many, care was taken by none.

The door at the end of the corridor was like a door in a private house, and when in answer to Sylvester's light rap upon it, it was opened at once by Helen, the room into which it led gave such immediate glimpses of light and colour, comfort and charm, that it was as if the public building in which they stood had vanished, and that instead the two young men were standing in a pleasant country house, looking over the threshold into one of its most charming and sunny rooms.

All that was wanting now was to hear a pleasant womanly voice bid them enter and seat themselves on the gay chintzed chairs that were the only definite features of the room that impressed themselves on Gabriel in the brief time that the door was held open.

In a minute after the door had opened, however, it had closed again, and Helen, who appeared then to be dressed for the street, was standing beside them in the hall, and pointing to a darker corner of the passage, under the staircase, to an assortment of statues, large and small.

"I have them all ready," said Helen, whose first words had been to thank Sylvester for coming to help her. "And are you coming to help too?" she asked, turning to Gabriel.

There was no mention of their entering the sunny room behind them, upon which the door had been closed so finally.

"I brought them out here for convenience," said Helen, and she began to drag one or two of them into the light.

"You should have left them where they were," said Sylvester, and to Gabriel's surprise he spoke harshly. "They were too heavy for you to lift."

"Oh, I couldn't carry them far," said Helen, "but I easily managed to get them out here."

She began to select those which were to make the burden of their first trip.

An unusual tenseness had come upon Sylvester as he made a selection among the statues of those that were heaviest and most awkward.

"Do you mean to say you lifted this out by yourself?" he asked, turning almost savagely upon her as he partially raised a huge block at the back of the group.

"The caretaker gave me a hand with that," said Helen, seeming to ignore Sylvester's tone, and if not changing the conversation at least giving it a turn sufficient to amount almost to a change. "I'm afraid it will be too heavy for you to carry far, Sylvester," she said. "Do you think we should try to get a handcart?"

Sylvester caught it up in his arms.

"It's not that heavy," he said irritably.

Gabriel looked at him in surprise. Sylvester's displeasure was never concealed, but it was usually revealed in sarcasm or sneers, and not as now in a very ordinary show of temper.

"Come, Gabriel," said Helen, who looked up and saw him staring at Sylvester. "What will you take?" And without waiting for him to reply, she suggested a piece of marble near his foot. "That's not heavy enough," he objected.

"Take two then," said Helen lightly, and she began to fill her own arms with smaller pieces of statuary that needed careful handling. He saw that although she was so calm she was not unaware of Sylvester's ill-humour, and that it had disturbed her.

The statues were sorted at last, and they were ready to depart.

"Are they all right there?" said Sylvester as they reached the door, looking back over his shoulder at those they had been forced to leave for a second journey.

"Oh yes, of course," said Helen, and then on an afterthought she stopped. "Perhaps I should ask the caretaker to keep an eye on them; someone might push a bicycle in there out of the way and knock some of them over. Just a minute."

She went back along the passage and they saw her press a brass bell that was placed in the wall about halfway down its length.

"Let's stand out in the air," said Sylvester, and adjusting their heavy loads they went out into the street and stood at the foot of the steps, waiting.

"Did you see the room?" said Sylvester, after a few minutes' silence had passed.

"I caught a glimpse of it," said Gabriel. After another minute he spoke again. "She didn't ask us to go inside," he said.

It was clear from his voice that his statement was not as simple and banal as it sounded, but that it wanted to draw out some comment upon it from his friend. As a matter of fact he hoped to hear that on their second visit when they went back for the rest of the statues they might expect to receive the hospitality that he had been so disappointed at not receiving on this occasion.

Sylvester, however, made no answer, or at least he allowed such time to pass that when he spoke it was hard to tell whether or not it was intended as an answer to Gabriel's remark. Helen was, at that moment, coming out of the doorway and down the steps so that Sylvester's words, as well as being obscure, were muttered so hurriedly that Gabriel was scarcely able to catch them at all.

"More of her stupid prudery," said Sylvester, and then he added more rashly still as she was almost within hearing, "I wish we had left her to haul her own junk."

Gabriel looked up at Helen and smiled. He was afraid she might have caught the end of Sylvester's words.

"We want something from you in return for our help," he said, to attract her attention upon himself, and also because he was determined that he would not let the morning pass without trying to further his own plans in some way, although Sylvester's interest in them seemed to be so slight and so easily tossed aside.

They had begun to walk down the street. Helen turned with interest towards Gabriel.

"What do you want from me?" she asked agreeably, but not without some amusement.

In a few words Gabriel explained his wish to find some way of supporting himself and Onny, and as he explained, Sylvester interested himself enough in the conversation to throw in the same confident remark with which he had first excited Gabriel's ambitions in Castlerampart.

"There ought to be several jobs he could get," he said.

"There ought to be. Don't you think?" said Gabriel, looking eagerly at Helen.

It exhilarated him to be at last discussing the matter seriously. But at the first glance he took of Helen's face his spirits were dampened. Instead of the easy confidence which Sylvester displayed, which he had undoubtedly expected to see upon her face too, he saw that she was wearing a very serious expression, and what might almost be considered a frown had gathered over her brow.

"There ought to be," she said at last, repeating the words that they themselves had used, but with such a different tone of voice, and with such an ominous emphasis on the second word, that Gabriel felt his heart sink. Helen continued: "There ought to be work for a young man who is willing and able, and whose education, if not very sound, is amply compensated for by natural intelligence."

Gabriel looked down at the ground. He felt the justice of her reference to the inadequacy of his primary education, but it hurt him, all the same, to hear it announced so casually. At the mention of his natural intelligence, however, he looked up with some confidence and was able to hear the rest of what Helen had to say without the distraction of any further emotion.

"The trouble is," said Helen, "that there is a very sharp line between manual work and the professions. A young man with good muscles and a will to work can find a job at any time, and on the other hand there are certain opportunities open to young men who want to start on a professional career. But for people who come in between there is sometimes difficulty in getting a chance to earn a livelihood."

Even in his inexperience, Gabriel felt the truth of what Helen said, but nevertheless he recalled all the brass plates and placards that he had seen in the hallways of so many of the buildings in the city when he and Onny had walked through it the day before, and it seemed hard to think that there would not be an opening in some of those firms and organizations whose numbers were so great all over the city. What he felt dimly Sylvester felt more strongly, and in expressing himself Sylvester had the satisfaction of entering into an argument with Helen.

"Nonsense!" he said. "What about all the offices and counting-houses? What about the organizations and agencies that set themselves up so fast it's hard for a person to get a room in this city? Look at those windows!" They were passing along the north side of the Green at this moment and Sylvester pointed upwards.

Almost every window had the bare appearance of an office window, and on many of them there were gilt letterings pasted against the glass announcing the nature of the transactions carried within. "Look here!" As they passed an open hallway Sylvester stopped and drew their attention to the brass plates and wooden placards that lined one whole side of the wall inside the door. "House Agent, First Floor," he read. "Accountancy Office, Second Floor," and without waiting to hear anything from them, he strode to the next doorway. "See," he cried, "another house agent, first floor, second floor insurance company."

He ran his eye over the plates on the wall, passing over those of solicitors and dentists, and those which announced the showrooms of different trade organizations, but pausing triumphantly every other moment to call their attention to some office, or agency far below the status of the professions, but yet with certain pretensions over the trades.

"He could get into some of these places," he said, as if in defiance of contradiction.

Helen did not contradict him.

"Yes," she said quietly, "as an apprentice!"

"Well?" said Sylvester. "He wouldn't always be an apprentice!"

"No," said Helen, again agreeing with him, "but how would he live in the meantime? An apprentice doesn't get any salary."

"Some of them do," said Sylvester. "In fact most of them get pay now:

371

after all they give as much as they get. Some of them have a dog's life. They're hardly treated any better than messenger boys, but are sent running here and there all over the city, as well as doing the most disagreeable jobs that are to be done in the office."

In his enthusiasm to make his particular point about the salary Sylvester overlooked the effect his remarks might have on the issue in general, but both of his listeners were themselves so eager to clear up the same particular point that they let his other remarks pass.

At this moment there was a slight interruption. They had reached the gallery at which the statuary was to be deposited. It was not until after the delay in carrying in the things and arranging them on the shelves provided that they were able to take up the conversation again. Helen, however, was so interested in what they had been saying that in spite of having spoken to several people in the gallery, and giving directions to her two escorts as often as was necessary, she was no sooner in the street again than she took up the conversation exactly as if it had never been broken.

"They may give pay in some offices," she said, and then almost taking the same words out of Gabriel's mouth she hurried to add, "but it's only barely enough for one. Gabriel must have enough for two. You must not forget Onny."

"Oh Onny!" said Sylvester, and, as if he saw a loophole for escaping from the tedium of the argument in which he was being worsted, he laughed. "Onny could support herself if she was put to it!"

Gabriel was not going to be put off like that.

"Don't make a joke out of this, Sylvester," he said. "It's a serious matter to me. Let us be practical."

"Practical?" Sylvester caught at the word. Here was another loophole out of this tiresome conversation. "Practical? Don't talk about being practical when the practical thing for you to do is to write home to your aunts and demand your rights from them."

All morning a growing feeling of enmity against Sylvester had made it difficult for Gabriel to keep his temper. This last remark, more insulting because it touched a point on which they had had hot words even in Castlerampart, showed him that Sylvester for some reason or other was no longer to be counted on for any assistance in this matter. Yet the matter was all the more urgent for that, because until it was successfully settled he would have to take from Sylvester the humiliating assistance of board and lodging.

"I see you have no real interest in either me or my problem," he said, turning coldly to Sylvester. "I see you have no understanding of my nature or of such poor principles as I hold. I had better go and see if I can find elsewhere the help and advice I expected to have had from you." Gabriel then turned to Helen. "Leave whatever you want me to carry under the stairs where the rest of the statues were, and I'll call later and carry them over to the gallery."

He turned on his heel and was about to walk away without further ceremony.

"Wait a minute!" Sylvester put out his hand. "There are at most only a few statues left to be moved, and two can manage them easily without further help. Since you think me incapable of assisting you, you had better stay and help Helen and I will go about my business. You can hardly complain that she has lacked interest in your affairs."

Quicker than Gabriel had done, Sylvester turned around abruptly, and making more certain than Gabriel that he would not be called back, he put himself out of earshot by jumping on to the platform of a tramcar that had at that moment come to a stop at the curb.

In the embarrassed moment after Sylvester left them, Gabriel was unwilling at once to take up the topic that had been interrupted. Instead he said impulsively what had been in his mind for some time.

"I can't understand Sylvester," he said. "Before he left home and in all his letters to me, he constantly urged me to come to Dublin, but ever since I arrived here on last Friday night his manner towards me has been changed. I think at times that he wishes I had not come. Yet, only for him, I would never have done so."

When he had said this, Gabriel, who had been staring after the tramcar, turned back to Helen questioningly. She returned his gaze seriously, but although she parted her lips as if about to say something that came to her mind involuntarily, she closed them again and said nothing, but walked along by his side looking reflectively down at the flagstones of the pavements as they vanished under their feet. At the next corner they turned down towards Helen's rooms. Gabriel spoke again.

"I would not have been surprised at his manner if I felt that he was annoyed with me for bringing Onny, but as it is he is far nicer to Onny than he is to me. In fact he pays her so much attention it amounts to insulting me at times."

Helen murmured a light protest.

"I do not think," she said, "that his manner towards Onny would necessarily be an indication of his attitude towards her."

"Why not?" said Gabriel, but without waiting for an answer he abandoned his question to ask another. "So you think he was disappointed when he heard I was not coming alone?"

"All I can say," said Helen, "is that he was full of enthusiasm about you. He often spoke of you. And, although he said that you protested that you would never join him, he knew you would break away sooner or later." She paused.

"Yes?" said Gabriel eagerly.

"From the day he got your letter saying that you were coming, and that there would be someone with you, he said no more about you except that he would give you the use of the studio if you were short of money for your holiday."

"Holiday?"

"Yes, you see at first he got it into his head that it was some girl named Agnes Finnerty who would be with you, and that you would make it up with your aunts after a few weeks and go back to Clewe Street."

In spite of the weight of other things on his mind, Gabriel noticed the familiarity with which she spoke of the old street in Castlerampart from which he had come. She might almost have lived in the town herself at one time. He put aside his irrelevant thoughts, and took up her last words.

"He must have been surprised to see Onny," he said, and he smiled with a faint return of the adventurous feelings that had stirred him when he and Onny first stepped out of the train on to the city platform.

"He was," said Helen, and Gabriel glanced at her. She had spoken the words with great deliberation.

"Do you mean he was unpleasantly surprised?" said Gabriel, himself surprised.

"I think so," said Helen, in a low reluctant voice.

"But that's ridiculous!" he cried. "If you knew Agnes Finnerty!" Then as if realizing that he might be giving a wrong impression he hurried to add another protest. "Why I hardly knew the Finnertys. They lived next door but they were away at boarding school most of the time, and although my aunts encouraged them to come in I didn't see much of them, at least no more than it took me to decide they were not my kind."

Gabriel spoke with unusual heat; he was determined that Helen should not think wrongly of him.

"Onny was the only girl I ever got to know so well," he said, and he looked up earnestly to see that he had convinced his hearer. No sooner, however, had he mentioned Onny than he felt awkward and confused. He remembered again all that Onny had said about Helen's strait-laced opinions and narrowness.

He recalled that less than an hour ago, Sylvester had called his attention to what he called her prudery. And here was he, alone with her, casually discussing his relationship with Onny, a relationship which according to all her standards must be sinful and vicious. On impulse, he suddenly decided to make matters better or worse in her eyes by a direct reference to the situation.

"I never intended to let any time pass before Onny and I were married," he said. "I thought we would get married as soon as we got to the city."

"There would probably have been delays in any case," said Helen, speaking in a low voice, but neither turning aside her head nor averting her eyes.

374

Yielding still further to his impulses, Gabriel fixed her eyes with his.

"I hardly think that you can like to associate with me," he said. "I understand your views are very rigid on most things."

Helen steadily returned his glance.

"I know you are sincere," she said, "that makes a great difference." She paused for a moment, and as he said nothing she went on slowly. "I think that you are like myself and that however strongly you may revolt against the superstitious growths that spring up around the codes of religion and morality, you would still respect those codes."

Gabriel listened thoughtfully. He felt that she was probably giving him credit for a discrimination that he did not possess a week ago, but it pleased him to think that she believed him sincere.

"It is just as if we were married," he said, "and we will be as soon as I can arrange things."

"I understand," said Helen, "you want to get a means of livelihood first."

"Yes," said Gabriel, "and I'm doubly anxious to do so now that I see the view Sylvester has taken of things." As another idea occurred to him he almost stopped up in the street. "Sylvester might think better of me if Onny and I were married. Perhaps he is afraid I will neglect her."

"Oh no," she said, "I don't think Sylvester is worried about Onny." After a pause she added another few words. "On the contrary," she said, "I think he believes Onny to be well able to look after herself and her needs." For the first time since they had begun to talk in this intimate manner, Helen turned her head aside. "Sylvester is a strange person," she said, and her thoughts seemed to have taken flight into some region of the past where he could not follow, and where she was apparently comparing this example of Sylvester's strange conduct with other analogous incidents of which he knew nothing.

Gabriel could not help a feeling of regret that Sylvester's name had been introduced to cause this diversion.

"Why do you say he is strange?" he asked, since he could not but take his part in the conversation no matter how much he regretted the turn it had taken.

"Don't you think he is?" asked Helen.

"Sometimes, perhaps," said Gabriel, "but why did you mention the fact now?"

"I did so because I cannot help being struck by his self-confidence in his own ideas. He thinks that you made a mistake in getting involved with Onny, and therefore he is annoyed and irritated at seeing you persist in the affair. Of your duty, of principles, he thinks nothing." She looked at him and this time her eyes were questioning. "That is strange, don't you think?" she said. "There are not many people who can let go the life-line of conventional opinion in these matters." Her face became animated and unusually coloured. "Now, I," she cried, "no matter how greatly mistaken I thought you to be, I could not free myself enough from the principles in which I was reared to think that you would be justified in any other course but the course you are going to take!"

Gabriel walked along a few paces in silence. Then quietly he turned towards his companion.

"So you, too, think that I made a mistake?" he said.

Helen, who had spoken with impetuosity, was startled and confused for a moment, but even so she did not try to get out of her difficulties by false denials and excuses. Instead, turning aside so that the rise of colour in her cheeks might pass unnoticed, she answered him in an offhand manner.

"What does anyone's opinion matter to you!" she said. "You have only yourself to please." After a minute she added as an afterthought, "No doubt you see qualities in Onny which others cannot see until they know her as well as you do."

All this was said in a low voice, as they walked along, but the next minute Helen raised her voice and in a different tone, pointing up the street a few yards, she exclaimed, "Here we are! Back again! And we haven't said a word about your plans."

They had indeed reached the house in Molesworth Street in which Helen lived, and going ahead of Gabriel she ran up the steps and pushed open the door.

"On the way to the gallery this time," she said, as they lifted up the few remaining statues, "on the way to the gallery this time we must let nothing distract us. We must talk about you and your chances of getting something to do as soon as possible." She stopped. "Have you a good hold of that one?" she asked anxiously, putting out her free hand to steady the larger of the two figures he held in his arms. "Now," she said, "that's all right," and she began to move towards the door again.

Gabriel followed. He would have liked to continue the conversation that had been interrupted, but he knew that he had been given more than a hint that his companion wished otherwise.

He began to speak again about the other matter. They spoke of nothing else until they reached the gallery, and there they parted, because Helen had to remain there to arrange and number her work for the exhibition which was to open next day.

Gabriel turned at once in the direction of Sylvester's flat. He felt that he had left Onny alone for too long a time. She would be lonely and perhaps anxious to hear how he had fared. He hurried his steps.

Although the time had passed in nothing more than discussion he felt that something had been achieved, for if they had not discovered something that he might do, they had at least eliminated several careers which he in his inexperience might have considered possible, and which he would have wasted time in investigating. Then also there had been one or two suggestions made by Helen which would never have occurred to Gabriel himself, and although he did not believe that he would have sufficient qualifications to succeed in the work suggested, it encouraged him to think that Helen did not agree with him. One of these suggestions was that he might try the large libraries, of which there were so many all over the city, and see if an assistant was needed in any of them. Another was that he might go around to some of the editors of the smaller journals and magazines and see if any of them had a vacancy on their staff that he might be permitted to fill.

The last suggestion seemed to Gabriel to be even more unlikely than the first to yield hope for him, but he was going to keep both suggestions in mind. He based his confidence however upon the third and last suggestion Helen had made, namely, that he should go down to the newspaper offices every day and look at the advertisement columns to see if anything appealed to him in the lists of employments that were vacant.

"You never know what might turn up," Helen said, and although she was doubtful and spoke without enthusiasm Gabriel grasped at the phrase, and he found it exhilarating enough to turn over on his tongue several times on the way back, with a view to using it as an encouragement to Onny as soon as he set foot in the apartment.

ഗ ഗ ഗ

When Gabriel turned into Kildare Street, his attention was attracted at once to the high window of Sylvester's apartment which was thrown up with a loud sound, and immediately Onny's head appeared as she thrust it out and glanced rapidly up and down the street.

Gabriel put up his hand to wave to her, but almost as quickly as it had appeared, Onny's head was withdrawn again and the window was closed with a louder sound than that it made upon being thrown open. It was probable that Onny had gone to the window in order to see if he was returning, but it was clear that whatever eagerness to see him had possessed her had been satisfied by the violent gesture of flinging up the window and sticking out her head, for had she looked out at all carefully she would have seen him. He smiled at her familiar impetuosity, and hastening his own steps he reached the apartment house and ran up the stairs.

Before he opened the door he heard Onny run across the floor.

"Here he is now!" she cried, and before he could turn the handle of the door she had flung it open with a flourish.

The first thing Gabriel saw when the door was opened was not Onny, because the flourish with which she had opened it had caused her to be eclipsed behind it for a moment. It was Sylvester, and on Sylvester's face there was an expression of quiet amusement that told him as clearly as Onny's excitement that something unusual had happened in his absence and that both of them were eagerly awaiting his return until they could relate it.

"What's the matter?" he asked, looking from one to the other as Onny came out from behind the door and closed it with a backward kick of her foot.

"Oh, you missed it, Gabriel!" she cried, as she leaned back against the closed door. "You missed it, didn't he, Sylvester?"

"It was a good thing you stayed out so long," said Sylvester. "If you were back an hour sooner you would have walked into the middle of it."

"The middle of what?" Gabriel wondered if they were teasing him.

"I missed it myself by five minutes," said Sylvester, "but I daresay it would have been worse for you than for me."

Gabriel was going to make another appeal to be taken out of suspense, but he was saved the trouble because Onny's eagerness to tell him everything could not be controlled a minute longer.

"Oh, tell him! Tell him!" she cried, impatiently, and overcome with excitement she began to jump up and down like a child and clap her hands together. "Tell him! Tell him!" she cried to Sylvester, and to Gabriel she cried with the same excited voice, "Wait till you hear! Wait till you hear!"

Sylvester however had no intention of telling the story.

"My dear Onny, the charm of the story lies in the telling of it. My own enjoyment of it was due entirely to the way in which you told it. I have no doubt that the facts themselves, if set down by anyone else, would sound quite differently." As he said this last sentence Sylvester looked at Gabriel with a peculiar expression in his eye, at once ironical and curious. Then, crossing his legs, he addressed himself to Onny again. "Besides," he said, "I want to have the pleasure of hearing you tell the story again. I could not hear it too often."

Onny needed no more encouragement. She ran across the room, and pushing Gabriel into a chair she stood over him exultingly.

"Well!" she cried, and she put her hands behind her back. "They were here! Could you believe it? They were here! Here!" And swinging around she pointed to the door. "Here," she cried, "at that very door, knocking and rapping and calling my name!"

Onny expected that Gabriel would be surprised as indeed Sylvester had been, but in the space of time between the first and second tellings she had become so familiar with what she had to tell that she failed to make her meaning as clear to her second listener as she did to her first, and

Gabriel's face when she stared down at him eagerly expressed only mystification. But this in itself delighted Onny.

"He doesn't know who I mean!" she cried, in delight, and she turned to Sylvester. "He doesn't know who I mean."

"Who was here?" said Gabriel, this time turning to Sylvester.

Sylvester shrugged his shoulders.

"I gathered that it was your aunts," he said, and he looked away as if it were not necessary to his enjoyment of the incident to watch Gabriel's flush of embarrassment.

"Oh, no! Here?" cried Gabriel, springing up from the chair. "When? Where were you? What did you say?" All these questions were addressed to Sylvester as well as a final and more urgent one, "Where are they now?" And almost as if they might be hidden in some corner of the room, Gabriel glanced around him distractedly.

"Don't ask me," said Sylvester. "Ask Onny. I wasn't here. It was she who received them."

As he said the last words, something caused Sylvester to smile again with an ironical amusement. Gabriel turned to Onny.

"Why didn't you tell me at once?" he cried, as if this made any difference. "When were they here? Where were you? What did they say?"

To the last one only Onny made an answer.

"I wasn't talking to them," she said. She answered in a less excited tone of voice than hitherto, because Gabriel's reaction was not exactly what she had expected. Sylvester, for instance, had behaved more as she would have thought natural. He had thrown himself down on the couch, and slapped his hands and begun to laugh for all he was worth, and to question her about what they wore and how they looked, as they went off after the scene was over.

But Gabriel had not smiled once. And now he was pestering her with all those questions.

"You weren't speaking to them, you say? How was that? I thought you were here?"

"So I was!" said Onny, her voice getting sulky.

Gabriel looked perplexed. Then, seeming to grasp the situation more clearly, he looked at Onny with surprise.

"Do you mean to say you didn't let them in?" he asked, and at the same time he looked back to see if there was a key in the lock of the door.

Onny looked at the door too, and she was quickened with the thought of the scene that she had enacted with the ladies on the other side of it. Her voice became somewhat spirited again.

"What did you expect?" she asked, and she tossed her hair, and looked to Sylvester for the approval that she was disappointed at not getting from Gabriel. But Sylvester was not looking at her. He was looking at the ground and about his lips there played the same smile that had been there when the door was first opened to reveal him.

Gabriel too had glanced at Sylvester, and with his whole heart he wished that he and Onny were alone, that he might hear this incident recounted simply, without affectation, and that he might allow his own reactions to it to be revealed in a natural way. As it was, he tried to hide his reactions, and to gain time he began to ask other questions which, however logical they sounded, were inconsequential to the logic of his heart.

"How did you know who was at the door?" he asked. "How did you get time to turn the key in the lock?"

This question defeated half his purpose, for in giving him the answer to it, Onny had to relate the first incident of the story, which had no sooner been uttered than the whole story poured out in an avalanche. Sylvester's smile of encouragement, and the fact that the story was twice as easy to tell upon the second occasion, were two more factors that contributed to the uncontrollable rush with which she spoke.

"I had just cleaned up the place," she cried, and she threw out her hand to show the result of that labour, "and I had the dinner all ready." Gabriel, glancing involuntarily at the table, saw that a meal had indeed been prepared and consumed and that a portion evidently intended for him was cold and dried upon a plate. "I had the dinner all ready, and it was a lovely dinner, and I said to myself it would be spoiled if you didn't get here soon. 'What is keeping them?' I said to myself several times, and then I said, 'What is the use of me letting mine get spoiled? I'll eat mine anyway.' But that seemed kind of mean, so I said I'd wait another while. 'I'll wait five minutes more,' I said, 'and if they're not here by then I'll eat mine anyway.' So I stood up and I went over to the window to see the time by that clock at the end of the street, and save my feet from having to walk into the other room." At this point she paused to draw a breath. "I went over to the window," she said then, repeating herself carefully, "and I threw it up, and put out my head. But instead of looking at the clock what do you suppose I saw?" This time Onny paused from the force of instinct. This was the climax of her narrative. "There! Under the window was a taxi, and who was stepping out of it but your Aunt Sara, and who was standing on the path tapping her foot with impatience but your Aunt Theresa, for all the world as if she'd like to catch Miss Sara with the crook of her umbrella and drag her out without waiting for her to put her feet under her on the step."

"Poor Sara."

Gabriel felt an involuntary pang at the vivid picture of the two women that was brought before his mind by Onny's artless little tongue. That tongue, however, was running on, and he had small time for private reflections if he was to hear the details of the story it told.

"There they were," said Onny, "under the window! And there was I hanging out over the window staring down at them till my eyes nearly fell out of my head. I never got such a fright in my life. If only you were here, or Sylvester. But I was all alone, and to make things worse all of a sudden before I thought of pulling in my head, your Aunt Theresa gave one of those turns she gives—you know, Gabriel, like as if she was swung around by the wind—and the next thing she was staring up at me!"

Onny at this point gave an imitation of Theresa, pressing her lips together and staring fixedly at Gabriel. Then she became Onny Soraghan again and went on with the story in a rush of words.

"Such a fright as I got! I pulled in my head and I banged down the window. 'Maybe she didn't recognize me,' I said to myself, but I knew well she did by the look in her eye. I didn't know what to do for a minute. I just stood in the middle of the floor with my heart jumping up and down inside in me, and the sweat rolling down off me with fright. Then I got an idea and I ran over and locked the door."

As Onny said this, Gabriel's face showed signs of some distress, but Onny was lost in the enthusiasm of her narrative.

"I only just turned the key in the lock when I heard their feet on the stairs, and the next minute I heard them on the landing, and I heard your Aunt Theresa telling your Aunt Sara to straighten her hat.

" 'Straighten your hat, Sara,' said she, 'I don't know how it is you always lose your head in a crisis!' "

Onny gave as good an impromptu rendering of Miss Coniffe's voice as her preoccupation with her own position allowed.

"I was standing just inside the door," she explained, "with my ear pressed against the wood.

" 'Well, Sara,' said your Aunt Theresa, 'what are you standing there for? Knock at the door.'

" 'Which door?' said your Aunt Sara.

" 'Which door do you think?' said Miss Theresa. 'Didn't we see the girl looking out of a front window? Move aside, and I'll do it.'

"But I think it was Miss Sara that knocked after all because the next thing I heard was a small rap on the door, but it was the wrong door. It was the one in there."

Onny nodded her head at the wall that divided the room in which they were from the small room in which Sylvester had his bed.

" 'There's no answer,' said your Aunt Sara.

" 'No wonder when you gave such a feeble knock,' said Miss Theresa. 'Give a good rap with your knuckles.'

" 'There's still no answer,' said Miss Sara after she gave another knock, a small bit louder than the first.

" 'Try the handle so,' said Miss Theresa.

"'Oh, Theresa, do you think that's proper?' said Miss Sara.

"'Proper!' said Miss Theresa. 'Do you think there's any need to be proper in a matter of this nature?'"

Here Sylvester interrupted.

"That's the part I wanted to hear again," he said, and he laughed. "Go on, Onny."

Onny glowed with the warmth of her triumph.

"'Go on,' I said in my own mind. 'Open the door. You'll get a proper surprise!' And the next minute they did.

"'There's no one here, Theresa,' said Miss Sara, and do you know I think she was glad? Anyway Miss Theresa lost no time in coming out on the landing again. I thought she'd try this door next but I suppose when she came out of the other room she was staring straight at the room on the other side of the landing.

"'Try that door, Sara,' said she, and this time there was no talk at all about rapping. But Miss Sara gave a rap all the same.

"'Try the handle,' said Miss Theresa, and I think she pushed Miss Sara to one side because I heard the door crashing back against the wall, and Miss Sara would never do anything in a rough way like that.

"'There's no one there either,' said Miss Sara, and I thought by her voice she was stretching up on her toes to look over Miss Theresa's shoulder.

"'No,' said your Aunt Theresa, 'but there's plenty to show we're not in the wrong place anyway,' and I heard her going into the room."

Gabriel frowned again at this point. He wondered if Onny in her burst of tidying had had time to cover the room they occupied, or if it was still in the state of disorder in which he had left it that morning. It made him feel bad to think that they should see evidence around the room of an intimacy that could only be offensive to them. In fact it was solely for their own sakes that he regretted their inspection of the studio.

"I wish they hadn't seen the studio," he said impulsively.

"Oh what do we care!" said Onny. "Anyway they didn't stay long in it; they came out again and this time I knew by the sound of her feet pounding the boards that it was your Aunt Theresa who was in front. She came right up to this door.

"'They must be in this room,' she said, and I suppose she had her hand out to grab the handle because Miss Sara called out to her.

"'Theresa,' she said, and then she began to whisper, but I heard her all the same.

"'I think we ought to rap at the door,' she whispered, 'because after all if they were in here all the time they mightn't have heard us knocking at the other doors.'

"'All right,' said Miss Theresa, and then before she rose her fist to the

382

door she turned to Miss Sara again. 'What do you mean by saying *if* they're in here? Aren't they sure to be here if they're not in the other rooms? Didn't I see Onny Soraghan with my own two eyes?' And I didn't laugh! I was fit to be tied. I rose up my fist, and I banged after she said that, she brought her fist down on the door with such a rat-at-tat, she might as well have given me a clip in the ear because my ear was right up against the wood." Onny put up her hand to this organ as if, even yet, she could feel the sting in it. "I think she must have been going to try the handle again then, because Miss Sara asked her to knock once more. 'Give one more knock, Theresa,' she said. 'Well, only one more,' said your Aunt Theresa, and you may be sure I didn't have my ear against the wood the second time, and it was a good job because she had no sooner given the door the second blow of her fist than she caught the handle and tried to turn it. 'It's locked, Sara,' she said, and with that she began to rattle the handle until the door shook like a sheet in the wind. If I had my ear against it then I might have been deafened for life!" Onny once again put up her hand to her ear. "I once had a cousin," she said, "and she got a blow on the ear that left her as deaf as a loaf of bread! You could get deaf in two minutes, did you know that?" Onny interrupted her story to put her question first to Gabriel, and then to Sylvester, but Gabriel brushed aside the interruption.

"Did you not let them in at all, Onny?" he asked.

"Well I like that!" said Onny, appealing to Sylvester. "Did I let them in? I did not, and what is more I wouldn't let them in if they were to stand there yelling at me for a week."

"Oh, they said something?" said Gabriel, who thought the story had more or less ended.

"Do you think your Aunt Theresa would go away with her tongue in her head?" asked Onny, and she turned to Sylvester. "I think he doesn't know his aunt like I know her," she said.

"Tell him what she said," said Sylvester, and he looked at Gabriel. "You'd better sit down," he said. "The story isn't half finished yet. The best part is coming. Now go on, Onny."

Onny looked uncertain and then she appealed to Sylvester.

"Will I tell him what I said?" she asked.

"Tell him everything," said Sylvester.

Gabriel sat down. In actual fact he felt at that moment a sensation of weariness that was as much of the body as of his spirit.

"Tell me everything, Onny," he said, repeating Sylvester's words, but in a very different tone of voice.

To Onny however the difference in tone was unimportant. She had two listeners; that was enough to encourage her to go on—two listeners who urged her to continue.

"Well," she cried, turning back to Gabriel, "there was another rap on the door, and the next thing your Aunt Sara called out :—

" 'Are you there, Gabriel?' she said.

" 'Stop your nonsense, Sara Coniffe,' said Miss Theresa, and you could just see her turning on the poor thing although you weren't looking at them. 'Bad and all as Gabriel may be, he was brought up better than to behave like a coward and skulk behind a locked door! There's no one in there but that wicked Onny Soraghan and I'm going to let her see that she can't treat me like this!' And with that she raised up the umbrella and she brought it down on the door so loud it's a wonder the people didn't come up out of the street to see what was happening.

" 'Onny Soraghan,' said she, in between the bangs of the umbrella on the door, 'Onny Soraghan! Open this door at once! I know well that you're in there. There's no use pretending you're not. Open this door at once!' "

Up to this Onny had been faced more towards Sylvester than towards Gabriel as she told the incident, and her interest in his reactions to it had been more keen than her interest in Gabriel's reactions, but now she suddenly turned to Gabriel. He alone could relish the full flavour of this scene.

"Oh, Gabriel," she exclaimed. "You'd die laughing if you were here. It was just like the night she was hammering on the kitchen door in Clewe Street: the night I kept them late for church! But I shouted back at her.

" 'You're not in Clewe Street now, Miss Coniffe,' I said, 'and you've no rights over me. If you stayed out there till you grew into the floor I wouldn't open the door a crack!' "

Flushed with the memory of her triumph, Onny tossed her head.

"I can tell you there were no more knocks after that. I heard a noise like as if Miss Coniffe was going to choke, and then maybe she was going to batter the door again because I heard Miss Sara begging her to go away.

" 'I wouldn't if I were you, Theresa,' she said. 'I think we had better go. There's nothing to be gained.'

" 'Well I must say, Sara Coniffe,' said Miss Theresa then, 'that it comes well from you, who were the cause of our coming in the first place, to talk now about going, without our having as much as said one word of what we came all the way to say.'

" 'I'm sorry, Theresa,' said Miss Sara, and I could hardly hear her this time. Then she said something else I couldn't hear at all, but whatever it was, Miss Coniffe started to scold her.

" 'Do you think I'm going to let Onny Soraghan get the better of me?' she asked.

"You should have heard what Miss Sara said then.

" 'The poor child,' she said. 'She is probably too frightened to open the door.'

"But this made Miss Coniffe ten times worse.

" 'A nice child!' she said."

At this point both Onny and Gabriel were startled by the shout of laughter which Sylvester gave.

"That's what I wanted to hear again," he said. "Miss Coniffe, in spite of her limitations, seems to me to be at times a woman after my own heart. It isn't everyone who would hit the nail on the head like that!" He laughed again, and looking at Onny he repeated musingly, "A nice child. A nice child," and then began to laugh again.

"Is that all, Onny?" said Gabriel, ignoring Sylvester.

"That's all," said Onny. "They went away after that. I saw them going down the street, your Aunt Theresa walking like the wind and your Aunt Sara hard put to keep up with her. At the corner of the street your Aunt Sara turned back and looked up at the window. I was going to pull in my head, but she turned away again so quick there was no need. I think Miss Coniffe was going to turn around and Miss Sara was trying to stop her, because she caught her by the arm and began to point across the road. And you know how she was always scolding me for pointing at things. 'Don't point, Onny!' she used to say. 'What will I do?' I used to say. 'Just indicate, Onny, indicate,' she used to say."

"Poor Sara," said Gabriel again, and he did not trust himself to say anything more in the presence of Sylvester.

Onny too seemed to have a soft impulse towards the younger of her late antagonists.

"If it was Miss Sara who came alone," she said, "I might have let her in, only I'd be afraid Miss Theresa might be waiting around the corner."

"I don't think my aunts would stoop to the level of a deceit like that, Onny," said Gabriel. "They have their faults, but they would hardly lower themselves in the way you suggest."

In this remark Onny seemed to see some criticism of herself, and instantly she took up her former position of defiance.

"They lowered themselves today, I can tell you!" she said.

Gabriel stood up.

"I'm not sure that they did, Onny," he said. "I think there was something to be admired in the way they came here openly."

"They came to give out to us!" said Onny angrily.

"I don't know," said Gabriel. "You said, I think, that Theresa blamed Sara, and said that it was she was the cause of their coming?"

"Yes," said Onny, sulkily, as if she knew what he was going to say.

"If it was Sara's idea to come," said Gabriel, "you may be sure that the idea was prompted by a good and a gentle instinct, Onny."

Onny's red underlip dropped open, and remained that way.

"Do you think they came to give us money?" she asked.

"I don't know, Onny," said Gabriel, "and what is more, we will never know."

Onny thought for a moment.

"Perhaps they'll come back again?" she said.

But before Gabriel had time to answer, Sylvester answered.

"They won't come back, Onny," he said, "I can tell you that." He turned casually to Gabriel. "I suppose they got the address from my mother," he said, "and guessed that you'd be here."

"I suppose so," said Gabriel dully. He didn't want to talk any more about the incident. "Is there any dinner?" he asked, going over to the table and sitting down at the end where the untouched plate of cold meat was conspicuous among the soiled plates and scattered knives and forks.

He felt ill at heart, and besieged by several conflicting emotions, foremost among which was a bitter disappointment at the way Onny had behaved. Onny too seemed to have become despondent all of a sudden, and sat with her eyes downcast on the floor.

"Come, Onny!" said Sylvester. "What would you like to do this evening?"

But Onny did not seem to hear him, and a minute later she sprang to her feet.

"Wait a minute, Gabriel," she said. "I kept some potatoes hot for you," and she snatched up the dish from the table. "Give me your plate," she cried, snatching it up too. "I'll heat it again. I won't be a minute."

Sylvester stood up. He said nothing for a moment, and then he went over and took up his hat from a chair by the window, and went towards the door.

"I'm going out," he said, and then, as he passed Gabriel, he stopped for a moment and with what was perhaps the first show of warmth that he had displayed since their meeting, he laid a hand on his shoulder. "So even Onny," he said, "is not without some of that complexity which disturbs us all. Five minutes ago, in as short a time, she displayed a vulgarity, vindictiveness, spite, and pettiness such as one would not expect from the lowest type of creature, and now—" Sylvester jerked his head in the direction of the door through which Onny had vanished—"and now, with the instincts of an angel, she is reheating your badly cooked dinner!"

Just then the door opened and Onny came back into the room.

"Don't close the door, Onny," cried Sylvester, and before she had taken her hand from the doorknob he had passed out into the landing and they could hear him running down the stairs.

༄ ༄ ༄

386

"What's wrong with him?" Onny asked, looking after him as she laid down a plate of potatoes in front of Gabriel. They were hot, but cooked in their skins and kept in the oven for so long that they were now crusted and hard and unappetizing. Involuntarily Gabriel thought of the meals he was used to at home, and a feeling of humiliation came over him at the thought that his aunts should have seen the squalor of his situation.

He began to eat the food without gust for it.

"Is there something wrong with you, too!" said Onny, seeing that his expression was dour.

"It's just that I'm tired, Onny, that's all," he said, because he felt it would be useless to try and explain to her his true feelings. She would think he was casting a reflection on her. As it was, however, she was ill-at-ease, and kept moving in and out of the room all the time he was eating.

"Do you think they might come back?" she said at last, hoping to please him by renewing the talk about his aunts. But he was soured by the whole incident.

"I hope not!" he said, and he pointed to the littered table in front of him.

"Oh, if that's the way you feel!" said Onny, and she turned around with a flounce. All the same she came back after a few minutes and without saying anything she began to gather up the soiled plates and carry them out to the sink on the landing.

Gabriel was left alone at last. He knew his aunts would not come back, and although he spoke in vexation to Onny when he said so, nevertheless it was true that he did not want them to come back. He had never at any time regarded the break with them as final, but neither had he imagined a meeting with them under the present circumstances. It made him feel sick at heart to think of how the apartment had appeared to them. He looked around him, and seeing his surroundings with their eyes it became even more repugnant than it had been at first, to think that he and Onny should be reduced to this level. For Sylvester it was all right. For him alone it would be all right. But for two people like Onny and himself starting their life together—it was different. They should have some place of their own, no matter how poor a place.

He would have to get out of the studio. In despair he made a mental calculation of the state of his pocket. More than two thirds of his money was gone between the expenses of the journey and Onny's finery. And even more would be gone if he had had his way, because he had thought to keep at least some independence for them by contributing something to the food. But Sylvester's generosity would not be curtailed.

"It's only a matter of a few shillings," he said once or twice. "People overestimate the cost of keeping alive," he said on another occasion.

At first Gabriel had been deeply affected by this generosity, but lately he had begun to feel that Sylvester got some peculiar satisfaction in having them dependent upon him. And now, considering it more critically, his doubts were greater. Might not this generosity that disclaimed gratitude be after all a subtle form of belittlement? One thing he knew: Sylvester relished subtlety. All at once he clenched his hands. The situation was getting intolerable. He would have to get money somewhere.

For the first time the implications of his aunts' visit came into his mind. Without doubt they intended to give him money, because they would not, he knew, have contemplated bringing him back to Castlerampart, with or without Onny. They would be the first to see the impossibility of that. Or was it impossible? In the despair of the moment he was ready to grasp at anything, but after another moment he sank back in his chair. It was impossible. And all at once, with a shock, he realized the intransigence of his acts, the finality of his departure from Clewe Street. The thought was so sobering that even his depression of a few minutes previous seemed irregular and intemperate. This was not a matter for feeling; it was a matter for reasoned consideration. How had he taken this aspect of the situation so lightly up to now? How had he not considered it in a more responsible manner? It was one thing to break free from the subjection of an Aunt Theresa. It was another thing to cut yourself off from the place of your birth, the town where your mother and father had made themselves known and respected, where before them your grandfather . . . Gabriel's thoughts were arrested by a remembrance of old Theodore, and he was overcome by feelings once more. He recalled his grandfather's pride of family, and his ambition. And he thought of something Mary Ellen had told him one time. She said that Theodore told her shortly before his death that he was not so sorry after all that things had turned out as they had, and that there was not a whole brood of grandchildren to divide and dwindle the property. It wouldn't be worth much to anyone if it was divided and scattered about among a crowd, but passing entire and undivided to one person it would be a nice patrimony.

Patrimony! The word struck at him out of the past. That was what he had disregarded. That was what he had thrown away; his patrimony. He spoke the word to himself out loud. It was heavy with meanings he had never concerned himself with before. Then, as he said it aloud, a smile of self-contempt formed over his face. His patrimony? Was this the exchange he made for it?

But suddenly he pulled himself together. There were other things to consider besides money. He must not let himself forget the indignities he had suffered at the hands of Theresa. He wondered what way she would have treated him if he had encountered her that afternoon. Would she have felt any necessity to alter her attitude towards him? Somehow he felt not. And how would he have acted? This question was not so easy to answer. Perhaps for more reasons than one it was just as well that he had not seen them. Perhaps, and it would not be for the first time, Onny, by acting on her instincts, had done the wisest thing. He would never cease to regret, however, that Sara had to be repulsed with Theresa. He felt a lump in his throat at the thought of how much this gentle aunt had been hurt. Perhaps he would write to her? He had almost started to his feet to do so at once, when he thought better of it. A letter from him might only give occasion to Theresa for attaching some blame to Sara. She might say that her sister had connived with him. It was better to do nothing rashly. He stood up. Onny was not in the room. Poor Onny. She had acted according to her understanding. He had been too hard on her. Where was she? He went out to the landing to look for her and make up to her for the way he had taken her story. He remembered the way he had seen her hanging out of the window to see if he was coming, and how she had rushed up to him when he came into the room, all excitement to tell him her adventure. Poor Onny! She thought he would find it funny. He began to soften. Perhaps if Sylvester had not been there he might not have been so rigid. The picture she had drawn of Theresa standing on the curb tapping her foot while Sara timidly alighted was undoubtedly funny. He was prepared to admit that.

"Onny!" he called out to her placatingly as he saw her sitting disconsolately on the floor of the studio turning over the leaves of one of Sylvester's art catalogues.

∽ ∽ ∽

Telman Young's party was to be held on the Wednesday of that week. At the last minute however it was postponed.

"He always does that," said Sylvester. "There are times when his inspirations fail him and rather than be seen wandering around idle, with his spiritual paucity exposed for all to see, he packs his tubes of paint and his palette and brushes, and telling everyone that he feels a driving urge to be in closer contact with nature he disappears to some hut in the mountains, and he does not return again until he has covered at least one canvas. He thinks that he deceives all, and that we are impressed with the compulsion of his genius."

"But the party?" said Onny, who was indeed bitterly disappointed.

"Oh," said Sylvester, "if this urge comes over him it does not matter what engagements he must break, or what contracts he must cancel. In fact the more the better, because this, he believes, will impress people all the more."

"I think he's very mean," said Onny, and her disappointment was so genuine Sylvester turned to her.

389

"Never mind," he said. "He'll be back in a week or perhaps less, and then he'll be in such good form the party will be all the better."

Gabriel, who had not spoken up to then, saw a point at which his thoughts converged with the conversation.

"Perhaps by then I will have found something to do," he said, "and if so we'll really enjoy ourselves." He turned eagerly to Onny, "Perhaps I will be able to buy you something new," he said.

"What will you buy?" cried Onny, satisfactorily distracted. "What? I'd love a necklace. I saw one made of shells the day we bought all the clothes. I'd love that. I could find the shop again. Will you buy me that?"

"I will, Onny," said Gabriel, and he felt that already the independence which the purchase would stand for was within his grasp.

Then Sylvester broke in again.

"And if he doesn't get it for you, Onny," he said, "I'll get it for you."

Gabriel winced under the implied doubt that was cast on his hopes, but in a moment he recovered. Telman would not be back for a week. That was a long time. A lot could happen in a week.

As a matter of fact, three weeks passed before Telman came back to Dublin, and appeared at Sylvester's apartment with a renewal of his invitation, fixing the date for the following Wednesday evening at eight o'clock. Yet in that time Gabriel had met with no success in his search for work, and the necklace that dangled over Onny's bosom was bought for her by Sylvester.

The suggestions that had been put forward by Helen had all been tried in vain. Every morning and every evening Gabriel had gone down to the city to the newspaper offices, and diligently read the advertisement columns, spending the day in between investigating any of them whose requirements it seemed at all likely that his limited abilities might suit. Day after day, however, brought nothing but disappointment, and these disappointments were the harder to bear because of the indifference with which his news was received each evening when he came back to the apartment.

Onny's indifference he could, to a certain extent, understand, and he was even able to turn it into a virtue, telling himself that it showed an attitude towards money that was fresh and unspoiled. It seemed quite natural to her that they should stay with Sylvester and accept from him all he was able to give them.

"He likes to have us," she said several times.

"But you wouldn't expect us to stay here indefinitely," Gabriel protested.

"Oh I didn't say we would," said Onny, who terminated many arguments that were going against her by means of this same phrase.

The necklace had been the cause of one of those arguments.

"I wish you had waited until I could buy it for you," said Gabriel, when he was called upon to admire it one day as Onny came back from an excursion into the city with Sylvester, wearing around her neck a string of large white shells that jostled together gaily as she moved, and made a gay tinkling noise.

"Oh I wasn't going to wait for ever," said Onny, whose pride in the necklace was not going to be spoiled by criticism, and who was learning the skilful trick of countering criticism by criticism.

"That's not a very kind thing to say to me, Onny," said Gabriel. "You can't say but that I am trying hard to find some way of making money. It's not fair to say what you said, as if I was lazy or indolent."

"Oh I didn't say that," said Onny.

"I know you didn't," said Gabriel, "but you implied it."

"I did not," said Onny, and put up her fingers and tangled the shells with a smile of satisfaction and pride. "Why didn't you buy them for me anyway?" she said, looking at him suddenly with a challenging glance.

"How could I, Onny?" cried Gabriel. "I couldn't let Sylvester see me spending the small amount we have left on things that, after all, no matter how you desired them, cannot be called anything but useless and unnecessary."

Up to this point Onny had divided her attention between her conversation and the shells that were the subject of it. She either fingered them, or glanced down at them, or paused in front of the chest of drawers in order to catch sight of their reflection in the small piece of cracked looking-glass.

Nothing had been said about the price of them, but from this preoccupation with them Gabriel was getting an increasingly greater opinion of their value, although as a matter of fact they did not appeal to him at first, and he thought them vulgar and showy. Yet when he spoke of being unwilling to spend his money on such things, Onny suddenly abandoned all interest in them.

"Oh don't talk about spending your money on them. You could have bought them for me if you wanted." She smiled a strange secretive smile, as if it had been her intention to withhold something that it now suited her to reveal. "They only cost sixpence," she said.

Sylvester's indifference was harder to endure because it was harder to understand. As long as he, Gabriel, failed to find work, Onny and he would have to remain dependent upon Sylvester. It could hardly be said that Sylvester's indifference was a deliberate exercise in courtesy and hospitality, since he must know that if they did not secure independent means in a short time, they would be compelled to admit defeat and leave Dublin altogether to return to Castlerampart.

The only person who showed a genuine interest in his search was Helen. He did not meet her often, but when he did she was concerned about him and, what was more, she associated herself with his disappointment.

"What can we do?" she exclaimed on one or two occasions. "I was sure you would have had some success before now."

It was Helen, too, who on another occasion made a remark which showed a peculiar insight into his difficulties.

"I know how disappointed you must be, day after day," she said, "but I am sure that you must find that downright disappointments are better than false hopes, and I am sure your hopes are sometimes falsely raised."

"They are indeed," said Gabriel, and he began to tell her some of the occasions when he had allowed himself to believe that success was within his reach.

At the time that he was talking to Helen, however, Gabriel had yet to experience the greatest disappointment of all, which, as Helen had said, was all the more bitter because it followed upon a trail of false hopes.

The suggestion that he should try the city libraries had been most unproductive of all, because it had been ascertained that they employed only trained assistants who had taken special courses in library training, and as for the suggestion that he might find some employment in the smaller editorial offices in the city, this too had been unproductive, because after a scathing interview with one or two editors his courage to interview others had vanished.

One day, however, when he returned to the apartment, Onny, who was sitting on the couch with her feet up on a chair reading a cheap magazine, stood up to get him his meal, and threw the magazine on the floor. Idly Gabriel picked it up, and as he turned the pages and saw the poor quality of the articles, he felt that it would not be too great a presumption on his part to think himself capable of filling some position on the paper, if such a position should be available. He ran over the pages again. There must be several activities in the offices of a magazine like this, apart altogether from the actual journalese. There were not many advertisements for the back pages. Perhaps he could persuade the editor to take him on as a canvasser for advertisements. In some capacity or other he might find work on this page. He glanced at the clock and sprang up. There was just time to get downtown again before the offices closed.

"Don't mind getting anything for me, Onny," he cried, as he paused on the landing where Onny was standing over the gas ring.

Onny swung around in surprise.

"A nice time to tell me!" she said, but her vexation at his departure was lost in her curiosity at its abruptness, and following him to the top of the stairs, she stared down after him, the saucepan in one hand, and the frying pan in the other.

Sylvester, who had heard the unusual haste in Gabriel's footsteps and the note of excitement in his voice, came to the door of the other room.

Onny and he exchanged a look of surprise. Onny went back to the gas ring, and turned off the flames. She and Sylvester exchanged glances again, and Sylvester raised his eyebrows.

∽   ∽   ∽

Gabriel's confidence had had time to slacken before he found the offices he was looking for in a short back street on the north side of the city. He was as downcast as ever as he went up the steps of the crooked stairway and knocked at a dilapidated door which was scored all over by initials and names and dates. There was no answer to his knock. He knocked again. This time he heard someone comment on the knocking, and he heard an indistinct reply, but there was still no effort made to open the door. He wondered if he should turn the handle and walk in, but he did not feel justified in this. He looked at the initials and began to wonder if they had been carved by people who were left waiting like himself.

He began to read the letterings, turning his head from side to side, deciphering those which were obscured, either by age or by newer initials scored over them. He had travelled over all the initials on the upper panels of the door and was unconsciously bending down to examine those on the lower panel, when the door opened suddenly. Blushing, he straightened himself, and looked up.

The door had been opened by a young girl who had apparently done so as a matter of routine, and without looking to see to whom she had opened it turned back and disappeared with a swirl of skirts into an inner room, leaving him standing on the threshold, little better off than before the door had opened. When he recovered his composure, he stepped into the room.

Every available table and chair was covered with bundles of papers. The bundles were all neatly tied with brightly coloured tapes, red, yellow, and blue, as if they had been newly sorted and classified. On the floor, all around the room, there were similar bundles, covering every inch of the floorboards. The paper in these bundles, however, was somewhat yellowed and the coloured tapes that tied them were somewhat faded.

A passageway between these bundles led up to a large desk in the centre of the room. Another passageway led away from the desk into the inner room. The desk was of yellow oak, very large, and liberally spattered with inkstains. It was laden with such a variety of objects that the small pot of paste with the brush in it, which was left on top of other things, looked like the successful termination of a conjuror's balancing trick.

The room smelled strongly of freshly made paste, but underlying this odour he detected what was probably the more usual odour of the room, a smell of damp and mildewed paper. Then there was a stir in the back room and a small stout man of middle age came out, closing the door behind him. His face was pale, and round in shape, and the top of his head was bald and glossy, but his hair, although it had vanished from the dome of his skull, had remained in a thick circle of corkscrew curls around the sides of his head. These curls sat as tight upon his skull as their wreaths of marble laurels sit upon the statued heads of the Roman Emperors. But Samuel Modell had bad sight, and the classic effect of the wreath of curls around his brow was somewhat spoiled by the fact that he had to wear spectacles. These spectacles had, moreover, such thick lenses that Gabriel could scarcely see the eyes whose sight they presumably aided, and he could not tell whether or not the editor had looked at him as he walked across to the desk. He certainly made no attempt to speak to him for a few minutes, as he sorted the papers in front of him, and made some notes with a pencil that he had some difficulty in finding in the confusion of the articles on the desk. Then suddenly, when Gabriel was least aware of it, it seemed that the editor was staring straight at him, because he shot out a question and sat back to await the answer.

"Well, what is your business, young man?"

Gabriel felt himself redden. He was very conscious of the fact that he had had no grounds for supposing that there was any vacancy on the paper.

"I suppose I ought to apologize," he began, but the older man cut him short.

"In search of a place on the paper?" he asked, as he settled down more easily in his chair, and it seemed to Gabriel at the time, and he remembered it afterwards, that the man suddenly became better disposed to him. Taking confidence, he spoke out more boldly.

"Yes, sir," he said.

The editor nodded his head, and speaking still more affably he indicated a chair.

"I don't know whether I can do anything or not for you," he said, "but sit down, young man. Looking for work these days is a tiring experience." He nodded his head again. "I haven't forgotten what it is to be young," he said.

Under the influence of this unusual sympathy, Gabriel relaxed and sat down. Suddenly, however, there was a slight change in the editor. He seemed to become more alert and businesslike again.

"What previous experience have you?" he asked, and there seemed to be a sharp note in his voice.

So this was where he was going to fail, thought Gabriel, and he explained that he had no experience of any kind. He was about to plead his case upon other grounds, and strove to remember some of the phrases he had planned as he came along the street, but the editor cut him short again.

"Who sent you here?" he said, and this time there was no mistaking the sharp note in his voice.

"Nobody sent me, sir," said Gabriel. "I just saw a copy of one of your magazines . . ."

Again a mercurial change came over the man behind the desk. All his affability returned.

"Ah, yes," he said complacently. "I see. Several young people have approached me after seeing the papers. Young people are quick to see the advantage of being associated with a progressive paper, run on modern lines and showing a policy of catering for varied interests." The editor clasped his hands in front of him and appeared to contemplate them. "What did you think of the editorials?" he asked, but Gabriel's mind had wandered and he did not reply at once.

Did the editor think he was anxious to get experience, and that he would be willing to take work as an apprentice?

"I am anxious to make a living," he said with awkward irrelevance, and he had no sooner spoken than he regretted his haste, and expected that the editor would terminate the interview with a caustic comment upon his lack of experience.

But the older man seemed to think his remark quite reasonable.

"Of course you must make a living," he exclaimed, "I understand that. I think I might say I am a man of a certain understanding. In fact I think I might go so far as to say that I am one of the few editors in this city who have such a thorough understanding of the difficulties that confront young people like you!"

There was a pause in which Gabriel wondered if he should say something, but the editor was only pausing for breath, and Gabriel became aware that he was slightly asthmatic.

"In general, my fellow editors," he continued, "will have nothing to do with a young man who has no experience, or else they will expect him to apprentice his time and youth to them, which comes to the same thing as driving him from the door. Isn't that so? We must all live nowadays. The epoch of the apprentice is gone." The editor leaned back in his chair, which he tilted slightly backwards against the wall behind him. "I must say I would not expect any man to give me his time and intelligence for nothing."

This was the point upon which Gabriel had been most worried, and once it was settled he felt more at ease in listening to the editor, who would seem to be somewhat garrulous—a small fault in the eyes of one who had suffered as much curtness as Gabriel had done in recent weeks.

"No," said Samuel Modell, "I would not expect any young man to work for me for nothing. After all, what is inexperience? It is something that can be remedied in a few days if—" and here the editor threw up a warning hand—"if a young man gets into the right office, and is under the supervision of the right kind of editor. Inexperience is not the worst fault a man can have. After all, how do we know but that when we turn aside a young man because he is untried we may be turning aside the very man who was destined to be the greatest asset to our business, the very man who might have revolutionized our foundations! Isn't that so? Isn't that so?"

This question, although it was repeated, was one to which Gabriel felt he could hardly be expected to give an impartial answer, and so he remained silent. Accepting silence for agreement, Samuel Modell took up the train of his thought again. "When a young man comes to my offices," he said, "and says that he is looking for assistance, I am sometimes, I must confess, tempted, like my weaker fellow editors, to tell him plainly and straightly that I am overstaffed, and that I cannot afford to hire any more young people. But before the words have been uttered, I hesitate. I ponder. I ask myself a question. 'How do you know,' I ask myself, 'but that you may be turning Genius herself aside when you turn aside this young man? You may be sending her out to starve in the gutter!' " Here his voice sank. " 'You may,' I say to myself, 'you may, worse still, be sending her out to hang herself in despair from an attic rafter!' " At the end of this sentence the editor's voice had sunk so low as to be almost unheard. He was silent, and Gabriel wondered if his eyes, behind the thick glasses, were staring at him, or if they were closed in inward contemplation. He moved uneasily on his chair. He felt that his case was being dramatized somewhat beyond its limits. Suddenly the editor allowed his chair to regain its normal position, which meant that it jerked forward with a violent rock that nearly precipitated him over the top of his desk and into the arms of his auditor, but nothing deterred, he brought out the sentence to which this change of posture was to have been the dramatic prelude.

"Few there are who possess genius," he said, "but fewer still are those who are willing to give genius a chance! If only men would realize that the next best thing to possessing genius oneself is to be possessed firstly of the opportunities for encouraging it, and, secondly, of the generosity to make use of the opportunity. I unfortunately am a poor man; I cannot give all the employment that I would wish, and when a young man comes to me, as you have come, I may not be able to give him work at once, as I would wish to do." Gabriel's face faltered in the hopeful expression that had rested upon it for the last few minutes, and seeing this the older man stood up, and coming around the desk he patted him on the shoulder. "I may not be able to give him work at once," he repeated, "but I have one thing I can give him—something I may say which no man should withhold from another when it is in his power to bestow it."

Gabriel looked up.

"What is that?" he said, almost rising to his feet.

"Hope!" said the older man, and as Gabriel sank into his chair with visible relief, the editor, clasping his hands suddenly behind his back, began to pace up and down the narrow aisle between the mildewed bundles of manuscript upon the floor. "Yes, yes," he cried, "I will not let you go away empty-handed. I will at least give you hope."

As he reached the middle of the paper aisle for the second time, however, the door of the back office suddenly opened again, and the girl Gabriel had first seen came out.

"Will you sign these?" she said, tossing a heap of letters on the desk in front of her employer, and disappearing again as curtly as she came.

Gabriel wondered at her lack of deference, and as he looked after her, he felt again that the eyes of the editor were fixed on him.

"I see you noticed her manner?" he said, and then leaning over confidentially he spoke in a low voice. "It has always been my policy," he said, "to encourage youth to give talent an opportunity to manifest itself, but—" he shook his head sadly—"I cannot say that I have always found gratitude in those to whom I gave a helping hand." He shook his head still more sadly, and then, indicating the closed door with his hand, he spoke more sternly. "Take that young woman," he said. "I may as well admit that she is a source of dissatisfaction to me."

At this point there was another interruption. This time a young man opened the inner door and, putting no more than his head around it, he broke into the editor's conversation without ceremony. He ignored Gabriel.

"The leader page is set up now, if you want to look at it," he said, and he withdrew his head again.

Gabriel felt embarrassed for the older man's sake. The behaviour of his staff was certainly peculiar. But the editor only shook his head from side to side sadly.

"Ingratitude!" he said. "Ingratitude!" Then he drew himself up again. "It is when they find no other return for their efforts than ingratitude and ill-will that men abandon the talk of helping others. But that is not my way! That is not my way. When I meet with ingratitude I do not turn aside. I tell myself that all the disappointments of a lifetime would be as nothing compared with the privilege of giving one deserving young person a start upon a career that would lead to fame and fortune." Just then he stopped again, because there were sounds beyond the far door that seemed to indicate that the people in the other room were impatient. "I will not keep you any longer," said Samuel Modell quickly, "but remember that I have not sent you away. Call again. Call in three days' time. And in the meantime: hope!" Just as he reached the door, and as Gabriel stood up uncertainly, the editor darted back, and bending down, almost in a whisper he said, as he glanced back urgently at the door of the back office, "I am thinking of making some changes in my staff," he said. And then, lifting up a finger again, he once more raised his voice. "Hope!" he said. "Hope!" And grasping the door handle he vanished into the other room.

◡ ◡ ◡

Gabriel did not intend to tell Onny about the comparative success of his interview with Samuel Modell when he came back that evening, but his high spirits were unusual and she suspected that he had news. She began to torment him with questions, but he resisted them. She was, however, quick enough to connect his sudden departure earlier in the day with the magazine that she had thrown on the floor and which she had seen him take up in his hands just before she went out of the room.

"I'm right, aren't I?" she cried.

"I won't say whether you are or not," was all Gabriel would reply.

Yet after all when she had ceased to torment him with questions, and had forgotten the affair, the information came out accidentally.

It was the evening of Telman Young's party and they were preparing to go out when, rushing across the studio to shut the window against a sudden whirl of rain that had spun through the air, Onny caught her silk stocking on the rough edge of a canvas that stood against the wall.

"Now look what I've done!" she cried, and bent down in horror to examine the tear.

When she looked up her face was flushed from bending, and also from her momentary anger. Gabriel, remembering her concern of old for the cheap yellow stockings that had annoyed his aunts so much, felt sorry for her disappointment.

"I'm very sorry, Onny," he said. "I know how you feel. Don't be upset. Have you another pair?"

"No, I haven't," said Onny. "I'll have to mend the tear. I don't believe I have a needle fine enough for this mesh. I don't believe I have mending floss of the right shade." She put the tip of her finger to her lips and wetting it she moistened the stocking around the place where it had torn. "That will keep the tear from getting larger," she said, and holding her skirt up in front of her in case the rough cloth might rub against the silk, she ran over to a box where she kept some of her private things and began to toss everything up in order to find the floss.

The box was a cheap affair that her grandmother had been given by some sweetheart at a bazaar when she was a girl. She had given it to Onny. At the time it was made it must have seemed hideously ugly to people of taste, but with the passage of time it had taken to itself a certain quaintness and novelty and had moreover that slight irregularity which indicated that, poor as it was, it had been made by the human hand. It was a cardboard box, covered with velvet in a shade of yellowish green which, having faded or passed out of fashion, is never seen nowadays. The actual pile of the velvet had been flattened by constant handling, which gave greater subtlety to the particular shade, for flattened velvet, despite feminine endeavours to prevent it from flattening, has a silvered gloss that is at times very attractive. The lid was decorated with pearly shells stuck on to it in rows all around the edges, and forming a design of true lovers' knots in the centre. These shells shone with a natural iridescence, but lest this should not prove brilliant enough, they had been lacquered over with some colourless enamel that made them glitter and gleam, seemingly growing brighter with the years, as the velvet under them faded.

From this shell-crusted box Onny began to turn out the contents, strewing the window ledge with pieces of ribbon, scraps of lace, remnants of silk, darning floss of several colours, and a variety of glass buttons, beads, and buckles, and even the faded silk petals from artificial flowers.

Gabriel, who had hitherto been denied a glimpse of the contents of the shell box, drew near in curiosity. The box was one of the few possessions that Onny had taken from home. It had bulked largest in the cramped space of the red carpet bag in which she had carried her things. Had Gabriel been observant, he might perhaps have felt a sense of familiarity as he looked at the scraps of silk and flosses, because although she was unaware of it, Onny could hardly have brought with her anything more impregnated with the spirit of the small rampart town; there was hardly a young lady in the town, or a fine matron for that matter, whose memory was not caught into this tangle of silks and fringes, for there was not one of the Soraghans, from Mrs. Soraghan down, through the long line of Judys, Chrissies, and Nonies, who had done odd jobs in the various houses in the town, who did not bring back the scraps of finery they found in the wastebasket for Onny, who, as a child, had set no value on toys, but who would hold out her small hands, and smile and sit contented all day with the smallest scrap of silk, the smallest strip of ribbon. She had treasured all these scraps in the shell box and she had treasured them so long and so carefully that time had given them a value in her eyes quite out of proportion to their real value.

Since coming to Dublin, and seeing the finely garbed women in the street, and the elegant gowns displayed upon silk cushions behind the plate-glass windows of the dress salons, she might perhaps have altered her values, but she still treasured the tangle of dressmakers' scraps. Where before she kept them for the sensuous pleasures afforded by their silken textures and gorgeous colours, she kept them now as patterns of the dresses she would herself possess in the near future.

Today, however, looking frantically for thread to mend the tear in her stocking, she threw the silks to right and left, tossing and tangling them further, until some of them, inextricably knotted, and twined together, trailed over the floor like carnival streamers. At the sight of this wanton disregard for a treasure-trove which he himself had been forbidden to explore, with even the most gentle fingers, Gabriel was impressed more, minute by minute, with the tragedy of the torn stocking. He longed to be reckless and say that they would buy another pair, but when he could not do this, he sought to soothe her like a child, and picking up the picture which had caused the damage, he made a pantomime of putting his foot through the canvas.

"For two pins I'd put my foot through it," he said.

Onny started. "Are you crazy?" she said, rushing to snatch the picture.

"I was only fooling," said Gabriel, taken aback.

"Fooling! How would it be if your foot slipped?"

She had taken the picture and inclining it on one corner was passing her hand over the surface as if there might be danger that his foot had actually come in contact with it.

"If I had put my foot through it I don't believe it would have mattered," said Gabriel. "After all, Sylvester couldn't have thought very much of it if he left it lying in here so carelessly, without giving us any particular warning about its value."

"Why should he warn us? We aren't children."

He was disconcerted at her anger but it created an answering anger in his own voice.

"No, Onny, but you must admit that it's a careless place to have left it, among articles which we know he regards as lumber." He pointed to a chair with three legs which lay legs upward on the floor, and to an old tin water ewer in the bottom of which there was a large hole. Undoubtedly there were other paintings there, and Helen's sculpture, but it was clear that in general the contents of the corner were not greatly regarded by Sylvester. He stared at them, and then looked back at Onny. "How can you be angry with me?" he said. "I was fooling to amuse you and I should think you would have sympathized with me, and not been angry. Onny, why are you so vexed with me?"

Onny's cheeks still blazed, and with a pocket handkerchief she was dusting over the entire canvas, and picking off with her fingers the strands of cobweb that had fastened upon the back of it, weighted and lodged there by an accumulation of dust that made their frail strands tough and resistant.

"I'm not angry," said Onny, with the rasping irritation with which this particular phrase is generally spoken. "But I often notice that you brush past these canvases as if they were worthless. You kick up against them going across the room. I didn't say anything, but I noticed it."

"I said before, Onny, that I don't believe they are valuable. I don't think that Sylvester would have left them in here if they were valuable. In fact, now that I come to think of it, I believe he asked me to have a look at them sometime, that he was thinking of scraping them clean for fresh work."

Onny placed the canvas back against the wall, reverently.

"Telman Young said that it is often the work that the artist considers worthless that is the best work he has done. He said the artist cannot be creative and critical at the same time."

Gabriel stared. He was amazed at this evidence of the way she had assimilated the conversation of Sylvester and his friends. His own mind had been so preoccupied with his plans that he had hardly noticed what Onny's reactions had been to the new life into which she had entered, but he had taken for granted that they were confined to her clothes and her appearance, the changes in which he certainly had noticed with both amusement and approbation.

"Why, Onny!" he cried. "Let me look at you! You are picking up strange ideas, aren't you?" He put out his hands to push her further from him to see her better.

Onny wriggled free of his hands. "I want to mend my stocking," she said, and she went back to the velvet box.

Gabriel smiled, and looking down at the painting on the floor he began to examine it. The painting represented a doe grazing. The doe was a soft dove colour with darker mottling upon its flank. The eyes and ears, and the forelegs, were dark brown, and the inside of the ears was a bright pink. The grass upon which it grazed was represented by vivid green stripes of the painter's brush. It was not a very successful picture, but it had a certain attraction which may perhaps have been the simplicity of an inexperienced but not incompetent hand.

At that moment his eye fell on the tattered copy of Samuel Modell's magazine.

"Painting is peculiar, isn't it? A painter sees a doe and paints it. If he paints it well it will be hung in public galleries; people will flock to see it. Younger painters will come and sit before it on canvas stools, studying it and making copies of it. It may even sell! Someone may pay out coins for it, and hang it over their mantelpiece where they will see it every day for the rest of their lives. Yet if I were to describe a doe, however perfectly, there isn't a single person who would buy it unless I made a jingle of rhymes upon it, or buried it under a mountain of other words to make it the bulk of an article. Now does that mean that painting is superior to writing, or that it is inferior?"

He was speaking idly, jocosely, without thinking of an answer, although possibly he was formulating for himself the first brief sketches of a question that would ripen in his mind and give rise to deep questioning when he discussed it with someone interested in the subject. He certainly did not expect an answer from Onny, least of all the vindictive answer which, turning around suddenly, she flung at him.

"I think painting is ten times better than writing. After all it isn't everybody that can be bothered with books, but everyone likes to have a picture hanging on the wall!"

The crudity of her judgment would have amused him perhaps if this vindictiveness of tone in which it was uttered had not startled him.

"Why, Onny! You are in a bad temper today. What is the matter? Surely a tear in your stocking is not the cause of all this anger and malice. You're being deliberately unkind to me."

Onny's head was bent. She was darning the stocking, taking long quick strokes with the needle and drawing out the thread, which was long, to a great distance in front of her. The gestures were so old, so womanly, so infinitely touching in their ancient symbolic character, that, casting his glance from Onny to the garish studio in which she sat, he began to wish that she had a room of her own, that could be brought into greater harmony with such domesticity. He blurted out his news.

"The accident shouldn't have happened at all. We shouldn't be here, Onny. We should have an apartment of our own." He wondered suddenly if he had stumbled on the cause of irritability. "Do you mind, very much, staying here? Do you think unkindly of me, for not having got a place of our own before now?"

Onny caught the thread in her teeth and broke it before she answered.

"You said you'd get one in a few days," she said, pouting her lips before parting them to wet the point of a fresh piece of floss to thread the needle.

"I know I did, Onny, I meant to do so. You don't know how sorry I am sometimes that we came here at all. I wish Sylvester had never suggested it."

Onny looked up sharply. The thread came out of the needle again.

"Well, that's a nice way to thank him for his kindness! What would we have done if he hadn't taken us in!"

"Oh, I'm not ungrateful for that," said Gabriel, "but I mean that I might have been more urgent to get work if there had been a rent bill waiting for me every evening when I came home."

Onny threaded the needle again. "I suppose you're regretting the money you spent on my clothes!" she said, bending forward to see the eye of the needle.

The situation was bad. Everything he said seemed to provoke her. His impulse was to desist and keep his news for a more auspicious occasion, but then, realizing that the news was good news, he felt that although he had made the wrong approaches in telling it, the news itself would please her and wipe away, at once, all the discord.

"You are undoubtedly in bad humour, Onny, but I have news that will put you in good humour. I should have told you earlier. I think that we may be able to leave this studio one of these days and get a place of our own."

Onny let her hands fall into her lap. Her lower lip slipped open and when she glanced up at him the silk stocking loosened from her grasp and began to slide slowly down her glossy leg, leaving her rosy knee exposed above her folded skirt.

"How is that?" she said faintly, her lip remaining open after she had spoken, and the tips of her lower teeth gleaming bright with saliva.

"I think that I have a chance of getting work at last." He went over eagerly and picked up the magazine. "I may thank you, Onny," he said, "for giving me the idea. I picked up this old magazine you were reading, and went straight down to the office and interviewed the editor. I am not certain yet, but I think that he was favourably disposed to me."

Onny continued to stare at him, with an almost frightened expression. "When will you know for certain?" she said.

"In a few days, I think," said Gabriel.

"How much will he pay you?"

"I don't know that either," said Gabriel, "but a beginning is a beginning."

Onny said nothing for a few minutes. Then she looked up with a worried expression on her face.

"I don't think we ought to go the first minute you get money. It would look very queer. It would be ungrateful, and what would Sylvester think?"

"He knew the arrangement was only temporary."

"Just the same!" said Onny.

"Surely you don't expect that we could continue living on Sylvester after I began to have some independent money?"

"No, I didn't mean that," said Onny, "but I thought that it would look as if we were dying to get out of here, if we went the very first minute you made a little money."

"Well, what else can we do? We must either do that or continue staying here at his expense."

Onny stooped down again and began to draw up the stocking over her leg.

"Perhaps we could make other arrangements with Sylvester."

"What arrangements could we make?"

"We could stay on here and pay him for the studio!"

"Onny!" Gabriel drew back. "But surely you wouldn't like that? Wouldn't you like a place of our own; one that you could fix up for yourself, decorate, make a sort of a home out of it?"

Onny said nothing; Gabriel went on.

"I will be working most of the day and you'll be alone. If we were here there would be nothing to do all day long for you, but if we had an apartment of our own you would find plenty to do."

"I thought you said when we left home that you were taking me away from drudgery!"

"I didn't think that you would regard keeping house for me as drudgery!" Gabriel's voice was filled with hurt surprise. Onny shrugged her shoulders. "Were you serious, Onny?" he asked. "You were joking! You didn't mean that you wouldn't like a place of our own. I can't believe that. There was another reason why you wanted to stay here. Did you think we would save money?"

Onny pondered the idea he had given her. "Yes," she said slowly, and then watching his face she added eagerly that there was another reason.

"What other reason?" said Gabriel.

"It would be all right for you. You'd be busy. You'd be out every day meeting people but I'd be all alone; I wouldn't know anyone and I'd never have anyone to talk to me."

"But Sylvester and his friends would call on us. We'd give parties for them, like the parties that Sylvester gives."

Onny hesitated.

"Well?" said Gabriel.

"I don't think I'd be able to give a party. Sylvester says it isn't everyone can give good parties. It's an art, he said."

"Oh nonsense!" said Gabriel.

"It isn't nonsense; after all what do I know about entertaining?"

"But, Onny," said Gabriel, "I have been watching you here in the evenings and only last night I was marvelling at how much you have learned since we came here. It was such a break from the life you were used to, and yet you look sometimes as if you had been brought up to this life."

"I watch the others," said Onny. "I wait to see what they are going to do."

"That's fine. That's fine," said Gabriel. "That's the way to manage."

Onny flashed a glance at him. "But I have a lot to learn yet!"

"Oh, I daresay," said Gabriel. "But you must walk before you run. It will take a certain amount of time."

"There!" said Onny. "And if we go away to an apartment of our own, how can I learn anything, shut up by myself most of the day!"

"But people will come and visit us! If they're asked they'll come. Sylvester will bring them. They'll come to us as often as we ask them to come. You can pick up all their tricks in your own apartment just as easily as you can pick them up here."

"How can I? In my own place I'll be busy all the time. Here I can just sit down and listen to the conversation. If I don't understand I don't need to say anything, but if it was in my own apartment I'd have to start the talk. They'd laugh at me!"

"Laugh at you! I'd like to see anyone laugh at you! As a matter of fact we don't have to depend on Sylvester's friends. We will make friends of our own."

"Sylvester's friends are good enough for me!" said Onny. "I don't hear you making many objections to Helen. You seem to like her company so well that it's a wonder you don't take some of these dirty old statues to bed with you!"

She jerked her foot in the direction of a Roman head bald at the dome and crowned with a wreath of laurel leaves. It was a copy of a classical piece, and was one of those famous heads which skilful workmanship, antiquity, and classical association have given an aura of beauty but which, taking it, as Onny did, upon its face value, was indeed rather ugly. There was about Onny's remarks a robust coarseness that made him smile, and he was misled into laughing at it against his will.

"I give in," he said. "We'll stay here a little longer, if you like, and if Sylvester is willing to have us, but we'll insist on paying him."

Onny instantly regained her good spirits. She ran back to continue her preparations for going out.

"Oh, Sylvester will be glad to let us stay," she said, leaning in close to the mirror and examining her eyes.

"How do you know?" asked Gabriel sharply. "You haven't been talking this over with him?"

Onny swung round, but her thoughts had flown forward. She gave him no reply.

"I'm nearly ready," she said. "It's long past the time that we said we would meet Sylvester. Do you mean to say you are still in that old dressing-gown?" Gabriel looked down at the shabby fleece dressing gown. "The first money you get," said Onny, breaking in on his thoughts, "you ought to get yourself some clothes. I wish you wore a suit like Sylvester or like Telman. Every time I look at you I feel that we are still back home. Did you see the lovely silk shirt that Telman had on last night, a pale blue one?" Onny giggled. "I'd love to see you in a blue shirt, Gabriel. You said that we'd make all kinds of changes when we came here. As far as I can see I'm the only one that changed." Onny stood away from the mirror. "Lord! How my mother would stare if she saw me now. And Judy, who used to think so much about her old plaid dress that was made by the dressmaker in Draghead!" She pulled out the hem of her skirt and elevated her head. "I'd like to walk up the town now and pass your aunts in the street without saluting them. I'd love to walk up the church and sit in the front seat. I'd wait till the service was started and walk in, late, up the aisle and sit on the cane chairs in front of the altar rails where

405

everyone would have to see me, because they're so mean they'd look the other way if they could sooner than give in that you were as good as them. They wouldn't please you to let you see them staring at you!"

Looking at her, in spite of the new clothes, and listening to the old tones that had sounded in her voice again, Gabriel began to think over what she had said about learning from Sylvester's friends. She had learned a lot, but he could see now that she had more to learn. What a strange mixture she was. She was so proud and headstrong in some things and yet she was not ashamed to admit humbly that she had a great deal to learn.

He began to pull off the dressing-gown and get ready, while Onny, ready and dressed and perfumed, postured at the mirror, mimicking in turn the Dublin ladies she had seen in the shops and on the streets and then, with a capricious twist, the ladies of Castlerampart.

"See!" said Gabriel. "I am ready. It isn't every man who can boast that he has a cabaret show in his bedroom to entertain him while he changes his shirt."

But Onny continued to mince around the room, one hand outstretched as if upholding a parasol, and picking her way with uplifted skirt. Her eyes were fixed upon the mirror where a reflected lady bowed and postured with her, gesture for gesture. The cabaret show was not for Gabriel. It was for her own delight.

"Come, you wanton!" said Gabriel.

Onny twirled around and, making a final pirouette, laced her arm in his, laughing up into his face.

"What does that mean?" she said. "I heard it somewhere before."

ᔕ ᔕ ᔕ

Sylvester was tired of waiting for them. When they arrived at the café where they had arranged to meet him, he was sitting with his legs spread out in such a way that he was as near to reclining at full length as it is possible for the human anatomy to be upon a stiff metal chair.

The waiters were put to great trouble getting past his table to attend to their other clients, being forced to alter their course and go behind him where the direct course would have been in front of him. As the café became crowded, however, such a detour was impossible, and they were soon excusing themselves profusely and stepping over his long legs. From stepping over them apologetically they had progressed to stepping over hurriedly, leaving their laden trays to make their own apology. As Gabriel and Onny came towards him between the tables Sylvester drew back his legs and shot into an upright position on his chair. Remaining in this position for a few seconds to create the impression that he had been in that posture all the time, he only rose to his feet when Onny was within a few yards of the table.

"I hope we didn't keep you waiting," said Gabriel, conscious of the café clock.

Sylvester looked at Onny.

"It's a lady's privilege to be late."

"That's not correct. It's a lady's privilege to change her mind," said Gabriel, irritated by Sylvester's easy adaptation of all things to suit his needs.

Sylvester, taking his bill from the waiter, appeared not to hear him, but a moment later, jingling the coins upon the glass-topped table, he looked directly at Gabriel, with a faintly sneering look.

"As you please," he said. "Shall we go?"

Onny, who had glanced at Gabriel crossly, was relieved at what appeared to be Sylvester's graciousness, and linking them both, she laughed.

"Hurry! We're late enough as it is," she said.

Telman's studio was in a remote street. It was on the top storey of a building which was unusually low, being unaltered since the days when this area was regarded as outside the city limit. The ground floor belonged to a laundress. This laundress had her ironing table placed in the window alcove, and all day long she was to be seen, passing her iron up and down over her wet, white linens, and thumping it down on the thick seams. As each article was pressed to perfection, she flung it up overhead on to a line that ran from one side of the window to the other, and from this line, as the day progressed, an increasing number of frilled and pleated garments, with hanging belts and dangling sleeves, hung downward over her head, gleaming white, and frostily crisped, until it seemed as if she worked in an icy cavern of white, where glossy icicles and stalactites hung down so brittle over her that with a jerk of her head they would crumble or crack into fragments.

In this window, passing her iron to and fro, she was a living emblem of her trade, and needed no sign or signboard to draw attention to her shop. At night, however, when her work was ended, she retired to her rooms behind the shop, and drew a stiff white curtain across her window. Her place was taken by a big black cat with a white nose and a white spot on the tip of the tail. This cat sometimes curled up in a ball and slept behind the glass, but more often it spent its time in making an elaborate toilet, stretching out its long hind leg, and beginning at the tip, would lick it from one end to the other. Like the laundress herself, the big cat was a symbol of cleanliness and fastidiousness.

On this particular evening as Sylvester, Onny, and Gabriel passed the window the cat was busy about her ablutions, and as usual she was unheeding of the passers-by however curiously they stared at her. But when, as they reached the window, Sylvester, casually, as a matter of habit, tapped the glass with his fingernail, lightly, the big cat at once raised her head, and, although still with her long black leg extended, opened her stiff pink jaws and closed them again three times in succession. And although they could hear nothing through the thick plate glass they knew that she mewed at them and recognized Sylvester.

"Another of my friends!" said Sylvester to Onny, and went to move on. Onny however could not tear herself away from the window. "Does he know you?" she cried. And when the cat made no response to her own tapping, or to Gabriel's when she insisted on his trying also, her face was a mixture of disappointment, wonder, vexation, and awe.

But at last they got her away from the window, and went over to the door at the side that led to the rooms overhead. The entrance to Telman's studio was separate from the entrance to the laundry, and the door was closed. Sylvester, however, drew out a key and opened the door. This would have surprised Gabriel and Onny at one time but they were accustomed to it by that time, for many of Sylvester's friends had duplicate keys to each other's rooms, distributed as symbols of the freedom and comradeship between them.

"I wonder what our Aunt Sara would think of this exchange of keys!" said Gabriel laughing. "There were so many bolts and bars, catches and locks, on the doors in Clewe Street, that it took my aunt a full quarter of an hour to close up the house for the night." He laughed again.

"At home our door was never locked," said Onny suddenly. "We often left it wide open on a hot night." She laughed. "We often woke up in the morning and found the birds flying around the room and picking up the dirt on the floor."

Gabriel was surprised. Onny had seldom or never referred to her own life, having left it to be inferred by her silence that her life at home had been in every respect the same as his—Gabriel's.

Sylvester stopped on the stairs.

"Is that so?" said Sylvester. "That is very interesting. It bears out what I have often said, that socially speaking the lower you were at home, the higher you are here!"

As they spoke they were advancing up the stairs upon which an ever-increasing accumulation of dust and burned-out match sticks indicated their advance out of the region of the laundress into the region occupied and accounted for in rental and condition by the painter. Onny was somewhat out of breath from climbing the stairs but she broke out eagerly.

"Did you know my grandmother was a tinker?" she said.

Gabriel heard her with astonishment. She had been at such pains always to gloss over her origin when talking to him and, for her sake, he had himself been so sensitive that he was always on guard against any reference that might be tactless. But Sylvester threw back his head and slapped his thigh.

"Of course I knew it," he said. "Everyone in the town knew it, but if they didn't they had only to look at you, at your brazen cheeks and your bold eye!"

He laughed again, and Onny, too, laughed excitedly, cheeks blazing brighter and her eyes lighting with some rich racial pride.

In the narrow space of the stairway their laughter echoed louder. At once a door on the upper landing opened with a crash and the sound of voices that had, although muffled, been heard before, broke over their heads like a thunderclap.

"What is the joke?" called Telman, leaning down over the banister rails. "Oh, it's you people! Come on up."

Several people had crowded out on to the landing.

"What was the joke? Share the joke!"

Faces that they knew, and many that were fresh to them, peered down. Their own necks were strained looking upward on the steep and dark stairway.

Sylvester put on a serious face.

"There is no joke, I assure you. In fact, quite the contrary. I am not only serious, but I hope that I have about my person the seriousness that should distinguish one about to confer a favour on posterity, one about to make a magnificent gesture to the Arts. In short, Telman, to you, Painter of the Epoch, I am about to give a suggestion which may make you immortal. You must paint Onny! You must paint her as Queen of the Tinkers! I'm surprised you did not think of this for yourself. Alas! You can undoubtedly paint, but you have no more idea than the brush in your hand of what is suitable and what is not."

By this time they had reached the landing and were crowding back into the studio. Onny had become the centre of attention. People were staring at her; those who did not know her standing a bit apart and staring at her. Those who knew her were eagerly turning her around, lifting her arm at one minute and discussing her frankly limb for limb.

As for Telman, it was true what Sylvester had said, he had an amazing native power in his brush, but he lacked a selective instinct, and was unable to choose suitable objects upon which to work. Since he was a man of about forty, of humble origin, who had stumbled upon his own abilities almost by accident, it was unlikely that he would ever cultivate a taste, even at second hand, which might take the place of this natural instinct. But he was an indefatigable worker. His superhuman energy and his abnormal capacity for work resulted in the acquirement of a faultless technique, which unfortunately showed up his spiritual deficiencies, since the ability and distinction of his workmanship drew attention to the mediocrity and sentimentality of the subjects upon which it had been expended. When he did a piece of good work, it was almost always discoverable that the subjects had been pointed out to him by another person. But unfortunately, since his vanity was towering, he did not often take suggestions from outside, and his studio was crowded with forgotten canvases.

As he looked at Onny now, however, it seemed as if he were about to accept Sylvester's suggestion. There was about her a robust beauty that seemed to leap forward to meet his robust talent, and as he watched her, Sylvester watched him, and catching Gabriel's eye directed him to observe the painter, into whose face there were coming the signs of mental excitement that denote the conception of a work of art, and beside which the actual working out of the idea is a dull and tedious affair.

All round him his friends were talking of the forthcoming picture.

"Why don't you keep her for yourself, Sylvester?" someone asked. "I thought that creative artists were as jealous of their models as writers are of their ideas."

"I know my type," said Sylvester shortly.

"Even so! I thought there was no pain greater than the consciousness that there was a subject one couldn't handle."

Gabriel all this time said nothing. His feelings were varied. He could not stifle a feeling of pride that they should all think Onny a good subject for a painting, but he was irritated at the way Onny was preening herself at the compliments. He wanted to change the conversation, but it had become too general to be affected by an interruption from one person. Just then, however, an interruption did occur which distracted the attention of most people in the room. The door opened and Helen came in.

"Ah, Helen!" cried Telman, rushing forward to meet her and giving her an elaborate welcome.

Telman was, as a matter of fact, somewhat in awe of Helen, with whom he never felt at ease, and as is not uncommon with people of his nature who are abnormally sensitive in their reactions to others but insensitive to the way in which they react upon others, he treated her with an almost insolent familiarity. Helen appeared to understand him, however, and never took offence. Her manner towards him was specially gracious and kind, and always had the effect of putting him more at ease. It was as if she ignored the awkward effusive hulk that gesticulated in front of her, mouthing flattery, and spoke directly to the simple, even docile, godlike soul that underlay the pretentious exterior.

"I can understand her manner," thought Gabriel, as he watched her smiling graciously at the fulsome Telman. "I can understand in the same way that I can understand her coldness to Sylvester although she likes him."

He looked around to see where Sylvester was at that moment, and saw that he was talking to Onny. Although he was talking to her, his eyes were wandering around the room, and now and then they came to rest on Telman.

"He cannot understand Helen's toleration of him," Gabriel thought.

The buoyance of his own hopes for the future made the evening more than usually enjoyable for Gabriel, and at the earliest opportunity he moved over to Helen.

"I have had a stroke of luck at last," he said, and his heart glowed warmly at seeing her genuine gladness in the news. "I'm not altogether certain yet, of course," he said, "but I think I have good reason to hope."

A slight shade of disappointment crossed Helen's face.

"I distrust uncertainty," she said. "Tell me more about it."

In a few words Gabriel told her of his interview with the editor of the magazine.

"That would certainly be congenial work," she said, "and it might lead to better things."

"That's what I thought," said Gabriel eagerly. "As a matter of fact the same firm controls two or three magazines of different kinds, all cheap publications, of course, but covering a wide field. There ought to be possibilities of expansion."

This phrase was one that he remembered hearing the editor use, and he felt that it gave extra weight to his own remarks.

"Yes, I suppose so," said Helen, still reluctant to become excited about something that was uncertain. "What makes you so sure he is going to make a place for you?" she asked.

"But I told you what he said, didn't I?" said Gabriel in surprise.

"Yes," said Helen, again reluctantly. "But talk is easy." She looked doubtful. "You didn't tell me the name of the magazine," she said then. "What kind of man was the editor?"

"Oh, he edits several small magazines," said Gabriel defensively.

"What did you say his name was?" asked Helen persistently.

"I didn't say what it was," said Gabriel, but feeling that he was acting childishly, he added the name instantly. "His name is Samuel Modell," he said.

"Samuel Modell!" At the sound of the name, Helen's face betrayed unmistakable signs of recognition. "I've heard something about him," she said, seeing that Gabriel was looking at her.

She would not say what she had heard, however, taking refuge in the plea that she could not remember what it was that she had heard. One thing only she would admit. She looked Gabriel straight in the eye.

"I don't think it was anything good," she said.

"I don't care what you heard about him if he gives me a job," said Gabriel, with an effort to appear undisturbed.

"I may be able to find out something about him for you," said Helen suddenly, and he saw that she was looking across the room at a pale young man in dark spectacles, who was talking earnestly to another young man a few paces away from them. "I see someone who might be able to give me some information. Excuse me." She was about to leave him, but she turned back. "If you are to get a disappointment," she said, "I'm sure—you will agree that the sooner it comes the better."

And having said this she went across the floor and after a short delay, during which she spoke to one or two other people, Gabriel saw her in earnest conversation with the pale young man. They both looked serious and once or twice the young man made a deprecatory gesture, and Helen nodded her head in agreement. Before she came back to him he knew what she would have to say.

"Don't tell me!" he said. "I know. It's bad news."

"Well, of course we may be wrong about him," said Helen, meaning herself and the young man with whom she had been speaking, "but as I thought, his reputation is not worth much. He may employ you, Gabriel, but if he does, it will be a surprise to me. You see he is well known to make a practice of giving false encouragement to young people, like you, or"—she looked around—"like that young man I was talking to just now. He can't be said to make any definite promises, he's too clever for that, but by hints and implications he raises false hopes."

"But why? Why should he do this?" cried Gabriel.

Helen shrugged her shoulders.

"I don't know," she said, "and really it doesn't matter. All that matters is that he is not to be relied upon."

"Still I can't see why he should do that to me!" cried Gabriel.

Helen shrugged her shoulders again.

"Why should he do it to anyone? Yet I understand it is a well-known practice with him, and that there are hundreds of young people whom he has treated exactly as he treated you, and some of whom he even deceived more culpably—gave them work to do for him, saying that he wanted to test their abilities, and afterwards made use of it in one of his papers with a few small changes here and there."

"I find it hard to believe," said Gabriel again. Then he added quickly that he did not doubt Helen. "It's just that I liked him so well," he said. "I can't imagine why he should do such a thing."

"I must say I'm not much interested in people like that," said Helen, "but if, as you say, you liked him, it may be possible that his faults are due to weakness. He may be one of those people who covet liking and admiration so much that they don't scruple what means they use to get it. Rather than send people away, when they apply to him, or come to him with manuscripts, he may wish to create a good impression by making these false promises. Then, once they are out of sight, he forgets them. I believe there is no use trying to get a second interview with him, and if you write to him he will not answer, and will keep the stamps if you send stamps for a reply."

"What about all the things he said about discovering talent?" asked Gabriel.

"Well, as a matter of fact," said Helen, "there is a rumour that he will have to sell out. For some time he has only been hanging on by the skin of his teeth, keeping one paper alive with the help of another, and depending solely on advertisements, which of course are falling off according as his sales diminish. I suppose he's to be pitied in a way. Then, too, he is overstaffed with underpaid assistants. The only chance he gets to make a favourable impression is on people like you, who don't know him." Helen softened somewhat as she said this, but she quickly resumed her disdainful attitude. "Let's not talk about him any more," she said, but before she changed the topic, she put her hand on Gabriel's arm. "I'm sorry to be the bearer of bad news," she said, "but do not lose heart. Something is sure to turn up one of these days."

Gabriel looked down at the hand she had laid upon his arm. In his gratitude for the kindly interest, he forgot the sting of his disappointment. When she had moved away, however, he recalled with regret that he had told Onny of his hopes, and the rest of the evening was spoiled by the thought that he must now tell her they were mistaken. He need not expect sympathy from Onny. She would have nothing but contempt for him.

It was late into the night when they finally left Telman's rooms, and after a long walk home, under the leafy summer trees, through which the lamplight streamed, they came to Sylvester's apartment, and on the landing they said good-night to Sylvester.

"Good night, Sylvester," said Gabriel.

"Good-night, Gabriel," said Sylvester, and he turned to Onny. "Goodnight, and good luck!" he said, and he opened the door of his own room.

The studio was bright with moonlight. It streamed down on the floor from the pale skylight. It lay on the white statues. Onny put her hand on the switch to turn on the artificial light. Gabriel caught her wrist.

"Don't turn on the light for a minute," he said. "I have something to tell you. I'd rather tell you before you put on the light. It's bad news, Onny. I was given to understand tonight that Samuel Modell was not to be relied upon. It is unlikely that I will get anything to do from him."

In the darkness he heard her draw in her breath quickly

"Are you very disappointed?" he asked.

Onny said nothing.

"But I have made up my mind to one thing, Onny," he said, speaking quickly, but deliberately. "I have failed to get the kind of work I wanted,

413

but from tomorrow on I'm going to look for whatever kind of work I can get. I will take any job I can find for which the pay will be sufficient to keep us."

"What kind of a job will you get?" said Onny.

"I don't know yet," said Gabriel, "I'll take anything I can get for a start."

Onny's voice contracted.

"I hope you don't mean that!" she said. "Sylvester's friends are all either literary or artistic."

"Do you mean that you would be ashamed of me if I took some humble work?"

"Oh, don't be silly!" said Onny, turning on the light and cutting short the conversation.

Gabriel remained firm in his determination to find a job. Onny's words did not shake him, but he resolved to use a certain amount of discrimination in his search.

∽ ∽ ∽

At the end of another month Gabriel had given up all thought of choosing work with discrimination. If he could have got work of any kind to do he would have taken it gladly, but there was none. He visited all the employment agencies, and all with the same result. He was without qualifications.

Meanwhile Telman Young was working on the portrait of Onny. He worked day after day. She went to his studio at regular hours, but sometimes he sent for her at odd hours when he felt an urgent need to work at the picture. Sylvester's idea of making Onny the centre of a narrative picture had been abandoned. Gabriel would not give his permission to use her as a model. He had consented, however, to let her sit for a portrait on condition that it would be a formal portrait, in a conventional pose. He further stipulated that although Telman might exhibit the picture as often as he wished, if it were to be successful, it was to bear the name of the sitter as sole title in the gallery catalogues. Neither was it to be sold without Gabriel's having the option to purchase it at the same price as that which would have been accepted from the outside purchaser. By making these rules, Gabriel felt that he had kept Onny from sinking to the level of a commercial model.

One evening, coming back from his weary search for employment, he was dispirited to find that Onny was out. A note left on the table informed him that she was at Telman Young's studio, and that, as Telman hoped to finish the picture that evening, she might not return until late. About an hour later, however, he heard her running up the stairs.

When she burst into the studio, letting the door bang back against the wall and dragging off her hat, there was about her, from her head to her feet, a look of having enjoyed herself. Her hair had loosened from the exertion of running up the long stairs, a slight moisture had come out on her forehead. Her breath came irregularly, and her breasts rose and fell. But almost at once, when she saw him sitting dejectedly at the window, her humour changed.

To express this change of humour all that was needed was a slight alteration of her facial expression, for her flushed cheeks and loosened hair, her moist forehead and her pulsing breast, were as suitable for the expression of anger as they were for the expression of joy, and bore witness to the fact that the passions are nearer allied one to another than we may like to believe.

"So you found nothing!" she said. "If you had any sense you'd let me take the job Telman offered, and then you could take your time about finding work."

Gabriel clenched his hands.

"I told you a thousand times that I will not let you become a paid model. If Telman wants to have you sit for a picture once in a while I can hardly be disagreeable enough to refuse my permission, although he knows I do not like to have you do it. But I won't let you take money. I want it to be made quite clear that you are obliging him, not he obliging you."

Onny tossed her head.

"You had great complaints some time ago about us being dependent on Sylvester. Now, when we have a chance of earning money of our own, now, when we could leave here, you make objections!"

"But, Onny, I could not live on your money!" said Gabriel.

"You can live on Sylvester's," said Onny. "I don't see the difference!"

ᔕ   ᔕ   ᔕ

Three weeks later Gabriel was still without work. Then one day he heard that a community of nuns, in a convent near Stephen's Green, were looking for a man to clean the convent windows. He applied for the job.

The sisters did not think that Gabriel was exactly suitable, but they were willing to give him a trial, although one of the younger sisters kept repeating over and over again that he would fall and be killed.

"He will fall. He will fall and be killed. It is better to get an older man." Whether the older man was less likely to fall, or whether his fall would upset the community less, Gabriel could not decide, but he tried to assure the young sister that he was agile and strong. They gave him the job.

As he came out of the convent he noticed that, although it was still early afternoon, the sky had darkened and there was a strange stillness over the city. The air was heavy. There was a thunderstorm threatening. He took a short cut through the Green and there he saw the people hurrying for the shelters. They had an intimidated air about them as they ran, casting rapid glances at the sky. The birds were silent in the bushes. Humans and animals were striving to efface themselves from the scene. But the green grass under them, and the green leafy trees above them, seemed, on the contrary, to glow with a fierce intensity of colour, as if they were rousing themselves to greet the oncoming storm. Gabriel's mind dwelt vaguely on the elemental bond of vapour that existed between these green things and the great storm clouds that were soon to open over them. The sap had risen in their veins. Every leaf and every blade of grass in sight had deepened to a vivid green that was shrill as a shout in the gathering dark.

He hurried home, anxious to be with Onny when the storm came on; anxious to tell her about the job he had taken. As he ran up the stairs he could hear her singing. He had no preparation for the almost hysterical nature of her opposition to his plans.

"How can you think of such a thing?" she cried. "It is bad enough to clean windows, but to clean the windows in a convent is ridiculous! Please don't mention it to anyone. Don't let anyone know that you even thought of such a thing. Above all don't mention it to Sylvester. He would make such jokes at my expense."

Gabriel caught her by the shoulders.

"I must do something, Onny. Surely you realize that? We cannot stay here in this studio any longer at Sylvester's expense."

"There is no need for us to stay here. I could have earned money any time, from Telman, and you would not allow me. But I was a fool to listen to you! Your objections were absurd. Everyone said they were absurd! I'm not going to listen to you any more. I am going to take a job with him. He is starting new classes tomorrow. He wants me to pose for three hours every day. For that I will earn enough to do a lot of things!"

She pulled herself away from him. Gabriel caught her arms again and shook her.

"I said I would not allow you to do that."

"How can you stop me?"

"I forbid you to do it!"

Onny laughed. She imitated him crudely.

"I forbid you! You sound like your Aunt Theresa!" Then she stopped laughing abruptly. "Who do you think you are talking to now? What right have you to say what I will do and what I will not do? What right have you to order me about? Let go my arm."

Gabriel stared at her. A silence fell swiftly between them, and moment by moment it spread until it became unbearable. The room too was darkening for the storm. At last Onny broke it herself constrainedly.

"I'm going to take the job!" she said, but her voice was weak and hardly seemed to affect the silence. The words seemed but the echoes of words uttered a long time back.

Then, on the brittle panes of the skylight, one after another, great drops of rain began to fall, with slow, steady, insistent tapping. The room darkened still more. Far away a low rumbling began; and as they listened it came nearer, as if some great supernal chariot trundled down the unseen cobbles of the sky. Then the sound was above them, right over their heads. It roared in their ears.

"Is that thunder?" cried Onny, and she remained motionless in the middle of a stride she had begun to make towards the door. She waited tensely for a repetition of the noise. Gabriel watched her. His own thoughts were eager for expression, and he wanted to continue the argument, but it was clear that Onny's thoughts had been swept asunder by the noise. Her attitude was unmistakable.

"Are you afraid?" he asked, in amazement.

"Wait! Listen!" she cried, not bothering to answer him, matching the stillness of the air with her breathless immobility. "Listen!" she commanded again, her face upturned and tense, as if she hoped to find that the sound had been but the rumble of some explosion far away.

But while she stood expectant, hopeful, the green panes of the skylight over her head were shot with a flash of lightning that lit up all the studio with a ghastly glare. After it, their eyes were dazzled for a moment, and the room became still more darkened by contrast. They could hardly see each other in the confusion that came upon their eyes, but around them the statuary shone with a startling whiteness.

There was another peal of thunder. It rumbled and rolled over their heads; it broke and crashed around them. Quickly they averted their eyes from the skylight before the green flash fell upon it, but this time they faced the small open window at the other end of the room, and through it the lightning flash seemed to enter the room like the crack of a whip. Outside the window, the light fell on the wet slates of the other houses and from their wet surfaces volleyed back at the savage sky.

Onny covered her face with her hands.

"Oh, God! We'll be struck!" she cried, and she ran blindly towards Gabriel, and threw herself into his arms, pulling the lapels of his coat across her face to shield her eyes.

"Onny, Onny! Are you frightened?"

She buried her face deeper in the darkness of his coat, and her fingers dug into his flesh.

"Shut the window!" she screamed. "Draw the curtains! Shut the window and cover the mirror. Oh, do it quick. Shut the window and cover the mirror. A mirror draws lightning!"

She withdrew her head from under the cover of his coat for long enough to glance wildly around the room.

"Put away the knives," she cried. "Are there any pins lying about? I hope my scissors are in the box. I hope they're not on the table?"

Then as another flash came, she screamed and clung to him again.

"Onny, control yourself," said Gabriel, wincing with the pain of the clutch in which she held his arm. "There is no need to be afraid. There's no danger, at least it is a million to one against anything happening to you"

But Onny wasn't listening to him. She screamed louder.

"Shut the window," she screamed, "shut the window!" And with her heels she began to drum on the floor with a frenzy that frightened him.

"I cannot do anything while you are strangling me like this," he said, dragging at her hands and trying to tear himself away from her. "Let me go, and I will shut the window; the rain is coming in on the floor. Let me go, and I will shut it."

Onny released him at once. He went over and slapped down the window sash with a crash that coincided with another great flash of lightning, and was echoed by another resounding peal of thunder. The rain had ceased to fall in single, heavy drops and was now pouring down in torrents, and rolling down the windowpanes in one unbroken sheet of water.

"I closed the window because the rain was coming in all over the floor," said Gabriel, "but I won't cover the mirrors, Onny; that is absurd."

"Cover them, cover them!" Onny stamped her feet. "They attract the lightning."

"Where did you hear that nonsense?"

Onny began to cry gulpingly, hysterical tears streaming down her face.

"Don't stand there arguing with me," she said. "Oh, Gabriel, please cover the mirrors."

Gabriel did not stir.

"You must control yourself, Onny," he said. "Use your reason. If we weren't here, the window would be open, and everything uncovered with no one to worry about them. Think of all the places all over the city with hundreds and hundreds of mirrors that nobody bothers about! Where did you hear such nonsense?"

Onny was wiping the tears away, and her face had become smeared with the grime of her fingers. Two or three times she made an attempt to carry out her own orders, and ran forward towards the mirror with her scarf raised as if to wind it over the glass herself, but each time the lightning flashed out over her head before she was halfway across the room, and, since she was staring straight at the mirror, each time the reflection of the light crashed and broke in the sky it was reflected in the mirror, until it seemed as if the mirror itself had cracked and broken.

"Oh it's struck!" she screamed on one occasion and, weakened with fear and with shock, she sank on to the floor, where in the comparative darkness she lay crouching and moaning.

Unable to understand such a sudden terror, particularly in one as brave and rash and reckless as Onny, Gabriel nevertheless began to see the necessity of obeying her as she became more and more hysterical, and, catching up the tablecloth which was lying across the back of a chair to dry a tea stain upon it, he flung it contemptuously over the mirror, from which, almost at once, it slipped and fell to the ground.

"It fell off," screamed Onny. "Put it on again."

Although she had her hands over her face, she was peering through the crevices between her fingers. Gabriel threw the cloth over the mirror again and, tucking it down behind the frame, he secured it there.

"Hide the knives," said Onny.

He began to collect the knives.

"Don't forget the scissors," said Onny. "Hide the scissors."

Gabriel took up the scissors. Onny glanced cautiously at him through her fingers. She began to talk quickly.

"My mother told me about a girl who was sewing at a window and she took up some scissors in her hand to cut the thread, and the lightning fell on the scissors, and travelled up them, and struck her dead! She was as black as a tree when they found her. Only for the scissors she would have been saved. If only she wasn't holding the scissors!"

By this time Gabriel had collected all the knives and forks and had taken up the scissors from the table.

"Is there anything else you want hidden?" he asked, noticing that Onny was quieter while he was taking these precautions. Night was coming on, and the flashes of lightning showed up more vividly in the darkness. Once or twice when it flashed into the room it seemed to run along the blue blade of the knives. And once, as he passed near Onny while he collected them, she screamed.

"Don't come near me with those things in your hand!" she cried, shrinking back against the wall.

"You little coward," said Gabriel, and he looked down at the glittering steels in his hand. "You don't care whether I'm struck or not, I suppose?"

"I do! I do care," said Onny. "If you're struck I'll be struck. If one person in a room is struck with lightning everyone in the room will be struck." She pointed to a box on the floor. "Don't keep standing there with the knives in your hand. Put them in that box."

"I'll stand here just to show you!" said Gabriel. "I'll stand here to let you see there is no foundation for your foolish fears."

He stood waiting for the next flash, and just before he judged that it was about to come, he held the knives out on the flat of his outstretched palms. Onny sprang to her feet. For a moment he thought that she was going to run and dash the things from his hands, but she ran past him, and flinging herself face downward on the bed began uncontrollably to hammer the mattress with her fists.

"You're cruel, cruel," she cried, her voice distorted by the bedclothes in which she had buried her face. "You want us to be struck!" She sat up for an instant, and pointed her finger at him accusingly. "That's it! You want us to be struck!"

Gabriel was absolutely unafraid of the lightning. Under normal circumstances he would have liked to stand at the window and watch it tear its way through the clouds, but he had weakened his own powers of reasoning by giving in to Onny, and covering the mirrors and the scissors, and so just before the flash came he put the scissors into the box and shut the lid. He went over and sat beside Onny, patting her shoulder and urging her to be quiet. But Onny, now that all the precautions she thought necessary had been taken, felt worse than before. While he had gone about taking the precautions she suggested, she had felt that he was in some way counteracting the evils of the storm. Now, however, with the mirrors shrouded, with the steel articles hidden away out of sight, and the window shut and the curtain drawn, she felt that there was nothing more that could be done against the forces of destruction, and they must only wait now until the storm abated, or destroyed them. Not till the last peal died away in the distance, and the last pale flash flickered dimly in the sky, would she feel safe. She sobbed louder.

The storm was bad. As day receded and the darkness of night thickened, its intensity could be measured more surely. Yet, to Gabriel night brought relief, for there had been something oppressive in the unnatural day darkness of the afternoon. For Onny the coming of night brought greater hysteria. Where in the daylight the lightning had been like a vast sheet flapped across the sky, it showed itself against the dark night sky in its true character. The ragged thorny branches of destruction switched the frail glass of the windowpanes, and remained for a moment etched in the air, like a crack in the glass.

Her fears had taken possession of her. She could sob no more, but her body convulsed and shook. She was almost suffocated with her head buried in the bedclothes, and when he persuaded her to lift her head for a moment to breathe, the moment always seemed to coincide with the moment of the lightning flash, and she threw herself back on the bed with a scream.

The heat of the room became unbearable at last.

"I'm going to open the window, Onny," he said. "I cannot breathe. If there was fresh air in the room you would not feel so bad."

"Are you mad?" She clung to him and held him so tightly that he was unable to stir. "You will not open the window."

He tried to free a hand to unfasten his collar. Finally he tugged at it and tore it open.

"If you won't let me open the window I'll have to go out on the landing to get a breath of fresh air out there. I'm smothering in here."

She did not answer, but she clung to him closer and, when he stood up, she herself was dragged into a sitting position.

"For God's sake don't go out there, Gabriel."

"If you are afraid to let me go, if you are afraid to be alone, come with me!" said Gabriel, and he stood up.

Onny was dragged after him again until she was almost on her knees.

"No!" she cried. "No! Don't go out of this room. I won't let you." Her eyes were wild and glittering. "We will be struck. Oh God! We'll surely be struck." And with the last exclamation she sank utterly to her knees in a suppliant posture, and, putting her hands up to her face, she began to pray in a babbling way, the words falling over each other as they tumbled out of her mouth.

"Oh, God, make it stop! Make it stop! Don't let it go on all night. Deliver us. Deliver us. Save us. I'm sorry for all my sins. I'll go to Confession tomorrow. I'm sorry for my sins. I didn't mean any harm. Oh, make the rain stop. Take away the thunder. Don't strike us! Don't strike us!" She looked up wildly at Gabriel. "If only we had a blessed candle! At home my mother always lit a blessed candle when there was lightning. If you have a blessed candle in your hand you'll get time to confess your sins before you're struck!"

Gabriel stared down at her with a mixture of pity and disgust.

"You're making a fool of yourself," he said coldly. "If you were out in the rain, in the dark, reduced to sheltering under a tree, I'd have some pity for you, although even then it would be a chance in a million if you were hit. And even then, I would expect you to be calm and dignified. After all, there would be nothing that you could do to save yourself. If it was to be your fate to die that way, you would die that way. But here, in the house, with the windows and the doors shut, I cannot understand this panic! Stop those hysterical prayers! What God do you suppose would be bothering listening to your last-minute ravings, even if He had demeaned His gigantic mind by plotting your small destruction. And this talk about a blessed candle! Don't be nonsensical! Do you expect God to save you because you hold a piece of smelling tallow in your blasphemous little hands!"

While he was talking, Onny had sprung up, and run over to him. She put up her hands and closed his lips.

"Don't say it. Don't say it," she said. "You'll draw down a curse on us." She was beside herself now with hysterical excitement. Her hair had loosened and her clothes had become moistened with the heat of her body.

421

"I wish I'd never listened to you," she cried. "If I never listened to you I'd be at home now, where I'd be safe. We never had storms like this at home. Oh!" She hid against him again as another vivid flash came across the room. "It's bad enough to have brought me here, to have made me commit a terrible sin, without standing there cursing God, and drawing down wrath on us. This is a punishment!" She fell on her knees again, but this time her prayers had subtly altered. "Oh, God, don't strike me. It wasn't my fault." She flashed a look at Gabriel. "It's all his fault. I wanted us to be married. I said all along that I wanted us to be married."

Wearied and hurt Gabriel went over to the window. He laid his face against the windowpane that the chill of the glass might cool his flushed cheeks. Suddenly Onny called to him.

"Hand me my bag," she cried, triumphant and excited.

He went over for the red carpet bag, and he gave it to her. Onny opened it and took out a thin roll of smoke-blackened paper. With clumsy fumbling fingers she unrolled it. It was a gaudy varnished print of some religious character, glossy and garish, crude in conception, wretched in execution. She caught it to her breast and began a new mumble of prayers. Gabriel put his hands over his eyes.

"I can't bear to look at you, Onny, making such a cowardly exhibition of yourself. To think that you secretly hoarded up that execrable picture."

"Don't say anything bad about my picture!" said Onny, screaming at him.

"I'd take it and burn it, only you're hysterical enough as things are without provoking you further," said Gabriel.

"Burn it?" she screamed. "Burn it? A holy picture!" And she held it closer.

A new understanding of her nature came to him, and with it a great pity.

"All right, keep your picture," he said, "if it makes you feel any better."

The storm would last all night. If she continued to react to it in this way she would be ill. Even her strong body would not stand the strain of such a night. And it seemed as if the storm were only entering into its first stage, and that it was gathering, instead of lessening, in intensity as the hours went on. She would not listen to reason. Blinded by primitive fear she was beyond help of words. They had no meaning for her. There was only one way to reach her consciousness, and with one primitive emotion to try to conquer another. Gabriel leaned over her and put an arm around her shoulder.

"Hush, Onny, hush!" he said, gently. "Nothing will happen to you. I promise you! Don't you remember, you said one time that you would never be afraid anywhere with me. Don't you remember?"

His hands moved across her forehead, gently, soothingly. With the other hand he drew her nearer to him and lay down beside her on the crumpled coverlet. Speaking as if to a child, he smoothed her damp hair. Before a flash came he pressed her nearer to him, but in the dark moments between the flashes he leaned away from her and moving his hand backwards and forwards created a slight stir in the air that gave her a chance of cooling her cheeks and breathing more easily.

"There now," he said. "It's not as bad as it was. It's getting better. The thunder is going further away. It's getting fainter. And the lightning is not as bright as it was, it's going further away too." As she raised her head he pressed his hand over her eyes. "Don't look up," he said. "I'll tell you how it is. There is a longer time between the peal and the flash. That means that the storm is going further away." He stroked the moist hair and spoke lower and lower. "It is very late too, Onny. Think of this great city, and all the thousands of people that lie under its roofs at this minute, as we are lying here." He pressed her closer. "Among so many thousands of people why should we be singled out for destruction?" He began to speak softer and softer, and there were longer and longer intervals between his words. "Soon it will be morning," he said, "and daylight will shine along the roof tops. The wind will rise and scatter the rain clouds, and then perhaps, just before the light, the stars may ride into view for a moment, bright and magnificent. The rain will be shaken from the drenched leaves of the trees. The blades of grass that have been beaten to the ground will begin to swell with the sap of the earth and they will unbend slowly, and straighten upwards like javelins of the light. In some places they will snap up into a straight position with a swift spring. And then, in the cool bright morning, of green skies and green leaves and green grasses, the birds will come out along the sodden branches and raising their sleek throats give clear calls to each other. One after the other the birds of the morning will begin to sing." He looked down at her. "Perhaps before that peaceful time comes you will have slipped away into the brighter valleys of sleep." As he spoke he felt the restlessness leaving her limbs. He felt the stiff-nerved limbs relax, and the fingers loosen their tight clasp. "Sleep, Onny. Sleep!" he said, almost singing the words, saying them over and over again. "Sleep! Sleep!" he said. "Sleep! Sleep!"

∽ ∽ ∽

The next day when Gabriel wakened he was lying in the same position as that in which he had fallen asleep in the earlier morning, but this time his shoes had been unlaced and laid on the floor beside him, and a light blanket had been laid over him, while, on a chair, pulled up near the bedside, was a plate with some sandwiches on it, and a glass of milk. The window was open again, and the sun was streaming in through it, the bright dazzling sun that comes after great rain, and on the floor in a corner of the room was Onny's dress thrown there, where she had stepped out of it. Of Onny herself there was no other sign. Gabriel remembered that she had said Telman was starting his classes on this day, and in his amazement at her concentration in remembering it, and wakening uncalled after such a scant and troubled sleep, his indignation at her flouting of his wishes was obscured. As well as that, his mind was troubled by the display of unreason that she had given in the thunderstorm, and he began to plan the words which he would use to show her the indignity of her panic of prayers.

He was frightened at the reversion to old superstitions which had taken place in a moment of fear, and he felt that it was his duty to explain to her that her display of panic was unworthy. He leaned up on his elbow and looked out at the sunlight glinting on the roofs. Then he looked at the glass of milk on the chair beside him. She was a strange person. As had frequently happened before, after some irritating scene with her, he was softened by some strange loving quality in her that drew him back against his will to the full strength of tenderness that he had formerly felt for her. He put out his hands and lifted the glass. It was warm to the touch. It must have been lying there for a long time. He looked at his watch, but it had not been wound and although it was still ticking, he knew that it was slow and that the hour was late. He didn't know how late it was, how far the day had advanced, but slipping out of bed he began to dress hastily. If there was still time, he would accept the job of window cleaning in the convent. Onny had gone against him. There was no reason why he should pay heed to her objections to his work. And thinking of the changes they would be able to effect with their joint salaries, small though either might be if taken alone, he felt his spirits rise and in the interests of the day's trivial details he began to forget the unpleasantness of the night. As he dressed, he watched the antics of some pigeons on the wet slates outside the window, and as he went down the stairs he felt gay and happy, and the day, at its brightest and best, was as natural a setting for his mood as the night had been for its mood.

An hour later he was out on the window ledge of an upper window in the convent, cleaning the glass vigorously, and planning what he would do with the money he was earning. There must be other institutions in which he could get similar employment. Everything seemed more hopeful.

ഗ   ഗ   ഗ

After the thunderstorm there were a few days of clear sunlight that sparkled on the leaves of the trees, and the skylight in the studio glittered with reflected light until the eye could hardly bear to glance upwards at it. Then, quite suddenly, the rain began to fall again, and it rained steadily from morning till night.

424

On the fourth day of this determined rain, Gabriel was preparing to go out, when his attention was drawn to a heap of brightly coloured scraps of paper, which were strewn all over the floor on Onny's side of the bed. Onny herself, already fully dressed, was sitting on the side of the bed with one shoe on her foot and the other shoe in her hand. Whatever her task, she was so absorbed in it that she was unusually silent and, missing her voice, Gabriel looked over at her.

Onny held the shoe firmly and attentively in her left hand, and with her right hand she was carefully lining the inside of it with pieces of coloured paper from the floor. These fragments she chose carefully, bending down and scrutinizing them closely, as if to get one exactly suiting her requirements. These requirements must have been exact because from time to time she set down the shoe on the bed, and with her fingers, and occasionally with the aid of her sharp teeth, she tore the edges of the paper scraps to alter their shape. Gabriel was amused.

"Is this a new invention?"

"My shoes are worn through," said Onny. "They let in the wet. I'm putting paper soles in them to soak up the water and keep my feet dry."

Gabriel's amusement died away instantly. He was humiliated that she should have to resort to such methods.

"I'm sorry, Onny," he said.

"Oh, I don't mind," said Onny, putting on the shoe and taking off the other one. She began to line it with the same paper. "They look all right as long as the uppers are good. Nobody knows they're broken. At home I often wore shoes with no soles in them. I stuffed them with paper, but it was different there because in the church when I knelt down the people could see the soles, unless I knelt at the back of the church, and the back seat was always filled."

"The first money that I can spare I will buy you a pair of shoes, Onny," said Gabriel, still feeling contrite and humiliated. "I want you to have nice things, not just to appear to have them." But as he said this, he lifted his own foot, and displaying the sole of his own shoe, he smiled, for it was worn as thin as paper, and just then, as his finger pressed against it, the leather gave way and left a hole the size of his thumb.

"I think perhaps I may have to get you to do some cobbling for me too, Onny."

"Give them to me," said Onny good-humouredly. "I'll cut up more of this," and she leaned across the table and, taking a large untorn piece of the same gaudy paper that lay already on the floor in fragments, she began to shape it to the sizes she needed, glancing at his shoe as she did so. But Gabriel was glancing at the paper scraps.

"Where did you get the paper, Onny?" He took up a bit. "It is good and strong." He picked up another scrap. The texture of the paper was so thick it was almost like parchment. The colours were rich and deep, and they had been glazed to give an appearance of oils. The first thought that came into his mind was that this glossy surface would not soak the wet as quickly as ordinary paper. She was full of clever notions. Then a second thought flashed into his mind. He turned around and glanced at her with suspicion. He half opened his mouth to ask a question, but instead he bent down and picked up another fragment, and then another, and another, examining them closely and placing them edge to edge to try to gain a better idea of their original appearance before they were torn.

The first two pieces he had picked up showed only patches of colour, a brilliant red and a glaring blue. Placed together they had no more meaning than separately. On a third piece however there was a garish pink colour that might have represented human flesh. He stooped and without speaking began to gather up more of the fragments. Upon one of them there was a distinct representation of a human limb, possibly the forearm of a figure. Upon another there was the fragment of a hand. Then, straightening up, without needing to pick up any more of the picture, Gabriel knew that it was the gaudy, cheap print of the Virgin and Child with which Onny had irritated him on the night of the storm, when she clung to it for protection.

He raised his head slowly and looked at Onny. She had ceased to work at the shoe. Although he had said nothing she had seen after a minute or two that his interest in the torn scraps was deeper than the mere casual curiosity he had expressed when he first stooped and picked up one of them. A feeling of antagonism entered her as she watched him. What was wrong now, she wondered. Without waiting for him to say anything she broke out angrily.

"What is the matter now?"

"Isn't this your picture, Onny—the picture you made so much fuss about the other night?"

"What if it is? It's mine, isn't it? I can do what I like with my own things, I hope!"

Gabriel frowned, waiting for her to stop before he spoke, but she could not stop. She had started an avalanche of words.

"If I had a decent pair of shoes I wouldn't have to put paper in them."

Gabriel came over and stood beside her.

"Hush, Onny," he said. "Hush! Don't say anything you will regret."

"I regret nothing."

"I'm not blaming you, you know."

"I should hope not!"

He put his hand up gently to her mouth to silence her.

"I am not blaming you," he repeated deliberately, "but I want to ask you why you used your picture in this way?"

"I wanted paper! I told you that!"

"There was plenty of ordinary paper you could have used. Why did you choose to use this?"

"It's stronger than other paper," said Onny, "and it will keep out the wet better because it is glossy!"

Gabriel nodded his head. That was true enough, but he was not satisfied.

"I still think that you could have used ordinary paper, or cardboard. Cardboard would have been as good and better than this." He looked around the studio. On the floor there was an old art catalogue, with heavy glossed pages, "You could have used this!"

He was disconcerted by the situation. He had received a considerable shock at seeing the picture upon which she had set such value a few nights before, put now to so base and undignified a use.

Onny stared at him fiercely, her cheeks blazing, and her fists clenched. With one foot she kicked at the scraps remaining on the floor, and scattered them far and wide.

"You said yourself that it was only an ordinary piece of paper!"

Gabriel drew a deep breath. That was true. He had said that. He remembered his words exactly.

"You said it was cheap! You said it was hideous! You said it ought to be destroyed!"

Gabriel listened in humility. Then he turned slowly. As he moved, the loose scraps slipped from his fingers and fell to the floor. He rested his hands on her shoulders. She tried to shrug his hands away, but he pressed them down firmly and gently.

"You have repeated the words I used, Onny. You have repeated them correctly. I said those things. I admit them. And I am ready to stand by them." He pointed down at the scraps of the picture. "That picture was cheap. It was ugly. It should have been destroyed. So much for that. It might, and no doubt would, bring a certain amount of happiness and consolation to ignorant and uncultured people, as a representation of religious doctrines that they were unable to visualize for themselves, and so it might be tolerated were it not that good and decent pictures by real masters could be reproduced and sold so cheaply. Apart altogether however from the hideousness of the picture, there was another reason why, whether it was good or bad, it was not right for you to attach such power to it as you did on the night of the storm. It was only paper! And it was absurd for you to think that by holding a piece of paper in your hands you could have saved your life, if it had been ordained that you were to be killed. If at that moment you had clutched to your heart one of the finest masterpieces of art, it would still have been powerless to save you. It hurt me to see you acting so blindly in your terror. It hurt me to see you letting your reason become so abased."

Onny's anger had not abated.

"You told me to destroy it!" she said, reverting to the picture.

"I meant that too, Onny. I said that you should destroy it because I felt if the material object upon which you based your superstitions was destroyed, the superstitious impulses that made you value it would be destroyed too."

"Well! I did destroy it, didn't I? What are you making a song about? Why are you looking so queer?"

Gabriel's face wore indeed a strange sad expression.

"Yes, you destroyed it all right, Onny, but it is a pity that you should have chosen this way to destroy it. Why didn't you put it into the fire and burn it? Can't you see that there is all the difference in the world between destroying it deliberately, with dignity, because you felt that it no longer had the significance or value for you that it had when you were a child, and desecrating it in the way you have done?"

"I don't know what you're talking about!" said Onny, but he knew that she did.

"Do you remember, Onny, how vexed I was one day at home when my aunt took a book I was reading out of my hands and said that it was not fit for me to read?"

"I do," said Onny, not seeing any connection between this remark and those that went before, but hoping that the subject was going to be changed.

"Do you remember that she tore out the pages and gave them to you to scour the pots and pans in the kitchen with them?"

Onny nodded, but she also shrugged her shoulders. She was beginning to see an analogy between this incident and the incident of the picture.

Gabriel continued. "My aunt had a certain authority over me then. I was, as a matter of fact, old enough to have been able to choose my own reading matter, but I could perhaps have brought myself to realize that, having reared me since I was a small child, she had not noticed that I was no longer a child. In other words, I might have been able to forgive her for taking the book away from me, I might even have forgiven her for destroying it, but I will never forget my revulsion at the cheap and vicious way she tore it up page after page and gave the pages to you to scour the greasy kitchen pots with them." He shuddered. Then he looked at Onny. "What you did with that picture was just as cheap and just as vicious. If you accepted what I said to you as true, the night after the storm, then it was right for you to destroy the picture, but I cannot, I absolutely cannot, understand how your instinct did not prevent you from destroying it in a way that would have offended anyone for whom it might still have the false value it had for yourself such a short time ago!"

428

"Oh stop!" said Onny, sticking her fingers in her ears. "I'm tired of hearing the same old thing!" She caught up her shoe and shook it by the heel till it let fall a shower of gaudy bits of paper on the floor. "I don't see why you're making such a fuss. No one saw me!"

"That doesn't matter," said Gabriel.

"Oh, you're too exact! It's true as Sylvester says, you're as complicated as a tree. Now, I won't go out at all. I hope you're satisfied. I'll stay in. I'll stay in till it gets fine, and the streets get dry. I'll stay in for a week if I have to do it!"

She shook out the paper insoles from the other shoe and then, one after another, she threw the shoes across the room, with all her force. One after another the shoes hit the far wall with a crash, and fell on the floor. Onny climbed onto the bed in her stockinged feet, and, curling her legs under her, she pulled over her shell box and began to root in it with an absorption that cut him out of her existence.

Gabriel was about to break into the silence, when there was a quick knock on the door, and before they had called out to tell him to do so, Sylvester had come into the room.

"Is there anything wrong?" he asked, looking anxiously at Onny's pouted lips, and at her spoiled capricious attitude on the bed. Then he looked at Gabriel who stood dejectedly among the scattered bits of paper. Lastly he looked at the two small black shoes that lay upon the floor, one leaning up against the wainscot and the other lying in such a way that the heel pointed upward and the ragged hole in the sole was displayed with abandon.

"Have you been having a quarrel?" he asked. He picked up a shoe. "I heard this hitting against the wall." He laughed. "Did she throw it at you Gabriel?"

"We weren't quarrelling," said Gabriel, stiffly.

"Don't tell lies!" said Onny crossly, from the bed, and she glared with equal defiance at them both.

"I am on your side, Gabriel," said Sylvester jokingly, and throwing his arm across Gabriel's shoulder. "Without hearing any more I am on your side. In quarrels like this I always take the man's part. I find it safer to be the friend of the man than it is to be the friend of the woman!"

Gabriel disengaged himself from Sylvester's arm. Sylvester shrugged his shoulders.

"Since I am not needed as arbitrator I may as well retire," he said.

Onny straightened up.

"Don't go," she said. "Gabriel has just been abusing me for doing something that he told me himself to do!"

Sylvester came back into the room smiling.

"I knew it!" he said. "My dear Onny, have I not told you that the supposed virtues are all very unprofitable, and that the supposed vices, upon close inspection, often show that they are worth cultivating in moderation. Now you have seen for yourself how unprofitable the virtue of obedience can be! I suggest, as I have done before, that you accept my tutelage in exposing the fallaciousness of some of the other supposed virtues! And now, may I inquire the cause of the dispute?"

Onny pointed with her finger to the bits of paper on the floor. The tears that had not made their appearance during the actual scene with Gabriel threatened to fall so copiously now that she could not describe that scene for Sylvester. He put his hand into his pocket and pulled out a white handkerchief. This handkerchief had a border of fine hem-stitching and a faint fragrance was released from its fold when it was opened, but Sylvester seemed unaware of any oddity in being its possessor. He wiped Onny's eyes with the handkerchief, sitting down beside her on the bed. Onny submitted to this attention, sniffed once or twice and showed signs of ceasing to cry, when suddenly she noticed the lace on the handkerchief. She caught the corner of it and began to examine it with a surprised expression. Sylvester laughed and pulled it from her. He drew in a breath of its faint scent and folded it and put it into his pocket again.

"Come! Come!" he said. "If you found this in Gabriel's possession you might be justified in examining it, but you have no such rights over me, madam!"

He winked at Gabriel, but to his surprise Onny had burst into tears again, and this time her tears were not only more abundant, but more noisy.

Sylvester turned to Gabriel. He indicated the paper on the floor.

"What masterpiece is that I see torn to shreds?"

Onny ceased crying instantly and sprang up.

"I'll tell you," she cried. "I'll tell you. It's a holy picture I brought with me from home. It was hanging over my bed. My mother bought it for me at the Mission stall the day I was confirmed."

Sylvester had been idly picking up the scraps as she spoke, and trying to piece them together. He was barely listening to Onny, but when he heard her mention the Mission stall he opened his hands and contemptuously let the pieces fall again.

"Gabriel told me to destroy it," said Onny, taking up the story. "And I did. But it seems that he has changed his mind and when he saw it torn up, he lost his temper."

"I thought she would burn it," said Gabriel, "but instead she tore it up and put the pieces inside her shoes to keep out the damp."

He looked at Sylvester entreatingly, as if to implore that his opinion of Onny's conduct would be the same as his own. Sylvester threw back his head and began to laugh. He caught Onny's hands in his, and clasped them with delight.

"What a pupil you are, Onny! How I wish I had undertaken the tutoring of your soul. He tells you to destroy, and you not only destroy but desecrate. Oh, Onny! Oh, woman!" He turned to Gabriel. "What is your complaint?" he said. "She has only done what any woman would do. Women are never content with abstractions. They must make physical changes as well."

Gabriel had begun to pick up the pieces carefully.

"I could understand that," he said, "but I should imagine that she would listen to me when I told her that she had done wrong, that she had behaved cheaply." He held the pieces on the palm of his hand. "Is the stove alight in your room, Sylvester?" he asked. "I want to burn the picture now at least."

"The stove is alight and at your service," said Sylvester. Gabriel went towards the door. As he closed the door he heard Sylvester whisper something to Onny, and laugh again. This time Onny's own laughter rang and rippled through the louder laughter of her companion. Gabriel closed the door on the disagreeable laughter, but as he crossed the landing he heard footsteps run across the floor of the studio he had left, running with the peculiar heavy thudding of bare feet, and then Onny threw open the door, letting a flood of pale light out upon the dark landing. She called after him with a loud triumphant voice.

"Do you know what Sylvester said? He said that you were a fool."

But as Onny began to speak Sylvester ran across the room after her.

"Shut up, you little devil," he said. "I whispered that to you. You had no business repeating it out loud."

Onny laughed. Sylvester looked at Gabriel's haggard face which caught the full force of the light as he stood in the landing looking back at them framed in the doorway. With a rough arm he thrust Onny aside.

"Get back into the studio," he said, and he stepped out into the hall.

Onny gave a sharp exclamation.

"You stood on my foot," she said angrily, lifting her bare white ankle in her hand.

"I'm glad I did," said Sylvester, and he closed the door on her. He followed Gabriel into the other room and began to speak hurriedly.

"I'm sorry you heard what I said; I didn't mean you to hear it."

"Why did you say it?" asked Gabriel.

"Oh, I only said it to please her—the little fool. I didn't think she'd repeat it."

Gabriel put his hand to his head wearily.

"I might have been able to guide her," he said, "but now she will quote your remark."

431

Sylvester sat on the edge of the table.

"Why do you want to guide her? Why can't you let her alone? Why do you want to change her and make her different? You have no influence over her!"

"I influenced her when I took her away," said Gabriel.

Sylvester sighed. "How absurd that seems to me. You might as well say that I influenced her life indirectly, because it was I who first gave you the idea of coming here. I did not influence you. If you did not have the desire for liberty within yourself I could not have put it there. Our characters are like stones. They do not alter. We may roll from one place to another, but we do not alter. For me it would take from the dignity of the human being to think that we had such reciprocating influence over each other. I should hate to feel that I had ever exerted such influence. I should hate to feel such influence had ever been exerted over me. I see myself alone always. You, on the other hand, you always see yourself in relation to other people. But Onny is not like you. She is like me. She sees herself always as an isolated person. She has never been influenced by you. Surely you must see that? Onny was always strong and selfish. She knew what she wanted always. You gave her the opportunity of breaking her bonds. But she had no intention of submitting to other bonds. She has her own ideas. She is determined to go her own way." Sylvester stood up. "I think I'll go back and see her," he said, his old manner establishing itself. "I think she said I stood on her foot. Did you hear her say that, or was I dreaming? The poor child. Do you know, Gabriel, I have an affection for that child that you are incapable of, with your high ideas for her spiritual welfare." He paused. "You see, to me she is just a little servant; no more or no less."

As he uttered these last words Sylvester stared defiantly at Gabriel, but Gabriel made no protest. He knew that under the rude words there were both compassion and common sense.

"Tell her I'm sorry I lost my temper," he said. "I won't go back to her just now. I don't want to see her until I feel calmer. I want to think things over. I think I'll go out for a walk."

The rain still fell as Gabriel crossed the street and went into Stephen's Green. The gardens were deserted and bare.

It is on a wet day that a public park is seen to the best advantage. Then only is it seen as the architect designed it, with its symmetrical arrangements of parterre and statuary. Then the cinder paths and alleyways gleam darkly, and show up their clear and definite design against the rain-washed grasses.

Clean and rain-washed, too, are the trees and fancy shrubbery, the shafted foliage of the plants, and the little green metal seats and benches. The flowers in their various star-shaped plots are bright with an almost

432

unbearable brilliance, and the eye seeks relief from the strain that is put upon it by such brilliance, and turns to stare at the black clay from which the flowers spring, and at the wet clay that has splashed halfway up their stems, even splattering the petals here and there. On the greenswards the black clay relieves the brilliance of the grass, and around the bases of the trees, where lovers have wandered and children have chased each other in rings, there are wide circles of the same wet clay.

On a wet day, too, the grey plaster statues, the memorial tablets, the ornamental fountains, the bandstands and stone seats, are clear to the eye in every detail of their carving and construction. Usually they are smothered with children clambering over them. Now they are washed and purified by the rain. But nowhere perhaps is the benefit of the rain more manifest than where it falls upon the black wooden shelters, so dismal in fine weather, but gleaming now like ebony. In fine weather these shelters are covered with dust and littered within with fallen leaves. They are made use of only by children, who run in and out of their dismal shade with such fleet flashing legs that they could not be said to waste any greater quantity of sunlight in their visits than do the skimming swallows when they dart under the barn eaves from moment to moment upon mysterious errands that are woven inextricably into the pattern of their blue flight. In fine weather, also, there is oftentimes a poor idiot sitting in the dismal depths of these shelters, crossing his thumbs, and smiling at the floor, the very fact that he sits there, while the sun radiates without, as sure a sign as his white face and swollen limbs that he is bereft of wits.

But in wet weather these shelters are empty. They gleam with rain. Their ebony boards are blacker than the wet clay around their entrance.

Gabriel wandered along, watching the rain as it fell upon the surface of the artificial lakes, striking the water irregularly as if invisible fingers played upon it as upon the keyboard of a pianoforte.

There was no sound except the light tinkle of the drops that fell through the trees. All else was still. There was an emptiness about the public gardens that suggested a stage setting in the breathless moment after the curtain has just risen, before the actors appear, when the audience is left for an instant alert with their expectancy of the events about to happen.

Gabriel walked along, heedless of the rain, his thoughts confused and weary. He went over in his mind the scene that had just been enacted in the studio. At one moment it seemed that he had made too much of a small matter, but another moment it seemed that the significance of what had happened was even more serious than he thought at first.

In the end, however, walking along the wet cinder paths, the drops of water falling from the trees, he decided that he must make some effort to divert the direction upon which he had set Onny's feet. If he had exposed her to danger, he must take her away from it again.

The rain ceased. It ceased suddenly. The clouds, which had not been very heavy, began to rift and break, and through them the blue sky shone. A brittle sun crackled over the drenched leaves. And at once, from different gates, all converging upon the centre of the park as if they were players who had been standing in the wings waiting their cue, came the laughing and gesticulating people of the city, the women in costumes of lilac and blue, paler than the flowers, fluttering and flowing; the nurse-maids with their white veils flying, the children with lolloping curls and flashing legs; and two Sisters of Charity leading a long line of orphans in black clothes with red belts and red caps. Gabriel could no longer think there quietly. He went towards a narrow path intending to go out by a side gate. On this narrow path the rain still dripped from the trees, and as it fell the sunlight glinted in the drops. Gabriel had only gone a few paces down this path when suddenly, at the end of it, he saw Helen.

Along she came, serene among the crowding people, set apart from them by the dignity of her gait, which instantly, even in the crowded gardens made her conspicuous among the hurrying people around her. She was dressed in blue, with a capelet of some white slippery waterproof over her shoulders. Her head was bare, and over it she held an umbrella of some pale dove-coloured silk through which the steel ribs of the frame were clearly seen. Over her face this umbrella cast its scalloped shadow.

It seemed certain that she would see him. When they both took another pace or two forward they would be within speaking distance. But, a moment after he had first seen her, Helen had become aware that she was the only one in the park with her umbrella open. She glanced up at the sky and while she glanced upwards she held the umbrella down at her side like a great upturned flower of tenuous silk petals. She had apparently been walking for some time, screened by her thoughts, and as Gabriel watched he saw that the front of her hair was sprinkled with fine rain that lay upon it like seed pearls. Satisfied that the rain was over, she picked up the umbrella, and, extending her hands in the long gesture of closing the umbrella, she gave her simple occupation all her attention, and unconsciously displayed that grace of body which results when every limb seems to co-ordinate in order to achieve the perfection of a gesture to which perhaps the hand alone might have attended with sufficiency.

Gabriel felt a piercing sadness enter his heart. There are some gestures, slight, unimportant, like the threading of a needle, the raising of an arm to draw across a curtain, the folding or opening of a parasol, or the gesture with which pins in the hair are adjusted by slight pressure of the palms of the hand to either side of the face, which, slight as they are, startle us by the new quality they take on with each individual who performs them, while the heart does not forget the pitiful universality of the common needs that underlie them. Such gestures, at once familiar and unfamiliar, pierce the heart with a double shaft. So Gabriel watched Helen, as her hands stretched outwards to close the silk umbrella. And it came to him in that moment, with a piercing, drenching sweetness, that he loved her. Instinctively he advanced towards her, but all at once he remembered himself, and he remembered Onny, and he stopped in his stride. For an hour he had been walking up and down, undecided as to what he should do about Onny; now in a flash he knew. Taking one last look at Helen, where she stood with bent head fastening the clasp of the umbrella, he turned on his heel and went back into the centre of the park to leave it by another path. He had been afraid that Onny would stray from under his protection. Now the danger was doubled; for he might be glad that she should stray. But the past was not to be undone so easily. He would marry Onny at once.

∽ ∽ ∽

When Gabriel reached the apartment, his excitement at the decision he had taken was almost overwhelming. The feeling of guilt that, unadmitted, hung heavy over him all the last few months had banished almost at once, as the summer trees, thick and coarsened with dust, had been washed sweet with the recent rains. He ran up the stairs, two at a time, the exertion and the excitement in his heart making him breathless.

When he reached the landing, before he threw open the door of the studio he was daunted for a moment by the thought that Sylvester might still be within, but he heard a sound of fat frizzling noisily on a pan, and through a crack in the door of Sylvester's room, the odour of Sylvester's evening meal came streaming.

Gabriel threw open the door of the studio. Onny was still on the bed, her legs curled under her, and her arms around her knees. She was doing nothing, and her eyes seemed filled with reflection, darkened and heavy. Even in the instant that he was crossing the room, he noticed their dilated appearance, but he rushed forward and took her hands in his. Onny looked up indolently.

"I hope you are going to apologize?" she said, and began to withdraw her hands.

They were moist and warm, and holding them, Gabriel thought impulsively of the cool white hands that he had watched so lately, as they fastened an umbrella. He thought too of the cold plaster hands of the statues in the park, wet with rain. But he held tightly to Onny's warm hands, and, looking from them to the eyes that were looking up at him sullen and resentful, he was again aware that in spite of her anger there was in her face a return of the warmth and richness that had characterized her in the old days. As he stared at her, a flicker of interest came into her eyes.

"Yes, Onny, I have come to apologize; but not for what happened this afternoon."

"For what then?"

A slight embarrassment came over him. He let her hands drop and looked down at the ground.

"I want to apologize for something that happened a long time ago." As he said the words they seemed inadequate and absurd. He was using the language with which he would have sought pardon for some trivial error of social life. He plunged on again. "I did you a great wrong, Onny. I should never have brought you here, but, since I did, we should at least have been married!"

Onny did not move.

"Onny, we must be married now." Suddenly he wanted to feel her arms around him. He stretched them out to her. He must shield her, and she must shield him from the dangers into which they had strayed together.

"We will be married at once; at once. Onny, you will be my wife!"

Over and over again he said the words that brought with them such relief. Over and over he said them, and stared, while he spoke, at her hands, her rounded childish knees, her hips and her full rich breasts, for with his intention to marry, it seemed that her limbs and flesh had been blessed, and that in them henceforth he would know a new sweetness. And then, he lifted his eyes to her face. To his astonishment her face was distorted with anger. Her lips were compressed and her eyes blazed. Unaccountably, before a word was spoken, a feeling of absolute terror came over him. He stared at her. Whatever had angered her? Onny was for a moment unable to move, her limbs were stiffened into a rigid cast. Then, suddenly uncurling her legs from under her, she sprang to the floor, and faced him.

"So, you know! You found out!" She was beside herself. She threw a glance of hatred at him. "Who told you?" she screamed. "You wouldn't have the wits to find out for yourself. Who told you?"

Gabriel, although used to her tempers, felt there was a depth of hatred in her words that he had never sounded before. He moved back from her. The bright saliva gleamed between her teeth and when she spoke it bubbled in the corners of her lips. Those lips were moistened like the petals of a poisonous flower. There are insects with exquisite colouring and markings, silver-skinned and dappled with jewelled scales, that appear beautiful and good, yet, let them but flick for a moment in the air the thin forked tongue of their venom, and then, strong as we are, healthy, and filled with the richness of life, and small, frail, and weak as the creature is, we recoil with suddenness, and a fainting of the heart comes over us, the blood flies from the flesh and the hands chill; for, stronger than reason, stronger than the evidence of the eyes, there is the lightning warning of the instinct that in that tongue there is lethal poison.

So Gabriel drew back from the venomous words that Onny spat at him. And only from a distance, staring fascinatedly at her in her paroxysm of anger, did he listen to the actual words that she hissed at him, the saliva winking and pearling on her lips and gleaming between her teeth.

"You knew it. You found out! And now you think you'll trick me!"

Gabriel stared in stupefaction.

"What do you mean?" he managed to ask.

"You think you'll marry me, and then you'll be able to order me about. You'll say you have legal right over me. Oh, I know your game!"

Gabriel did not know what was in her mind, but was resolved to find out.

"Why should I want to order you about, Onny?"

Onny was trembling with anger. Her face worked with rage.

"Try to pretend that you don't know!"

"Don't know what?" Gabriel's voice rose on the last word.

For one moment it occurred to Onny that he was sincere and that her secret was still safe, if she said no more, but she had lashed her anger forward and could no longer now control it.

"You needn't try to pretend you don't know. I suppose Sylvester told on me."

"What does Sylvester know that I do not know!"

"Sylvester isn't the only one that knows. Telman knows! Everyone knows!"

"Knows what?"

"That I'm going to have a child."

Onny spat out the words with the last breath that her rage had left in her tightened body, and then she threw herself on the bed again, and burst into a fever of crying.

Gabriel stood silent, heart-struck. Before the great gust of emotion that rushed over him unprepared, he felt a weakness in his limbs that made him look around for somewhere to sit. He sat down on the edge of the bed where Onny lay, dipping the thin sagging mattress down to one side. Overwhelmed, unable to speak for a moment, he looked at the sobbing Onny, and in his strange curiosity at the new life concealed within her, he felt no curiosity at the way she had announced her news to him, nor at those terrible strangling tears that now shook her. He put out a hand to her.

"Onny dear, I don't know what to say."

At his words she sat up suddenly, her face wet and blotchy, and her eyelashes matted and sticky with tears. She wanted to see the effect of her

437

news upon him. It appeared to be the effect that she had anticipated. With a hand, wet still from her tears, she struck at his outstretched hand and beat it back.

"It doesn't matter what you say," she said. "Oh, I know what you'll say all right. I was warned. Sylvester and Telman and the others, they all told me what to expect. They knew how you'd take this. They said you'd be glad!"

Gabriel let pass the fact that those others were in her confidence before himself.

"Can it be possible that you are not glad yourself, Onny?" he said, half rising and sinking back with a return of the dread he had first felt when he came into the room.

"Glad? Glad?" Onny almost shrieked the words. Then in a different tone, sinking to a level so calm that it was like a dead voice, she stared at him straight between the eyes. "I'm not going to have this child! Do you hear? I'm not going to have it! That's why I wasn't going to tell you anything about it. Everyone warned me that you'd act like a fool, that you'd be delighted, that you'd go against me." Her voice rose again, and she rose herself, towering over him. "But you have no control over me. Do you hear? I'm not your wife! You have no rights over me; I am free. I can do what I like." She came closer to him. "You thought you'd play a cheap trick on me. You thought you'd get me to marry you, and then, when you had legal control over me, you'd make me do as you said. You'd make me have this child, and get ugly and lose my figure, and have to give up modelling, and give up earning money. You've been jealous of the money I earned. But I was too clever. I saw through you." Slapping him suddenly on the side of the face she ran across the room and, pulling out the carpetbag from under the couch, she began to run around the room, gathering up her clothes and her possessions and pushing them, crushed and unfolded, into the bag. "You're no more to me than those plaster heads!" she said, as she kicked one of them out of her way. "I'm going to leave here. I'm sick of this place anyway. I'm sick of you. You promised so much! What did you give me? I thought we were coming here to be out of the way of the old interfering preachers that we were sick of hearing at home. I was going to tell you so today when you were preaching about the picture. I was going to tell you a hundred times, but I'm glad I waited till now. I'm glad I waited till I told you about the child. So, you'd love to have the child, would you? Well, you won't. I'm glad you won't. I'm glad I can do that much to you, because I hate you. I hate all men!" She threw another handful of soiled linen into the carpetbag.

"Onny, you cannot do this." Gabriel went across and tried to drag the bag out of her hand. "You cannot leave me. Married or not you belong to me. You cannot do this."

"Let go." She dragged at the bag. "I have my mind made up. You couldn't stop me. If you had arms of iron you couldn't hold me."

Gabriel let go.

"It's not with my arms I want to hold you, Onny. I want you to think of the awful thing that you are doing. What you are thinking of doing is so terrible that I cannot bear to think of it. I am confused and bewildered. I am not able to think of arguments with which to prevail over you. But surely your own instinct tells you it is a terrible sin?"

Onny knelt down on the floor to fasten the clasp of the carpetbag.

"Who are you to talk about sin?" she cried, flashing a look of scorn at him. "According to you there was no such thing as sin a year ago. A year ago it was a sin to get married. Now it's a sin not to get married. A little while ago it was a sin to look at my holy picture, that I had over my bed, and kiss it; then it was a sin to destroy it. Who are you to talk about sin? You don't know your mind for two minutes."

Gabriel bowed his head. The truth of her words stung him so that tears came to his eyes.

"You have a bitter tongue, Onny. It finds out the sore spot and stings. But there is truth in what you say. Your accusations against me are just, but I was very young. We were both very young. Oh, Onny, we were so young!" She shrugged her shoulders. He stood up. "But we are still young!" he cried. "And all that we have done wrong so far is remediable. I beg of you, Onny, do not do anything that cannot be undone. This thing that you have in your mind to do can never be undone. All the days of your life will be embittered by useless remorse. Think! Onny, think! What you are going to do can never never never be undone."

"I'll never want it undone!"

"I beg of you to wait. If you believe that I have no claim over you I declare before God that I will let you decide that for yourself freely, if only you wait. Wait and think. Wait I implore you, and do not act rashly."

When he said that he declared before God, she sneered with her lips, but when he begged her to wait, and to take time, she lost her temper again.

"I can't wait," she said. "If I wait much longer it will be too late. I've waited too long as it is!"

At these words he lost heart.

"Oh, God!" he cried, and he put his head down upon his arms. "Oh, God! Onny, can you not see that this is terrible?"

"What is so terrible about it? It's done all over the world. It's quite common."

"It's a most deadly sin!"

"Sin! There is no such thing as sin!"

"Don't say that, Onny. You don't know what you're talking about!"

439

"I know as well as you do!"

"Onny, if you will not believe me when I tell you that what you are doing is a terrible, foully evil deed, will you not think of the way this deed will come between us? How can I ever look at you again? How could I ever bear to see the sight of you, if you did this thing? Think of these things. Think of the future. I will do anything you ask me if only you do not do this evil deed." A new idea struck him. "We will go home, Onny. I never thought that I would go back, but everything is different now. Now I would go back for your sake, for the sake of our child. My aunts will forgive me. All the old objections to you will be forgotten. You look so nice, Onny. Our visit here has done a great deal for you. We need never regret it. And before we go back I will buy you beautiful clothes and some brooches and rings; whatever you like. My Aunt Sara will send me money. I know she will. She would have sent it at any time, but I was too proud to take it. Now, I would not be too proud. Now I would do anything for you! And when we go home we will have a fine house, and I know it will be a long time yet before I come into my grandfather's property, but we can have money advanced to us. And anyway, we will not feel the time passing and we can bring up this child to a wonderful life, a much better life than either of us ever had!"

Onny listened to him, as if she measured her price with every word, but when he had finished, her lips curled downwards and she looked at him contemptuously.

"I wouldn't go back to that little town now, for all the money in the world! No, Gabriel Galloway! I'm finished with that life. I'm never going back there! Never! Never! Do you hear that? Never!"

Her voice had risen to such a pitch that it seemed as if the thin green glass of the skylight over their heads shivered and tinkled in its cracked putty frame. She rushed across the room and, opening the carpetbag, she dragged a coloured handkerchief out of it and tied it over her disordered hair. Then she picked up the bag, but a minute afterwards, capriciously, she threw down the bag on the floor, kicked it, and without any luggage ran to the door, and opening it ran out onto the landing, giving the door a violent push so that it shut with a crash behind her as Gabriel rushed to follow. When he opened the door she was running madly down the flight of steep, dark steps to the street. Gabriel rushed headlong towards the stairs himself, but before he reached them, an arm shot out of the darkness and Sylvester, barring his passage with one arm, caught him around the waist with the other, and with all his energy held him pressed back against the wall.

"I was waiting for this all the week," he said, ignoring Gabriel's struggles. "I tried to warn you this afternoon. I knew how things would be. I warned Onny too!"

"Let me go." Gabriel struggled more fiercely.

"Why?"

"I must stop her!"

"How can you do that in the street, if you could not do it in there?" He nodded with his head towards the open studio. "She would call assistance. She would say that you were following her, that you were annoying her. She might even say that you were a stranger, that you were nothing at all to her, and in a sense she would be right. She is nothing to you." As Gabriel tried to speak Sylvester continued hastily. "And if you did succeed in stopping her today she would only sneak away from you another day. She will not have this child. On that she is determined. Nothing you can say or do will alter her decision."

Gabriel felt that Sylvester's words were only too true. He relaxed a little and leaned back against the wall for support.

"If she had been my wife it would have been different," he said, weakly.

"Don't be a fool," said Sylvester. "If she was married to you ten times over she would do what she had gone to do. I know her type. I know it inside out!"

In spite of his feeling of exhaustion Gabriel asserted himself in her defence.

"I cannot listen to you speaking about her like this," he said.

"Why not?" said Sylvester. "Be honest! she is nothing to you. She has repudiated any claim you had on her! She has flaunted her defiance of you. She has shown you that you have no authority over her. She has shown you that she is nothing to you! A selfish woman; she wants her pleasure at small cost." He lit a cigarette. "But it is my belief that the experience she will go through today will chasten her. She will be a different girl when she comes back to you!"

Gabriel started. "When she comes back? Do you think I would tolerate her under the same roof with me after this?"

Sylvester smiled. He moved over towards his own part of the landing and laid his hand on the knob of his own door.

"How complicated everything is to you idealists! A little while ago you were belabouring me with your cries that she belonged to you, and that neither book nor bell nor priest, pulpit, jury, or judge, could make her any more yours than you considered her to be before God. Yet, at the first transgression, you are ready to cast her off from you with a shudder. Now I, for my part, would have regarded the whole thing differently. I would have found the problem simple, and the solution of it still more simple. I would have said, 'To hell with her! She is a human being, as strong and free as I am myself. Let her go her way. Let her make her choice. Let her damn herself in her own way!' But you say that she is bound to you, that her sins are your sins, that her actions are due to your influence, and so on, and so on! In that case, if you are to be consistent you should take her back. Remember too that when she returns, probably greatly disillusioned and frightened, she will need your help as she never needed it before. Then she will need love. Then she will need, above all, a roof over her head." Having said this, Sylvester turned abruptly on his heel, and opening the door of his room went in, banging the door.

Gabriel turned back into the empty studio and sat down on the couch, looking at the litter of clothes and odds and ends that Onny had left strewn about the room, and at the red carpetbag worked with pink roses in crude cross-stitch, which gaped open on the floor, some of its contents spilled out on the floor since she had rooted in it for the handkerchief she had tied over her hair.

ᔕ ᔕ ᔕ

As the day passed and Onny did not return, Gabriel gradually began to worry about her in spite of himself. Late that night, when there was still no word of her, a thousand regrets sprang up within him: that he had opposed her so bitterly, that he had not tried to show some sympathy with her, and win her confidence, before he reasoned with her. He should have considered her weaknesses and appealed to her emotions. And where he had previously recoiled from seeing her again, it now seemed unnatural that she should not return to him.

"Why didn't I tell her to come back to me? Why was I so hard?"

These and a thousand other questions he hurled at Sylvester twenty times in the day, and again in the long cold night that he sat at the window in Sylvester's room while Sylvester, although not sleeping either, lay in his shirt sleeves on the coverlet of the unopened bed.

As the second day came without any news of her, Sylvester began a long worried vigil on his own account. He was baffled at her complete disappearance. On his own account too, profiting by knowledge that Gabriel did not possess, and which he had spared him from acquiring, Sylvester made inquiries all over Dublin, in the hope of getting some news of Onny. But he could not find her, and his difficulties were increased by the fact that those from whom he sought information were unreliable, those who were quickest in assuring him that they knew nothing of her being the least reliable of all. Then, too, whatever chance there had been of getting information in the beginning, as time passed those chances grew less. People did not want to be associated with an affair that might prove unlucky.

Although he had not seen her, Gabriel knew that Helen's help had been sought by Sylvester. He knew that she had been to the studio several times, but he had not met her. Each time she had come he had been out walking the streets. He only came back to the studio when he was too exhausted to walk any more. And when he came back he always made the same inquiry.

"Did you hear anything?"

On these occasions Sylvester was sometimes able to persuade him to eat something, but never able to make him rest. On the evening of the third day Gabriel had just gone out again when Sylvester heard Helen's footsteps on the stairs. He went out to the landing. She was white-looking and tired, but she had come with a suggestion.

"I think we should go to see Telman again," she said.

"We were there already today," said Sylvester.

"I know that. But I have been thinking it over. Telman would be sure to have seen her condition before anyone; he has a quick eye, and, painting her, he would notice the least change in her, even a psychological change in expression. It's most likely that he would have flown into a temper if he had planned a picture for which she would be an indispensable model. And if Onny too showed disappointment, he might easily, through selfishness, have given the information she unconsciously sought. Or she might have got that information from another of his models. Such information is common enough with them."

Sylvester nodded his head in curt agreement with the last sentence. He had seen that Helen attached some importance to her suggestion, and that a faint ray of hope shone in her face. It was more to preserve that pale hope for a time, than from any conviction that it was justified, that he had nodded his agreement with her words. After a moment's thought he stood up. Her suggestion would give them something to do anyway, which was better than sitting down waiting for they knew not what.

"Come, so!" he said. "We will go over to Telman's studio right now and question him more closely. We could watch him more closely too, at the same time, and see if he is telling the truth!"

She nodded her head, and they went down the stairs together.

They walked along, jostling the crowds on the pavement, their own silence supplemented from time to time by the scattering fragments of other people's talk that floated on the air, and the broken chords of music from indoor cafés when the swing shutters swayed open for a moment to let someone in or out. Voices and faces, phrases and tunes, smiles, leers, and jostling elbows seemed to fill the world.

Once, as they walked along, Sylvester spoke.

"So many people!" he said. "In this small quarter of a single city, so many people! It hardly seems reasonable to spend so much energy and time looking for one single soul where so many abound."

Helen said nothing.

"One time you would have reacted violently against such a remark," said Sylvester. "Now you are unmoved. Now you are indifferent."

They were getting near to Telman's studio. Sylvester slackened his pace. Helen, however, continued to walk briskly.

"There is no need to talk about ourselves," she said.

Instantly Sylvester increased his pace. His face expressed a momentary irritation, but it was irritation with himself, not with her. A moment later he spoke again, casually, as if indeed he were at that moment breaking the silence for the first time.

"This fellow may not be in his studio," he said.

But there was a light high up. Telman was there. They turned into the doorway that led up to the studio, and ran up the stairs, impatient to question him.

Telman was working on a picture, and when they came in he asked them to excuse him while he finished a detail that was giving him trouble.

"We can't wait!" said Sylvester. "We're in a hurry. We want to ask you a few questions."

"What have I to tell you?" said Telman challengingly, turning back from the easel, but immediately turning towards it again, and wielding his brush furiously upon a different corner of the canvas from that upon which he had been working a moment before.

The glimpse they got of his face was sufficient for his visitors, however, for in that momentary glimpse they read the facile face, and knew that there was something on the painter's mind. From the nervous way his eyes searched their faces they knew that he suspected the object of their late visit. The planned phrases with which they were to trap him into a betrayal of his knowledge were unnecessary.

"We came to ask you about Onny," said Helen at once. "You have heard some news of her?"

"Onny? Why should I hear news of her? Why should I know anything about her? Gabriel was here a while ago asking the same question. Why are you all pestering me about her? What do I know about her? I am at work on an important picture. I don't want to be tormented in this way. I cannot work unless I have peace!"

Sylvester stepped forward. "The quickest way to end your torment, the quickest way to get peace, is to give us the information we want. In the name of God what are you afraid of, Telman? Nobody is going to blame you. If anything has happened to Onny you will not be involved. Indeed it might be said that, according to your lights, you thought you were doing her a good turn!"

As Sylvester said the last words he put out his hand and patted Telman on the shoulder encouragingly. He did this for a variety of reasons: partly because he wanted to encourage him to confide in them, partly to create an atmosphere of casualness, but partly also for an involuntary feeling of pity for the man. This pity was justified at the moment for at the touch of the friendly reassuring hand the great creature went to pieces at once. He snatched Sylvester's hand and held it in his own great iron grip, till Helen saw the white streaks radiate from Sylvester's knuckles as the blood fled from the surface of the skin under the violent pressure of the clasp.

"Yes, yes, that is it. That is true," he cried, snatching at the excuses that had been put into his mouth. "As long as you guessed the truth I may as well tell you. It was she herself who made me promise not to tell. As you say, I thought I was doing her a good turn. She was in a terrible state. She was crying and stamping her feet."

"When?" said Helen, quietly.

Telman turned towards her quite naturally and answered :

"When I said that she wouldn't be any more use to me as a model."

Sylvester glanced swiftly at Helen and saw, as he had expected, that her contempt was beginning to express itself on her face. With the tip of his shoe he gave her an admonitory tap on the ankle. He himself turned to Telman and took up the job of questioning him.

"She stamped her feet, you say? She cried?"

Telman spread out his hands.

"I have never seen anyone so upset. I pitied her so much. She was so young! She was so unhappy! She begged me to tell her something she could do to get out of her difficulties."

As, with his great ability to paint, he was nevertheless unable to choose suitable subjects for his brush, so now, having been unable to find a way to treat this affair, the way being once given to him, he entered into it with his whole heart, and where before he had been uncertain, shifting, frightened, he was now wholly and entirely a victim of the moods he had induced in himself, and as he spoke the tears came into his eyes, his voice thickened with feeling, and he kept glancing involuntarily at the empty dais where Onny evidently sat when she posed for him. Involuntarily Sylvester and Helen turned towards the dais too, and staring at its empty blocks, on which a few rags of dirty gauze drapery lay discarded, so vivid were the words of the painter that they too could almost imagine that they saw Onny crouched there, as she must have done upon the day which he was describing.

"Why didn't she tell Gabriel?" asked Helen. "Was it by your advice that she did not?"

"Ach, Gabriel!" said Telman. "He would have put some obstacle to the arrangement."

"Don't you think that he had the right to put such obstacles?"

"Why?"

Telman looked around at Helen. It seemed for a moment that he was going to ponder upon this. Sylvester took a hand again. He must be played on through his feelings and through visual memories of the day in which they were interested. If he began to think, he might regain some cunning.

"She wouldn't have listened to Gabriel anyway. She was very headstrong," said Sylvester.

The danger was past. Telman grabbed eagerly at this further exoneration of himself that he saw in the character of Onny.

"Ah, yes. She was very headstrong. I knew that. I told her what she was going to do was very dangerous. I told her there might be trouble. I told her she mustn't blame me if there was trouble; but she was very headstrong. She shouted at me. That was the time she stamped her feet. 'Give the address to me, you fool!' she said."

In a quiet voice, almost as if he had lost interest in the story, Sylvester spoke again, walking over to the dais as he spoke, and lifting the pieces of drapery.

"What did she say when you gave her the address?"

He moved back to Telman again. Telman was staring at the dais.

"She snatched it from me. It was written on a piece of paper. She snatched it from me, and stuck it in the neck of her dress."

"And then?"

Sylvester's voice was getting quieter and quieter. Raising her head, Helen listened to the noises out in the street. There, too, the silence was gathering. The revellers were departing, some to their homes, and those who were still intent on turning night into day were departing to the places where they might be sheltered from the chill that had come into the night air.

"Then she took her coat from the back of the door," said Telman, and he pointed to the empty nail.

"Did she say anything?"

"She said 'Good-bye till the next day.' "

He stared at the door and then his gaze, heavy and weary, came back to the dais and rested there. Sylvester looked at Helen. Having made great progress, they were almost afraid to venture further, but they had not yet extracted the information they needed.

"Where did you send her?"

Telman remained staring at the dais. He did not answer.

"Did you hear me?" said Sylvester.

Telman spoke in a low voice. They bent their heads to hear better, but he was muttering something that did not seem to concern the matter.

Helen pulled Sylvester's sleeve.

"He thinks he's talking to her!" she said, in an awed voice.

"To whom?"

"To Onny! He thinks she is there." Helen shrank back and clutched

Sylvester's arm. "Oh, Sylvester, he sees her there, where we see only the empty dais!" Helen put up her hands to her face. "I always felt that his vision was abnormal," she said, shuddering again, "that he did not see things as other people saw them!"

"Do you mean that he is mad?" said Sylvester, speaking out loud, as if there were no danger that Telman would either understand or hear him.

"No, not exactly. But his imagination is so terrible. Do you remember how he painted things in different colours from the colours we saw them? I used to think at times it was affected and showy, but now I believe that he really saw them in those colours, while we saw them as thousands of others saw them."

"And now?"

"Now, at this minute he sees Onny there, because all these days and nights he has been thinking about her with such concentration; because he has been frightened in case anything happened to her."

She looked with distaste at the muttering man, and began to back towards the door. Sylvester hesitated for a moment as if he would follow her, and then he became firm again.

"We must make him give us that address," he said. "We can't go yet!" He went over to the artist and threw his arms around him. "I'm sorry for you, Telman. You thought you were doing the girl a good turn. I understand. We can't always be the best judges of our own actions."

Staring into his eyes to catch the first return of normal gaze in them, he began to pat him on the back, increasing the pressure of the slaps upon the great bent shoulder until he set up a certain activity in the circulation of the great body, and a certain glow began to appear in the pale bloated face. The muttering stopped, and the eyes became brighter. Quietly Helen had gone to the window and thrown it up till the chill air came into the room. Then, going into the back room, she found a glass and filled it with water. Bringing this out she went over to Telman smilingly and held it out to him.

"Take a drink of this, Telman. It's cool and fresh."

Stretching out one hand Telman took the glass, his hot hand instantly misting the outside. At once, upon contact with the chilled glass, he gave a sharp shudder and a minute later he regained the normal attitude with which they were familiar.

"Hello, Helen," he said, as if seeing her for the first time, and then, looking intently at the glass of water before raising it to his lips and sipping it, he turned to Sylvester. "Have I been ill? I don't seem to remember clearly. Why are you and Helen here?" He glanced at Helen again, and made a vague gesture towards the other end of the room. "There are chairs," he said. "Please sit down. Will you have something to drink?" He looked again at the glass of water in his own hand. "Did I take a weakness?" He glanced rapidly at the easel that stood idle. "I often get faint after painting too long."

"Sit down. You're all right," said Sylvester, and he himself sat down on the edge of the dais. Helen remained standing. "You weren't painting," said Sylvester. "We were talking about Onny. You were telling us about giving her an address. I want to get that address from you, Telman."

Telman, with the glass held up to his mouth, paused and lowered it.

"You needn't be afraid," said Sylvester. "You won't be drawn into it."

Helen held her breath.

"They won't like being pestered with questions," said Telman at last, in a tone that implied that he was going to give them the address, but that he was first warning them how to treat the addressee.

"Leave that to me," said Sylvester.

"It's no place to bring Helen," said Telman, glancing around at her.

"It was no place for Onny," said Helen.

Telman shrugged his shoulders. Sylvester made a sign to Helen.

"Hurry and get the address," he said. "It's getting late."

Telman went into another room, and came back a few moments later with a stump of red pencil and a piece of wallpaper torn from the wall, where it had flapped loose.

"Here is the address."

Sylvester stretched out a hand for it, calm, casual.

"Keep my name out of this," said Telman, as they began to go towards the door. And then, as he held the door open, as an afterthought he caught Sylvester's sleeve. "Why are you interfering in this? Why don't you let it drop? What do you want to get mixed up in it for? They won't give you any information when they didn't give it to me."

Already out on the landing, Helen swung around. Sylvester gave an exclamation.

"Why didn't you say that before? What did you hear? When did you get in touch with them?"

Telman retreated into the room backwards.

"Today," he said, retreating more and more.

"What did they say then?" said Sylvester, following him step by step.

"They said she left there yesterday," said Telman. "They didn't hear anything more about her." And then, with a hideous relapse into his previous mesmeric state, he turned back towards the dais. "I only did what I thought was right. I only wanted to help," he said, but they felt he was not speaking to them.

Helen and Sylvester went towards the door. Before they went out on to the landing they looked back over their shoulders once. Telman was still talking, oblivious of their presence, and his great hands were outstretched as he advanced nearer and nearer, with words of placation and endearment, to the empty dais, with its vacant drapery and its pale treachery of shadows.

When they were outside, Helen spoke.

"Yesterday? Where can she be gone? Oh, Sylvester, if she didn't go back to Gabriel something dreadful must have happened to her!" Then her hope rose again. "Perhaps she might not have liked to go back to him. She might have had some delicacy of feeling about it."

Sylvester sneered. "What delicacy of feeling could she have had after doing what she did? No, I'm afraid that Onny would not have hesitated to go back to him if it had suited her to do so. I'm afraid that something must have happened to her. I don't like the way Telman urged us not to interfere. He must have been given the same warning himself by these people"—he indicated the name which was scrawled on the paper in his hand. "They must have felt unsure about her condition when they let her go."

"But if they were unsure about her condition, they would not have let her away, alone, through the streets!"

"Helen, don't you realize that they would be anxious to get her out of the place, out into the anonymity of the city streets, where anything that might happen her could not be laid at their door?"

"Anything that might happen her." Helen put her hands to her face. "What will we do now?" she said.

"We can do several things," said Sylvester, stirring himself. "We can call at the emergency wards of the hospitals, and we can inform the police that she is missing."

It was on the tip of his tongue to say that they could inquire at the city morgue, but he was sure that that would be the counsel given at the hospitals if they had no news of the girl, and he felt that from the impersonal mouth of a hospital porter it might be less shocking to Helen than it would be from his lips.

They began a search of the hospitals that lasted until their limbs were weary, but still they went from one to another. In all of them, although they interviewed the porter in his cubicle off the main reception hall, they were forced to witness sights and sounds that gave an ever-increasing emphasis to their own suffering. Once it occurred to Sylvester that he should send Helen home! Then it flashed into his mind that such gradual and consistent review of the various sufferings of mankind might prepare her in some way for what he now believed would be the ultimate information that, at one or another of these places, they would receive of Onny.

They tried progressively those hospitals situated within a radius of the evil place where Onny had gone in her degradation, and then they tried all those that lay within the direct course from that place to Sylvester's apartment, for whatever pride might have kept Onny from going home in health, under the influence of pain and humiliation she would surely have sought refuge there. But they found no sign of her.

At last in their wanderings they found that they were once again back in the vicinity of the apartment. Suddenly Helen halted and put her hand on Sylvester's arm.

"Why are we searching for Onny?" she asked, her voice suddenly sharp and urgent. "It is only for our own peace of mind that we have been trying to find her. Wherever she is, she is receiving the attention she needs —whatever that may be."

As she said the last few words, her voice was low and sad, and Sylvester nodded, knowing then that he had no need to shield her from the worst possibilities.

"I am thinking of Gabriel," she said. "Where is he? Oh, Sylvester," she cried, and she caught at the lapels of his coat. "I feel that Gabriel is in some danger. We must look for him. It is him we must find."

Sylvester, listening to her, felt his heart surge with a vague sadness.

"We'll see if he is in the apartment," he said, and although she said nothing, he felt conscious that she was grateful for his prompt compliance with her demand.

ဢ ဢ ဢ

The apartment was silent and dark when they reached it. Gabriel was not there.

"Oh, where can he be?" cried Helen, and again Sylvester felt a pang of sadness in his heart.

"I'll light the light," he said. "He may have left a message for us."

Almost at once when the light filled the room, he heard Helen exclaim again, and he saw her lift up a paper from the table. It was a page of the evening paper and a small paragraph at the bottom of it was scored with pencil marks.

"He must have left this for us to see," she said, and she began to read it. She read it in silence and then she held the paper down at her side.

"Well?" said Sylvester.

The tears had come into Helen's eyes.

"An unidentified woman," she said, "found in a state of collapse in Stephen's Green. She died this morning." She raised her head and looked at Sylvester. "It may be some other person!" she said. "It may not be Onny."

There was a questioning hope in her voice. Sylvester stretched out his hand for the paper.

"It's her colouring," he said, "and her height, and the description of her clothes is correct." Here his voice faltered for a moment as he thought of the day that he and Gabriel had taken Onny to buy her finery. Then, reading the rest of the paragraph, he spoke lower and less distinctly. "The rest of the information is correct also," he said, and he put the paper down on the table.

"Gabriel?" said Helen, again. "We must look for Gabriel."

"Yes," said Sylvester abstractedly.

He lifted the paper again and ran his eyes over the end of the paragraph. The usual information was given. The unidentified woman was at the city morgue, where an inquest would be held upon the following day. The police would welcome any efforts on the part of the public to assist in the identification of the body.

"He may have gone up to the morgue," said Sylvester, and as she was about to suggest that they would go in that direction, she was startled by the suddenness and violence of an exclamation from Sylvester. "The fool!" he said. "It's a good thing it's night-time." He went over and put out the light. "Can you see your way?" he asked. "We'd better hurry and find him."

Helen was conscious of a certain feeling of perplexity, but she put it aside. Whatever the motive that lay under it she was glad to see Sylvester show anxiety and a desire for haste. There was for the first time a note of urgency in his voice.

They made their way out on to the landing and descended the steep dark stairs.

"Are you sure you want to come?" asked Sylvester. "I think you ought to get some rest." He tried to see her face in the darkness. "I think I'll take you home," he said.

"No, no," she cried impatiently. "Time is precious."

Sylvester hesitated, and still did not move.

"I wonder would you think it improper of me," he asked, with a faint return of the mocking tone that had been conspicuously absent from his voice in the last few hours, "I wonder would you think it improper of me to suggest that you go back to my rooms, and lie down there?" But almost at once a note of tenderness came back into his voice, and he didn't wait for an answer. "I hate to think of how tired you must be; how cold; how weary!" His voice sharpened again. "And for what?" he demanded. "What is Onny Soraghan to you?"

He bent his head as she murmured an answer.

"It is for Gabriel's sake!" she murmured.

Sylvester jerked his head upward again.

"Come along, then," he said. "Why are we wasting time!"

Instead of following him, however, he felt her hanging back, and almost immediately she caught his arm and with her other hand she pointed.

"Look!" she said. "Isn't that Gabriel?"

451

At the end of the street, coming into solitary prominence under the light of a street lamp, was a thin figure that unmistakably resembled Gabriel. Their hearts leaped at the recognition of him, and catching hands like children they ran forward eagerly to meet him; but when they came within speaking distance of him they were checked with a sudden embarrassment. Gabriel, however, had seen them, as they had seen him.

"Did you see the paper?" he asked, and then as they nodded miserably he spoke almost to himself in a voice they could hardly hear. "It said that she was found in Stephen's Green," he said. "She must have been on her way home to me."

Helen nodded sympathetically, and even as she did she was aware again of the same inexplicable impatience that Sylvester had shown already once before that night. She said nothing, but she looked at him, her expression puzzled and hurt.

"Let's go across the street," said Sylvester curtly. "There's a seat there. We can sit down."

Dully the other two followed him, as he led the way, and as these few extra steps took them within sight of the dark silent foliage of the Green, which was locked and barred for the night, Helen shuddered. They said nothing as they crossed the street, but when they reached the metal seat that was set on the outer edge of the pavement, facing away from the park, they sat down.

One of the strangest things about tragedy is the simplicity of its setting; the banality of its *décor* and dialogue. Leading up to the climax of a tragedy the playwright is wrought to a pitch of frenzy in his efforts to create a dialogue so heightened in its style that it will evoke the emotion of the protagonists in the breast of the spectators. Yet, in real life, how often the setting is like this, a metal bench in a public park, where others have suffered before, and where others will suffer again. And the dialogue? Even in moments of trial and strain the pitiful human heart is still solicitous for its fragile frame.

"Are you cold, Helen?" said Gabriel. "You look so pale."

"She's all right," said Sylvester, feeling her hand with his, but unable through the lifeless chill in his own fingers to perceive the condition of hers. "She's all right, but you must be cold, Gabriel. The night air is bad, and you have no coat."

"I had one when I left the apartment," said Gabriel. "I must have left it somewhere."

"Your coat? Oh, that's too bad," said Helen. "We must make a search for it tomorrow."

"It doesn't matter about it," said Gabriel. "Not much, anyway; it was very worn. It was time I gave it away."

"All the same, we may as well get it in the morning," said Helen, feeling that if she continued this dull talk some gain would be theirs, she knew not what.

Just then the street lamps over their heads went out, and instantly it was seen that day had thrown its first radiant ribbons of light across the eastern sky line. She did not want that day to come. But Sylvester, raising his head, rejoiced.

"Morning!" he said, and his eyes fastened on that rift of radiance. "The daylight is coming."

Gabriel sprang into life.

"Is it day?" he cried, and he looked in despair at the bright rim of the sky. "I must get ready. I must go back to the apartment before I go to the morgue."

Helen started and looked at Sylvester with apprehension. Sylvester stood up. He did not seem surprised.

"Are you going to go there?" he asked. "Do you think it wise? Hadn't you better let me go? I could bear it better than you."

Gabriel simply did not understand such suggestions.

"What do you mean?" he asked.

Helen looked from one to the other of them. For some reason Sylvester did not wish Gabriel to go to the morgue. This was the cause of his uneasiness earlier in the night. She did not know why he didn't want it, but looking at his stern face she put her trust implicitly in him and was about to urge Gabriel to do the same, when, looking at Gabriel, she saw that it was waste of time to argue with him. She turned back to Sylvester.

"You can't stop him if he wants to go," she said. "Naturally he wants to see her."

"He'd be better away from there," said Sylvester doggedly, and he bit his lips with vexation.

"Poor Onny," said Helen. "What an end! The city morgue!" The tears rushed into her eyes. Gabriel turned.

"Will you go home, Helen?" he said. "Go home and try to get some rest." He turned back to Sylvester. "Will you come with me?" he asked.

Helen leaned over and whispered something to Sylvester.

"I'll go certainly," said Sylvester. "But I want to give you a warning, Gabriel. I know how you feel, but I want you to promise me that you will keep yourself under control when you see her."

Helen, who had been crying gently, stopped, struck with a new significance behind Sylvester's words. She began to understand what was in his mind.

"Will there be an inquest?" she asked, her face expressing concern.

"Hush!" said Sylvester, and he turned to Gabriel again. "It would be better for you not to go, but if you go, you must do as I say. You must keep yourself under rigid control."

"Why?" said Gabriel.

"Have you ever been in a city morgue?"

"No."

"You have no idea what it's like. The dead, God help them, are inoffensive. But there are others there besides the dead, journalists in search of a story, art students, sensation-mongers, morbid old hags that come there to gape. And if you betray any feeling at sight of Onny they will see it at once, and their curiosity will be roused. They will link you together at once. You must not let it be seen that you knew her. You will have to appear indifferent; to school yourself to look at the other poor creatures laid out there, and when you come to Onny you must look at her with equal indifference."

Gabriel did not seem to understand.

"Why?" he said again.

Helen stepped over. She laid her hand on Gabriel's arm, and spoke in a voice of infinite sadness and gentleness.

"Onny is dead. Nothing can alter that, but the fact remains that the manner of her death was unpleasant. There is no reason why you should become involved in the investigations or an inquest."

She felt that he was drawing away from her. She tightened her fingers on the hard cloth of his sleeve.

"It can do no good," she said, urgently, despairingly, having read already in his eyes that he was not listening to her arguments. "It can do no good. She is dead and nothing you do can affect her."

Sylvester's mind was busy with more practical problems.

"I don't suppose she had any letter, or papers on her person that would indicate where she lived; and even if it was found out that she lived in the apartment we could explain that easily enough. We could say that she had hired the studio from us; that we both occupied the other room. It would be just as well to make a few adjustments anyway, just in case there would be inquiries. You could attend to that, Helen. And I'd have to have a few words with the caretaker to make sure he'd keep his mouth shut."

While Sylvester was speaking a look of understanding came over Gabriel's face, but it was rapidly succeeded by a look of horror and disgust. Helen, intent on what she had to say, did not look at his face however; she was intent on convincing him.

"We know how you feel, Gabriel," she said, "but you have to conquer your feelings."

Gabriel tore her hand from his sleeve.

"How can you know what I feel?" he said. "You say that you are my friends. Then why are you urging me to do something that would make me for ever ashamed of myself? Do you mean to look me in the face and

454

tell me that you want me to keep out of this; to pretend that I never knew her; to let her be passed over by a few formal words of empty inquiry and put down into a nameless grave?"

Sylvester shrugged his shoulders. "One grave is the same as another."

Gabriel took up the words.

"One grave may be the same as another if you die in your bed, but Onny will lie in a dishonoured grave."

Helen put out her hand vaguely, as if she would take his hand in hers, but when he made no response she let it drop to her side. Sylvester made a more firm gesture. He took Gabriel by the arm. .

"Personally, as you know," he said, "I have my own ideas about honour and dishonour, but even if you feel differently from me in this matter, the fact remains that there is very little you can do about it. Poor Onny, she made her bed and she lay in it, and now she has dug her grave and you may as well let her lie in it too. What can you do to alter things?"

"I can associate myself in her dishonour. I can take the blame that I deserve, not perhaps for the deed she committed, but for the events that led up to that deed. You said the other day that she had a bad streak in her nature. I think, now, that there may have been something in what you said, she could not otherwise have acted as she did. In the light of all that has happened since that conversation with you I have changed my opinions on many things. But I do not blame myself less, because I know that the superstitious interpretation that Onny had put upon her religion acted as a safeguard to the weakness of her character. Rather than bring upon herself the punishment of fire and brimstone that she believed would attend iniquity she would have lived within any code, although she did not understand it. I begin to see some value in the externals of religion. I begin to see that for people of lesser moral fibre they are necessary, and that there are few who can dispense with the safeguard they provide against temptation from within and without. Poor Onny! Poor, poor Onny! What an evil day it was for her when I first came into her life."

While he spoke Helen stared at him, and into her face there came an expression of admiration that dispelled her former concern, but when she glanced in Sylvester's direction, she saw that Gabriel's words had only angered him.

"Fine words!" said Sylvester. "But what do you plan to do next?"

"I will go to the inquest, of course," said Gabriel. "I will claim her, and take upon myself whatever share the court considers should fall on me of that dishonour that would otherwise fall on her alone."

Sylvester clenched his hands as if he could strike him.

"Do you know what this will mean?" he asked. "I do not know myself what attitude the courts take to cases of this sort, but I think there is a chance that you may be regarded as an accessory to murder!"

"I am prepared for that!" said Gabriel.

Sylvester ignored his interruption.

"In any case whatever happens you will never live down the disgrace. I implore you to think of everything."

"I have thought of everything," said Gabriel. "Onny's people, my own people, can say that I led Onny astray, but at least they will not say that I deserted her when the day of punishment came. I must go now."

But Sylvester called after Gabriel.

"I want to ask you a question. If Onny had left you after you came to Dublin, and if she lived with someone else, would you still feel yourself responsible for her, just because it was under your influence that she made the first step in leaving home?"

Gabriel was about to answer, but he suddenly looked at Sylvester, and instead of giving an answer he asked a question himself.

"Why do you ask that?" he said, and he looked from Sylvester to Helen, to see if, in her more mobile face, he might read more than was betrayed by Sylvester. But Helen, too, was staring at Sylvester with a look of curiosity. She did not know what he had in his mind.

"Is it as the father of this child that Onny was carrying that you take the blame upon yourself for her death?"

Again Gabriel was about to answer, when all at once, recoiling a step from Sylvester, he stared at him suddenly, as if he read his mind.

"What are you trying to tell me?" he said, in a terrible voice, low and steady, yet filled with pent-up anger.

"I am not trying to tell you anything that I have not been trying to tell you all week," said Sylvester: "That you have no moral obligation towards Onny Soraghan in this affair."

"Are you trying to tell me that Onny was unfaithful to me?"

Gabriel's eyes blazed with fury and indignation, but Sylvester seemed cooler than ever. For him at least the tension of the situation seemed to have utterly vanished. It was as if for him the drama had ended, and he was merely winding up the tiresome details of the dénouement.

"I thought, my dear Gabriel, that you had your own suspicions at the time you were so determined against letting her model for Telman!"

"How dare you! How dare you suggest such a thing! Her relations with Telman were perfectly innocent."

"How do you know?"

"I trusted her!"

Sylvester raised his eyebrows.

"Speak plainly!" said Gabriel. "Stop your hateful sneering. I don't believe you. I thought you were a man, but to make an accusation against a girl who is lying dead and cannot defend herself is a form of caddishness that I would not have expected, even from you." His resentment was passionate and bitter. It seemed that at any minute he would strike Sylvester. "I can put that lie down your throat, Sylvester. Onny may be dead, but I can bring you face to face with Telman, and make him deny it!"

Sylvester for some time past had been staring up at the lime trees over their heads. He now reached up and tried to tear a leaf, but he could only reach high enough to catch the tip of one green leaf which tore with a sharp sound like tearing silk, and left a fragment of green in his hand. This he put to his lips and began to chew. The gesture was infuriatingly casual and indifferent, but his yellow eyes were fixed on Gabriel, alert and calculating.

"I'll make him deny it," said Gabriel again.

"That I think would not be difficult," said Sylvester. "Far harder, I should imagine, to make him admit it."

Gabriel, realizing the truth of these words, was halted for a moment, but then he rushed ahead.

"You never see any good in anyone. What more could I expect from you? It is easy for you to raise doubts about others; but you can't expect me to believe the man is a blackguard because you say he is one."

Sylvester's small even teeth bit into the leaf and the green sap began to stream out from the veins of it, and stained his teeth, but again, his quick darting eyes were watching every line of Gabriel's face.

Then, suddenly, he took the leaf out of his mouth and threw it away, and either because of his gesture of throwing away the leaf, or because of the fact that he gave a rapid glance at Helen before he spoke, he created a strong impression that his next words would be significant, yet when he spoke his voice was as casual as before, and his words even more elaborately casual.

"There may be something in what you say " said Sylvester. "After all who am I to throw the first stone?"

Helen's head lifted with a swift startled movement. Gabriel's entire expression changed. Over his face came an expression of indescribable bewilderment.

"You! You!"

He put his hands up to his face and pressed them against his eyes. For a time he stayed this way, and they were both silent, waiting. Then he lowered his hands, and turning on his heel, without a word he walked away from them, a moment later breaking into a run, as if he fled the very city itself, swift, blind, intransigent.

ᔥ   ᔥ   ᔥ

Gabriel ran down the vacant, early morning streets between the vacant buildings lit with the early morning light. The streets were corridors of confusion, opening one out of another, and the buildings rose up sheer to either side of him.

Where was he going? He did not know. He had some vague idea that if he ran far and fast enough he would at last flash out of this labyrinth of streets into a cool place of green fields and open sky.

Yet what respite could he hope to find there; or anywhere? What was the use of running forward? He carried the same body with him, the same mind, the same heart, the same sorrows. Still he felt as he ran through the clear air that his mind was becoming refreshed, and the confusion was falling away from it. The questions that had swarmed in his mind sang singly now. He longed to cry out in the empty streets.

"What have I done? What have I done?"

And in his heart he cried out still more bitterly. "How did these things come to happen?"

He was at one and the same time filled with a sense of degrading guilt and yet upheld by a feeling that he did not deserve his punishment in the form in which it had come. He was like one who had seen a bright road ahead, and had rushed along it recklessly, but when he came to the bending of it, and found that it led to a dank and evil-smelling place, could not believe that it was still the same road, and looked back to see where he had taken the wrong turning. But it was indeed the selfsame road upon which he had set out so gayheartedly. Yet, what matter about him! He could still turn back. But oh, if he had only trod that road alone! If only he had not taken the trust of another's hand, he, who was so young, so blind, so ill-equipped himself for the journey to which he set his face!

Blindly he ran forward, not caring or seeing where he went, and gradually the tall buildings that rose up like walls to either side of him became more widely spaced, with broader alleyways between, and above the walls of courtyard and garden green trees began to appear spreading their foliage out over the pavements. He was getting to the outskirts of the city, nearing the wide spaces of the Phœnix Park, from which, being situated on a certain eminence above it, the whole city could be seen stretching away to the bay beyond.

But Gabriel was unaware of it. He still went forward. At last, however, the first early traffic began to sound in the streets, and carts laden with fruit and vegetables rattled down the cobbles on their way to the morning market. Not until then did he come to a stand. Where was he going? What was he going to do? He pressed his hands to his temples, and as he did so he recalled his former miseries as a child in Castlerampart. Miseries! The word seemed a mockery of him. Compared with all he had suffered in the last week, they had been no more than slight irritants at which another might have merely laughed.

In his perplexity and bewilderment the old town of Castlerampart appeared suddenly to shine with the golden innocence that for some time past seemed to have shone over his childhood, and he forgot that in that innocence the seed of this moment was sown. And further it suddenly seemed to him that if he could go back to those old scenes, he would step again into that golden innocence. A violent longing surged over him to return to the old town where he was born. If he could go now, at once, without even going back for one moment into that intolerable city from which he had fled! If he could, now, at this moment, be back there in that old town, running down the old and crooked length of Clewe Street! How he would burst open the old hall door! He would make a clean breast of everything. Like a child he would throw himself on the mercy of his aunts. He would fling himself into the arms of Sara; arms that would be stretched out to him, he knew, no matter what he had done. And Theresa! He would throw himself upon Theresa's mercy, and ask her to help him, to tell him what to do, as she had always told them all what to do, long ago—his mother, and Sara, and the little boy Gabriel that he longed to become again. To Theresa, even more than to Sara, his mind turned in its anguish and he yearned for her strong hand jerking him to her side more even than he longed for Sara's soft palm on his forehead, for now in a flash he came to the knowledge that had been denied to him in all the years, that whatever his Aunt Theresa might think of him she would stand by him against the world. No matter how great his guilt she would take his part against his accusers. And no matter how fierce the onslaught of his retribution, she would stiffen herself to oppose it, and behind her dominating figure, austere and hard, neither the importunities of the Soraghans nor the inquisitiveness of outsiders would be of any avail.

How had he been so blind to the virtues of those two women? Now that his eyes were opened his heart yearned to see them again, and image after image of them rose before his mind, abrupt as shadows rising up on a wall: Sara, standing at the foot of the stairs with the lamp held over her head and the slanted light falling on her sad and gentle face; Theresa, sailing down the passage with her black skirts pinned to her sides and her hair plastered back as sleek as wings to her head. Sara, with her cloud of hair crushed under her Sunday best hat, clasping her umbrella in one gloved hand while with the other she tried the back door for the thousandth time to see that it was secure before she joined Theresa in the hall; Theresa, in the doorway, tapping her foot impatiently in the familiar fashion while she waited for Sara, watching out of the corner of her eye all the time to see that the Finnertys or Molloys made no stir to leave their houses before her and rob the Coniffes of their proud example over them. Face after face, one more familiar and intimate than the other, came up before him—the Molloys, the Finnertys, Hannah, Agnes, Mary

459

Ellen, Packy Hand. And his heart leapt at the thought that soon he might see them real and solid before him.

But suddenly among those faces out of the golden past, radiant with life, Onny's face rose up, and her glorious bold smile shone over him, effacing all else.

A great shudder passed through him. How could he have forgotten her and the duty he owed her? The rash hope of escape that had flashed through his mind died away. It had been a meretricious light leading him astray from the path of honour. He could not leave this city yet; this dreadful city in which had been enacted the terrible scene of Onny's tragedy, and in which he had yet his own tragic part to play. But how would he bring himself voluntarily to return to those places of darkness and sin through which he had wandered all night in despair, when, just beyond the sky line, it seemed the golden sunlit walls of the old rampart town seemed to offer him their sanctuary?

Suddenly his mind fastened on something he had forgotten. Sylvester's accusation; what of that? Did it not exonerate him? As the ignoble impulses stirred in his heart, however, a sure feeling came over him that Sylvester was lying. And what did it matter whether he was lying or not; his, Gabriel's, duty was clear. He must go back and face whatever punishment it would be decreed he deserved.

Another violent shudder passed through him as the physical implications of his decision came home to him. Then deliberately he turned around, and an exclamation of surprise escaped from his lips at the loveliness of the sight before his eyes.

Dublin lay outstretched below him, its pinnacles gleaming in the morning mists like the pinnacles of a dream. Nothing was seen from this height of the lower reaches of the city—the shops, the tenements, or the busy pavements. They were all huddled together out of sight in the low levels between the tall buildings. But up into the bright air, the steeples, spires, and domes, the lancing pinnacles and towers of church and court and college, rose resplendent, as the city carried aloft her triumphant testimony of man's mighty struggle to cut through ignorance and doubt a path of sane philosophy.

Of this city he knew nothing; he had never seen it, never for one hour been a part of it. He stared down at the fair vista, and at the shining sea beyond it, and for the third time hope rose in his heart, a faint ray perhaps, wan and pale, but as pure and true as the first white javelin of light that pierces the darks of morning.

He held up his head, and strode forward.

AFTERWORD

AFTERWORD

The Irish novel is remarkably deficient in bourgeois experience. Before the arrival of Kate O'Brien and Mary Lavin one could hardly have deduced from Irish fiction that there was a settled upper middle class either in the cities or the provinces. The nineteenth century, from Maria Edgeworth to George Moore, had been rich in what Yeats called the "dream of the noble and the beggarman". The big house of Sommerville and Ross carried on its ambiguous traffic with the mud cabins of William Carleton. The landed Catholic found expression in Banim and Griffin. But few seemed interested in the substantial population of the merchant and professional classes who supplied increasingly the backbone and ballast of what social order there was throughout the country.

With the new century everything changed except that. Joyce gave a voice to Dublin's chancers and corner boys, its drinking classes and its shabby genteel, but apart from a couple of passages in the *Portrait* and "The Dead" he skirted the milieu from which his own parents, the Joyces and the Murrays—"Dedalus" and "Goulding" had declined. Stephens moved from slum realism to prose fantasy. Moore continued to deal in priests, peasants and artists. Corkery launched the "Cork realists", O'Connor and O'Faolain, on a world of insurgent guerillas, Irish-speaking farmers and fishermen, dubious clerics and the social drama of Cork's back streets. Elizabeth Bowen negotiated between the ancestral Irish manor house and Regent's Park. Liam O'Flaherty found his imaginative world on the islands of Ireland's western sea-board.

Mary Lavin's fiction, from the start, tended to bypass the turbulent or the exotic in Irish life and centre upon the permanent, upon those patterns of continuity that animate a settled order. It has been pointed out that her second novel, *Mary O'Grady*, told the story of a woman who lived in Dublin during the Great Lock-Out of 1913, the Easter Rising, the Black-and-Tan War and the Civil War, without any of these events appearing to enter her consciousness. Similarly when, in 1944, Sean O'Faolain was opposing in his journal *The Bell* what he called the disabling myths of Irish consciousness, "the Gaelic Myth, and the other Myths like the Noble Peasant, and a host of susceptibilities born of History", Mary Lavin was putting the finishing touches on *Clewe Street*, a book tranquilly immune from all that ideological pother. Its only turbulence is a hilarious race to the graveyard between two rival funerals wherein the hearses and carriages take on Homeric proportion, and where the author perpetrates an Irish bull that would have made Edgeworth envious: "It's easy seen that the man that is dead is no longer alive ... When a person came to ask a favour of Theodore Coniffe he was civilly received." Apart from that a young husband dies in a fall from a horse, a girl gets pregnant and the hero, Gabriel, temporarily leaves home. The real drama of the novel, as always with Mary Lavin, is in the tensions of inter-personal relationships: the human heart ranging for love in a world dominated by class, property, and a religion that finds its chief expression in the demand for social conformity; the strange forms love assumes when it is denied its small opportunities—Theresa's hardness, Sara's meekness, Onny's wilfulness, Gabriel's thwarted solicitude.

The novel is, therefore, well named: Castlerampart with its moral epicentre at the house in Clewe Street is the chief character in the action. It imposes its will on the destinies of the human characters who give their names to the novel's three books: "Theodore and Cornelius", "Gabriel" and "Gabriel and Onny". Even more so it stamps its authority on the lives of the three women whose private destiny leads them to conceive of it as a world in itself, with no considerable universe outside. Cornelius arrives in the town from somewhere or other, in answer to some vague planetary pull. The honeymoon couple go off somewhere and return home with horses and carriage. The hero's friend, Sylvester, is introduced as the son of "the new visitor at the Central Hotel". When Aunt Theresa steadfastly refuses to send Gabriel to a boarding school the tyranny of the town and its stultifying values become animate in her interior monologue:

> Wasn't he the grandson of Theodore Coniffe? Wouldn't he inherit his grandfather's position of eminence and authority in the town? What need was there for him to go away to school and put on false airs and graces? Above all, had they themselves gone away to school? They had not! Yet who was more highly respected in the town than the Coniffe sisters?

The progress of the reverie with its primly mounting self-righteousness is comic, while its implications for the young hero, given the inoffensive decency of his character, are tragic. The reader senses that he must smother in the embrace of Castlerampart or get out. But this is no Joycean *Bildungsroman* of rebellious self-assertion and flight. This novel opens with the patriarchal figure of Theodore Coniffe gazing down the street which he practically owns, and it ends with the prim prodigal, Gabriel, coming home after his traumatic adventure in Dublin:

> A violent longing surged over him to return to the old town where he was born. If he could go now, at once, without even going back for one moment into that intolerable city from which he had fled! If he could, now, at this moment, be back there in that old town, running down the old and crooked length of Clewe Street! How he would burst open the old hall door! He would make a clean breast of everything. Like a child he would throw himself at the mercy of his aunts. He would fling himself into the arms of Sara; arms that would be stretched out to him, he knew, no matter what he had done ... whatever his Aunt Theresa might think of him she would stand by him against the world.

When measured against such heroic predecessors as Stephen Dedalus saying goodbye to his native city or young Rastignac looking down upon Paris at the end of *Old Goriot* Gabriel cuts a plaintive figure; but in his circumstances, the reader is well aware, it is braver for him to go home than to run from the consequences of his action. His, at the end of the day, is a conscience shaped by Castlerampart with its puritan sense of duty as well as its intimidating sense of sin: "his, Gabriel's duty was clear. He must go back and face whatever punishment it would be decreed he deserved."

His father, Cornelius, had been similarly punished. A shrewd social climber he had worked his way into the willing confidence of old Theodore and his three daughters. Hesitating between the equally eligible and willing older girls he is caught, ambushed as it were, by an impulse of romantic love, and later by an unsanctioned ambition to break out of the bourgeois ambience of his adopted family. Each of these gestures calls forth from the author some of her most vivid and memorable prose, the kind of intense evocative writing that make her short stories so haunting and memorable.

When Cornelius, on his return from the city, steps into the twilit garden where the youngest daughter, Lily, is sitting, the scene is laid for that moment of enchantment and transformation that is to alter, fatally, the pedestrian course of life at Clewe Street. The girl, poised on the brink of womanhood, is resentful that her sisters refuse to let her have a long dress for the Annual Outing. Cornelius, acting with an ingenuity that is typical and an impulsiveness that is not, "lifted the hem" of her short dress "slightly" to discover that its ruffles can be let down. When the cutting and unstitching—the symbolism barely surfaces—have been completed everything is, for a moment, transfigured:

> Slowly, and as if conscious that in shaking out the folds of the heavily creased tucks in her simple dress she was shaking out the lottery of the years ahead, Lily stood up, and catching the ends of the skirt shook it slowly ... the tucks began to give way, heavily and slowly opening, like the tucks in a concertina, and little by little the hemline went lower and lower and lower until at last it reached her ankles and some of the longer, taller grasses reached up as far as it and striped and etched it like a dark embroidery.

In the exchanges that follow it becomes even clearer that into the "simple garden there had come some new influence".

The new influence lasts while Cornelius lives—survives in the new elegance of carriages, presents, gowns, thoroughbreds. But the household gods take their vengeance when Cornelius's attempt to break out of his class into that of the gentry ends in a fatal hunting accident. In a passage, different from the garden scene in everything but its sensuous particularity, the author conveys the precise inflection of Cornelius's error. Old Theodore while looking at the dead body of his son-in-law remembers Colonel Fanshaw's earlier remark that "a man must be bred to horses".

> When those words came back to his mind, with them there came a remembrance of the odours that had emanated from the clothes of the huntsmen, and even of the grooms; a slightly scented, slightly camphorated odour of cloth preservative from their coats, mixed with odours of valet cream, saddle soap, and the faint but not unpleasant smell of sweat from a clean body. These odours began to symbolize something unattainable, for when the body of Cornelius was brought home covered over with the jackets and coats, gladly volunteered by members of the Hunt, from these coats there exhaled

the same odours, while from the splattered clothes that were taken from the dead man, despite the racking they had received, it seemed to Theodore, as he threw them in a heap in the kitchen, that there was only an odour of newness, the smell of some tailoring establishment.

With her husband's death Lily fades into insignificance and the disappointed Theresa comes forward to ensure that the dead man's son, Gabriel, will not repeat his father's misdeeds or nourish his vain aspirations. Old Theodore's will, which makes his grandson wait till twenty five for his inheritance, provides her with the ideal conditions for shaping the boy to her own joyless ethic.

Theresa, arguably the best characterization in the book, is the chief focus of its tragedy and the medium of its moral irony. Having been denied a real childhood by her mother's death—with her sister, Sara, she must act as nurse and governess to Lily—she enjoys a few months of tentative romantic love in expectation of Cornelius's proposal. When she is rejected in favour of her teenage sister her love hardens into resentment, religion into righteousness, virtue into respectability, justice into vengeance. Her portrayal, though largely unsympathetic, is not without understanding: it is clear that within the world of Castlerampart, and given her upbringing, a character as strong as hers has few other options. She is further corrupted by the power given her as executrix of her father's will. Ironically, in wielding that power, in expelling, gratuitously, the sensible housekeeper Mary Ellen, she lets in the unwitting enemy of all her values, Onny Soraghan.

The action of Onny within the novel's development is managed with great subtlety. While the rituals of death are being administered at Theodore's funeral, young Gabriel is enjoying unaccustomed rituals of life at the home of the Soraghans. The large unruly family has suddenly noticed that their youngest daughter has wandered off somewhere, and when she is discovered the effect is quietly apocalyptic. Well aware of the commotion her absence is causing the little girl is sitting naked on the grass in a patch of sunlight:

She sat on the grass and with one hand she pulled out a curl of golden hair as far as it would go from her forehead and then she let it slap back against her face. Every time she pulled out the curl she stared at it with fierce concentration, but every time she let it slap back into its tight gold coil again she turned her head and stared at

Gabriel's face and peered through the chinky leaves. Her big eyes were wide and blue and she neither smiled nor blinked.

This apparition of innocence and daring occurs in the first quarter of the novel, and it has the effect of a moral time-bomb in the reader's consciousness. The image of life-affirmation in the person of a bold baby girl is a frequent motif in Mary Lavin's short stories—the eponymous heroine of "Posy" is a triumphant re-incarnation of the tragic Onny—and here it stands over against the values of rigour, prudence and piety that are embodied in Theresa. In time the chemistry of Onny's presence in the Coniffe household—despite and sometimes because of the contempt with which she is treated by her employer—subverts that entire world. She carries with her a complex aura of nature, the sky, the garden and the river, and her spontaneous joy and energy even downface the images of decay in the churchyard and the old castle where she eventually trysts with Gabriel.

When the Soraghan children surround young Gabriel in the school yard taunting him with the refrain "Who's afraid of the river?" we have a proleptic image of his eventual fate. He breaks out of his middle-class morality—downwards whereas his father had tried it upwards—risks the challenge of the natural life, fails, and returns at the end to his Clewe Street sanctuary. Having been twice shocked into admiration at Onny's scorn for convention—once in the grass, again in the churchyard when she misses Mass—Gabriel encounters her, momentously, in the back garden, and by the river. It is the same garden as provided the setting for his father's infatuation, but the allure of Onny is significantly distinct. Dressed in her bizarre finery, on her way to the crossroads dance, she pauses to take her handkerchief from the bushes. When he teases her for not ironing it she replies:

> "I never iron my handkerchiefs because I like the smell of the bushes on them! So there!"
> ... he took the piece of crumpled linen from her pocket and pressed it to his face. He breathed in the sweet wild scent of the air that clings to clean-washed cool linens as it clings to nothing else, and in breathing it a new sense of sweetness and simplicity in life seemed suddenly to come to him, and Onny, herself, as she stood, with her toes turned in, upon the dampening grass, seemed nearer and more in harmony with the earth than anyone he had ever met.

It is another of these intense moments in the narrative that convey so much through symbolic gesture and the evocation of atmosphere that authorial comment is superfluous. The wilful, uneducated little kitchen maid is transformed temporarily into a sort of wood nymph. And immediately both of them dare the river, crossing perilously on the stepping stones so that Onny will be in time for her dance. It is at the same point of the river, several chapters later, that he rescues Onny from possible death and their pact against the house in Clewe Street is fatally sealed.

The third book of the novel, "Gabriel and Onny", must constitute one of the strangest culminations to a *Bildungsroman* in literature. In it the unlettered kitchen maid takes to Dublin's artistic colony as to her natural element while her middle-class lover becomes more awkward, priggish and defensive as week follows week. Sylvester, once the *alazon* of Gabriel's Castlerampart days becomes the *eiron* of his Dublin exile, ultimately betraying him, or so it seems, with Onny herself. The challenge of a bohemian life style intensifies Gabriel's bourgeois prejudices. He is hag-ridden by the desire to earn his living, contemptuous of the suggestion that he might mortgage a little of his substantial inheritance so that he and Onny may survive in comfort. As Onny throws herself with increasing recklessness into the artists' milieu Gabriel finds himself turning towards Helen, the Mass-going sculptress who most resembles the Agnes Finnertys of Castlerampart with whom his aunts had wanted him to associate. Walking down Kildare Street on their first Sunday beside the sulking and mutinous Onny, Gabriel insists that there are "three things I must do tomorrow ... write to my aunts ... look for work ... see about getting some priest to marry us". Onny's response is ominously characteristic:

"There's only one thing I have to do," she said, "and I'm going to do it right now." And leaning her weight on Gabriel's arm, she stooped down and drew off one shoe and then the other, and slinging them together by the laces, she laughed up gaily into Gabriel's face, and ran up the stairs ahead of him in her stockinged feet.

Increasingly the reader wonders whether her love for Gabriel is securely founded, and not a convenient illusion to get her out of an intolerable home life. Conversely Gabriel's exasperated constancy seems more and more a desperate resolve to do the right thing. Thus the tragedy of Onny's abortion—an extremely daring event in an Irish novel of the time—seems to symbolize the emptiness and folly of an affair dictated

469

not by genuine passion but by the spiritual poverty of an environment which makes it the last desperate expedient.

Commenting on her first novel forty years on, Mary Lavin professes herself puzzled. In the first place there is not a character in the novel remotely like herself, nor, except for such an incident as that of the "blood oranges", is there a line of autobiographical material in its three books. The only character, she claims, who gripped her imagination was Onny. This is understandable; as remarked above, the life-enhancing energies of Onny are re-incarnated in a succession of characters in the short stories, characters whom she portrays with especial affection. She concedes, however, that the three aunts, the righteous and manipulative Theresa, the meek, self-effacing Sara, and the frail, precarious Lily, may be types for an array of female characters in the later fiction. They are typical of the "refined" milieu of any country town like Castlerampart then and even now. But the town itself, she insists, is altogether authentic.

The nicely chosen incidents that make up the novel's leisurely opening seem to prepare us for a sort of Irish *Cranford*: the patriarchal Theodore surveys the street he virtually owns, scans the houses, the bridge, King John's Castle with its stone ramparts; the social stratum above Theodore is deftly introduced by the chat with Colonel Fanshaw on his hunter and subtly underlined by the Colonel's "Give my respects to the bride", a polite but impersonal reference to the fact that Cornelius and Lily are returning from their honeymoon that day. He talks with the bank manager's wife—mother to Agnes Finnerty who will be vainly eligible as a bride to the unborn Gabriel—about ivy and flowerpots; he talks to Mrs Molloy of the Central Hotel and greets Mary Ellen, his housekeeper. In the flashback that follows, Theodore is holding the ladder while one of his workers, Murty Rod, mends the roof of a tenant's house. Their easy-going banter is interrupted by the arrival of the doctor with the news that Theodore's wife, Katherine, has become unexpectedly pregnant in middle age, a delight to him and an acute embarrassment to her. The narrative proceeds in the ambience of local humours: "I'll split my sides laughing at old Theodore's face when he sees it's a girl", a woman called Packy remarks to the postman and the thatcher as the birth is awaited. Katherine dies giving birth to Lily, later mother of Gabriel.

From that point on the sense of a shared and salutary community recedes: the fictional cosmos splits into the interior world of the house at Clewe Street and the outside world of the streets, the church and the cottages. The town which had been almost idyllic in its easy social intercourse becomes sinister at the death of Cornelius and the rise of Theresa. Young Gabriel becomes an outsider in the community, derided for his timidity and staidness by his school mates; later he is denied community with his peers at boarding school. From the moment of her nakedness in the fields Onny is destined to be an outsider to the town's values, and more particularly to the bourgeois, Catholic values of the Coniffe house.

Significantly these unlikely lovers meet in a world of exclusion, outside the church while the others are at service. Their courtship takes place in exterior darkness, amid the shades of the old castle. They are outlaws from the town and the house. The house cannot contain his passion, the town will not tolerate their affair. Given the atmosphere the reader himself can hardly approve. When the lovers escape it is not towards each other they are journeying but away from provincial Catholic Ireland. When Dublin is reached their flight resolves itself into an escape from each other. For Onny it ends in death, for Gabriel defeat and return. In the end Castlerampart rules.

This conclusion seems inevitable from the manner of the novel's ending, about which some readers, including the author herself, have reservations. Gabriel, to still his emotional tumult and to clear his mind, walks out of the city in the early morning. In the course of his walk he resolves, as we have seen, to take the moral responsibility for Onny's tragedy, to go home and face the consequences. He must first return to Dublin. Walking towards the city—an archetypal progress in the life of so many novels—he sees it with an Wordsworthian sense of its hitherto unnoticed beauty, "the steeples, spires, and domes, the lancing pinnacles and towers of church and court and college, rose resplendent, as the city carried aloft her triumphant testimony of man's mighty struggle to cut through ignorance and doubt a path of sane philosophy". The final passage is a curious reversal of Hardy's Jude and Christminster, Balzac's Rastignac and Paris, Dickens's Pip and London, Lawrence's Paul Morel and the "city's phospherescence":

Of this city he knew nothing; he had never seen it, never for one hour been a part of it. He stared down at the fair vista, and at the shining sea beyond it, and for the third time hope rose in his heart, a faint ray perhaps, wan and pale, but as pure and true as the first white javelin of light that pierces the darks of morning.

He held up his head, and strode forward.

Middle class morality has its own virtues, and there are few writers in the mid-twentieth century who, like Mary Lavin, have dared however ambivalently to allow them at least a momentary triumph.

Augustine Martin, University College, Dublin, 1986

VIRAGO MODERN CLASSICS

The first Virago Modern Classic, *Frost in May* by Antonia White, was published in 1978. It launched a list dedicated to the celebration of women writers and to the rediscovery and reprinting of their works. Its aim was, and is, to demonstrate the existence of a female tradition in fiction which is both enriching and enjoyable. The Leavisite notion of the 'Great Tradition', and the narrow, academic definition of a 'classic', has meant the neglect of a large number of interesting secondary works of fiction. In calling the series 'Modern Classics' we do not necessarily mean 'great' — although this is often the case. Published with new critical and biographical introductions, books are chosen for many reasons: sometimes for their importance in literary history; sometimes because they illuminate particular aspects of womens' lives, both personal and public. They may be classics of comedy or storytelling; their interest can be historical, feminist, political or literary.

Initially the Virago Modern Classics concentrated on English novels and short stories published in the early decades of this century. As the series has grown it has broadened to include works of fiction from different centuries, different countries, cultures and literary traditions. In 1984 the Victorian Classics were launched; there are separate lists of Irish, Scottish, European, American, Australian and other English-speaking countries; there are books written by Black women, by Catholic and Jewish women, and a few relevant novels by men. There is, too, a companion series of Non-Fiction Classics constituting biography, autobiography, travel, journalism, essays, poetry, letters and diaries.

By the end of 1988 over 300 titles will have been published in these two series, many of which have been suggested by our readers.

Also of Interest

MARY O'GRADY
by Mary Lavin

With a new Afterword by Augustine Martin

In the early 1900s Mary O'Grady leaves behind the countryside and the family she cares for, to be with her husband in Dublin. Here she puts down new roots and looks forward to the day when she will return to Tullamore with her own sons and daughters. Marriage and motherhood sustain Mary, gradually the memories of her own childhood fade and her life revolves around the secure home she has created. But as her children grow, they seek the freedom of adults as she had done. Slowly Mary comes to realise that a mother's love cannot protect them, as it could not protect herself, from the sorrows and tragedies of life. First published in 1950, this sensitive novel is a compelling record of one woman's love and the strength of her silent faith. Mary Lavin has 'not only a delicate understanding of human beings, but also a great gift of lyrical expression' – *Daily Telegraph*

THE FLY ON THE WHEEL
by Katherine Cecil Thurston

With a new Introduction by Janet Madden-Simpson

Isabel Costello's return to Waterford causes a stir in the Carey household when Stephen, an upstanding lawyer, hears that his impecunious brother has become engaged to her. Outraged by Frank's attachment to a woman with few material prospects, Stephen intervenes. But his actions are the prelude to a far more devastating entanglement—he and Isabel fall in love. As a married man with children, Stephen faces the full weight of society's moral and religious opprobrium. For Isabel the consequences are equally circumscribed: a beautiful and reckless woman with no inheritance has little freedom in turn-of-the-century Ireland. This vivid portrait of social behaviour among the Catholic middle classes, originally published in 1908, is also a moving story of illicit love.

Katherine Cecil Thurston (1875–1911), born at Wood's Gift, Cork, was married to the writer E. Temple Thurston. The author of six novels, she became a celebrity in Britain and America on the publication of her outstanding bestseller, *John Chilcote, M.P.*

Irish Modern Classics

Margaret Barrington
MY COUSIN JUSTIN (forthcoming)

Brigid Boland
THE WILD GEESE (forthcoming)

George Egerton
KEYNOTES & DISCORDS

M. J. Farrell
DEVOTED LADIES
FULL HOUSE
LOVING WITHOUT TEARS
  (forthcoming)
MAD PUPPETSTOWN
THE RISING TIDE
TAKING CHANCES
TREASURE HUNT (forthcoming)
TWO DAYS IN ARAGON
YOUNG ENTRY (forthcoming)

Maura Laverty
NEVER NO MORE
NO MORE THAN HUMAN

Mary Lavin
THE HOUSE IN CLEWE STREET
MARY O'GRADY

Janet McNeill
TEA AT FOUR O'CLOCK
  (forthcoming)

Kate O'Brien
THE ANTE-ROOM (forthcoming)
THE LAND OF SPICES
  (forthcoming)
THE LAST OF SUMMER
  (forthcoming)
MARY LAVELLE
THAT LADY
WITHOUT MY CLOAK

Katherine Cecil Thurston
THE FLY ON THE WHEEL

Irish Non-Fiction Classics

Elizabeth Bowen
BOWEN'S COURT AND SEVEN
  WINTERS

Countess Markievicz
PRISON LETTERS OF COUNTESS
  MARKIEVICZ

Kate O'Brien
FAREWELL SPAIN